'Stric

Stacy, lost to everything, resembling,
but known it, her father in one of his rare and formidable tempers, raged at him. 'You *can* speak strictly, then? I had thought insolence was more your line. But pray continue,' she added, poisonously sweet, as she saw him open his mouth. To explain presumably. But what explanation could mend this?

She no longer wanted her bed. She wanted to see m'lord whoever-he-was grovelling before her. Nothing less would do.

Paula Marshall, married with three children, has had a varied life. She began her career in a large library and ended it as a senior academic in charge of history in a polytechnic. She has travelled widely, has been a swimming coach, and has appeared on *University Challenge* and *Mastermind*. She has always wanted to write, and likes her novels to be full of adventure and humour.

DEAR LADY DISDAIN

Paula Marshall

Harlequin Mills & Boon

SYDNEY ❀ AUCKLAND ❀ MANILA
LONDON ❀ TORONTO ❀ NEW YORK
PARIS ❀ AMSTERDAM ❀ HAMBURG ❀ MILAN
STOCKHOLM ❀ MADRID ❀ ATHENS ❀ BUDAPEST
WARSAW ❀ SOFIA ❀ PRAGUE ❀ TOKYO ❀ ISTANBUL

First Published 1995
This Edition 1998
ISBN 0 733 51355 7

Published by
Harlequin Mills & Boon
3 Gibbes Street
Chatswood, NSW 2067
Australia

Printed and bound in Australia by
McPherson's Printing Group

CHAPTER ONE

'What! my dear Lady Disdain, are you yet living?'
Shakespeare

'So, LORD AXFORDE didn't suit?'

Miss Louisa Landen's question came out idly as she applied herself diligently to her canvaswork. It seemed almost to be an afterthought.

But was it? Stacy Blanchard, seated at her desk in the main office of Blanchard's Bank, situated in the heart of London's financial centre, raised her dark head suspiciously.

'Was that a question, Louisa—or a statement?'

'Whichever you please, my dear,' Louisa returned placidly, without taking her eyes from the peacock she was stitching. 'I must say that I wasn't surprised that you refused him—you have refused all offers made to you so far—but. . .' And she stopped, apparently lost in confusion over the important question as to whether the wool she now required was light or dark blue.

Stacy wrote down the date, October 24th, 1818, before flinging down her quill pen, fortunately now empty of ink. 'But what, Louisa? Lately you seem to have developed the most distressing habit of not finishing your sentences.'

Louisa looked over the top of her work at her one-time pupil, now a handsome woman in her late twenties. Not pretty, or even conventionally beautiful perhaps, but something better. She possessed the oval ivory face of the Blanchards, their brilliant green eyes, and their dark, lightly curling hair, even if the curls were severely drawn back into a large knot at the nape of her neck—

which merely served to enhance the pure lines of a classic profile.

'But, my dear, Lord Axforde is, after all, such a tulip of fashion, seems to possess a considerable understanding, and is so rich in his own right that one could hardly claim that he was marrying you merely to get at the wealth of Blanchard's Bank. All in all you could scarcely do better. A handsome, reasonably clever man, and a marchioness's coronet—what more could you ask?'

It was no more—and no less—than the answer Stacy had expected. Louisa had, indeed, made something of a litany of lamentation of it, repeating it, with variations, over Stacy's last six offers—except the one made by Beverley Fancourt, of course. Now *he* really had been an open fortune-hunter.

Louisa might be her oldest, indeed, if truth were told, her only friend, but that didn't give her the licence to choose Stacy's husband for her. She was perfectly capable of doing that for herself—if she wanted a husband, that was. She rose from the desk and crossed the beautiful room, more like a great house's salon than an office, a room which her late father had created and which she had left unchanged.

She stopped before the window to pull back deep green velvet curtains, the colour of the dress which she wore, and to stare at the dome of St Paul's, before saying a trifle satirically, 'Really, Louisa, really? D'you know I gained the distinct impression from the manner of Lord Axforde's proposal that it was to the Bank he was making it, and not to me as a woman?' She gave a short laugh, and continued to inspect St Paul's as though she had never seen it before.

'Do not exaggerate, my dear.' Louisa's reply was coolly judicious. 'I told you not to do that as long ago as the nursery. I am sure that Lord Axforde said everything that was proper.'

Stacy's lips thinned, and, unseen by Louisa, her fists clenched. 'Oh, quite proper, I assure you. A regular commercial transaction was taking place—no doubt about it. Why, I half expected that he would ask me whether the Bank's interest rate would continue to remain high if we married!' She shook her head at Louisa's pained expression. 'Worse, from his expression—that of a man taking medicine—I thought that he was prepared to pay any price to get at Blanchard's money to buy himself a dukedom—even if that price included marrying someone as undesirable as myself!'

'Oh, come!' Miss Landen at last looked up from her stitchery. 'You do not do yourself justice, my dear. You misunderstood him, I am sure. Few prospective brides are as handsome and as *comme il faut* as you are.'

'And few lack as much pedigree as I do,' retorted Stacy briskly, returning to her desk and sitting down again. The desk was another of her father's innovations; previously the office had been furnished with an old-fashioned lectern at which one stood.

She looked across at a row of oil-paintings on the opposite wall. The older ones were hack-work, done by travelling colourmen for a few shillings; the last two were fine things, one by a pupil of Gainsborough and the other by Romney.

'My great-grandfather began life as a Huguenot pedlar who turned himself into a prosperous back-alley money-lender.' She waved her hand at the oldest painting. 'My grandfather built up the business until he was able to found Blanchard's Bank, and my father transformed it into the richest bank in England.' Now she waved at the Romney. 'His father sent him to Harrow, and he had the manners and tastes of a gentleman and married a lady of aristocratic birth, but that does not make us gentry. And they do not really accept us, however much they and the nobility fawn on Blanchard's—when they need the Bank to lend them money to carry on their gambling and their follies.'

Opening a large red and gold ledger which stood on her desk, she said almost savagely, 'Would you like me to read to you the loans we have made to the flowers of English society—and tell you how many have reneged on them? No, I am merely the cit's daughter, who has the bad taste to behave as a young man might, and run Blanchard's—successfully, too.'

She closed the ledger again. 'Do you know what he said to me, Louisa, in the middle of his pretence of loving and admiring me? That he expected that once we were married I would give up the foolishness of running the Bank and put in a manager to do it for me, so that I could give my mind to being a wife fit for a person of his station.'

Miss Landen stitched for a moment in silence, before replying, 'Most husbands would expect you to do that, my dear.'

'Yes, I know that, Louisa, and that is why I promise never to marry. Father didn't train me to run Blanchard's in order to stop doing so once some handsome popinjay decides that he might like my money while consigning me permanently to the nursery or to talk nonsense to fine ladies.'

Louisa sighed, before saying gently, holding up her work to inspect it the better, 'I thought you told me not long ago that you would like to have children of your own, my dear. You are leaving it rather late to marry—you are already twenty-eight years old—and husbands do not grow on trees.' And she gave her one-time charge a sideways look.

So even Louisa was full of sententious piff-paff, it seemed, and she, Stacy, was condemned to live in a childless desert because in order to have children one must first have a husband. How much better if one were a plant, fertilised at a distance by a passing bee—with no idea where the pollen came from!

This ridiculous notion was enough to restore her good humour and bring a wry smile to her face. It was the kind of nonsensical idea which she could never share with kind Louisa but which would have amused her father. Tears pricked at the back of her eyes. Hardly a day passed but she missed him—her father, her tutor, her mentor, her friend, the parent with whom, improbably, she had shared her jokes.

It occurred to her that it was too long since she had made one, or heard one, and meantime Louisa deserved an answer. But she would not like it.

'Oh,' she said, the hint of unexpected laughter in her voice bringing Louisa's head up, 'never fear, my love. When one is as rich as the heiress who owns Blanchard's Bank, husbands forsake the trees and spring out of the ground! There will be no shortage of offers for the richest prize in England! The shortage lies, Louisa, in men whom I might wish to accept. And that is enough of that. I have work to do.' And she opened another ledger and began to write as briskly as she had spoken.

If Miss Landen was thinking sadly that her one-time charge was such a strong woman, both mentally and morally, that it would need a man of equal strength to contain and perhaps tame her, she did not say so. It was all her stupid father's fault, she thought ruefully as she watched Stacy's quill drive across the paper, bringing her up as he had done.

It had been the failure of Louis Blanchard's wife to give him boy children who could survive birth which had done the damage. He had married Lady Rachel Beauchamp, of a poor and noble family, and he had loved her in his aloof fashion, but constant childbearing and miscarriages had made her sickly and ailing.

It had been a miracle that she had carried her one girl

child to term—another miracle that the child had been born large and healthy—but the birth had killed her mother, and left her father, for a time, resentful of the child who had taken his wife from him.

And then, as she grew up, her bright intelligence had begun to impress him. The child was christened Anastasia, but he had early shortened her name to Stacy, not Anna, because Stacy sounded more like the boy he had wanted to continue the Blanchard dynasty. Louisa remembered the first time she had met Louis Blanchard and Stacy.

'I'm not hiring you as a governess,' he had told her bluntly in the rich study of his home in Piccadilly. 'I want her to have the manners and appearance of a fine lady, even if she has the brains and mental accomplishment of a clever man. I have hired male tutors to educate her. 'Why,' he boasted proudly, 'she can calculate a percentage and draw up a bill better than any of my clerks, and she still but a child.'

Louisa had risen from her chair, said severely, 'I do not wish to undertake this task, Mr Blanchard. You are doing the poor child no favour and I ought not to abet you.'

He had given her the smile which transformed his hard face, and which immediately won him Louisa Landen's heart.

'And that is exactly why I am hiring you,' he had told her warmly, 'to keep her still a woman, and a modest one, for all her accomplishments.' He had seen Louisa hesitate. 'I will send for her,' he had said, and had rung the bell, 'and you may see that I am not asking you to care for a hoyden or a female pedant.'

What Louisa had seen when a lady's maid brought Stacy in was a shy, dark little girl, the image of her handsome father, who, for all her shyness, was thoroughly in command of herself, and who took one look at Louisa Landen and thoroughly approved of what she saw.

'My dear,' her father had told her, as coolly as though

he were addressing an equal, 'this is Miss Louisa Landen, who I hope will agree to become your companion and teach you the conduct and etiquette of a lady.'

Stacey had looked at the ladylike figure before her, and had seen through Miss Landen's modest exterior to the kind heart beneath it. She had made a short bow and said in a pretty voice, quite unlike anything which Miss Landen might have expected of the child prodigy whom her father had described, 'Oh, I do so hope, Miss Landen, that you will become my companion. I really do need someone to talk to and tell me exactly how a young lady should behave.'

Such composure in a ten-year-old Miss Landen had not met in her long career as a governess. She had bowed in her turn and murmured gently, 'And I shall be pleased to do just that, my dear,' and had begun her long association with Stacy and Louis Blanchard.

And if she had fallen a little in love with Louis Blanchard on the way, no one was ever to know. Occasionally she had remonstrated with him over his daughter's odd education, telling him in no uncertain terms that it was quite improper and that he was doing her no favour by insisting on it.

He had smiled at her and announced, 'I am not here to do her favours. I am here to secure for Blanchard's someone of that name who can run it when I am gone, and if that someone is a woman, then I must make do with what the Creator of us all has sent me!'

And that had been that. Louisa had never raised the matter again and here was the end of it, Louis Blanchard having died suddenly at a comparatively early age, leaving Stacy, still unmarried, to run the Bank, and waiting now for her right-hand man Ephraim Blount to come in to discuss the day's news and doings with her.

It grew increasingly likely, was Louisa's last sad

thought, that Stacy would never marry now, and her unlikely situation was the cause of it!

Stacy didn't feel sad, however, and the arrival of Ephraim Blount, carrying a pile of papers and demanding some immediate decisions, served to invigorate rather than depress her.

He bowed to her, before he stood and presented each problem to her—he never consented to sit by her while they worked together, for Ephraim, although only in early middle age, was a man of the old school. Everything must be done exactly so, as Louis Blanchard had taught him, which was sometimes a disadvantage rather than an advantage, as Stacy had often found. Imagination was not his strong suit. He was often mournfully depressed, rather than happy, when some of her wilder innovations proved to be fruitful. 'So daring for a young woman,' he was given to murmuring to his own assistant, the young Thomas Telfer, who worshipped Stacy from afar, 'but I have to admit that up to the present Miss Blanchard's judgement has never let herself, or the Bank, down.'

Prim, starched, his thinning yellow hair brushed stiffly over his forehead, he was the perfect right-hand man. Now he was saying, his voice melancholy, as though announcing a death, 'Things are not going well at the York house, madam. All seems to be at sixes and sevens since Poxon was appointed. I fear that he is not up to snuff. Something needs to be done, or Blanchard's reputation will suffer. May I suggest that, given your agreement, of course, I myself go there to try to put matters straight?'

Stacy propped her chin in both hands—a gesture of her father's which always brought that formidable thruster to Ephraim's mind. She looked steadily past him at the opposite wall, to where, before the blazing fire, Louisa was now gently sleeping. She no longer took her chaperonage of Stacy, when the latter was entertaining the Bank's employees—all male—seriously.

'D'you know, Ephraim, I have my doubts about the wisdom of that? I think that one of the things which may be wrong at York is that no Blanchard has visited there since my father died. I wish to remedy that. My aunt and uncle Beauchamp have asked me to spend Christmas with them at Bramham Castle, which is only a few miles from York. We have not met since Father's death, and to agree to their wishes would mean that I could combine business with pleasure—and leave you here in sole charge. You would like that, I think.'

If such a dry stick could be said to glow, Ephraim glowed. Stacy noted with amusement that he thought it politic to demur.

'Are you sure, madam? Think of the time of year. To travel to Yorkshire in mid-winter—is it wise?'

'Before the snows, I think,' Stacy murmured gravely. 'It is what my father would have done, I am sure.'

She had struck exactly the right note. Louis Blanchard had been Ephraim's god, and he bowed down before his very name. 'Oh, indeed, madam, yes, madam. Of all things the most suitable. You will take one of our senior clerks with you, I trust, to act as a secretary and aide?'

'Greaves, I thought,' murmured Stacy, happy to have got her own way so easily, 'unless you have any objections?'

'None at all, madam. The very man.' He was trying to contain his pleasure at the prospect of taking sole charge of Blanchard's for at least two months—something which he had longed to do since his late master's death. 'I will write at once and set all in train.' And he bustled importantly out of the room.

Stacy lay back in her chair and contemplated the prospect of a few weeks' freedom from the daily grind of running Blanchard's. Lately she had begun to feel strangely restless, rewarding though her work was, and the power that came with it. A change of scene, the challenge of putting York straight would renew her spirits, she was sure. All that remained was to waken Louisa up and shock her with the news.

'God rest you merry, gentlemen,' she hummed to herself. Perhaps I may hear the waits singing in the northern snows, she thought, and perhaps. . .perhaps. . . I might meet someone more interesting, more to my taste, than Lord Axforde and his not so merry gentlemen-friends!

She walked across the room and bent to kiss Louisa gently on the cheek. She was sure that after her first shock was over Louisa would approve of what she was about to do—and would start to wonder what handsome and eligible young men, of whom her charge might approve, lived in and around York!

'Damn my father,' said Matthew Falconer violently to the lawyer who had been speaking of his parent's wish to be reconciled with his long-estranged son. 'I haven't crossed the Atlantic in order to please him—simply to end my associations here by disposing of all that I own, including this estate which my great-aunt has thought fit to leave me.'

'But, m'lord——' the lawyer began, in a feeble attempt to pacify the massive man who stood opposite him. Matthew Falconer was over six feet tall, and gave the appearance of being nearly as broad. His harshly handsome face, leonine beneath tawny hair, with matching golden eyes, bore the marks of his having worked in the open. His hands, Lawyer Grimes had already noticed, were those of a man who did much physical work with them. His nails were cut short, and there were calluses on his long fingers and on his palms. He was dressed like a farmer—plainly—with nothing of the man of fashion he had once been remaining to hint of his lineage, or of his newly acquired title.

Which he didn't want. He hadn't come to England to be called by his detested brother's name. He interrupted Grimes to say, 'I will not be addressed as Lord Radley—nor will you call me m'lord or sir,' he added as he saw the lawyer's mouth shaping to say it. 'You will address me as Matthew, Matt, Mr Falconer, or Falconer, as you please, or earn my instant displeasure.'

He saw Grimes close his eyes before he replied in a long-suffering voice, 'I will do as you ask, Mr Falconer, but that does not make you less the Viscount Radley, your father, the Earl Falconer's heir, now that your older brother has died so prematurely.'

The man standing by the window, staring sardonically at both Matt Falconer and the lawyer, gave a rolling chuckle before saying in a thick American accent, 'Y'all better learn soon, Mr Lawyer, sir, that what Matt Falconer wants Matt Falconer usually gets. That so, Matt?'

Matt noted with grim amusement the lawyer's wince away from them both, particularly from Jeb Priestly, who, in his determinedly Yankee garb of black and yellow checked trousers, tight at the knee, flaring at the ankle, his black frock-coat extravagantly cut, and his battered black top hat, which he had refused to remove in defiance of all English custom, stood for everything which Benjamin Grimes deplored. A mannerless rebel come to mock his late masters.

Worse, Matthew Falconer was allowing this creature, who was merely his valet-cum-secretary-cum-man-of-all-work, to address him as familiarly as though they were both of the same rank, and made no effort to check his rudeness to Grimes himself.

'I say again, Mr Falconer, before we even begin to dispose of your late great-aunt, Lady Emily Falconer's estate in Yorkshire, that you ought to consider the olive-branch which your father is holding out to you. You are, after all, his only remaining son. . .'

Matt found all this boring beyond belief. 'Why, sir, do you persist in telling me things I know? I am well aware of my position *vis-à-vis* both my father and Lady Emily. So far as the Earl is concerned you may tell him, with my compliments, *timeo Danaos et dona ferentis*. I am sure that he will know what I mean.' This last came out in a mocking drawl reminiscent of the young rattle-pate about town he had once been, so different from the large and sombre man he now was. He could see the lawyer registering shock again.

Priestley saw fit to put his oar in once more. 'Well, your pa might know what you mean by that gibberish, Matt, but, sure God, I don't. Try translating it into good American, would you?'

Matt knew that Priestley was, in his words, twisting the lawyer's tail. Uncouth he might look and sound, but his knowledge of the Classics equalled Matt's own, he being an alumnus of Harvard. Nevertheless, Matt decided to join in Jeb's game.

'It translates, Jeb, being said by a Trojan with whom the Greeks were fighting, into, "I fear the Greeks even when they bring gifts", or, in other words, It is dangerous to accept presents from an enemy.'

'Tro-jans,' drawled Priestley. 'An' which are you, Matt?'

'A Trojan, of course,' smiled Matt, 'ever since I was born to be my father's curse. Isn't that right, Mr Grimes? How many ultimatums had you the honour to face me with until the final one before I left England? No, don't answer; it would tax your memory to recall them all.'

Grimes' face flamed scarlet. He looked away at the shelves of law books on the wall behind his desk, and said in a low voice, 'I suppose it is useless to tell you how much

I regretted m'lord's treatment of you, Mr Falconer, but I must also tell you that your father is a broken old man. . .'

'Only that, I suppose,' returned Matt, his eyes wicked, 'could bring him to wish to see me again—and Rollo's death, of course. That must have been the final facer.'

'You are pleased to be heartless. . .'

'My father cut my heart out long ago,' returned Matt carelessly. He was suddenly regretful of his baiting of the old man who had been the scourge of his childhood, youth and young manhood, until he had finally left England nearly twelve years ago, and added, a trifle stiffly, 'I am wrong to allow my dislike of my father to take the form of tormenting you. You were kind to me, I remember, when I was invalided out of the Navy after Trafalgar, and no one else was.'

'You brought your own doom on you,' Grimes could not help retorting, 'when you ran off with your brother's wife. My sympathy for you died on that day.' He saw Priestly's face change, and knew that here was something Matt Falconer's impertinent shadow had not known.

Matt Falconer was not nonplussed. He was no longer the eager boy who had yearned for his father's love and whom his father's lawyer could patronise.

'Leave that,' he ordered in his quarterdeck voice. 'It has nothing to do with you, or with the business I have come to settle.'

But Grimes must have thought he had found a chink in Matt's armour, although Matt was not conscious of possessing one, for he continued, although in a lower tone, 'And her death does not lie on your conscience, Mr Falconer?'

Oh, the old man did have weapons to fight with after all! Matt closed his eyes, only for a sad and beautiful long-dead face to swim before them. The memories that face recalled had him swinging away from both men. For the first time in the interview he was struggling for self-control.

'I lost my conscience with my heart,' he asserted stiffly. 'And if you refer to my late sister-in-law again, I shall leave this office and England within the day, and you, my inheritance from Lady Emily and my father may all go to the devil. Is that plain enough for you, sir?'

Matt was himself again—cold, strong and unshakeable, the man whom Jeb Priestley had always known, and whom the lawyer had never met. After that they returned to the business at hand, Grimes recognising that the man before him would never agree to any of his father's demands, and consequently now wishful to settle the matter of the inheritance as rapidly as possible.

Pontisford Hall, his late great-aunt's home on the borders of Nottinghamshire and Yorkshire, was the last reminder of Matt's childhood, and the only happy one. He had a sudden burning wish to see it. He remembered warmth and love, and a place where he, as well as his older brother, had been welcome. Before he had reached England, on the boat over, re-reading the letter which told him of his great-aunt's death and his inheritance, he had resolved to sell the Hall and its contents, to raise capital to enlarge his Virginia plantation, and partly rebuild and beautify the stark house which he called home.

But stepping ashore in England, travelling to London, seeing that great city's sights, smelling its unique smell, had reminded him agonisingly of his past, of his youth, before the world had fallen in on him. He had a sudden yearning to revisit the scenes of his childhood—if only to say goodbye to them before he parted from his homeland for the last time.

He said nothing of this to Grimes, merely, 'I shall travel to Yorkshire, sir, to pay my respects to Lady Emily's tomb in Pontisford church, and to visit the Hall for the last time.

She was kind to me, and I must not let her go without a proper farewell. You will inform the staff there of my proposed arrival. I shall set out as soon as I have completed other urgent matters here.'

Matt could imagine Jeb's raised and mocking eyebrows at this rare display of sentiment, and the silent cynicism of the old lawyer, but damn that for a tale. When he had reached his middle thirties a man had the right to say goodbye to his youth.

And so it was settled. Mr Grimes did not pry into his client's life. He assumed that Matthew Falconer had not married while in the United States, for there was no talk of a wife. He assumed that he had had some success as a plantation owner, but made no move to discover how much of a success. If the grim man before him wished him to know these things he would have told him. Once or twice he sighed for the carefree young man he had once known, who had faced life with a smile despite his father's displeasure, but it was plain that that man was long gone.

Business was done, and done quickly—after the fashion of Yankees, Grimes presumed. The old Matt Falconer had never been businesslike, or hard. Now he was both. He even kept his insolent man on a tight rein while he and the lawyer went through the necessary business of establishing identity, examining Lady Emily's will, and signing and witnessing the necessary documentation.

It was soon all over, and Matt and his man were in the street, holding their top hats on, braving the keen wind of early November, before Jeb spoke again.

'Well, there's a fine tale, Matt. Did you really run off with your brother's wife?'

'Yes, but not for the reason you might think.' For once he was short with Jeb. Revisiting England must have made his memories keen again. He thought he had been rid of that old pain long ago.

'Why, what other reason is there?'

Which, of course, was what everyone had said at the time. Matt replied, in what Jeb always thought of as his 'damn-your-eyes' aristocrat's voice, which he had rarely used in the good old United States, 'Nothing to do with you, Jeb. You may have the rest of the day to yourself. I shall meet you for supper at Brown's this evening. We shall set out for Yorkshire as soon as I can organise suitable travel arrangements.'

There was no brooking him in this mood. Jeb rearranged his face, pulled a servile forelock, bowed low, mumbled, 'Yes, massa, certainly, massa,' a ritual which usually drew an unwilling grin from Matt. But not today. Today he was unmoved, immovable, and his shadow, wondering where his master was going, would have been surprised to learn that he ended the afternoon in a church, before a marble memorial consisting of an urn held by a weeping Niobe whose inscription simply read, 'To the memory of Camilla Falconer, Lady Radley, 1785–1806, cut down in her youth. . . "Cometh forth like a flower".'

Naturally there were no pious words chiselled into the marble about loving wives or grieving husbands, and she was buried far from her home and friends, forgotten, probably, by everyone except the grieving man who had come to pay her his last respects too.

CHAPTER TWO

EVERYTHING, but everything, had gone wrong from the moment they had left the confines of the Home Counties. Stacy thought that there must be a curse on the journey, her first of any length since her father had died.

And it had all gone so beautifully right at first— inevitably, with Ephraim and herself arranging things. She was to travel incognito; it would not do to let possible men of the road know that the enormously rich owner of Blanchard's Bank was travelling nearly the length of England in winter. Safety lay in anonymity. She was to be Miss Anna Berriman, to match the initials stamped on her luggage and entwined on the panels of her elegant travelling coach. Polly Clay, her personal maid, and the other servants had been carefully coached for the last fortnight before they set out to address her as, 'Yes, Miss Berriman', 'Indeed, Miss Berriman', 'As you wish, Miss Berriman', until Stacy had almost come to believe herself Miss Berriman in truth.

They were taking two coaches to accommodate Stacy, Miss Landen, Polly, James the footman, young Mr Greaves and his man, a coachman, and a spare footman, Hal, a big strong man, to act as yet another guardian to the party. It occurred to Stacy, as she watched the two post-chaises being loaded with luggage and impedimenta, that throughout her life she had rarely been alone, and for a moment she wondered what it would have been like truly to be not-so-rich Miss Berriman, who was no more and no less than an ordinary, unconsidered spinster. She decided that the uncomfortable truth was that on the whole she would not have liked it. She had grown used to being in command in exactly the same way as a man would have been.

It was while they were crossing from Lincolnshire into Nottinghamshire through heavy rain, after an unpleasant night in a dirty inn, that Greaves' cold, which had been merely an inconvenience to him, became much more than that. From her seat opposite him Stacy watched his complexion turn from yellow to grey to ashen, tinged with the scarlet of heavy inflammation round his eyes, nostrils and mouth. Her concern grew with each mile that they jolted forward, until she ordered the coach to stop when they reached Newark.

'Greaves,' she said, genuinely troubled, 'I do not think that we should go further today. You look very ill.'

Louisa nodded her head, agreeing with her, while Greaves muttered in a hoarse voice—his throat was badly affected—'I feel very ill, madam, but. . .'

'No buts. . .' Stacy was both brisk and firm. 'We shall stop at the first good inn in Newark, put you to bed and send for a physician. I do not think that you are in any condition to continue.'

He didn't argue with her, nor, a day later when the physician had said that his fever was a severe one and he must not rise from his bed, did he or Stacy argue that anything other was to be done than leave him at the inn, with sufficient funds, one of the coaches, his man and James, the senior of the two footmen, to follow after Stacy's party as soon as the physician pronounced him well enough to travel. 'Which will be some days yet, I fear,' he said.

So now the single coach toiled onwards towards York, through the East Midlands counties and beyond—land which Stacy had not seen since she was a small girl. Alas, the further north they went, the worse the weather grew. The rain turned into an unpleasant sleet, and even the stone hot-water bottles and travelling warming-pans, wrapped in woollen muffs and kept on all the travellers' knees, were hardly enough to keep them warm as the temperature continued to drop.

Ruefully Stacy privately conceded that Ephraim Blount had been right to worry about her going north in winter, until, at the beginning of the stage where they were due to pass from Nottinghamshire into Yorkshire, her party woke up to find a brilliant sun shining and the sky a cold blue. Everyone, including Stacy, felt happy again.

Everyone, that was, but Louisa Landen, who had endured a bad night and suspected that she had caught Greaves' cold, but, being stoical by nature and knowing that it was necessary to make up the time lost in caring for Greaves, decided to say nothing of it to Stacy. The cold might not grow worse—and besides, the day was fine.

Except that the landlord of the Gate Hangs Well had shaken his head at them, and before they set out had said gloomily to John Coachman and the postilion they were taking on to the next stage, 'Fine weather for snow, this, maister.' John Coachman, however, who wished to press on to make up for lost time, had decided that such country lore was not worth the breath given to offer it, and that he would ignore the warning.

It was a decision that he would come to regret.

Stacy was already regretting her ill-fated winter journey to York. She was to regret it even more as, towards noon, when they were still far from journey's end, the weather suddenly changed; the sun disappeared, it became cloudy, dark and cold, and the bottles and warming-pans grew cold too. Louisa began to cough, a dry, insistent cough, which had Stacy at last registering her companion's wan face, with a hectic spot on each cheekbone.

'Oh, Louisa, my dear!' she exclaimed, taking her companion's cold hand in hers. 'I have been so selfish, wishing to make good time and not thinking of anything but my own convenience. You have caught Greaves' cold, and we ought not to have journeyed on today. You should have told me.'

Louisa shook her head and croaked, 'My fault—I said nothing because we are not so far from our journey's end, and I knew you wished to make good time today since the weather seemed to have taken a turn for the better. I must confess I did not think that I would feel so ill so soon.' She had begun to shiver violently, and it was plain that she was in a state of extreme distress.

The shivering grew worse, almost in time with the snow which had begun to fall, turning into a regular blizzard. By the early afternoon they were making only slow progress into territory where it was plain that snow had fallen during the night, and only the fact that a few carriages had passed earlier, leaving ruts for them to drive in, kept them going at all.

John Coachman had consulted his roadbook, and had already told Stacy bluntly that they would be unlikely to find a suitable inn to stop at before Bawtry, which they had originally planned to make for. They were now, he said, in an area where hostelries with beds were few and far between. 'We'd best be on our way, madam, or night will fall or the road become impassable before we reach the inn.'

The prospect of being trapped by the snow and spending the night in the coach was not a pretty one. Polly's lip trembled, but the sight of Louisa lying silent in Stacy's arms kept her silent too.

Night fell early, and John Coachman was now gloomily aware that he must, in the dark among the snowdrifts, have taken a wrong turning, for he had no idea where they were, only that they were lost—something he didn't see fit to tell his mistress. He called for directions to the postilion who was riding the near horse, who shouted back, 'I'm as lost as you are, maister. Mayhap we're nigh to Pontisford,' which was no help at all, as there was no Pontisford in John's book.

Worse, the road was growing impassable, and only the sight of the lights of a big house, dim among trees, gave him some hope that he might be able to drive them all there safely—perhaps to find shelter for the night.

He had no sooner made this decision, and told the postilion of it, than the horses, tired by their long exertions, slithered into a ditch which had been masked by the drifting snow. The coach tilted and was dragged along for a few feet before toppling slowly on to its side.

Hal, the footman, who was riding outside, was thrown clear. John, less fortunate, was caught up in the reins, and before he could free himself completely one of the falling boxes of luggage which had been stowed on top of the coach struck him a shattering blow on the arm, fortunately not breaking it.

Somehow avoiding the plunging horses, he fell across poor Hal, who was trying to rise, winding him all over again. The postilion had also been thrown clear, only to strike his head on a tree-trunk and fall stunned into the freezing ditch-water. They were later to discover that one of the horses had been killed in the fall, breaking its neck instantly.

The three passengers inside were flung from their seats to land half on the floor, half across the door next to the ground. Stacy, when everything had subsided, found herself with Louisa still in her arms and Polly, on top of both of them, gasping and moaning, her wrist having been injured in the fall.

Stunned and bruised, but happy to be alive, Stacy could only register that their ill-fated odyssey was at an end, and that she was somewhere in North Nottinghamshire, but where she had no idea. . .

* * *

Matt Falconer was wishing himself anywhere but in North Nottinghamshire. He and Jeb had arrived at Pontisford Hall two days earlier, after a hard and uncomfortable journey in a hired post-chaise which had stunk vilely of tobacco and ale.

All the hard and jolting way to North Nottinghamshire he had sustained himself with the thought of the comfortable billet which was waiting for them at journey's end. The sardonic mode which ruled his life these days had told him later that if it were better to travel than to arrive then he might have guessed what he would find!

He had dismounted from the chaise in the dark of the November afternoon, the first snow of winter beginning to fall, to be greeted by an ill-clad bent old man whom Matt, with difficulty, had identified as Horrocks, the butler, whom he had last seen fifteen years ago as a man still hale and hearty.

'And who the devil may you be, sirs,' he had quavered at them, 'to stop at Pontisford? There are none here to entertain you since my mistress died—only a few of the old retainers who cared for her are still living at the Hall.'

Matt had blinked at him. 'Don't you recognise me, Horrocks? It's Matt Falconer. My aunt left me the Hall and I have come to claim my inheritance.'

The old man lifted the lantern he was carrying to inspect his face. He shook his head. 'Master Matt, is it? Lord, sir, I would never have known you. You've changed.'

'So have we all,' Matt told him gently. 'Are you going to let us in?' He pointed at Jeb and the shivering driver.

'Aye, but I warn you there's little to eat and little to warm yourselves with,' mourned Horrocks as he led them indoors. 'No money's come in since Lady Emily died, and we had little enough before that.'

Grimes had said nothing of this. Matt asked urgently, 'And Lady Emily's agent, where is he?'

'Gone, Mr Matt. With the money. He upped and left

two months ago, his pockets well-lined with all he'd stolen from the estate. But Lady Emily wouldn't hear a word against him. Wandering in her mind, she was. I wrote to Lawyer Grimes, but by chance the letter went astray.'

Matt could only suppose that it had. He didn't suspect Grimes of wrongdoing, only carelessness about matters taking place so far from London. He heard Jeb giving suppressed snorts of laughter as they entered the derelict house of which Matt had talked with such enthusiasm on the way north. It was plain that Lady Emily must have fallen into her dotage unable to control her life, for Horrocks' lantern showed the entrance hall to be dank and cold, the statuary and furniture covered in filthy dust-sheets, the chandeliers empty of candles, the smell of must and mould everywhere. And the whole house was the same. There was a scuttle of rats in the wainscoting of an unheated drawing-room which Matt remembered as full of warmth and light and love.

His aunt had died earlier in the year in her late seventies, and, by what Horrocks had said, having been pillaged by her agent. Her mind wandering, she had seen Pontisford as it had been, and not as it was.

'Turned nearly all the servants away, didn't he?' quavered Horrocks. 'Only left enough to keep m'lady fed and bedded. Short commons, we was on, while he lived in comfort in his cottage with his doxy—you remember miller's Nell, Master Matt?'

Yes, Master Matt remembered miller's Nell. She had educated him in the coarser arts of love the year he had reached fifteen, on the edge of the park not far from the ford in the Pont from which the Hall and village took its name. He shook his head, avoided Jeb's eye, and asked to go to the kitchen. Which was, as he had expected, the only warm room in the house.

The cook, a blowsy fat woman, stared coldly at him, bobbed an unwilling curtsy when told who he was, and grudgingly hung the big cauldron, which he remembered from his childhood visits, above the fire to make them tea. Bread was fetched from a cupboard, and a side of salt beef from which she carved coarse chunks of meat to fling at them on cracked plates. It was all as different from Matt's memories as anything could be.

A thin-faced serving-girl peered at them before being bade to 'Take the master's food into the drawing-room as was proper'.

Jeb finally broke at this point, spluttering with laughter, and said, 'By God, she'd better not do any such thing. I've no mind to freeze to death while sharing my meal with the rats.'

Matt would have joined in his laughter except for the agonised expression on Horrocks' face—he shamedly remembering other, better days.

'Right, Jeb, we'll eat before the fire. At least this room is warm.'

The kitchen door was flung open and a hard-faced woman bounced in. 'What's going on in here, Cook? Entertaining chance-met strangers, are we? Not in my house.'

It was Matt's turn to break. Bereft of his childhood's dreams, unknown in the house where he had been known and loved, he said as coldly as he could, 'Your house, madam? You are, then, Lady Emily Falconer?'

The woman drew herself up. 'I was the late Lady Emily's housekeeper, I'll have you know, and as such it is my duty to see that the servants here do their duty. I'll thank you to leave.'

Matt walked to the window to pull back the ragged curtain and reveal the snow falling relentlessly outside, 'No, madam. It is you who must leave. Were it not for the weather I should turn you out this instant, for it is all you deserve if you say that you are responsible for the state which the Hall is in. I am Matthew Falconer, Lord

Radley, and my aunt has left me this house and her estate.'

He was aware of Jeb staring at him, jaw dropped, aware that he had never sounded more like his stern and detested father, and that, for the first time, he had laid claim to the title which he had vowed he would never assume.

The woman before him clapped her hands to her mouth. 'M'lord, if I had known who you were. . .'

'You had no need to know,' Matt returned savagely. 'On such a night as this it was Lady Emily's habit to care for any lonely travellers who might need shelter. The fact that I am your master is neither here nor there. You will see, at once, that beds are prepared for Mr Priestley and myself, and a fire will be lit in the drawing-room and candles provided, and if there are any able-bodied men about they will begin to clear out the rats which have invaded the house. You will work until the weather allows you to leave, madam, taking your wages for the present quarter with you. See to it.'

He had turned his back on her as she'd run to do his bidding, but as he was saying now to Jeb, two days later, 'It is of no use. Cut off by the snow as we are, with only one half-witted boy besides Horrocks and the cook, and two young girls as maids, and little in the way of food and means to make fires and warm the place. . .' He shrugged. 'There is little that can be done to improve the condition of Pontisford Hall. It needs time and an army of workers, and I have no mind to organise it. Sell up and go back to Virginia, I say.'

The shivering Jeb nodded agreement. They were huddled over the drawing-room fire, with two small tallow candles to give them light, wax ones being unknown at Pontisford. Matt had insisted on using the room for part of the day, carrying wood and coals through himself to light the fire to ease the burden on Horrocks and the half-witted boy, Jake.

'We shall leave when the snowstorm stops, and I shall put the Runners on the track of that damned agent, and see him swing before I leave England.'

Jeb said, his teeth chattering, 'And then you can turn back into cheerful Matt Falconer again. I can't say I care much for Lord Radley.'

'Nor do I,' returned Matt. He walked restlessly to the window to look out at the grim scene. The snowstorm had abated and the moonlight showed a white and icy world. 'I'm sorry for anyone out on a night like this. . .' And then, 'What the devil's that?' For someone was beating a tattoo on the big front door and shouting above the noise of the gale.

He seized the second candle, said, 'I'll go. Poor old Horrocks will take an age to answer the door and the poor devils outside will be dead of cold before he gets there. You stay here and try to warm yourself.' He crossed the dim entrance hall, shouting, 'I'm coming, I'm coming,' as the knocking redoubled, and then as those outside found the bell it began pealing vigorously—as Horrocks said in the kitchen,

'Enough to wake the dead.'

Afterwards Stacy could hardly remember how her small party had made its way from the fallen coach to Pontisford Hall. One horse was dead, and another, which Hal and John released from its traces, escaped from their numbed hands and bolted into the distance.

They were more careful with the other two, and they and the recovered postilion put John and Louisa, now barely conscious, on the third horse, and Hall, with the injured Polly riding precariously sideways behind him, on the fourth. Stacy, oblivious to Polly's wails that it wasn't fitting for her to walk, helped the postilion to lead them along the lane and up the winding drive to the Hall, trying to avoid ditches and other obstacles, unseen because of the blanket of snow.

Fortunately the snowstorm was gradually abating and a wintry moon came out, which seemed to make the cold worse. None of the party was dressed to be outdoors in such cruel weather. John had put a horse-blanket around Louisa and had covered Stacy with the blanket from the box, which, even if it smelled dreadfully of horse, gave her a little warmth.

The one thing which kept Stacy on her feet and walking was what awaited her at journey's end. A warm house, a comfortable bed, food and succour, perhaps even some inspiriting conversation after the trivialities of the past few days. The very notion made her blood course more rapidly, kept her head high and her spirits from flagging.

Hal slid off his horse as they reached the steps leading up to the entrance of the Hall, which the moon had already revealed to be a massive and brilliant structure, built in the Palladian style. It was a smaller version of the Duke of Devonshire's villa at Chiswick, although by now Stacy was incapable of registering such architectural niceties.

She followed Hal up the steps, leaving John still cradling poor Louisa in his arms and trying to keep her out of the wind. It seemed to take ages for the door to open, and when it did she eagerly walked forward to say to the butler who had answered it, 'My name is Miss Anna Berriman. The chaise taking us to York has broken down and we are in need of shelter and succour for the night, and men to rescue the chaise tomorrow morning, check the damage and arrange for it to be repaired. Please inform your master of our arrival.'

All this came out in her usual coldly efficient manner, the manner which set everyone at her home and at Blanchard's Bank scurrying about to do her bidding without argument. For a moment, however, the man before her did and said nothing. By the light of the dim candle he was holding she could merely see that he was very large, and only when the moon came from behind a cloud was she able to see him fully for the first time.

He was not wearing any sort of livery but a rough grey country coat and a pair of black breeches. His cravat was a strange loose thing, black, not white, made of silk, with a silver pin in it. The only immaculate thing about him was his boots. A butler wearing boots! His whole aspect was leonine; tawny hair and eyes, a grim, snapping mouth—she was sure it was a snapping mouth. Who in the world would allow a servant to dress like this?

He seemed about to say something, and his mouth quivered, but he simply waved a hand and enunciated—there was no other word for it—curtly, 'Enter. We have little enough to help you with, but what we can do we will do.'

Well, on top of everything else he was certainly the most mannerless churl it had ever been her misfortune to meet! His harsh voice was as strange as the rest of him. There was an accent in it which she had never heard before. Now he was turning away, without so much as a by your leave to her, and motioning them in.

For a moment Stacy had a mind to reprimand him, but then she remembered poor Louisa. It was no time to be training servants.

'My poor companion has a bad fever,' she told the broad back before her, making her voice as commanding as she could—she was not used to being treated in such a cavalier fashion by anyone, let alone a servant—'and I think she ought to be put to bed in a warm room immediately.'

The butler turned around, to show her his leonine mask again. He really was the most extraordinary-looking creature, strangely handsome, almost. 'That may be a little difficult, *madam*.'

Was it her imagination, or had there been something unpleasantly sneering in the way in which he had said the last word? Stacy, followed by her small party, who were looking about them in astonishment at the decayed state of the entrance hall, continued to walk on until she said, 'I find it difficult to believe that your master would refuse warmth and shelter to forlorn travellers. . .' She stopped, indicating that she wished to know his name, and as he turned around just as they reached a large baize-covered door he apparently read her mind for he said, head bowed, almost in parody of a servant, 'Matt, madam. You may call me Matt.'

May I, indeed? was her inward angry thought, but, about to say something really sharp, she was stopped by Matt—could that really be his name?—checking his stride to say to John Coachman, who was carrying Louisa and was staggering with weariness, 'You're out on your feet, man; give me the lady,' and he lifted poor Louisa out of John's arms to carry her himself.

He waved at Hal to open the door. Hal was nearly as shocked as his mistress by this strange ménage and even stranger servant—as he was later to say to the assembled staff at Bramham Castle, when Stacy finally reached there, 'I were fairly gobsmacked by it all, and no mistake.'

At last, Stacy thought, comfort and succour. The whole party felt as though their life had been suddenly renewed—but what was this? They were in the kitchens, where, although they didn't know it, for the first time in years the great fireplace had been properly cleaned. Jeb had retreated to its comfortable warmth when Matt had left the drawing-room.

Behind her Stacy felt her party shuffle their feet and begin to hem and haw. The butler laid Louisa gently down on a settle in the corner of the huge, high-vaulted room, and, taking a blanket from a cupboard, put it over her. She surfaced for a moment to say blindly, 'Where are we?' before lasping back into semi-delirium again.

'You have brought us to the kitchens,' announced Stacy dramatically. 'Kindly inform your master of our arrival. I am sure he will order you to prepare somewhere more suitable for us.'

She was uncomfortably aware that not only were her feet frozen, but that her light boots were soaked as a result of her long trudge through wet snow. Approving of being shown into the kitchens or not, she found herself holding her skirts before the huge fire in an attempt to dry them. She would wait to remove her boots until she finally reached a comfortable bedroom. The rest of her party were clustering round the fire, which was large enough to heat even this most cavernous of kitchens. Steam was beginning to rise from their wet clothes.

Jeb, who was finding life in the frozen wastes of northern England even more amusing than he had anticipated, if not exactly comfortable, gave a snort of laughter on hearing Stacy's orders. Horrocks, whose wits seemed to decline daily, began to speak, caught Matt's stern eye, and thought better of it.

Matt Falconer offered the stone-faced termagant who was speaking to him so brusquely his hardest stare. All the pent-up anger created by this wretched visit to England, compounded by what he had found at Pontisford Hall, was making him behave in a manner totally unlike that of his usual good-humoured self.

Oh, yes, he's Lord Radley to a T, thought Jeb gleefully, guessing what was passing through Matt's mind as he was addressed so peremptorily, and this icy-faced bitch had better watch her step. He's had a hard time lately, has our Matt, and someone is going to pay for it.

Matt was thinking the same thing. What a shrew! She hadn't even the decency to enter the house before she was throwing orders about like confetti. She deserved a few lessons in good manners, if not to say due humility. Never mind if she had had to endure the storm and a wrecked coach—that was no reason for her to carry on like a mixture of the Queen of Sheba and Catherine the bloody Great rolled into one.

'There are no warm rooms other than this one,' he announced, his voice as cold as the snow outside. 'We shall all have to sleep down here tonight. By tomorrow some of the bedrooms may be fit for habitation, and if so I shall arrange for them to be made ready for you. Kate,' he told the little maid, who was helping Polly into a chair and exclaiming over her damaged wrist which Stacy had bound up with a length torn from the bottom of her petticoat, 'go and fetch Mrs Green from her room. And Cook, the soup left over from dinner can be heated up to stop these poor folk from dying of the cold.'

He stretched out a booted foot to kick one of the logs on the fire into a more useful position. 'And you, madam,' he added, drawing up a tall Windsor chair, 'may sit here—unless, that is, you care to make yourself useful. You seem to have come out of this accident more fortunately than the rest of your party. Instead of shouting the odds about what we are all to do, you would be better employed doing something yourself.'

Matt watched with a wicked delight as the shrew began to say something, then bit her tongue before the words could fly out. Stacy wanted to scream at him that she and the postilion, who was now on his knees before the fire with his frozen hands held out to it, had trudged more than a mile through the snow while the rest of the party had ridden, but her pride forbade it. She would not bandy words with servants; she would not.

If the half-conscious Louisa Landen had ever wondered how her wilful charge would fare when faced by someone with a will as strong as her own, and who did not give a damn for her name and fame, which he didn't know in any case, she was soon to find out.

Hal walked up to her, his face worried, to say in a low voice before she sat down, 'He should not speak to you as he does, mistress. Let me tell him who you are. That should silence his impudent tongue.'

'No, I forbid it,' Stacy whispered fiercely at him. 'On no account—and you may tell John Coachman and Polly the same. We shall not be here long, I trust, and I do not bandy words with servants.'

Hal was doubtful. 'As you wish, mistress.'

'I do wish, and now go and sit down. You have had a hard day.'

She sat down herself, in the chair which the butler had earlier offered her, and began to pull off her ruined boots, seeing that she was not going to be offered a decent room of her own in which to do so, only to discover that her stockings were as wet as they were. Which did not improve her temper, for she could see that there was no way which she could pull them off surrounded as she was by staring underlings, some of whom seemed to be taking a delight in her discomfort. She put her boots before the fire to dry after first helping Polly to remove hers; her damaged wrist was making life difficult for her.

The little maid had set out coarse pottery soup bowls and an odd assortment of servants' hall cutlery on the big scrubbed table, and presently the cook ladled out a thick vegetable soup for them all. Stacy's party set to work with a will, being hungry as well as tired. Even Stacy swallowed the greasy stuff, although it nearly choked her. Matt had left the kitchen for a short time, to return with blankets and pillows which he put to warm before the fire before making up an impromptu bed for Louisa.

Jeb had accompanied him, saying with a grin as he helped to collect bedlinen, 'Come on, Matt, put the poor bitch out of her misery and tell her who you are. She's in an agony about having to argue with a butler.'

'Not. . .likely,' Matt had sworn. 'She's just the kind of useless fine lady I thought that I'd left behind for good. Full of her own importance and fit for nothing but embroidery and spiteful gossip!'

He had said this with such venom that, not for the first time since he had heard of the scandal in which his master had been involved, Jeb had been curious about the details of it.

'You'll have to tell her some time—and soon,' he had argued.

'But not yet. Let the shrew sweat.'

Jeb had shrugged, and later he was a little surprised to discover that it was the fine lady herself who fed Louisa, whom the kitchen's warmth had restored to consciousness, sitting by her on her impromptu bed and spooning the soup gently into her unwilling mouth. 'Come on, my love. You won't help yourself by starving,' she coaxed, to be rewarded by a watery smile.

After that Stacy insisted on looking after Polly's wrist, rubbing goose-grease salve on it which the cook had grudgingly fetched from her store-cupboard. Matt watched her with a puzzled expression on his face—he had not expected so much practical compassion from such a proud piece—only for him to lose it when Stacy said curtly to him, 'I would like to speak to your master now. At once, if you please!'

What on earth was the matter with the man? This perfectly ordinary request produced such an answering spark in his golden eyes, and such a savage twist to his lips, that it almost had Stacy stepping back in fear. She was trying to imagine what kind of master would tolerate such a. . .wild animal. . .as a butler. A dilatory one, obviously, who in his idleness let his servants do just as they pleased, for after a second's hesitation this most unlikely butler came out with, 'Oh, I daren't disturb him just now, madam. More than my job's worth, I should say.'

For some reason, after he had offered her this piece of insolence, the uncouth and strangely dressed Jeb—and what was his position in this zoo, if not to say menagerie, which apparently comprised the Hall's staff?—saw fit to fall into a fit of the sniggers. He had previously been engaged in flattering Polly, who was simpering and grinning at him in the most unseemly fashion. Were her own servants becoming infected by this disorderly crew?

Not Hal, who said bluntly to the butler, who had turned away to begin placing the used pots on the massive board by the large stone sink preparatory to beginning to wash them, 'Have a care how you speak to my mistress, man. What your master requires of you is one thing. What she deserves in respect from you is quite another.'

The butler turned to stare at Hal, who was belligerently squaring up to him. Big though he was, he was by no means a match in size for the butler who, now Stacy came to think of it, resembled a prize-fighter rather than an indoors servant.

'Oh,' he came out with, a faint smile on his face, 'but she doesn't pay my wages, does she?'

Which produced another snigger from Jeb, who, to stir this delightful pot even more, added, 'I doubt whether she could afford them.'

Hal turned on Jeb, enraged by his attentions to Polly, on whom he was sweet himself. 'Oh, and who the devil are you to tell me anything? And as for my mistress's ability to pay this yokel. . .'

'Hal!' Stacy used her very best voice on him, not loud but stern and compelling, the voice with which she had dragooned the employees of Blanchard's Bank into realising that here was no girlish and innocent chit to be ignored, but Louis Blanchard's true heir in person. 'Be quiet. I will not have any brawling here on my account.'

'What a wise conclusion,' the yokel—and what a splendid description of him that was—drawled amiably, beginning to wash pots with what even Stacy could see was exemplary speed and precision. 'Hal shouldn't begin on an enterprise which he can't win.'

This had the desired effect on Hal, of starting him off all over again. He had begun by defending his mistress from discourtesy, but he was now defending his own prowess. He advanced on the smiling butler with his fists raised. 'I'll have you know I work out at Jackson's gym. I've never seen you there, and that's a fact. Put up your dukes—or shut up.'

The only things the butler raised were his wet and soapy hands, which didn't stop Hal. 'Any excuse to dodge a fight,' he sneered, and threw a punch in the butler's direction.

For a moment Stacy was frozen by the unlikely revelation that Hal was not only her loyal servant, but also saw himself as her champion. At all costs she must not allow him to fight with the butler. Desperately she threw herself between the the two men to expostulate with them, to do anything which might stop the coming brawl.

All she stopped was Hal's fist. By good fortune she was struck only a glancing blow, but it was enough for her to see stars before she sat down, ignominiously and humiliatingly, on the kitchen floor. Through her swirling senses she heard Hal's cry of distress. 'Oh, mistress, God forgive me.'

She also heard the butler cursing under his breath, 'Oh, hell and damnation, what next?' as he put his soapy hands under her armpits and hauled her to her feet again.

Oh, God, what next, indeed? Would this dreadful evening never end? All that Stacy wanted was to be in her own comfortable bed, Polly in attendance, kind Louisa well and on her feet again, somewhere near by in loving attendance.

But what she got was something else entirely. The kitchen door opposite her opened abruptly to reveal to her dazed eyes a tall woman with a thin, hard face, decently dressed in black. The housekeeper presumably.

The woman took one comprehensive look at them all. At Stacy, white-faced and trembling. At Hal, now on his knees, agonised, begging forgiveness of her for his unintended blow. At Jeb, leaning against the wall, convulsed and chortling, 'Oh, Matt, boy, this is your finest turn ever. Better than a play.' At the assembled servants, both the Hall's and Stacy's, all either shocked or amused according to their preference, and lastly at the butler, a canvas apron round his waist, his soapy hands just releasing the now furious Stacy.

'And what,' the woman roared, happy to have a chance at getting back at the uncouth monster who had disrupted her easy life, and knowing that now she was under notice to leave she had nothing to lose by saucing him, 'is the meaning of this, m'lord? And why are you wearing Cook's apron and doing the washing-up?'

CHAPTER THREE

EVERYTHING, but everything, went into a weird kind of paralysis, as though time itself had stopped. For a long moment no one moved and no one spoke.

M'lord? Thought Stacy and all her party. *M'lord*? She must mean the butler. She can't mean the butler, can she? Can she?

But she did.

Stacy turned to face him. M'lord. Of course, she should have known. Everything about him radiated authority—which she had mistaken for insolence. For whatever goddamned reason—and really, her internal language was growing more impossible by the minute—the coarse brute had chosen to lie to her from the first moment that he had spoken to her.

She did something which she had never expected to do, something which no lady should ever have done—but then, she told herself grimly afterwards, I am no lady, and for sure, for all his title, he is no gentleman! She slapped him across the face with all her strength.

Her blow broke the paralysis which had afflicted them all. Hubbub ensued. Hal rose slowly to his feet, staring at this unlikely lordship. Jeb gave a whistling roar into the silence which followed Stacy's blow, and then began to clap his hands slowly. 'Well struck, madam,' he called to her from his post by the wall.

For his part Matt Falconer held his flaming cheek, and slowly admitted to himself that he should never have allowed his hot temper, long reined in during his years in the United States, to take him over now that he was back in England again and incite him to taunt this heastrong shrew—however much she had deserved it. And now least said, soonest mended. He picked up a towel and began to dry his hands.

He didn't immediately address Stacy but said, almost mildly, to the triumphant woman who was defying him, 'I told you not to call me m'lord, and I meant it. I am Matt, Mr Matt, or Mr Falconer to you.'

Stacy, overwhelmed by her own unladylike behaviour, conscious only of poor, sick Louisa's reproachful stare, murmured hollowly to him, 'She called you m'lord. Was that another lie in this house of liars, which you, the biggest liar of them all, are supremely fit to head?'

Matt held on to his temper. A hard feat, since he could see that the cross-grained bitch in front of him now had the upper hand, the moral hand, and would use it to provoke him further. She had a tongue like a striking adder, and no mistake.

'Strictly speaking, madam. . .'

Stacy, lost to everything, resembling, had she but known it, her father in one of his rare and formidable tempers, raged at him. 'You *can* speak strictly, then? I had thought insolence was more your line. But pray continue,' she added, poisonously sweet, as she saw him open his mouth. To explain presumably. But what explanation could mend this?

She no longer wanted her bed. She wanted to see m'lord whoever-he-was grovelling before her. Nothing less would do.

Matt decided not to bandy words with her. They had an audience, fascinated by the sight of their masters engaged in a ding-dong, knock-down quarrel in front of them, instead of it taking place decently in private. What a rare treat! And all the time in the world to enjoy it, since it was plain that they were all, except possibly the housekeeper, trapped in the kitchens for the night.

'Strictly speaking,' he said between his splendid teeth,

his eyes still defying her whatever his tongue might say, 'I am Matthew Falconer, Lord Radley—Earl Falconer's heir. I prefer, however, to be known as Matt Falconer.'

'Oh, I thought your preference was to be known as the butler,' returned Stacy nastily, green eyes flashing, while inwardly she said to herself, Matt Falconer—now wasn't he involved in some massive scandal when I was barely out of childhood? And no wonder, carrying on as he does.

'Something wrong with butlers, is there?' gritted Matt, his own eyes shooting fire as he immediately forgot the resolution which he had just made, that he would be unfailingly polite to this icy hellcat—could hellcats be icy?—and giving her what his old nurse had used to call 'what for' again. 'Unconsidered serfs, are they? I had sooner be a good butler than a bad nobleman any day.'

'And, of course, being who you are,' Stacy shot back, all discretion, all decency gone, now completely the true descendant of the rampantly outrageous pedlar who had made the Blanchard fortune, '*you* know all about bad noblemen, I'm sure!'

Jeb, who was busy counting the score for each side as though he were the referee at a boxing-match, saw that red rage was overcoming his employer. He had experienced it rarely, but he knew the signs. And for once Mad Matt had met his match in a woman whose icy deadliness equalled his fiery temperament.

How he mastered himself Matt never knew. Each fresh insult she offered him had him wishing that he could teach her a lesson, put her across his knee. . . Added to his rage was his sudden shocked horror at the knowledge that, of all dreadful things, he was becoming sexually roused.

What he really wanted to do was to take her in his arms, bear her to the floor and show her who was master. . .

He shook his head to clear it, rebuked his misbehaving body, and ground out, 'No useful purpose is served by our being at odds in this situation, madam. I apologise to you for my deception.' Which, had he ended there, might have done the trick, but the sight of her small contemptuous smile had him adding, 'Although you must admit that you did come on too strong from the beginning.'

Behind them Jeb gave a groan, and Hal, forgetting his mistress's orders, grew angry with the arrogant swine all over again. Lord he might be, but his mistress was right. He was no gentleman.

Stacy was also ready to restart the battle. Just because he was a man, an aristocrat, was big and strong, and, it must be admitted, in an odd way handsome, that was no reason for him to think that he could speak to her as he pleased, but as she opened her mouth to deliver another broadside she was stopped by her companion.

Louisa Landen had watched the affray with growing horror, and total surprise at seeing Stacy, who was usually so cool and controlled, so completely and utterly lost to all ladylike as well as decent behaviour. At first she had felt too weak to intervene, but was now so shocked by the behaviour of both parties that she cried feebly, 'Stacy, oh, Stacy. I feel so ill! Do leave off wrangling, my love, I need you.'

This had the effect of Stacy exclaiming remorsefully, 'Oh, Louisa, forgive me! I had quite forgot how ill you are.'

While Matt Falconer remarked nastily, 'Stacy? I had thought that you had informed me that your name was Anna!'

Stacy dodged this question, which proved that he was not the only liar in the kitchen, by running over to Louisa, putting a hand on her hot forehead and murmuring, 'Oh, dear, you have a strong fever.' She looked across at the housekeeper, who, amused by what she had provoked, was standing there mumchance, being, like the rest of the servants, content to leave her betters to their quarrel.

'Have you no willow-bark, madam, which we may infuse to break my companion's fever?'

A learned shrew, was Matt's grim inward comment as he turned his attention to the cooling water in the stone sink—to have the little maid twitter at him, 'Oh, you should not be doing that, sir. Allow me,' and try to push him to one side.

'Nor he should,' drawled Jeb. 'Even if you were the butler, Matt, you wouldn't be washing up. Most remiss of you. Should have given you away immediately—if everyone was in their right mind, that is.'

Taking this remark as a reflection on herself, Stacy, her language deteriorating further, pronounced in her most deadly manner, calculated to bring idle clerks to heel, 'And who the devil may you be, to speak to both me and Lord Radley so impudently?'

Before Matt could answer Jeb executed a low bow. 'Matt's man, ma'am, right hand and factotum. Adviser, too, as you may have gathered.'

'Your man, m'lord!' Stacy was all indignation. 'And you allow him to speak to you so insolently? Did you learn your manners from him, or he from you? No matter,' she added hastily, as Matt flung down his washcloth and began to advance on her. 'Pray do not disturb yourself; you will never finish the washing-up at this rate!'

Only Louisa Landen, throwing a conniption fit—Jeb's words—at this point, stopped both Matt and Stacy from prolonging their slanging-match into the night's watches.

As Stacy, remorseful again, bent over Louisa, that good lady hissed at her, 'For shame, Stacy, and use your common sense if it hasn't quite flown away. You do no good bandying words with him. He has an answer for everything.'

'And so do I, madam,' retorted Stacy between her excellent teeth, 'so do I.'

'Quite so, and that is what I complain of. He is a

dangerous man, and, for him, you appear to be a dangerous woman. A quiet, ladlylike refusal to join in his games would end all.'

His games! Was he playing with her? Perhaps so. He had returned to his duties, to fling over his shoulder at her, 'I am late from the United States, Miss Stacy, or whatever your name is, and we have no masters and servants there, only equals working together.'

Forgetting all her resolutions and Louisa's wise advice, Stacy shot back at him, 'Which country, sir, since you are no gentleman, must be an eminently suitable place for you to live. I recommend that you return there.'

'And by the same token, madam, since you are no lady, you should surely accompany me. Except that in the States your haughty manners would soon earn you a reprimand from everyone unfortunate enough to meet you.'

Behind her, Stacy heard Louisa wail her name, and how she refrained from answering him back she never knew. She knew only that her common sense, which seemed to have taken flight from the moment she had set foot in this accursed place, told her that she must consider poor, stricken Louisa, and try not to disgrace herself before her own people, who, apart from Hal, were staring open-mouthed at her. Who would have thought that their cool and haughty, if kind mistress could behave so wildly?

Astonishingly, bending over Louisa again, Stacy found tears pricking at her eyes. No, I will not cry, she told herself. This vile bully, who, as I recall, is no better than he should be, shall not make me cry. I will see him in hell first! And what on earth was happening to her that she should think such dreadful thoughts, use such language?

She straightened up, turned towards her tormentor, and said in a more normal voice, 'You have said that we must sleep here tonight, sir. Are you sure that you have no rooms in this vast house sufficiently warm for us to sleep in them?'

That's more like it, madam, thought Matt grimly. A little due humility works wonders. He forgot that he hadn't been humble either. But he replied more gently, 'I arrived here only two days ago, and no one has lived in most of the Hall's rooms for the past fifteen years, nor, I fear, have they been heated during that time. We also face a shortage of fuel, so I am afraid that we are all doomed to spend the night in the kitchen – where it is at least warm – or die of cold in one of the bedrooms. I have already moved the servants from their attic bedrooms – I wouldn't stable beasts in them.'

Jeb was nodding agreement, as well as old Horrocks, who, by what was being said among the servants, really was a butler. But what a butler! Physically frail and in his dotage, he was nearly as unsuitable in his way as Matt Falconer had been in his.

That gentleman was now asking Hal to accompany him and Jeb into the linen-store, which was kept upstairs, to fetch down sheets, more blankets, pillows and pillow-cases, and air them before the fire, which he kept going by fetching logs from a store in a lean-to against the kitchen's outer wall. It was plain that 'm'lord' he might be, but he was performing menial tasks to the manner born.

It wasn't only the logs which were almost in the open, but also the very necessaries of life. And, since the earth closet used by the servants had become frozen, Stacy was soon to discover that relief was only to be obtained by using the buckets and pails in a small storeroom with a door which didn't shut properly and a broken window through which the keen wind whistled.

Trying to keep her voice reasonable, a difficult task, Stacy returned indoors after she had visited it to address Matt Falconer, who was now using blankets to rig up impromptu partitions to separate the women from the men during the hours of sleep. 'I would like to wash myself, and Louisa would probably benefit from being sponged. Where shall I do so. . .please?'

To Matt's grim amusement he saw that it almost choked the haughty bitch to be polite to him. And well might she ask. 'The kitchen pump,' he told her agreeably, 'will supply you with cold water. Use the big iron cauldron which stands by the fire to heat it. Cook will help you.' And then, seeing that Cook was already engaged in making up beds on the floor, he added, 'No, allow me to assist you.'

Never in her life had Stacy ever contemplated having to do any such thing as haul buckets and pails about, or to wash herself in the full view of Cook, the little maid and Polly, whose right wrist Jeb had placed in a makeshift sling. It was quite plain that anything she needed she would have to supply herself! And the beast knew that, and was waiting to see her throw a tantrum at the prospect of having to be her own servant, as it were. Well, damn him, and his ready sneer too. If Stacy Blanchard couldn't learn how to do the simple menial tasks which so far others had performed for her, she wasn't worth the signature she wrote on the cheques and accounts of Blanchard's Bank.

'Very well,' she replied crisply, avoiding his satiric eye, and walked across to the cauldron, which she lifted with some difficulty before placing it beneath the pump which stood by the sink. Not only was Jeb watching her, but also her servants, their jaws dropped at the sight of madam being so meek and obliging.

But, alas, when she came to try to lift the cauldron with water in it it was too heavy for her, and presently, as she struggled, she found a large hand pushing her own smaller one to one side, and Matt Falconer was lifting it with ease to hang it from the great hook above the fire.

His hands, Stacy noted, were long and shapely, but the

strange thing about them was that they were the hands of a workman, not a gentleman. They were brown and scarred, with calluses on them, like Clem's, her gardener, and his nails were cut short, quite unlike those of the men who had danced attendance on her since her first season, begging her to marry them.

Matt saw her eyes on them, smiled wryly, but said nothing. Later he ladled warm water for her into a bowl, and she retired behind one of the screens to give Louisa and herself what passed for a wash.

'Oh, my dear, you shouldn't be having to do all this,' murmured Louisa ruefully, after Stacy had draped blankets round her and helped her outside to what they all referred to as the conveniences, although John Coachman forgot himself once by asking loudly before all the company, 'Where are the jakes?'

'Well,' replied Stacy incontrovertibly, 'Cook can't do everything, the maid is useless, Polly's wrist prevents her from assisting us, all the able-bodied men have gone outside to shovel the snow away from the fuel-store and the path to the conveniences—such as they are—so who else can help us, I should like to know?'

Louisa patted her hand. 'You are a brave girl, my dear. Try not to mind too much the pickle we have found ourselves in. After all, we might be freezing to death in a ditch, or killed or maimed for life in the accident. And I am beginning to feel so much better after your ministrations.'

Which was no lie. The willow-bark had broken Louisa's fever, and presently Stacy tucked her up for the night before going back into the main part of the kitchen to find the men all sitting round the scrubbed table drinking good ale. The other women were already in their beds behind the hanging blanket.

Jeb waved a hand holding a pewter pot at her.

'Ah, Miss Berriman, what can we do for you?'

There was bread and cheese on the table, she saw longingly, and from somewhere Horrocks had found bottles of port as well as the ale. Matt, who was seated at the head of the table, stared coolly at her and said, 'There's food here if you want it.'

Did she want it? Of course she wanted it. She had been too strung up to eat much earlier, but she had done a lot of unaccustomed physical work during the day, and hunger gnawed at her. Pride as well as etiquette said, No, it is not possible for you to sit here, the lone woman among a pack of men, all but one your social inferiors, and tope with *him* and Hal and the rest; it wouldn't be proper. They had already unwillingly dragged themselves to their feet on her arrival.

'Sit, sit,' she said imperiously, meaning to tell them that no, of course she wanted nothing.

Then *he* said mockingly, 'I think that the fare here is too coarse for m'lady, perhaps.'

Was it, indeed? And was she to starve because she was too finicking to sit down with them on the worst night of the year, and please *him* by starving herself?

'No, indeed,' she shot back. 'I find myself ravenous, and ale and bread and cheese, after a day spent in the snow, seem just the thing!' She sat down by the amused Jeb and stretched out a hand for the loaf and cheese, to cut herself a good share of them and place them on one of the pewter plates which Matt had set out.

And if that broke up their damned masculine drinking-party, so much the better. They would have clearer heads in the morning, when, with luck, the storm would have abated, the coach and their possessions would be rescued from the ditch, and she could be on her way again.

A pewter pot of ale was pushed in front of her by Jeb, who, she could see, now that she was close to him, was quite a personable man despite his strange accent and even stranger clothes. She took a defiant swig from the pot and said, as though she were conversing at dinner with Lord Melbourne himself, or perhaps the Duke of Wellington, with both of whom she was on terms of friendship, 'Pray tell me, sir, how do you find England after the United States?'

Jeb nearly choked into his ale at the sound of such ineffable condescension. He surfaced to say, 'Cold, ma'am, damned cold. Nigh as bad as a Virginia winter, eh, Matt?'

Matt drawled, his lion's eyes hard on her, 'Oh, I don't think that Miss Berriman really wishes to know about the States, Jeb. She is merely making dinner-party small talk, to put you at your ease.'

His man—or whatever he was—considered this unlikely possibility solemnly. Since Jeb was always at ease, whatever the company, high or low, the notion of a spinster lady putting him there seemed rather odd. He was about to reply, but was unable to do so, for Stacy put down her pot of ale with a defiant bang and threw loudly down the table in Matt's direction, 'When did you take up mind-reading, sir? Recently, I hope, if your present failure to perform it correctly is any guide. I am most intensely interested in. . . Jeb's. . .impressions of his ancestors' country.'

'So there', would have been a nice ending to that piece of defiance, but Louisa had long cured her of that trick. Now let him trump that ace, if he could!

But of course he could. He threw back his head and laughed, and damn him, why did he have to look exactly as she had imagined the dashing hero of every delightful Minerva Press novel which she had ever read, when she disliked him so? 'Tell her why your ancestors found themselves in Virginia, Jeb, and then Miss Berriman will understand why your impressions of the old country are hardly likely to be favourable ones!'

Ever willing to oblige, and putting on his best smile, Jeb

offered a trifle tentatively—for, while he was not ashamed of his ancestors' behaviour, he was not exactly proud of it either—'Why, Great-granfer Priestley was transported to Virginia as a convict, ma'am, having taken part in the Monmouth Rising, when his sentence of hanging was transmuted to penal service in the colonies.'

Stacy, overcome by what she had provoked, and angry with herself as well as with Matt, said as firmly as she could, 'Well, Mr Priestley——' for she now knew his name '—a man is not to blame for what his ancestors did. I own that if I had to answer for my own great-grandfather's actions I should be hard put to it to excuse them. And Mr Falconer should not have compelled you to answer me thus, but that doesn't surprise me, since he obviously gave up the pretence of being a gentleman long ago.'

Matt, who was a little surprised by this generous offering to Jeb from someone whom he had thought was steeped in pride of birth, still could not prevent himself from asking, 'And what, pray, Miss Berriman, did your ancestor do which was so scurvy? Entertain us, please.'

She had entertained them enough, Stacy thought. She had behaved like a vicious termagant in the stews or in an alehouse, and in front of her own servants too! What Louisa would have thought of her sitting at a kitchen table with a gang of men swilling drink she couldn't imagine. At least she had avoided the port, of which Louisa always spoke in shuddering horror as the corrupter of men. But she had drunk heavily from the pot which Jeb had mischievously refilled several times, and the effects of the ale, tiredness, and the increasing warmth of the kitchen were beginning to overcome her.

'Certainly not,' she told him firmly. 'I will now retire.' And she stood up, to find the room going around her. Her face paled, and Matt Falconer, moved by an impulse he refused to recognise, swore to himself and as swiftly as he could ran round the table to catch her and prevent her from falling. Cold bitch she might be, but she had had a hell of a day, and behind the autocratic and imperious manner was a woman with a lot of guts—he had to grant her that. She had cared for the welfare of all her people before she had so much as sat down herself.

He picked her up, to find her strangely light for such a tall female, said softly, 'Allow me, madam. I think that you are not accustomed to drinking strong ale,' and carried her, unprotesting and already half asleep, to her bed, which was made up between those of the sleeping Polly and Louisa.

Stacy, unaware of anything but that she was in someone's strong arms, was back in her childhood again, being carried to bed by her father. Without thinking, eyes closed, she kissed the man carrying her, on the cheek which she had earlier struck, murmuring drowsily, 'Goodnight, Papa,' and by the time the surprised Matt had lowered her to the bed she was soundly and sweetly asleep.

CHAPTER FOUR

STACY started awake as a dim early light began to steal into the kitchen. She had been dreaming that she was on a wide plain, quite alone, no friend or companion with her. There was a brilliant sun overhead, and on the far horizon there was a stand of strange trees, quite unlike anything which she had seen before.

On impulse she looked down at herself, to discover that she was most oddly dressed—or rather undressed, since she was wearing nothing but a short garment made of skin, which left her arms and her legs bare. Her hair streamed, long and unruly, down her back.

Where can I be, and whatever am I doing here? she thought rather than said, looking around for help and succour. But there was no one in sight. A strange terror seized her, which deepened when from out of the stand of trees a male lion emerged, his back rippling as he moved slowly towards her, his mask inscrutable, his golden eyes blazing.

Paralysed with fear, Stacy could neither run nor speak, but stood there, staring back at him, waiting to be eaten, she supposed.

Only. . .only. . .something weird happened. The nearer the lion drew, the more he began to change, his shape shimmering, so that when he reached her it was not a lion who stood before her but a man, dressed in skins like herself; his tawny hair, like hers, flowed down his back, his strong jaw was bearded like the lion's, and his eyes, a golden-brown, were lion's eyes. . .

The lion-man gave her a brilliant smile, revealing his splendid white teeth, his eyes flashed, and, before she could register anything, whether fear or desire, she was in his arms, his mouth was on hers, his hands about her body. . . And she was sitting up in bed awake, panting, sweating. An ecstatic sensation which she had never before experienced was sweeping through her body, its passing leaving her weak and shuddering, as though she had run a race.

A fever! I must have caught Louisa's fever! she thought. But when the shudderings had subsided they left no sensations of illness behind, only those of shock. It was *him* she had been dreaming of, and in her sleep she had allowed him to begin to make love to her.

She must be going mad. Or had gone mad the night before, for she was wearing all her clothes except her shoes, and she had no memory of how she had reached her bed. And what a bed! Memories of the previous day came flooding back, all of them unpleasant.

The kitchen was quiet except for the occasional groan, cough or snoring of the humans who occupied it. She had a strong desire to relieve herself—all the ale she had drunk, doubtless—but she had to drive herself to visit the outhouse, only dire necessity compelling her to do so. She must try not to wake the sleepers on her way there and back.

Stacy found her shoes on the floor beside the bed—who had taken them from her feet and placed them there? Was it. . .*him*? Her memory failed her again, but as she picked her way cautiously out of the kitchen it came back. Yes, *he* had carried her to bed, and had stopped short of stripping her of everything, had merely removed her shoes.

It had begun to snow again, and the wind had risen during the night, so that using the inadequate convenience was even more of a pennance than she had feared, but needs must. She pulled the blanket she had thrown about her shoulders more tightly around them before making her way back. With luck she would be in her bed again before anyone was up and stirring.

But the kitchen door opened even as she put a hand out to open it, and, of course, it was *he* who was up and about. He would be. Matt closed the door carefully behind him before he saw that she was there, and for a heart-stopping moment they stared at one another in silence.

She was right: he *had* been the lion-man. He was carrying a heavy greatcoat and his perfect boots, the only dandified thing about him. Otherwise he was, all things considered, lightly dressed, wearing only his shirt, unbuttoned almost to the waist, to show a tawny pelt extending from his neck to his middle, and his black breeches, with his legs and feet in black silk socks. If anything, he looked even larger and more massive than he did when he was fully dressed. And she had been right about him looking like a prize-fighter: he was fully as muscular as she had imagined him to be.

His firm jaw showed a light, tawny stubble, and a pang shot through her. She had a dreadful, insane desire to run her fingers along the strong line, to feel his growing beard's roughness. His eyes, the most compelling thing about him, were on her, as avidly as hers were on him. Yes, this place was driving her mad to make her think such thoughts.

Matt Falconer, for his part, saw a transformed woman. The softness of sleep was written on Stacy's face; all the stern lines, together with the strong set of her mouth, were quite gone. She looked like a woman ready to entertain her lover. Did she know, or was she quite unconscious of what she looked like when she wasn't playing Lady Disdain? Her black hair had come loose during the night so that it was no longer strained away from her face, sharpening it, but tumbled in soft, curling waves almost to her waist, adding to the impression of soft abandon which the rest of her gave.

The stasis which held them both paralysed passed. Stacy said in a whisper, 'You are out and about early, sir.'

Matt shrugged, replied prosaically, 'Someone must look after and feed the horses.'

The horses! She had quite forgotten about the horses in worrying about everyone and everything else. Matt was now sitting down on a low stool which stood by the door and was beginning to pull his boots on. *He* was going to feed the horses. How odd. Why not Jeb, or one of the other menservants—Hal or John Coachman, for instance, or even the postilion? She could not think of one of the many men who had passed through her life, offering for her hand—no, for the Bank—who would have gone to the trouble of caring for and feeding the horses when there was a kitchen full of menservants who could be ordered to do so.

The wind struck her keenly and she began to shiver, with cold this time. 'I ought to help you,' she offered.

Matt, now booted, stood up and began to pull on his heavy many-caped coat. 'No,' he told her curtly. 'Not that I couldn't do with your assistance, but you are not properly dressed for the task. If it becomes too much for me I shall fetch that tall footman of yours, the one who is so keen to defend you, to help me. He will probably be awake by then. Now go indoors before you die of cold, and if you really want to be useful make up the fire and put water on to boil for the breakfast porridge.'

His coat was on and fully buttoned, and without further ado, and certainly without any of the usual empty politenesses with which gentlemen usually favoured ladies, he was gone, struggling through the driving snow to the stables. What a strange creature he was! One moment insulting her by talking so of Hal, the next off to save Hal and the others trouble, after speaking to her as though she were a servant!

Anger flooded Stacy as she made her way to the big

kitchen fire, to find Cook there, already beginning to work, but grateful to the fine lady who insisted on helping. In the daylight she could see how large the kitchen was, and also that, over the years, it had been allowed to deteriorate. The walls were black, the copper pans were dull, overgrown with verdigris, and the tables looked as though they had not been scrubbed since the Domesday Book had been written.

Which was probably due, thought Stacy disgustedly, to Matt Falconer's easy way with servants. No wonder he orders me about as though I were a kitchen maid if he is so willing to do the menial work himself—but how can he bear to live in such a pig-sty? This was a puzzle which occupied her until the next time she crossed swords with him.

Matt Falconer, feeding the horses, throwing extra blankets over them, was occupied in trying to solve another problem—that of Miss Anna Berriman, known to her companion and servants, when they weren't thinking of what they were saying, as Miss Stacy.

He had met many women in the United States who carried themselves with a frankness usually reserved for men, and who often, out in the fields of Virginia in the poorer plantations, did the work of men. But Miss Berriman was another thing altogether. It was plain that all her people were, if not frightened of her, ever-ready to jump to her orders. She had an unconscious arrogance, giving her orders as though it were the only thing in life she existed to do. But she was, he was coming to see, much more than your usual domineering fine lady, who took her rank as *carte blanche* to be as unpleasant as she could to all around her while doing nothing herself.

She organised her affairs in a wholly practical way. There was nothing frivolous about her. And she was ready to do things herself. She had helped to feed Louisa and had bound up Polly's wrist, and although she had bridled and tossed her head at his orders she had carried them out once she saw that her assistance was necessary if they were going to get through the night without undue distress.

And Hal, the young footman, once the ale had begun to work on him the night before, had roared belligerently at Jeb, who had said something deliberately provocative about Miss Anna Berriman, calling her 'your typical idle fine lady', and suggesting that she was more decorative than useful. 'You just watch your manners, sithee. Miss Stacy ain't no useless fine lady. Why, tonight she not only took the lead in getting us all out of the pickle we were in when the coach overturned, but she walked more than a mile through the snow herself, helping the postilion so that poor Polly, who was injured, could ride pillion with John Coachman, when by rights *she* ought to have been sitting there with him.'

Well, now, that was a surprise. Eager to discover more about this odd young woman, who annoyed him every time they met—and partly, he acknowledged, by not conforming to any of the expectations he had of women—Matt had commented sardonically, 'And is that her sole claim to not being a fine lady? If so, it's little enough.'

Hal had just been about to retort hotly, Well, she runs Blanchard's Bank as well as any man, when he had belatedly remembered Miss Stacy's injunction that no one was to reveal who she was until they reached York.

So he had consoled himself by sulking until Matt, still pushing at him, had asked, apparently inconsequentially, 'And what is her real name, Hal? She says she is Miss Anna, and you and the rest sometimes call her that and sometimes Miss Stacy. Which is it?'

Hal had muttered sullenly into his ale, 'Her pa used to call her Miss Stacy, and it stuck. Something to do with her ma, I think.'

'Oh, and who and what was her pa when he was at

home?' asked Jeb, who, like Matt, found Miss Berriman intriguing as well as annoying.

'A gentleman.' Hal had enough sense left to be evasive. 'His pa left him money, they say.'

One of the *nouveaux riches* created by the late wars, then, thought Matt. Which might explain the hauteur as a form of defence, in a society which tolerated rather than approved of them, although the explanation seemed thin. He wanted to ask, How much money? but he thought that any more questions and Hal would be waving his fists at him again, and the last thing he wanted, with the women sleeping at the other end of the kitchen, was a brawl.

Just before they finally retired for the night Jeb came up to him and muttered, so that the others couldn't hear what they were saying, 'Hot for her, are you?'

Matt drew back, almost assuming the aristocrat again. He stopped abruptly. He didn't like the effect being back in England had on him. The very air breathed social difference and unwanted deference. He was used to being a man among men, not a demi-god among men.

'Now what should make you think that? I don't even like the woman, as you must see.'

Jeb shrugged. 'Liking has nothing to do with it, as well you know. Wanting to wipe that don't-touch-me expression off her face by having her on her back was more what you were thinking of by your own expression, I should say.'

There was such a grain of truth in this that Matt turned away, saying irritably, 'For God's sake, Jeb, have you nothing better to do than try to talk me into bed with a noisy termagant? And now off to your own bed before I lose patience with you.'

Well, he hadn't convinced Jeb that he didn't want Miss Anna Berriman, if that was her name, beneath him, that was for sure, if the knowing expression on his face when he crawled into his makeshift bed was any guide.

And what did he think of her? Nothing, of course, only that she was someone chance-met and now in his house, and he wanted her out of it.

Which, he now recognised wearily, wasn't going to be soon. If the worsening weather was any guide, they might be penned in the Hall for days. The sooner they could warm up some of the bedrooms so that they were all spared her dictatorial presence the better.

Later on in the day he found that trying to heat some of the many bedrooms was a mammoth task, and no mistake. Matt, Jeb and all the able-bodied men lent a hand, including the postilion, who, when he moaned that this was no business of his and he wasn't paid to lug coals and logs about for free, was rapidly informed by Matt that to do so was some part of his payment for his board and lodging.

On his second trip upstairs Matt found Lady Disdain, as he was coming to think of her, toiling along the landing with a full scuttle of coal.

'Come, madam,' he told her roughly, 'allow me to take this from you. Carrying coals is men's work. What are you trying to prove?'

Stacy looked him firmly in his blazing amber eyes. Her eyebrows rose, and she evaded his reaching hand, swinging the scuttle away from him. 'Men's work, you say? How many maidservants have carried scuttles full of coal up and down these stairs, do you think? That poor child in the kitchen can barely lift a pan on to the fire, and Horrocks was commanding her to see that this was taken up to the master. You mean, I think, that ladies don't carry coal. But you have already informed me that I am no lady, so have done, I pray you.'

There was no telling her anything.

Stacy saw that she had scored a hit, a palpable hit.

He shrugged. 'As you will, but remember that the servants are trained to do this work, and you are not.'

'Then I collect that I must learn, m'lord,' was her smart riposte to him, and she swept by him, a slow and laboured sweep, she thought afterwards ruefully, for it was true that her whole body was beginning to protest at the back-breaking work she had been doing since she had arrived at Pontisford Hall.

The coals were for her bedroom, one of the smaller and less well-appointed ones, since its size would make it easier to warm up quickly. The fire was alight, but there was more smoke than flames rising from it, and Jeb was poking at it in an uninformed way, she saw. Doubtless he was more used to squatting half-naked in a wigwam and nursing a few sticks to life, was her acid inward commentary.

'Allow me,' she said briskly and, wrenching the poker from his astonished hands, she stirred the fire vigorously, producing a blazing flame which she presently fed with a few coals, before standing back to look at her room.

And what a room. No lady's bower, this. The dust-sheets had been ripped from the bed and the furniture and were lying discarded in the corner. Grey fluff and cobwebs were everywhere. Clean linen, ready for the bed, and a great quilt had been placed on a chest under a window whose only view was of snow, and yet more snow.

'I can't sleep in this,' she told Jeb. 'The room needs a thorough cleaning before it is habitable.'

'So it does.' Jeb's grin was sly and he lifted his shoulders in a massive shrug. 'Poor Polly's wrist is worse than ever this morning, the cook isn't paid to clean bedrooms and the little maid has woken up with a fever. So, who's to do it?' He was being particularly insolent because he wanted to see how far the woman opposite him would go if provoked. A long way, it seemed.

'If there is no one else able to clean this room, and the one which is being prepared for Miss Landen,' Stacy told him, wondering how long she could keep up her iron determination to show him, and his impossible master, that there was nothing, but nothing this fine lady would not do to prove herself as willing as any high-nosed man, 'then I shall clean them myself.'

Jeb bowed to her, and whether he meant the bow to be one of admiration or derision he wasn't sure. 'Ma'am, I think that you may be ill-prepared for such a task.'

Up went Stacy's eyebrows again. 'Oh, you are an expert on housewifery, Mr Priestley? It seems to me that nothing but diligence, common sense and a strong back are needed to carry out most of the duties I see done around me. But if I fail in the doing, be sure that I shall come to you for advice.' And this time she did sweep out, a real sweep, not an arthritic one, since she had no bucket of coal to discommode her.

'Oh, Miss Landen,' wailed Polly, later in the day, 'I wondered what Miss Stacy was doing, running in and out all the time, and now Jeb tells me that with the maid's help she has been scrubbing, cleaning and dusting the bedrooms which are being warmed for us. On her knees, Miss Landen. It cannot be proper. She should not be doing that. What would her late pa have said to such goings-on?

'And he,' she added, nodding at Matt, who was falling asleep after a hard morning moving furniture, feeding horses, hauling logs and coal and ashes up and downstairs, and trying to keep a pathway cleared to the back door, 'he don't make no effort to stop her. "Do her good to do a bit of hard work," he said to Jeb and me.'

'Good God, Polly,' murmured Louisa faintly, 'you cannot be telling me the truth.'

'As God's my witness, Miss Landen, I would not lie to you. And he's as bad,' she moaned, waving a hand at the semi-conscious Matt. 'He does more work than his man or his butler. He's the strangest lord I ever met.'

And Miss Stacy's the strangest mistress, was her unspoken gloss.

Stacy, her colour high, her back aching, her hands like coarse crêpe from being constantly immersed in water, entered, carrying a bucket and a scrubbing-brush in time to prove the truth of Polly's unlikely tale. Louisa sat up in bed, and, using the voice which had brought the childish Stacy to heel, called to her, 'Anastasia! Whatever do you think that you are doing?'

Her first word was so loud and shrill that it woke the dozing Matt in time to hear the rest of the sentence.

Stacy sat down plump on one of the Windsor chairs to rest her protesting body and replied as cheerfully as she could, 'I don't *think* that I'm doing anything, Louisa. I have been making our rooms habitable. But, of course, if you would prefer to remain in the kitchen until the weather changes, then I will stop.'

'It is not fitting, it is not proper,' the agitated Louisa wailed. She turned to Matt, a useless ally, she was to find. 'Tell her m'lord, tell her that it is neither fit nor proper for a young lady of her great position to be carrying out menial tasks.'

'Oh, no,' returned Matt placidly, sinking even further into his chair and putting his booted feet up on to a bench. 'I shall tell her nothing, for she never takes the slightest heed of anything I say—or of anything anyone else says, for that matter.'

Jeb gave another of his snorts of laughter, and Hal, aware that his mistress was being criticised again, sat up straighter, ready to do battle on her behalf.

Stacy, rising and carrying the bucket to the sink to empty it, to wring dry the swab she had been using and to clean the scrubbing-brush, merely said over her shoulder in the general direction of everybody, 'I shall always listen to anything of sense which is proposed to me, Louisa, as you well know. But I take no note of nonsense, however great the station of the person who offers it to me. Lord Radley would do well to keep his opinions to himself—

the neglected state of his home is no testimonial to the soundness of his judgement or of his organisational abilities.'

Louisa, by now deprived of any ally, told herself miserably that she might have known that if Stacy was uncontrollable in her own home and at the Bank, then it was not to be wondered at that, given the circumstances at which they had arrived, she should be uncontrollable here too. Only the prospect of a comfortable room where she might be ill in private could console her for Stacy's total abandonment of all the decencies which made up a genteel female's life.

'And when,' Stacy queried briskly, drying her poor damaged hands on a coarse towel, 'will luncheon be ready? All this hard work is making me feel uncommon hungry.'

Cook looked up from the fire to announce that if madam cared to bring over one of the crockery soup plates she might have a couple of ladlefuls of vegetable broth. As for the bread, butter and cheese, that was laid out on the table, and she could help herself to them.

This was so unlike her normal life, where a deferential butler served her exquisite and delicate food in fine porcelain on a damask tablecloth, offering her a noble French wine to go with it, that Stacy almost laughed aloud. Instead, she said, without thinking, 'You see, Louisa, you always said that I worked too hard, but I assure you that a morning spent in cleaning is harder than a week spent in figuring. Never reproach me again. But, as you only live to reproach me, I fear that that is probably a vain hope.'

And she carried over Louisa's bowl to hand to her before fetching her own share of the soup and sitting down at the table with Hal and the rest to eat it.

Figuring? A week spent in figuring? Now, whatever could be meant by that? was the thought which crawled like a maggot through the brains of both Matt Falconer and Jeb Priestley. What figuring could Miss Anna Berriman possibly be doing? And what did Louisa Landen mean by Miss Anna—or Anastasia—Berriman being a lady of great station? Who and what was her family? Berriman was not a name which sprang to Matt Falconer's mind as carrying a great weight in Society!

Only too well aware that she had made a slip of the tongue, Stacy decided to say nothing further, but instead to eat her luncheon as quietly as she could, avoiding the sardonic gaze of Matt Falconer and his shadow.

Later, going over to take Louisa's empty soup bowl from her, she said quietly and reproachfully to her, 'You must understand, Louisa, that without my active help we are both condemned to live here in public until we leave. May I also remind you that your comfortable life with me is built upon the daily work which I do at Blanchard's and which brings us our profits? I don't think that you quite understand that Papa left Blanchard's to me to run because he didn't believe that, faithful though they may be, either Ephraim Blount or any of his associates possess either the skill or the foresight to steer Blanchard's Bank in the direction in which he thought it ought to go. That is my last word on the matter, Louisa. You may advise me, but you will not issue orders to me. Now I will give *you* an order. Rest a little, I beg of you, before we carry you upstairs to your room.'

She had never spoken so to Louisa before, although occasionally she had spoken even more sternly to members of the Bank's staff who had failed to carry out her orders efficiently. It was not a tone which Louisa approved of or liked, but it was one which she had heard before—when Louis Blanchard was alive. She was truly her father's daughter, thought Louisa sadly, and as she had loved the father, for all his faults, so she loved the daughter. But from now on she knew that their relationship would have changed. Stacy had cast off the last bonds of her childhood.

She wondered what Matt Falconer would have made of Stacy's little speech if he had heard it. That gentleman was now fully awake, eating his luncheon, and directing a quizzical stare at his most unwanted guests as he did so. He was wiping his mouth with a much darned napkin which Horrocks, who was trying to carry out what his poor old brain hazily told him were the duties of a good butler, had given him a few moments earlier.

His meal finished, he walked over to Louisa and said in a kind voice, 'My dear Miss Landen, I trust that you will be delighted to learn that in a short time we shall be able to carry you to a warm bedroom, where you may recover from your malaise in peace and comfort.'

He finished this pretty speech with a short bow, bringing a blush of pleasure to Louisa's wasted cheek, and also bringing a sardonic curl to Stacy's lips. But she said nothing—safer so.

Nor did she speak again to any of the company while the arrangements to move herself and Louisa to their new rooms went ahead, but contented herself with sitting comfortably before the fire, falling into a doze which eased her aching back and legs. It might be true that the hard menial work of servants was not difficult, but oh, it was exhausting.

Jeb watched her with amusement, whispering to Matt, 'Looks a proper gentle fine lady when she sleeps, don't she? Nice and quiet! Pity she don't sleep all the time!' To which Matt said nothing. He too had come to the conclusion that least said was soonest mended.

Stacy's sleep was a happy one. She was dreaming again of the lion-man, although this time it was not bright day but dark night, with a big moon and stars overhead, and the lion-man was sitting opposite her, tending a fire. A bird was calling somewhere, and she was lying on skins.

The lion-man was looking at her, the firelight making his amber eyes glow, and presently he rose in one lithe movement and walked over to her, to sit beside her. She knew that he was going to embrace her, and delight shuddered through her.

Alas, as before, even as he touched her she was sliding awake, a smile on her face—to hear Matt Falconer's taunting voice in her ear. 'At least, madam, I see that you are happy in your dreams—if nowhere else.'

Stacy looked up at him, and knew at once that he was the lion-man of her dreams—indeed, momentarily she didn't know whether or not she was awake, or whether she was still lost in her dreams.

She was now awake, that was for sure, and why should she dream of *him*? Simply to think of her dream caused a hot and betraying colour to flood her face. Jumping to her feet and turning away from him to avoid his mocking amber gaze, she muttered in a stifled voice, 'The warmth made me sleepy, I fear. Does it still snow?'

By asking the last innocent question—anything to take her mind off what her dreams might be telling her—Stacy hoped to turn the conversation into channels which would neither embarrass her nor cause him to attack her. This ploy seemed to work, for he told her mildly, 'Yes, I'm afraid that the storm shows little signs of abating as yet. Jeb and I have carried Miss Landen upstairs to the room we prepared for her earlier, and where Polly will be able to look after her during the day—if that is agreeable to you?'

'Of course. And my room—is that ready too?'

Matt nodded gravely. 'Jeb and I are agreed that it is sufficiently warm for you to retire there as soon as you wish. Supper will be served at six of the clock. Cook is making tea for us all, and you might like to share a cup with us before you go—if you don't object to being without either your companion or your maid, that is.'

Was he offering her an olive-branch by speaking to her so steadily and calmly? If so, she must try to respond in kind, and accept the offered tea before she took herself out of his disturbing presence. She seemed to have taken leave of her senses since she met him, and as for dreaming of him in such a dreadful fashion. . . She was only too happy that dreams could not be shared. Who knew what might happen if he knew that he walked so intimately through hers?

For in the last dream he had been stripped to the waist, and how could such an innocent maiden lady as herself know that the rough pelt of tawny hair which covered his chest would arrow down into his stomach? It must be the Greek statuary which Papa had purchased for the gallery in their country home outside London which had produced such immodest thoughts!

'A cup of tea would be most welcome,' was her even reply, eyes downcast so that she could avoid looking at him, and she took from him the porcelain cup and saucer, two fine and delicate pieces, which Matt told her had been rescued from a glass case in the ante-room off the dining-hall.

For a moment Stacy considered asking him how he could have allowed such a splendid place as Pontisford Hall must have been to fall into neglect and ruin, but prudence said, Do nothing to provoke him, and after she had drunk her tea in silence she allowed Matt to take her arm and escort her upstairs. And that was worse than ever, for his very touch seemed to scorch and burn her skin as the lion-man's had done in her dreams. But no matter; she must control herself. They walked upstairs as decorously as though all the fierce words they had so recently hurled at one another had never been uttered. On the way to her bedroom they passed through what had once been a noble gallery hung with portraits, now hidden in canvas bags, and in which statuary of all periods stood, also hidden away under dust-sheets.

Matt felt her arm stiffen beneath his hand and, because touching her was affecting him almost as strongly as his touch was affecting her, with the difference that Matt Falconer knew what the spark which was being lit between them meant and was determined to stifle it, remarked coolly, 'You are strangely quiet, madam.' He couldn't be attracted to such a strong-minded, strong-willed termagant; he couldn't. She was everything which he most disliked in women, so he made his tone as cold as possible to demonstrate that he tolerated her only—which was a damned lie if ever there was one! Every moment he spent with her only served to magnify his growing and unnatural desire to have her in his arms, or in his bed.

His tone undid Stacy's resolution not to provoke him. She replied, her voice sharp, 'You have given me the distinct impression that you prefer my silence to my speech, so I was duly obliging you. If, on the other hand, you wish me to say what I think without fear of offending you, then I will cease to keep my thoughts to myself.'

They were by now at her bedroom door. Matt threw it open with an elaborate gesture. 'Your bower, madam. I regret that I cannot deck it about with the nettles which your mode of speech deserves.'

Stacy walked by him into the room, turned, and hurled at him, 'And I regret that I have to be in this benighted hole at all. You will forgive me if I don't come down to supper. I would rather not eat at all than owe my bread to someone whose only wish appears to be to insult me.'

That's better, madam, was Matt's unholy thought. Nag at me like that and I shall soon lose all desire to teach you what men and women can do together besides talk! But again he was lying, for he was beginning, unwillingly, to understand that what attracted him was not only her fiery spirit but the wit and intellect which fuelled it. She was gradually destroying all his easy expectations of women and their behaviour. He had always told himself that he was attracted only to women like poor Camilla had been—small, delicate, shy and—yes, admit it, Matt—innocently worshipful of any man they might love.

There was nothing of any of that about Miss Anastasia Berriman. She was certainly not ready to worship any man! He almost resented her for it, for she was beginning to tell him something about himself which he was not sure that he wished to know. That he had changed fundamentally over the years since Camilla's death. He pushed the thought away from him, to say curtly to his tormentor, 'I cannot allow that. The cold is such that you must eat, madam. I have no desire to nurse you on a sickbed. If you are as demanding as this in rude health, I can scarce imagine what you would be like when ailing.'

Stacy turned. 'I shall not,' she blazed at him, 'come down if I do not wish to.'

'Madam, if I have to carry you down by main force to compel you to eat, I shall do so. Do not provoke me to act thus, I beg of you. It is for your own good, I assure you.'

They were face to face now, like two duellists. Stacy knew that he meant it. That he would do as he said. The lion's eyes told her so. His whole demeanour told her so. A strange excitement coursed through her. She would defy him! And then, dismally, she asked herself, Is that what I want? For him to manhandle me, lift me up, carry me down, while I try to stop him? Does the notion excite me?

Dreadfully, only the thought of what the servants downstairs would think if she were to allow any such thing stopped her from trying Matt Falconer to the point where he would physically overcome her.

'You leave me no alternative,' she muttered. 'I will come down at six, but under duress, mind. It is not my wish.'

'With or without duress, it is all the same to me, so long as you do as I wish,' he told her arrogantly. And if, thought Stacy after he had gone, he sees me as Kate in *The Taming of the Shrew*, then, damn him, he's as cross-grained as Petruchio!

She sank on to the bed, clutching her hot cheeks. How can I think such things, for how did Kate and Petruchio end? In one another's arms, and she agog to please him. I must be going mad. I'll be damned before I let the unnatural circumstances in which I find myself lead me to believe that I could ever have developed so strong a *tendre* for such a damned domineering oaf as to wish myself in his arms.

On his way downstairs Matt was thinking similar thoughts. But the play of Shakespeare's which he appeared to be trapped in was *Much Ado About Nothing*. My damned Lady Disdain, was his fiery thought, and then, But by God I'll not be Benedick, for he ended in his lady's arms, and I'll see her in hell before I give way to such a ridiculous impulse. She's just another woman, after all.

But he knew that he lied.

CHAPTER FIVE

'NO SIGN of a thaw, my poor Louisa,' announced Stacy on the fourth morning of their stay, looking out of the window at the featureless white world which was Pontisford Hall's park. 'But even if there had been I do not think that we ought to have attempted to continue our journey today—you still look a trifle wan.'

'For all that,' returned her companion, pleased to see Stacy more like her usual equable self, 'I shall rise from my bed today. My fever seems to have broken during the night.'

'But you must promise me not to overdo things. We shall leave Pontisford instanter the thaw does begin and the coach is rescued. Even if it proves to be too damaged for us to continue in it, I shall arrange either for Mr Falconer to allow us to borrow his, or send to the nearest inn for a post-chaise to speed us on our way. I have quite taken this place in disgust. I find Mr Falconer and his impudent servant to be intolerable beyond belief.'

Louisa held her tongue. She thought that Stacy's behaviour had also not been beyond reproach. But Stacy had also made it plain that she was not in Louisa's charge any more, so caution in speech must be the rule.

Polly came in while Stacy was helping Louisa to dress to tell them that breakfast was ready—did Miss Stacy wish to eat it in the kitchen, or should she bring it to her room?

Louisa said briskly, before Stacy could reply, 'I should prefer to eat in the kitchen. I must recover my sea-legs and my strength.'

Stacy would have preferred to remain where she was. Her room was now sufficiently aired and warm for Matt

Falconer to be unable to demand her presence in the kitchen, and to go there might now look like conceding him some right to dictate what she did. But Polly's wrist was still painful, and she couldn't have her carrying trays several hundred yards through all the long corridors and up the great winding staircase of Pontisford Hall.

'I shall eat in the kitchen too,' she announced. 'Come, Louisa, give me your arm. We must not keep the company waiting.'

But, of course, when they reached the kitchen no one had waited for their arrival and breakfast was in full swing—Matt Falconer, indeed, had already finished, and was shrugging himself into his big coat preparatory to taking buckets of mash to the horses.

'Good morning, madam. You have condescended to breakfast with us, I see.'

Trust him to come out with some disparaging remark. Well, she had a suitable answer for that. 'Good morning, sir. I had hoped that a night's sleep might improve your manners, but I see that I was wrong!'

Louisa closed her eyes at this. Stacy, head high, having reproved insolence, picked up two pottery bowls and went over to the cauldron of porridge hanging over the fire and ladled the steaming oats into them. Carrying them back to the table, she looked for milk to put in her tea and over the porridge but found none. Matt Falconer, who had ignored her cutting response to his curt welcome, remarked drily from the door, 'We have run out of milk, I fear, but there is plenty of honey, Cook says, so you may use that instead.'

No milk. Well, she could not reprimand him for that. In all fairness, it was the sudden arrival of Stacy and her party which had depleted Pontisford's supplies so rapidly. Jeb had told her the day before that most of their store of fresh food came from the home farm from which they were now cut off.

She spooned honey over the oatmeal and began to eat it. She was so hungry that the coarse stuff tasted good, and she said so.

Jeb, who sat astride a bench mending tack, said brightly, 'Well, that's a good thing, madam, seeing that we have run out of bread, butter and smoked bacon too, and shall be reduced to eating oatmeal and vegetable soup at alternate meals.'

'Better that than nothing,' she riposted. Louisa gave a faint groan, porridge not being her favourite food. Jeb offered Stacy his impudent smile as a reward for her stoicism—never say the haughty bitch had other than a gallant spirit. If Mad Matt hadn't set his heart on having her—for Jeb had no doubt that he had, even if he refused to acknowledge it—he might have tried to give madam the time of day himself. Such spirit augured well for her performance in bed.

Something of this showed on his face, so Stacy gave him her most haughty and repressive stare before she carried the bowls over to the sink. Jeb put his tack down and followed her there. 'My dear Miss Berriman,' he murmured, 'pray do not be over-hard on Matt. We had a difficult journey here from Virginia, unwelcome news for him when we reached London, and another long haul before we arrived at Pontisford. Now, as to the Hall's condition. . .'

'I should worry about your condition, Jeb, if you choose to gossip about my affairs,' Matt Falconer's hard voice ground out. He had returned earlier than expected from his task, having taken Hal and John Coachman with him to finish examining the horses to see how they were bearing up under the cold.

Jeb turned an unrepentant face on his master and friend. 'Why, Matt, I but thought to put Miss Berriman wise about our reason for being here. . .'

Matt said harshly, throwing down his wet greatcoat

before the fire, 'I shouldn't trouble yourself overmuch. I doubt whether Miss Berriman thinks that anyone could put her wise about anything.'

'Oh!' Stacy rose to her feet to excoriate him. 'Enough, sir. I shall retire to my room at once, where I may read in peace.' Yesterday she had found and explored the dusty library, and had discovered there Sir William Blackstone's great treatise *Commentaries on the Laws of England*. Just the right corrective, she thought grimly, to the lax goings-on at Pontisford Hall. In any case, the owner of Blanchard's would do well to be *au fait* with her country's legal system.

'As you wish,' was Matt's curt answer, while Louisa closed her eyes again. Her eyelids were going up and down like a shop's awning on a showery day, but what could be wrong with Stacy? It was not like her to be so cross-grained and downright rude. Why, she'd even flounced like a reprimanded parlour-maid when she'd walked out of the kitchen.

Blackstone, Stacy found, might be useful, but was hardly riveting. She visited the kitchen again for luncheon: soup without bread. Cook had unearthed some withered potatoes and had roasted them in the front of the fire, and Stacy found herself eating them as though they were manna, trying to avoid Matt Falconer's satiric eye while she did so. Later, after several more stunningly dull, if instructive, pages of Blackstone, she found herself supping off porridge, with more honey than seemed advisable.

Her ill-temper, something which she had never known that she possessed before she had arrived at Pontisford Hall, was not improved by having read Sir William's pompous dismissal of the Rights of Women, who were, he wrote, fit only to be the handmaidens of men, and who, once they were married, were dead to law and lost all the rights which they had possessed as single women!

Worst of all, Blackstone solemnly asserted that this proved how favourably the law regarded women! At this point Stacy had closed the book with a bang, sending dust flying about her room and making her sneeze. 'The man is a fool,' she had announced in ringing tones to no one at all, 'if he can believe anything as stupid as that.'

After enduring Sir William Blackstone's vapourings it was the outside of enough to watch Matt Falconer striding about the kitchen, giving orders to all and sundry and doubtless regarding her as a member of an inferior species. Papa had not brought her up to be the instrument of fools. No, she would never marry—to be the appendage of a husband, no more than his tail. . .

This unlikely thought brought on a fit of the giggles, so that she almost choked over her porridge. Louisa clapped her on her back and the whole table, masters and servants, admired her scarlet face. Matt Falconer seemed particularly to enjoy her discomfiture. For some reason this enraged Stacy so strongly that a red mist rose before her eyes, a response out of all proportion to the offence. Later she dismally conceded that it had been reading Blackstone which was responsible for her anger, but, whatever the cause, she was lost to everything.

'Laugh on, sir,' she threw at him furiously. 'It becomes you, who, I collect, have little care or respect for women so to enjoy a woman's discomfiture. I seem to remember that Society cast you off for your disgraceful conduct. It has seldom made a better judgement. You had done better to remain in the savage country you chose to settle in, where you might exploit women as you pleased, rather than return to these more civilised shores.'

The silence which followed this public denunciation could almost be felt. Matt's face became truly a lion's mask of fury, as Stacy's was a Medusa's, all hateful condemnation. Then Louisa gave a wailing cry. 'Oh, Stacy, Stacy, you forget yourself.'

'On the contrary, madam, I have never remembered myself more. I bid you all goodnight.' And for the second time that day she flounced out of the kitchen.

Jeb read the signs on his master's face. He had risen, stood with his hands flat before him on the table, his expression a rictus of anger. Oh, madam had tried him beyond endurance—and what delightful consequences might flow from this to entertain a man of sense! Which Matt Falconer at that moment plainly was not. He was all Lord Radley, with a vengeance. And vengeance was what he wanted.

He snarled at Jeb, 'See to the horses for me, man,' and strode out of the kitchen after the shrew who had at last succeeded in smashing his fine control. 'I shall be down presently.'

The door banged shut behind him; the company all let out its collective breath, and began to talk frantically about anything but the conduct of their betters—although later, when Louisa and Polly had gone to their beds, speculation and sly amusement ran rife among the men—except for poor Hal.

Stacy reached her room, shaking at the enormity of her behaviour. Louisa was right. Of course she was right; never more so. What would Papa have thought of her? She had always been, until she had reached Pontisford Hall and met Matt Falconer, absolutely in command of herself—icy cool, reserved, correct at every point of her behaviour, almost a joke in the eyes of Society for her determined rectitude. And where had it all gone? And how could she have behaved so dreadfully? Whatever would the servants think of her? What did *he* think of her?

She was soon to find out. The door to her room flew open, and he stood there, either an avenging archangel or a demon come from hell to devour her, whichever version of him you preferred.

He kicked the door to behind him and advanced on her, the amber eyes shooting sparks at her. Stacy almost expected to see a lion's fangs appear when at last he spoke. She found herself retreating before him, until the wall stopped her from retreating further.

'Damn you, madam, who gave you leave to speak to me thus so publicly? You are exactly the kind of high-nosed bitch I most detest.'

Shivering and shaking at the sound of him, Stacy said through her teeth, all her recent remorse flown away in the face of his insults, 'And you, sir, are the most boorish oaf it has been my misfortune to meet.'

'Then it seems, madam, that in terms of dislike we are quits.'

'Quits, sir, quits? Indeed not,' she flashed back at him. 'We can never be quits, nor do I wish to be so. You are beneath my consideration, sir. I beg leave to continue disliking you more intensely than you dislike me.'

'On the contrary. I shall make it my good fortune to be the winner in this contest.'

They were eye to furious eye now. Stacy, who was standing on tiptoe in an effort to be level with him, was trembling, and so, she saw, with fascination and trepidation equally mixed, was he.

Matt's jaw was clenched, the muscles standing out on it. His eyes devoured her, as a lion by doing so might hypnotise its prey before sinking its jaws in it. The whole room was warmed by their wrath. He began to speak again, hissing at her through his clenched teeth, causing Stacy to walk sideways along the wall to try to escape him as he stalked her, step by ruthless step. 'What unkind God sent you here to plague me? A woman lacking in all the womanly arts which give your sex grace. A disputatious, loud and unlovely shrew. By God——' and he raised his hands '—I have a good mind to give you a lesson in decent submission, a lesson which your father should have given you long ago.'

Stacy found herself, improbably and to her complete astonishment, to be in a condition of intense and quivering excitement. Her whole body hummed and throbbed, and, far from fear at the sight of Matt's ferocious mask so near to her own, a mask which resembled the face of the battered Hercules which she had seen in the gallery, she felt a strange exhilaration.

She felt more alive than she had ever felt before. His anger and fury, added to her own, had broken the icy shell in which she had been living since her father had made her his aide and his confidante at Blanchard's.

'Touch me, sir,' she panted, 'and I promise you that you will live to regret it sorely.'

'Touch you? Why should I touch you, other than to chastise you? What man in his senses would wish to touch you?' But he continued his slow pacing alongside her, and now Stacy had reached the wardrobe and could move no further—other than towards him.

From eye to eye they were breast to breast. Green eyes met golden-brown ones, flashing an equal fire. The whole world had shrunk down to the pair of them. Matt stood back a little and Stacy slipped by him, only to have him catch her by the shoulders and turn her, so that now she was trapped against the bed curtains, and to retreat further was impossible—unless she wished to take him with her on to the top of the bed.

Excitement made her reckless—she felt that she lived only to provoke him. To do what. . .? She put up her hands against his chest to push him away from her. Immediately the strong and rapid beat of his heart, matching his breathing, assaulted her. Her touch, light though it was, served only to excite him. His heart beat more rapidly still, his breathing grew shorter, the very pupils of his lion's eyes dilated.

'You challenge me with your body, madam, after challenging me with your tongue. Is that it? Is this what you have wanted all along, the cause of your provocation? To be beneath me, in my arms? If so, I accept the challenge!'

So saying, he grasped her wrists to pull her to him so that she could feel the power of him, to feel—for Stacy was not so ignorant that she was unaware of what a roused man might feel like—the hard evidence of it stark against her stomach.

Stacy gave a tiny sob, quite unaware that her own face betrayed to her enemy, who was rapidly becoming her lover, the strength of the arousal which their mental and physical struggles had created in her.

His mouth was hard on hers, his hands clasped her head, and now that she was free to fight him off Stacy made no attempt to do so. Rather, she clutched him to her, and was returning his kiss with interest, finding his mouth again when for a second he raised his away from hers for very breathing's sake.

They stood like this for a long moment before he whispered into her ear, 'And this too, madam, this too,' and he was lifting her on to the bed before joining her there, where her hands became as purposeful as his as they continued their busy work about her body.

He was unbuttoning the bodice of her dress, to find her breasts fashionably unbound, to release them, to stroke them, to take them in his mouth, while she moaned and whimpered in his arms, before imitating him by unbuttoning his shirt and stroking the tawny pelt which she had seen before only in her dreams. It was as though her body, quiescent and dormant for so long, had been released from a long sleep. Each touch of his lips, hands and body stoked the fire of passion which was rising within her.

She was on her back, her arms around his neck; his mouth was now on hers again, his tongue found its teasing way inside, and they were touching there too as her tongue learned what to do from his. The acute pleasure this created in them both had Stacy half lifting herself off the bed and Matt pulling away to groan fiercely, 'And this, madam, and this?' and his hands were inside her skirts and were stroking her inner thighs. Oh, God, such sweet delight!

And where, in all this maelstrom of lust, was icy Miss Anastasia Blanchard? Disappeared quite in the gasping maenad on the bed. And when, finally, Matt lifted his body above hers, it was her hands and body which helped him, rather than repelled him, on towards the final act of love.

Above him, for a fleeting second, Stacy registered the grimy and cracked plasterwork of the ceiling, before her eyes closed, to seal the sensation of being apart from her body; Stacy Blanchard had disappeared from the moment she had surrendered her will and her reason in her desire to be one with the man who was rapidly fulfilling that wish.

He was pulling up her skirts and she was unbuttoning his breeches' flap to stroke him—or was it the other way round, and she was taking the lead. . .? Her principles seemed to have disappeared with her clothing and his—she was too busy enjoying the new sensations which coursed through her to trouble about them. Afterwards she was to ask herself how in God's name they could have changed from blistering hate to an equally blistering passion in the blinking of an eye. So blistering that the only thing which mattered was their ultimate union, as though all their life had simply been a preparation for what was happening upon the bed. . .

In this, in passion, as in all else between them, they were equals. In no way afterwards could Stacy excuse herself, call what had happened between them rape. She had connived at her seduction—nay, asked for it, by provoking him until he had lost his self-control. Afterwards she was to ask herself from what depths of womanly knowledge, untaught, never before plumbed, she had fished up the skills which had enabled her to pleasure him as he pleasured her.

Strangest of all, although they had begun by making love with the same ferocity with which they had warred, gradually, as they lay naked together, tenderness followed, and although desire never slackened it became channelled into softer kisses, gentler stroking, so that when, with a groan, Matt entered her, there was nothing violent in his actions. The only pain which Stacy felt was the momentary tearing pang which told of virginity gone.

And if for a moment Matt hesitated at the enormity of what he had done, was doing, it was lost in Stacy's cries as she clutched him to her, tighter than ever, until the ecstasy took them both higher and higher, to deposit them, satisfied, on the further shores of love, where they lay quiet in one another's arms.

Downstairs, as time passed and Matt did not return, Jeb began to whistle thoughtfully. Hal sprang to his feet, shouting, 'I shall go upstairs to protect the mistress' but Louisa pulled him down, saying gently,

'I think that Miss Stacy can protect herself.' But what she really thought was, I dare do and say nothing, for if I do she might cast me off, with a pension, no doubt, and I shall die alone and friendless, which I do not want—and nor, I think, does she. She has made her bed and she must lie on it, which, I fear, is exactly what she is doing.

She looked around at the assembled company and defied them to say anything as the clock ticked on and they were all left masterless. . .and mistressless.

CHAPTER SIX

THE inhabitants of Pontisford Hall slept on until the dawn. Jeb, imitating his master, though unable to sleep with the woman he had—against all the odds—begun to admire, contented himself with Polly in his bed instead.

Louisa passed Stacy's closed bedroom door, wondering whether she and Matt Falconer were still together, before resignedly shrugging and retiring to her own empty bed—to enjoy the first peaceful night since she had arived semi-conscious at Pontisford. Stacy had declared her independence of all restraint, and she must live with that decision.

Inside Stacy's bedroom the strong man and the strong woman slept in one another's arms. Shortly after their first coupling, while Stacy had lain temporarily replete, in the dim light from the dying fire, Matt had slipped from her bed to renew it. She had watched him walk naked through the shadows, a Greek statue come to life, and instead of feeling shame or regret had felt only admiration of the superb body which had so recently pleasured her.

His return had found her slipping her arms and body around him to warm him, so that presently they were making love again, slowly this time, Stacy exploring sensation while Matt explored Stacy.

After that sleep had claimed them. They had defied winter by celebrating the renewal of life, and outside a steady dripping sound told them, had they been inclined to listen, that winter had been temporarily routed and the Blanchard party's forced occupation of Pontisford Hall would shortly be at an end.

Matt woke first. Momentarily he wondered where he was and whose head it was which lay so confidingly on his broad chest. Memory revived, to have him sitting up, his heart hammering again, but not with passion. In the cold light of early dawn the euphoria of bliss which he had shared with Stacy was dissolved, and all that he was left with was a strong and strange sensation of shame.

What in God's name had he done? And why had he done it? To put it bluntly and brutally, in the plainest terms, he had lost his temper to such a degree that he had set upon and ravished a maiden lady of mature years. He was at last worthy of all the reproaches and insults which had been heaped upon him at the time of poor Camilla's death. If he had been innocent then, he was assuredly guilty now.

He looked down at Stacy's sleeping face. It was soft in the harsh light; all the lines of strain, of hauteur, which he had seen upon it since he had first met her, had vanished. Peace surrounded her like a halo.

This almost made matters worse, not better. He remembered the passion with which she had so freely offered herself to him throughout the long night, and closed his eyes at the memory of it. He wanted to deny what he had done, what their loving meant. He wanted to deny that he had been strongly attracted to her, for he had long told himself that after Camilla he could give himself to no woman other than as a temporary lover.

He put out a hand to stroke her into life—then drew it back. Shortly, when she awoke, she would remember too, and, being what she was, she could only do so with the deepest regret for what she had done. She would hate him for being the cause of her ruin, her surrender of virginity, honour and chastity, all things which a virtuous woman would hold most dear. He put his head in his hands; what to do?

He could ask her to marry him—but what would that mean to her? She didn't even like him, and he certainly didn't want to lose his freedom, or so he told himself. No, the best way was for him to leave her bed, and by his actions help her to pretend that last night had never happened. That she was still untouched icy Miss Anna Berriman, who would leave Pontisford Hall as chaste as she had been when she had arrived.

But the servants must know what had passed, surely? He hadn't returned, and Jeb at least would be aware that Matt Falconer had not slept in his own bed that night. No, they could not *know*, they could only suspect. Let him return to his room, to be found there later, and there could be no certainty attached to their suspicions.

So thinking, he gave his sleeping love one last gentle kiss, pulled on his shirt and breeches, picked up his other clothes and walked to his bedroom. To find Jeb already there.

The two men stared at one another. Matt said violently, as he saw Jeb begin to speak, 'Not a word, you understand. Not a word. I spent the night in this room, and you must bear me out. Whatever happened last night was my fault, no one else's, and no one else must pay the price.'

'If you say so, although I find difficulty in believing that whatever you got up to was not most vigorously consented to by the lady in question. I am certain that she knew her own mind, and exactly what she was doing.'

Matt flung his clothes on the bed. 'Damn you, Jeb, be silent. I gave you an order. Obey it. She deserves your consideration as well as mine.'

'And shall surely have it. I take it, then, that officially nothing happened? Is that what she wants?'

'How the hell do I know?' groaned Matt. 'I left her sleeping. And why am I discussing this with you? I said silence, and I meant it.'

'Ah, but can you guarantee her silence? No, don't strike me——' as Matt raised his fist '—it is surely a consideration. Is she likely to come after you, through a relative, with a pistol, to redeem her honour—or does she want a permanent mate, not a fly-by-night?'

There was no silencing him. 'You are not my conscience,' snapped Matt. 'Look to your own. Whose bed did you spend last night in?'

'Oh, "a hit, a very palpable hit"!' quoted Jeb. 'But I have never claimed to possess a sense of honour—you do. What made you lose it?'

Matt closed his eyes, turned his back on Jeb who had, strangely and uncharacteristically, apparently constituted himself Miss Anna Berriman's defender.

'Go and join Hal,' he said as he pulled off his shirt to change into a fresh one. 'The pair of you are lost in the wrong century. Chivalry is not dead while you and Hal still live!' After which unkind remark he refused to speak again. But he thought a great deal, and none of his thoughts was pleasant, and all of them reproached him.

Stacy awoke, her right hand questing to find Matt's. Unlike him she had no doubts about where she was, or with whom she had shared her bed and spent the night. Nor had she any regrets—as yet. The first of them surfaced when she found him—and all his clothing—gone.

It was only when she sat up and full consciousness had returned that the full enormity of what she had done struck her. Her hands rose to clutch her flaming cheeks. How could I? No, I must have dreamed it, she thought. But the hard evidence of a night spent in loving was all about her: her swollen mouth, her face reddened where his beard had caught it as they had kissed and clutched at one another. Her nipples were sore and tingling, and the very thought of what he had done to them brought them erect again.

She had been shameless, quite shameless, and whatever would he think of her? Simply, of course, that she was as loose as any whore, not even offering him a token resistance. When he had come to his full senses he must have been disgusted by her, and that was why he had crept away without so much as a kind word or a last caress.

It had never happened. Yes, that was it. If she thought and said so, then it must be so. Had not Bishop Berkeley, whom her father had admired, said that nothing existed except in the mind of the beholder? If so, then all that she had to do was wipe last night's madness from her mind until it no longer existed. There was no beholder. He was only a part of her mind, not she of his.

The boldness of this notion brought a sad smile to Stacy's lips. And if he tried to pretend that something had happened, then she would deny it, firmly and truthfully, since such an unlikely happening as Stacy Blanchard taking a man to her bed was, of course, unimaginable.

But it had happened. Worse, not only had she enjoyed it, but she had found inside herself a cauldron of passion like the one which boiled and bubbled above Cook's fire. Which reminded her that she was hungry, and she must go downstairs and face the assembled servants, persuading them by her iron control that nothing, absolutely nothing had happened and that she was indifferent to him.

But inside herself, as she was dressing, something shrieked and wailed, Oh, but I am not indifferent to him, and I want him back in my bed and in my life, and without him I am but of a barren stock, and always will be!

A timid knock came on her door. She called, 'Come in,' as she brushed her hair back into its most severe mode, having smoothed down as best as she could the deep green woollen travelling-dress in which she had been living since the coach had broken down five nights ago.

It was Louisa, looking better, but also looking timid, bleating anxiously, 'I trust I see you quite well this morning, my dear?'

Her brush still battering her curls into smoothness,

Stacy lied boldly back, 'Of course, Louisa. Why should I not be?'

'I thought Mr Falconer seemed rather annoyed by what you said to him last night, Stacy. I feared that he might reproach you.'

'Oh, he did, Louisa, he did. But you know me, I trust. I gave as good as I got.' Which was the literal unspeakable truth, was it not?

'I fear that you are too bold with him. He is not one of your bank clerks, my love, nor does he take kindly to strong-minded women. Most men don't.'

She couldn't resist speaking out after all, only to have Stacy reply briskly, 'Which doesn't worry me in the slightest, seeing that I have no interest in what any man, let alone most men, think of me. They must take me as I am.'

Which he had last night, even if he apparently regretted it afterwards. But it had been lovely while it lasted.

'All the same —— ' began Louise.

'All the same, Louisa? Nothing has been the same since we arrived at Pontisford.' And that is telling the truth with a vengeance, she added silently.

She swept downstairs in what Louisa was dismayed to see was her haughtiest mode. She made Jeb a languid bow as he emerged from the drawing-room, also on his way to breakfast; she wondered what he had been doing there. She missed the admiring glint in his eye as he watched madam brazenly throw open the kitchen door to sweep in and equally brazenly carol, 'Good morning all,' as though she were the town crier wishing everyone well.

Sure God, Matt had pleasured madam last night to the top of his and her bent—she was on even higher ropes than usual. It was to be hoped that she didn't fall off them.

Louisa was thinking the same thing in slightly different terms.

All the servants gave her a slightly stunned, 'Good

morning, madam,' including Hal, who was relieved to see that his lady, far from looking subdued and downtrodden after a rating from that unpleasant bastard Matt Falconer, or Lord Whoever-he-was, was, on the contrary, more pleased with life and herself than he had ever seen her. Unlike Jeb, he and the rest of her servants did not draw the correct conclusion from this.

The cauldron supplied her and Louisa with porridge. Ten minutes of time supplied her with Matt Falconer, who entered the kitchen after having overseen the horses, feeling that he was either about to be beheaded or would behead. He wasn't sure which.

All his expectations were confounded when his late bed-mate looked up from her porridge to announce briskly, 'Good morning, sir. I trust that you spent a pleasant night? It was my first comfortable one since arriving at Pontisford, and I do believe that a thaw is setting in, which will be a great relief to all of us.'

So that was to be the way of it. Nothing had happened. She had made the same decision as himself, so all would be well, and all manner of things would be well.

So why was it that, far from being happy, his own spirits took a nosedive? Could madam dismiss him so easily, then? Why, had he not pleasured her as few women had been pleasured, and had she not screamed beneath him in ecstasy, not once but several times? It almost demeaned a man that his doxy could be so airily non-committal after such a night of bliss.

'Middling,' he growled back at her, 'middling. I have known better.' And there, that should hold you, madam, if nothing else does.

Jeb was enduring another fit of the chokes, a real one this time, as the late lovers' double-edged conversation flew above his and everybody else's head. Stacy pounded his back vigorously. She had begun to have her suspicions of Jeb, and if she couldn't strike his conniving master, who had loved her and left her, why, then, she would strike his man—hard.

She took Matt's dismissive comment in her stride. 'I am sorry to hear it, sir. Such hard work as you indulge in deserves a better reward. You will, I am sure, be relieved to find that the weather has changed. I trust that as soon as possible labourers may be fetched to lift our coach from the ditch into which it has fallen, and, if it prove unroadworthy, that we may hire—or borrow—a post-chaise so that we may soon be on our way? You may rest a little easier then.'

The bitch, the magnificent bitch! She was taunting him before them all. What a nonpareil she was, to lose what no woman should lose before marriage and then to dismiss so casually the man who had done it, and defy him, publicly, to say or do anything which might betray both him and her. He was in no doubt that it was her behaviour which had caused, and was still causing, Jeb's splutterings.

Stacy rose, to recommend sweetly that Jeb consult a physician. 'You have these spasms far too often for your own good,' she informed him, and said to Matt, 'I'm sure that I need hardly remind you to act with all speed to arrange our departure. "Welcome the coming, speed the parting guest" is a maxim that I can recommend to you. It is one which I have always followed.' And this time she didn't flounce out of the kitchen, but moved like a Spanish galleon, carrying all before it in state and majesty. My dear Lady Disdain in person. Nothing, but nothing, anyone could do would ever be able to overset her.

Even Louisa was open-mouthed. Jeb was having convulsions again. Matt Falconer looked at them and the smirking servants with exasperation. 'For God's sake,' he bawled in their direction, not being able to vent his anger on Stacy, 'rattle your hocks. The sooner Pontisford is rid of you all, the happier I shall be.'

Which was just about the most curmudgeonly thing that

he could think of to say, when all that he really wanted to do was to pelt after madam and have her on her back again, welcoming him, but where in the world that would lead to scarcely bore thinking of!

What *did* bear thinking of was the rapid thaw, and the arrangements for Pontisford Hall's unexpected guests to leave. Matt, Jeb, Hal, John Coachman, the postilion and the dull boy, the last two having watched all the goings-on open-mouthed and uncomprehending, trudged through the slush to rescue the luggage from the coach. They were watched by Stacy from the window of her room. She had resolved to remain there until they left. She would have nothing to do with him ever again. Nothing! He was a vile seducer, that was all.

Louisa had come to her, later in the day, when it was decided that Matt would lend them his post-chaise to take them on the final stages of their journey to York, their coach being beyond immediate repair. Louisa's face was grave. 'I believe that we may be able to leave tomorrow, my dear, or so Mr Falconer seems to think.'

Stacy looked up from reading Blackstone to say coldly, 'He has not the good manners, then, to come to tell me himself?'

Louisa hesitated, and said placatingly, because she had rarely seen Stacy's face set in such uncompromising lines, 'I think that he will, my dear, when all the arrangements are made and it appears that the present milder weather will hold.' She hesitated again. 'I have remembered a little about what the scandal in which our host was involved consisted of. Your own remarks to him, in the circumstances, could scarcely be more unfortunate.'

'Indeed. And am I to be allowed to know?'

No, Louisa had never known her so icy, so withdrawn. 'I think that you ought. You will then be able to guard your tongue a little.'

The cauldron inside Stacy almost boiled over. Somehow she controlled herself, said, 'Continue, pray. I am agog.'

Louisa sighed. 'It seems that when he was a very young man he fell in love with and ran away with his brother Rollo, Lord Radley's wife. She died shortly afterwards, while quite young. The details of what happened were hushed up.'

'And that's it?' Stacy's voice was stifled. She had tried to keep it level, but could not.

'Isn't that enough? To run off with his brother's wife? He was cast off by his family, as you may imagine, and fled England to farm, his man Priestley tells me, in the Virginias on some land settled on him by his mother—her mother was an American. He worked alongside his men, I collect, which perhaps explains his strange behaviour here, working alongside the servants. . .'

'And expecting me to do so. Thank you, Louisa; I wish that you had told me the details of the scandal before.'

Louisa nodded. 'It was remiss of me, I own. But I thought. . . I don't know what I thought. . . That it would not be helpful. I was wrong.'

Stacy sat on the bed. 'Leave me, I beg of you. I wish to make ready for the journey.'

Which was a monstrous thundering lie. She wanted to face the fact that she was not the first woman he had ever seduced—as though she had ever thought that she was. But worst of all was that he had dishonoured his brother.

And I? Stacy suddenly thought, springing to her feet to put her hands to hot cheeks. Suppose I have been left pregnant? And what has possessed me that I should never think of such a possibility, either before, during or after what we did? Yes, I have truly run mad ever since I set foot in Pontisford Hall. God help me, but I must leave as soon as possible, and also trust in God that I may not pay a price for what I have done. What could I have been thinking of or, rather, not thinking of? How could my wits have gone so far astray?

And he? Should he not have considered what might be the inevitable end of. . .last night? And I was a virgin, too. Oh, yes, after our night together nothing was left of any maidenly modesty I might once have possessed.

Stacy's whole body was burning and shivering as though a fever afflicted it. The knock on the door in the middle of her torment had to be repeated before she pulled herself together and called, 'Come in!'

It was Matt Falconer. He had the effrontery to look and speak as though nothing untoward had passed between them. He bowed, said, 'Madam, I am come to inform you that with luck, and the thaw holding, you and your party should be on your way by first light tomorrow morning. Your luggage has been brought from your coach. Hal will be carrying your boxes up so that you may change for the journey should you wish to do so.'

Stacy inclined her head graciously, looking away from him as though the sight of him hurt her. 'I thank you, sir, for your consideration and the hospitality which you have shown to me and mine.'

Matt could not help himself; he started forward, said impetuously, 'Do not look at me so, madam. I do not know how to express my regrets for what occurred here last night——'

Her smile was frozen. 'A little late, wouldn't you say, sir?' And then putting up her hands as if to ward him off, 'No, do not say anything further, sir. Your departure this morning, without a word, tells all. I do not wish to dwell on what should never have happened. I pray that we do not meet again.' And she gave him her back.

'Miss Berriman,' Matt found himself saying hoarsely to that forbidding sight, 'I can only ask your forgiveness, and ask you to marry me. That is the least a man can do who behaved as I did.'

So, 'the least a man could do' was all that he had to offer her! And why not, pray, the most? Had he, then, felt nothing of the burning passion which had overwhelmed her, allied to the feeling afterwards, as she'd lain in his arms, that she had come home, had found the lost half of herself?

Apparently not, so coolly had his proposal been made. A proposal plainly made to salve his conscience rather than because he had felt anything but a passing lust for the woman he had bedded so casually. Desolation, followed by rage, overcame her.

'Marry you, sir? Marry you? I had as lief marry one of the apes from the zoo at the Tower. Or lead them in hell, as our forefathers said spinsters did! Marry a man, chance-met and chance-bedded? Indeed not. Take your proposal away, to offer it to someone less discriminating than I!'

Face on fire, he was almost on her again. Mastering himself, he stopped without touching her. 'That was not what you felt last night, madam, when you sighed and moaned in my arms. Where was your discrimination then?'

'Lost, with my wits,' she hurled at him, near to tears, near to breaking down, to clutching at him and howling, Say that you care for me a little. That what we felt in our transports was more than mere pleasure, was an identity shared.

Pride forbade it. And he, conscious of the enormity of what he had done, and that, excuse himself as he might, he deserved no more of her than the scorn which she was pouring over him, could not believe other than that was all that she felt for him.

She was splendid in her anger, splendid in her straight-backed independence, which offered neither him or any man quarter.

'Think again, madam. I have a title to offer you, if that

might please you. And a good name, even if I have done little to cover it with glory. . .'

'I would not have you,' lied Stacy, 'if you offered me the Crown of England.' But oh, if you offered me your love, I would have you though you had not a penny, and I not a sou to my name, and we walked ragged through England.

No, he was not about to offer her that. He was backing away, saying as he reached the door, 'You will not reconsider?'

'You have had my answer, sir. I am accustomed to my yea being accepted as my yea, and my nay as my nay. Nay it is. You should have considered what you were doing when you set upon me.'

For the second time in two days she had broken through his usually iron control.

'Oh, madam, do but you consider. I may have begun our bout of love but, by God, you joined in it so lustily that you had my breeches off before I had your skirts up!'

She should have fainted, died away, at having anything so gross thrown at her, but dreadfully Stacy had only one impulse overcome. . .and that was to laugh. She was hard put to it to stifle her giggles at the picture this conjured up, which was unfortunate, because had she laughed things between them might have been mended immediately, they being so equal in all that mattered between a man and a woman—in humour as in everything else.

Instead, she lifted her hands primly before her face and said in a fainting voice, 'Oh, for shame, sir, for shame! I did not know what I was doing I was in such shock.'

'But I think you did, madam, I think you did—to succeed in your objective when so stricken! But no matter I will leave you with my apologies, and with my offer. It stands, madam, it stands. Remember that.'

She shook her head at him, and he was fain to take her in his arms, to say, For God's sake, woman, for no reason on earth you attract me, sharp-tongued though you are, as no woman has ever done, not even my poor Camilla. We should deal well together, you and I, so let us deal well for life.

But, like Stacy, life had made him fearful of expressing himself, of betraying his emotions. If she distrusted men because all that they had ever wanted of her was Blanchard's Bank, then he distrusted not women, but the wretchedness which loving one woman had caused him. Better not to love them but simply to enjoy them. What distressed him over his treatment of Miss Anna Berriman was that he had taken her into his bed at first without her consent, even if by her conduct she had freely given it to him afterwards.

Stacy turned away from him. The word 'remember' rang in her head. She would always remember him, but she dared not trust him. Besides, duty and Blanchard's called, York awaited her, and she would not exchange her free life to be a man's slave, not for all the love he might have offered her but hadn't, and certainly not for his title—which he apparently didn't value anyway.

It was over. Useless to continue. He said, 'Remember,' again, and stalked out of the room, having bowed to her. Nothing was left to her but to open her boxes, change into clothes which she had not spent five days a-wearing, and leave for York. To resume her character as the passionless owner and ruler of Blanchard's Bank, her father's true daughter.

Matt walked downstairs, and only later, when the chaise was being driven through the slush of the drive on its journey to York, did he think to rebuke himself for not taking madam in his arms and convincing her that, chance-met or not, he and she could make a pair to withstand the world.

But by then it was too late.

CHAPTER SEVEN

'THANK goodness it's behind us,' sighed Stacy dramatically as the turning road, which for a fleeting moment had offered them one last glimpse of Pontisford Hall, took it away from them.

She had to admit, inwardly—not outwardly, that in the distance, beneath the clear blue of the November sky, Pontisford Hall, set in a landscape which was rapidly changing from an engraving in black and white to a dramatic oil-painting, looked singularly lovely. Its severe classical façade gave no hint of the horrors within.

Louisa nodded. 'So neglected,' she sighed, 'I wonder at Lord Radley allowing it to fall into such decay, I really do.'

Polly, sitting opposite them, not sure whether she had been using her common sense in allowing Jeb Priestley into her bed with her two nights ago, interrupted her betters pertly.

'Not Mr Falconer—I mean Lord Radley's fault,' she announced knowingly. 'He and Jeb—I mean Mr Priestley—only arrived there a few days before we did. Inherited it from his great-aunty, Lord Radley did, who was too old to care what condition she lived in. They were as shocked as we were by what they found.'

Which only goes to show, thought Stacy resignedly, that the servants often know more than we do. And, of course, Jeb was trying to tell me so that time when Matt came in and stopped him. She wriggled a little—she had misjudged him over that at least, but it was his own fault that she had done so. But I won't think about him, I won't. With luck I shall never see him again, she told herself.

Then why did she give an odd little shiver at the very idea that he had passed out of her life for good? She shook her head to clear it, and remarked briskly to Louisa, 'It is to be hoped that we reach York without further delay. They will be wondering what has detained us—unless, of course, they shared our bad weather.'

As if to make up for the disasters inflicted on them in the earlier part of their odyssey, Stacy's party reached York without further trouble, to find that the rooms taken for them in a house in the shadow of the great Minster were as warm and comfortable and as unlike Pontisford's filthy splendour as rooms could be.

The landlady welcomed them with open arms—pleased that her lodgers had taken over the whole house, saving her the trouble of looking for more—exclaiming, 'At last, madam! I had quite given you up. The weather here has been atrocious.'

There was a splendid meal soon made ready for them, comfortable beds in warm bedrooms, a footman of the landlady's own to help poor Hal carry in their boxes and other impedimenta, and maidservants to assist Polly, whose wrist still pained her. Louisa, face grey, was helped to her room where her dinner was sent up to her, daintily laid out on fine porcelain on a silver tray, while Stacy dined in lonely splendour off food which she had only dreamed of while half starving at Pontisford.

So why did she feel so desolate, so full of ennui at being, as she usually was, alone? At Pontisford she had been compelled to share her life with others, to sit at table with a pack of dependents, to listen to Matt and Jeb and the others laugh and talk companionably when she had retired to her bed behind the makeshift partition. And she surely couldn't be missing the rough fare which was all that Pontisford had supplied.

But she had never felt so lonely, she who had never felt

lonely before. And could she also be missing the sound of masculine voices in this house of women?

Enough of that, she told herself briskly. Tomorrow she would visit the York branch of the Bank, to discover what had been going wrong there and try to put it right. She would have preferred to have Greaves with her, not because she wanted him to assert authority over the men whom she would have to face, but because he would have been an ally, and she might need an ally.

Poxon, the manager, when he finally met her, thought that she not only needed an ally but a keeper, she having evidently escaped from a madhouse. . .

Remembering her father's wise advice, Stacy had given the staff at Blanchard's, York no warning that she was immediately to descend on them. Oh, they knew that a party from the London headquarters was on the way, and that it would include Miss Blanchard herself, but they had no idea of exactly when that party would arrive—or that, improbably, it would be Miss Blanchard who would head it.

Stacy dressed herself carefully in a black gown of sober cut, with small Mary, Queen of Scots-style fine linen ruffles discreetly edged with lace at her throat and wrists, and a black leather belt with a silver buckle and a small chain hanging from it, to which was attached a tiny notebook and a pencil. Over this she wore a long black coat, caped and cut like a man's. A black fur busby completed the ensemble. The impression of cold and competent austerity was completed by her hair, which had been pulled straight back into a giant knot; a black velvet band was wound round her head and across her forehead to restrain any curls which might wish to spring loose. A single pearl depended from its middle.

The whole effect was formidable in the extreme, as was intended.

Thus accoutred, with Louisa and Hal in attendance, Stacy set off on foot to the Bank's premises, situated not far from the house which she had taken. All seemed fair outside, and inside too, as she entered, her acolytes a little behind her.

The clerks behind the gilt grilles and the mahogany counters stared a little at this procession, particularly as no gentleman seemed to be in attendance. Hal, wearing the green and gold of the livery which Louis Blanchard had designed in one of his more creative moments, was the only male in the party. He was carrying a large leather bag which held all the business papers relating to the York branch which Stacy had brought with her from London.

The clerk whom she approached stared the hardest of all. She stripped off her long black gloves and said, without giving the man behind the counter the slightest notion of who she was, 'I would like, sir, to speak to your manager—as soon as possible.'

The clerk bowed and said, 'Oh, madam, I am afraid that might be difficult. Perhaps you could inform me of what business you wish to transact? Although, forgive me, it would perhaps be better if I, or the manager, spoke to your brother or to your husband about financial matters.'

'Now that would be difficult——' Stacy smiled at him '—seeing that I have neither. Pray escort me to your manager. The business which I have with him is serious in the extreme.' And as she saw him hesitate, 'Come, sir, I have my companion with me, and my footman; it will be quite proper for him to see me with them as chaperons.'

The clerk gave way; he came from behind the counter, bowed again, and asked, a shade of insolence in his expression, 'What name shall I give to him, madam?'

'Why, sir, I prefer to name myself to him.' And as he prepared to argue with her Stacy added lightly, 'Come, I have a deal of money to dispose of, and your bank has been recommended to me as a sound one. You would not wish to lose my account, surely?'

'Indeed not,' sighed the clerk dubiously, beginning to lead the way to the bank parlour, watched with intense interest by the rest of the staff, business obviously being poor at Blanchard's that morning. By the papers in Stacy's bag, it was never other than poor.

The clerk knocked on the door, heard the answering, 'Come in,' before bowing and escorting Stacy through it, saying, 'A lady to see you, Mr Poxon, sir.' He walked by Stacy to stand at the rear of the room, his master's aide, it would seem.

'A lady?' The manager, a gross man, with the signs of heavy drinking about his face and body—he was so red-faced and barrel-stomached, put down a large glass of port and said, 'Good morning, madam. You wish to do business with me? Forgive me, but——'

'You would rather do it with my husband, father or brother,' Stacy finished curtly, refusing the chair he was offering to her. 'No, I prefer to stand.' Perforce that left him standing too, but she was unable to prevent him from seizing her hand and planting a wet kiss on the back of it. Unattended ladies—for he obviously regarded Hal and Louisa as non-existent—were fair game.

'Yes, thank you, I should care for a glass of port,' she intoned in response to his lack of an offer of it, 'seeing that you appear to be out of Madeira,' and, when he stared at her nonplussed, added sweetly, 'I will have the one which you would have offered my father, brother or husband. It is, I understand, the custom for managers to offer those who visit the bank parlour a glass of something or other and a sweet biscuit. I see that you have anticipated my arrival and favoured yourself with one. On examination you seem to have a deal of liquor and a marked lack of sweet biscuits!'

Behind her Hal gave a curious snort, rather like the

ones which Jeb Priestley had been accustomed to give when his betters were entertaining him. The clerk looked as though the sky had fallen in on him.

'I had not thought. . .a lady. . .' stammered the manager, beginning to pick up a decanter, to pour a hefty share of port into a large glass. 'But if madam wishes. . .'

'Madam wishes,' returned Stacy. She was beginning to enjoy herself. After five hard days of battling with a man whose wit was as ready as her own, to cut this poor fool down to size was a pleasure. It might be cruel of her, but perusal of her papers back in London, Ephraim assisting, had proved to them both that if the manager was not on the take his incompetence bordered upon genius! Seeing him, Stacy didn't think that he displayed genius in any department; he was most likely a crude swindler.

'You would care for a glass too?' she asked Louisa, who shook her head determinedly.

'Not in the morning, my dear.'

'Very wise of you,' commented Stacy, draining her glass at one go, in imitation of all the men she had seen doing the very same thing when business was under discussion. 'A clear head is most necessary when one talks business. I'm sure you agree, sir.' And, as he picked up the glass he had refilled, 'Oh, no, I couldn't possibly advise you to drink further. I fear that you will need all your wits about you in the next few hours.'

She placed her glass on his leather-topped desk, walked around it and, before he could remonstrate, took his glass from his astonished hand and sat down in his high chair.

'I think that we ought to begin our business immediately. I have little time to waste,' she informed him sweetly.

The manager stared at her as if she had lost her wits. Louisa, used by now to Stacy's methods, designed to destroy confidence even before she began a merciless interrogation, sighed internally. She should have been a man, that was plain. The manager, poor fool, reached fo the bell standing on his desk, to ring it to summon help. ' will have you removed, madam. The madhouse is you proper destination, not the parlour of a bank!'

Stacy put her hand over his before he could use it. 'No so, sir. Now, were I to be here to open an account, should require a full and frank statement from you as t the solvency or otherwise of this branch. But, seeing tha that is not my business with you, we shall come to tha which is. Hal! Pray hand me my bag, if you please.'

'Certainly, madam.' Hal placed the bag on the desl before her.

The manager, face now purple, went to pick it up, t remove it. Stacy looked at him and said, her voice cool 'Pray leave the bag where it is, Mr Poxon, or I shall asl my man to restrain you.'

'Burtonshaw!' thundered the manager at the stupefie clerk. 'Either assist me to dispose of this madwoman o fetch a constable to do so!'

'Oh, I shouldn't do that,' smiled Stacy, all deadl charm. 'Were you so unwise as to summon a constable, should feel compelled to ask him to charge you with frau and embezzlement, for the papers in my bag seem t suggest that you have been engaged in both, and wouldn't like to do that until I had given you a chance t defend yourself. Besides, I wouldn't want Blanchard's t have an open scandal which might cause a run on the banl in York and damage the London house too. No, M Poxon, let us keep this in the room for the time being. She paused. 'Oh, I forgot. I didn't inform you of m name, did I? Most remiss of me. I am Miss Anastasi Blanchard, come from London to discover what has bee going wrong in York.' She eyed the decanter before he with distaste. 'I think that I may already have discovere part of the reason.'

She began to pull papers out of her bag, fixing th

stunned manager with a basilisk eye before handing him the letter of intent which she and Ephraim had jointly signed. He took it with a nerveless hand, and collapsed into a chair as though his legs had failed him.

'And now,' Stacy contrived, holding up the first of the papers from her bag, 'we shall begin to discuss your last balance sheet, and you may endeavour to explain to me how you have managed to achieve these remarkable figures. . .'

'You've never seen anything like it,' a grinning Burtonshaw told the rest of the clerks in the alehouse that evening. 'She had it all off pat. Knew more about how the house ran than he did! Sat there figuring away in her head, as though she had worked in a counting-house all her life, catching him out whenever he tried to fudge an answer. *And* she did something I've never seen afore—added all three columns up at once, pounds, shillings and pence in one go—*and* got it right—while poor old Poxon was still stumbling over the pennies! Like a trick in a fair.' He mimicked a woman's voice. '"But oh, pray, Mr Poxon, how can that be? Your figures distinctly prove otherwise, unless you are keeping a second set of books for your own pleasure, of course."'

He took an almighty swig of his ale. 'Never thought I should ever see old Poxon done down by a lady who looked as though butter wouldn't melt in her mouth. Halfway through he started some tale of it not being proper for a *real* lady to be adoing all this, and why hadn't she sent Ephraim Blount to see to things? So then, so then,' he went on, relishing his tale, 'she snaps the ledger in front of her tight shut—did I tell you she had all the ledgers in *and* mastered them before you could say knife?—and says, as sweet as pie, "Very well, Mr Poxon, if you prefer not to deal with me, and seeing that Ephraim has more to do than tour Yorkshire in winter, let me go to the magistrates this afternoon and swear a warrant for your arrest." And *then* she says, "And if you can't see that I'm saving of you from being transported, and saving Blanchard's name too, then you are an even bigger fool than I take you for!"

'That finished him, I can tell you. And she's a-going to speak to us all tomorrow morning, afore the bank opens. I ain't never seen such a high-stepping goer in my whole life, I ain't.' In his excitement he had reverted to the coarse speech of his youth, before he had gone to the grammar school and had become one of Blanchard's clerks aspiring to be a manager himself.

One of the younger men said, 'What right has she to behave like that, though, eh?'

'Owns the bank, don't she? And she told Poxon that while he had been making a loss in York she had been making a handsome profit in London, and so he ought to attend to her, and not the other way round. . .'

That silenced everyone, for the time being at least, and not forty-eight hours had gone by before all York laughed and buzzed over the doings at Blanchard's, and a small crowd gathered outside the bank each morning to see the forward hussy who had had the temerity to tell Bob Poxon what was what, and turn him off as well, before the week's end.

Even the drawing-rooms of the Minster's clergy hummed discreetly, Mrs Canon Gunter saying to her husband, 'Pray, my dear Alberic, can it conceivably be true that some unsexed creature came down from London to dismiss poor Mr Poxon and publicly address the bank clerks in the bank's parlour?'

The Canon nodded his grey head, adding mildy, 'Although you might be surprised if you met her, my dear, as I was, when she discussed with me Blanchard's loan to the Cathedral of a sum of money to repair the stained-glass window broken in the recent storm, to find that she appears to be a perfect lady.'

'My dear Alberic, I have not the slightest wish to meet her.'

But the very next day, while she was dining with the Bishop, there was the Bankeress, as York society had begun to call her, being introduced to her! It appeared that she was a relative of the Beauchamps of Bramham Castle, in whose company she had arrived, and, after her work in York was ended, was to stay with them over Christmas, her mother having been Lady Beauchamp's late sister!

'It was a wonder,' Mrs Canon announced later, 'that she wasn't turning in her grave, her daughter's conduct being so unladylike.'

York society at the dinner was all agog. The more so because of the remarkable cold beauty and composure of the woman who had set the town's gossips a-roaring. If Stacy was aware of the impression she had made, she gave no sign of it. Inwardly she was less sure of herself than she had ever been.

Earlier that day she had dismissed Poxon, with the pay owing to him. Her work with the bank's ledgers and her discussions with the clerks involved had made it apparent that he had, in addition to running the bank into the ground financially, been looting it for years. Greaves, who had at last arrived in York, cured of his malaise, was in full agreement with her.

Poxon had first paled, and then gone purple. His chief clerk, Robson, who had always disliked him and had remained honest—although many had not—was, at her order, standing by, waiting to be appointed in Poxon's place, with Greaves to help him during his first few weeks.

'You hard-hearted bitch!' Poxon had ground the words out between his teeth. 'I might have known this would be the end of it when I first met you—a woman who doesn't know her place in the world. But, by God, what place can you have, other than to turn men away from their rightful employment? What man worth his salt would want to touch you, I ask myself, other than to get at your money? What mercy could I expect from such an unsexed creature as you are?'

She had heard Louisa gasp as, ruined and frustrated, the wretched Poxon had continued to pour verbal filth over her, even as Hal began to draw him away and young Greaves started forward, thinking that she might need his protection as well. But, by God, madam had courage, one had to grant her that! She never moved, her colour never changed, and when Hal had wrestled Poxon to the door, preparatory to throwing him out of the office he had once ruled, she said, her voice peremptory and as impersonal as she could make it, 'Wait!'

He fell silent. Stacy rose to her feet and, disguising her inward tremblings, said coolly and clearly, 'The mercy I have offered you, Mr Poxon, is that I have not called on the magistrates to arrest you for offences for which you might either hang or be transported to New South Wales. It might be what you deserve, but would neither benefit your poor wife, who would be thrown upon the parish, nor Blanchard's Bank. Be thankful that I have spared you that.'

He made her no answer, but allowed Hal to drag him from the room. Once the door had closed behind him, Louisa rose, went over to Stacy, whose self-control was on a knife-edge, and cried forcefully, 'You see how wrong you are to try to take your father's place. No lady should have to endure what you did just now.'

Stacy closed her eyes. 'You are more troubled than I am by it,' she said severely, which was not quite the truth. 'Allow Hal to escort you home when he has finished with Mr Poxon. Send him and Polly back for me—I have more instructions to give Mr Robson before I leave.'

Later, after she, Robson and Greaves had gone over the changes which she had ordered in the Bank's administration, she walked out of the York branch's big mahogany front doors into the narrow street. Her feet took her towards the Minster, whose towers dominated the little town which was barely changed from what it had been in medieval times.

None of the Blanchards could ever have been called truly religious, even though the founder of the line had been compelled to flee Paris because he was a Huguenot, but Stacy suddenly felt that she needed more than mortal help. She realised that during her reign at the London bank she had been cushioned from the stark unpleasantness of dismissing those who had behaved criminally. Louis Blanchard had run his business on a tight rein, overseeing everything, leaving little chance for dishonesty to flourish, so she had not encountered the more distressing aspects of business life. For the first time she understood what Ephraim Blount had been trying to tell her on the day before she had left London.

'You must be strong, madam,' he had said, blinking at her over his gilt half-moon spectacles. 'You must be aware that the York branch's poor performance is due to more than simple neglect and idleness. Dishonesty is involved, and you must deal with it as firmly as your father would have done. The Bank expects it of you.'

'Oh, never fear,' she had told him impatiently, 'I am ready for anything.' Which had not, after all, proved quite true. Worse, Poxon's accusations that she was unsexed had touched a nerve which Matt Falconer had touched before him.

It was growing dark as she walked along. Hal was carrying a flambeau on a pole before her and Polly walked by her side. 'Wait for me here, if you please,' she told them, before she entered the Minster's porch which gave access to the nave. 'I shall not be long, I trust.'

There was a brazier burning in the street before the porch, and a man was stirring the coals into flaming life. Hal and Polly warmed themselves at its welcome heat, but the Minster struck cold as Stacy entered it—to hear the choir singing and find just sufficient light for her to glory in the sight of the great window, The Five Sisters of York, of which she had often heard tell.

Alone in the all-enveloping gloom, Stacy had never felt so lost and isolated. Every rule by which she had lived since her father's death seemed to be under challenge, not only because of what had happened to her at Pontisford Hall—and what she had done with Matt Falconer—but also because of what loyalty to the Bank had compelled her to do in York. Poxon had earned his dismissal, but she could take no pleasure in her part in it, even if, at the end, she had shown him a mercy which neither her father nor Ephraim would have done. They would have had him before the magistrates and on his way to Botany Bay without a second thought.

She needed grace. She needed to feel that what she was doing, to others as well as to herself, although harsh, was just. Most of all she needed to come to terms with her own passionate nature. Until she had met Matt Falconer she had not known passion, had, indeed, denied that she could ever experience it. A few short days had shown her how wrong she was. The memory was with her still, and to her horror, instead of being remorseful for what she had done, she was waking each morning to regret that he was not in her bed. Instead, in his guise as the lion-man, Matt Falconer visited her nightly in her dreams. Dismayingly she also knew that her body burned, not with shame but with frustrated desire.

Kneeling down, hands covering her face, Stacy prayed for help, for guidance. For the first time she—a Blanchard—almost wished that she were a Roman Catholic, so that she might confess her sins and receive absolution. Perhaps after that the memory of his lips and hands would fade away and disappear.

After a little time she rose, to see Canon Gunter standing in the aisle, dressed not as he had been in the bank's parlour but in his robes. He spoke hesitantly to her. 'You are not ill, I trust, Miss Blanchard? You are alone. Do you need help?'

What to say? Simply, 'Is it enough for us to try to do good, sir, even if our frailty means that we not only find it hard, but sometimes impossible? And if we backslide, may we be forgiven, however gross our sin?'

'If we truly repent, my dear. Yes.'

Stacy closed her eyes. How could she truly repent her night of love with Matt Falconer, however much she ought to do so?

'Repentance is hard, sir.'

'Oh, but consider, to do right and to repent is never easy. To be easy is the way of the sinner.'

That, at least, was true. She had fallen into bed with Matt Falconer with such consummate ease, but to repent of her sin seemed impossible. She tried again to discover whether the Canon had an answer for her, but since she could not tell him why she needed absolution she doubted whether he could help her.

'And does God forgive us our sins, even if we find it hard—nay, impossible—to repent?' Stacy heard her voice shake as she spoke.

The Canon considered her for a moment, doubtless, she later thought wryly, wondering what improbable sins Miss Anastasia Blanchard might have committed that she should so desperately ask him for help and absolution.

'I think that He would prefer us to repent, but I believe that, knowing our weak natures, He might be inclined to forgive us if we had tried to do so, even if we found it difficult.'

It was plain that he was not one of the new Evangelical

clergy, who would have thundered at her about hellfire and damnation lying in wait for those who sinned and did not repent. Would she have preferred him to do so? Stacy wasn't sure. As though he had divined her thoughts he added gently, 'I can only advise you to throw yourself on the infinite mercy of God if you are troubled, my dear Miss Blanchard.'

She bowed. 'I will remember that, sir, and I thank you for your help.' And she walked on, aware that he was gazing thoughtfully after her as she moved away from him to rejoin her waiting servants.

Polly said to her as they crossed the deserted road, 'Only think, madam, we thought we saw Jeb Priestley while you were in the Minster. Hal and I went a little way down the road—keeping an eye on the porch, a-course, in case you came out—and we thought we saw him going into an ale-house.'

This confidence had the improbable effect of cheering Stacy up. 'Well,' she said briskly, 'I can imagine that if you did see Jeb Priestley he would most likely be making for an ale-house, but I also think it is highly unlikely that either he or his master is here in York. I distinctly remember Mr Falconer saying that he intended to return to London as soon as his business was ended at Pontisford, and that he did not wish to remain there any longer than he needed.'

'Hal thought it might have been him,' offered Polly pertly.

Doubtless Polly's wish to meet Jeb again was father to the thought! Well, she, Stacy, didn't want to see him or his arrogant master again.

But what if, said a little voice in her head, he has made you pregnant? What then? To which the only possible internal answer was, I'll think about that if it happens, which, pray God, it won't. After all, we only spent one night together, and I am constantly hearing tales about persons who have been married for years failing to have children when they most desperately need them to provide a succession for a title or for estates, so one night's madness would surely not be enough. Would it?

The truth is, she admitted to herself, and it was something which she could never have confided in Canon Gunter, I might repent of the possible consequence of the sin of becoming Matt Falconer's mistress for one mad night, but I don't repent of the night itself, even if I wish that it had never happened—especially seeing that I don't even like the man!

And what did such an admission make of the once virtuous Miss Anastasia Blanchard?

CHAPTER EIGHT

'YORK?' queried Jeb Priestley, thunderstruck. 'We are going to York? I thought that you said when we reached Pontisford that we should return to London as soon as our business here was done, which it is, and take a passage back to Virginia post-haste. What are we going to York for?' And then, staring at his master, 'Oh, never tell me! You are haring after Miss Anna Berriman.'

'Not at all.' Matt made his voice as rough as he could. He was standing in his bedroom at Pontisford Hall, packing his bags, a task which was, by rights, Jeb's, only somehow he always managed to avoid doing it. 'I had quite forgotten the woman existed.' Which was a thundering lie; he thought about her every time he went to his lonely bed, and frequently in the daytime too. Which was a nonsense, considering what a cold-hearted bitch she was—except when she was in his bed. He would never have thought that a woman could show him two such different faces—as well as such a splendid body.

He swore at a recalcitrant shirt before stuffing it any old how into his bag. 'I need to see the lawyers there about some property in the town which my great-aunt owned—or so some papers I found seemed to hint—something which that ass of a lawyer in London appeared to know nothing of.'

Which was the truth. Or part of it. The real truth being that he would have taken the papers back to London with him, told Grimes to get on with sorting the whole business out, had they not provided him with the most splendid excuse for 'haring after Miss Anna Berriman'—Jeb's words—but he had to admit the truth of them. The woman haunted him. And, after so many years of loving them and leaving them, that was almost a bad joke.

'Well, I must say, I don't mind seeing Polly again, and for God's sake, m'lord, Mr Falconer, sir, or Mad Matt, whichever you prefer today, allow me to pack your bag for you before you ruin everything. You're showing a rare impatience to be off, I must say. Good in bed, was she?'

Even for Jeb this was insolence indeed. But how could you rebuke a man who had once saved your life for you, albeit you had already saved his? And who, despite his wagging tongue, was as faithful a friend as a man could have?

'Matt will do,' he told Jeb mildly, 'as I've informed you often enough before.'

'They don't like me to call you Matt here, though,' mourned Jeb, folding m'lord's fine cotton underwear. 'That poor old man Horrocks closes his eyes every time I fail to call you m'lord, and then "m'lords" you at twice the normal rate for the rest of the day to make up for my impudence, I suppose. They like bowing and scraping here, and no mistake. "Yes, m'lord, no, m'lord, pray walk all over me, m'lord, do," he mimicked savagely. 'You'll need a new pair of boots when you reach York. These are on their last legs. And a new coat and shirt and stockings and hat, if you hope to impress the lady. There was money there, you know. An heiress, do you think?'

'No, I don't, and I'm not going to,' retorted Matt cryptically, leaving Jeb to work out what he meant and aiming a half-hearted blow at him at the same time, which Jeb dodged dextrously. 'And for your information, Miss Anna Berriman is most definitely not the purpose of my visit. I thought that I might ride over and take a last look at my childhood home.'

And that was another truth, and an unwelcome one. Whether it was the passing years or the sense of having lost something which he had not known he had treasured until it was gone, he had been experiencing a burning desire to see The Eyrie again. And what a terrible name that was for the beautiful Jacobean mansion which the first Earl Falconer had built after doing some dirty diplomatic business for James I, and which had been paid for by one of the few grants of money made by that miserly king to a deserving subject.

He could ride over from York to see it, if only from a distance. He had no intention of accepting the olive-branch which his father had offered to him. Too much water had flowed under too many bridges for him ever to set foot in The Eyrie again. It astonished him that he should experience such a sharp pang at the very thought of its loss.

A flash of memory showed him the room which he had occupied after he had graduated from the nursery and before he had been packed off to be a midshipman. He had been the third son, highly unlikely to inherit, but Frank, the second son, had died at a badly taken fence in the hunting field shortly after he had reached thirty—and a mercy for the estate that he had, since his career had been one long debauch. He had been drunk on the day of his death, unfit to ride, but had insisted on doing so.

And Rollo, the heir, who had looked as though he might live forever, had departed this life a year ago; how, Matt didn't know, nor did he want to know. Grimes had started to tell him something of it, but he had stopped him with a sharp, 'So far as I am concerned Rollo died for me twelve and more years ago; what happened to him since means nothing to me.'

But, astonishingly, The Eyrie did. He could see the plain of York from the turret window, he remembered, and sometimes, on a clear day, he could almost convince himself that he saw the Minster's towers rising from it.

So he told himself that it was neither Miss Anna Berriman nor his aunt's property in York and outside it which drew him there, but one last chance before he left England forever to see that window again. Even if it was only from a distance. Memory told him of the bookcase beneath its leaded panes, his treasures ranged along the top of it, and on the facing wall the old print which showed Charles II's ships firing on the Dutch fleet in one of that king's few naval victories. A Falconer had commanded a ship there, he remembered.

Only, when he reached York and discovered that his aunt had owned a house in the town, and a small manor house outside it, he decided to open the town house and stay there for the Christmas season—he might catch a glimpse of Miss Berriman. Each time that he walked the streets he looked for her—but had no luck at all. One might almost have supposed that he had imagined her, and the night that they had spent together.

He had casually asked the lawyer he had found in York, Hayes, someone jovial and rubicund, quite unlike Grimes, whether he had come across a Miss Berriman who had lately arrived in York, but that gentleman did not connect her with the Miss Anastasia Blanchard, the Bankeress, who had recently scandalised York, and had shaken his head.

'You might,' he had offered, when Matt had told him that he wished to find the lady, 'take the opportunity to visit the Assembly Rooms for the Christmas Ball. If, as you think, she is a person of consequence, she is almost certain to attend.'

Well, yes, he might attend the Christmas Ball at the Assembly Rooms, Matt told Hayes as well as himself, but not simply to meet Miss Berriman. Oh, no, that was not it at all—on the other hand he found it difficult to understand why exactly he *did* want to attend something which was the kind of event which he always avoided—the small beer of living! But how to attend, when he knew no one of consequence in York who might introduce him to the Master of Ceremonies who ruled the Assembly?

Fate was on his side, after all. By chance, walking along, admiring the Minster's east window, he met Jack Vernon, an acquaintance from his days in the Navy. Matt hailed him as though he had been his oldest and dearest friend, and Jack immediately invited him to join the party he was escorting to the Assembly Ball. Matt had remembered Jack as a man of the most undiscriminating goodwill, and his memory had not deceived him.

'I shall be escorting my wife and her sister to the dance—a classy little filly, my sister-in-law Phoebe—you not hitched yet? No? By Jove, she's just the girl for you, then, and a little fortune comes with her—not that you mind that it's little now, eh, seeing that that ne'er-do-well brother of yours has gone to meet his last rest?' And he gave Matt a poke in the ribs which left him bruised for days.

But he accepted the invitation all the same, had Jeb dress him to a turn, as he hadn't dressed himself for years, and found himself in the Assembly Rooms, part of Jack's party. He dutifully made a leg at Phoebe, who wasn't to his taste at all, thanked Jack, and was introduced all over again to Jack's cousin, Viscount Trotternish, whom Matt remembered as plain George Drummond before he had inherited.

'Matt Falconer! I do believe you haven't changed a bit since we fought together at Trafalgar!'

It was as though the scandal had never happened, or Jack and George were being tactful. Matt rather thought that they weren't. Neither of them had ever been tactful when they had been young, and they hadn't changed much with age, only grown fatter. He supposed that being a hard-working farmer himself had kept him in trim.

What Trot, as he insisted Matt call him, was interested in was heiresses.

Matt asked him impulsively, as though they were young naval lieutenants again, 'What the devil are you doing here, Trot? Not your sort of thing at all.'

'Might say the same to you, Matt. And where have you been all these years?

'Farming in Virginia.'

'Haw-haw, you always did like a joke! But I suppose you've come here for the same reason I have. Like to get your hand on the dibs even if you do have to take the great heiress as well! Now, I'd prefer little Phoebe, but she ain't got enough tin to keep the old home in lead for the roof, whereas this one —' and he raised his eyes prayerfully to heaven '— is rolling in it.'

'Now what great heiress is this, Trot? I'm not up to snuff about such matters these days.'

'Must be behindhand, then, Matt, eh, not to know the Bankeress, the Blanchard heiress? That's why there's so many unattached bachelors here tonight, and all sober. She's supposed to be coming with the Beauchamp party. Rumour says that they're all staying overnight at her place in York—and then she's off to Bramham with them tomorrow. You remember the Beauchamps, eh, Matt?'

Yes, Matt did remember the Beauchamps—just. He didn't, however, remember any rich Blanchard family in York, and twelve years out of England meant that he had little idea of what was what in the society line.

'The Blanchard heiress who is a bankeress, Trot? And what, pray, is a bankeress? You have me all agog. I don't remember any Blanchards around York.'

'Why, she owns Blanchard's Bank, Matt. You do remember Blanchard's, surely? She's old Louis' daughter. He died suddenly two years ago, left it all to her—to run! Imagine, a female owning Blanchard's! And run it she does. She arrived at the York branch three weeks ago, and came down on old Poxon the manager like a ton of bricks. Found out that he had been robbing the bank blind, and had her footman throw him into the street. Sacked half the clerks for helping him, and read the Riot Act to the rest in the bank parlour. They say she ran the bank herself for a week before she handed it over to the new man.'

Matt might have made the inevitable connection with Miss Anna Berriman immediately, before he had so much as seen her, if Trot hadn't grabbed him by the arm, exclaiming, 'Good God, yes! There she is, with the Beauchamps. Some might say she's a stunner, but she looks a cold fish to me. Still, the Blanchard millions would make up for that, eh?'

And, like Jack Vernon, he abused Matt's ribs all over again. Not that Matt noticed—he was far too busy staring at Miss Anna Berriman, who was Miss Anastasia Blanchard, and saying to himself grimly, of course, of course. The Bankeress. I might have guessed.

Stacy had had to admit that meeting her aunt Beauchamp again had revived memories and feelings which she had thought she had forgotten. Louis Blanchard had never cared for his wife's sister, but Stacy had always found her a loving aunt until the final quarrel with her father had occurred over his training Stacy to succeed him.

She had corresponded with Aunt Beauchamp, secretly and against her father's wishes, but she had not seen her aunt or her uncle again until two days ago when they had arrived at her York home and her aunt had thrown her arms around her, crying, 'At last, my love. Let me look at you. You are as lovely as I thought that you would turn out to be! But oh, my dear, what is this I hear of you? Running the bank in York? That might have pleased your poor, dear father but I cannot say that it pleases me! And you are still unmarried. I blame your father for that.'

'Dear Aunt,' Stacy had murmured tearfully, 'do not let us quarrel, rather let us agree to disagree. I have my life and you have yours. And from now until I leave Yorkshire I shall take a holiday from work. Mr Greaves has finally arrived, quite cured of the illness which overtook him on the way here, and will look after the Bank for me until I return home.'

With that her aunt had to be satisfied, and her uncle too, that amiable, jovial man, quite unlike Louis Blanchard—or Matt Falconer, for that matter. All the same, once her aunt was alone with Louisa Landen they had sadly agreed that poor Stacy had been done no favour by her father when he had trained her to succeed him in the Bank. 'But at least she is willing to attend the Ball,' Aunt Beauchamp had said, and had looked with pride at Stacy when she'd walked downstairs to join the party ready to leave for the Assembly Rooms.

Stacy's only regret was that Louisa was not coming with them. 'You do not need me now that you have your aunt,' she had told Stacy, 'and I am growing too old for such junketings.' She had never really recovered from her illness at Pontisford, and Stacy was beginning to realise, with a pang, that the safe world in which she had lived for so long, with Louisa always by her side, was beginning to disintegrate. Change was all about her.

To her surprise she found herself looking forward to the Ball. She had dressed herself for it with great care, and walked into the Assembly Rooms conscious that she was looking her best. She was wearing a dress of pale green silk with the slightly lower waistline that fashion now demanded, trimmed with seed-pearls on the bodice and skirt, and a splendid pearl collar around her long and swan-like neck. Her fan was large, decorated with arabesques of seed-pearls and tiny emeralds. The whole ensemble served to emphasise the glowing green eyes set in an ivory face of classical purity.

Her cousin Anthony Beauchamp, who was her escort for the evening, bowed over her hand, looked into her eyes and said, 'My dear Anastasia. If only you would allow us to introduce you to Society I am sure that you would become all the rage.'

'Oh, as to that, sir,' she replied, tapping his arm gently with her fan as though she had been coquetting with men all her life, instead of doing so for the first time, 'I have no time to be all the rage; my presence is required elsewhere.'

He bowed again, his eyes hard on her. 'You must allow me to suggest that you should reform your ways to accommodate Society's demands and allow us to enjoy your charming presence.'

Well, that was as may be, and Stacy was about to answer him as kindly as she could, for she had absolutely no intention of transforming herself into a copy of one of his sisters. Their conversation appeared to centre on balls, their latest *toilette*, and handsome young men — in that order. Shrugging a little, she glanced across the room — only to see, gazing at her with a face like thunder, Matthew Falconer, Lord Radley! And where had *he* sprung from? And why was he looking at her like that? It was he who had wronged her, not she him. Worse, he was advancing towards her with that empty idiot George Trotternish by his side.

Anthony Beauchamp, staring at his magnificent presence, said involuntarily, 'Who the devil's that?' to have his mother reply,

'Why, I do believe it's Matt Falconer — Matt Radley, I suppose we ought to call him now — and goodness, how he has changed. I'm not surprised that you didn't recognise him. But what is he doing here?'

'Matt Radley?' Anthony sounded as stunned as Stacy felt, and she could not be surprised at his astonishment. Beside Anthony's bland and civilised charm, Matt Falconer looked more than ever like some pirate out of a Minerva Press novel, come to life in all his barbaric glory.

His superb clothing only served to enhance his savage appearance: he was more leonine than ever. His coat and breeches were skin-tight, revealing the muscularity of a body which put that of every other man in the room to shame. His face was so stern and strong that ordinary canons of handsomeness seemed unnecessary—nay, even a drawback. And every woman's eye was on him.

Stacy could not tear hers from him either. Especially since his were fixed so determinedly on her that she had the unwelcome impression that she had lost every article of clothing which she was wearing. Worse still, she realised that she was looking at him and seeing his remarkable torso naked, as it had been that shameful night, in all its splendidly muscled glory, his clothing too having fallen away.

George Trotternish was, as usual, sublimely unaware, as was Jack Vernon behind him, of the sensation which their friend and guest was causing. To add to the hum of excitement which ran round the room, many of the older persons present remembered both Matt and the scandal, and were busy reminding one another of it.

Stacy saw with rising desperation that Matt neither knew nor cared about the brouhaha he was creating, only bowing impassively when Trot said eagerly, 'Dear Lady Beauchamp, do allow me to present to you my old friend and fellow sailor, Lord Radley.'

Aunt Beauchamp said faintly, 'Oh, I have known Lord Radley since he was a child—but we have not met for many years. I am surprised to see you here, sir.' For some reason she felt unable to put down Trot or cut Matt. Possibly Matt's tremendous presence and his ignoring of the fact that he was officially *persona non grata* because of his disgraceful conduct so many years ago accounted for her consenting to receive him—which meant that everyone else at the Assembly Ball would.

Matt was taking Aunt Beauchamp's hand and bowing

over it. 'I have inherited property in and near York, dear Lady Beauchamp,' he told her gravely. 'I have been in the United States since we last met. I remember, though, that you were kind to me when I was a boy and sailed kites with Anthony here.'

Aunt Beauchamp said feverishly, 'Oh, he was much younger than you, and I recall that it was you who was kind to him. I must introduce you to my party,' and she began the civilities which ruled the social world over which she presided.

Matt was behaving politely and modestly, quite unlike the savage Stacy remembered from Pontisford Hall. And now it was her turn to be presented to him, and he was bowing to her and saying, as smoothly as though he were meeting her for the first time, 'An honour, Miss Blanchard. I must admit that I have heard so much about you that I feel that I know you already.' And his eyes were defying her as he came out with this splendidly ambiguous statement.

'Oh, Lord Radley, there you have the advantage of me,' she threw back at him, for if he wanted to play games with her, then so would she respond to him, 'for I am sure that had we ever met before I could hardly have forgotten doing so.' Her eyes were sparkling at him, sending him a message that she was quite unaware of.

Aunt Beauchamp was saying, as the music began, 'My dear Matt, if you have no partner for this dance then I am sure that my dear niece would be willing to oblige you,' ignoring the black look with which her son was favouring her.

Indeed, as Matt led the unwilling Stacy on to the floor for the cotillion, for she was unable to refuse her aunt's wish, Anthony turned on his dominant mother.

'I do not understand you, madam. You know perfectly well that I wished to begin the evening by dancing with my cousin. Instead you have handed her over to a man of such ill fame that I am surprised that you even deigned to receive him, never mind commit an innocent young woman into his care!'

Aunt Beauchamp watched Stacy and Matt take their position in the set and begin to move through the dance's intricate pattern. She was a woman of great character, even if that character had no real depth, and she went her own way with little consideration for what others might think — even her own son.

'My dear Anthony —— ' she smiled at him over her fan '— I have no wish for you to marry your cousin. Cousins shouldn't marry — bad for horses and even worse for us — and you would never be able to stand up to Stacy. Not that I want her to marry Matt Falconer — but as to receiving him, that is a different matter. I thought that he was badly treated years ago, and it is time that story was forgotten. Both Rollo and Camilla Falconer are dead, and the scandal should die with them. Now, why don't you ask pretty little Phoebe Whatever-her-name-is, Jack Vernon's sister-in-law, to dance with you? She's the sort of child you ought to marry — pretty and biddable.'

So now he had madam almost in his arms again! But she was intent on keeping him at a distance. Her hand might be in his, but that was all. Matt tried to look her in the eye, make her acknowledge him, but she resolutely kept her own gaze modestly fixed on the floor as though she were a young girl at her first ball. The result was that he was prey to the most dreadful and conflicting emotions.

From the first moment that he had seen her, tall and graceful at the other end of the room, her long neck elegantly inclined towards the young popinjay to whom she was talking, he had been unable to stop looking at her.

Really, madam was superb. As always, she carried herself with such damnable unconscious pride, but, more than that, tonight there was a glow, a radiance about her which he could not remember her possessing at Pontisford.

She even laughed lightly once, and as he moved nearer to her in the dance he could not prevent himself from mentally stripping her beautiful gown from her so that he could once again visualise her splendid breasts. He could remember only too well that he had held and caressed them with both his hands and his mouth. And as she advanced and retreated towards him, head modestly inclined, Matt was suddenly agonisingly aware that his body, constrained as it was by his tight clothes, would, if he was not careful, betray to the whole world his rampant and aroused desire for her.

Lust! That must be what he felt for her, and why he should feel it for the Bankeress, a cold, calculating machine, according to York gossip, he couldn't imagine. Down, Fido, down, he told his treacherous body, for the mere sight of her was proving his undoing. He tried to turn his mind to other things, took his eyes away from her face, only to see that now she had raised hers and was studying him as though, he thought angrily, he were an insect laid out for her to dissect.

To no avail. The memory of the night when he had wronged her, and she had so enthusiastically helped him to do so, was as sharp and clear as though it had happened only a few hours before, instead of a few weeks. He must be going mad. Even when she turned away from him, and all he could see of her was the long and lovely line of her back, the thing which held him most was the smooth elegance of her graceful and rounded behind as it moved beneath her light clothing—and the memory of his hands stroking it!

He was turning into a satyr and it was all her doing. Desire, lust, whatever it was which held him in thrall, also demanded that he needed to speak to her, so that he might hear that enchanting if disdainful voice, provoke her into saying something, anything, even if it was only something to put him down.

'You are enjoying yourself, madam?' he asked her, his voice glacial.

'Indeed, sir. And why should I not?' Stacy was retreating away from him even as she spoke, only to meet him again, hand extended, and say, 'You appear uncomfortable, sir. Do I take it that you are not enjoying yourself?'

The bitch! She was mocking him, he was sure. Did she guess the pother that he was in? Surely not. She was a maiden lady of impeccable virtue, after all—or had been until Matt Falconer had seized hold of her and thrown her upon her bed!

He felt himself breaking into a sweat while she, the cold-blooded doxy, was raising her eyebrows at him as the music brought her back to him, so that he felt constrained to say, 'A gentleman's clothing, especially a cravat, seems especially designed *not* to dance in, which explains my discomfort a little.'

Only to have her remark when next they met, 'Oh, I suppose that in the wilds of America you are more accustomed to perform clad simply in war-paint and feathers. This must make a most unwelcome change, I do agree—but you could hardly expect us to accommodate your more savage desires.'

'If I were to accommodate my more savage desires,' he told her between his teeth as he spun her around, 'you would be on the floor with me, and the company would retreat screaming.'

Well, I asked for that, was Stacy's inward response. She supposed that she ought to be shocked, but the picture which he had conjured up was such a wickedly amusing one that she was hard put to it not to laugh, especially when her next partner in the dance, her cousin Anthony, growled jealously between clenched teeth, 'If that fellow is annoying you, Cousin Stacy, do tell me, and I shall see that he ceases to do so.'

She shook her head at him and turned around, to meet Matt going the opposite way. She offered him her hand, wondering why, as he took it, a strange thrill always ran through her body when he touched her, or she him. Nothing like that had ever happened when Anthony Beauchamp took her hand in his.

Matt said, as they moved together, also through clenched teeth, she was amused to note, 'I see that you have a smile for that fribble who was entertaining you when I arrived. I suppose that you save your scowls and curses for me.'

'Of course,' she told him sweetly as the music stopped and they bowed at one another, 'for you deserve them, and he does not. After all, it was you who set upon me as though I were some lightskirt who prowls the Haymarket, while he has always behaved towards me with perfect rectitude.'

This goaded Matt into further unwise speech. 'Seeing that he is only half a man, I am sure that perfect manners are all he is left with.'

'True, and as you have no manners at all he must have inherited your share.'

'And who has inherited yours,' he asked her savagely as the music ended, 'seeing that we are an excellent match in the land where bad manners reign? My memory of your conduct at Pontisford is still fresh.'

'And I of yours, sir,' she said as they walked back to where her aunt's party was seated. 'But then, what can one expect of a savage who is accustomed to dancing clad only in paint and feathers?'

'The same as from a shrew who possesses a calculating-machine instead of a heart!' he ground back at her.

'Then we *are* well-matched,' Stacy informed him sweetly. She was astonished to find that, as before when she was with him, she had never felt so alive, every nerve in her body tingling and a strange excitement growing in the pit of her stomach. It was almost as though she wanted him to fall on her again. And, judging by his expression, if they had not been parading themselves in such a public place, fall on her he would have.

She could feel the tension in the strong body which walked so proudly beside her, and knew that it matched her own. When he looked at her the amber eyes grew ever more golden, the pupils enlarged—but she was unaware that as he betrayed the signs of sexual arousal, so did she.

He handed her into her chair, and, after the most polite fashion, as though he had not been insulting and assaulting her with every word, asked, 'You would care for a drink, madam? You look a trifle heated.' And she knew that he was tormenting her, was recognising what her body was telling her, and was taking a subtle delight in letting her know that he knew—and that he was breaching her defences.

Stacy could no longer bear to have him beside her. She was in danger of saying and doing something which she would later regret.

'Indeed, sir, a cooling drink would be most welcome,' she replied, and she watched him leave her, moving through the company as though he were a panther prowling, and truly would be more at home wearing merely paint and feathers as she had mocked him.

After that the evening became a blur for both of them, but a blur against which each saw the other plain and clear. Even when Aunt Beauchamp engaged him in conversation, trapping him into agreeing to visit Bramham Castle to bring in the New Year, leaving Stacy to be surrounded by a crowd of admirers, all astonished that the Bankeress was such an unusual beauty, they remained completely aware of one another and no one else.

'I think, Matt,' Aunt Beauchamp admonished him as they watched Stacy performing in the quadrille with Anthony, Matt with something like murder in his heart at the sight, 'that it is time that you took my niece on the floor for the next dance. For you to ask her twice would not occasion comment. More would occur if you were not to dance at all. It is the waltz, but I think that her advanced years would save her from scandal.'

'Her advanced years!' burst from Matt involuntarily. 'Pray, madam, what years does she have? And why has no one yet claimed her in marriage? One would have thought that inheriting the Bank would be a great attraction.'

'Alas,' sighed Aunt Beauchamp, 'she insists on running the Bank, and few husbands would allow their wives to continue doing so after marriage—and she is naturally fearful of fortune-hunters. To be in her late twenties and have such gifts—I blame her odious father for encouraging her to follow a course more suited to a young man than a young woman.' And she rolled her eyes to heaven as Stacy, her hand on Anthony's arm, walked towards them.

Jealousy, pure and simple jealousy, roared through Matt at the sight. He could have strangled poor Anthony, whom years ago he had found a good friend and a kind and biddable child. Now he saw only a rival. But a rival to what? Bedding madam? Ravishing the Bankeress again? What in God's name was possessing him? And how could such a cold-hearted creature as Lady Beauchamp had just described arouse such passions in him? He felt sure that the strength of them was written on his face! He had not been in such a lather since he had first become aware in his early youth of why women had been placed on earth, and what delights a man could share with them.

Perhaps, however, nothing showed. For madam seemed coolness itself. Anthony Beauchamp, ever the gentleman, bowed unwillingly at Matt as Aunt Beauchamp announced officiously, 'I believe that Matt wishes to ask dear Stacy to waltz with him. Do you waltz, Stacy?'

Yes, she *was* matchmaking, thought her son angrily, whatever she said. And why should his mother think that his cousin ought to be handed over to such a savage disguised as a gentleman? For a moment he thought of objecting, of challenging the brute, but from long ago he remembered Matt Falconer's strength, his cold courage, and decided against it.

Which was just as well, for before Stacy could manage, Oh, dear Aunt, I am tired; I fear that waltzing is beyond me. Pray excuse me, Lord Radley, there was a sudden and excited stir around the ballroom as a party of late arrivals were bowed through the door by an obsequious Master of Ceremonies. Some great personage led them, no doubt.

Some great personage did. Quizzing-glasses were raised, ladies chattered excitedly behind uplifted fans, and by the time that the great personage had crossed the floor he and the object of his sudden interest were the only unmoved people in the room.

For once Stacy lost her own cool control a little as she saw first Aunt Beauchamp's face set in an agonised smile, and then felt Matt Falconer's whole body stiffen beside her. The newcomer, attired in the black silk court dress of the late eighteenth century and followed by a small group of splendidly turned out friends and relatives, seemed sublimely unaware of the stir he was causing.

He was making straight for them, Stacy realised, and as he did so, as he drew near, so that he was under the full blaze of the great main chandelier above them, Stacy saw him fully for the first time – and also saw something else.

Not only was he as tall as Matt Falconer, but, although a trifle stooped, he had also once possessed as splendid a body. Facially he informed her of what Matt would look like if he lived into his late sixties.

She turned querying eyes on both Matt and Aunt

Beauchamp as the newcomer paused a little short of them and said involuntarily, for she could almost feel the pain radiating from the man beside her, 'Matt?'

It was the first time that she had used his name in other than despite, and he answered her distantly, not using her name as a weapon, his attention fully engaged by the man before him. 'No need to worry, Stacy. It's only my father. I present to you, Miss Anastasia Blanchard, the most noble the Earl Falconer, KG.'

CHAPTER NINE

'AND what, Radley,' asked the Earl Falconer of his son, after he had done the pretty with Stacy, Uncle Beauchamp, Aunt Beauchamp, the Honourable Anthony Beauchamp, Viscount Trotternish, Jack Vernon and wife, little Phoebe and the assembled nobility and gentry, and the music had started again, and Trot had carried Stacy off, Matt having been cornered by his parent, 'brings you here?'

'I would prefer, sir,' was Matt's stiff reply, 'not to be addressed by that name. I am plain Matthew Falconer.'

'But I, on the other hand, would prefer to use it,' was his father's reply to that. For a moment father and son, staring at one another, were as alike as two new-minted coins, showing heads with the profiles of eagles, or lions, or whatever animal or bird of prey you preferred.

'Come, Radley, you have not answered me. I asked you why you were here. Grimes distinctly informed me that you intended to leave England as soon as your business at Pontisford was over.'

'I changed my mind,' Matt returned coolly. He could hardly bear to look at his father. All his young life he had worshipped him, but nothing he had ever done had pleased. With the benefit of maturity he now saw that they were too much alike, not only in appearance but in character. Neither man brooked being controlled by others, or bending to another's will.

'But why York? And, seeing that you have chosen to visit York, could you not bring yourself to oblige me for once, and visit The Eyrie as I asked you?'

Matt's expression was a grim one. 'Now, sir, you of all

people should know why I never wish to see The Eyrie again. And have you forgotten that, on the last occasion I visited you, you ordered your footmen to beat me from the door if I tried to enter?'

The Earl's face twisted. 'If you must know, Radley, I regretted that order almost as soon as it was made. . .'

'I will beg leave, sir, to doubt that. I am coming to wish that I had left Pontisford only to take passage to Baltimore again. My home now is not The Eyrie but a plantation in Virginia, where a man is judged by what he does, and not what others think that he might have done, or by the bedroom he was born in.'

The old man before him, Matt saw with a savage pleasure, winced at this.

'Suppose I were to confess, Radley, that I have recently come to believe that I might have been mistaken in my beliefs about your conduct twelve years ago, that I might have been over-hasty?'

Matt, hardly able to credit what he was hearing, stared back at his father.

'Why, sir, I would be compelled to answer that such a re-examination of your prejudices is at least twelve years too late in coming. The Matt Falconer you knew then died long ago, and the new one does not need your belated forgiveness—should you feel inclined to offer it.'

His father bent his grey head in acknowledgement. 'Nevertheless, Radley. . .'

Matt could not bear to be addressed by that name; he said violently, 'Come, sir, I asked you not to call me Radley, and I meant it. I only knew one who bore the name, and I do not wish to be reminded of him. You say, or appear to say, that you are now prepared to question your long-established beliefs as to what happened between my brother, myself and my poor dead Camilla. That being so, I am astonished that you did not see fit to inform me earlier of your change of mind, in view of the speed with which you threw me off at my brother's lying behest.'

'Allow me to say that it is only since the circumstances of your brother's death that I began to question myself. The letter which I sent to you asking you to return to England so that we might discuss the possibilities of a *rapprochement* most probably arrived in Virginia after you had left for England. I am now in hopes that together we may review and reassess the past.'

Matt acknowledged this with a slight dip of the head, and said, 'Well, that being so, sir, I am happy to learn that you acknowledge that you *might* have been mistaken. And that, if you please, should cease correspondence between us. Twelve years ago you disowned me, and since then Matt Falconer has become an American farmer, and that is what he wishes to remain. I do not wish to discuss the dead past with you – ever. Let it remain dead.'

His cold impassivity contrasted with the pain on his father's face. That father remembered the days when this son had been famous for his youthful impetuosity, not for his cold self-control. The long years apart had brought great changes. The man before him possessed a strength of character which was beginning to convince the Earl that he might truly have wronged him. He tried again to reach beyond the cold mask which confronted him.

'Nevertheless, I must remind you, Radley, that you stand heir to a great name, and a great estate.'

Matt shook his head in wonder. 'Why, sir, as to that, I want neither. I almost changed my name from Falconer but, since that carries no burden of unwanted tradition or inheritance in my new country, it hardly seemed worth the trouble.'

The old man said grimly, seeing that the younger one refused to bend before him, 'Nevertheless, sir, like it or not, one day in the not too distant future you will be Earl Falconer.'

The music which had been playing as an accompaniment to their cold and painful conversation was coming to an end. Behind his father Matt could see Stacy in Trot's arms, being whirled into a series of spinning turns. He wondered why he could endure her being in Trot's company when the sight of her with Anthony Beauchamp filled him with jealous rage. He decided ruefully that it was because he thought that Trot was no real threat to him where the Bankeress was concerned, while Anthony Beauchamp was.

His father was saying painfully, 'You are not attending to me, sir.'

'I beg your pardon.' Matt was suddenly compelled to admit his gracelessness, if only because the desolation in the old face before him matched that which he had felt for so many years. 'But I was watching Miss Blanchard. Lord Trotternish is hardly the most suitable companion for her, I fear.'

The Earl turned to see Trot and Stacy exchanging final bows. 'Miss Blanchard? Do I understand that she is the young woman who now runs Blanchard's Bank? Are you acquainted with her, Radley?'

Was he acquainted with her? Of course he was. Had they not lain in one another's arms all night?

'Yes, sir,' he rejoined stiffly. 'I am acquainted with her.'

'Then I would wish to speak a little more with her. I knew her father—a most remarkable man. I am told that the daughter is equally so. You will do me the honour of presenting the young lady to me again. I was not fully aware of who she was when Lady Beauchamp introduced us.'

Why, the old goat, thought Matt derisively, he thinks that I may be interested in her, I do believe, and would not object to having Blanchard's Bank and Blanchard's money added to Falconer wealth! He wondered what his father would say to him if he told him the truth. That he had misjudged his son over the sad affair of his brother's wife, but if he assumed the worst in the relationship between the Honourable, the Baron Radley and Miss Anastasia Blanchard, spinster and ex-virgin, he would not be going far wrong!

'The whirligig of time brings in his revenges,' Shakespeare had once written, and Matt, reintroducing Stacy, most unwillingly, to his father, wanted to shout at him, You had better send for your footmen to attack me with their whips again, Father, for I have ravished a virgin—and the truth is I do not regret having done so. Far from that, I would have her in my bed again instantly if she would consent to come, for in it her sharp tongue and sharper mind are stilled, and she uses her intellect to promote our bodies' pleasure and not to make money!

But he said nothing at all, and watched with satiric amusement his father using all his undoubted charm on his son's late bed-mate.

'I knew your father,' the Earl was saying to Stacy, quite unconscious of the nature of his son's thoughts, thinking himself that Miss Blanchard was a fine-looking woman and that any man could do worse than marry her, seeing what a fortune she brought with her, 'and he and I were good friends. I always found his advice most useful.' He paused a moment, then added, 'I believe that I met you once, many years ago when you were quite small.'

Stacy bowed, murmured a trifle mischievously, 'I do not remember the occasion, sir, but I do have the honour of being well-acquainted with your account with us, if I may raise such a matter on the occasion of a Christmas ball!'

Clever as well as beautiful, a rare combination, and no wonder that his son was interested in her, was the Earl's conclusion. He had seen a certain look in Matt's eye when Miss Blanchard had walked towards them, and he had read it aright. He was as aware as she was that the encounter between first Matt Falconer and the father from whom he was estranged, and now his obvious interest in the Bankeress, was causing universal comment and interest among the spectators which almost transcended common politeness. But like his son—and the woman before him—he never allowed such considerations as that to affect him.

'You know my son, Radley, I believe?' he asked her.

Now, how should she answer that? Suppose she gave him the correct answer—in the biblical sense of the word 'know', only too well! But that would never do. Some truths were best not uttered, so she remarked, a trifle undiplomatically perhaps, 'Well enough to know that he does not like to be called Radley.'

Far from antagonising the Earl, this amused him. He laughed a little. 'Yes, you do know him. I should have collected that Louis Blanchard's daughter would be blessed with judgement beyond the common run.'

Aye, thought Stacy wickedly, but what judgement did I display when I allowed your son to bed me so incontinently? She was unaware that such forbidden thoughts as these were beginning to melt the ice with which she had always surrounded herself, so that more than one man watching her wondered how anyone could ever have dubbed her cold.

They talked easily on neutral matters for a few more moments, until the Earl said, 'As a matter of interest, Miss Blanchard, although it is perhaps a question which I should not ask you, how did you come to meet Radley? On business, one supposes?'

Well, here was one truth Stacy could offer m'lord which could offend no one. 'Oh, you may certainly ask me, sir, and I shall equally certainly respond. On my way north to York, where I had some business at the Bank and where I also intended to spend Christmas and the New Year with my aunt Beauchamp, my mother's sister, my coach broke down near Pontisford Hall during the recent great snow, and Lord Radley most graciously gave me and my entourage shelter for several nights until we were able to travel north again.'

Which was, when all was said and done, one way of telling a thundering lie so that it sounded like truth. The Earl took what she said at face value.

'You reassure me, madam. Most gratifying that my son has learned to conduct himself with such propriety. Gracious, indeed! Virginia must have had a civilising effect on him. I shall be delighted to observe it in action, for I am invited to Bramham for the New Year, and Lady Beauchamp informs me that she has also asked Radley to join us.'

The room swung about Stacy for a moment. How in the world was she going to be able to bear the constant presence of Matt Falconer in her life? She had never for one moment thought of having to dodge around him at Bramham. The effect that he had on her was so powerful, so disturbing, that she could hardly contemplate being able to endure it. The ice around her was melting with a vengeance.

More melted during the evening. She was relieved that Louisa was not there to watch and judge her. For some reason it seemed imperative that she show Matt that she made nothing of him at all, by making a great deal of such empty fools as poor Trot and the beaux from York who thought that they might have a chance of netting the Bankeress.

So light-hearted was she, so gay, that later on, after she had shared supper with Trot, Anthony Beauchamp, and a galaxy of young men who vied for her favour, Matt, who had spent most of the evening propped against the wall, looking morose and drinking over-much weak-minded punch, growled at her as she arrived back after dancing the minuet, 'A word with you, madam.'

Breathless, rosy, her lips parted, strands of her dark

hair curling loose around her face, so that she gave the impression of a woodland nymph who was only waiting to be caught by her satyr, Stacy nodded in his direction. 'Of course, sir.'

'What has happened to the cold-hearted mermaid who froze us all to death at Pontisford, madam? Are you intent on snaring every man in the room, married and unmarried? Oh, yes, I saw you cavorting with my sister's husband, Bibury.'

'For shame,' retorted Stacy spiritedly. 'I only dance where I am asked.'

Matt could not help himself. The man who had vowed never to commit himself to any woman was now in the thrall of the last woman on earth who he would have thought could move him.

'It is not your dancing I take objecton to, madam, but the way you conduct yourself before, during and after the dance.'

'Oh!' Stacy blazed at him. 'Who the devil are you to act as my chaperon? Recollect how you behaved yourself with me, and learn that all the men with whom I have stood up tonight have conducted themselves towards me with perfect propriety.'

He could not help himself; the words flew out before he could stop them. 'It is not their propriety which concerns me, madam, but yours.'

'Hypocrite!' she flung at him. 'Oh, base. Recollect your own lack of propriety where I am concerned before you animadvert on mine.'

'Animadvert?' he flung back, as thought it were a ball which they were tossing between them, his amber eyes glowing. 'Did you learn that at the Bank's desk? It might be better if you had remained in the Bank's parlour, and then we poor devils would all be safe from your lures.'

Had they not been in so public a place that they were compelled to exchange insults in so pleasantly polite a manner that they might have been exchanging words of the deepest love, Stacy would have cracked him across the face again. Instead, she lifted her fan and turned to Aunt Beauchamp, who, slightly alarmed by she knew not what, was coming towards them. 'I am a trifle warm, madam; perhaps we could take a turn in the ante-room where I understand it is cooler.' And she gave Matt another view of her magnificent back and bottom, which had him lusting after her all over again.

Decidedly the devil was taking a hand in matters at York's Christmas Assembly Ball, and there was still the New Year to get through. He would doubtless be ready to run mad before 1819 was well on its way if he was to be exposed to the constant temptation which Stacy Blanchard presented to him when they were thrown together at Bramham Castle!

Which was Stacy's conclusion as well as his.

After that, Christmas Day was something of an anti-climax for Stacy and Matt. Particularly as both of them desperately tried to avoid thinking of the other, but both, for quite different reasons, failed in their objective.

Stacy woke up on Boxing Day at Bramham Castle feeling strange and feverish. Polly, who was herself looking a trifle green, helped her to the small bathroom off her bedroom and held her head while she vomited into a porcelain washbowl decorated with flowers, before letting go of her mistress to be violently sick into the bowl herself.

Sweating gently, her skin feeling so sensitive that merely to have had Polly's hand on her forehead was distressing, Stacy sank back into a nursing armchair standing by the big tin bath which would shortly be filled with warm water so that she might wash herself all over in it, and wondered briefly whether any of the Christmas food which she had eaten had caused such an unwanted effect.

Oh, but she knew only too well that that was not it, not it at all. What was wrong with her was that she was missing her second set of courses. Not only was her skin sensitive, but her breasts were swollen and sore, and she was not so unversed in her knowledge of the world as to be unaware that one night of passionate love with Matt Falconer had resulted in the inevitable. She was pregnant.

Once Polly had finished, and had sunk into a chair opposite to her mistress, they looked at one another ruefully.

'Oh, Miss Stacy,' Polly began, 'I hates to 'ave to say it, but I am a fallen 'oman.' Like the clerk at Blanchard's, faced with a crisis, she had reverted to her normal manner of speech before she had been trained to be Stacy's personal maid by Louisa Landen herself.

She looked half slyly, half shyly at Stacy. 'And you, Miss Stacy?'

It was a direct question, and one which Stacy was compelled to answer truthfully. 'Alas, I fear that I am breeding too.'

Servant and mistress for once shared a common predicament, and Polly, her eyes big with wonder—for were they not now bound by more than the ties of domination and servitude?—asked, 'Oh, Miss Stacy, is it Mr Matt's child you are a-carrying of?'

Stacy answered this not with a reproof for insolence but with a wry nod, followed by, 'Seeing that it cannot possibly be anyone else's, the answer must be yes. And you, I suppose, are carrying Jeb's?'

Her maid's answer was a mute nod of the head, and then a *cri de coeur* which Stacy shared with her. 'Oh, Miss Stacy, whatever are we a-goin' to do? We are both ruined—and on the same night, too!'

And that was undeniably true, and there was no answer

which she, Stacy, could make to it. Instead she asked gently, 'And if Jeb Priestley asked you to marry him to make an honest woman of you, would you agree to do so?'

Polly nodded her pretty head vigorously. 'Oh, yes, indeed. I liked him famously. He made me laugh, and he treated me like a lady, which is more than any of the other servants who came a-courting ever did.'

Treated her like a lady, indeed—by giving her an unwanted present, no doubt. And how did Matt Falconer treat me? Like a servant, perhaps. And how did I behave with him? No, I cannot answer that.

Polly felt bold enough to ask, 'And you, miss. Would you marry Mr Matt?'

'Indeed not,' was her vigorous answer to that.

'Oh, but you must marry *someone*. Think of the scandal.'

Stacy thought of the scandal and closed her eyes. Yes, she must marry someone, she supposed—but not Matt Falconer. Never Matt Falconer. Why, she hated him, did she not? And not only because he had ruined her.

You did your share of that, her conscience reminded her.

She stifled its unwelcome voice by saying to Polly, 'If Mr Priestley does not wish to marry you, then I can arrange for you to go to some farm to have the baby, and I will see that it is loved and cared for.'

'Aye ——' Polly was bolder than ever '—and what about yours, Miss Stacy? Who is going to love and care for him—or her?' she amended.

Him, thought Stacy. I know it's a him.

'I shall think of something,' she announced grandly.

'Then you'd better do so soon,' returned Polly practically. 'There's not much time left before we both start showing.'

Rising rapidly to her feet and beginning to feel much better, Stacy ordered briskly, 'For the meantime we say nothing,' taking it for granted that Polly would obey her. But the peasant shrewdness which Polly possessed in abundance was telling her quite another thing. For was not Mr Jeb Priestley a bigger catch than she could ever have hoped for? And she knew instinctively that Mr Matt Falconer would see her right—aye, and Miss Stacy too.

It wasn't like Miss Stacy to be so airy-fairy as to think that she could keep a love-child from the world's knowledge.

CHAPTER TEN

THERE was more than that which Miss Anastasia Blanchard could not keep from the world's knowledge, but that hammer-blow to her name and fame was yet to descend on her. For the present she contented herself with allowing Polly, once she had recovered, to help her to dress for the day. Afterwards, she went downstairs, pretending that all was well both in her private and public world.

Hardest of all to bear, she was to find, when the company arrived to celebrate the New Year, was not having Matt Falconer steadily watching her and steadily avoiding her, but the unwanted and admiring attentions of her cousin Anthony, who seemed determined to defy his mother and father's wishes by paying her the most insistent court.

The more he did, the more sardonic Matt's gaze grew. It was almost as though, across the room, she could read his mind. But what she didn't know was, could he read hers? Was he, could he be aware of the fact that she carried his child? Unaccustomed to being idle, to speaking only the nothings of polite conversation as carried on by gentlewomen, Stacy found life increasingly hard to bear. She most passionately wished that she could be back in London in the Bank's parlour, discussing policy with Ephraim, signing letters, and carrying out all the minutiae of the commercial life which had been her world since her father had first discovered her capacities when she was in her mid-teens.

Boredom rode on her shoulders. Matt found her, late one afternoon, in the gloaming hour, standing before a window which looked out over the gravel sweep which led to the front portico, watching the carriages which held his father and his father's party arrive.

'At last, madam,' he said softly in her ear, 'I have found you alone, without your cavaliers around you.' For not only Anthony Beauchamp, but Trot, who was also a fellow guest, and several other men, young and not so young, had been clustering around her like bees around honey.

Stacy did not turn to speak to him but addressed the window instead. 'I fear that I have little to say to you, Lord Radley, and you can have even less to say to me.'

He leaned forward, whispered into her ear, 'Ah, but we went beyond speech, did we not, madam?'

Her reply was a frozen one for, if she unbent at all, she could not trust herself to be able to hold him off. Even to know that he was behind her when they were not even touching was to have her shaking and quivering inside. 'I wonder you care to remind me of that, sir.'

'Unfortunately,' replied Matt a trifle bitterly, for he had never been so undone by a woman before, 'I cannot bring myself to forget what passed between us.'

'Nothing passed between us,' Stacy told the window as she watched Earl Falconer descend from his coach, Matt's sister Caroline, and her husband, Lord Bibury, following him and beginning to make their way into the house.

'I would not have thought the Bankeress's memory worse than mine,' was Matt's retort. 'Or is it reserved solely for the adding up of columns of figures or the examination of the balance sheets of failed businesses?'

Nettled, Stacy finally swung around to confront him. 'I wonder at you, sir. If I choose to forget what happened that night then the least that you can do is respect my wishes. What never happened cannot be regretted or remembered.'

This remarkable statement silenced Matt, if only for the

moment. For cool pragmatism he felt that he had never met its match! Not only had the woman a mind like a knife, she also had the cunning deviousness of a politician.

He could not help himself; he finally came out with, 'By God, madam, with such deviousness at your command you should be a member of the Cabinet at the very least. More's the pity that a woman cannot sit in Parliament; you would grace the Treasury Bench itself. No ploy would be beyond you!'

Goaded, Stacy shot back, 'And is that supposed to be a compliment, sir?'

Equally goaded, Matt almost snarled, 'You may take it as you please.'

'What I please is to ask you to allow me to pass, sir. We have nothing to say to one another—let it rest at that.'

I shall never rest while I remember the night we spent together at Pontisford Hall, was Matt's secret thought. *She* may be able to forget it; I cannot. Thank God that the world has no knowledge of what happened there, else we were both ruined—and, whatever else, I do not want that for her, though, sure God, madam seems equipped to withstand anything—even that.

He took the thought downstairs with him to greet his sister and his brother-in-law; his father had already retired to his rooms. He thought Bibury, a rather dour man, if kind, looked a little sideways at him, but supposed that that was due to the reputation which had clung to him ever since Camilla's death.

Caroline kissed him warmly on the cheek and said, 'Dear Matt, how much better it is for us to meet affectionately in private, instead of having to be all formality in public. You look well. I cannot remember that you were so large and brown when we were last under the same roof together.'

Matt smiled, and kissed her back. 'Hard work, Caroline. I have been a farmer since we last met, and not a gentlemanly one, either. Hard labour is responsible for my increased size, not idleness and eating and drinking.'

Bibury, whose expression was still oddly quizzical, Matt thought—and why should that be?—drawled at him, 'You look strong enough to go several rounds with Gentleman Jackson himself, Radley.'

Well, it was useless to ask people not to call him that, Matt supposed, and when, a few moments later, Caroline took herself off to her room to change, Bibury drawled again, his hard advocate's face still quizzical, 'I should like a word in private with you, Radley, if you please,' Matt readily agreed. He did wonder, though, why his brother-in-law should be quite so formal with him. The fact that he had begun his early life as a lawyer, before his elder brother had been killed in the Peninsular War and he had inherited, was, he supposed, responsible for such a hanging-judge's manner.

They walked into the library, deserted at this hour, where Bibury sat himself down before a blazing fire and thrust his booted legs towards it, before drawing a paper from the pocket of his coat and handing it to Matt.

'I thought you ought to see that before anyone else at Bramham does,' he began without preamble. 'It will be all round London by now, and should reach York any day. Neither Caroline nor your father is aware of it yet—but they will be.'

Matt took the paper in his hand. It was a Radical newssheet devoted to scandal and innuendo about the doings of the mighty, both in Government and out of it. Bibury had run an ink mark down the side of a couple of paragraphs on the front page, headed 'Doings at Pontisford Hall—the Bankeress and the Bear'. It was brief and brutally to the point.

A country correspondent tells us that Lord R, fresh from the wilds of Virginia, while domiciled in his country home at Pontisford Hall entertained Miss A. B., commonly known as the Bankeress, to bed as well as board, when she was trapped there by the snow on her journey north. One supposes that the Snow Queen, as Miss B is also known, succumbed to the attractions of the Northern Bear and was thawed into submission. Are we to expect a baby Banker or Bankeress?

Matt stared numbly at the paper, aware of Bibury's cynical eye on him. How, he wondered, could anyone in London have learned of what had been done at Pontisford? And then he knew. He remembered the housekeeper, and her vow that he would regret turning her away. She must have gone straight to London and to the printers of the scandal sheet. She must have been told by the other servants his nickname, given to him because of his size, while he was still little more than a boy in the Navy.

He crumpled the paper in his fist and looked blindly across the library and through the windows at the wintry scene outside, avoiding Bibury's eye as he did so. 'Is this commonly known?' he asked.

Bibury shrugged. ''Fraid so. It was the talk of the Clubs.'

'And believed?'

'Oh, of course.'

'No use my denying it, then?'

'No, indeed. Silence is always the best weapon in these cases. One may hope that it will be a nine days' wonder, and then will die down.'

'But in the meantime. . .her reputation.'

'What reputation?' replied Bibury cuttingly and brutally. 'A female who pretends to be a man must always expect criticism. I suppose the scandal sheets have been waiting for such an opportunity to cut her up. Particularly since up to this time her reputation has been one of unbending virtue.'

He had not asked whether the rumour was true. Nor, he must have noticed, had Matt directly denied it.

He could only think of Stacy. Of his own reputation he thought nothing, for he had none. He waved the paper at Bibury. 'I may keep this?'

Bibury's face was wry. 'Oh, indeed, Matt, by all means.'

Matt was at the library door before Bibury spoke again. 'My dear fellow, you are by way of being my brother, so I feel compelled to warn you. Pray do not embark on anything rash — that can assist neither you or the lady.'

He made no answer to that, for there was none that he could make.

He found Jeb in his room, which overlooked the park at the back at the house. It was beginning to snow again. Jeb was folding his clothes. He had a shirt in his hand and an expression similar to that of Bibury's on his face. It seemed that everyone knew something which Matt Falconer didn't.

'You were saying?' he enquired politely of his unruly servant, although he felt far from polite.

'I wasn't saying anything.' Jeb was aggressive.

'No? Then you were thinking it. Out with it, man.'

'Oh, we are indeed Lord Radley today,' observed Jeb nastily.

The joke palled. Matt was too exercised by the paper in his hand to enjoy it. 'You will do me a favour by answering me.'

Matt might not be quite Lord Radley in manner yet, Jeb thought, but he was hovering near to being so.

'Very well, m'lord. It's Polly. She had some news for me this morning . . .' He paused.

'Had she, indeed? And is it something which should exercise me?'

'Both of us,' returned Jeb, his face one huge grin. He

doubted whether m'lord would be quite so hoity-toity when he heard his news. On the other hand, he didn't feel quite so hoity-toity himself. It looked uncommonly as if Jeb Priestley might have to settle down at last.

'Polly tells me that she finds herself in the family way. We. . .uh. . .climbed into bed together the night that you and—'

Matt interrupted him. 'You are sure that it's yours?'

'Aye, and Polly's a lively lass. She'll make a good wife. I've a mind to make her Mrs Priestley—if that's all the same to you.'

'I agree with you.'

Matt found himself holding the scandal sheet as though it were contaminating him. He put it down on an armoire. Jeb picked up another shirt and began to fold it, saying, 'That's not all.'

'Not all?' Matt sank into an armchair in an attitude resembling that of Bibury—although without Bibury's obvious ease. 'What more can there be? You haven't given another wench a little packet, have you?'

Jeb snorted, rather as he had done at Pontisford when his betters amused him. 'Oh, not I, Matt. Polly's my lass, no one else. Haven't touched a wench since. No, begging your pardon, *Lord Radley*, it's you she was speaking of.'

'Me?' A dreadful suspicion struck Matt. He jumped to his feet, caught Jeb by the lapels of his coat, ground into his face, 'What the devil are you trying to tell me, man? For God's sake spit it out. I've had quite enough to try me today without you dancing me round too.'

Jeb pulled himself free, laughing, saying between splutterings, 'It's Miss Blanchard, Matt. Like master, like man, they say, and it seems that we both hit the target together—and on the same night too. Who'd have thought it?' And he continued to laugh uncontrollably, wishing that there were others with whom he could share such a splendid joke.

Matt's face was grey granite. 'You're quite sure? This isn't your idea of a joke?'

'No joke. Polly says that the Bankeress is even more overcome by her present than she is, but is carrying it off well. Of course, even the Bankeress can't carry it off forever. What suggestions do you have, *Lord Radley*, to help her out of her unfortunate situation?'

He would have to marry her to make matters right. He couldn't leave her to the tender mercies of a society which had already agreed to despise her, and would despise her the more when this news broke. He had thought that the existence of the scandal sheet was bad enough—but this. . . How could he have put her into such a compromising situation? What madness had overtaken them both that night at Pontisford?

He pulled himself together. Jeb was saying, 'I've already asked Polly to be my wife, and she's agreed. Says she doesn't mind going back to America with us—that is if *Lord Radley* still wants to return there.'

Lord Radley didn't know what he wanted. He bit back at Jeb, 'Lord Radley isn't likely to be as fortunate as you are. Somehow I doubt whether Miss Anastasia Blanchard will fall into my arms as quickly as Polly has fallen into yours. And as for returning to Virginia—what you have just told me is likely to alter everything.'

'Well, as to that,' remarked Jeb agreeably, 'I would be prepared to say that if she has any common sense at all Miss Blanchard had better make up her mind to be Lady Radley well before another month is out.'

Which was all very well, but Miss Anastasia Blanchard's version of common sense might not be the same as Mr Jeb Priestley's. Matthew Falconer, Baron Radley, didn't know whether he had any common sense left at all!

Stacy was taking tea with Caroline Bibury, whom she was finding an agreeable soul, ready to discuss matters other than dress and scandal, being happy to comment on Lord Byron's *Manfred* which she, like Stacy, had just finished reading. She had met him, Caroline told her, during his short and unhappy marriage to Annabella Milbanke, and he had struck her as a man of intemperate passions, exactly like those heroes of whom he wrote. 'The very model of *The Pirate*,' she finished laughingly. 'Just the kind of handsome and passionate reprobate whom we all ought to avoid, for who knows how we might behave if confronted by such a charming monster?'

Who knows better than I, indeed? thought Stacy ruefully, watching Matthew, Lord Radley, enter the drawing-room, remembering the passionate reprobate with whom she had shared a bed, and the consequence which had flowed from *that*. She also thought that Matt looked *distrait*, not at all like his usually damnably controlled self, and wondered what was troubling him. She knew only too well what was troubling her.

He came over to sit with them, and to drink tea as though it were wormwood which he was consuming, so that even Caroline noticed his strange manner and asked him whether he was ailing.

Matt shook his head. 'No, indeed. I find England strangely dark after the clear bright air of Virginia.'

Caroline questioned him about his life in the United States and he began to answer her with passionate enthusiasm. 'And you work, yourself, in the fields?' she exclaimed.

He nodded, and when he spoke his eye was on Stacy, not his sister. 'I would not have it otherwise. There is a cleanliness of spirit and a satisfaction about manual labour when it is performed for the love of it and not as a duty, enforced on one by others. I do what I choose, and what I please, and no one there thinks my labours odd. Imagine the brouhaha there would be if I toiled with my hands in the fields around the Eyrie!'

Stacy suddenly saw him, stripped to the waist, his tawny head blazing beneath a golden sun, his big body etched against a clear blue sky. The sensation this unexpected vision produced was so exquisite that she could almost have cried aloud. Ever since she had known that she was carrying his child the sensations of faint nausea which she occasionally felt were linked with a heightened sense of awareness of everything about her.

And the thing that she was most aware of was Matt Falconer. It was almost as though she were a part of him, so that for a moment she shared his memories of the life he had left behind him. She listened, also aware that Matt Falconer was talking to her, rather than to his sister, reminding her that he had a life of which she knew nothing, and to which he wished to return.

Or so he said.

Later, when Bibury and the rest came in, and Matt's father looking tired from his journey, Matt took the opportunity to ask her to examine some of the family portraits on the walls of the corridor which led to the drawing-room, a pretext so nakedly obvious that Stacy smiled at it.

'Come, sir,' she asked him as soon as they were alone before the portrait of an Elizabethan Beauchamp, gallant in huge ruff, pearl-sewn doublet, and trunks and hose of pale pink, 'what is it that you wish to say to me?'

Matt smiled ruefully—rueful seemed to be the only word which fitted his thoughts these days.

'I'm sorry if I appeared clumsy,' he began.

Stacy's exasperation showed. She was used to being spoken to directly, not to having men make pretty speeches to her on the way to being direct.

'I doubt whether anyone else noticed,' she returned, 'but I could not help being aware that you were becoming increasingly impatient at being constrained to speak to me before others—that you wished to speak to me privately. Something is troubling you, I collect.'

She did not say that where he was concerned she had acquired a sixth sense.

'Well, then, madam——' and Matt was suddenly savage, and as direct with her as she could possibly have wished '—allow me to tell you that I would have preferred that you had informed me that you were carrying my child, rather than have discovered it from the lips of Jeb Priestley. I'm not sure what etiquette governs these matters, but I cannot but believe that, as the child's father, I should have informed him, should I have so wished, rather than he me.'

'Oh!' Stacy was enraged, and could not help but show it. 'I particularly instructed Polly that she should keep that piece of news to herself, not go tattling it around Bramham.'

'Just so, madam. Did it not occur to you that you had a duty to inform me even before you informed Polly?'

'Etiquette, you said. What book of etiquette exists to assist an unmarried pregnant woman on the right line to take with the man who so incontinently made her so?'

'Oh, madam——' and Matt's smile was deadly '—the same book which instructed you so well in how to fall incontinently into bed with the father!'

Now what could she say to that? Nothing but, 'Your being the father is an unfortunate accident. My child will be rich enough to be able to dispense with a father.'

'Would that matters were so easy, madam. I fear that any hope you might have entertained that you could somehow have your child and its origins remain anonymous have already been dashed. You had better read this.' And he handed to her the Radical broadsheet which Bibury had given to him.

If he had thought to overset her, he was mistaken. She took the paper from him and read it without so much as changing colour. She might as well have been casually examining something as innocuous as the latest *Book of Beauty*.

'So?' she remarked, handing it back to him.

'And is that all you have to say, madam?' His face was suddenly suffused, Stacy was fascinated to notice. He looked as he had done that night when he had fallen on her—and she on him.

'What is there to say?' she answered, her heart thumping, but determined to stay as cool as he was hot. 'It is the truth, is it not? Or are you prepared to dispute it?

She was prepared to drive him mad, that was it. Regardless of the fact that they might be interrupted at any moment, Matt seized her by the shoulders, ground out between his teeth, 'Are you determined to destroy yourself as well as me? That you care nothing of what is written there is one thing—but what of others who read it? That paper will reach Bramham in the next few days—and what reputation shall we have then? How shall we—you—face our fellow guests? If it were not for the fact that you are carrying the consequence of our madness, then we could deny what is written there, say it was concocted out of spite—as I believe it was. But nothing to that, madam, nothing to that. Our guilt will shortly be obvious to the whole world—unless you are prepared to say that the child is not mine—which would brand you a slut, as well as careless. Is that what you want?' And he began to shake her.

They were back at Pontisford, before they fell upon the bed. He had only to touch her and she was lost. Oh, she had dreamed of him in her arms night after night, as he had dreamed of her. Only the fact that a few yards away the assembled guests sat, innocent of the passions being released in the corridor outside, kept them from falling on to the floor to consummate those passions.

Both of them had been solitary beings so long, denying

themselves, enduring passionless lives, telling themselves that fulfilment was not for them—each for their own different reasons—that they found it difficult to surrender, to admit what was burning so fiercely inside them.

Eye to eye, breast to breast, heart to heart again, wishing only to be united, but strongly denying the wish, they breathed and trembled together.

Finally, Matt released her, to lean against the wall shuddering with the force of passion rejected. He lifted his head, muttered hoarsely, 'There is nothing for it, madam. You must marry me and soon—before you grow big and all is lost.'

It was the most ungallant, unloverlike proposal a man could have made. But it was not that which enraged Stacy; it was his cold assumption that she had no choice.

Shuddering herself, burning, caught in passion's toils, Stacy murmured, her voice so low that Matt could hardly hear what she was saying, 'I suppose I should have expected that. You may keep your proposal, sir. And what you say of that paper's news is yours to say. I shall say nothing.'

'Mad,' groaned Matt, 'you are mad. You cannot refuse me. Ruin lies before you, not me. I am already ruined—and you are a fallen woman. You will be a pariah.'

'I am already a pariah, so that is nothing new.' She came out with this splendidly, as though she were carrying a flag with the words emblazoned on it into battle. 'I am tolerated only for my fortune and the Bank. Men want to marry me only for my fortune and the Bank.'

'I want neither your fortune nor the damned Bank,' Matt growled at her. 'I want him—my child—to have a name, and his mother not to be called a whore. Is that so wrong?'

'Him?' And Stacy's voice was a reproach, even though her secret wish was that the child should be a boy—and look like him. 'Him? It might be a girl.'

'Boy, girl, whatever it is,' gritted Matt through clenched teeth. 'I won't have it farmed out.'

' I have not the slightest intention of farming my baby out. It will be brought up as a Blanchard—and, boy or girl, it will inherit the Bank.'

'It will be a pariah, too. You are a clever woman, Stacy. How can you be so stupid as to deny your child a name and an inheritance? Unless you marry me your child—our child—will have no name. Can you really want such a thing?'

Stacy. He had called her Stacy, not madam. And did she really want such a thing? If only he had shown her some affection, had put an arm around her, had said, I understand how you feel. Marry me and all shall be well. But he hadn't. He was worrying about the child, and her good name, not about Stacy Blanchard herself.

But what he had said about the child having no real name had struck her hard. Was she being fair to this unborn creature which she carried beneath her heart?

Her expression changed, softened. Matt saw it, and pounced. 'You will consider my offer,' he said eagerly, and put a hand on her arm, showing her for the first time some small sign of affection. Afterwards he was to ask himself why he had been so hard with her, but somehow the passion which ruled him whenever they met so appalled him by its strength that he wished to deny it, and denying it he denied her.

A mute nod was Stacy's only answer. He followed up this small advantage. 'We need marry only for show,' he assured her, for he was certain that she could not love him, since she never unbent to him, only showed him her indomitable will. 'I shall apply for a special licence. We can remain married until after the child's birth, give it a name, and then we may part on agreed terms—you to the Bank and me to Virginia. There, I cannot say fairer than that.'

Before she could reply they heard the door open and footsteps come towards them. Matt seized her by the arm, half ran her along to examine another portrait, so that the advancing party, seeing them thus engaged, could have no idea of the passions which had ravaged them the moment before, and which were plainly written on both their faces.

Only, when he handed her towards the stairs, Matt whispered hoarsely in her ear, 'And you will give me an answer, madam, and soon, I hope..

To which Stacy answered, 'Yes,' which was saying anything—and nothing.

Nor would Stacy say anything more, merely mounted the stairs to talk to Louisa, who was still a semi-invalid, as though nothing in the world had happened to overset her. Matt must wait for an answer—but what answer she would give him was as unknown to her as to him.

CHAPTER ELEVEN

'AND Mr Anthony Beauchamp, who dances such attendance on you, Stacy, my dear— what would your answer be to him if he were to propose himself to you? He would be so much more suitable a husband for you than Lord Radley—as I suppose you realise. Such a charming and pleasant gentleman!'

Louisa and Stacy were seated together, each of them stitching away at a pair of tapestry cushions, before the blazing drawing-room fire at Bramham Castle. Caroline Bibury had been playing Haydn to them, a pleasing, tinkling piece, light and airy, not at all matching the dark and troubled thoughts which lay behind Stacy's apparently composed countenance.

Louisa had asked her question in a quiet voice, so that no one should overhear her, although she and Stacy were seated well away from the rest of the company, who had begun to play spillikins as though their life depended on it. The noise that they were making quite drowned out anything which Louisa might care to say—or Stacy, when she replied to her.

She jabbed her needle viciously into the likeness of a hen pheasant and murmured, almost below her breath, 'I have no mind to marry anyone, Louisa, as I have so frequently told you. I like my cousin Anthony, but not as a future husband.'

'I can see that there is no pleasing you,' sighed Louisa sadly.

No, indeed, thought Stacy. Sooner or later I must give Matt Falconer an answer, for sooner or later my condition will betray itself, and I still cannot make up my mind as to the best course of action to follow.

It had begun to snow again and a group of gentlemen who had been riding earlier came in, exclaiming at the cold, the hard ground, and the inclement nature of the weather, as though every January did not find them saying the same thing.

Matt, walking beside his father, was wearing his usual expression these days, Stacy noted clinically. He glowered. He was waiting for the unwelcome news in the scandal sheet to reach Bramham. So far it had not done so, but so far his Lady Disdain had refused to make up her mind to accept the inevitable and marry him.

Yesterday, catching her in the library, he had said, 'If you accept me, madam, before the scandal about us breaks here, then it cannot be scandal. You understand me, I'm sure. Cannot you give me an answer now? To do so would be to the advantage of both of us. Every time that the post arrives I live in a sweat of fear that all will be revealed.'

So did Stacy. So why was it that she could not say yes to him? He was so unloverlike, that was it! But why was that it? Had she not scorned all talk of love and romance these many years? So how was it that now she was like a green girl waiting for her beau to shower her with compliments, promising her moonlight and roses? Instead he showered her with practical, rational, logical advice, plainly, almost rudely offered, with no intent to deceive her by pretending that he loved her—the kind of behaviour which she had always told herself that she expected, and would welcome, from a man. But, alas, now that she *was* receiving it, she found that she didn't welcome it at all!

A coach was being driven along the sweep, passing the drawing-room windows on its way to Bramham's superb front door, with its noble flight of steps. Bramham, although still called a castle, had been rebuilt in the classical style in the 1770s. Matt watched a uniformed flunkey alight and begin to unload the boxes and sacks of mail which it was carrying in lieu of passengers. No, there was one passenger, a black-clad lawyer—Grimes. He of the rueful countenance and impudent disapproval of Matt Falconer and all his works. What the devil was he doing here?

No need to ask, Matt thought dismally, and no need to worry this time what the sacks of letters, newspapers and parcels might contain. He gave a short exclamation, rose from his seat and walked over to where Stacy sat, the picture of virginal and untouched innocence. A picture which only he knew was false. He was aware that Anthony Beauchamp was watching him sourly, and knew that, whatever Anthony hoped, Stacy would never accept him—least of all now that she was pregnant by another man.

Ignoring Louisa, after a brief polite nod to her, he murmured, almost below his breath, so that only Stacy could hear him, 'The time grows short, madam. It may be already too late for us to emerge from this with any credit. Give me your answer. Now.'

Had the man no manners? Stacy saw Louisa's head lift itself sharply from its concentration on her work, and said reprovingly, 'I have no idea of what you speak, Lord Radley. As to the answer I promised to give you—that will arrive in due course.'

He leaned forward to hiss into her ear so that no one else might overhear, 'At least before the child arrives, I hope!'

'We are watched,' Stacy told him severely on hearing this sally. 'You grow indiscreet.'

'*Our* indiscretion is about to be announced to the world. I am sure of that, madam. You have left us no way out.'

He watched Grimes being ushered into the room by a footman, watched the tea-board accompany his entry, to be set out for him on a low table, saw his father speak to him, saw Grimes bend his head deferentially to say—what?

Lifting the silver teapot to pour both himself and his powerful patron a cup of tea, Grimes was muttering quietly, 'It is of all things essential, sir, that I speak to you in private, and soon. You ought also to ask Lord Radley to be in attendance to be called in to consult with us when we have finished.'

'And what, pray, has Radley done this time?' queried the Earl, a look of extreme anger on his old face.

'That I cannot speak of here. Later.' And Grimes drank his tea and ate a ratafia biscuit with all the appearance of extreme enjoyment.

Matt Falconer felt no enjoyment. Instead he put out a large hand to grasp Stacy's small one, to prevent her from continuing with her stitchery. As usual her extreme composure was driving him rapidly, not slowly, mad. Added to his thwarted desire to bed madam again, her refusal to give him an inch was the most exquisite form of torture she could have devised for him.

'Attend to me, madam,' he whispered fiercely, aware of Louisa Landen's horrified eyes on him. 'We have but a few minutes left, and your refusal to face facts is becoming dangerous.'

'Unhand me, sir,' hissed Stacy.

'No, indeed,' he told her, his voice rising a little, 'not until you answer me plainly.'

'Here is your plain answer, sir,' she told him equally fiercely. Before he could stop her she used her left hand to pull her needle from her right hand and stabbed him with it in the back of the hand with which he was gripping her.

This was so unexpected that Matt, taken unawares, let out a roar of anger, mixed with surprise, and, yes, admiration for her spirit. She was looking him full in the face, and was smiling at him. Yes, dammit, the bitch was smiling at him! No, dammit, she was laughing at him! At the predicament he was in, and at his inability to retaliate against her for what she had so incontinently done.

Every head in the room had swung towards them at the sound of Matt's bellow. Louisa, unbelieving, frozen with horror, watched Stacy throw down the offending needle and take Matt's damaged paw into her hand, to dab at it with her tiny lace handkerchief.

'Oh, sir!' she exclaimed, all innocence. 'Pray forgive me. I had not seen that your hand was in the way. Allow me to stanch your wound.'

The wound was light, and the pain was small. It was surprise which had wrenched the cry from Matt's lips. He saw his father's cold eye on him, and then Anthony Beauchamp was beside them, saying sharply, 'Cousin Stacy, is this fellow troubling you again?' and the look he gave Matt was a malignant one.

'No, not at all,' Stacy carolled, having discovered inside herself a fount of mischief which she had not known that she possessed. 'I wouldn't say that you were troubling me, would you, Lord Radley?'

Matt, holding her handkerchief over his damaged hand, looked up at Anthony, who was eyeing him as though he were some mad animal which ought to be shot on sight.

'No, not at all, Miss Blanchard, rather the contrary, I would say.' Which masterly and devious reply nearly overset Stacy, and had Anthony puzzling over its meaning. There was no doubt about one thing, was her inward judgement—Matt Falconer liked to sail close to the wind. She forgot that she was inclined to do the same.

Fortunately for decorum, for Anthony had just worked out the true meaning of Matt's reply and was squaring up to him again, the little lawyer came over to them, bowed, and said in his dry way, 'Miss Blanchard, Mr Beauchamp, sir, you will forgive me for intruding, I trust, but the matter is urgent. Your father, Lord Radley, would like you to accompany us for a discussion in m'lord's private suite.'

He bowed so obsequiously that the company forgave him on the spot, particularly since he was rescuing them from a situation which was rapidly becoming embarrassing. Matt allowed himself to be led away, promising himself grimly that dear Lady Disdain would pay for her pin-prick if it was the last thing she did.

But she was already having payment exacted, first by Anthony Beauchamp and then by Louisa Landen.

'My dear cousin——' Anthony was all indignation '—I cannot understand what you see in that rude fellow. I collect that he works like a peasant in his fields in Virginia, and now he has come over to behave like a peasant in polite drawing-rooms. If he is really troublesome, pray let me know, and, as I offered once before, I will deal with him.'

'That is very noble of you.' Stacy was all sweetness and light, having put Matt in his place and now being determined on putting Anthony in his. 'But I am well able to deal with Lord Radley myself. Pray do not exercise yourself over the matter. Should I ever need assistance, I would ask for it. You may be sure of that.'

He was a little mollified, spoke to her for a moment about a variety of things in an effort to soothe her, though she needed no soothing, and then left her to Louisa.

Louisa, shocked to the marrow by the wild behaviour of both Stacy and Matt, moaned gently at her, 'Oh, my dear, however could you conduct yourself so outrageously? I own that Lord Radley spoke a trifle brusquely to you, but that was no reason to assault him with your needle. I am beginning to think that all the wildness which you should have worked through in your earlier years is being expressed in your maturity instead. Is it not enough that your conduct already attracts attention because of your running the Bank, without you behaving like a hoyden and thus attracting even more censure?'

'Oh, pooh to that, and to everything else.' Stacy was on her high ropes, and had no idea why that should be so. She had seen Matt's face immediately after she had stabbed him, and she knew that had they been alone he would have inflicted the most condign punishment on her. And oh, how her body ached and wished for it. Yes, she *was* going mad, and it was all much more exciting than being continually staid and proper as she had been for so many years.

At the same time she could not help wondering what Grimes and the Earl were saying to Matt—and then it struck her, so that her face paled, and she swayed a little. What a fool I am! They have seen the scandal sheet—and everything which Matt has repeatedly told me would happen will happen.

Louisa caught her arm, said feverishly, 'Stacy! You are not ill?'

'Oh, no,' she told her old companion. 'I can't afford to be ill now, Louisa. Most injudicious of me. But I should like a cup of tea, and would wish you to ring for one for me. That should set me up to be ready for anything.'

She was not wrong. Grimes, who for all his dried-up manner and appearance relished the more scandalous aspects of his work, had given the Earl the scandal sheet to read, and when m'lord threw it down, disgusted, said, 'I have spoken around London and it seems that they did spend a night alone together at Pontisford. I thought it might be my duty to inform you before anyone else did, remembering that Lord Radley has been involved in a similar brouhaha once before.'

'But I have been recently led to understand that we might have been mistaken over that.'

'Indeed.' Grimes was smooth. 'As there may be a

mistake over this. I would advise you to discuss the matter with Lord Radley immediately. He may not be aware of this——' and he flicked a finger at the sheet '—and the talk which is going around London. There will be others who will find this in their post today.'

'No doubt.' The Earl rose and paced to the window to look out of it. The snow had stopped, but before it had done so had created a white world. The bridge over the lake, the little pavilion to which it led, the trees beside it were ornaments of silver filigree against a blank landscape. 'I had hoped that Radley and myself were coming to some kind of understanding—but this. . .' And he shook his head, began again, 'To destroy the honour of a young woman who has always possessed a reputation for extreme virtue. . . This is too much, and this time must be remedied.'

'There may, of course,' murmured Grimes smoothly, 'be a reasonable explanation. Might I advise that you speak to Lord Radley before reaching a final judgement?'

'Exactly so. You said that he was outside. Pray ask him to come in at once.'

Matt was in the ante-room. Restless, unable to sit quietly, he had been pacing the floor, examining cabinets containing rare china and curios from a dozen countries in the near and far east. He knew perfectly well what news Grimes had brought his father, and for the life of him he could think of nothing to say in extenuation of the conduct which the scandal sheet imputed to him.

If Stacy had already accepted him, then that would have been that. But she had not, and doubtless his father would put the worst interpretation on what he was supposed to have done.

Supposed? He had done it, and therein lay the rub. So, when Grimes beckoned him in, he squared his shoulders as he had done when a boy at Eton, waiting for old Keate, the headmaster, to beat him. And now, in his middle thirties, he was still in no better case!

Grimes withdrew with a bow and his father thrust the paper containing the record of his delinquency at him. 'I should like an explanation of this, Radley. I understood from you that you were not at your old disgraceful games again, but I see that I was wrong to believe you.'

This was easier to answer than Matt had thought possible. 'Hanged, drawn and quartered before I say a word in my defence, eh, Father? Still the same old story? Except that the old story was a lie, all of it, as I tried to tell you to no avail.'

'To the devil with the old story,' growled his father. 'It is this new one which exercises me now. Were you aware of this, sir?'

Matt said as coolly as he could, 'Aware that this sheet existed, yes. But I must tell you that I am not prepared to discuss with you, or with any man or woman, my relations with Miss Anastasia Blanchard.'

His father's face grew slowly red. 'You are not denying this vile libel, then, I see —'

Matt interrupted, 'Neither affirming it nor denying it. It is no affair of yours — or any man's.'

'This — this,' exclaimed the Earl violently, waving the paper about, 'makes it my affair! If a lie it impugns your honour, and the lady's. Hers most of all. If true then I have no words for you, sir. No words at all. Indeed, true or false, words fail me.'

Impudence was all that was left to Matt, and, dismally, he knew that it was the only weapon in his arsenal which he could use. Stacy's refusal to accept his proposal had deprived him of all others.

'Why, sir, that comforts me — to know that there are to be no more words from you on the matter. In that case, I will leave you, unless there is anything further of moment which you *are* prepared to discuss with me?'

For one moment he thought that he had gone too far. Behind his outward bravado he could hear the inward bells of regret tolling. Since he had met his father again in York it had almost come to seem that they might become father and son once more, Camilla and Rollo's ghosts no longer coming between them. But now it was Stacy who had replaced them as a living and breathing barrier.

The Earl's hands curled into fists. He was a young man again. Had he a whip in his hand he would have struck his son with it. Lacking a weapon, he used the only one he had left to him: his tongue.

'You are no son of mine, sir, if your answer to this gross libel is silence, and a refusal to defend a lady's honour. How will she be able to withstand the inevitable shock of scandal when this. . .becomes known to the company?'

Matt couldn't defend himself. He couldn't answer his father's just anger as he might have wished by saying, The lady and I intend to marry. What is printed on that paper is neither here nor there. We both ask you for your blessing. Then and only then would gossip be silenced, and his father not be shamed by his son.

He bowed. 'I will leave you, sir.' He refrained from saying, Reflect that, as you were wrong about my behaviour towards my brother's wife, you might also be wrong about this, because the paper was telling the truth.

His father said heavily, 'Yes, you may leave, Radley. I have nothing more to say to you. Except that I am sorry for the lady. Her life is difficult enough, I understand, without this.'

He could have said, Her choice, Father. She has left herself open to scandal by refusing my honourable offer of marriage. But no decent man could interpose a woman between himself and obloquy. In any case, the whole business had been his fault, and no one else's. The affair had been precipitated by his act of folly in pretending to be the butler, and had been further compounded by his falling upon her that night when they had been alone in her room. That thereafter she had co-operated with him most willingly and lustily did not lessen his own guilt—he was the older, the more experienced and the stronger. He should have stopped. . . He was suddenly aware that merely to think of being in her arms was to excite him. . .

He turned to let himself out, trying not to hear his father telling him that he was no son of his, that, after all, he had come back from America more unregenerate than when he had left, and that the best thing he could do would be to return there.

But none of that would help Stacy.

She knew. Oh, yes, she knew. The post had arrived and been distributed. There were letters for her, all dealing with business. Reports from Greaves at York, longer ones from Ephraim Blount in London, and a letter from Hamburg where the Bank had been doing business with some merchants of the old Hanseatic League, and her opinion was wanted on certain matters of importance.

But the letters of those around her were quite different. They were from friends and relatives, and their letters were chatty, gossipy, retailing the *on dits* which flew around London, or the great houses to which the nobility and great gentry—or, as it was sometimes known, the cousinry—retired during the winter months. And with the letters came newspapers, and among them, she knew, would be the sheet retailing the scandal about herself and Matt Falconer.

Even if the story had been a lie it would have stuck to them. But it wasn't a lie, and what Matt had forecast was coming true. More, the moment she walked into the drawing-room she knew that many there had already learned the delightful news: that Matthew Falconer, the renegade Lord Radley, already the leading player in one delightful scandal, was now the leading player in another.

And, even more than that, the other player was the eccentric Bankeress, long known as an icy virgin, but who had been melted not by the summer rain but by the winter's frost!

Matt they had called the Bear. Quite wrong. He was her lion-man, and she was coming to understand that by refusing him she had been selfish, for it was he who stood to lose the most, just when the old scandal which had ruined him had finally died.

She sat on her own. None came near her. She had dressed in virginal white, as much to defy everyone as to proclaim to the world what was no longer the truth. She wore her collar of pearls again about her long and graceful neck, with one giant ruby, set about with seed-pearls, depending from it above her bosom. The dress itself was of the most elegant simplicity, with floating panels of gauze depending from the high waist above the smooth satin of her skirts. Her fan was white, her gloves and shoes equally so, and the small circlet in her hair was again of pearls.

Louisa came over to her, her face agitated. 'My love,' she began, her eyes brilliant with shock, 'I feel that you ought to know. . .'

Stacy leaned forward, put a gentle finger on Louisa's lips as though she were the old and wise one and Louisa her charge. 'Shush, my dear, I already do know, have known for some days. And so, I fear, does everyone else. We will not speak of it.'

'But. . .' began Louisa when the finger was removed.

'No buts, dear Louisa. You must be brave as I will be.'

How could she be so cool? was her companion's only thought. Caroline Bibury came in, moved straight to Stacy, took her hand and said, her eyes swimming, 'My dear, I am so sorry. I would have such creatures who write filth about us shot if I were in the Government. Bibury says that I must not exercise myself. He told me that you have known for some days. . . What can I say or do but offer you my most profound sympathy, and my admiration for your moral courage? We, by virtue of our rank and station, stand to be attacked, but this. . .this is the outside of enough. And poor Matt. . .'

Stacy's eyes filled with tears as the most extraordinary mixture of sentiments warred in her breast. For she knew that she was not innocent, and Caroline was assuming that she was, and she felt a cheat and a rogue for deceiving her. She was not sure how much Louisa knew or guessed, but kind Caroline was a different proposition altogether. She pressed the sympathetic hand which held hers. Looking about her, though, she noticed something odd. Only the senior men of the party were present. Earl Falconer, whose old face was so sad that she knew that he too had read the scandal sheet, was seated by the roaring fire. Beside him was Uncle Beauchamp, pulling his watch out to examine it as the normal hour for dinner had passed by and half the company were not yet present. The lawyer, Grimes, was sitting mumchance in a corner, watching, his eyes sardonic. And night was beginning to fall as the afternoon wore on.

She stood up, worried by she knew not what.

'What is happening, Caroline? Where is your husband and Anthony Beauchamp, Trot and the rest? Where are they? What is to do?'

Caroline, Lady Bibury, who had never run a great bank, watched for signs of change in the money market, picked up hints and ideas from the movements of stocks and shares and the contents of speeches by members of the Government, had noticed nothing untoward. She looked puzzled, stared about her, said slowly, 'I only know that Bibury told me to go ahead. You are right. All of the younger men are absent. What can it mean?'

Stacy said, in the voice which she had often employed to dominate Ephraim Blount, Greaves, assorted bank clerks and the thieving manager at York, 'I don't know. But I intend to find out.' She picked up her fan. Louisa made to follow her, to have Stacy say, still in that cold, businesslike voice, 'No, stay where you are, I beg of you. I don't want anyone to follow me.' She waved down Caroline, who was beginning to rise, her face anxious.

Every female eye was on her as she crossed the room, straight-backed, head high, making for the door which led to the great entrance hall. Opening it, she saw at the bottom of the main stairway all the young men of the party. They had been lying in wait for Matt, who had just reached the last turn of the stairs before they opened on to the ground floor.

Anthony Beauchamp, his back to her, stood a little in front of the main group. He advanced on Matt, saying in a loud voice, 'Damn you, Matt Falconer. I want satisfaction from you for the slur you have brought on my poor cousin. I should have asked my father to have had you beaten from the door by the footmen before you ever set foot in Bramham. As it is, take this,' and before Bibury, who was plucking his sleeve and advising caution, could stop him, he struck Matt as hard as he could in the face, knocking him to the ground, and when Matt tried to rise was on him again.

Bibury and Trot pulled Anthony away. He was still raving, his face purple. 'Satisfaction,' he roared at Matt. 'I want satisfaction from you, Falconer. You may choose what weapons you like. I shall take pleasure in killing you whatever the means I have to use.'

Matt had made no effort to defend himself. He was conscious of his guilt, of the misery which he had brought upon himself and Stacy by his own rash and ill-considered action. He rose slowly, said, his voice low but steady, 'I don't wish to fight you, Beauchamp, but I shall, and it will not be my own honour I shall be defending, but Miss Blanchard's.'

Which had Anthony raving again, shouting, 'You are not to name her. I will not have her named.'

Bibury said sharply to him, 'Be quiet, man. You heard what he said. Now let him choose his weapons, and we will decide the time and place for the action. Until then, all must be decorum. You must name your second, Radley—as must Beauchamp—and if you have no one here who will stand your second, then I shall do so, for form's sake.'

Stacy watched them, mute for once, and shaking inwardly, aware that her own delay had caused this. She decided to stop the folly being enacted before her. She might play a man's part when she ran the Bank, but she thoroughly disapproved of the whole code of honour which governed the lives of the men who belonged to the gentry and aristocracy. In the moment of silence which followed Bibury's statement she chose to speak.

'There will be no need for any action to take place. You, Cousin Anthony, are quite mistaken if you choose to provoke Lord Radley to a duel. He has already asked me to marry him, and I have agreed to accept his proposal. No one's honour is at stake here, least of all mine or Lord Radley's.'

All the men had turned and were staring at her, a different version of shock on each face, shock that not only should she have been present, but that she had chosen to speak so publicly before a party composed only of men. And of men engaged in an affair of honour—an occasion where women had no place.

Bibury released Anthony Beauchamp, who said hoarsely to Stacy, 'Cousin, you should not be here. It is neither fit nor proper. I am about to teach this fellow a lesson he will not live to remember.'

Stacy could see only one face, and that was Matt's. She had begun to shiver internally, but quelled the shivers, said in her best Bankeress voice, 'Oh, what nonsense,

Anthony. Why should I not speak when I collect that the matter between you and Lord Radley is that of my honour, and that you are quite mistaken over the part he has played? Lord Radley and I have been grossly libelled, but it is no matter. We were waiting until we left Bramham before we announced our betrothal to the world but, seeing the misunderstandings that our natural desire for privacy has created, I release him from his vow of silence on the matter. We shall be married by special licence when we reach London, shall we not, my dear sir? No need for duellings and bravado; you may all wear wedding wreaths instead.'

She saw Matt walking towards her, the bruise on his face where Anthony had struck him slowly turning purple. He wore a small bandage on the hand which she had stabbed. He went down on one knee before her, said, 'Miss Blanchard, I honour you for your courage in speaking for me after such a public fashion. I respected your wish for silence, and respect the reason why you have now reversed it.'

A small hum of sound ran round the watching men. Anthony opened his mouth again, to protest, to reproach, no doubt. Bibury took him by the arm and said loudly, 'No need for bravado, indeed, Miss Blanchard, nor any need for a duel. Let us all go into dinner. I, for one, am hungry.'

Anthony, his face white, hissed something in Bibury's ear as they all walked towards the drawing-room door, Matt and Stacy leading, her hand on his strong arm. Bibury shook his head and said mildly, 'You heard the lady, Beauchamp. There can be no grounds for reproaches, none at all. The first toast at dinner shall be to the prospective bride and groom.'

He threw open the door, and escorted Matt and Stacy through it. Matt had taken Stacy's arm, and led her to where Caroline, her face white, sat with Louisa Landen and Earl Falconer, all looking equally troubled.

'Caroline, my love,' Bibury told her gently, 'I think that your brother and Miss Blanchard have something important to tell you and your father.'

CHAPTER TWELVE

THE announcement that Matt Falconer, Lord Radley, was to marry the Bankeress, and soon, was exactly designed to set the Bramham house party alight. It would not be true to say that everyone was pleased by the news: Anthony Beauchamp, for one, was not, and it was to be supposed that Trot and the other young hopefuls were afflicted by the dismals once they realised that England's richest heiress outside the ranks of the nobility was denied to them.

Among those who were pleased was Matt's father, who was quite bemused by the news, coming as it did on the heels of the distressing interview with his son. Why in the world could Matt, once he had been challenged so ruthlessly, not have told him that he had proposed to, and been accepted by, the very lady whose virtue he had accused him of tampering with? He would never understand his wilful son, never.

It was perhaps as well that the exact truth was never revealed to him. Questioned by his father later that night, once they were alone and Stacy had retired, Matt offered no explanations, no extenuation for his strange behaviour. The fact that Anthony Beauchamp had secured the backing of the younger members of the party, before publicly challenging Matt over the insult offered to the woman to whom he was already secretly betrothed, could not be concealed from the rest of those at Bramham who were not in the know, and added to the Earl's confusion.

Anthony Beauchamp and Bibury were both reprimanded by Uncle Beauchamp, Anthony for his rash hot-headedness, Bibury for not having the sense to hold him in check. 'But by God, sir,' Anthony had exclaimed, exasperated, 'their betrothal having been secret, how could anyone be expected to know of it? As her nearest young relative it was my duty to defend her name. And, come to that,' he added, his blue eyes bright with suspicion, 'when *did* they become betrothed? They have hardly met since Pontisford, and what occurred there must be a matter for conjecture.'

'Then let it remain so,' his father instructed him. '"All's well that end's well", as the Bard once said, and for Radley to settle himself so well must be a source of congratulation to his father and all his relatives. As for the lady you and she are not suited to each other. She is older than you are, and doubtless a self-willed man like Radley will be better able to hold her in check than you would have been.'

'But I love her,' grumbled Anthony, half beneath his breath. 'And I doubt whether Matt Falconer does.'

'And that is no matter, either. There are plenty of pretty, biddable young girls who would be delighted for you to make them your wife.'

Again below his breath Anthony muttered, 'I don't want a pretty biddable young girl, I want Cousin Stacy.'

Cousin Stacy didn't know what she wanted. Somehow she had endured the polite uproar which had followed the announcement of her betrothal to Matt. His father had come over to her and said, 'Madam, I could hardly have expected my son to have made so worthy a choice. I understand that you both wish to be married as soon as possible. It is fortunate that Grimes is here. He may set all the legal formalities in train straight away. But it is not that which exercises my mind, it is my pleasure at welcoming you into my family. As I told you before, I knew and respected your father. I hope to love, as well as respect, his daughter.'

Whatever might be said in private, all that was said in public was as proper as could be. Poor Trot, poor in every way, could only moan inwardly at the wretched luck that had handed the Blanchard wealth to a man who would be as rich as Croesus without it when he finally inherited the Falconer estates. But he, too, said all the right things on that interminable afternoon and evening which followed the revelation at the bottom of Bramham's stairs.

The only person to whom Stacy did not speak at any length was Matt himself. They were being watched so closely that they both, being a man and woman of some maturity of experience, in order to give nothing away, said as little as possible which was not light and innocuous. The private meat of their conversation, so to speak, would have to wait for the public hors d'oeuvres of it to be over.

Louisa, walking with Stacy to their suite of rooms, said timidly to her before they parted for the night, 'My dear, exactly how long is it since you accepted Lord Radley? I must say that I was as surprised by your news as the rest of the company.'

'I accepted him at exactly the moment at which it was proper for me to do so,' returned Stacy elliptically, and Louisa had to be content with that.

The servants were, as usual, wiser than their masters, knowing more of the truth than they did. Stacy and Matt's insistence on such a speedy wedding ceremony came as no surprise to them.

Matt, weary in body and soul, tired at having to behave in public with such circumspection, entered his bedroom to find Jeb there, laying his nightwear on the covers of the big four-poster bed which, he had been told, had once been slept in by the great Duke of Wellington himself.

Jeb, who would have had no more respect for the Duke than for Matt, said, 'So, you are to be turned off at last? Do I congratulate the Bankeress for capturing you? Or should my felicitations be more properly addressed to your good self? My own regret is that you didn't put a bullet into that pretty young fellow who calls himself her cousin.'

'My good self,' grated Matt, beginning to pull off the skin-tight clothing which was the current fashion, 'has only one wish at the moment, and that is for a good night's sleep. As for my future bride's cousin, however many bullets *he* had put in *me*, she would never have married him. Had she done so she would have eaten him in a week!'

'But you will eat her—or will the meal be mutual?' Jeb enquired suavely. 'At least your child will be legitimate now.' And he began to laugh. 'Is that why she accepted you?'

Matt, now naked, began to sponge himself down from the bowl of warm water which Jeb had poured out for him. He said, his voice muffled a little by the towel which he was using to dry himself, 'I don't think that she thought once about whether her child would be legitimate. It's my belief that she announced our engagement to stop an unseemly duel—for which I am grateful. I suspect I am more than a match for Anthony Beauchamp with either pistols, swords or fists, but honour alone would have prevented me from proving that I was.'

Jeb began to laugh uncontrollably. He threw Matt his nightshirt, spluttering, 'What a woman to win. By God, I'm reasonably happy to marry my Polly. She's a good girl, or was until I cozened her into bed, but she ain't a patch on the Bankeress for guts. I shall purely admire watching her tame you!'

A tawny head emerged from the ruffled neck of Matt's nightwear. He said gruffly, 'I shouldn't take any bets on that. I suspect a draw will be the result.'

Jeb wasn't the only man that night to discuss the outcome of such a bet. The comments of the women were more discreet, but followed roughly the same line. And, naturally, the question of whether the marriage was a forced one also exercised many minds.

The only response to gossip, Stacy felt, was to behave as normally as possible, to eat her breakfast, to talk briefly in the drawing-room to Caroline, and finally to retire to her own rooms—to sit by the fire, wondering what exactly she had done in handing herself over to Matt.

There was a knock on the door, not a timid knock, and of course it was Matt, looking larger and sterner than ever. He bowed to the rapidly departing Louisa—who was acknowledging that a betrothed couple might, ever under the strict etiquette then prevailing, safely be left alone together.

'I have come,' Matt told Stacy stiffly, 'not only to thank you for honouring me with your hand, but also to thank you for saving me from having to allow your cousin Anthony to put hole in me which might have proved fatal. I couldn't have put a bullet in him when he was in the right and I was in the wrong. I shall always remember, and treasure, your courage in speaking out.'

Stacy had never respected him more. She was suddenly aware that behind Matt's unconventional exterior was a man of impeccable honour—which made the details of the scandal which had destroyed his social position in youth even stranger. Stranger still was the manner in which he had behaved to her at Pontisford.

She murmured, 'It was the least I could do for you, sir, seeing that it was my dilatoriness in accepting your proposal which had brought you to such an unfortunate pass. I hope, also, that our betrothal has restored your credit with your father.'

None of this was what she wanted to say, it was all so stiff and stilted. And he was as stiff, too, running a hand under his carefully tied cravat and saying in a distant voice, 'Of course, the condition on which I offered our marriage still stands. One of convenience only, until our child is born—and after that we may honourably agree to go our separate ways. I have no particular wish to marry, as I am sure you have not——'

Oh, dear! Stacy's heart fell into her elegant kid slippers. She should have known. He didn't really want to marry that strange and eccentric creature the Bankeress. He must have had a syncope at Pontisford, and ravished her in the middle of it. He didn't, couldn't, care for her at all.

'I didn't want to marry in the first place,' she snapped at him, 'but, things being as they are, and seeing that for some reason which I cannot fathom we both ran mad at Pontisford, marriage is what we are doomed to. I must tell you that I have no intention of giving up my management of the Bank until my coming child compels me to do so. What you care to do with your life is of no consequence to me.'

And oh, what a damned lie that was! She cared most desperately, but if he was going to speak to her as bloodlessly as Ephraim Blount did, then she could not let him know that, whatever else he had done at Pontisford, he had caused Anastasia Blanchard to fall in love with him. She could no longer blind herself to that unwelcome piece of knowledge. And he, plainly, felt nothing for her—he cared only that their child might be legitimate.

'Nevertheless,' pursued Matt doggedly, wishing that his dear Lady Disdain would offer him something better than the cold face which she probably used when she was having thieving managers thrown into the street. He was a fool to think that she might care something for him—other than the moment of lust which had overcome them at Pontisford. 'Nevetheless, I have a duty to tell you what my plans will be once we *are* married.'

'Oh, that,' said Stacy as carelessly as she could, 'yes, that would be a piece of common courtesy, I agree.'

He wanted to jump on her, lift her out of the chair

where she sat surveying him as coldly as if he were an insect—a stare he remembered from their earliest encounters—and shake her and kiss her until she lay panting against his heart.

And what a savage she would think him if he did any such thing. No, he must be as cold as she, and resign himself to having had her as his love, even if only for one night, only to lose her to the kind of marriage which he had always despised. A man and a woman tied together simply for the sake of two pieces of land and a son and heir to them. It was only too grimly appropriate that the busiest set of people involved in their marriage would be their lawyers, working out the details of the settlement of her estates and his. Grimes would be in his element.

'My plans,' he began, dragging his mind away from the cheerless prospect of an arranged and convenient marriage, the reason for which—an heir— had already been accomplished, 'are as follows. I regret that I shall have to leave England as soon as is decently possible to return to Virginia to settle the management of my estates in the United States. It is being borne upon me that my future, now that my brother has died, lies here. I shall be Earl Falconer one day, and the duties of a great estate will devolve upon me. I cannot neglect them, even though I might like to. I shall leave Jeb behind to be the overseer of my farm. I don't think that he wishes to stay here. His spiritual home is across the Atlantic.'

He did not say, As is mine, although he was thinking it. He had not wanted Rollo to die, however much he had disliked his brother, because alive he would ultimately have become Earl Falconer and Matt would have remained a simple American planter. That dream was as dead as Rollo.

'I am sorry,' Stacy said truthfully. 'I know how much you love your adopted country.'

Matt waved a dismissive hand. 'No matter,' he told her.

'My one regret is having to leave you so soon after marriage, but I wish to be with you when our child is born, and to do that I must leave speedily, so that my early return is assured.'

He was speaking to her in the emotionless language of the world of banking and commerce—a language which Stacy had once thought was the only one which she would ever use. Pontisford had briefly introduced her to another, but that language seemed fated to be denied her in the future.

What would he say if she cast herself at his feet, crying, Damn everything, your and my duties, the Bank and the Falconer estates, and take me to Virginia with you, to stay there, for all I want is to be your true wife, and everything else can go hang?

Almost she did so, only unfortunately he continued, still emotionless, 'I know how much this marriage irks you, that you have no wish to surrender your independence. You may depend upon it that I shall make it as easy as possible for you to live as though it had never happened.'

His face was averted a little when he spoke, for he could not bear to look at her, knowing that they would be parted so soon and for so long. He remembered Camilla, thought bitterly, are all my loves to be doomed? But at least this love of mine is a strong woman, so I must be strong too.

Unknown to him, his strength was written on his face. Stacy, seeing it, stood up, began to move towards him, to say something of what was in her heart—and then, if he insisted on denying her, she would accept that denial, and learn to live with it.

She compelled him to look at her by the simple process of standing before him, her green eyes earnestly on his tawny ones. To be so near to him started her inward tremblings again, as though the child within her were already able to move, to tell her of his presence—

something which she knew would not happen for another few months.

Unknown to her Matt begn to tremble too. Her scent, a compound of lemon and spices from the little bags of herbs which Polly had made up to store between the folds of her clothes, and from which the laundress at her London home had created the soft soap which she daily used, was temptation itself to him.

'Stacy,' he said hoarsely, putting out a hand to touch her chin, to lift it. His tawny eyes were suddenly glowing, the icy manner in which he had been speaking to her was suddenly gone. 'Oh, God, Stacy. . .'

He got no further. The magic moment which they were beginning to share, with Stacy turning longing eyes up towards him as he started to speak, was shattered. The door was flung open, to reveal Polly.

'Oh, Miss Stacy!' she exclaimed, taking in the scene before her as Matt stood back and the light which his impulsive action had lit in Stacy's eyes began to die. 'I'm so sorry. I thought that you were downstairs. I came. . . no matter. . .' And she shot out of the room as quickly as she had entered it.

Too late. Both Stacy and Matt had lost the impetus which was suddenly bringing them together. They were apart again, the spell broken.

Stacy put her hands behind her back and clenched them tightly. A lifetime of obeying her father, of suppressing her emotions, was preventing her from telling Matt what he would most have liked to hear. As for Matt, he was so afraid of coercing her, a legacy of what had happened at Pontisford, that his usual forthright nature was strangely subdued.

He took up where he had left off, was busy outlining his—and her—future plans. 'We must, I fear, leave for London as soon as possible. My father will also be making plans to open Falconer House, off the Strand. I have spoken to Lord Beauchamp and I understand that he wishes to be present at the ceremony, and be responsible for you as your nearest living relative. I collect that you have no Blanchard relatives.'

Stacy was fascinated by this passionless and businesslike recital, which seemed to be leaving so little to chance. 'Only a very aged great-aunt,' she told him, 'who has had nothing to do with either my father or me since I was a baby. She is now in her late eighties, lives at Bath, and has not left that city for these thirty years!'

'As Lord Beauchamp informed me. My father wishes us to be married at Falconer House, but I believe that your uncle and aunt Beauchamp would prefer the ceremony to be at their place in Bedford Square. I think that the decision should be yours.'

Stacy would have married Matt over the anvil at Gretna Green if she had believed that he loved her, but, seeing that he was all business, then so would she be.

'If Aunt and Uncle Beauchamp wish to extend such a kindness to me, then let it be Bedford Square.'

Matt nodded, still passionless, she noted sadly, the spark which had been so nearly lit between them quite extinguished. 'Most proper of you, madam, but no more than I would have expected of you.'

'You did not always think me proper,' Stacy offered a trifle dejectedly.

'You have my word,' he returned earnestly, 'that I most truly regret my wretched behaviour to you at Pontisford and elsewhere!'

Which wasn't what she wanted to hear from him at all. She remembered the burning fire which had raged between them from the moment that she had mistaken him for the butler, and which had consumed them both on that fatal night. Whatever could have happened to it? Oh, it still raged in her heart, but it could find no outlet, no way in which it could light a similar fire in him.

The rest of their conversation was conducted in the same sad and emotionless tone. They would live at Stacy's home in London until Matt took ship for the States. Polly and Jeb were to be married quietly on the same day as Matt and Stacy, and would accompany him to Virginia. Stacy would work at the Bank until she grew too big for decorum and would then settle herself wherever she thought proper—in the country, he hoped, where she and the child could breathe the pure air, so unlike London's smoke and fumes.

At last they were finished. There was another knock on the door. This time it was a footman carrying a silver salver with coffee for them, and all that he interrupted was an icy exchange of courtesies.

Matt became a little more human, said, as Stacy poured coffee for them, 'I see, madam, that you are looking more in health than you were when you first arrived at Bramham. The child does not yet discommode you?'

The child, the child. He would never have offered her marriage if it had not been for the existence of the child, living proof of their scandalous behaviour which would, without marriage, effectively have ruined them both.

She replied, her throat closing as she did so, 'No, I am well now. I had some sickness when I first came to Bramham, but that has passed. If, once we are married, I do experience distress, I shall be able to send for a doctor. At the moment common sense must be my guide, since no one must yet know that I am already pregnant!'

'Ah, yes.' Matt was almost satirical. 'Common sense! That has always been your guide, I believe.'

'Except once!' she could not help shooting back at him. 'Except once!'

And that, Stacy was dismally aware, was enough to stop any further conversation between them, other than on the most neutral matters such as the probable date of their departure from Bramham, the wedding, and her own plans to notify her lawyers to meet Grimes and his cohorts as soon as possible. The impossible marriage was to be put in train.

CHAPTER THIRTEEN

'So,' Matt remarked halfway through dinner on their wedding-day, 'it is accomplished. For good or ill you are Lady Radley now. I offer you a toast, madam. To you and our future.'

Stacy raised her glass to him and, as cool as he, offered him a toast in exchange. 'And to you, sir, and any child which may spring from our union.' Which was as plain as she dared be, surrounded as they were by servants who might suspect why they had married so precipitately but could not actually know.

He smiled a trifle ruefully at that, and later, when they had moved to the drawing-room, a stately place which owed everything to Louis Blanchard's taste and nothing to Stacy's, she said to him, looking around at its ornate splendours, 'Had you ever thought of visiting this room, I doubt that you could have anticipated the reason why you might find yourself in it!'

At last she had provoked his stern face into something resembling genuine amusement. 'Perhaps, madam, the speed with which I have arrived here after our first meeting is as remarkable as the reason for my being here at all.'

Stacy's response was a mute one, a nod of agreement. Indeed, long afterwards, looking back at her wedding-day and the events which led up to it, she always marvelled at how short a time it had taken to turn her life upside-down. There she was at the beginning of November, living the life which she had led since her late teens and then, in a few short weeks, all was changed, and changed forever.

She had thrown her reputation to the four winds, been

initiated into the delights of the bed, become pregnant and accepted marriage from a man whom in the terms of their world she had barely become acquainted with and wasn't sure she even liked—lust being a different thing. After that she had been united to him in the most hurried wedding-ceremony, although their union was merely a legal one, the body having nothing to do with it, and in consequence had seen the old Stacy Blanchard disappear to become Lady Radley—and who was she?

Always, when thinking of it, her thoughts became as breathless as that time itself, as though, the grammar of her life having been destroyed, the grammar of her expressing what had happened to her had disappeared as well!

Their wedding-day had been fine at first. Later, after the ceremony, a winter thunderstorm had followed, out of a clear sky, as though the gods were expressing their anger at the hollowness of what she and Matt had done. They were to spend their empty honeymoon at Stacy's London home, which Matt had visited for the first time twenty-four hours before the wedding. The cool nature of their first meal together as man and wife was to set the tone for their married life before Matt left for Virginia, taking a tearful Polly and a happy Jeb with him.

On that last late January day, when he came to see her before leaving London to take ship, Stacy was seated at her desk in what had been her father's study. She had cancelled her visit to the Bank, but was working on some proposition which Ephraim Blount had put before her. She was trying not to think of what Matt's departure meant to her.

He had been scrupulously kind and distant in manner to her from the moment that the Bishop had made them man and wife. No one could have been more considerate. Only afterwards, when he had gone, did she realise that since the ceremony he had not so much as touched her, indeed had scrupulously avoided all contact with her.

And so things had remained. In front of others they were charmingly polite, the very picture of a newly married pair. But once alone the politeness remained, and some of the charm, but the rapport which Stacy had hoped that they might somehow find was missing.

So now he was standing before her, dressed for travelling. She thought that he looked gaunt, that since their marriage he had lost weight, so that the cheekbones in his face were starker than ever, adding to its strength.

'Madam,' he began, and then fell silent. There was nothing of the semi-bantering, semi-mocking manner which he had adopted with her before they were married. All was deadly seriousness. Stacy thought that she preferred the lighter manner of their illicit relationship to the gravity of their legal one—but she could not say so.

Over the few weeks of their marriage she was coming to understand that, however much her father's tuition had made her ready to run the Bank, it had done nothing to enable her to express the feelings of her heart.

'Yes?' Stacy prompted, trying to help him, but in the doing she remained so calm that Matt, who had thought that before he left her he might fall on his knees before her and tell her how much he had come to love her, how little he wished to leave her, was quite daunted by such cold composure—the composure that Louis Blanchard had bred in his child, unaware that it might act like a killing frost quelling an unspoken but truly felt love.

Also, at the last, he didn't want to leave her—and miss how much she would change and blossom as the child grew in her. Some intuition, foreign to the hard man he usually was, told him that the coming child would change her, was already changing her, and this he would miss—although he fully intended to return well before their child was born. Would she always remain his dear Lady Disdain, so cold and controlled that his heart wept within him, that heart which he had once thought that he had left in the grave with his dear, lost love Camilla?

'I have to tell you, madam,' he said, as cold and controlled as she was, for he would not force himself on her, as that would be to behave as Rollo had behaved to Camilla—with such shocking results—'that all is ready for my journey to Virginia. Jeb, I need hardly inform you, can scarce wait to be gone. Polly, now, is a different matter. She wails that she does not like to leave her dear Miss Stacy to the ministrations of a half-trained girl, but she knows that her duty to Jeb, and to their child, demands that she make a new life for herself in Virginia.

And I, thought Stacy, screaming inside herself, could not I make a new life for myself in Virginia? For there is only the Bank to keep me here, but you have never once expressed the wish that we might settle there as Jeb and Polly are doing. But I suppose that true love lies between them, and it is plain that you regret what we did together at Pontisford, since now you can scarce bear to touch me.

She forgot that she was giving him no reason to believe that she felt for him anything other than mere tolerance for someone who thought that he owed her reparation for having forced himself on her and caused her to commit an act which she had subsequently bitterly regretted. The loneliness which had been the constant companion of both of them throughout their lives had only been endured by their proud rejection of any form of surrender in the way of asking anyone for love and pity. Even Louisa had never broken through the shell of pride which had hardened around Stacy's heart.

Matt, likewise, had taught himself to depend only himself—to love was, in the end, he discovered, to experience punishment and pain, and his heart shrank, as Stacy's did, from commitment to another. Worse, ever since he had married her he had feared to touch her, for he knew that to do so would result in rousing him to the degree where he might force himself upon her as he had done at Pontisford. And that he had vowed never to do again.

Stacy, still a prisoner of her upbringing, said, in that deadly polite fashion which had Matt hungering to smash it, but not knowing how to do so without injuring them both, 'I hope that you have fair winds on your journey, both to the Americas and back again. I shall write to you in the hope that some of my letters may reach you.' For she knew how untrustworthy communication was across 'the steep Atlantic stream', as the poet Milton had it.

'Indeed——' Matt bowed '—and I know that you will look after yourself, and our child, for the one thing which I most admire in you, madam, is your practicality—a trait few women share with you.'

Well, doubtless he meant that for a compliment, but Stacy would have traded it for any sign of true affection, however small. But, asking for nothing, she received nothing. She rose, accompanied him to the door, to the entrance hall where Jeb and Polly were waiting, and Louisa stood in the shadows.

Polly was tearful again, flung her arms around Stacy and sobbed her farewells. Jeb bowed before giving her his hand, as though she were a man, and then, suddenly, impulsively, as though they were equals, not mistress and almost-servant, he took her in a giant bear hug—of the kind she would have liked from Matt. He whispered in her ear before he released her, 'I will look after him for you, madam, and see that he returns in one piece, and by then I hope that you will have the wit to find one another, for you were meant to be the two halves of a broken coin brought together, or a split apple, if only you and he had the wit to see it!'

Matt, astonished, watched as, impulsively and warmly, Stacy kissed his friend on the cheek, thinking jealously, Why could she not favour me like that? But, like Stacy, asking for nothing, he received nothing, and she watched him follow Polly and Jeb out of the ornate front door and into the waiting chaise which was to take them on their journey north to Liverpool, where they would take ship for Baltimore.

The chaise was driven down the short avenue which led to the iron gates which separated them from the road to central London. Stacy's eyes followed it. Outwardly she stood calm and composed beside an anxious Louisa, who was worried for her charge. Inwardly she was shrieking, He is my love, and I have been cruel to him, and I have sent him away. If he could but have granted me one word of love, or had asked me properly, I would have gone with him to the ends of the world, shoeless and in rags, rather than live here in my meaningless wealth and comfort.

All the years of her father's instruction were being stripped away from her, and the final words which haunted her as, straight-backed, she walked into the house with Louisa were, Too late! Too late!

And Matt Falconer? Looking out of the chaise window as he was whirled away out of her life, he also was consumed with the most bitter regret, that he had left her without telling her of his love, and the same words echoed in his head, even to the moment when he boarded ship and watched England's shores slide away into the distance.

Too late!

Inexorably the world swung around the sun, and the seasons changed, and with those changes Stacy changed too, the child growing big within her. The day finally came when she left the Bank's office, not to return, she said, until the child was born. Nothing came from America, which was no surprise, until one day in late May a packet arrived containing letters from Matt, Jeb and Polly. They had docked safely at Baltimore, and were on their way to Virginia.

'I trust, Lady Radley,' Matt had written in a hand as big and bold as himself, 'that you and the child thrive, that my business here will soon be conducted, and that it will not be long before I see you again. I remain your most devoted husband and servant, Matthew Falconer.'

'Devoted husband and servant'. Well, they were hardly words of love, Stacy thought, but they were better than nothing. The rest of the letter was like himself, straightforward, telling of the sea journey—that Polly had been ill, so that her coming child had been feared for, but that she and the child had survived the crossing, and were now well and fit. Jeb and Polly's letters were like themselves too. Polly's was full of ill-spelt excitement, and her sadness that 'Miss Stacy'—and who was she now?—had not travelled with them. Jeb's entertained her by its impudent bluntness.

> Mad Matt is madder than ever, and I know that it is because he regrets that we are not all of us, including Mad Matt's wife, returning to settle permanently in Virginia. When I taxed him over his desire to return to the land of the unfree, his reply was as stiff as you might suppose it: that he had his duty to perform to all his vast estates in England now that he was the heir, and now that he himself was on the way to having an heir. I made so bold as to suggest that he might as well have put a deputy in charge of what he owned in England as easily as he was putting me in charge in Virginia, and stayed in Virginia himself! I then had to endure a sermon on logic-chopping for my pains.

Almost as an afterthought, with a different pen and in different ink, he had written:

> I pray you, madam, for the love and gratitude I bear him—he having saved my life—that when he returns to you you prove kind to him, or shall I advise him, that

failing that, he must return to Virginia and I will make a burnt offering of myself by returning to run Falconer lands in England! You see what a sacrifice I am prepared to make for you both.

Tears gathered in Stacy's eyes as she put the letter down. She rose and walked to the window to see coming up the drive, towards the house, a coach with the Falconer arms on its side—a white shield with a black falcon, its wings outspread on it, a ring in its silver beak. She knew that Caroline Bibury was due in town, and had written that she would visit as soon after her arrival as was possible, but surely she would have come in her own carriage, not her father's?

She turned away from the window, but not before she had seen the footmen jump down from the box, one to throw the door open and the other to hand down the Right Honourable the Earl Falconer, Matt's father. Now, what was he doing, visiting his errant son's wife?

Stacy was soon to find out. The butler came to enquire whether she was receiving and, on being told yes, presently escorted my lord in, alone, no Caroline with him. She thought that he had aged since she had seen him at Christmas, was a little more stooped.

He bowed over her hand, and then Louisa's—Louisa being fully recovered from her Christmas malaise. Once again Stacy saw the resemblance to Matt, and saw that in his youth he had been as vibrant a man as his absent son was.

'It is good of you to receive me,' he told her, before taking a seat. 'I arrived in town but two nights ago, and I do not intend to stay long. I am merely here to do some necessary business. I visited Blanchard's this morning to pay you my respects, only to be told that you will be away until after your child is born. I trust I see you well?'

Stacy smiled at him. 'Very well, sir. And you?'

'Tolerably, madam, tolerably. As well as one of my advanced years is ever well in London. I shall not be truly well until I am back in the Yorkshire countryside again. It is of that which I wished to speak to you. I cannot think that being in London during the summer is good either for you or for my coming heir, and since it has been the practice these many years for the Falconer heir to be born at The Eyrie – most fitting a name in the circumstances – I am here to ask you to remove to Yorkshire until the birth is over.

'My dear Caroline and her husband will be returning with me, and it would please an old man to look after his son's wife in his son's absence. It is commendable that not only does his duty demand that he give up his home in Virginia, to devote himself to his life as the Falconer heir, but that also his duty demands that he return to see that his affairs are wound up there in proper form.'

He had been speaking with great conviction and great formality, and then, suddenly dropping all formality, he said, almost as blunt as Jeb would have been, 'Oh, madam, my son and I have been at outs these many years, and it is now my one wish that we shall be at ins again, and what better thing can I do than care for his wife? I shall send for the best doctor from London for you, well before my grandchild is born, so have no fears on that score.'

What could she say? The old Stacy, if she had accepted his offer at all, would have made a cool and distant answer of acceptance, not letting her emotions show, but the months of carrying his grandchild and Matt's child had changed her, had softened her. Impulsively, her eyes filling with tears, she put out a warm young hand to take his cool old one which lay loosely on his black silk-clad knee.

'Oh, sir,' she told him, 'you do me a great honour. Of course I will come. I have never been part of a family, you know, have only ever had my dear Louisa to care for me. I am sure that Matt. . .Lord Radley. . .would be happy to learn that I shall be staying in his childhood home. He said before he left that he hoped that I would leave London to have our child in the healthy country air.'

This pleased the old man, she could tell, almost as much as her agreement to go to Yorkshire did. She would form part of his train when he travelled home again, he told her, 'And I have already sent word to The Eyrie that all must be made ready for you by the time we arrive.'

All the way north Stacy could not but think of the last journey she had made through the cold and the snow, and that the result of it was that she arrived at The Eyrie under the summer sun, a woman who was happy to live in idleness, so that her child might be born safely—even though both the Earl and Caroline protested a little when she insisted on walking out each day, as she had always been accustomed to.

Her rooms looked out over a lake with a folly in the shape of a miniature temple before it. It was there that she walked each day, sometimes with Louisa in attendance and sometimes Martha Williams, Polly's successor. There she sat in a large armchair, or reclined on a sofa fetched from the folly, watching the ducks paddle by, dozing a little, doing tapestry-work, reading, and altogether being as idle as a fine lady was expected to be, instead of being the Bankeress, that unfeminine model of diligence. It was as though she was making up for all the years of hard work which she had spent first with her father and then alone, after his death.

The only thing lacking was Matt himself, and, as if to remedy that lack, after many months' absence from them he suddenly began to walk in her dreams again. He was the lion-man, golden against the blue of the sky, tawny all over, skin and hair both. Sometimes he was walking and sometimes he was running on a parched and sun-baked plain, a dog, a large one, something like a wolfhound, following him. Sometimes he crouched by a cave at night, feeding a fire, the dog now lying beside him. Always the dog was present and always the dream ended in the same way. He would suddenly see her. His eyes would light up, she would run towards him, and he towards her, to take her in his arms, to. . .

And then she would wake up, to find herself alone, the ready tears about to fall, asking herself whether when. . . if. . .he returned she would still be able to be as frank and free with him in reality as she was in her dreams.

'Did Matt ever have a dog?' she asked the Earl one evening when they sat together talking after they had finished playing a rubber of whist.

The Earl answered her, looking a little puzzled by her question, 'Oh, I don't think so, no.'

Caroline, who was helping her husband to put away the impediments of the game, looked up to say, 'Oh, but he did, Father, don't you remember? He had a wolfhound, Prince; he was very fond of it, and Prince was very fond of him. When Prince was. . .killed Matt was broken-hearted, said that he would never have another dog. I would have thought that you would remember how he grieved over him.'

'Killed?' Stacy's voice was almost that of the Bankeress again, cold and hard, detecting a false note in something which she had been told. She saw the Earl change colour, saw that Caroline's own colour was high. 'How killed?'

Her voice was so peremptory, so commanding that Lord Bibury looked curiously at her, and Caroline answered her unthinkingly. 'It was an accident,' she said slowly. 'Rollo shot Prince by mistake. . . Matt took it very badly.'

So Rollo, the brother whom Matt never mentioned, whose wife he had supposedly run off with, had shot

Matt's dog—and the Earl had chosen to forget that he had done so.

'How old was he?'

'Who, the dog?' Caroline appeared to be genuinely bewildered.

Stacy's sigh was impatience itself. She was the Bankeress again, questioning a prevaricating clerk, and the whole company, which included Caroline's other sister, Georgiana, and her husband, Dean George Tranter, were staring at her, good manners forgotten.

'No, Matt, I meant. How old was he? And Rollo—how old was he?' Stacy had thought it odd that no one ever spoke of Rollo, who had after all been their eldest brother and the heir, and had died comparatively recently.

'He was thirteen. Rollo was twenty-one. Matt was the youngest of us.'

Georgiana, a handsome woman, a little thrusting, determined one day to thrust her husband into a bishopric, exclaimed decisively, 'Oh, come, Caro, you were always too tender-hearted! You knew perfectly well, even if Papa didn't, that Rollo shot Prince because Matt loved him so. Matt and Frank could never have anything without Rollo wanting it. Rollo asked Matt to give him Prince and Matt refused. A week later Rollo shot Prince—accidentally, of course.' Her sneer as she said the last sentence was palpable.

An appalled silence followed. Stacy had got the answer she wanted and had, intuitively, half known was coming. Or was it the dream, where Matt roved a strange countryside, always with a dog beside him, which had told her? She had never seen him with a dog in real life.

She shivered involuntarily. The Earl saw her do so and said, 'Georgiana, I am surprised that you should make such an accusation about a brother who is dead, and cannot defend himself. If Rollo said it was an accident, done when we were all out shooting, as I now remember, then an accident it was.'

Georgiana sat down, picked up her canvaswork, abandoned for the game of whist, shrugged, and drawled, 'He never lacked a defender so long as you were there to defend him, Papa. Even now he's dead you can't acknowledge what a beast Rollo was. It's time you faced the truth. I heard him laughing about what he'd done with that groom of his. If he couldn't have Prince then he'd make sure Matt wouldn't, was the gist of it.'

The Earl's face was grey. He turned to Caroline, who was twisting her hands nervously together. 'Do you believe this to be true, Caroline?'

She nodded reluctantly. 'Yes, Papa. I was with Georgie when we heard him telling Yates—that was his groom's name, I remember—what he had done.'

Another silence fell as the Earl digested a bitter truth which he had long refused to recognise as a truth. Stacy was suddenly horrified at what she had uncovered, even if the sad story which she had just heard might make his father think a little differently about Matt. She avoided everyone's eye, cast off the mask of the Bankeress, picked up her own canvaswork and began to stitch as though her life depended on it. Silence fell again as each member of the party took refuge in some occupation, however trivial.

The Earl rose heavily, looking old. 'I should not be ungrateful to you, Caroline and Georgiana, for at long last telling me something which I should have known before. I think I will retire early, if you would all excuse me. I would like to reflect over what I have just learned when I am alone.'

Everyone, including Stacy, stood—to watch him walk slowly away, his years suddenly pressing heavily on him.

George Tranter began to reproach his wife, 'No need for that, my dear——' only for her to interrupt him spiritedly.

'Nonsense, my love. It's time he faced that, and even worse truths, about Rollo. Matt was always Rollo's victim, and it was not the worst thing which Rollo did to him, by any means —— '

This time the Dean managed to silence her by thundering, 'My love, *no*. You have said enough. Matt's wife is here. You will distress her.'

Stacy shook her head, replied as steadily as she could, 'No, it was my own insistent questioning which provoked this. . .incident, and I apologise for it.'

Lord Bibury, who had had a soft spot for her ever since the night when she had publicly proclaimed her betrothal to Matt, came over to sit beside her and take her hand — she had laid her embroidery down. 'No, my dear. You must not reproach yourself. You naturally wished to learn about your husband's past. It was your bad luck that you hit upon something which had long been hidden.'

No, it had not been bad luck at all. She had, after some curious fashion, known what she was doing, even as she had badgered Caroline. She often knew when people were lying, or concealing the truth from her, as Caroline had been doing when she had spoken of Matt's dog. It was a talent which she had inherited from Louis Blanchard, and of which, when she had spoken to him of it, he had said, 'All the Blanchards have possessed it, my dear, and whether it is a blessing or a curse, who is to say?'

Later, in bed, she asked herself what the real truth was in the story of Matt's running off with his brother's wife, for there was a false note in that tale, she was sure, and one day, for Matt's sake she would try to find out what it was. Meantime, she must watch and wait for him.

Several days later Stacy was doing exactly that in front of the little temple. Martha had wandered off — doubtless to meet an off-duty footman, she was sure — and she was quite alone, a book of Lord Byron's earlier poems on her knee—all her reading was frivolous these days; she had no time for Blackstone now.

The afternoon was warm, she was reclining on the sofa which had been carried out for her, and she could see the ducks on the lake, and one small rail, who had left the water and was skittering about in front of her. The sun and the silence lulled her into the easy sleep of a woman who was now more than seven months gone. She realised with a sense of shock, just before consciousness left her, that Matt had come back into her dreams on the very day when she had felt his child stir within her.

So it was natural that he should come to her again, as she lay sleeping in the grounds of the home that he had loved, and that she should, in her dream, stretch her hand out to his dog, and call him Prince, and that Matt should smile at her as she did so. This time he didn't embrace her, but took her hand, the dog walking along behind them. And how had she known that Matt had once owned a dog and had loved him? She had never seen him with one, which was strange for a man who loved animals and the countryside.

This afternoon his embrace came at the end of their walk, and as he took her in his arms she awoke, as she always did—to see him standing there, tall and bronzed, an expression almost of awe on his face at the sight of her, big with his child. . .

CHAPTER FOURTEEN

Busy though he had been during the short time he had spent in Virginia, Matt had found that he could not banish Stacy from either his daytime or his night-time thoughts. Camilla's death, and the manner of her dying, had made such a strong impression on him that he had told himself that he would never marry; any dealings he had with women would be both passing and superficial. He had never deceived his partners: he always made it plain from the beginning that any liaison he entered into would be temporary.

And now, in any pause in his work, when his mind began to wander, he found Stacy there with him. Always she was as she had been on that fatal night: wild-eyed, face aflame, her whole body vibrant and ready for him. Oh, he hungered for her as he had never hungered for anyone. With Camilla he had been her knight—protective, always ready to defend her, his love a gentle thing, as she had been gentle. He had been little more than a boy, after all, and chivalry as much as love had motivated him from the first moment he had ever seen her, shy and out of her depth at a grand ball, waiting for someone to rescue her—which he had done.

But Stacy! From the first she had been as fierce with him as he had been with her. She had traded him word for word, had stared him down, and when finally they had fallen into bed together it had been a contest of equals. As for shyness and needing to be rescued. . . He chuckled to himself a little wryly whenever he thought of the night when *she* had rescued *him* from the unwanted duel with Anthony Beauchamp. She had faced everyone down, had turned the whole business around, had been as bold in public as she was reputed to have been in private in York when dealing with her dishonest manager. She was quite the last kind of woman whom he could ever have imagined himself as finding attractive—but being absent from her told him that he loved her to distraction, that what he had felt for Camilla, although sweet and true, paled beside it.

He had concluded his business as quickly as he could, seen Jeb and Polly settled into the home which had been his, and had taken the first boat back to England on which there was a spare passage. All the way from Southampton to London he had had but one thought in his head and that was the hope that she was waiting for him. He had never thought of the child at all. It was as though once he had left Stacy behind in England she had turned back into the Amazon she had been at Pontisford, defying and mocking him every time they met.

By God, she was a woman in a thousand, and so he would tell her, and when he had done so they would celebrate his return in the most time-honoured way. He was burning as his coach turned into the drive of her home. . .

Only to discover that she was no longer there, had travelled to Yorkshire, to The Eyrie, of all places, to have her child. So there was nothing for it but to go and see Grimes, to discover that the improvements which he had asked to be made at Pontisford so that it would be habitable again had all been set in train, and then to race north to be reunited with her.

Impatience rode with him until The Eyrie came into view, and he was being welcomed into the entrance hall. Servants had gathered to strip his chaise of his luggage, to escort him to his room, except that that was not the thing which was most on his mind.

'Lady Radley,' he said eagerly, waving aside enquiries about his journey from Talbot, his father's secretary. 'Will someone please inform Lady Radley that I have returned?'

It was his father who, drawn by the noise of his arrival and coming to discover what was toward, told him that his wife was in the grounds by the lake, as was her wont on fine days.

Matt found himself so impatient that he was barely able to be civil to anyone, either his father or his sisters. Habit and long training rendered him apparently so. He allowed himself to be exclaimed over, congratulated by his brothers-in-law on his healthy colour—which his sisters deplored—and answered his father's questions on how he had fared in Virginia.

Finally he allowed himself to say, 'Pray send no messenger to Lady Radley. I will inform her myself of my return,' and was out of the door, still in the clothes in which he had travelled from London.

The Earl raised expressive eyebrows, but said nothing. If there were times when he had had doubts about the depth of his son's feelings for the remarkable woman whom he had married, then Radley's obvious desire to be with her again as soon as possible went a long way towards dispelling them. He had assumed that the marriage was that strange thing in their world, a love-match, by the unorthodox way in which it had come about, and Radley's conduct seemed to bear this out. What his son's wife felt for her husband was another matter.

Half running across the park to find Stacy again, Matt remembered himself and settled down into something resembling a determined stroll. With his good long sight he could see that she was alone, lying on a sofa, unmoving, a book upon her knee. Neither Louisa nor any other escort appeared to be with her.

His last few strides brought him before her. She was asleep, but it was not that which knocked the breath from his body, but the sudden sight of her, big with his child.

He shook his head disbelievingly. How could he have thought that after all these months he would find her as he had first seen her, tall and virginally slender? Instead, lying before him was no airy nymph but his wife, a fulfilled woman. . .who opened her eyes to look at him at the very moment when the reality of her condition smote him hard.

Matt had thought often and often of how he would fall on his knees before her, to tell her of his love, of the passion which he felt for her, and would shortly hope to demonstrate. . . What a fool he had been, for here was a woman who carried his child, who was smiling at him, trying to sit up and finding it difficult because of her condition. How graceless of him it would be to babble of love and passion to a woman who was carrying the result of it—she would think him a heartless boor to try to force himself upon her in her present state. She deserved his care, his compassion, more than anything else.

'Matt!' she exclaimed as he bent over her solicitously to kiss her rosy cheek, his face tender.

'Oh, madam——' and his voice was thick with emotion '—do not discommode yourself, I beg of you. Lie still. There is no need for formal greetings between us, no need at all.'

Stacy smiled, but her answer to him was as forthright as anything which the Bankeress would have said before she had met and surrendered to the man in front of her. 'Oh, Matt. I am not ill. I am having a child, and that is a condition which most women endure, and I have no desire, no desire at all, to be carried about before it is necessary. And now let me tell you how well you look, and, in return, you must tell me all your news.'

He was drinking in the soft lines of her face as she settled herself back on the pillows. She had blossomed and matured since he had last seen her. Her beauty was no longer so sharp, so haughtily dominant; there was a touching quality about it; at least, it touched him. Was this what happened to a woman when she ceased to add up columns of figures, or was it the effect of the child within her?

But Stacy's outward appearance, he noted with amusement, had not changed the cutting edge of her mind. She was as keenly intelligent as she had ever been. She listened to him as he told her of his adventures, saying as he finished, 'You remind me of what Shakespeare said when he wrote of Othello telling Desdemona of *his* adventures at the beginning of their tragedy: "She lov'd me for the dangers I had pass'd, And I lov'd her that she did pity them." I hope our play has a better ending than theirs!' And her green eyes teased him.

'Loved, madam, loved?' he repeated softly, bending forward. 'You said "loved". Is that a current description of your feelings for me, or a forecast?'

Stacy trembled beneath the intensity of his tawny gaze. He was more leonine than ever. He had pulled his cravat loose and she could see the bright golden hairs at the base of the powerful brown column of his throat. For once she regretted the child—which leaped inside her to reproach her for her desire to be slim and graceful again so that she would be able to demonstrate her love for him without having to wait.

'Time will serve to reveal all. Of that I am sure,' she began, her eyes mischievous, but before she could continue the child kicked her again, so that she cried out.

Matt's eyes widened; all thoughts of love fled at once. 'You are in pain?' he exclaimed. 'You must tell me if it is too much for you to sit here talking to me.'

To his surprise, Stacy smiled gently, even as her mouth twisted a little at the end, as the child reminded her of its existence. 'Oh, no, the pain is light, but it comes unexpectedly, without warning, so that I cry out with it. Your son and heir wishes to remind me that I must not give all my attention to his father. See——' and, to his surprise and astonishment, as well as his pleasure, she took his large hand and placed it on the curve of her stomach so that he could feel the wave of movement which a tiny kicking foot was creating.

They sat thus for a moment, eye to eye, Matt's wide. He thought that her forthrightness was so admirable that he wished that there were some tangible way in which he could reward her, other than by a passionless kiss. The lack of passion was for his sake: he was still afraid to touch her for fear of what that touch might do to him, especially after so many months of abstinence.

To walk his mind into neutral ground he told her gravely, 'By the by, madam, I forgot to tell you that Mr Jeb Priestley asked me to give you his respects.'

Stacy blinked naughtily at him. 'Now *that* I do not believe. Jeb has never respected anyone.'

'Oh, but he respects you. He told me that had I not existed, and he had met you, he would have done his best to convince you that despite the difference in station between the pair of you a marriage with him would have been made in heaven.'

For a moment Stacy was silent, contemplating a world in which Matt did not exist and Jeb Priestley pursued her. What a strange might-have-been that conjured up!

'But he has Polly,' she offered gravely.

'So he has, and she is good for him. She ignores his flights of fancy, and her only care is to look after him.'

'Now that might be a text for me to follow with you, when once our little monster is born,' she told him, her eyes closing.

No matter what she had said, Matt thought, looking at the delicate mauve shadows below her eyes and the white line around her mouth, carrying his child was tiring her, and he could suddenly understand why she had found refuge in The Eyrie.

To his astonishment he saw that she had fallen gently

and sweetly to sleep again, even as they spoke, and when Martha returned he ordered her to look after her mistress while he walked back to the house to find the chair in which his mother had been pushed around the grounds when she was carrying him. He would push Lady Radley home, he said. 'And you must be sure to await my return,' he told Martha a little severely, 'for I know that your mistress will try to walk back: her will is stronger than her body at the moment.'

His head was awhirl, as Stacy's was when she awoke to find him and the wheeled chair waiting for her. There was such tenderness in his strong face that she wanted to cry gently at the sight. Tears had come easily to her during this last stage of her pregnancy, and the reality of Matt's presence was so much stronger than the image of him which walked her dreams that she was almost overwhelmed by it.

Matt was surprised by the transformation which the Bankeress had undergone. He had thought that she might resent her coming motherhood; he had not imagined that she would embrace it with such passion. But then he remembered how hard she had worked under difficulties at Pontisford. . . Yes, his heart told him, she puts *her* whole heart and mind into everything she does. And, knowing that, I also know that if she is to be a mother, then she will, no doubt, be the best of mothers.

Another thought struck him, an unpleasant one. And shall I see her after the birth, or will she insist on the strict letter of our agreement, that once the child is born and settled we part? In the joy of seeing her again he had quite forgotten the conditions to which they had agreed before he had gone to Virginia!

Unaware of all these seething emotions boiling about her, Martha trotted happily beside them, holding a parasol over Stacy's head to shield her from the sun. Together she and Matt helped her from the chair and into the house. Stacy had found walking troublesome these last few weeks for the child was large, and she had begun to worry that the birth might be difficult because of it.

Matt, however, seemed determined to save her from all discomfort, for once she was out of the chair he carried her into the house to the drawing-room, where, although dinner would shortly be served, Caroline Bibury had ordered tea for them as soon as their small procession had come into sight, and had had the big glass doors to the garden thrown open so that they might sit in the shade of the awning above it.

The warmth of early July enveloped them. Caroline had tactfully left them alone. Stacy gave a small sigh of pure contentment. Matt leaned forward, said softly, 'Did you miss me, Stacy? I missed you. How strange it is that I calculate that we have spent less than a month in one another's company, that in our early time together all we did was quarrel, and yet every day I turned to say something to you—and you were not there.'

Stacy's heart beat in time with her child's. Now it suddenly beat in time with his words. Surprisingly she found her throat thick with tears. She remembered words he had said then, and also Poxon's, flung at her in rage and contempt on his last day at the York bank. Was it possible that Matt could truly feel for her what she had come to feel for him?

She could not help herself; she muttered in a low tone so that Matt had to strain to hear her, 'You do not now consider me a high-nosed bitch, then? A woman lacking all the womanly arts which give my sex grace?'

As his own words, spoken early on that fateful night at Pontisford, came back to haunt him, Matt's face twisted in pain. 'God forgive me,' he told her, his own voice low and broken. 'It was my rage and temper speaking then. I could not forgive you for tempting me so, for calling to me, albeit unwittingly, in a way which no woman had ever done since. . .my first and only love died. No, whatever else you are, Lady Radley—' and he tried to speak lightly to lessen his pain and hers '—you are not lacking in womanly arts.'

His reward was a watery smile, and the words, 'Yes, I missed you,' but behind those simple words Stacy was registering 'my first and only love'. What, then, does he feel for me? And if it is only friendship, a meeting of minds, and, yes, of bodies, but not love, then I will accept it, and not bore him with my love.

Which was exactly what Matt was thinking as they moved away from the dangerous ground which lay between them—and which each was refusing to explore.

So, in the happy days which followed, when they laughed and talked together, and Matt pushed her around the grounds or drove them in Rollo's curricle, a magnificent thing, picked out in scarlet and gold, as far as the boundary wall, neither spoke openly of the love which might lie between them. They talked of everything—and nothing. Both of them usually silent souls, found in the other a partner whose tastes and attitudes matched their own.

Forthright himself, Matt began to love Stacy's forthrightness. A hater of shams and hypocrisy, Stacy found Matt's similar attitude towards them admirable. They liked the same books and the same music, which Caroline played for them in the evening.

So much were they at evens that they began to wonder how they could ever have been so much at odds. Except that Stacy, laughing, raised the matter as they sat alone one evening in the dusk, before the candles were lit, by saying, 'I suppose the reason why we were so fierce with one another when we first met is because we are so much alike, both determined to have our own way, and in those days our ways differed,' and then, looking at him almost shyly, 'I wonder why they don't differ now?'

Matt drew a sharp breath, took her hand to kiss it, and answered her, with an admirable lack of sentimentality, 'That, madam, is because the coming child constrains you. When he has arrived, and you are bounding about, full of *joie de vivre*, you will be as harsh with me as you ever were, and I shall be compelled to point out once again where you are going astray!'

Was that true? Stacy wondered. Or, now that they were coming to know one another, were they both beginning to find in the other virtues that they were not previously aware they possessed? Could it be that they might come to love one another? Perhaps the coming child, which she had once resented a little because Matt had seemed to consider it more important then herself, was responsible for bringing them together? Or was it the long months of separation which had revealed to each of them that they had, as Jeb would have put it, lost their other half?

She was not to know that Matt was thinking the same thing! For strong-willed and determined people they were strangely diffident towards one another, even now, so far as their emotions were concerned, Matt because he was still afraid of commitment, and Stacy because she had not completely cast off the shackles which Louis Blanchard had bound around her. Neither could quite say to the other those magic words: I love you. To do so would be to surrender, and neither of them had ever willingly surrendered anything to anyone. But those about them saw more than they did, as onlookers often saw more of the game than the players did.

The Earl had summoned his son to his study soon after his return, to speak to him of the duties which he, as the heir, must take on, and of the way of life which Matt must then follow. As he had wryly said to Matt, 'The land owns us as much as we own the land.'

Afterwards, as Matt had prepared to leave, his father

had said slowly, 'Stay a little longer, Radley; there is something which I must say to you.'

Matt, who had risen, sat down again, to hear his father continue, his face grave, 'I have learned a lot, during the year which has passed, of the true nature of my late son and heir, your elder brother, and what I have learned has not been pleasant. I know, for example, and I think that you ought to be aware of it, that he died a shameful death in a brothel, in a fight over a whore when he was drunk, and that he had squandered the fortune which came to him at your mother's death. I am ashamed to admit that I arranged that the cause of his death be hushed up.

'Because of what I have subsequently discovered about his mode of life, I fear that I may have misjudged you over the matter of Camilla, his wife; that what you said in defence of your behaviour at the time was most likely the truth.

'I have no proof of this, nor do I wish to seek any, for to set agents on your and Rollo's trail after so many years would be demeaning to you. I believe, from all that I have seen of you since living with you again, that you have a strong sense of honour, and your choice of a wife demonstrates that you possess common sense too. Shall we agree to put the past behind us—if you can forget my wilfulness in misjudging you—so that we may start again as father and son, living in harmony, if not always in agreement?'

This speech was so remarkable and so unexpected that Matt was almost stunned by it, and said so.

His father smiled sadly. 'Let us shake hands on it, sir, and then you may believe that I am sincere, and the past may no longer haunt us.'

Well, that was something which he had not expected. Time and chance had done their work, and now he might walk about The Eyrie with a sense of pride again. Matt no longer cared what the world thought of him, but his father's opinion was quite another matter.

From that day on one of the ghosts which had haunted Matthew Falconer, now Lord Radley, for so many years passed from his life. He would try to remember Rollo as he had been when Matt was a boy and Rollo was in his teens, before drink and dissipation had begun to destroy him. But the other ghost, that of Camilla, still walked with him. His father's forgiveness could neither exorcise her nor make him forget the manner in which she had died.

'I do believe, sir, that you are at last becoming civilised! The lion has ceased to roar, and the bear to rove the hills.' And Stacy moved her backgammon counter along the board to take her a little nearer to victory.

Matt muttered something rude beneath his breath about calculating women who could play chess and backgammon better than most men he knew, before he rattled the dice-box again.

'I should have known better than to play with you,' he told her ruefully a few minutes later, when victory became inevitably hers.

'But you lose so much more nicely now than you were wont to do when we first met.' And Stacy lay back against her pillows. She was now into her eighth month, and the doctor who was to supervise the birth was due to arrive at the Eyrie before the weekend. He was to take over from the one who rode twice-weekly from York to stare at her, and comment that 'Lady Radley is in great fettle, and by all appearances preparing to give birth to a fine boy'. He was to be the London man's assistant when he arrived.

'I can't recall that we played backgammon together when we first met,' retorted Matt, who was busy gathering up the counters and the dice. He thought that she looked particularly well that afternoon, with a fine colour on her—the pallor which had been hers before she had conceived seemed to have disappeared.

'No, indeed,' riposted Stacy, 'but we played other

games, as you well know, and losing them appeared particularly galling to you.'

'But I can't recall losing any kind of game,' he replied, grinning at her as he carefully replaced the backgammon board in the ornate inlaid box which held it, the dice-box and the ivory counters. 'On the contrary, I distinctly remember winning.'

'Oh, yes, the last one.' Stacy's tone was careless, and the eyes she lifted to look at him as he towered over her were full of shameless mirth. 'I grant you that. For, behold, as a consequence of it you have reduced me to a condition in which I am fit for nothing but to be carried about and petted.'

'To make up for all the years in which you weren't,' he told her briskly, and bent down to kiss her warm and rosy cheek. Yes, madam looked particularly fine today, fine enough to drive a man mad, particularly a man who hadn't touched a woman since he had last taken the woman before him to bed.

The rapport between them was so strong now that Stacy leaned forward to take his hand and kiss it, being unable to lift herself up to kiss his cheek. 'I do believe,' she had said that morning, 'that I am about to give birth to a veritable giant. It must be a boy; I could not wish a girl to be so large.'

'You wish to renege on our bargain?' he asked her now quietly, so that Caroline and Georgiana, sitting on the other side of the room and chatting about a ball which they were due to attend at York, could not hear them.

'Bargain?' Stacy repeated dubiously, as though she had never heard the word before—and when had she learned to be so teasingly naughty, so that she was provoking him with every word she uttered? 'I can't remember a bargain, sir. On what piece of paper was it written? Remind me, so that I may refresh my memory as to the details of it.'

Matt had dragged up a chair, to sit on it facing her. He

leaned forward and took her happy face in both his hands. 'You witch, to tease me so! You know perfectly well to what bargain I refer. The one to which we agreed before our wedding—that our marriage would be in name only, and that we would part after a suitable interval, once our child was born.'

He was still holding her face and gazing into her eyes, regardless of what his sisters might think, when she answered him. 'Oh, that bargain! I believe it was one which you proposed. I cannot remember any countersigning on my part.'

Matt drew in his breath sharply, and took his hands from her face. He leaned back, said hoarsely, 'Have you no idea, madam, of the effect which your words have on me? And that I am helpless before you in your present condition. Stop playing the Bankeress with me and remember that you are my wife, and that you promised to love, honour and obey me! Did none of those words mean anything to you, madam?'

Stacy decided not to taunt him further. There was a look almost of agony on his strong face. The lion seemed to be wounded. She murmured softly, 'As much as you wish them to mean, Matt. As much as you wish. . .'

The air between them vibrated, was full of a strange magnetism. It was as though they were completely on their own, out of space, out of time. The room they were in, the people near them, had gone. Everything but the other disappeared.

'Are you saying, madam, what I think you are saying?' Matt finally ventured, only to have Stacy return,

'Now who is playing with words, sir?'

'You taught me,' he answered her, all brevity.

'Then you are an apt pupil, sir, who does credit to his teacher.'

'And if the pupil told his teacher, and the client told the Bankeress, that he wished to renege on the agreement, and wondered what strange maggot had invaded his brain that he could have ever conceived of such a thing, what then?'

'Why, then the teacher, as well as the Bankeress, would answer that the same maggot must have invaded her brain to cause her to agree to such a proposition, and furthermore that an agreement entered into by two persons whose sanity was in doubt at the time could hardly hold—so let us agree to forget it.'

It was, Stacy afterwards thought, typical of them both that they could declare the love they had come to feel for one another in such a roundabout and oblique fashion—the magic words were still unsaid.

But Matt's response to her invitation was not oblique. He gave a sudden shout of laughter so that Caroline, being timorous, started and dropped her needle, and Georgiana, being fiery, glared at him. ''Pon rep, Matt,' she exclaimed, 'think of your poor wife! You will overset her with your noisy ways.'

'Overset her?' choked Matt, taking Stacy's hand and covering it with kisses. 'By no means, never. My dear wife is never overset—least of all by her husband. No, she makes a practice of oversetting him! And now, to celebrate her latest feat, I will, like the magician in the fairy-tale, tell her that I will grant her any wish she cares to make, seeing that she has granted me my dearest one. Come, madam, wish!'

He was transformed. Usually stern, and a little forbidding in his bearing, like his father—as that father was coming to recognise—he was suddenly all playfulness. Georgiana was to say afterwards to her sister and her father that marrying Miss Blanchard was the strangest thing that Matt could have done, but was quite the best. 'She is turning him back into the man he was before he lost Camilla, and for that we should all be grateful.'

'I have no wishes left,' Stacy told him, 'since my one wish has been granted.'

'Come, there must be something. A diamond necklace, perhaps?'

Stacy shook her head. There was one thing which she *had* come to wish for in the last few days as they had driven about the park, and perhaps, if she asked him nicely, he would agree to grant it, even if it was only a small thing.

'No, Matt, I have enough jewellery to make the Tsarina of all the Russias envious. What I would really like is to leave the grounds, for you to drive me, not around the park, but into the open country. Pleasant though it is here, I have begun to feel a little imprisoned.'

Matt said, laughing, 'Is that all? A most frugal request for the Bankeress to make. But are you sure that you are fit to undertake such a drive? You would not be overset?'

'No, indeed. I would like a breath of the wide world. and so, I think, would you.'

'When I think what you might have demanded of me! A fortune perhaps—and all you wish is an extended drive. So be it. Tomorrow, then, if it be fine, and, if not, the first fine day. We must celebrate, must we not?'

Georgiana overheard this last. 'Celebrate, Matt? What's to celebrate?'

He could hardly tell her that they had just agreed to be truly man and wife, seeing that they were already married! Instead, he answered her airily, 'Why sister, we have just decided that if the child is to be a boy, then he will be Henry, after our grandfather, I believe, Adolphus after my father, and Louis, after Lady Radley's. Is not that a splendid thing?'

'Well, I think so,' agreed Stacy, to whom Matt's fertile invention had come as a surprise, almost as big a surprise as to learn that he had been thinking of what to call his future son, if son it was. 'Especially since he has left to me the choice of names if it is to be a girl—but I have not yet made up my mind what they are to be. He is before me there.'

'Bravely said,' replied Matt, thinking that once again Stacy had trumped his ace so to speak; after having had a boy's name sprung on her she had counter-attacked by claiming the right to decide on a daughter's name. Oh, he could see that life with madam was going to be lively, full of surprises. He wished with all his heart that their child would soon honour them with his or her presence so that they could start living that life as soon as possible.

And if she wished to go on being the Bankeress, then so be it. Somehow he would arrange to let her have her wish—if that was what she truly wanted.

That night they were more loving than they had ever been, and Matt came to Stacy's room after she had retired, and sat by her on the bed, holding her in his arms, enjoying the sweet torment which that provoked in him, and thinking of all the sweeter ecstasies which were to come. . .

CHAPTER FIFTEEN

'You are quite sure that you are well enough to undertake such a long ride in the country?' Matt asked anxiously. 'After all, so far we have stayed inside the park on easy roads and pleasant ways. You will not find the motion too distressing?'

He had already lifted Stacy into her seat in his curricle; grooms were holding the horses' heads to prevent any chance that they might rear before he was fully in control of them and cause her discomfort—he did not think that she would be frightened, for nothing seemed to frighten her.

She shook her head as he sat beside her, taking up his whip. 'No, indeed. I ailed a little in the first few months, but of late I have felt most amazingly well. Today I feel that, if it were not for the burden which I carry, I could move mountains. Truly, I have never felt so well in my life.'

She gave him an enchanting sideways glance, which had him trembling again, before adding, 'Why, I do believe that you are going back on your word.' Stacy was still revelling in her new-found powers of mischief and of teasing gaiety, which she had been unaware she possessed until she had met Matt. It was as though he was getting the benefit of all the flirting which she had never done, but now felt able and willing to do.

'Never,' he told her, with a grin, as the grooms released the horses and they started off. 'But if you *do* feel any discomfort you must tell me so immediately and we shall return home at once.'

Home. Matt had spent many years denying that the

Eyrie had ever been, or could ever be, his home. As for Stacy, it was odd to think that she could call somewhere home which she had only known for a few months, but she had already come to love The Eyrie, which would one day be truly hers and Matt's.

It felt strange to reach the big gates and turn out of them on to the York road, and then to make not for York itself but for the open plain. The Eyrie was situated between York and Selby, in open country criss-crossed by small lanes and ditches which were even more primitive than the road on which they were travelling, the one which the mail-coaches took.

They had taken no groom or tiger with them—not that Matt possessed a tiger—something which he was later to regret—but he did not intend to be out for long, and he had become accustomed to living informally during his years in Virginia. It had taken him some time to grow used again to the press of servants who were needed to make The Eyrie run smoothly. Once he had taken them for granted, but after Virginia he would never do so again.

'He's a good man to serve, the new lord,' the staff at The Eyrie had agreed, 'not like the bastard, his older brother.' There were those who remembered Matt as a boy, and thought that he had grown into someone who commanded affection as well as respect.

'Oh, do let us go along there!' Stacy suddenly exclaimed as they came to a side-road which led gently down to a small valley through which a stream, a tributary of the Derwent, ran beneath over-arching trees. 'I would love to be able to paint it.' Then she added wistfully, 'There are times when I wish I had not given up painting, but Father said that, like music, it was a waste of time best occupied by more serious matters.'

It was unguarded disclosures like these which told Matt something of the rigorous life which Louis Blanchard had inflicted on his daughter. If it had made her a strong woman, it had also deprived her of many of the small pleasures of living. He had already made a private resolution that once their child was born he would encourage her to enjoy herself by indulging in all those innocent amusements which one by one her father had vetoed in favour of the stern regime which had come to dominate her life.

Matt shook his head, murmured, 'I am sorry to disappoint you, my darling, but we have already come quite a long way from The Eyrie. I think that we ought to turn for home. The plain of York is a lonely place.'

'But peaceful,' said Stacy, and then, 'It also seems a long way from the Bank. Please, Matt, let us go just a little further before we turn back.'

She accompanied this plea with such a charmingly wilful expression that he felt compelled to give way. 'Very well, my naughty minx, just a little further. I see that having our child is making you lose all your high-minded caution.' And he touched the horses lightly with his whip and they turned into the narrow lane. Any narrower and he would have refused to go down it at all.

Here, among the scents and smells of the open country, Stacy found it hard to believe that the Bank existed, that it had been the centre of her life for so long. Her father had become a distant figure, no longer the demi-god who had dominated her, and he was fast receding into the past. It was not that she no longer loved him, or his memory, but she was at last freeing herself from the prison of lovelessness into which he had unintentionally thrust her. Ephraim was sending her regular reports, and she dutifully commented on them and wrote back suggestions, but it was like posting letters to Mars, or the outer planets, she sometimes thought.

She turned to share this odd notion with Matt after he had negotiated a bend in the lane and was turning for home again—he had already told her that the road, such as it was, was growing too poor for them to go much further — when disaster struck.

They were bowling happily along when they disturbed a large nye of pheasants, which, the cock-bird leading, exploded out of the bushes which lined the lane, straight into the path of the horses.

Neighing and snorting, both horses reared and stumbled. That alone might not have caused an accident, but the nearside horse, despite all Matt's efforts, lost his footing, tried to recover it, lost it again, and, as he did so, took his companion down into the ditch with him, the curricle and its occupants following. The nearside horse broke his neck immediately, his fellow his leg. Matt, half stunned, landed among the ruins of his carriage, with Stacy beside him. She lay there unmoving. One moment she had been enjoying the afternoon sun, the next she had been flung sideways, and now was hardly aware of where she was.

After a little time, through the almost pleasant haze she was lying in, she heard someone say hoarsely, 'Stacy, oh, my darling Stacy. I have killed you in my folly. Dear God, not twice. I could not bear this to happen again.'

In her dazed condition she thought that she was lying in the wreck of her coach in the November snow, and she could not imagine why Hal should be saying such strange things to her. A horse was making a dreadful noise, as though it was in great pain.

She tried to sit up, but found that she could not, and then someone was freeing her, lifting her and carrying her some little distance to lay her down on the ground — in the snow? What a strange thing to do. Someone — could it possibly be Hal? — had his arms around her, and was holding her tenderly. She looked up to find out who it was, but at first all that she could see was the sunlight shining through the trees — and then she saw Matt's agonised face — and remembered everything. . .

It was not November, it was July. And she was no longer Anastasia Blanchard, but Anastasia, Lady Radley, expecting her first child, and it was her husband who was holding her, and begging her to speak to him, if she could. Yes, they had gone for a drive, they had driven down to a stream, and then away from it, but after that. . . nothing. . .

Her head began to clear. She said, weakly at first, then more strongly, 'Matt, what happened?' And now she could see him properly. His face was white. There was a great bruise on his cheek, his coat was torn, but otherwise he didn't seem to be hurt.

'Pheasants flew at us,' he told her, 'frightened the horses. I couldn't control them—I doubt whether anyone could have done. . .which is no excuse. . .' He held her tightly to him. 'Oh, God, Stacy, what have I done to you?'

Her voice muffled, because he was holding her so tightly against him, she answered him, 'Nothing; I don't think I've taken an injury. . .' She paused, then continued doubtfully as he released her a little, 'I must have caught my head on something, for it feels very odd, but it is growing better now. And I have a pain in my back. I think I must have twisted it when we fell. But what about you?'

'Oh, me,' he answered her dismissively. 'I think I might have damaged my ankle—we're both lucky to be alive. Fortunately neither of the horses fell on us, or kicked us. Unfortunately one is dead, the other badly injured, and the curricle is done for.'

That must have been the horse which had been making a noise and was now silent. She was to learn later that while she was still semi-conscious Matt shot it with one of the horse pistols which he always carried when not riding in the park.

'God forgive me for not bringing a groom with us, but I have grown out of the habit of having servants trailing around after me. Forget that,' he said anxiously. 'I can see a cottage not far away. If I can get you there you can shelter in it, and we can send someone to The Eyrie for help. Do you think that you could manage to walk?'

Her head was still misbehaving, but Stacy said, as bravely as she could, 'If you will help me up I shall try.'

It was almost a question of the blind leading the blind, for Matt was limping badly—his ankle was more sprained and swollen than he had admitted—and the pain in Stacy's back was so severe that she found difficulty in walking.

She could tell that he was in pain, so she tried not to lean on him too much, but as they made their way up the track, to where a cottage stood on a small rise in the ground, she felt such a sharp pain in her back that she gave a little cry, and sat down abruptly on the ground.

Matt was squatting beside her immediately, his face more drawn than ever through pain and worry. 'Stacy! What is it?'

She looked up at him, trying to control herself. 'Oh, Matt, I'm sorry to make a fuss, but the pain was so strong and came so suddenly, without warning. . .' She gave another small gasp. 'It's not continuous, it's coming and going, which makes it hard for me to bear it.'

Stacy had not thought that Matt could grow any paler than he already was, but he did, and she felt the arm which he had put about her shoulders tighten, but he said only, 'Try to walk, my darling, but if the pain grows too bad, then I will carry you.'

But she didn't want that, and somehow, half leaning against one another, they drew near to the cottage.

Matt, who was not suffering as Stacy was from the after-effects of a blow to the head, saw before she did that something was wrong. The cottage looked neglected; it had once possessed a garden, but it had been allowed to run wild. A dirty child in ragged clothes played in it, casting feral looks at them as they approached, before running through an open door. No, not a door, but an opening where one had been.

His heart sank. He helped Stacy into the garden and laid her down on a small patch of rank grass beside some bedraggled fruit bushes which had run wild. The child reappeared – it was difficult to tell whether it was a boy or a girl. He asked, trying to keep his voice gentle and steady, 'My dear, is either your mother or your father at home?'

Matt thought wryly that he might have been speaking Greek for all the impression he made on the wild creature before him. He started for the doorway in order to enter the cottage, to see if anyone was there, but the child ran before him, darting in, to come out again dragging with him a woman, as ragged and dirty as he was. The woman stared at him. She was as feral as the child. For the first time he saw that a tinker's cart stood near to the cottage, but there was no sign of the tinker.

The woman said slowly, in an accent so wild and strange that he could barely understand her, 'What's up, maister?'

Nothing in Matt's life had prepared him for such indifference as she was showing him. Even as he spoke to her her eyes ranged away from him to stare into the distance while he tried to explain what had happened, that he was Lord Radley, and that he would like someone to go to The Eyrie to fetch help, for he did not wish to leave his wife on her own. To his dismay she didn't answer him, but shouted unintelligibly at the boy, who stared at him again and then began to run away from the cottage, towards the lane from which they had so painfully walked.

He saw that Stacy was sitting up, and was holding her back. The woman walked over to her, said something which Stacy could not understand, and then she put her hands into Stacy's armpits, pulled her erect, and began to walk her into the cottage. She said to Matt as she passed him, 'Coom in, then. Thy missis is having thy child.'

'Having thy child!' The world spun around Matt. he cried hoarsely, 'No!' Time turned in on itself. He was in an inn, and a woman was saying fiercely to him, 'Couldn't you see that the girl you have brought here is about to give birth? Shame on you for dragging her around the countryside in such a state. . .'

He was back on the plain of York again, walking into a small, dark room. There was a table, a bench, a rude fireplace without a fire in it, and something which passed for a bed in a corner. His brain told him that the tenant farmer who had lived here was long gone, and that a tinker's family had taken over the derelict cottage. Where the tinker was God only knew. All he knew was that he had brought Stacy to this terrible place, and history was about to repeat itself. . .

The woman sat Stacy down on the bench and fetched a clean blanket from a wicker basket which lay on the dirt floor before the empty hearth. Matt joined Stacy on the bench. She turned a white face towards him, exclaimed feverishly, 'Oh, Matt, she says that I am about to birth the baby! Do you think that she can possibly be right?' Even as she spoke her face contracted again, as the pain in her back struck harder than ever this time, and she said numbly, once it had subsided, 'Oh, I do believe she is, but surely the pain is in the wrong place?'

All that Matt knew about the birth of babies was that Camilla had died trying to deliver one—something of which even now he could barely think. He pushed the thought away. The woman came over and put the blanket on the bed, saying to Stacy as she passed her, 'Coom on, then, gal. On to the bed wi' ye. Stay there while I fetch old Grandam Outhwaite to help yer. He—'and she jerked her thumb at Matt '—will 'ave to look after ye until she cooms.'

Stacy looked wildly round the room. The bed did not appear to be particularly dirty but, apart from the blanket which the woman had just laid down, wasn't particularly clean either. Whenever she had imagined having her baby she had never foreseen anything like this! She had seen herself on the large bed in her room back at The Eyrie, servants coming and going, perhaps faithful Louisa sitting in a corner, Matt striding along the corridor outside as Georgiana had told her her husband had done when her first child had been born. One of England's most famous doctors would have been in attendance; the best doctor in York was to have been his faithful aide.

But the only person attending her was Matt, and all that she was being promised was some peasant midwife, who was probably having to be fetched from the nearest village—wherever that might be. This was certainly not how she had visualised giving birth to the heir to all the Falconers!

For once even her brave spirit faltered. Matt saw her face change and came to sit beside her on the makeshift bed, to lift her up a little, to hold her against his chest, to say anxiously, 'Oh Stacy, my darling, what a time to tell you. I should have told you before, but for some odd reason I never found the courage to do so. . . I love you so dearly that I can hardly bear to see you suffer. I think that I have loved you ever since I opened the door at Pontisford and saw you standing there, so brave and defiant, and look at you now, at what I have done to you. . . How can you love me after this?' His voice broke on the last words and she could feel his poor heart beating furiously as he held her against him.

They were the words which Stacy had always wanted to hear him say, and what a time to choose to tell her! Even through her pain and rising fear she felt that she had to reward him by saying, her voice hoarse and broken as she fought the all-consuming pain, 'Oh, Matt, you must surely know that I have loved you since Pontisford, and what we did there was done together — together we made our child, and I was as willing and eager as you were. . .'

And then the pain took her, and this time it was he who held and comforted her, not she him, and he felt with her the pain which was tearing her apart. After it had passed they rested in one another's arms, until Matt said tenderly, trying to control his own rising fear that he was in danger of losing his wife and child just as they had found each other, 'Is there anything I can do for you? Have you any idea how soon it is likely to be before the baby arrives?'

Before she could answer him another pain — they were coming thick and fast now — tore through Stacy with such force that she could not prevent herself from writhing and crying out, putting her fist into her mouth to stop herself from screaming. This time the pain was in the front, and when it had passed she told Matt what she thought the woman had said: 'It won't be long, me duck.'

'Won't be long!' Matt muttered something blasphemous under his breath, and then, 'And how long before she returns with this old wise-woman, and how useful will she be?'

Stacy didn't answer him; she was too busy trying to cope with other things — one a great gush of water which she knew, from questions which she had compelled the York doctor to answer, was the breaking of the waters which preceded birth.

'Oh, really, Lady Radley, I do not think it my place to discuss such matters with you, nor would it be proper for you to know of them,' he had twittered at her.

To which she had replied in a voice of steel, 'Well, it is I who am having this child, sir, so kindly do as I ask. I have no wish to die as the result of ignorance like the late lamented Princess Charlotte.'

He had also told her that the pains she would feel would come more and more rapidly as the time for the birth neared, and there was no doubt that this was beginning to happen. Once the latest pain had subsided a little she told Matt so, adding, 'You are going to have to help me if you wish your son and heir to be born alive, for there is no one else here to do so.'

She could not have anticipated his reaction to this news. She had felt him shaking when he had taken her into his arms, and now she felt him begin to shudder violently. She twisted her head a little to find that he was not grey, but yellow, and looked as though *he* was about to faint.

'For God's sake, Stacy,' he muttered, 'do not say so. It is not half an hour since the accident, and I always understood from what I heard of my sisters' talk, and from the women on the plantation, that birthing a baby usually takes a day at least.'

One thing was certain, he learned immediately, and that was that Stacy's fiery spirit had not been quenched by what was happening to her.

'Well,' she told him bluntly, 'you had better pray that the baby does come soon, for one thing is certain—a day of pains such as these would be the death of me—' and then she was writhing again in such agony that he gently laid her down on her back again, thinking that that might ease her.

He remembered being present after Camilla's agony, and after the birth of one of the black servants on his Virginia farm, and that on both occasions there had been blood everywhere—although the black servant's child had lived and Camilla's had not. Stacy would need some clean linen, and water. She had begun to sweat heavily, and he used his fine cambric handkerchief to wipe her face tenderly—but she would need more than his handkerchief if the child was coming.

'Listen,' he murmured urgently, during the interval between her pains, 'if the baby is coming soon, which God forbid, then I must try to find some water—there will almost certainly be a well at the back of the cottage, or a running brook nearby. Do you think that you could hold on for a moment or two while I reconnoitre?'

It was the last thing Stacy wanted, to be left alone, but there was no help for it. She offered him a twisted smile and a murmured, 'Yes,' while she concentrated on preparing to withstand the next pain.

When it came she closed her eyes, gripped the corner of the blanket and thrust it between her teeth to stop herself from screaming at its force, so that on Matt's return some little time later, carrying a bucket of water and a battered pewter cup, she was able to offer him a brave face.

'There *was* a well,' he told her, 'and the water looks and tastes sweet. Would you like to drink some?' For he thought that she was now beginning to show the effects of severe pain added to the shock of the accident.

Stacy took the offered water, drank it greedily, and then watched with some astonishment as Matt took off his jacket, untied his cravt and pulled off his fine linen shirt, which he began to rip apart, creating from its back one large piece, and tearing off long strips from its sleeves and front. He put his jacket back on again, and offered her one of the strips. 'To bite on,' he told her, 'when the pain become too great to bear. That's what the surgeons did on board ship after a naval battle when they were looking after the men. The others will do for later, when the child comes.'

Taking the linen strip, and doing as she was bid, Stacy didn't inform him that she had already used the blanket for that purpose. He looked so ill and worried that one might almost have thought that he was about to have the baby himself! Surprisingly, even through her pain, the thought made her want to giggle.

For a time nothing changed, the pain came and went, but after about an hour, by which time the pains were coming continuously and she could no longer suppress her screams at their strength, Stacy's body began to tell her that the baby's birth was imminent. She was now half sitting up again, Matt was holding her, and when she turned to say to him, 'Oh, Matt, I think that the baby is about to come,' it was at this point that he broke.

He laid her down on the bed, put his head in his hands, and groaned, 'I can't, Stacy, I can't bear this, not again, not twice. Oh, God, I don't think that I shall be able to help you!' He had, unknown to her, gone back more than ten years. He was in another room, the bedroom of an inn, and he was looking down at poor, dead Camilla, at her child who had been born dead, and the ghastly evidence of a painful, mismanaged birth all about them. It had unmanned him then, and he had tried to suppress the memory of it, but, faced with Stacy in a similar situation, he was unmanned again. Was he to lose another, and stronger love in the same painful way as the first?

Stacy, overcome by surprise as much as by shock when Matt buried his face in the blanket on her bed, stared at him, even through her agony. She was sweating, her hair had come down and hung in wet tendrils around her face, and the man whose strength and courage she had always admired, the man who had saved Jeb's life, rescuing him against fearful odds when his farm has been attacked by roving brigands, was telling her that he was unable to help her to bear their child. Whatever could be the matter with him?

'Matt,' she almost shouted over the pain which was destroying her, 'you must help me. Look at me, Matt, look at me! Of course you can help me. How many mares have you helped to bring their foals into the world?'

He lifted his head to show her a face nearly as agonised as hers. 'But you are not a mare, Stacy, you are my wife, and——'

'And bosh,' she roard at him rudely, the Bankeress *in Excelsis Gloria*, as an irreverent wit had once named her.

'What am I now but a two-legged mare, about to let her foal slip into your hands? Would you do more for your horse than you would do for me?'

Slowly, unwillingly, as the memory of Camilla's deathbed faded from his mind, driven away by the strength of his wife's words, he gave a slow and reluctant grin at her unquenchable spirit.

'By God, madam,' he told her softly, 'you rightly rebuke me. Yes, we will birth our foal together.'

'Then see to it at once, Radley, do you hear me? For I shall shortly have little more reason left than your mare, and it is you who will have the greater burden —— Ah, God, Matt ——' and she gave a shrill scream '– I believe he is nearly here.'

This time he was ready for her, his courage restored, and for the next few hectic minutes, as Stacy panted and pushed their child into the world, Matt was helping her and encouraging her, as though she were the mare she had claimed to be. And when at last the baby emerged into the cruel world, crying its protests at being born at all, it was Matt who caught him in his large hands, who wrapped him gently in the remains of his father's linen shirt – for yes, he was the boy whom Stacy had always claimed that she was carrying. And it was Matt who showed him to his mother and let her hold him for a moment, saying, 'Hal, my boy, you must meet your mama at last. Stacy, my darling, here is your foal.'

To which she replied weakly, but with a smile, 'Oh, no, Matt, he is my lion-cub. See, when his hair dries it will be as tawny as yours!'

Matt thought that he had never seen anything so beautiful in his life as his wife as she lay there, cuddling their child, never mind that she bore about her all the stigmata of a difficult, if rapid birth. And so he told her, the pair of them sharing broken endearments over the head of their child.

And finally it was Matt who carried the protesting Hal over to place him in the wicker basket from which the blanket on the bed had earlier come.

As he bent down there were shadows and noise at the door, and the woman who had earlier gone for the wise-woman entered. Behind her came an older woman, bent and wrinkled, who took in the scene before her—the large man holding the howling baby, the exhausted woman on the makeshift bed.

Grandam Outhwaite said in a cracked voice, 'Why, I believes as 'ow yer didn't need me arter all,' before she went over to Stacy to finish the business of birthing, finally washing both her and the baby down with an infusion of herbs which she had brought with her in a little blue bottle.

The heir to all the Falconers had been successfully born, on a blanket in a deserted cottage in which a family of tinkers had been squatting, with only his father and mother to help him!

'I am sure that something must be dreadfully wrong!' Caroline Bibury was wringing her hands. It was late afternoon and Matt and Stacy had been gone for some hours. They had been expected back long before. 'Matt would surely not have taken Stacy on a jaunt as extended as this in her condition.' And she looked helplessly around at the assembled company.

Earlier that afternoon the Beauchamps had driven over from Bramham, and Anthony, still smarting from losing Stacy to 'that fellow', muttered ungraciously, half beneath his breath, that, 'Nothing that Radley did would surprise me.'

His father cast warning glances at him, so he subsided, but if he didn't speak again he thought a great deal. The Earl ordered the grooms and stable-hands to ride out in the direction which Radley had gone, but so far no one had returned with any news. Aunt Beauchamp persuaded Uncle Beauchamp to stay longer than they ought to do before returning home, in the hope that they might see Stacy safe before they left, but even so they finally had to make ready to take their leave.

The Earl and his family, by now seriously worried, walked to the stable-yard to see the coach for the Beauchamp parents driven out; Anthony had ridden over on his horse. The Earl did them the honour of coming out himself. He was leaning on his stick, his mind in turmoil as a result of Radley's non-return, when a ragged child who had been lurking about the yard suddenly sprang at him, howling something incomprehensible.

Thwaites, the head groom, who was busy supervising operations, leaped forward to remove the child bodily. 'Danged little tyke bin a botheration to us all arternoon,' he grunted. 'Shouting and roaring his nonsense at us. You mind your manners, lad. 'Tis the Earl you're saucing.'

At the mention of the Earl the child howled again, trying to escape Thwaites' strong arms. This time the Earl thought he heard something familiar.

'You heard that,' he said to Anthony Beauchamp who was making ready to mount. 'He distinctly said Radley. Now how would he know that? Let him down, Thwaites. Let him come and speak to me, since that is what he wants.'

Thwaites, muttering, put the child down. He immediately ran to the Earl, fell on his knees before him, and began to speak. The name Radley was now distinctly heard by all of them in the yard.

'He's trying to tell us something about Radley,' the Earl announced incredulously. 'Slowly, lad, slowly.'

The child nodded his shaggy head, mouthed at the Earl so that he could make out that Radley had had an accident and, ''E's at whoam, 'e is. At whoam.'

'And where's home?' the Earl asked him gently.

The child pointed towards where Selby lay, took the Earl roughly by the sleeve and began to pull him in that direction. There was no doubt that he was trying to tell him that he knew where Lord Radley was, and that he was to go with him to find him.

'Is Lord Radley injured? Hurt?' he added, when he saw that the child had not at first understood him.

The child shook his head, said something incomprehensible, and repeated it when he saw that the Earl had not understood him. This time, 'Nay, the ooman,' came out quite plainly.

Anthony Beauchamp said feverishly, 'My God, it is Stacy who is hurt. We must go to her at once. Cannot the child show us the way? If necessary I will go alone.'

The Earl shook his head. 'No,' he said, 'I will ride there, and you may accompany me if you wish.'

And so it was that they came at last to the lane below the cottage, the child riding with Thwaites and pointing out the way, the Earl and Anthony Beauchamp following. They passed the ruined curricle and the dead horses lying in the ditch. Anthony swore blackly below his breath and the Earl's heart sank within him. But when the boy slid off his horse and began to run up the track to the cottage, he dismounted and set off after him, fearful of what he might find.

He and Anthony had not reached the cottage before Matt came out to meet them, after hearing the sound of men and horses. He had been helping Grandam Outhwaite to undress Stacy and put her into a coarse but clean nightgown, after giving her a draught from yet another blue bottle—'Poppy,' she had told him briefly. ''Er 'll sleep soon.'

He had such an expression of joy on his face as his father had never seen. The grim, rather dour man had gone: he had the manner of the happy boy he had once been. 'Father!' he exclaimed, and there was joy in his voice as well. 'I knew that you would come to find me if the lad could only find the way.'

'Your wife?' panted the Earl, sinking on to a bench beside the door.

'Stacy—what have you done to her? We saw the ruins of the curricle on our way here,' burst from Anthony, who was privately vowing to kill Matt Falconer if any harm had come to Stacy.

Matt was still wearing that queer look of triumph. 'She's as well as can be expected,' he said. 'Come.' And he waved them into the cottage.

To their astonishment they saw Stacy lying propped against a pillow, covered by another coarse blanket. She was half asleep, already under the poppy's influence, and gave them only a distant smile, while Matt bent down to a basket by the hearth, to lift from it his son, who, roused from peaceful sleep by his father, gave a howling welcome to his grandfather.

'Your grandson greets you, sir. Allow me to introduce Hal Falconer, not yet an hour born. He came so rapidly into the world that his mother and father were hard put to see him into it properly.'

Anthony looked aghast. 'Here!' he almost moaned. 'The poor child had her baby here—with only you present!'

'Aye,' said Grandam Outhwaite, bobbing an indifferent curtsy to the gentry, more as a mere token of respect than anything else, 'an' what better place to have it, wi'out a pack o' useless noddies dancin' around her, but wi' her own true love helping her, and me to see her right when 'twas all over? Sleep now, me duck,' she told Stacy firmly. 'Tek no notice of 'em. The maister and I will look after ye until ye are fit to travel 'ome agin.'

Stacy's last sight before she fell into a black pit of healing sleep was of the Earl's half-amused face and Anthony's outraged one as the old woman ordered them about. The last sound she heard was that of her protesting son, whom Matt was still holding as though he never intended to lay him down again. He was to ask himself afterwards whether the fierce pride he had felt for the boy-child in his arms was because he had assisted at his birth, not been fetched in when all was over and shown a spotless baby lying in a spotless cradle covered in lace, as though he had been dropped from heaven clean and washed and clothed in the finest garments!

Instead little Hal Falconer wore nothing but the remains of his father's shirt, and was to do so until Thwaites rode back to The Eyrie with the news of his birth. He carried with him a request that many of the baby-clothes wrapped around bags of lavender and lying in the drawers of the waiting nursery should be brought to the poor cottage where the latest Falconer had been born, along with his mother's nightrail and enough bedlinen, towels, soap, perfume and other etceteras to make the cottage a more suitable place for the Falconer heir until he and his mother were fit to be carried back to The Eyrie.

The small, dark room seemed smaller and darker still, filled as it was with more people than it had known for many a day. The Earl looked round it and said, 'I believe that a yeoman used to live here, but he died some years ago, unmarried, leaving no children behind. The land being marginal and hard to farm, I never let it out again. I take it that this poor woman and her child are squatting here, for want of anywhere else to go?'

'Then, whoever you are, you takes it wrong,' a harsh voice told him as the owner of it stepped into the room. 'And who the devil are all of ye to be in my whoam? And who the devil's she?' And he was pointing at Stacy, happily asleep, all her problems solved, dreaming that she was roving across a great plain, Hal in her arms, Matt by her side, and a large dog following them. . .

CHAPTER SIXTEEN

'WELL, one could hardly blame the poor man for being surprised. To step into such a galaxy of great men, all sitting in his one small room, and me asleep on the only bed in it, must have been a great shock for him!' Stacy was responding to Matt's tale of what had happened while she had been happily unconscious after Hal's birth. 'I hope you were all suitably kind to him for the shelter his wife gave us. Otherwise Hal might have been born in the open!'

'Oh, Father is arranging that,' responded Matt, who had been on his highest ropes ever since Hal had been born and Stacy had survived his birth, 'and if he hadn't done so I would. After all, you were given bed and board there for several days until the York doctor allowed that you might safely be moved.'

Stacy laughed again as she remembered the great man's shock on hearing how Hal had come into the world, and a letter had been sent to the even greater man in London telling him that his services were no longer needed.

She had been back at The Eyrie for some days, in her own bed again, and was waiting to feed Hal, reluctant to disturb him while he was sleeping peacefully. Louisa was distressed by Stacy's insistence that she feed Hal herself, and was constantly worrying her over it, 'Are you sure that you would not be better with a wet-nurse, my dear?' being her usual refrain.

'Perhaps I should,' Stacy had told her robustly, 'but seeing that master Hal arrived so incontinently into the world that there is none available, nor will be, I am told, for another few weeks, he is going to have to be content with his mama.'

Whether it was Matt's ministrations during the birth, or Grandam Outhwaite's herbs, potions and care after it that did the trick, as Matt was fond of saying, Stacy recovered amazingly quickly from what Anthony Beauchamp, Caroline and others persisted in calling her 'ordeal'. Far more rapidly, Georgiana said acidly, than *she* had ever done with her more conventional *accouchements*.

It had seemed like an ordeal at the time, Stacy thought, but afterwards, well, that was quite a different thing. Like Matt she thought that she loved young Hal the more because they, and only they, were responsible for his presence. Not simply in creating him, but in seeing that he was safely born.

'So brave, Stacy,' everyone said, but Stacy always maintained that Matt had been the brave one. Anthony and others had tried to blame him for taking her to such an out-of-the-way place when she was so near to her time, but she wouldn't have that either.

'Why, I was the wilful one,' she always said, 'not Matt, seeing that it was I who insisted on going down that final lane where the accident happened, when Matt had wished to turn for home earlier. So, there's no more to be said.'

But there *was* one more thing to say, and when Matt came into her room to see how she and Hal were faring she patted the bed and asked Matt to come and sit by her. 'For,' she told him, 'there is a question I must ask you, sir.'

'Oh,' said Matt, gazing at her fondly, 'and what question is that?' He thought that since Hal's birth she looked more beautiful than ever. Motherhood had softened her, put a faint blush in once pale cheeks, had rounded her even more delightfully in every direction. Only her sharp intelligence remained unchanged, which was all to the good, he thought, for he was coming to treasure it, and could not imagine why so many men wished to have fools for their wives.

'I am curious,' she said, speaking slowly, 'as to why a man whom I know to be brave out of the common run – no, do not contradict me, sir, Jeb Priestley told me of your exploits in America – should behave so strangely when his wife was having their child. I thought at one point that you were about to faint. Most unlike you. I would have imagined, beforehand, that you would have taken all in your stride.'

To her surprise he changed colour, and then rose to walk to the window and look out of it at the golden afternoon, before he turned to speak to her.

'If I said that most men of any sensitivity would be distressed at the sight of their wife giving birth then I should not be speaking the entire truth. There was more to it than that. . .' He paused.

After a time Stacy said, 'Yes, I thought so. You said something odd at the time. "Not twice," you said. "I can't bear this, not again, not twice."' And then swiftly and tenderly she added, 'Oh, my dear, if it distresses you to speak of it, then pardon me for having raised a matter which might hurt you.'

He came back to the bed to sit by her again and take her hand before saying quietly, 'No, it doesn't hurt me now. Not like it did. Indeed, I think it might be better if I told you why I was so distressed.' He paused again. Stacy pressed his hand, and he pressed hers back. Since their child's birth they had been more tender and loving with each other than she could have believed possible. One day, soon, when the pains of the birth were behind her, they would celebrate their love as it deserved to be celebrated, wildly and fiercely, no doubt, as it had been that night at Pontisford, but for the present simply to be together, and Hal not far away, was enough.

'I was a happy child,' he began slowly. 'I was the

youngest and a little spoiled. I never knew my mother; she died when I was only four years old—she had never been strong, they said. And while I was very young Rollo seemed not to resent me. I realise now that when they grew up he resented both his brothers, as though we were somehow his rivals. So when I grew older he changed towards me. I was given a dog, a wolfhound. Prince, I called him. Rollo wanted Prince, simply because he was mine, I now think. He asked me to give him Prince. I said no, Prince was mine. I loved him and Prince loved me. He said nothing when I refused, only softly, "You'll be sorry."

'I didn't really understand what he meant by that. I did about a week later. We were out on the moors shooting, the dogs were with us, and Rollo shot Prince dead. He always claimed it was an accident. Only he and I knew it wasn't, that it was quite deliberate. After that I was careful never to show that I cared much for anything when he was about, for I knew that if I did he would do something like that again, or would take it away from me.

'And then I met Camilla. It was at a ball at York Assembly Rooms. She was not at all like you. She was a little thing, with silky blonde hair, eyes like cornflowers and a tender, delicate face. She was shy, and was seated quite alone, with an old aunt by her side, while the young men fought over her three elder sisters. I fell head over heels in love with her. I wanted to protect her, to make her smile. I asked her to dance, and, seeing that I couldn't dance with her more than twice or cause gossip, I sat by her and talked to her. She seemed to like talking to me.

'She was the youngest daughter of a family of gentry who had lost their money through unwise speculation in the late wars. They lived in a tumbledown manor house near York. All the older sisters married early and, if not well, quite decently. Her parents were naturally overjoyed when I began to show that I was serious in my intentions towards her. After all, I was Earl Falconer's son, even if only a younger one, and he would see that we had a decent living one way or another.

'My way was to go into the Navy, and before I left for my first service in it it was agreed that when I came home on leave the arrangements would be made for us to marry. Both our parents thought that we were a little too young to rush into marriage straight away. I suspect that for some reason my father delayed it – her parents were much more eager.

'At first she wrote to me quite regularly, although as was the way at sea I often got a whole budget of letters at one go, after receiving nothing for months. Suddenly the letters stopped altogether, until one day I received one from her. . .' He stopped, turned his face towards Stacy, and she could see that he was not with her; he was reliving the pain of that day again.

'It said, quite simply, that she no longer wished to marry me, that what we had shared was a boy-and-girl love – that Rollo had proposed to her and she was going to marry him! It was the story of Prince, and a score of other hurts, all over again. She wasn't the sort of girl whom Rollo had ever shown any interest in before. He liked them big and showy. It was just that she was mine, and he was taking her away from me. I learned afterwards that her parents brought enormous pressure on her to throw me over. After all, if they had thought Earl Falconer's younger son was a great catch, imagine what they made of it when his heir offered for her, a virtually dowerless girl. Perhaps she was a little dazzled by him, too; he was considered to be very handsome. Although now I think not. I don't think that she ever cared for him, but she dared not defy her parents.

'I'm not sure what my father thought. Probably that all she and I had shared was puppy-love, as they say, and Rollo at that time was the apple of his eye; he could do no wrong. Later was a different matter, but by then it was too late.

'They were married when I was at sea. I didn't come back to The Eyrie for a long time after that, not until I was wounded at Trafalgar and they sent me home. I was put on half-pay, so I lost even my navy career, the thought of which had been something of a consolation to me after losing Camilla. Father wanted me to go into the *Corps Diplomatique*. He had a lot of influence then, but what subsequently happened put an end to that.

'When I went home all that I could think of was that I would see Camilla again. What I never thought of was how much she might have changed. She had always been delicately pretty, pink and white, with a charming manner and what I had thought was an enchanting laugh. Nothing of that was left. She was sallow and haunted-looking. When I met her again she turned her face away and could hardly look at me.

'Rollo's manner to her in public was always correct and loving. He claimed to be puzzled as to why she was so constantly ill. She was breeding, he told me carelessly, and that was probably why she looked such a fright.

'"I hope to God she looks a little more *comme il faut* when she has had the heir," he drawled at me. "I can't stand all this weeping and wailing; she's forever having the vapours, and never seems fit enough to perform her wifely duties." I think that he talked like that about her to taunt me.

'I wasn't feeling very well when I first got back to Yorkshire, but as I recovered my strength Camilla's condition worried me more and more. Seeing her again had revived all my old love and compassion for her. Oh, I know now that it was quite a different sort of love from that which I feel for you—there was no passion in it, and what would have happened if we had married sometimes worries me. But then, I was ablaze with anger at what I clearly saw was Rollo's mistreatment of her. And my father couldn't seem to see it.

'Matters came to a head one day when I came across her in the gardens; we had been avoiding one another. She was sitting in the small gazebo, looking away from the house, not the folly you used to sit in before Hal was born. She had been crying. I remember that it was a warm day and she was wearing quite a heavy shawl. She was so different from the little fairy that I had fallen in love with that I could hardly believe that she was the same person.

'I remember that I asked her if there was anything I could do for her, since she was so plainly unhappy. She shook her head and said no, nobody could help her. She couldn't help herself. She had made a mistake in marrying Rollo, and that was that. I couldn't help myself; I put an arm around her. God knows, I meant nothing by it; she was big with my brother's child and I was only trying to comfort her.

'She gave a great cry and pulled herself away from me, and half-shrieked, "No, don't touch me, don't." I don't know why I did it, but as gently as I could I pulled the shawl away, and then I saw. All the great bruises down her arms, and even on her neck. I knew then why she wore long sleeves in the height of summer, and dresses with high collars.

'I remember sitting there trembling, saying to her one word—"Rollo"—because her condition explained so much. She put her thumb in her mouth and whispered through it, "He mustn't know you know. He'd kill me." I asked her why she hadn't told my father, and she said that she was afraid of him. Not that he had done or said anything unpleasant; he was always kind to her, but he thought the world of Rollo. . . I could see that it was hopeless; Rollo had broken her spirit.

'I didn't know what to do. I was still little more than a boy, only twenty-one, and despite my hard life in the

Navy, and all I had seen and done there, I was still inexperienced in the ways of the great world. For several days I debated what to do to save my lost love, and then events took their own course. My father went away to London—he had a minor post in the Cabinet—which gave Rollo the freedom to practise even more cruelties. That last afternoon he drank too much at dinner, snarled at me, snarled at Camilla—I remember how she shrank away from him—until finally he took her by the hand and dragged her off to their rooms. He shouted at me as he left that he was tired of seeing my hanging-judge's face, and couldn't wait for me to leave.

'I went to my own rooms. About an hour later I heard noises, running feet, Camilla's voice raised. She was outside, in the stable-yard—my room overlooked it—talking to one of the grooms, a boy who was always ready to do things for her.

'He was doing something for her, something he should not have been doing. He was readying one of the small chaises for use. I saw that Camilla had a bag in her hand; she was calling feverishly to him to hurry. Finally she climbed into the chaise, the groom was on the box and they were off, clattering out of the yard. There was no sign of Rollo.

'I picked up my coat and ran downstairs. I ran into the yard and roared at Beckett—he was Thwaites' predecessor—Where is Stephen taking Lady Radley?

'He looked at me as though I were witless. "He's not taking her anywhere, Mr Matt."

'I said something like, Don't treat me like a fool, Beckett, and then Sim Farrell came running up. "He's taking her down to London to her folks, Mr Matt, and about time too. We all know what m'lord's been a-doing to her!"

'Beckett was as nonplussed as I was, and roared at Sim, "You fool, Sim, that's your job gone!"

'I stood there, my head whirling. She was very near her time, and setting off for London with only an ignorant boy with her was the last thing that she ought to have been doing—and where was Rollo?

'Beckett was so shocked he was almost witless himself. As well he might have been—he was turned off for not having the gumption to stop Stephen—even though he had no idea what Stephen was doing.

'I had only one thought in my head; to go after her and help her. Saddle my horse, I flung at Sim. I'll ride after them, try to get her back.

'That ride passed in a dream, a nightmare. I finally caught up with them after changing horses at Selby. I nearly rode past the inn where they had stopped to change horses again, but fortunately, or unfortunately, I recognised the chaise as I rode past the inn-yard.

'Camilla was sitting in the parlour. She looked worse than ever. I ran over to her, said something wild about whatever did she think that she was doing.'

He was suddenly not with Stacy any more. He had gone back in time. He was in the parlour, holding Camilla's hands.

'You must come back with me, Camilla. You're not fit to travel to London when you're so near your time.'

She looked up at him, the once cornflower-blue eyes dark with suffering. 'I won't go back, Matt. I will kill myself rather. You have no notion of how dreadfully he treated me. This afternoon he started to beat me so cruelly I began to fear for my baby's life. I fought him. He was so drunk he found it difficult to overmaster me. I hit him over the head with one of the bronze statuettes from Pompeii. He fell down and didn't get up again. I know that I didn't kill him, for he was still breathing. He was only stunned. I can't stay with him, Matt. Don't make me go back. I want to go home to my father and mother. I know that they're in London.'

She said all this in a tired, matter-of-fact voice which had Matt trembling. 'You must go back to The Eyrie,' he told her desperately, for he knew that her father and mother would not stand by her. They had sold her to Rollo, and that was that. 'I shall go to my father and tell him the truth.'

She began to shiver and shake, her hands writhing together, her face ghastly. 'I won't go back. I would rather die in a ditch than go back. I have an aunt in Chelsea; perhaps she will take me in.' Then she added almost inconsequentially, 'You know, Rollo often told me that he only married me to take me away from you. He said that you wouldn't want me when you saw what I had turned into.'

Matt took her into his arms as gently as he could and told her the truth. 'I shall always love you, Camilla, and I shall always try to help you.' But he had never felt so helpless. In the face of her determination and her suffering he could no longer argue that they should return to The Eyrie.

Stephen came in. Matt said wearily, 'I suppose you know that you'll be turned away for this?'

'So?' Stephen shot back at him. 'A fine sort of man I should be to stand by and see what I have seen without doing something. I'm surprised at you, Mr Matt. Want her to go back for him to beat her again, do you?'

'No,' he said, and made up his mind. 'I'll take her to her aunt at Chelsea, if that's what she wants.'

He told Stacy, whose face was now as white as his as she listened to his long and painful tale, 'But, of course, we never got to Chelsea. Twenty miles further on her pains started. I had left my horse at the last stop and was travelling with her. The postilion was driving, Stephen beside him on the box. I stopped the coach at the next inn and carried her in, as I carried you into the cottage where Hal was born.

'But Camilla's baby was born dead. It had been dead for some little time. And Rollo had probably killed it, if what Camilla said to me in her delirium after his birth was true. I cannot tell you how much she suffered while her child was being born, and how long it took.

'I was not with her. But I sat on the inn stairs and could hear all her agony. The landlady thought that we were eloping; she was certain something discreditable was happening and she raved and shouted at me for making a woman in such a condition travel at all.

'They let me in to see her when it was all over, and even now I can hardly bear to think of it. I had seen what a warship looked like after a battle, but what I saw in that bedroom beggared description. And my poor Camilla lay there dying, killed by my brother as surely as though he had run a sword through her heart. . . So now you know why I was not brave when Hal started to arrive, and why I thought that I was going to lose you. That I would have two loves and would lose both of them in the same cruel fashion.'

'But you were brave in the end,' riposted Stacy, squeezing his hand lovingly. 'Without you Hal might not have survived. And, now that you have shared your story with me, I understand why you felt and behaved as you did. The only thing that I don't understand is why everyone blamed you, why you had to leave home and were given such a bad name. After all, you only went after Camilla to save her.'

Matt's smile was a twisted one. 'Oh, when Rollo came to, and found out what had happened and started after us, he arranged everything so that the blame fell on me. Stephen and Sim were turned away and told that if they betrayed what had actually happened he would make sure that they would never work again, which was enough to silence them. Beckett, too, was bought off. By the time my father was informed and arrived on the scene, several days later, it was fully established that Camilla and I were running away, that we were guilty lovers. Rollo couldn't pretend that Camilla's child was mine, but everything else which could blacken me was thrown at me.

'The landlady at the inn didn't help; she blamed me for making Camilla travel when her time was so near. Nobody helped me, or would listen to anything I said in my defence. My father believed every word Rollo said. Camilla's parents accused me of killing her. If I hadn't persuaded her to run away with me, they said, then the child would have been born alive at The Eyrie and Camilla wouldn't have died.

'No one thought to ask themselves where in the world I could have been taking Camilla to, without a penny in my pocket, and no home of my own. I didn't help myself much. I was incoherent with grief and anger. When I tried to tell anyone—even my father—the truth of the matter concerning Rollo and Camilla I was called even worse names for attempting to blacken the character of the grieving widower. One of the reasons I was so harsh to you at first, at Pontisford, was because you reminded me of all the fine ladies who had torn my poor Camilla to pieces after her death.

'She was given a hole-and-corner funeral, which I was not allowed to attend, and when I said that I wanted to leave the Navy—the Navy didn't want me anyway—and go to the small estate which my mother had left me in Virginia everyone was only too happy to see the back of me.

'So there you have it. Until I met my dear Lady Disdain, organising and managing everyone's affairs, driving me mad because I could see that beneath her icy exterior there were fires of passion blazing in which I wished to immolate myself, I never felt true affection or love for a woman again. I think that I was afraid to. . .' There were tears in his eyes as he finished.

For a moment there was silence in the peaceful room. Stacy gently stroked the hand which held hers. 'Oh, Matt, what a terrible story. Poor Camilla, and poor you. I can quite understand that when I began to give birth so incontinently, and in such an isolated situation, it revived all your most painful memories and fears. I am astounded that you found yourself able to help me at all.'

She stopped, and for a moment they were silent again, Matt remembering his lost first love and Stacy seeing a young Matt, quite alone, desolate, and his life lying in ruins about him. It explained so much that had puzzled her. She told him so, adding, 'And will it be too painful for you to stay in England, my love? I know how much you loved your American home.'

Matt shook his head vigorously. 'If I were still the younger son, with no ties, then I would take you back there, but I am not. I am the heir and I have my duty to do, and will do it cheerfully, I hope, with you by my side.'

He leaned over to kiss her cheek. 'And now I'm not afraid to give my heart to you, to risk you having another child, thanks to your bravery while you were bearing Hal. And to some extent I think that I have my father's affection back again. He may never know the whole story of Rollo's treatment of Camilla, but I could not wish him to. Let us leave him with some of his illusions. As to the future—well, I only hope that for our next child there will be a warm, comfortable bedroom, a doctor and nurses standing by, and that I may be allowed to pace outside in the corridor with my shirt safely on!'

Stacy kissed him back with interest. 'Well, I hope that you may have your wish, sir, and that we may soon set about fulfilling it. But, I warn you, I shall also expect Grandam Outhwaite to be present, with both of her blue bottles, for, although you and I birthed the baby, she made sure that we all recovered from it afterwards.'

At that moment there was a series of loud squawks from

the nursery next door. Stacy laughed up at her husband, whose face had lightened appreciably since he had at last rid himself of some of the burden which he had carried for so many years.

She said mischievously, 'One day I shall tell you why I call Hal our little lion-cub, but in the meantime you must fetch him to me so that I may feed him, and while I do so we shall discuss buying a wolfhound for you, to replace Prince, for life is about renewal as well as death, my dear.'

Her husband did as he was bid, and sat and watched her feed their 'little cub', as she called him, and thought that on the day on which he had opened the door to the Bankeress he had opened the door to a new life for them both as well.

Hero could see his face now.

Craggy with lines of harsh experience. No smile to lighten and transform it. Grey eyes which no longer laughed but regarded her without expression. He had given no sign of recognition and neither did she. The man she remembered so vividly did not resemble this creature in the slightest. How could she have been so mistaken? wondered Hero despairingly. Her childish dream had no part to play in the real world of a young woman past her prime with no valid hope of marrying except for purely worldly reasons.

Dear Reader

Sarah Westleigh has enjoyed a varied life. Working as a local government officer in London, she qualified as a chartered quantity surveyor. She assisted her husband in his chartered accountancy practice, at the same time managing an employment agency. Moving to Devon, she finally found time to write, publishing short stories and articles, before discovering historical novels.

FELON'S FANCY

Sarah Westleigh

Harlequin Mills & Boon

SYDNEY ❀ AUCKLAND ❀ MANILA
LONDON ❀ TORONTO ❀ NEW YORK
PARIS ❀ AMSTERDAM ❀ HAMBURG ❀ MILAN
STOCKHOLM ❀ MADRID ❀ ATHENS ❀ BUDAPEST
WARSAW ❀ SOFIA ❀ PRAGUE ❀ TOKYO ❀ ISTANBUL

First Published 1995
First Australian Paperback Edition 1998
ISBN 0 733 51355 7

Published by
Harlequin Mills & Boon
3 Gibbes Street
Chatswood, NSW 2067
Australia

Printed and bound in Australia by
McPherson's Printing Group

CHAPTER ONE

THE Honourable Hero Langage stared at her sire in blank astonishment.

'Wed?' she cried, her utter disbelief echoing around the library, the threadbare carpet and few books gracing the shelves powerless to absorb and soften the outrage in her voice. 'You wish me to wed, Papa?'

Baron Polhembury glowered across the desk, intent upon subduing his daughter into obedience. 'That is my command, miss.'

'Why now?' Hero demanded abruptly. 'Since Mama died and I left the schoolroom you have refused to introduce me into any society where I might meet an acceptable suitor, for it served your purpose to keep me here at Polhembury Hall as your housekeeper. Why now?' she repeated, and added indignantly, 'And to a creature I have never met? Whose reputation is of the lowest kind?'

'Would you rather see me ruined?' blustered her father in return. 'What would become of you then, miss, a lady no longer of tender years cast adrift upon the world? Without a penny piece to your name?'

'And whose fault is it,' raged Hero, shivering at the thought but determined to fight for her future happiness, 'that I am almost three and twenty and still unwed? Or that you are threatened with ruin for debt?'

'Mine, daughter, I freely acknowledge my guilt, but now I am making amends,' declared the baron grandly, thrusting aside the past with a wave of his hand. 'I have found a gentleman of considerable rank and substantial means willing, nay, demanding to wed you! In return for your hand he will settle my debts, thus setting both matters of which you complain to rights.' The baron heaved his considerable bulk to his feet, put his fists on the desk and leant repressively towards her. 'I will brook no more arguments, miss. You will wed the Earl of Calverstock,' he ordered heavily.

'But I can never come to love such a man!'

The cry came from her heart. For an instant Hero was back in the village, seeing the hard, harsh features of the man she had met so suddenly in the doorway of the grocer's, the collision between them making her drop her basket. He had given an apologetic smile as he stood back, which had softened the lines of his face and held so much charm that Hero's heart had lurched and confusion had brought colour to her cheeks.

'My apologies, ma'am! How infernally careless of me!' he'd murmured, making an impeccable bow.

Although a gentleman of means and taste by the cut of his blue superfine jacket, he had wasted no more time on pleasantries but set about gathering up her scattered fruit and putting the plums back in her basket. His grey eyes had twinkled down at her as he had handed it back. She had been able to see the admiration in them, won despite the old faded blue dimity gown she wore and the rather shapeless chip bonnet upon her head, and the knowledge had brought a deeper blush to her cheeks.

'Thank you, sir,' she had managed to utter, dipping a small curtsy of appreciation.

Instinctively, she had known he was a man she could

come to respect, admire, even love. She had never met his like before and, incarcerated in Polhembury, was unlikely to do so again.

'Love?' scorned her father, breaking ruthlessly across her thoughts, which had, since that afternoon a few days ago, possessed a distressing tendency to stray in the stranger's direction whenever not otherwise occupied. 'What has love to say to anything? It is high time you put all that foolish schoolroom nonsense behind you, miss! Ladies of your rank wed for duty, for fortune and position, not for love. You have been reading too many of those rubbishy novels you borrow from the vicar's wife.'

'Miss Austen is not considered rubbishy,' muttered Hero, not because she felt the need to defend her reading but because she must keep arguing with her father or submit.

Lord Polhembury glanced down briefly at a letter lying open on his desk. Hero noted the crest embossed at the head of the page, the bold decisive writing beneath and the self-confident signature.

'His lordship is coming here tomorrow,' Lord Polhembury informed her curtly. 'You will provide hospitality and present yourself in your most attractive gown.'

'The old green velvet riding habit? 'Tis too hot for this weather,' said Hero, scornful in her turn. 'I will wear my yellow sprigged muslin if I must. Matty can iron it up for me. But I do not promise to accept the gentleman's offer.'

'You will have no choice,' her father informed her, his heavy features grim. 'Be about your business, child.'

She was no longer a child, thought Hero rebelliously

as she mounted the stairs to find the sanctuary of her room. There had been something ominous in her father's tone as he'd told her she had no choice which worried her considerably. What plan had he hatched with this ex-convict who had inherited an earldom and an immense fortune to go with it? She would put nothing past *him*, or her father either.

She could not, would not submit. She would run away rather.

As the idea came to her a slow smile lit up Hero's anxious face, bringing a gleam to eyes which she had long ago decided matched the colour of the hazelnuts growing in the hedgerows despite the darker patterns etched into the light golden-brown iris. Her determined chin set firmly. It would be difficult, but she could do it.

Matty, knocking sixty now and crippled with rheumatism, was too old to go with her, though. Could she travel alone? And how? She had no money of her own to pay coach fares and the month's meagre housekeeping allowance was already spent. Otherwise she might take the stage to London, if she could manage to make her way to Exeter. Her late mother's sister lived in Dorset Square and there had been talk of Hero's staying with her Aunt Augusta for her come-out, but talk was all it had been. Her father had had no intention of depriving Polhembury Hall of her valuable services. Not until now. He must be desperate to have his debts repaid.

Well, he would have to manage in the future, whether she wed or ran away. Even if she had to walk, she determined, she would get to London somehow. Perhaps Bessy Foster, the youthful maid of all work, would go with her. Hero no sooner thought of that solution than she discarded it. Bessy had no education and little sense. When Hero's plums had scattered on the ground all she had been able to do was first shriek and then cry out embarrassingly, 'Oh, Miss Hero! After all that risk us went to to pick they, too!' while the gentleman had immediately responded by grovelling around retrieving them. Grovelling extremely elegantly, she remembered with a pang. Though his hands had been strong, had looked no stranger to hard work, unusual in a gentleman, they had handled the ripe plums with exquisite care.

But Bessy would be nothing more than a hindrance on the journey. The young maid had lost what little wit she had once possessed after her brother was caught stealing produce from the gardener's store and been transported for seven years for the offence. Hero had pleaded with her father not to prosecute the lad—he was young, worried sick because his father had been stricken down and his family near starving, unable to survive on his pittance of a wage. But Lord Polhembury had ignored her entreaties.

'Let Ben Foster off?' he'd snorted. 'You are too soft-hearted, Hero. 'Twould only encourage others to become criminals. We'd be stripped bare in no time!'

Ben had been sent to the penal colony of New South Wales on the other side of the world. Bessy's father had died and her mother and the younger children been reduced to paupers. Hero had taken them food whenever she could and eventually the older children had found employment in the village. Then, a year or so ago, their fortunes had improved considerably when Mrs Foster had been offered a position as housekeeper to a widow living in Gloucestershire. How she had come by the appointment was as much a mystery to her as it was to Hero, but she had gone, and had taken all her children with her except Bessy, who had asked to stay. The cook, Mrs Blackler, was kind to the girl, who adored Miss Hero. Besides, she knew where she was at the Hall, she didn't want to leave for somewhere strange, even to be with her mother.

Lord Polhembury had been reluctant to keep Bessy on after Ben was convicted but in this Hero's arguments had prevailed. The girl was not responsible for her brother's crime, they had no reason to suspect her honesty and her labour was cheap.

But none of this helped to solve her own immediate problem. Mrs Blackler, Matty and Bessy were the only servants still resident at the Hall apart from a boot boy who acted inadequately as footman, answering the door and running messages. Many of the rooms in the house were disused, the furniture languishing under dust covers. The heavy housework was done by women from the village, who came in daily. They could not be called upon to accompany her. A groom and boy lived over the stables and a gardener and his wife occupied a cottage on the estate, for the baron would not consider giving up his horses whatever other economies he might demand, and the services of a competent gardener were imperative to keep the kitchen provided with vegetables. But she could not call upon any of them for help, either.

Young ladies were not supposed to travel alone, but Hero reckoned she was old enough to take care of herself and strong-minded enough to disregard what people might say. In any case they would soon forget, provided her aunt received her kindly.

That, of course, could not be guaranteed. She could not even remember what Aunt Augusta looked like, not having seen her since her mother's death. She vaguely remembered a rather formidable lady, not at all like Hero's mother, who had been kind and loving.

But she would cross that bridge when she came to it. Definitely, she refused to remain at Polhembury Hall to be forced into a marriage for the convenience of her father and on the inexplicable whim of the unknown Lord Calverstock.

'You can't, Miss Hero,' said Matty worriedly some time later. 'It wouldn't be right for a young lady like you to travel all that way alone.'

She had come to help Hero change for dinner and found her busy packing her things into a bag ready to leave that very night. Now Matty stood twisting gnarled fingers together in distress.

Hero spread her hands in a helpless gesture. 'I must, Matty, don't you see? Papa is threatening to force me to marry a man I don't even know.'

'You might not find him so bad, my chick,' ventured Matty reasonably.

'A convict?' retorted Hero, frowning at the elderly woman who had been nurse, maid and friend for as long as Hero could remember. 'A man who has inherited a fortune and appears set upon squandering it on gambling and high-flyers?'

'You shouldn't talk like that, Miss Hero,' reproved Matty. 'And 'tis all gossip anyway.'

'I'll wager 'tis true enough,' said Hero, not to be deflected from her opinion.

'Ben Foster is a convict,' reminded Matty. 'He was a decent enough lad. Maybe some of the others must be, too. What was this lord's crime?'

'I don't know,' admitted Hero, thrusting slippers and a nightgown into the bag with unnecessary energy. 'But he was no Ben Foster, he was the grandson of an earl. It must have been something bad for him to end up on a convict ship.'

Matty hesitated. Then she spoke with unusual decision. 'If you must go, then I'll come with you. I'd never forgive myself if anything happened to you, my chick. I promised your blessed mother to look after you, and I will!'

'Oh, Matty!' Impulsively, Hero took the old woman into her arms and drew her close. 'I would never have managed without you! But I can't ask you to make such a long, uncomfortable journey, I really can't, it would be too great a sacrifice. Papa wouldn't have you back, you know, if I couldn't keep you with me. But once I'm settled, I'll send for you if I can, I promise!'

'You're not asking me, I'm telling you, Miss Hero! I'll come with you. But must you go tonight? Why not wait and see what this Lord Calverstock is like? That can't hurt, can it? Then, if you won't have him but your papa still insists on the match, we'll leave tomorrow night. How about that?'

'I don't know.' Hero felt uneasy about that arrangement yet couldn't really fault Matty's reasoning. In the end she nodded. 'All right. As you say, it can't do any harm to wait and meet the man. Truth to tell, I'm curious to see what he's like!'

Matty beamed. 'I'll press your yellow muslin, then, shall I, chick?'

'Yes, all right. But I shall not unpack my bag. For I believe that in the end I shall be forced to seek sanctuary with my aunt in Dorset Square.'

'Is that where you were going?' Matty looked relieved to discover that her mistress had not intended to entirely discard her family, but nevertheless pursed her lips doubtfully. 'She has daughters of her own, I believe, but whether they are wed or not I do not know. You are a beauty, Miss Hero. If they are not already settled...'

Hero chuckled. 'You are prejudiced, Matty! I am far from beautiful! My hair is brown not golden, my eyes hazel and ordinary, not large and blue! And besides, I am practically at my last prayers.'

'But your eyes glow, Miss Hero, and your hair is thick and wavy and when it is just washed, as it is now, it shines like polished mahogany. Don't you put yourself down. You're beautiful all right, even if it isn't in the fair, simpering way folks seem to think is fashionable these days. And you're not too old to wed, that's certain. Otherwise the earl wouldn't be asking for your hand, now, would he?'

Matty was used to speaking her mind and often did it forcefully. But she'd never before been so outspoken about her appearance. Perhaps she did have some semblance of looks, thought Hero, who had never suffered from vanity but rather the reverse. And she did have a reasonable sort of figure, she supposed, tall but not too tall, well-covered without being exactly plump, and it went in and out in all the right places. The yellow sprigged muslin suited her colouring and the tight band beneath her generous bosom allowed the skirt to fall gracefully about her hips and legs. The fashion was out of date, of course, for waists were lower now. But still, with its lowish neckline and tiny puffed sleeves it was just right for summer and it did make her look her best.

Just as her father had ordered, she thought ruefully, and almost determined to wear something else. But in the end she decided to comply with his wishes for the moment. Rebellion could come after her meeting with the earl. She did not relish the prospect of being examined like a prize pig going to market, but two could play at that game. She wondered how his lordship would react to her critical scrutiny of him.

His lordship was due to arrive in the afternoon, after the light nuncheon Hero normally had served at two.

Having partaken of very little, she repaired to her room to change. The day was hot and airless and windows were open throughout the used part of the house.

'I swear, I am glad I am not a gentleman,' Hero declared, going to the casement and drawing a deep breath. 'How they manage not to dissolve from the heat inside their coats I shall never comprehend!'

''Tis a different story in the winter,' remarked Matty as Hero returned to sit before her mirror to have her hair dressed. 'They are warm while the ladies shiver in their muslins.'

Hero laughed. 'Right as usual, Matty, though we can always carry a shawl!' She sobered as she watched the maid pile her abundant hair on top of her head and secure it in a becoming topknot with a few curls arranged to frame her face. Matty's gnarled hands could still work wonders, thought Hero affectionately.

Her hairstyle was out of date too, she knew, short hair being all the rage at present, but she had been reluctant to part with the luxuriant growth when she came out of the schoolroom, and still was.

'He won't like my complexion,' she stated critically. 'I have been too much in the sun. Perhaps he will not take to me and then I shall be free of this odious business.'

In sudden frustration she turned to Matty, who gave a 'tsk' of warning. 'Be still, Miss Hero, or you'll spoil your hair!'

'Much I care,' declared Hero forcefully. 'I could do without this charade!' Her voice rose in her indignation. 'How could Papa do this to me? Expect me to wed with a *convict*!'

'He is an earl, my love,' Matty pointed out placatingly.

'Faugh! By some unfortunate quirk of fate! He is the son of a common woman and is an ex-convict to boot! What can Papa be thinking of?'

''Tis not like you to be high in the instep, my chick,' muttered Matty reprovingly. 'No doubt his mama was a gentlewoman, if not one of high degree.'

Hero sighed and went on more moderately, 'I expect you are right, Matty. I am being excessively rude to a woman I do not know—if she is still alive.' She glanced at the clock ticking on her mantelpiece. 'He should be arriving soon. Since I am Papa's hostess, I should go down to the morning-room ready to receive him. No doubt he will think it strange to be entertained there, but the drawing-room is under covers and the notice was too short to bring it back into use.'

'Then you'd better put your gown on,' said Matty dourly. 'Come here, Miss Hero, and stand still. There!'

Matty fastened the last hook, straightened the ribbon streamers flowing from the bow beneath Hero's breasts and stood back. 'You'll do, my chick. He'll be a fool if he doesn't want you for a wife.'

'It seems he does,' muttered Hero. 'Unseen. I wonder what possessed him to pick on me?'

'You will inherit the estate when your father dies,' suggested Matty.

'But he has land enough and the estate is not worth anything now!'

'Maybe it could be.'

'It'd need a lot of money spending on it first.'

'He has more than enough by all accounts.'

'True.' Hero twirled in front of the cheval mirror, hardly aware of the reflection of herself in it, her mind obsessed with what seemed to be an insoluble puzzle. Why had the Earl of Calverstock demanded her hand in marriage? There must be plenty of doting mamas in London who would overlook his deficiencies in order to secure a title for their darlings.

Braced for the coming interview, one hand on the worn handrail, Hero descended the curved oak staircase, one of the beauties of Polhembury Hall which she kept lovingly polished around the threadbare carpet running down the centre of the treads, and made her way to the morning-room, which she used as a sitting-room.

As she approached the door, which was open a crack, she heard voices. Her stomach muscles tightened. Her father's accents were unmistakable and the chilly tones now addressing him must belong to the earl. A quick glance at the hall table, graced by a top hat and riding crop, confirmed her suspicion. He had already arrived.

'I think you will agree that the sum of ten thousand pounds which will be required to clear your debts is an excessively generous payment to make for the hand of your daughter, my lord. You will oblige me by including the horses in your stable in the settlement. Despite my generosity you will not have the means to keep them without incurring more debt, I collect.'

'But——' blustered the baron, but before he could say more the earl interrupted.

'You may keep a hack, of course, for you will need one to see to your estate, which is in a sad state of neglect. Since it is your only source of income, you will doubtless feel obliged to bring it back into productivity. The only alternative to the course I have proposed is incarceration in a sponging-house prior to being thrown into a debtors' prison. The choice is yours.'

Hero stood rigid in the doorway, the shiver shaking her nothing to do with the breeze from the window issuing through it as a draught. The cooling air would have been welcome. But much as she herself had often wished to set her father down, to hear this upstart treating him with barely concealed contempt made her furious. Her papa was in a financial hole caused in no small part, she was convinced, by the man now dunning him. She drew a deep breath and prepared to fling the door back and confront this cold-blooded felon who had bargained so cruelly for her hand.

Even as she did so, she knew that she would have to

save her father, undeserving as he was, painful as it would be. Ten thousand pounds! He had gambled a fortune and lost. She was his only remaining asset, for the run-down estate was not worth half that sum.

Head high, indignation ousting all thought of nervousness, Hero pushed the door wide and stepped into the room.

Her father stood by the empty fireplace, his protest at having his horses taken from him frozen on his lips. Hero scarcely glanced at him. Her eyes focused immediately on the tall stranger standing with his back to the open window, his features in shadow.

The shock almost made her faint, but she was not given to the vapours. Even without a clear look at features imprinted on her mind, she knew it was he. The blue coat was the same, as were the buff pantaloons and the gleaming boots, which must have been dusted off if he had been riding, which it seemed he had.

'Hero!' exclaimed her father, attempting to regain his composure and at the same time project his authority over her. 'There you are, miss! His lordship has already arrived, as you may see. Your lordship,' he turned to the silent man at the window and performed the introduction, his voice hoarse. 'This is my only daughter, Hero. Hero, Lord Calverstock, the man I have decided you shall marry.'

The gentleman moved. He took a step forward and bowed. 'Madam,' he intoned, his voice tight.

Hero could see his face now. Craggy with lines of harsh experience. No smile to lighten and transform it. Grey eyes which no longer laughed but regarded her without expression.

Hero wanted to spit into those chips of ice but breeding won. She inclined her head, made her curtsy and murmured, 'My lord,' her voice as devoid of warmth as his eyes.

He had given no sign of recognition and neither did she. The man she remembered so vividly did not resemble this creature in the slightest. How could she have been so mistaken? wondered Hero despairingly. Even the slight, unlikely hope of meeting him again somewhere, that one faint vision of possible felicity, had been ruthlessly exposed for what it was: the childish dream of an adolescent which had no part to play in the real world of a young woman past her prime with no valid hope of marrying except for purely worldly reasons.

'I trust everything is now satisfactory to you, my lord?' blustered Lord Polhembury, giving his daughter a repressive stare. 'The matter is settled?'

'Provided Miss Langage is agreeable. Have you any objection to the match, madam?'

His voice held an undercurrent of anger Hero could not understand. It made her own hackles rise and she wanted to hurl her defiance in his face but knew she could not. Her rebellion had been short-lived, she thought wretchedly. How she wished she had run away last night, as planned. Yet she could not have remained away, knowing what it was costing her father. She would rather suffer at this man's hands than see her father thrown into a debtors' prison.

Hero lifted her chin and met his eyes, her own full of contempt. 'None, my lord,' she said.

'Good! Capital!' Baron Polhembury's manner became effusive and as a knock at the door echoed into the room he exclaimed, 'That will be the admirable Reverend Cudlip! You have the licence, my lord?'

Calverstock nodded and reached into his breast pocket to produce an official-looking document.

The boot boy announced the vicar. As greetings were exchanged and introductions made Hero realised that she was to be left no time to change her mind. In a few moments, for good or ill, she would be wed.

The preliminaries were short. The vicar, knowing nothing of the tensions in the room, took the proffered special licence and prepared to proceed with the ceremony.

'We shall need witnesses,' he observed, peering through his spectacles first at one and then at the other of those about to be joined in holy matrimony. They were standing stiffly yards apart but he apparently saw nothing strange in this, nor did he sense anything amiss.

His wife would have been immediately aware of her own mutinous discomfort, thought Hero. She and Mrs Cudlip had become friends over the years, for Hero had found the kindly young matron a congenial companion on her visits to the poor and sick in the neighbourhood and she knew her as well as anyone apart from Matty, who probably knew her better than she knew herself. What must Mrs Cudlip be thinking now, presuming she knew the nature of her husband's mission to Polhembury Hall? And Matty. She must be wondering what was going on.

The thoughts flashed through her head as her betrothed's voice answered calmly, 'My man will do for one. He is in the kitchen with Lord Polhembury's cook. She can act as the other. They may also witness your signature to the marriage settlement, my lord. My lawyers witnessed my signature,' went on Calverstock relentlessly, indicating a document already spread upon a nearby table, no doubt the subject of their earlier discussion. 'I shall require yours before the marriage ceremony proceeds.'

Hero opened her mouth to suggest they call Matty instead of Mrs Blackler but closed it again without saying anything. Matty would wonder, be uneasy for her chick, who could do without waves of sympathy flowing over her at the moment. Later she could cry her heart out in the security of Matty's motherly arms.

Her father sent the boot boy to fetch the witnesses but the entire indoor staff, who had been gathered in the kitchen wondering what their betters were up to, presented themselves to ask that they be allowed to witness Miss Hero's wedding. A strange man, grave yet pleasant-looking, presumably the earl's servant, followed them in.

Matty looked anxiously at Hero, who returned a reassuring smile, wondering how long she could hold back the tears which threatened at sight of her maid. In one way she had been right not to want Matty near, yet her presence was a comfort.

The elderly maid then turned her attention to the earl and an expression of relief washed over her lined face. She did not know the half of it, Hero thought bitterly. All Matty saw was a strikingly elegant gentleman of some thirty years whom any girl might be happy to wed at first glance. Bessy had stared blankly at Calverstock with no sign of recognition in her eyes, thank heaven.

After only a slight hestiation her father signed the

marriage settlement. Hero wondered what terms Calverstock had laid down, what provision had been made for her should she become a widow. But really, what did anything matter except that she was about to wed this cold-blooded devil who had her father in his power?

The ceremony proceeded. Hero made her responses in a firm, cold voice, as did her bridegroom, whose given names she discovered to be Drew Wystan. His family name she already knew. Drew Wystan Challoner, fifth earl of Calverstock, became her husband in a matter of minutes.

'You may kiss the bride,' said the Reverend Cudlip benignly the moment he had pronounced the blessing.

Calverstock obliged, doing what was expected of him with no sign of emotion. His hard lips touched hers in a brief salute which lasted no more than a second but it sent such a *frisson* of distaste shivering down Hero's spine that she almost gasped. Heat rose in her cheeks and her vision was momentarily impaired as she saw everything as if through a dark, eddying mist.

'A drink!' her father cried and Hero could sense the relief beneath his false cheerfulnes. 'We must have drinks to toast the happy couple! Mrs Blackler, you may pour ale in the kitchen!'

Mrs Blackler bobbed her thanks and addressed Hero. 'We all wishes you happy, Miss Hero. We'm sorry to lose 'ee, that we be, but we be that glad 'ee've found a good man at last.'

'Thank you, Mrs Blackler,' choked Hero, appreciating the sentiment while doubting its accuracy.

Matty, taking advantage of her long service and

special position, came over and kissed Hero before addressing Calverstock.

'I'll be coming with my lady,' she announced firmly. 'I hope you make her happy, my lord. She deserves the best.'

Calverstock did not react with anger to what could have been considered an impertinence but eyed Matty gravely before inclining his head in acknowledgement of her concern. 'Much will depend upon Lady Calverstock herself,' he said. 'Her eventual happiness lies in her own hands.'

Matty gazed at him steadily and then nodded, as though satisfied. 'I'll go and pack her ladyship's things,' she said.

'No need for undue urgency,' murmured Calverstock with a faint shrug. 'My wife will remain here tonight. Have her things ready by morning. I will be here with the carriage at six.' He turned to Hero, who stood by listening to the conversation unable to believe it was taking place. Matty must have gone light in the attic to be taken in so! 'We will travel to my London house tomorrow,' he told her. 'I trust you have no objection, ma'am?'

'None,' returned Hero faintly, her main emotion other than astonishment at the conversation which had just taken place one of immense relief.

He obviously did not intend to claim his marital rights that night.

Their servants left to partake of ale in the kitchen. A glass of sherry was placed in her hand by the earl's inscrutable man, who then served her father, the vicar and Calverstock himself. A toast was drunk. Hero barely allowed the liquid to touch her lips.

Calverstock was chatting quite amiably with the vicar, whose fawning manner Hero had never noticed before. His living was in the gift of her father and she knew Cudlip would do anything to please him, but he had no need to curry favour with the earl. Except, she supposed bitterly, that he might hope to be well paid for conducting the wedding at such short notice. But, dear lord, they were actually laughing together over some stupid joke of the vicar's as though nothing in the world were wrong!

The stifling room had become overpoweringly hot. Hero moved towards the open window, seeking air and solitude in which to recover her composure. She became aware that the earl had come to join her.

'It will be a long journey tomorrow,' he informed her formally, as though he had never laughed in his life, 'for I do not wish to make more than one overnight stop. Have your maid pack a small bag with the things you will need at the inn.'

Hero nodded, the merest acknowledgement of his words.

'Then I will take my leave, ma'am. I engage to be here at six tomorrow.'

Realising he would receive no further word from his bride, Calverstock turned to her father.

'I will take the horses now, Polhembury. Two hunters and a useful road horse, as agreed.'

'You drive a hard bargain, Calverstock,' muttered the baron with renewed hostility. 'They are all prime cattle, and you leave me with but a broken-down hack. But,' he waved a petulant hand, 'they are yours. Do with them what you will. Good day to you, my lord.'

Hero noted bitterly that the loss of his precious

horses seemed to distress her father rather more than the prospect of losing her.

Calverstock addressed the entire company with a supremely elegant bow and left, his man following closely upon his heels. If the earl noticed the vicar's bemused expression he made no sign.

'I must be on my way too,' murmured that gentleman, at last perceiving that all might not be quite well. 'I wish you happy, Lady Calverstock. Mrs Cudlip sends her felicitations and trusts she will have the pleasure of seeing you when next you visit Polhembury.'

'I do so regret that I shall be unable to bid her goodbye. I should account it prodigiously kind of you if you would return this book to her?' Hero had just remembered the collection of Lord Byron's verses she had been reading only yesterday. It seemed an age ago, when she had been a different person. She picked up the volume from the table on which it lay and handed it to the vicar. 'Tell her I shall write.'

Alone with her father at last, Hero turned to him with a resigned, helpless gesture which was yet full of outraged hurt.

'You see what a fine mess you have landed me in, Papa? What possessed you to play with Calverstock and allow him to fleece you of money you did not have?'

'I did not, daughter. Oh, yes, I play deep when I visit London but have the sense never to engage in a ruinous contest with a single opponent. I own to several large debts of honour and had run up the usual tradesmen's bills, my tailor and so on. And it costs a great deal to keep this place going,' he added self-righteously.

'We have been living in penury for years,' snapped Hero. 'You cannot blame the bills here for your journey up the River Tick!'

Polhembury glared back. 'The horses—'

'Were an extravagance,' cut in Hero fiercely. 'How many times have I pleaded with you to sell them? You could not afford to keep such a stable.'

'Well, they are gone now, so I collect that you will be satisfied at last, miss!'

'Madam,' bit back Hero, 'by your own contrivance, Papa!'

'But I owed no one person enough to put me at *point non plus* and it was deuced unlikely that all those to whom I had lost at the gaming tables would decide to call in my debts at the same time,' growled her father. 'I'd have managed if Calverstock had not bought 'em all up, gambling and otherwise. The total staggered even me,' the baron confessed in a more conciliatory tone.

'Calverstock did that?' breathed Hero, her fury rising not against her father now but against her husband. 'And asked for my hand in repayment? Why?'

'I know that no more than you do,' said her father heavily. 'He demanded the money knowing I could not pay and said that if you would wed him he'd save me from a debtors' prison by cancelling my vowels and settling my tradesmen's accounts. God knows why he wanted you but, devil take it, Hero, I'm confoundedly glad he did, for you're no great catch!'

CHAPTER TWO

'I HAVE no objection to travelling to London with His Lordship,' Hero declared later, alone in her room with her maid. 'It is where I intended to go to escape him.'

'But you're wed now, my chick. You can't go running away from your husband,' protested Matty.

'I shall if he drives me to it.'

Matty sucked at her nonexistent front teeth. 'I can see no reason why he should. He seems a nice enough gentleman to me.'

'Matty!' cried Hero in exasperation. 'Don't tell me you have not seen what he has done to my father! Why should he treat me any better?'

'Because you're his wife,' said Matty stubbornly, 'and I do not think he is indifferent to you. If he treats you badly it'll be because you ask for it, Miss Hero—my lady,' she corrected herself quickly.

'He has bamboozled you,' snorted Hero, hiding the tightening of her nerves at Matty's remark and wondering what had induced her maid to make it. For Matty did not know that she and Calverstock had met before, that on that occasion she had sensed his interest to be as great as her own despite the brevity of their encounter. 'Did you not see the way he regarded me?' she demanded, her heart crying out to know what had happened to change his attitude so. 'As though I were beneath contempt!'

'The way you were acting you were,' said Matty

roundly. 'All right, my chick.' She held up a placatory hand as Hero turned on her indignantly. 'I'm not saying you did not have reason according to what you have told me. But the sooner you find out why he did what he did and stop driving yourself into a frenzy, the better.'

Hero was not ready to hear such sound advice. 'I am not in a frenzy!' she denied hotly. 'But after what he has done to my father and the way he treated me, can you wonder that I have taken him in dislike? To him I was no more than a sack of coals to be bargained over! And if you are going to vex me so by taking his side then perhaps it would be preferable for you to remain here.'

'You don't mean that, Miss Hero,' cried Matty, immediately contrite for taking her mistress to task when the child was so upset. 'I was just trying to make you see it would be wise to make the best of the situation, that's all. After all, he is a fine, upstanding-looking gentleman despite his past. His family is an old and respected one. But of course I'm on your side, my chick.' She gave her gappy smile. 'Here, let me brush your hair. That will soothe both of us.'

Under Matty's ministrations Hero began to relax. She was, as she had said, quite willing to accept her new husband's escort to London; she had never been there and would enjoy seeing the capital. What gave her unease and a certain *frisson* of fearful excitement was what might happen when they reached the inn where they were to lie overnight. He had not pressed his claims on her immediately. Would he be so forbearing tomorrow? And the night after, in his London residence? He had regarded her with disdain but there had been something in his expression which echoed the admiration she had seen in his eyes in the village. Only, admiration had changed to a cool, rather derisive assessment of her charms. The scrutiny had proved every bit as offensive as she had anticipated but she had been too shocked, too overcome by the treatment meted out to her father, to answer him in similar coin.

Now, as she sightlessly contemplated her own reflection as Matty stroked the brush through her crackling waves, she acknowledged that she had had no need to examine his face or figure. Both were indelibly imprinted on her mind. And even at his most chillingly austere, despite the detestation in which she now held him, his hard features and commanding presence had the power to excite her in the most extraordinary way.

Long after she was tucked up in bed Hero could hear Matty rustling about packing the few things she intended to take with her. Most of her clothes were too old and worn to be much use but she must have something to change into. In London, perhaps, she would be able to ride again, so she had told Matty to pack the green velvet habit, unused since her much-loved mare had been sold, together with the carriage horses and the carriage itself, since the baron considered them unnecessary to his own pleasures.

He had kept the two fine hunters Calverstock had now claimed in order both to hunt and to race them; the road horse to journey to local friends and acquaintances, and the hack for the groom to ride. None was trained to a lady's side-saddle. Hence, unless she could beg a lift or cared to ride on the carrier's cart, for the past few years Hero had been unable to travel further than she could walk.

But now, she supposed, she would have a carriage at her disposal and no doubt a dress allowance. The prospect held a certain charm. She would, she decided, as the maid at length pinched out the last candle and retired to her own room, take Matty's advice, make the most of her new circumstances and use her allowance to help her father if she could. And ignore her husband as far as possible.

On this comforting note she finally slept, to be awakened, it seemed, mere moments later.

''Tis time you were up if you are not to keep his lordship waiting,' Matty told her as she set a cup of chocolate on the table by the bed.

'What time is it?' yawned Hero, gathering her wits as fast as she could. His lordship! Her stomach turned a somersault and she was suddenly wide awake. Of course, today she began the journey to London with her new husband.

'Gone five, my chick. I've got your hot water here.'

Hero was up, dressed and ready to leave when she heard the sound of a carriage approaching the door. Six of the clock precisely, she thought with irritation. His lordship was prompt, if nothing else. Had he been tardy she would have been equally provoked, she acknowledged wryly. In her present mood nothing the wreteched creature did was likely to please her.

She rose from the breakfast table, having swallowed no more than a mouthful of bread and butter, which had almost choked her, and went through into the hall.

'I must say goodbye to Papa,' she declared as the boot boy sped to answer the door.

'He should have been down to see you off,' muttered Matty, who looked lined and tired beyond her years that morning. Hero felt a pang of guilt. Matty could not have had above three or four hours' sleep.

'You know he seldom rises before ten unless he is hunting,' she retorted, hiding her deep disappointment that her father had made no effort to see her off. News of her departure had reached the outside staff and everyone except her father had gathered in the hall.

'I'll go up and fetch him,' muttered the groom, Ned Tribble, who, when occasion demanded, acted as the baron's man. Her father's valet proper had left a year or so before and he had never replaced him.

'No,' said Hero. 'I'll go.' She had not yet greeted her husband, who, a sidelong glance told her, stood in the doorway blocking the light from outside. The sun had risen to silhouette his figure against its brightness: tall, straight and menacing in its dark immovability. She made a slight inclination of her head in his direction and addressed him formally. 'If you will excuse me, my lord, I must bid my father farewell.'

She did not wait for his answer but mounted the stairs to hurry to her father's room. Receiving no reply to her knock, she opened the door and went in.

Baron Polhembury lay on his bed, fully clothed, snoring. An empty brandy bottle on the floor near his limp, drooping hand betrayed the cause of his insensibility.

Tears rose to Hero's eyes. Perhaps he did care after all and had been unable to face the prospect of her leaving. Or, more likely, she acknowledged cynically, blinking back the signs of her ridiculously sentimental distress, he simply wanted to forget all his troubles. They would surely multiply without her to see to the running of the household. He would be far less comfortable, be unable to ride as he wished, to visit his cronies whenever he liked. Much as he irritated her and had abused his power over her, she discovered that she did still hold him in some affection. As she lifted his flaccid hand and placed it on his chest she determined to send Tribble up to put him to bed.

As she took her leave of Mrs Blackler and Bessy she instructed them to look after the master well in her absence. 'I'll see he's fed, never you fear, Miss Hero,' promised the cook comfortably.

Ned Tribble stood a little apart, dressed in his best, Hero noted. As she moved towards him she detected a certain unease in his manner.

'Goodbye, Ned,' she said and added softly, so that Calverstock should not hear, 'Go up and see to the baron, will you? He needs your help to get to bed.'

Tribble's discomfort grew. 'I'm sorry, miss. . .my lady, but I can't do that. Popping up to fetch him was one thing, but serving him's another, if you'll forgive the presumption, my lady. You see, I'm to travel to Ashworthy with Lord Calverstock's head groom to help deliver the horses there. I work for the earl now, my lady. Lord Polhembury won't need more than the boy to look after the hack and there was no proper job for me here any longer, so I accepted his lordship's offer of employment.'

Hero looked at the man in disbelief. Then she turned to her husband, who had entered the house in her absence upstairs and now stood waiting, none too patiently, she observed.

'You are ready, ma'am?' he enquired icily.

'No,' denied Hero furiously. 'I am not! Not only do you steal *me* from my father but Ned Tribble, too! He was groom and valet to Lord Polhembury. How will he manage without Tribble's services?'

'Well enough, I imagine,' returned Calverstock with an indifferent shrug. 'He no longer needs a groom and valeting was never intended to be part of Tribble's duties. His love is of horses. He will be happier serving in my stables.' He turned to Tribble. 'Once the horses are safely delivered to Gloucestershire, you will proceed to London by mail coach, as we arranged.' As Tribble touched his forelock in acknowledgment of the order, Calverstock addressed Hero again. 'My head groom, Cuthbert, is of more use to me supervising the stables at Ashworthy than in London. I needed another experienced groom and Tribble will suit me perfectly.'

'And you do not care what becomes of my father!' accused Hero angrily.

Calverstock bowed, his expression unreadable. 'As you say, ma'am. Shall we proceed?'

He gestured towards the door. Hero controlled her temper, knowing the staff stood gawping. It would do no good to slap that infuriating face, although she longed to do so. For the moment she was helpless. She was his wife, his chattel, sworn to obey him. And her father was not ill, not incapable. He could pick up the pieces of his life, find a new valet, set the estate to rights, if he wanted to. She just doubted whether, left to himself, her thoughtless, selfish, profligate father would have the determination to succeed. Even with her to chivvy him he had fallen further into idleness and debt.

Instead of giving vent to her feelings in the way she truly wanted, Hero tossed her head, sending the yellow ribbons on her best bonnet dancing. She wore the sprigged muslin again, since it was the only decent dress she possessed and would be cool in the heat of the day. At the moment she had it covered with a pelisse, for the early-morning chill still lingered in the air.

'Come, Matty,' she said, stalking past Calverstock without another glance, twitching her skirt aside as she did so to ensure that it should not touch his immaculately booted leg.

Their meagre luggage was already strapped on the back of the carriage with Calverstock's trunk and his man's bag. The step had been lowered. The earl's man opened the crested door and helped her in, his face still impassive though she detected a hint of disapproval in the downward curve of his mouth. No doubt, like most valets, he resented the intrusion of a wife into his master's life. Her presence was scarcely her fault, thought Hero, and he would have to adjust.

Tribble had joined a man she presumed to be Cuthbert, since the latter was leading a string of horses, one a fine bay gelding, two more obviously for the servants to ride and three she recognised as her father's. To have his own riding horses with him, Calverstock must have been staying somewhere in the neighbourhood, she deduced. Somewhere where he had been able to house his carriage and stable her father's horses as well as his own. But why take Papa's yesterday when today would have done? Simply to rub in the fact of his possession, she imagined. Indignation threatened to overcome her again as she settled into the comfortable, padded interior of the earl's coach and watched the two grooms take cheerful though respectful leave of him.

Matty followed her into the vehicle and silently took her seat beside her. To Hero's surprise and relief Calverstock did not enter the coach to seat himself opposite but climbed up on the box. His man, having closed the door and raised the step, got up beside him. The whip cracked and she heard the earl give the horses the office to start. Presumably he intended to act as gentleman coachman and drive the four post horses himself.

As the carriage moved forward Hero clutched at a strap, hoping Calverstock could manage the four-in-hand. She peered backwards through the window. Cuthbert and Tribble had mounted up ready for their journey. Behind them stood the old house, familiar and beloved in its neglected greyness of stone and slate, the only home she had ever known. A lump formed in her throat as she saw Mrs Blackler and Bessy standing on the step waving and realised that Matty was returning the farewell salute, tears wending a convoluted course down her wrinkled cheeks. Matty had lived at Polhembury Hall for longer than she, for she had come with Lord Polhembury's bride, been nurse to the Polhembury heir, the brother Hero had never known, who had died soon after her own birth. Matty had been the one to whom Hero had run with all her troubles for as long as she could remember. At her mother's death she had been scarce fourteen and had wept out her grief in Matty's arms. Matty's pain must be almost as great as her own, she realised. As the building disappeared round a bend in the overgrown, weed-studded drive she reached out to take Matty's knotted hand in hers.

'It is a wrench,' she said softly, 'but truly, we have both lived there for far too long. We must consider this an adventure.'

'I'm glad to hear you say so, my chick.' Matty sniffed and patted Hero's hand with her free one, then broke away to clutch at the nearest support as the earl wheeled the team out of the gates with such expertise that Hero, clinging to the strap and swaying with the vehicle, began to relax. He did know what he was doing.

During the miles into Exeter, where she guessed he would change the horses, Hero watched the high-banked hedges speed past. Now and again she glimpsed a panorama of the lush, hilly countryside through a gap but more often than not the view was blocked. She could not help wondering when she would next see the familiar scenery. London seemed a world away and Gloucestershire distant enough, with the whole of Somerset to traverse before one reached it.

Despite her brave words to Matty a pang struck through her. She was leaving everything she knew and loved. If only her husband was a man she could admire! Then she might not have felt apprehension, might have eagerly anticipated exploring his establishments and estates instead of already feeling heartily homesick.

Matty was not one to speak much unless encouraged and dozed quietly in her corner, making up for her lost sleep. At least the carriage was well-sprung, thought Hero, glancing at her maid affectionately. Perhaps the journey would prove less trying for Matty than she'd feared. If the elderly woman could sleep for most of the time she would scarcely notice the miles being eaten up under the horses' hooves.

As she had predicted, the horses were changed at the Half Moon in Exeter. Calverstock had sent a groom ahead to arrange for fresh teams to be waiting at post stables along the way. She declined the opportunity to descend and stretch her legs, though she did remove her pelisse, wishing the coach were an open one, for the day promised to become uncomfortably warm for travelling. Matty stirred as ostlers bustled about the coach, hooves clattered on cobbles and the carriage swayed as the new horses were put to.

'We shall swelter in here,' Hero grumbled as they set off after the next brief halt to change the horses. 'I wish his lordship had provided a barouche or a landau.'

'We'd only get smothered in dust,' Matty pointed out. 'I've always heard it said that an open carriage is no good for travelling long distances. If you are too hot we could lower the windows, though, lord knows, that would let in enough dust.'

'Perhaps just a little would be all right,' Hero suggested. 'We can always shut them again. But this is the main London road and doesn't seem quite so dusty as the lanes.'

'Do you know where his lordship intends to spend the night?' asked Matty as she resumed her seat after pushing down the glass in the windows.

Hero shook her head. 'Somewhere like Salisbury, I should think. He is driving the horses hard and wasting no time at the post houses. If we alight to stretch our legs we are off again before we've had a chance to so much as solicit a drink from the waiter!'

'It's all stop and go,' grumbled Matty. 'Besides changing the horses every hour or so there are all the toll gates and barriers to stop us in between. I'd forgotten what it was like to make such a long journey.'

'I never have, so it is all new to me. Still,' Hero remembered, 'it used to take Papa a week to travel to London. Now we shall do it in two days.'

'Aye, the roads and the coaches have improved, there's no disputing that. I remember when I came to Polhembury Hall with your mama. Bumping and lurching all over the place we were, no springs and terrible lumps and ruts all over the road. Couldn't put the horses to more than a walk in those days.'

'But his lordship is able to keep his at a fast trot all the time. It doesn't get dark until late and he will not stop early, I collect.'

Matty sighed and settled back into her corner. 'I hope he will stop for a nuncheon.'

'I could not eat a thing.'

'You haven't eaten more than a morsel since yesterday morning,' chided Matty. 'You'll be making yourself ill, my chick. That won't do you or anyone else any good.'

When they stopped in Axminster in the late morning, she declined his lordship's invitation to join him for refreshment in the inn.

'I will partake of a drink out here and walk a while,' she declared. 'The fresh air will do me more good than sitting in a stuffy inn parlour.'

'I cannot allow my wife to starve herself into a decline,' said Calverstock coolly. 'You will come inside, eat a small meal, relieve your thirst and refresh yourself, ma'am. The next decent inn is some thirty miles distant and we shall not reach it until mid-afternoon.' He held out his hand to help her alight. 'Come; my man, Benbow, is ordering our repast.'

It was a command Hero could not dispute. The inn yard was full of people and she had no wish to make a spectacle of herself. But she ignored the outstretched hand and prepared to descend from the carriage with dignified independence.

Had her skirt not been so unfashionably tight and the cobbles been better laid, all would have been well. As it was Hero's ankle turned on an uneven stone and her skirt prevented her from regaining her balance. She stumbled and would have fallen but for the two strong hands that grasped her and set her on her feet again as though she were a child.

'Did you hurt yourself?'

There was a definite trace of concern in his voice but Hero was too mortified to notice it. 'No!' she snapped, wrenched herself free from a touch which seemed to scorch her bare arms and marched ahead into the inn.

An obsequious landlord showed them into a private parlour. His wife, on Benbow's instructions, was loading the table with cold meat pies, cold chicken, cheese, bread, butter and some fruit tartlets. A flagon of wine and another of lemonade soon followed. Having seen their master and mistress served, Benbow and Matty retired to a corner of the parlour to consume the victuals provided for them.

Hero's initial reluctance to enter the inn had been lost in the interest the incident afforded. She had never passed inside the portals of a hostelry before and she was enthralled by the experience despite the stench of stale beer and the noise coming from the taproom. And truth to tell she was hungry as well as thirsty and privacy to attend to her personal needs would be most welcome. Were it not for the disagreeable presence of her husband she would have enjoyed the novelty immensely.

'You are not finding the journey too uncomfortable, I trust?' enquired Calverstock politely as they began to eat.

'The carriage is most comfortable, as I am certain you are aware, my lord. I did not feel in need of refreshment, apart from a drink.'

'So you said.' He smiled slightly, seeing the relish with which Hero bit into a slice of fresh white bread liberally spread with butter. 'We will lie in Salisbury overnight and be on the road again by seven tomorrow. We may take nuncheon at Basingstoke and should reach my residence in Kensington by seven in the evening.'

Hero inclined her head. 'Thank you for informing me, my lord.'

After that they ate in silence. Hero consumed both chicken and cheese with the new bread spread lavishly with butter and washed it all down with lemonade. Calverstock chose pie followed by cheese and drank deeply of the red wine.

'Would you like coffee?' he asked at length, breaking a silence which had become oppressive.

Hero nodded. 'Yes, please.'

Benbow left to order the drink and while it was being brought Hero excused herself and took Matty to the room set aside for the convenience of ladies. She returned to the coach feeling comfortable and replete.

Somewhere between Axminster and Dorchester, warned by a blast from the guard's horn, Calverstock was compelled to slow down to allow the Exeter mail coach to pass in the opposite direction without hindrance. Hero, her interest aroused, watched the fine-looking vehicle flash past, just managing to glimpse the royal crest in its door. She almost envied the two outside passengers their enjoyment of the fresh air and remarked on how exciting it must be to travel in that way.

'Uncomfortable,' said Matty sourly, speaking from bitter experience. 'And dusty. Especially if you've been up there since last evening.'

'I didn't think of that,' confessed Hero.

They stopped briefly at Dorchester, this time merely for a drink. Hero found herself dozing alongside Matty as Calverstock tooled the carriage across Salisbury Plain. Without hills to tire the horses he made excellent time, lingering at the post stables only to change the team, though late in the afternoon he extended the enforced wait while they again partook of refreshment.

By the time they reached Salisbury that evening Hero was almost too tired to eat. Calverstock sent her straight up to her room with Matty, promising that a tray would follow in half an hour.

Hero wanted to thank him for his consideration but as she looked up into that hard countenance, despite the lines of tiredness she detected about his eyes, brought on no doubt by the strain of driving so far and so fast, the words died upon her lips. Instead, she acknowledged her approval of the arrangement with a curt nod.

'We will breakfast in the parlour before we leave,' he informed her. 'I have ordered it served at six-thirty of the clock. I depend upon you to be ready on time. You will be roused with a cup of chocolate at six. We leave at seven.'

'I shall be ready,' said Hero grimly, uncertain whether to be relieved or offended at his evident reluctance to sample the pleasures of the marriage bed. For her own part, she had no desire so to do, she told herself firmly as she followed mine host's ample wife up the narrow stairs to the room she was to share with Matty.

The next day followed a similar pattern to the one before. Calverstock stopped for refreshment at Basingstoke and Bagshot and crossed to the north bank of the busy, sluggishly flowing Thames at Staines. Hero was glad to stretch her aching limbs on its banks at Brentford and accepted a cup of coffee at the inn before mounting the step into the coach ready to cover the last stages into London.

If her own limbs were so cramped, what agonies must Matty be suffering? Yet the elderly woman had made no complaint as she struggled down from the carriage, assisted by a Calverstock bent on charming her into the sort of devotion offered him by Benbow.

But Hero was really too tired to resent his wiles as she should. The countryside passed by in a blur until the coach reached Kensington on the western outskirts of London. The traffic was heavier here but Calverstock threaded his equipage through the midst of carts, horses, donkeys and pedestrians with assurance and expertise until, having passed an inn called the Halfway House, he suddenly swung through gates already standing open and sped along a sweeping drive to pull up before an imposing mansion. Calverstock House, she soon learned, had been built in Kensington Gore, one of the residences erected there at the end of the previous century, and commanded views over Hyde Park.

Benbow sprang to the horses' heads as the coach drew to a halt beneath the portico, the great double doors opened, footmen hurried down the steps and grooms came running through an archway leading to the stables. Before she knew it Hero was being escorted up to the entrance by her new husband, leaving the bustle of busy footmen and grooms behind. Benbow followed, bringing Matty with him.

Calverstock must have sent word ahead. The staff had gathered in the vast, vaulted hall to greet their returning master and new mistress. The butler stepped forward to greet them.

'Welcome home, my lord,' he murmured with a respectful bow.

'Thank you, Grindley.' A firm hand in the small of her back propelled Hero forward. 'This is my wife, the new Lady Calverstock.'

How could the butler contrive to look both well-fed and complacent yet at the same time austere? wondered Hero, eyeing his expressionless face with some misgiving.

'Good evening, Grindley,' she murmured.

His expression did not change yet a spark of curiosity lit eyes which were by no means hostile. 'Welcome to Calverstock House, my lady. It will be my pleasure to serve your ladyship to the best of my ability.'

Hero's lowered spirits raised a little at this but quickly sank down again as she was confronted by an intimidating woman of mature years, dressed in black from cap to toe, who must be the housekeeper. She curtsied stiffly with a rattle of keys, a bunch of which hung from her waist by a chain. Her badge of office, thought Hero wryly, flaunted like a challenge. But perhaps she was being over-fanciful.

'My dear,' said Calverstock, holding Hero's elbow in a vice-like grip which belied the pleasant mildness of his voice, 'this is Mrs Deacon, my housekeeper. I am sure you will do all in your power to make her ladyship feel at home here in Calverstock House, Mrs Deacon.'

As her eyes left Hero to rest upon her employer, Mrs Deacon's rather grim features relaxed into a smile that softened the set line of her mouth.

'Indeed, my lord. The mistress will not lack for guidance from me.'

'Capital,' said Lord Calverstock inanely, smiling at the woman in a way that Hero could have sworn brought a blush to her sallow cheeks. She supposed Mrs Deacon to be another of his conquests.

Beside the housekeeper stood a small, foreign-looking man wearing a chef's hat, introduced as Monsieur Vodin. His lordship employed a French cook, then. He looked the most friendly of the upper servants, bowing with a flourish and offering her a wide smile of welcome that showed all his yellowed teeth.

'I shall cook like ze dream for you, madame,' he

promised, kissing the tips of his fingers at her in an expansive gesture of intent.

The minions were dismissed. Calverstock instructed Mrs Deacon to take Matty up to the chamber her ladyship would be using so that she could unpack her ladyship's things. Their luggage had already been carried up the superbly carved, winding mahogany stairway by a procession of footmen who had disappeared from view. Hero's threatened headache now held her head in a vice every bit as strong as that with which her husband continued to grip her elbow. He turned to Grindley.

'Have supper brought to the small drawing-room,' he instructed. 'A tray of tea for her ladyship, brandy for me. Come, my dear.'

The grip on her elbow tightened as Calverstock urged Hero towards the staircase. Her feet sank into the luxurious softness of thick pile and for an instant she longed to be treading the threadbare carpet at Polhembury. But a new awareness was growing upon her. An awarness of wealth such as she had never known. She would be a fool to let her grudge against her husband, the provider of all this luxury, spoil her enjoyment of it.

They reached the next floor and Calverstock guided her towards a pair of open doors. The stairs went on up and Hero imagined the bedrooms would be above. He was not taking her there, she decided with relief.

'The main drawing-room,' he announced softly as they entered the huge mirrored and gilded apartment. 'We will use the smaller room leading from it. When I entertain it becomes the card-room.'

It was still light. The open windows overlooked a

long garden in which sweeping, sloping lawns, surrounded by shrubs and flower beds, led the eye out over the southern landscape. Away to the left, behind the stables, lay a walled garden. Immediately beneath the window a terrace led down to a small flower garden laid out with paths and seats. The pungent, flowery perfumes of evening wafted on the air to invade the room, obscuring the odour of the stables, which Hero felt certain would obtrude at certain times. Not that she objected to the clean smell of hay and horse dung. It would remind her of home.

Drew had released her elbow as soon as they entered the smaller room. She stood by the window, inhaled a refreshing breath and turned to her husband.

'This is a most pleasant room,' she acknowledged, 'but I would prefer to seek my own.'

'All in good time,' he returned easily. 'Give Matty a chance to make things ready for you. We shall share the master suite.' As he saw the sudden tightening of her features his voice hardened. 'One of the bedrooms is mine, and so is the dressing-room. You will have the use of the other bedroom and the boudoir. I shall expect to visit you to consummate our union later tonight.'

The words had been spoken in brisk, unemotional tones. Hero swallowed. 'I am very tired.' Surely he would not press his attentions upon her immediately?

He bowed. 'As am I. But supper followed by a hot bath will revive us, I am certain. And I have no wish to delay matters further. This marriage will be a true one, madam, despite its inauspicious beginning.'

CHAPTER THREE

Hero consumed little of the cold dishes Grindley brought to them, all too conscious of the silent man in the chair opposite, who ate with obvious appetite. But she had to admit that two cups of tea did much to remove her headache and later, having excused herself to her formally polite husband, luxuriating in the comparative privacy of her splendid bedroom, she found that the warm bath eased the aches from her limbs.

She sent Matty away to find her own bed as soon as she could, insisting on brushing her own hair.

'You are even more weary than I, Matty. You must be stiff as a board. Call a footman and I will instruct him to order you a bath. You need one every bit as much as I do.'

The young footman looked only slightly put out at this strange request. Matty left her mistress with a chuckle. 'They won't like waiting on a maid, my chick.'

'But they will do it or I'll know the reason why. You are my personal maid, Matty, a lady's maid. You must demand respect from the other servants. Only Mrs Deacon can claim to be above you.'

With Matty gone, Hero brushed desultorily at her hair, despising the shaking of her hands. But how could she expect to be anything else but nervous? He had said he would come to consummate their union and there was no way, short of feigning illness, that she could escape the consequences of her agreement to wed him, however reluctantly it had been given. And pretending to be ill would only serve to delay the inevitable.

The throbbing in her head threatened to return as a dull ache behind her eyes. Anticipation stretched her nerves, clenched her muscles into knots. She had thought that stroking the brush through her hair might relax her but if anything the mild activity was having the opposite effect.

Disgusted with herself, she threw down the brush and sprang up, her slippered feet silent on the deep-piled rug that almost covered the floor as she paced around the room. Paced round the great tester bed with its mahogany canopy, deep feather mattress, snowy linen and lavish silken cover and curtains.

She thought about climing in and trying to go to sleep before her husband came but discarded that idea almost as soon as it occurred to her. She was far too strung up; she'd never be able to lie still, let alone manage to fall asleep.

Why had this happened to her? Why could God not have sent along a rich, kindly gentleman whom she would have been happy, if not delighted, to wed, who would have rescued the baron from his debts because he loved her?

For the hundredth time her eyes strayed to the door through which Calverstock would come. The door which communicated with his dressing-room. On first coming up she had investigated, wondering whether to assert her own preference by locking him out, only to discover that although there was a lock there was no key to turn in it. Just as there was no means by which to fasten the door between the dressing-room, with its many dark oak cupboards, its shaving chair and mirror, and Calverstock's bedroom. All the rooms in the master suite intercommunicated; there was nothing to bar either of them from invading the other's privacy.

Having strained her ears to make sure Benbow was not about, she had peeped in, ready with an excuse should she be wrong and find him there going silently about his business. Someone had been up to light the candles, which added a soft flickering, shadowy glow to the otherwise austere apartment, but to her relief there was no one there. Curious, she had stepped inside, careful to make no sound on the bare, polished boards. His bed was as large as hers and looked as comfortable but whereas her room was decorated in palest pastel spring yellows and greens, with white lace and patterned damask at the windows and a silken bedcover to echo the theme, his was done out in deeper, more sober hues, plain or striped greys and blues, the dark oak of the furniture boldly obtrusive, not softened by drapes like the mahogany in hers. A splash of white marble round the empty fireplace and a pale cream rug by the side of his bed were the only signs of lightness, of softness. A room fit for a man who had no room for weakness in his life, she had concluded, retreating.

Since then she had heard vague sounds coming from beyond that door but, listening attentively, had decided it was only Benbow preparing his master's bath. Calverstock himself had not yet come up.

She could have retreated to her boudoir and waited there but the adjoining room held no attraction for her, being altogether too pinkly fussy, frilly and garish for her taste. The decorations and furnishings there were at odds with those in her bedroom and Hero wondered who had been responsible. The embellishment of her bedroom looked recent and might reflect Calverstock's taste, albeit so different from that to be found in his own room, while that of the boudoir appeared to have been executed on relatively old-fashioned lines.

Arms crossed beneath her breasts, clutching her old cambric peignoir about her, Hero continued to pace. It seemed the only thing to do to ease the strain while waiting for her husband to keep his promise.

Drew sat as long as possible over his brandy. Benbow had his room ready, probably his bath, too, by now. Before long he would be down to warn him that the water was cooling. He sighed. If only things had turned out as he had planned. But those scathing words he'd overheard through Miss Langage's open bedroom window had killed his budding regard, withered forever the eager hopes he'd had of entering into a felicitous alliance. The woman he had chosen to wed evidently had no conception of the ease with which desperate people could find themselves condemned to the horrors of transportation and the possibility, almost certainty, of suffering extreme hardship and cruelty under the Draconian laws regulating their existence in a penal colony. Had he detected one scrap of softness in her voice, had she not gone on to scorn his mother's birth and his own worthiness to inherit the earldom, he would have considered explaining his actions to her. But she was as bad as her father. He should have expected nothing else. As a result of one moment of dazzled weakness he had leg-shackled himself to a selfish, unfeeling woman with whom he could expect to enjoy no true intimacy of communication or understanding.

How could he have been so misled? He had bumped into her and spilled his plums from her basket. They were his plums, he was assured of that, for he had been inspecting the orchard attached to the estate he had recently acquired only hours earlier and seen them hanging on the trees. He had not begrudged her fruit which would otherwise have gone to waste or allowed such a minor offence to dim the instant attraction he had felt for the young woman carrying them. When he'd heard her maid address her as 'Miss Hero', his heart had leapt, for he had realised that the delightful creature must be Lord Polhembury's daughter. The idea of demanding her hand in marriage had sprung into his mind as though by magic. It had seemed such an eminently suitable solution. Baron Polhembury would be left with his estate, though penniless, while he gained the desirable Miss Langage as his wife.

Desirable. Yes. Still desirable despite her contempt. His body craved her so badly that he feared it might betray him into revealing his need. Which explained his present reluctance to do what he most wanted to do—take the distracting creature into his arms and make her his.

He would do it, of course, he had told her so. But first he had to gain complete control over his emotions, for he must take her as coolly as he was certain she would respond to his advances. He must not give the impression that he was making love to her. Not that he felt so inclined, given what he now knew about her.

But in the throes of passion his guard might drop. He might imagine her the creature he had thought her to be, the young woman who had gazed at him with wide, dazed eyes while plums spilled unheeded about her small feet. That girl would have responded. . .

But there could be no profit in indulging in dreams. He had to face reality. He had made his offer on the most slender of evidence and must live with the consequences of his folly.

He drank down the last of the brandy in his glass and stood up, just as Benbow arrived to inform his lordship that his bath was ready.

Hero heard the voices, the splash of water. Her stomach clenched in a tight knot. Not long now. She should get into bed. Be ready for whatever might ensue.

Of one thing she was quite certain. She would give her father's unfeeling persecutor nothing, would not allow him the satisfaction of resisting his demands. Would lie still and endure. She was, of course, almost entirely ignorant of what went on between a man and woman in the marriage bed. Matty, the only woman she could have asked, was a spinster. Mrs Blackler, too, despite her honorary title. Mrs Cudlip must know, but Hero doubted whether she could have broached the subject to the vicar's romantic but genteel wife even had there been time. She took a last glance in the mirror, placed her frilly cotton nightcap over her cascading hair and tied the strings firmly under her chin. Huge, frightened eyes in a white face stared back at her. She tightened her lips impatiently. Why should she be afraid? She was no green girl! After all, every woman who wed endured the attentions of her husband. If they could do it, so could she.

With this determination held firmly in mind, Hero extinguished all but one candle, the one on a table by what she had decided should be his side of the bed, and threw off her peignoir, revealing the cotton nightgown beneath. Her best, with the smocking and embroidery at the shoulders, insisted upon by Matty. Finding nothing further to delay her, Hero at last slid in beneath the covers, pulled them up to her chin and lay rigid, awaiting the advent of her lord and master.

It seemed a long wait while her thudding heart beat out the seconds against her ribs but at last she heard the door handle turn. Her fists clenched and she shut her eyes, not knowing what to expect, afraid of what she would see, reluctant to look at the man who might have embodied all her dreams of a husband had she not discovered his true nature.

His feet brushed across the carpet and stopped by the side of the bed. She heard the rustle of silk, a quick puff of his breath followed by the acrid smell of a smoking wick. The bed sank under his weight, threatening to roll her across to his half. She resisted the movement, clutching the wooden edge of the bed to keep herself in position.

'Well, my dear,' his voice drawled, 'I trust you are not asleep?'

Hero's eyes snapped open. She turned her head to look at the shadowy figure leaning up on one elbow studying her face. He must have known by her breathing that she was not.

'Far from it, my lord,' she answered tartly. 'I have been awaiting your lordship's pleasure this age.'

His hand came out and touched her cheek. 'Did it seem so long?'

Suppressing an involuntary shiver at his touch, Hero jerked her head away. 'Long enough, my lord, after such a journey.'

'Then,' he said softly, 'I must apologise and waste no more time. Come, wife. Since I trust you are virgin I will endeavour to be careful. Believe me, any pain you suffer will be unavoidable.'

'Pain?' choked Hero.

'When I break your maidenhead, my dear.'

Hot shame rushed to Hero's cheeks. How dared he mention such a delicate subject, even to his wife? Even to explain something of which she was ignorant.

'I did not realise your activities would be painful on top of everything else,' she muttered resentfully.

'What else?' he enquired, his voice soft and silky.

Ignoring the warning implicit in his tone, Hero clenched her teeth and spoke through them. 'The indignity,' she informed him fiercely.

'Ah!' The exclamation sounded like a jeer. 'You find it an indignity to be touched by an ex-convict, my lady?' His hand deliberately sought her breast and squeezed it through the fine cotton while his thumb teased her nipple, which immediately hardened, thrusting itself against the pressure with mortifying abandon.

The shock sped down to her vitals. Hero's breath caught in her throat but she made no sound, no movement. She hadn't actually meant the indignity of being touched by a convict but of being in such a situation at all, of being at the mercy of any man apart from one who loved her as she loved him. That must surely make all the difference, she thought wildly as his hands, warm despite the insulating layer of cotton, went to work on her body, stroking, teasing, arousing sensations she distrusted because they were so enjoyable.

Still she lay immobile, tense under his experienced exploration. Even when he lifted her nightgown and found the most secret, unmentionable part of her she made no protest.

'It will hurt the more unless you relax.'

His voice came in her ear as he moved above her. She could feel hot, throbbing flesh against her thigh. Instead of relaxing, she tensed the more.

He did not kiss her. Had not done so once, except for that brief touching of her lips with his after the ceremony. She thought he should, should do something other than thrust himself into her unwilling body so that, despite all her resolution, she did cry out in pain.

He did not apologise, merely grunted. After allowing a moment for her to recover he began to move, swift, sharp, abrasive thrusts which gave her more pain, though now she was able to suppress her cries and endure as she had promised herself.

It was over quite quickly. An extra-hard drive, a few gasping breaths and he rolled aside and from the bed. While Hero watched through eyes glazed with unshed tears he picked up his gown and draped it over one arm instead of putting it on to hide his nakedness. Distraught as she was, dim as was the light, she could still appreciate the splendid proportions of his physique. A fine, upstanding-looking gentleman, Matty had described him. He looked it even unclothed.

'I will see you at breafast, ma'am. I trust you will sleep well. Goodnight.'

Hero had no answer to give him. She turned over on her side and curled herself into a miserable ball.

The tears trickled from her eyes to seep into the pillow. If that was marriage, she wanted no more to do with it. And Matty had been wrong, Calverstock was no gentleman to have treated her in so cavalier a fashion. She never wanted him to touch her again.

The next morning Hero, aching and sore in places she could not mention, decided that she would not present herself downstairs for breakfast but have a tray brought up to her bedroom. She ate scrambled eggs, hot rolls and butter and felt the better for having a full stomach. The previous night's events seemed less gothic in broad daylight, as did the boudoir she had scorned the previous evening.

Even if it did reflect the tastes of a bygone age, it breathed luxury and femininity. Perhaps Drew's grandmother had had it done in accordance with her taste. The pink was not quite so overpowering when seen in the sunlight and much of it was sadly faded. The curtains needed renewing and she could choose delicate stripes to blend in with the brocade of the giltwood cabriole chairs and the matching sofa. The mahogany sofa table, banded with satinwood, was exquisite and the upholstered window seats with high, curving ends looked promising, as did a comfortable *chaise-longue*. Hero wondered why she had taken such a dislike to the room the previous evening. She must have been feeling particularly jaundiced. It could be made her own, a room where she could retire to be private. Calverstock need never enter it, certainly not without her invitation.

Absorbed in plans for the future, all of which excluded the presence of her husband, Hero was interrupted by Matty with a message relayed by a footman.

'His lordship desires your presence in the library, Miss Hero.' She grimaced. 'Footman says immediately.'

'Does he?' muttered Hero, the quick colour staining her cheeks. Defying him would only delay a confrontation which must come sooner or later. 'Very well, I am as ready as I shall ever be, I suppose.'

She had donned the only other dress she had brought with her, an elderly blue muslin much faded from washing. But Matty had done her hair in a stylish chignon and covered it with a pretty cap, one of the late Lady Polhembury's things she had kept tucked away rather than lose all trace of the old mistress she had loved.

'You must wear a cap now you are a matron,' she had told a reluctant Hero, but once the cap was on her head Hero had admitted that it suited her and added dignity to her appearance. A dignity of which, that morning, she felt in need. 'His lordship will expect it,' Matty had added, almost aborting her victory, for the last thing Hero wanted to do was what his lordship expected. However, she had kept it on for her own reasons and now followed the footman down to the library, situated at the rear of the house on the ground floor, secure in the knowledge that the servants, at least, would have no cause to criticise her for appearing without one. They would probably look askance at her gown, though, she thought ruefully. But what couldn't be helped must be endured. Henceforward, that must be her motto.

When she entered Calverstock was sitting behind a huge desk in a room lined with an impressive array of books, except where long windows, partly opened to encourage a cooling draught and framed by tobacco-brown velvet curtains, gave on to the fine prospect she had seen from above. A door opened on to the terrace.

Her husband's polished boots, thrust through the kneehole by his long legs, withdrew from view as he looked up from some document he was studying, sprang to his feet, and moved round to meet her.

'My lady.' He took her hand and bent over it in a graceful manner but his lips failed to touch her skin. Despite this, the touch of his fingers, the warmth of his breath was enough to send a tremor of awareness streaking through Hero. She had hated last night but this morning, waking alone in the bed, reliving the moments when she had shared it with her husband, her mind had skittered between revulsion and a sneaking feeling that had matters between them been different the experience might have been extremely pleasurable.

She dipped a slight curtsy. 'You wished to see me, my lord.'

He stepped back and leant against the edge of his desk, crossing his arms over his chest. That morning he had chosen to wear a brown superfine coat, of much the same shade as the curtains, with buff pantaloons. The lapels of his shot cinnamon-coloured waistcoat framed a snowy neckcloth tied about the high collar of his equally pristine shirt with admirable dexterity.

Benbow knew his job, even if his haunted eyes and large hands did not immediately suggest him to be entirely suited to the position he graced with such an outward show of inscrutable dignity.

But now was not the moment to speculate over the earl's man. Her husband was scanning her person with blatant interest, his expression hovering somewhere between knowing enjoyment as he studied her figure and disparaging amusement as his eyes took in the nature of her apparel.

Hero felt her colour rise in an angry, embarrassed tide. How dared he mortify her so? She smoothed the cotton of her freshly ironed if unfashionable and faded skirt, and met his mocking gaze without flinching.

'My dress displeased you, my lord?' she enquired sweetly. 'I acknowledge that upon your countess it scarcely does your lordship's present noble status justice, but you must accept much of the blame.' One darkish eyebrow rose and she hastened to make her point, not attempting to keep the sarcasm from her voice. 'You should not have wed the daughter of a man you knew to be so far up River Tick.'

The eyebrow descended and he bestowed an amused smile, but not before she had noted the momentary tightening of his lips. He uncrossed his arms and ran a hand through his carefully arranged hair, of a lighter hue than her own mid-brown and laced with tawny streaks. Funny, she thought, eyeing the disarray he had created in his coiffure, that he should have darkish eyebrows and such seductively long, sweeping lashes to frame his grey eyes. The style achieved had suited him but he looked decidedly more human with his hair rumpled. Besides, the gesture revealed that he was not quite so coolly in possession of himself as he would wish her to believe.

But his next words disabused her of any idea that he might be softening towards her.

'You are correct, madam, your present apparel does your new status no justice at all. But it is not beyond my means or capabilities to redress the situation to my own, if not to your, satisfaction. One of London's foremost modistes will wait upon you in your boudoir at eleven. She will bring with her samples of fabrics and a number of sketches from which you may select a suitable wardrobe with which to enter London society. At twelve, a milliner will join you and at twelve-thirty a ladies' shoemaker will attend upon your person. After some refreshment you will descend to the music-room, where, at three of the clock, a master will attempt to teach you the rudiments of dance.'

Hero stared at her husband in disbelief. He had arranged all this without so much as mentioning it, let alone seeking her agreement. She sighed and put the back of a hand to her forehead, allowing her shoulders to droop in artistic fatigue.

'I do not believe I have the energy for so full a programme today,' she uttered in a weak voice. 'I fear these worthy persons will be making a fruitless journey. Perhaps next week. . .'

She let her words trail off and glanced at Drew from beneath fluttering lashes which were neither so long nor so dark as his, curse him. The lines about his mouth deepened ominously and his brows knitted together.

'It is of no use your practising foolish female wiles on me, madam. You appeared perfectly rested when you walked into this room a few moments ago. You will oblige me by adhering to my timetable. By the end of September, a mere six weeks ahead, my wife must be fitted to move in London society. Meanwhile, since there are still a number of my acquiaintances in residence here, you will exchange cards and morning calls. You will,' he insisted, his voice grim, 'take your place as my countess, accompany me to any function I wish to attend and entertain as necessary. Is that clear?'

Hero dropped her languid pose, straightened her shoulders and lifted a defiant chin. 'Perfectly, my lord. But I would remind you that, although I have sworn to obey you as my husband, I am neither slave nor convict labour and refuse to be treated as such. Do I make *myself* clear?'

'Indeed, madam.' His voice took on a harsher note. 'You will be neither flogged nor condemned to solitary confinement in a scorching tin shed.'

Hero's eyes widened with shock. 'Were you. . .?'

'No, ma'am. I managed to avoid such barbaric treatment. Benbow was not so fortunate.'

'Benbow?'

Drew inclined his head. 'Benbow was transported, too. He rebelled against the conditions a cruel master imposed and suffered the consequences.'

'Oh,' said Hero flatly. There were some things, she found, that she would rather not know. 'Very well, my lord. I will allow these tradespeople to attend me. And I will do my best to learn to dance, if that is your pleasure.' She did not think it necessary to tell his lordship that she could dance quite adequately despite the lack of society in Devon. The vicar's wife had been only too happy to teach her the steps she had been used to perform before her marriage. Nor did she choose to inform him that she could play the pianoforte and had an adequate voice. A small devil seemed to be driving her. 'Do you wish me to take music lessons?' she enquired. 'And mayhap a singing master would not come amiss.'

'Later, perhaps,' said Calverstock. 'You cannot be expected to learn everything at once. But dancing is an essential social skill.'

The devil in her made Hero give an awkward curtsy before leaving the room. His frown seemed to her like a reward. 'I must go and make myself ready,' she said, backing towards the door. 'I will bid you good-day for the present.'

'We will meet for dinner,' said Drew, returning her inept curtsy with an elegant bow. 'Mrs Deacon will have ordered it served at six of the clock.'

Hero frowned and stayed her departure. 'I am used to ordering my father's household at Polhembury,' she said.

'I am certain Mrs Deacon will take note of your wishes, my dear. I will instruct her to wait upon you tomorrow morning. But she is an excellent housekeeper; I could not wish for better. You will have much to occupy your time here. There is no need for you to concern yourself with the running of this establishment.'

Now it was Hero's lips which compressed into a tight line. She was not to be allowed to interfere in the daily running of his life. So be it. But she must make the housekeeper understand that her wishes, as well as Calverstock's, must be obeyed.

She inclined her head. 'She may wait upon me in the morning-room at eleven,' she said, turned about, and swept out.

Drew watched her straight back disappear and the door close. Only then did he move. Wearily. And sighed. What a disaster. And yet he still wanted her, had even thought for a moment last night that she might respond to him as he might wish. But, just as he had set himself to keep his emotions under control, so she had quite clearly determined to allow him his rights and nothing more. But she had been virgin, with no experience to draw upon and so had not understood the instinctive response he had elicited from her body, had tensed up and made the entire act difficult and painful.

He could not, in all honesty, blame her. Perhaps, when she had had time to adjust to her new life, to her status as his wife, things might change. Upon his return from Australia it had been devilishly difficult for him to come to terms with a civilised existence, let alone life as a member of the *ton*, but he had done it. So would she, he assured himself with sudden confidence. She had spirit and grace, despite that absurd curtsy she had given him. An unwilling smile tugged at the corners of his mouth. She had been determined to overcome any embarrassment she might have been feeling and to give as good as she got. He had to admire her for that. Perhaps, one day, he would be able to resurrect that lively, delightful young woman he had met in Polhembury village. She must be buried somewhere inside the new Countess of Calverstock. Just as the true Drew Challoner, gentleman, grandson of an earl, had lain buried inside Drew Challoner the convict for all those years, waiting his chance to emerge.

She had been shaken by his mention of the treatment Benbow had endured. Most people back home had no idea of the harsh conditions experienced by those transported to the other side of the world. Certainly, there were hardened criminals among them, men and women who deserved severe punishment, pickpockets and thieves who were a menace to honest folk and needed to be isolated from decent society. But most, he had soon found, were bewildered petty offenders unable to understand why they had been condemned to spend weeks in stinking hulks moored off Portsmouth, with iron weighing a stone riveted to an ankle, awaiting passage to Botany Bay or Sydney. Or why they should be chained together and daily made to shuffle through the town, a spectacle to all observers, to work in the dockyard. That, for him, had been hardest of all to bear. Like him, all most had done was try to feed their loved ones and to survive.

His mind shied away from the memory of the seemingly endless days at sea, chained four to a six-foot-square bunk in a fetid hold, most suffering agonies of seasickness, dosed with lemon or lime juice on doctor's orders but only allowed to see daylight, to breathe fresh air, to take exercise, for an hour here and there. It had taken them over three months to make the traumatic voyage. More than a few had not survived.

A tap on the door came as a welcome interruption to his unpleasant memories. A footman entered at his command to announce the arrival of Viscount Harrington.

'Archie!' he exclaimed. 'My dear fellow, I cannot tell you how glad I am to see you!'

CHAPTER FOUR

HARRINGTON entered the library, a smile of greeting on his pleasant but unremarkable face. Dressed, like Calverstock, in the height of fashion while managing not to appear dandified, he had nevertheless developed a languor of manner which amused Drew, who had no time for false airs and graces when applied to himself.

'Mornin', Drew. Saw the knocker back on your door. Everythin' go according to plan?'

Drew waved his visitor into one of the deep armchairs by the screened Adam fireplace and sank down in the other. He and Harrington had met by chance while riding in Hyde Park and found themselves in immediate rapport despite the difference in their circumstances. Archie Dalmead, a couple of years younger than Drew at almost eight-and-twenty, was still dependent upon an allowance from his father, Earl Dalmead, and would be until such time as he inherited the title. He had done much to help Drew to acquire the town bronze necessary for him to move easily in society.

Benbow and Harrington were his only confidants in the enterprise he had set himself. He looked across at his friend's expectant face and shrugged. 'More or less.'

With a well-kept nail, Archie flicked a speck of dust from his maroon sleeve. 'Do I collect that somethin' went wrong?'

'Yes and no.'

Archie's black brows rose over deceptively sleepy blue eyes. 'Bein' uncommon reticent, ain't 'ee, m'dear fellow?'

Drew laughed, though without humour. 'I suppose I am. I found my newly acquired estate of Wanleat in precisely the neglected state I imagined it would be, given the empty state of its late owner's pockets and the fact that he hadn't honoured the place with his presence for years. My stay there was primitive to say the least and it took Cuthbert all his time to keep the horses comfortable in almost derelict stables. Polhembury was in slightly better case thanks to the daughter, who had done her best to keep the place going.' For a moment he allowed his mind to dwell on the poverty Hero had been unable to hide. The faded elegance, the old, gleaming wood. The pride with which she had faced him in her outmoded gown. 'I married her,' he added abruptly.

A look of complete incredulity spread over Archie's face. 'You what?' he uttered faintly.

With a grim smile, Calverstock repeated his words. 'I married her.'

'You're leg-shackled?' demanded Archie, displaying such an anguished aversion to the very idea that Calverstock had to laugh, this time in genuine amusement.

'It did not seem such a bad notion—she is attractive, well enough born and I need a wife.'

'But her papa ain't a feather to fly with and it is common tattle she ain't in possession of a dowry,' frowned Archie. 'When you left here you had no such notion in mind.' He waved an expressive hand. 'We were agreed that even if she weren't a complete antidote, Miss Langage's chances of makin' any kind of a decent match were slender. We even wondered what the poor creature would do when you took possession of Polhembury!' He eyed his silent, pensive friend and comprehension dawned. 'I vow you're too devilish soft-hearted, Drew! You wed her because you felt sorry for her! You could have married any chit you liked, secured a sizeable settlement—'

'But I don't need more money,' pointed out Drew, shrugging. 'Polhembury will come to her upon her father's death. I shall secure the estate, but somewhat later than I had envisaged. And I'm not addle-brained enough to wed someone unsuitable out of mere pity, you should know me better than that. I now have a wife to grace my table—and my bed,' he added, with perhaps a little more grimness in his tone than he had intended.

Archie was quick to spot it and darted Drew a look which belied his indolent manner. 'Everythin' not quite right in that department, eh?' His only answer being an incomprehensible grunt, he went on, 'Well, there's always the beauteous Alicia. What d'you intend to do about her? Does she know?'

'No. And I haven't made up my mind,' admitted Drew sombrely. But courtesy demanded he warn her before the announcement appeared in the papers tomorrow. He'd have to call on her later in the day. When he had conceived the idea of marrying Hero Langage, part of the attraction had been the prospect of nullifying the need to continue the liaison with Alicia. Now, with his wife so obdurate, so unwilling to accommodate him, he was having second thoughts, for he would not plead and last night's experience had been more torture than pleasure. Alicia, Lady Willoughby, although approaching forty years and therefore ten years his senior, satisfied his needs with generosity. Sir Arthur, her elderly husband, was complaisant, since she had already provided him with two sons to secure the succession to his baronetcy and a daughter to charm his old age.

'Did Miss Langage turn out to be a beauty?' probed Archie. 'If you didn't marry the creature out of pity there must have been somethin' else, though you ain't much given to swoonin' over a pretty face...'

Drew stirred uneasily, remembering the instant attraction he had felt, the grinding disappointment on discovering her true nature, the desire the mere sight of her aroused in him, a desire he had barely been able to control last night. If he didn't keep away from her he'd be caught in her web, behave like a callow youth, a supplicant for her favours. And that he could never allow.

'No,' he denied abruptly. 'Not a beauty. She has more than beauty. Character.' Even if he had discovered it to be one he could not altogether admire. 'Grace. Spirit.'

Archie grinned. 'I wish I might see this paragon. Must pay me respects to your wife, y'know.'

'All in good time,' promised Calverstock abruptly. 'She is engaged with the dressmaker, milliner and shoemaker this morning. She will be available to receive callers in a day or two. She had no clothes fit to be worn.'

Archie pulled a face. 'That short of blunt, eh? Poor girl.'

'Yes,' agreed Calverstock. But she had not refined over her fate and sunk into a gloom. Neither the laughing girl he had met in Polhembury nor the scornful creature he had married had appeared as an object of pity.

'Comin' to St James's?' asked Archie idly, his interest in Calverstock's new wife satisfied for the moment.

Drew looked at the papers strewn over his desk, then shrugged. 'I might as well. Brook's or White's?'

Arguing amiably as to which club to visit, the two men left the house to step up into Archie's curricle and tool along Knightsbridge to Piccadilly and St James's Street. Fleetingly, Drew wondered how his wife was faring. He could safely leave her in Madame Ernestine's hands. A foremost modiste, she dressed Alicia. She was, of course, discretion itself. She would never mention the fact that he had paid for several of Lady Willoughby's gowns over the two years she had been his mistress.

Madame Ernestine, small, dark, voluble, dressed entirely in black, took one look at Hero, tut-tutted in dismay and ordered her client to remove her gown. After twenty years in London, having fled the revolution in her own country, unless she became agitated her French accent was slight.

'That is better!' she exclaimed, eyeing Hero's neat figure, scarcely hidden at all beneath her cotton chemise. 'Now I can decide what will suit you, madame.' She eyed her client critically, her bird-like head on one side, her dark eyes bright with enthusiasm. 'You will pay for being dressed well, my lady. I shall make you the sucess of the little season, you will see! His lordship is a generous gentleman. He will not begrudge the cost.'

Hero stood still, Matty hovering near by, rather amused by the antics of the little modiste. It did cross her mind to wonder how Madame Ernestine knew her husband to be generous but decided it would be unwise to dwell upon the subject. Most gentlemen, particuarly unmarried gentlemen, bought gowns for their mistresses. Her father not only gambled to excess but spent lavishly on women, money he did not possess. Calverstock would be no different to any other in his position and—a blush threatened to betray her and she fought it down—he was certainly experienced. He could keep as many mistresses as he liked as long as he did not trouble her again, she told herself fiercely. The mental picture she conjured up of his making love to some unknown woman sent a most peculiar feeling through her. Since it could not possibly be jealousy, it must be disgust.

Madame Ernestine ran a tape over her figure, dictating measurements to her pallid assistant. 'Such lovely proportions!' she enthused. 'Neither too tall nor too short. Good hips—thirty-seven inches——' she muttered in an aside '—an excellent bust—thirty-six—well-covered bones but scarcely any surplus flesh to be hidden, certainly about your waist—twenty-five—and with the new lower waistline that is a great advantage.'

Under such critical yet enthusiastic scrutiny, Hero began to gain confidence. She determined to show Calverstock that she was more than able to carry the role he had assigned to her. She would not sink under the weight of his scorn.

Madame Ernestine had brought swatches, even bolts of material with her, which she spread about over the furniture. It seemed that pale muslins were beginning to go out of fashion except on very young girls, particularly for grand occasions. Certainly, such gowns would be suitable for wearing in the house in summer but, for the evening, gauze over silk or satin was much in fashion, with wider skirts and ribbon trimmings. For mornings her ladyship should consider gowns of various patterned materials in deeper shades which would suit her admirably...

So it went on. And Hero, entranced by the billowing swaths of sumptuous materials despite her annoyance at her husband's uncompromising attitude to her appearance, decided to stop concerning herself over choice or cost, to accept madame's advice and spend lavishly on new day dresses with matching pelisses, several exquisite evening gowns, shawls, cloaks, and a splendid ballgown of glowing amber satin with an overskirt of old-gold gauze.

And a new riding habit. The material, though green, was of a different shade to that of her old one and the style would be modish. Her husband kept a stable of horses. If no suitable lady's mount was numbered among them then he must purchase one. She would most definitely ride as soon as possible.

Hero donned her old gown again with some reluctance, not realising that, despite its age and madame's exclamations of horror, it had a simple charm her new gowns would never equal. Before the modiste had left the milliner arrived. Together the two women decided on a saucy top hat for riding, a number of bonnets and hats which would go with the day dresses, all lavishly trimmed with ribbons, feathers and flowers, and several headdresses for the evening.

'No caps,' decreed the milliner. 'Your hair is too beautiful and you are too young, my lady. I will create becoming confections from ribbons, flowers and beads.'

Gloves, muffs, reticules and fans were discussed. Hero felt her presence to be somewhat unnecessary, except to nod her approval of a purchase. By that time she would have agreed to almost anything they suggested. They were the best in their fields and who was she to argue if they felt that seed-pearls must decorate the bodice of her ballgown, long curling ostrich feathers were essential on a particular hat, or finest carved ivory the only possible material for a fan?

Hero felt rather like a doll being dressed up for the benefit of its owner. Calverstock! she thought grimly. Well, he would soon discover that clothing his wife in the style Madame Ernestine thought suitable cost dearly. She dared not think what the bill would come to. But he had set no limit, given no indication that he cared how much she spent. What use was it to be married to one of the wealthiest men in England if she could not disregard expense? It was a new and rather seductive experience to be able to forget money problems, to purchase anything she fancied. And it would serve Calverstock right if she spent more than he intended.

The others had scarcely left when the shoemaker presented himself, a rotund man who bowed obsequiously, eyed her with approval, and experienced some difficulty in getting down to measure her feet, huffing and puffing as he did so and having to be helped up again by his assistant. She chose shoes in finest kid or morocco, slippers in various shades of satin to match the swatches madame had left with her, riding boots in strong, supple hide.

By the time a small procession of footmen arrived at her boudoir door to serve a light nuncheon, Hero was exhausted. She ate the game soup, cold ham, rolls and butter with good appetite. The dinner hour here was set much later than that to which she was used at Polhembury and if she did not eat now by six she would be starved.

After her meal she stretched out on the pink *chaise-longue* and discovered it to be surprisingly comfortable. The gold was peeling off the woodwork in places and she wondered idly about having it restored before tiredness took over and she dozed.

Matty woke her an hour later.

'There's a Mr Reynolds waiting for you in the music-room,' she told Hero. 'Footman says he's here to give you dancing lessons.'

The outrage in Matty's voice made Hero smile, despite her reluctance to be disturbed. She sat up with sudden energy.

'I was expecting him, Matty, I forgot to say. His lordship informed me that he was coming. He may be able to teach me a few new steps, don't you think? You'd better tidy my hair.'

Matty's expression softened as she fetched a comb and began to tease some loose strands back into position beneath Hero's lacy cap. 'It'll be good to see you dancing and enjoying yourself at last, my chick. With the gowns you've ordered this morning you'll not lack for partners, I'll vow.'

'I can't imagine what Mr Reynolds will think of this gown and my old slippers. But still, they are the best I have for the moment. Maybe I'll be able to surprise him the next time he comes. Madame Ernestine promised that some of the dresses will be delivered within a couple of days.'

Mr Reynolds, a man in his late thirties, badly in need of a new suit of clothes and looking as though a good meal would not come amiss, greeted her with the greatest courtesy. He had brought a young girl of about sixteen with him, his daughter, Hero suspected, to play the pianoforte. She inspected Hero with large, anxious eyes, noted the elderly gown she wore and the quick smile with which Hero greeted them, and visibly relaxed.

'My eldest daughter, Lizzie,' Mr Reynolds introduced her, confirming Hero's suspicions. 'She is a good pianist and keeps excellent time.'

'Capital,' said Hero with another smile especially for the girl. 'Please make yourself at home, Lizzie. Perhaps you would like to try the instrument while your father tells me what he intends.'

'I have been engaged to instruct you in the dance, my lady,' murmured Mr Reynolds as Lizzie dropped a curtsy and made for the music stool. He spoke in cultured tones which indicated a good education and had good address. Perhaps a younger son down on his luck and without the prospect of even a mortgaged estate to inherit, guessed Hero. 'Do you have no experience at all?'

'Some,' she admitted, speaking over the sound of Lizzie's experimental scales, 'although because I have been living in secluded circumstances in a Devon village, my husband assumed that I had not. He failed to enquire before engaging you.'

Disappointment clouded Mr Reynolds's face. Clearly he had been relying on the money to be earned over a lengthy period of tuition. 'I see,' he said.

'I doubt it,' she rejoined, enjoying the prospect of conning Calverstock. 'I am certain I still have much to learn,' she went on encouragingly. 'I have had very little practice. Virtually none in the quadrille or the waltz.'

Relieved, Mr Reynolds beamed. 'Then we will concentrate on those dances, my lady. But first, allow me to join you in some steps from one of the older, more familiar dances.'

An hour later, flushed, happier than she had been for a long time, for she enjoyed dancing, Hero beamed at both Mr Reynolds and his daughter.

'I enjoyed that so much!' she exclaimed. 'Lizzie, you are a most accomplished pianist! I wish I could perform half as well!'

'Should you wish tuition I could recommend...' began Mr Reynolds, but Hero shook her head.

'No, not at the moment at least. I believe I can do well enough.'

She wanted to surprise Calverstock when the occasion presented itself. He had such a poor opinion of her that it would do him good to be proved wrong.

By the time it was needed, the yellow sprigged muslin had been washed, dried and ironed. Changing into it, Hero could not prevent a keen sense of anticipation. In only two days' time she would be able to dine wearing a real evening dress, provided Madame Ernestine kept her promise. Hero could imagine the team of cutters and sempstresses already engaged in producing her gowns, perhaps working late, sewing by the dim light of candles to finish the rush order in time. Older needlewomen often suffered from bad eyesight; it was a hazard of the job. Of course, plenty of other people had difficulty in seeing clearly, even members of the *ton*. But they did not have to rely on their eyes to earn a living and in any case could afford to buy a pair of spectacles should they wish to work or read. Or so Mrs Cudlip, who had connections with the minor nobility, had reliably informed her.

The five-minute gong reverberated throughout the house. Hero drew a deep breath and prepared to walk down to the floor below to meet her husband once again.

The kitchens occupied the semi-basement of the service wing, with store-rooms below. The vast entrance hall and staircase area took up much of the ground floor, though the library was located there, as she had discovered that morning, together with the morning-room and breakfast-parlour, reception-rooms, anterooms and a garden-room where impedimenta and boots were left. The first floor held all the formal rooms, the ballroom, the salon, the withdrawing-rooms, dining-rooms and the music-room.

The top floor housed the master suite at the front of the building and enjoyed an extensive view over Hyde Park and the Serpentine river. Other bedrooms were located at the back of the house and on the far side of the staircase. An empty nursery suite at the far end of the building included a schoolroom and rooms for nurse and governess. Benbow's and Matty's rooms were located near the staircase to be close at hand. All the other servants were quartered above the kitchens in the service wing, where the upper servants had their own sitting-rooms.

Hero had not yet inspected her new home in detail. Her information had come through Matty. Tomorrow, she determined, Mrs Deacon would show her around the domain she ruled, whether she wanted to or not. She, Hero, was the mistress and should be aware of everything the house contained. But things looked in such good order and seemed to run on such smooth wheels that she anticipated, as Calvestock had hinted, that there would be little need for her to exert herself in the ordering of the household. Which might be a pleasant change after the struggle she had had to keep Polhembury in even half-decent trim.

Hero descended to the elegant salon adjoining the dining-room, annoyed with herself because her legs felt weak with nerves. Calverstock stood by the window gazing out over the park, a glass in his hand. He turned at her entrance, his gaze appraising and wintry, his lips barely moving in a smile of greeting.

'Madam.' He inclined his head. 'May I pour you a sherry?'

'I would prefer a glass of ratafia if there is any, thank you,' returned Hero. For that evening she wished to keep a clear head, and did not feel the need for false courage.

He made no remark but his lips tightened as he turned to the side-table holding an array of decanters and jugs, and poured a small glass of the almond-flavoured cordial. Perhaps he thought she had asked for it to test the catering efficiency of the housekeeper, though she had not.

He walked back and handed it to her. 'Your ratafia, ma'am. We must not be long. The dinner is ready to serve.'

Hero drank quickly, set her glass down and stood up. 'I am perfectly ready, my lord.'

Drew tossed his own drink down, brandy by its aroma, disposed of his glass, and offered his arm. 'Then let us go in.'

Touching him had such a disastrous effect upon her nerves that Hero wished she could ignore the invitation. But, without showing herself to be completely without conduct, she could not. She therefore allowed her fingers to graze the sleeve of his informal evening coat, scarcely touching him but still aware of the flexed muscles beneath the dark blue cloth.

He was garbed impeccably but not extravagantly, wearing trousers rather than knee breeches for dining at home. He had, in fact, chosen to dress down and a tendril of gratitude threaded its way towards her heart. A more elaborate choice could have made her feel dowdy, have emphasised the poverty of her own attire.

Though they were to dine alone, the table glittered with crystal and silver. They took their places at either end of a table reduced to its minimum length but which still set them some ten feet apart, making conversation, even had they wished to indulge, difficult. Footmen carrying the dishes appeared from a small adjoining servery.

Hero frowned. She judged the kitchen to be below and to one side. She had not observed the food being brought up. It would be stone-cold if it had been waiting in the servery all that time.

The covers were lifted. Hero was offered a choice

between baked trout, roast fowl, and a steaming steak and kidney pudding, together with dishes of fried celery and oyster loaves. She realised she was unexpectedly hungry. The aroma rising from the pudding was irresistible. Having started with a small portion of the trout, she took a large slice of pudding packed with meat and running with thick gravy, and added some celery to her plate.

Drew chose a portion of pudding, too. As Hero sampled it she exclaimed over its delicious taste and its warmth. 'Yet it must have left the kitchen long ago.'

Drew laughed. She liked the sound. It held no hint of scorn, but simply genuine, proud amusement. 'Not so, my lady. After the meal you must take a look in the servery. The food is hoisted up from the kitchen by lift.'

How stupid of her to show her ignorance, thought Hero. Of course, she should have remembered Mrs Cudlip talking of the wonders to be found in the residences of the rich. Calverstock House would be equipped with every amenity, of that she could be certain. Although chamber pots concealed in night tables still abounded in the bedrooms, Hero had been introduced to a water closet which took the waste straight down to a cesspool in the garden. A closet had been put in on each floor, tiered one above the other. Although convenient, they tended to smell and Hero preferred to use her close-stool, which was emptied at frequent intervals.

'I shall be most interested,' she acknowledged, relaxing somewhat and offering a tentative smile. 'I expect to become better acquainted with the amenities

Calverstock House has to offer when Mrs Deacon takes me on a tour of the establishment tomorrow.'

'I trust you will approve. Would you like me to accompany you?'

The offer seemed genuine yet Hero could not imagine he really wanted to traipse about the house on her heels. Besides, she wanted to become acquainted with the housekeeper.

'It is kind of you to offer, but Mrs Deacon might prefer to show me heself,' she pointed out. 'I shall manage perfectly well.'

'I am certain you will.'

His flat tone told her she had, in some way, disappointed him. But that was absurd. She concentrated on her meal, following the pudding with an oyster loaf. The roll had been buttered and crisped in the oven, the oyster fried and tucked inside. It was delicious.

The second course was delivered. Chicken in a cream sauce this time, jugged pigeons and a variety of syllabubs, tarts and pancakes. Drew took some chicken and a spoon of potato pudding but Hero moved straight on to something sweet, choosing a pancake rolled round strawberry jam, which she followed with a raspberry syllabub. Drew finished with anchovy toast.

Wine had been served with each course. Although she had refused the sherry, Hero did accept a glass of wine, which she found both pleasant and stimulating. Perhaps it was that which loosened her tongue.

For when he asked her, politely but casually, how her consultation with Madame Ernestine had gone, she found herself giving a witty account of the little Frenchwoman's antics and a more enthusiastic description of the fabrics and styles than she intended. She had thought to be restrained, off-hand about the luxury being lavished upon her, for his reasons for generosity were not worthy of true appreciation. But something in the atmosphere, some strange contentment at sharing a pleasant tête-à-tête meal with her husband, made her forget her resolution to treat him with the contempt he deserved for ruining her father and claiming her hand as part-payment of the debt.

Drew looked along the length of the polished table, bare now that the cloth had been removed. Above the bowls of fruit and decanter he saw a charming girl in a faded blue gown, saw in her eager, animated face, her suddenly softened manner, the delightful female he had deluded himself into thinking her. If he did not watch himself she would succeed in seducing his senses again. It was the money being lavished upon her she appreciated, not him. He gripped the stem of his glass and sent her an icy stare.

'I trust the account for all this extravagance will not exceed your dress allowance,' he remarked coldly.

Hero's ease slipped abruptly back into tension. 'Allowance?' she enquired. 'What allowance?'

'Did it not occur to you, my lady, that you would receive an allowance? You cannot expect to have your every whim satisfied from my pocket.'

'I will cancel the order, ' said Hero through gritted teeth.

'No.' The denial was final. 'I will not have Madame Ernestine, the milliner or the shoemaker inconvenienced.' He had no intention of preventing her from making a show in society. He intended to be the envy of every blade in London. And scuttle the fond hopes of all the mamas at one go. As well as discourage other bored women, like Alicia, who pursued him with unflagging energy. For the first time the thought of Alicia brought with it a feeling of slight distaste. The interview this afternoon had not been pleasant. Alicia had flown into a jealous fury; then she had begged. He had given her no definite promise for the future and had left without taking her to bed.

Damn the creature he had made his wife! Was she to spoil even that pleasure for him? His voice when he continued sounded harsher than he intended.

'I will meet these first bills in full. But hereafter you will receive a quarterly allowance, which will be available from my bank. You will be issued with a chequebook. I think you will find the sum adequate but I would advise you to keep within it and to spend it wisely.'

'I have learned to do that the hard way,' gritted Hero. All her pleasure in the new gowns, the intimate meal, had disappeared. For a while she had forgotten Calverstock's ruthless nature. It would be a long time before she forgot it again. 'If you will excuse me, I will retire to my room. I have spent a tiring day.'

Calverstock rose as she did, bowed over her hand and wished her goodnight. He did not mention coming to her later.

Hero prayed he would not. Yet she lay for hours wondering whether he would and when she at last heard him come up prepared herself for his invasion of her privacy and her body.

But he did not trouble her. And she was not at all sure whether the tears she shed before falling into a restless sleep were because she was glad or sorry that he had not.

CHAPTER FIVE

THE announcement that a marriage had taken place between the Earl of Calverstock and Miss Hero Langage took the beau monde by storm. Teacups clattered as tongues wagged. No one had seen the new countess and curiosity was high. Before the day was through cards had begun to appear on the tray in the hall of Calverstock House.

Hero remained unaware until late in the afternoon when, her tour of the establishment completed and a satisfactory relationship with Mrs Deacon established, her nuncheon consumed and boredom set in, she descended to the library in search of something to read.

She gave a cursory knock before entering, not expecting to find Calverstock there at that hour, but he was, busy with the papers he had neglected the previous day.

He glanced up and then swiftly rose to his feet as she hesitated in the doorway.

'You wished to see me, ma'am?'

'No—I came to find a book to read, but it is of no consequence.' She half turned as though to go.

He made a sweeping gesture. 'You are at liberty to choose any book you wish. What kind of reading interests you?'

'History, geography—anything. I wish to improve my knowedge,' Hero explained somewhat breathlessly.

Calverstock's unexpected presence had confused her. 'The library at Polhembury was limited for choice. This one looks more promising.'

He nodded. 'It is reasonably extensive. But if you find nothing to your taste here I suggest you join a subscription library or visit Lackington's bookshop in Finsbury Square.' He appeared to hesitate for a moment before indicating copies of various newspapers, which lay on a table near the door, folded open at the announcement he had paid to have inserted. 'Have you read the papers today?'

'No. I did not know they were here.'

'You did not breakfast in the parlour,' he observed, a faint note of censure invading his tone. He had been irritated by her non-appearance. Not that he particularly wished to see her, of course, but her avoidance of him rankled. 'They are first available there. The announcement of our marriage is in them.'

After a startled glance at him Hero looked down to see the paragraph, boldly marked in pencil. She read the short, bald statement of fact and looked up again, her cheeks slightly flushed.

'So the world now knows.'

He acknowledged her statement with a slight bow. 'And in consequence many of those still in town have already left or will shortly be leaving their cards. Once Madame Ernestine has delivered suitable apparel for you we will begin to return the courtesy and make our calls. Everyone is eager to meet my wife.'

'You will accompany me?' asked Hero faintly, not sure whether she wanted him to. She had been nervous of making the necessary morning calls on her own, but his presence at her side could surely do little to diminish her apprehension.

'I think it would be wise.'

'Very well, my lord.'

He waved an expansive hand around the book-lined room. 'Please feel free to make your choice.'

As she moved forward he seated himself again and began to write. Hero remembered that she wished to ask him about the possibility of riding while in London. She cleared her throat.

'Excuse me, my lord, but there is something I wish to ask you.'

He looked up, a slight frown marring his forehead. 'Yes?'

Don't be so idiotish, Hero scolded herself silently as agitation threatened to overcome her. You are only making an enquiry! He cannot eat you! Besides, it was too lowering to acknowledge herself unnerved by the prospect of her husband's displeasure.

'I wished to ask if there is a horse in your stable suitable for me. I have ordered a new habit in the expectation of being able to ride. Exercising on horseback was something I enjoyed at Polhembury until Papa had to sell most of his cattle.'

Calverstock's expression relaxed. He actually smiled and Hero felt her own tension dissolve.

'There is bound to be. I keep a horse trained to a lady's saddle for the use of a possible guest. You may use that until I can find a suitable mount to purchase for you.'

Hero's face glowed. 'Thank you! And. . .may I order a carriage should I wish to go somewhere—Finsbury

Square, for example?' she added quickly, remembering his earlier suggestion about the purchase of books.

He nodded. 'Naturally, my lady. You are my wife. The servants are at your command, the amenities at your disposal. I shall not always be available to accompany you on your social calls.'

'You are most kind,' murmured Hero, and meant it. He seemed in a most accommodating mood. 'I will not disturb you much longer,' she promised. 'It should only take a moment to choose a book.'

'You do not disturb me,' he returned coolly, returning to his letter.

But he did disturb her, thought Hero as she quickly scanned the shelves for a likely title. She was far too aware of his virile frame, of the way his capable hand moved down the sheet, filling it with his bold, decisive script. In the end she chose almost at random, took the book from its shelf and made her retreat.

That evening at dinner conversation flowed more easily. He enquired about her tour of his establishment and she was able to enthuse over the general size, layout, furnishings and convenience of Calverstock House. He looked gratified. 'How did you find Mrs Deacon?' he enquired.

'Efficient but a trifle stiff,' acknowledged Hero. 'I think she imagined I might wish to usurp her authority. I managed to calm her fears. We have agreed that she will present herself for a consultation each morning, immediately after breakfast. She will receive my instructions regarding any entertaining we may do and seems willing to include in the menu any dish I may suggest. Provided, of course, Monsieur Vodin agrees to cook it!'

This she said with a wry grimace which brought a brief smile to Calverstock's lips. 'Inform me should you encounter any difficulty,' he said.

Hero silently decided to ignore that suggestion. She would manage the cook without his help. She went on to inform him of the book she had chosen, an amusing account of a gentleman's travels around England. He asked her when Madame Ernestine hoped to deliver her first gowns.

'Tomorrow,' said Hero. 'She promised both a morning and an evening gown delivered by noon.'

'Then you may tell Mrs Deacon that we shall be entertaining tomorrow evening—a single gentleman,' he added quickly, seeing the consternation on Hero's expressive face. 'My particular friend, Viscount Harrington. He wishes to meet you.'

Hero relaxed again and nodded. 'I will inform her.'

'And now, my lady,' he said as he finished his port. 'Shall we retire to the small drawing-room? I will not linger at the table this evening. I am engaged to attend my club in an hour's time but we may drink tea together before I leave.'

He was, thought Hero, offering a small olive branch. She would not reject it. They might never achieve closeness, even friendship, but if they were to share the same house they could not exist in constant enmity.

Hero descended to dinner the following day endowed with a new confidence. Madame Ernestine had delivered the two simple gowns promised, had brought them herself and insisted upon a fitting before she would allow Hero to appear in them. She had brought tacked-up editions of several of the more elaborate garments, too, and her visit had developed into a full-scale session. Her assistant had made minor alterations to the two finished dresses—a tuck here, an adjustment to a seam there—while the modiste gave more detailed attention to the fit of the other, more complicated designs.

The evening gown Hero wore as she entered the salon to greet her first guest as Calverstock's countess, though simple, suited her to admiration and displayed her figure to advantage. The soft rose-pink silk clung lovingly to her generous bosom before falling in elegant folds to the floor, the colour lending its glow to her creamy shoulders and face. Sprigs of artificial flowers decorated the neckline and hem. Matty had taken care over her hair, which was piled on top of her head, displaying the slender length of her neck. In lieu of a headdress not yet delivered by the milliner, Matty had substituted a bow of dark pink velvet ribbon, the ends of which trailed fetchingly down the back of Hero's head.

The man lounging in a chair talking to Calverstock sprang to his feet as she entered, as did her husband. Their guest was a little shorter than Drew, slim, dark and handsome in an aristocratic way. He looked nice, thought Hero as she braved the scrutiny of his lazy blue eyes and answered the slow smile which spread itself over his face as she approached.

'My dear,' said Calverstock formally, 'allow me to introduce Archie Dalmead, Lord Harrington. Archie, my wife.'

Archie made a most elaborate bow to which Hero responded with a deep curtsy. A graceful one, Drew noted wryly. Seeing her dressed in the manner to which she was entitled, albeit simply, had taken his breath. If he had thought her verging on beauty before, how much more must he admire her looks now. He longed to be able to take her hand without embarrassment, to go to her bed without guilt. Guilt for desperately desiring a woman who despised him.

The emotion had kept him from her since that first night. How could he so debase himself? Yet. . .

Through a haze he heard Archie congratulating him, and responded automatically. The butler offered him another glass of brandy, which he took. He seldom drank deeply, having too much respect for his dignity and a deep desire to keep in possession of keen faculties which had stood him in good stead on many an occasion. Others in the penal colony had chosen to drown their sorrows in any rot-gut they could lay their hands on and here men at the gaming tables indulged freely as they risked their fortunes upon the turn of a card, the fall of the dice. But he had always resisted the urge and had no intention of changing his habits now and certainly not over a woman.

Hero, despite a certain nervousness, enjoyed the evening more than those she had so far spent in London solely in her husband's company. Archie Dalmead, despite his indolent manner, supported an interesting conversation, recounting anecdotes of members of the *ton*, setting the scene for Hero's entry into society. Before the meal was over she felt she already knew many of the people she would be meeting in the next few weeks.

'You'd better keep an eye on this clever, fetchin' countess of yours,' drawled Archie with a mischievous glance at Hero. 'Just the sort to take the beau monde by storm, I'll warrant. Have all the gentlemen about town eatin' out of her hand, I wouldn't be surprised.'

Hero blushed and glanced uncomfortably towards Drew, who eyed her, she thought, disparagingly—no change—before saying in his most top-lofty manner, 'So they may. I anticipate that many men will admire Lady Calverstock once she is introduced into society. But, should my wife be tempted to betray me, when it comes to pistols at dawn I fear no man.'

Hero went cold. She had a dreadful feeling that he meant it.

'I say, old man, doin' it a bit brown, ain't 'ee?' enquired Archie with a lazy grin. 'Wasn't what I meant at all. Just tryin' to pay your delightful wife a compliment, that's all.'

Watching her husband's expression relax, Hero felt a sense of relief. Until that moment she had been truly enjoying herself for the first time since leaving Polhembury. She liked Archie and in his company Drew had behaved more easily towards herself. Not that he had ever shown her other than the outward courtesy good manners demanded, but beneath the surface she had sensed disdain, even anger in his attitude. Perhaps because of his friend's presence he had relaxed that evening and the underlying censure had been muted, as had her resentment towards him. The two men were comfortable in each other's company and she had discovered a side of her husband's character which had previously been hidden from her. With Archie acting as a buffer, a kind of rapport had been established between them. Until that unfortunate turn in the conversation.

But the incident was soon forgotten and the evening

proceeded in a most pleasant manner. The men lingered at the table for a short period while Hero retired to the small drawing-room to await them and the arrival of the tea tray.

Drew's reaction to the merest hint of the possibility of her infidelity had not only chilled, but also amazed her. He did not love her, did not even want her were the last few nights any indication of the depth of his desire, yet he had shown himself ready to demand her fidelity and challenge any man rather than play the cuckold. Yet she was certain he would think nothing of keeping a mistress himself. A gentleman could behave in the most blatantly indiscreet manner and his wife could remonstrate in vain. But let that wife step only slightly out of line and she would be condemned by both husband and society, become an outcast unfit to be received. It did not seem fair.

Not that she had the slightest desire to flirt or dally. Her husband's absence from her bed was welcome. Although. . .his indifference to her charms was inclined to make her feel rejected, and that was not a comfortable state in which to live. In truth, she scarcely knew what she wanted.

But she would give the matter no more thought. Drew had married her for some mysterious reason of his own—he could have ruined her father without insisting on making her his bride. She owed him nothing more than duty demanded. She would otherwise live as she pleased, enjoy the chance to explore London and to attend the routs and balls, the theatre and the opera, perhaps obtain a voucher for Almack's, that pinnacle of acceptance, of which she had heard so much. She would, in fact, make the most of the chance to sample the delights of living in town. After being buried in Polhembury for all her twenty-three years she would enjoy spreading her social wings for once.

Over the next weeks Drew gradually introduced his wife into the society which had, at first, regarded him as an interloper. His manner, but above all his fortune, had soon secured his acceptance. As it would that of his countess.

Most of society had returned to their country estates well before the first of September for the partridge shooting. Many would remain there until after Christmas, even until the start of the next season. But others preferred to return to town in October and arrange routs, dinners and balls before departing again for Christmas. Calverstock escorted Hero to make morning calls on all those currently residing in town and who mattered, and arranged to attend her when the calls were returned. At the fashionable hour he sometimes drove her in the park in his curricle, where she was introduced to yet more of the beau monde. It rather amused Hero to think that she had become part of the procession of smart carriages she had watched from her window.

A couple of weeks after her arrival in town, with her new habit delivered, Hero ordered a mount and groom to meet her next morning for a ride before breakfast. To her surprise and pleasure she was greeted by a beaming Ned Tribble. She had forgotten he was to travel to London to take up the duties of head groom and coachman there. Despite still holding him in some displeasure for leaving her father's employment, she nevertheless felt warmth spread through her at sight of a familiar face.

'How are you, Ned?' she enquired as he gave her a lift to mount.

'I'm fine, miss. . .my lady,' he returned.

He looked fit and healthy, happier than she had seen him for some time.

'The new position suits you, I collect.'

'Indeed it does, my lady. And, no disrespect, but my wages are paid regular.'

Arrested, Hero gazed down into his weatherbeaten, open face. 'They were not paid regularly at Polhembury?'

He flushed beneath his tan. 'No, my lady. I was owed a full year's pay. I couldn't have carried on much longer.'

'You should have applied to me,' said Hero grimly.

Since their steward had been dismissed because the estate could no longer support his salary, at about the same time as her horse had been sold, she had undertaken his duties. She had collected the rents, accepting them from the farmers on quarter days, and from the cottage tenants, visiting them in their homes once a month. She had kept the books of the estate, retaining just enough of the rents she collected to pay the household bills, including the wages, and then handed the remainder to her father. Ned and the boy's remuneration had been included in her careful calculations but she had given the cash to her father and trusted him to pass it on, since the horses were his and the running of the stables the only thing of interest to him. It had been a mistake. She had not believed her father capable of such blatant dishonesty.

And Ben Foster. Had he been driven to steal garden produce because he had not received his wages? If so, why hadn't he told the magistrate?

'I didn't like to complain, my lady,' said Ned awkwardly as he mounted his hack and they began to walk the horses towards Hyde Park Corner.

Probably Ben Foster hadn't liked to tell, either, for fear of retribution should he be acquitted. He would certainly have lost his job and most probably been driven to commit far worse crimes in his efforts to help his family. She wondered where he was and how he was faring in that far-off land. Poor Ben.

'You were too loyal,' she told Tribble, the last of her resentment towards the groom disappearing. Her father had brought Ned's defection upon himself, like so many of the troubles which had resulted in her own unhappy marriage. And now the staff at Polhembury had no one to look after their interests. Were they being paid? A new worry occupied her mind.

She had already written to the vicar's wife, as promised. Now she determined to write again to ask her friend Mrs Cudlip to investigate her father's and the servants' welfare.

She had to wait two weeks for an answer and when it came she did not know whether to be glad or infuriated. Now that she was no longer there to do it, her father had taken to collecting the rents and so far had paid the servants their wages, but as far as Mrs Cudlip could discover he did nothing else. The tenants informed him of their complaints and worries, but the baron did little about them, and he kept Mrs Blackler desperately short of housekeeping money. He paid the wages rather than be deserted, thought Hero bleakly.

Perhaps losing the services of Ned Tribble had taught him a lesson. And she could guess at how her father spent the rest of the money he collected: on brandy, gaming and women, in that order.

The report was not reassuring. She made up her mind to send Mrs Cudlip a draft every quarter to cash at the bank and give to Mrs Blackler to augment the housekeeping and make up any shortfall in the wages should her father fall behind. She felt her solution far from satisfactory but it was all she could do. The worry did not go away.

She rode out most fine mornings, as did Drew, but they never arranged to ride together. On a couple of occasions they met in the park and he turned and accompanied her. On those rare occasions they engaged in an exhilarating canter, to their mutual enjoyment. So far there had been no sign of the new mount he had promised to purchase for her but since the one she rode suited her well this did not trouble her and she did not mention the matter again.

October proved a busy month socially, so Hero should have had little time to feel sorry for herself, yet she did. She was lonely and bored, mainly for lack of anything useful to do, she thought. She had been kept busy at Polhembury, had found no time to repine over her lack of friends, her limited social life. But she had no wish to interfere with Mrs Deacon's smooth running of Calverstock House and possibly cause an upset. So she had nothing to do all day but socialise with people she scarcely knew and did not particularly like and, now that many of the *ton* had returned to London, attend hot, stuffy receptions and routs, listen to indifferent performances on the pianoforte and endure the trilling of those with no pretension to a voice. And feign an interest in all the latest, scandalous *on dit* flying about town.

She now had a score of acquaintances but not a single friend. And she had met no one she wished to cultivate. The ladies appeared so superficial, interested only in gossip and fashion, except for some of the government ministers' wives, like Lady Castlereagh, married to the foreign secretary. But she could scarcely expect to make a friend of her, despite the cordial relations existing between their husbands.

The new wardrobe had been delivered in good time. Drew had called her to the library and spoken harshly, shaking the resultant sheaf of bills under her nose.

'Your extravagance is far worse than I had anticipated. Did you not question the need for all these gowns?' he demanded coldly. 'No less than five evening and ballgowns, several morning gowns and house dresses, two riding habits, numerous walking gowns and pelisses, hats, gloves and headdresses by the dozen, not to mention unlimited underwear and enough shoes and slippers to equip an army—'

Hero cut in acidly, 'I offered to cancel the orders, but you would not hear of it. You instructed me to be guided by Madame Ernestine and the others you had called upon to attend me. They considered the gowns and accessories no more than an adequate wardrobe for someone of my rank.'

'And you did not question the opinions of tradespeople?'

'No, my lord,' said Hero, wide-eyed and innocent. 'Not since you had placed me in their hands. I accepted their advice as being yours and did not question the cost. After all, you are reputedly an exceedingly rich man.'

Drew's normally shapely lips compressed into a thin, straight line of annoyance. The chit had hoist him with his own petard. 'I will, of course, meet these accounts,' he stated haughtily. 'But many a gentleman has been ruined by his wife's extravagance. You will, in future, keep your expenditure within the allowance I promised you.' He turned back to his desk to throw down the bills and retrieve some other documents, which he handed to her. 'Here are the details. You may draw cheques as you please, but the bankers have instructions not to allow you to exceed the sum deposited each quarter.'

Hero glanced down and almost staggered as she read the size of her personal allowance. Just in time she regained her poise. He must know it was far more than she had had at her disposal with all the expenses of Polhembury to meet. But she would not give him the satisfaction of seeing her surprise. Since he was grumbling about her initial expenditure, it must have been immense. A trickle of guilt entered her mind but she forced it out. He had deserved nothing less.

She inclined her head. 'Maintaining my position in society will no doubt be expensive, but now I need merely to augment my wardrobe from time to time and occasionally replace damaged or worn items. This,' she tapped a careless finger on the written sum, 'should prove adequate, I believe.'

The merest twitch softened the severe line of his mouth. She had accepted his generosity with complete poise and calm. Only the faintest tinge of pink in her cheeks had given her surprise away. She was, he thought with admiration, a worthy opponent. A woman he could so easily admire and love.

'I am confident it will,' he said, repressing the urge to take her in his arms but unable to resist a compliment. 'The gowns you chose become you. I have been proud to present you as my wife.'

Hero glanced at him, almost overset by his sudden change of attitude. The gleam of appreciation in his eyes suggested that his initial severity had stemmed from a desire to punish her. In fact she had long suspected that he held some grudge against her, something more than simply the fact that she was her father's daughter. A grudge that had not been there during that first encounter in Polhembury village, although then he had not appreciated who she was. Just as her grudge against him had been absent then, for how could she have known him to be an ex-convict and a man who bought up debts and used his power to ruin his victims?

For her father was not the only peer he had brought to ruination. Despite the favour he had found in many quarters she had discovered one or two ladies who held him in deep disgust for what he had done to someone of their acquaintance. They had not spoken openly, but, knowing what she did of his dealings with her father, she had realised immediately the cause of their disparaging remarks. Yes, she knew why she nursed an underlying resentment against him, although when he behaved as he was behaving now it became hard to sustain. He was such a difficult man to understand. But the cause of his antagonism to her remained obscure. Could it be due to something her father had said or implied?

She wished she knew. Wished they could return to ignorance of each other, return to being the two people who had met as strangers in Polhembury and instantly felt an affinity.

But dreams were for green girls. She swept him a graceful curtsy. 'I am glad you are not altogether displeased with our bargain, my lord. I shall do my utmost to perform my part of it.'

'Capital. We shall deal well enough together, I collect. Perhaps you would like to take a drive in the park?'

'I would account it a pleasure, my lord.'

'Then we will leave in half an hour, if that will suit?'

Hero smiled. 'I shall be ready, sir.'

Only one incident since then had broken the cool truce existing between them.

Shortly afterwards, as she presented herself dressed for an evening's entertainment, Drew had given her coiffure a critical stare. 'You must employ a skilled lady's maid,' he had decreed abruptly. 'Matty is not competent to turn you out in a manner due your station.'

Hero stared at him, dismayed. Did he wish to break her last close link with her past life? And, after so many years of faithful service, what would happen to Matty?'

'Matty knows me and I know her,' she protested. 'I have no desire to change her for a stranger. And there would be nothing for her back at Polhembury without me there.'

Drew threw her an exasperated glance. 'I did not itend to deprive you of Matty's company. But the little season is about to begin and you need to acquire more town polish, my dear. Matty may remain as your companion, if you so desire, but I insist that you employ a woman skilled in the art of dressing someone of your rank. I will advertise tomorrow.'

'In that case, thank you. Matty has been like a mother to me. I could not bear to lose her.'

'I know.'

Relief that Matty was to remain made Hero more complaisant over the appointment of a new maid. She smiled her acknowledgement of his consideration. 'And I may make the final choice?'

'Naturally. All those sent along will be competent. You have only to decide who will be most congenial to you. I shall not interfere.'

They had departed for the evening's entertainment in amity once more.

The dancing classes had proceeded smoothly but it was not until November that she attended her first ball. They had been invited to attend the banquet given at the Guildhall to mark the inauguration of the new lord mayor of the City of London and a ball was to follow. How Drew had come to be invited remained a mystery but he did know Mr Vansittart, the chancellor of the exchequer, and they had attended the Countess Bathurst's drum the previous week. The earl, her husband, was the minister responsible for the colonies and both would be present at the Guildhall. Plenty of official guests had been invited but, for the first time, Hero would be mixing with those men who had made their money rather than inherited it. Perhaps Drew's banker had invited him. The bank must be keen to keep such a wealthy client, whatever his history.

That evening Hero knew she looked her best, resplendent in cream satin trimmed with seed-pearls and with fine gold lace about the neck and sleeves. The elaborately decorated hem, which trailed the floor behind, was designed to be lifted to facilitate the dancing afterwards. Jackson, her new maid, was indeed proficient at her job. Hero's hair, arranged in smooth pleats behind with ringlets about her face, gleamed with health. Jackson, however, refused to place in position the headdress the milliner had created to match the gown.

'I have received instructions from his lordship to leave your head bare, my lady,' she excused herself when Hero commented. 'He wishes you to wear a jewel, I believe.'

'His lordship must, of course, be obeyed,' said Hero, hiding a certain bitterness, for she had thought the confection of gold ribbon and lace became her. She almost decided to challenge the whim of her husband which decreed she must adorn her head according to his dictates, but decided that it really did not matter. It was his overbearing manner which rankled, not what she wore on her head, and her complaint against him could be dealt with at leisure.

At first Matty had watched with jealous eyes as Jackson wrought her transformation, but she had long since accepted her own limitations and found a greater pleasure in her role as Hero's companion. Her duties were lighter, which suited her age and rheumatism, and she, too, had acquired a wardrobe more suited to her new status.

'Enjoy yourself, my chick,' Matty admonished as Hero prepared to descend to join her husband.

As Hero entered the room where he waited, he looked up from his contemplation of his shoe and stood to receive her. She approached swiftly and as she did something stirred in the depths of his eyes. Could it be admiration? Hero hoped so. For the limbo in which they were living irked her. He was meticulous in his attentions when necessary, but for the remainder of the time he disappeared. He dined at home when they entertained, but that was seldom. Otherwise, unless they were invited out, he went to his club, leaving her to share a tray with Matty in her boudoir, for neither of them fancied eating in the stilted atmosphere of the dining-room. Once or twice he had absented himself for two or three days—called away by urgent business out of town, he said, but Hero wondered.

'Congratulations,' he murmured after making his customary bow. 'You look very well. Come here.'

His tone was neither curt nor cold, the instruction an invitation rather than a command. Perhaps, after all, he did not intend to be provoking. Maybe he had a good reason for the order he had given Jackson. If so, then his manner of transmitting it to her left much to be desired.

So Hero complied, though the constriction in her throat brought on by the sight of her husband arrayed in full evening dress threatened to deprive her of breath. His black cutaway coat revealed a narrow margin of white satin waistcoat, a high-collared frilled shirt and cravat tied with Benbow's usual expertise. White satin breeches clung lovingly to his muscular thighs, descending to meet white silk hose held up by ribbon ties fastened by diamond clips which matched the buckles on his black pumps. She had never seen him looking so fine.

He reached behind him to pick up a piece from a jewel box lying open on the table.

'Turn round.'

Hero tore her eyes away from the sparkling stones spilling from his palm and tried to ignore the *frisson* of awareness that ran through her at the touch of his fingers on her nape as he fastened the necklace about her throat. His hands on her shoulders turned her back to face him and she saw that he held another piece of jewellery. He inspected her hair, and smiled. 'This will suit you to admiration,' he decided, placing the gold hoop with its swirls of colour on her head and tucking the ends securely in the folds of her hair. 'These are but two pieces I picked out from among the family heirlooms. The most valuable are set entirely with diamonds but I thought, since your gown was decorated with pearls, this mixture of stones and pearls would suit it best.'

Hero moved to stand before the mirror placed over the mantel. The colours, set in gold in both necklace and tiara, were exquisite, a mixture of aquamarine, amethyst and beryl set off by an interweaving of pearls set in finely wrought gold scrolls. The necklace rested about her throat, the drop at its base nestling into the hollow between her breasts; the tiara framed her face and set off her hair. Both could have been designed for her.

'They are beautiful,' she said, touching the fine workmanship of the heirloom necklace with loving fingers.

Drew's face appeared behind her in the mirror, his

features softened, his eyes smiling and holding a gleam she was unwilling to interpret.

'*You* are beautiful,' he murmured.

'Fustian!' cried Hero turning, blushing with pleasure. 'You are bamming me, sir! I fear I shall never be a beauty.'

'Ah,' he responded quietly, 'but beauty is surely in the eye of the beholder.' He grinned. 'I dare you to call me a liar.'

Embarrassed, not knowing how to deal with this new, flirtatious man she called her husband, Hero giggled. 'You will turn my head, my lord. I think we should depart!'

He immediately offered his arm. 'The carriage awaits you, your ladyship. Let us hope the streets will not be too crowded, or we shall be late.'

CHAPTER SIX

In this amicable mood they descended to the carriage and began the journey into the City of London.

On first passing through the streets of the capital, Hero had been stunned by the number of buildings, the quantity of traffic. Carriages and carts, horses, drays, donkeys and pedestrians jostled for room. Many of the vehicles melted away to make room at the approach of so splendid an equipage as the earl's town chariot, crested and gleaming, drawn by a pair of matched greys, with Tribble and a groom wearing beaver hats on the box and two bewigged and uniformed footmen up behind. For Drew insisted that when she travelled without him she was as well attended as when he accompanied her.

Even with the carriage windows shut, new and unwelcome odours had assailed her nostrils. The rattle of iron wheels on cobbled streets, despite being muffled by the malodorous layer of dung and slime, had threatened to add a headache to a turned stomach the first time she went calling in Mayfair. Although she was by now accustomed to it, she always returned to Kensington Gore thankful that the Calverstock residence had been built in several acres of grounds on the outermost limits of London and overlooking a vast open space where the air was fresh and the noise of traffic too distant to be heard.

The heart of the City was new territory for her. She

therefore peered out of the windows of the carriage regretting November's early advent of darkness, for she could see little. The gas lamps, already lit, supplied only fuzzy pools of muted brilliance because of the mist, which almost completely obscured her view. Buildings lined the streets and the carriage appeared to be moving through a murky canyon filled with ghostly crowds, people who, having earlier watched the lord mayor's procession proceed along the Thames, disembark and drive through the City streets, now hoped to catch a glimpse of the dignitaries arriving for the banquet. Unused to the conditions, afraid of losing his way, Tribble drove carefully.

Despite its being a City rather than a society occasion, plenty of the *ton* attended the function, if the number of crested carriages caught in the crush of vehicles attempting to set their passengers down at the steps of the Guildhall was any indication. Hero found the arrival at functions a tedious business, but nothing had prepared her for the frustrating wait while Tribble edged their coach and pair into the waiting line and inched forward as one after another of the carriages discharged its load.

Arrived at length, they were greeted by the new lord Mayor, Mr Alderman Atkins, and his lady, before being ushered through to the council chamber, where the guests, including members of the government, foreign ambassadors and other dignitaries, many in the livery of famous London guilds, were gathering prior to processing through to dinner.

'Allow me to introduce you to our prime minister, Lord Liverpool,' said Drew, and Hero found herself curtsying to the head of His Majesty's government.

Faces and names flashed past her after that, Lord Bathurst, Lord Sidmouth and Mr Vansittart, all members of the cabinet, among them. She was by now quite used to being introduced to some of the cream of London society and made the appropriate responses without nervousness. Drew entered into a deep conversation with Earl Bathurst, presumably discussing the state of the colonies, leaving Hero to be entertained by Mr Vansittart, the chancellor of the exchequer.

She was not sorry when that gentleman was called away, for, charming as he was, they had no point of contact and making small talk had been difficult for both. Before leaving her he introduced her to the man on whose arm she was to enter for dinner. Mr Rudge, although not currently an Alderman, was an important man in the City and proved to be a round, cheerful draper of middle age, who dealt in woollen materials and was reputed to be vastly rich.

To him she could talk easily about cloth and fashion and he urged her to visit his main emporium, where she could command his personal attention. While they spoke he escorted her on a tour of the paintings hung in the chamber, some of historical interest, others of more contemporary importance. For a rich cit Mr Rudge showed considerable address and an agreeable degree of knowledge of the topics on which he chose to expound.

'Our prosperity depends upon the Navy's mastery of the sea,' he explained when Hero wondered why so many admirals featured among the portraits. 'Without men like Nelson, Howe and Rodney to command and ensure that our shipping lanes are kept open through war and peace, trade would suffer. The City owes them much.'

The pageantry outdoors had been, by all accounts, lavish; indoors high ceremony was maintained. The dining hall itself, Gothic in its architecture, almost defied description. As she went in to take her place, just one of some nine hundred invited guests, Hero marvelled at the brilliant lighting provided by myriad candles and lamps, at the glittering decorations, the livery banners, the lavish table ornamentation, the silver and glass, all displaying the wealth and importance of the City.

They stood while a band slowly led in a procession which included all the ancient symbols of the City's history and power.

Aldermen, sheriffs and judges in full regalia were followed in by the lord mayor in his, which included several heavy chains of office. The mayoress wore court dress, a hooped gown of the last century. Once they had all taken their seats grace was said and the banquet began.

'The men wearing the armour have to be small,' explained Mr Rudge as they took their seats, 'for, although that is King Henry the Fifth's armour, it would fit no one larger. And the City presented the helmet the other knight is wearing to Henry the Seventh. Can you believe, it weighs fourteen pounds?'

Hero tried to imagine such a weight of iron enclosing her head and resting on her shoulders and failed.

'I should not like to have to don it,' she acknowledged with a smile. 'But, if those are full-sized suits of armour, men must have been smaller in those days.'

'Undoubtedly,' put in Drew, sitting opposite with

Mrs Rudge. He smiled encouragingly, obviously pleased with her perception. Hero silently fumed at his condescension.

Mrs Rudge was, she thought when she had recovered from her pique, rather overwhelmed by finding herself partnered by an earl. The pairing had elevated the Rudges from their normal order of precedence. Mr Rudge, secure in his ability, his wealth and his influence, suffered from no such susceptibility.

The dinner was much like others she had attended, although so much larger and more lavish. Each course, the food of superlative quality, was carried in and removed by an army of footmen. Fortunately she was not required to speak much, for the noise level in the hall rose as the meal progressed and to make herself heard she would have been forced to shout. Her partner seemed content to enjoy his food and wine, pausing only to serve her and speak an occasional word of approbation of a dish. Drew gave his attention to Mrs Rudge, who, like her husband, had a well-padded figure, and her colour soon became high. This did not prevent Calverstock from exerting his charm to put her at ease, Hero noted, and he soon had the woman hanging on his every word. Hero did not know whether to admire his manners or feel jealous of the attention being lavished on such a creature. Sharply she caught up her thoughts, reminding herself that how Calverstock behaved to other women was of no consequence to her, none at all.

She was not sorry when toasts were given, for the noise level fell. Once they were over and the speeches made—they seemd never-ending—everyone rose from the tables to make their way through to the splendid ballroom.

Drew immediately claimed the first set of dances. He smiled slightly as he said, 'I must check on the skill of Mr Reynolds in teaching his art.'

'I have enjoyed the lessons,' said Hero truthfully and, unwilling to allow overt discord to obtrude that evening, said no more. He would surely discover for himself that the instruction had been unnecessary. She had known the steps since leaving the schoolroom and made no attempt to appear clumsy or awkward, allowing her natural grace to carry her through the movements with accomplished ease.

If Drew was surprised he made no comment. As the music stopped he made his bow and escorted her back to the chair she had found. He bowed again as he prepared to leave her sitting with Mrs Rudge for company.

'I shall claim you for the first waltz,' he informed her, his eyes intently quizzical. 'I am certain you will not lack for partners, my lady, but I must look to my duty elsewhere.'

'Of course,' assented Hero, strangely forlorn at the idea of his leaving her side.

Drew stood up next with Mrs Rudge, and Mr Rudge claimed Hero's hand. Like so many stout people, the merchant proved light on his feet and perfectly at home with the steps. As, thought Hero, watching her husband and his partner whenever the pattern of the dance allowed, did Mrs Rudge, who, despite her plebeian accent, appeared to be as good-hearted and well-mannered as her husband. Drew, she saw with amusement rather than scorn, was still bathing his partner in soothing, courteous charm. As he would every female he danced with. Even her.

Between dances, Hero chatted with Mrs Rudge and was introduced to some of that lady's friends. Isolated as she had always been from the company of matrons whose husbands were in trade, Hero had never realised how unjustified most of the *ton*'s criticisms of their manners and behaviour was. They did not possess quite the polish of the pampered ladies of the nobility and quite possibly many vulgar, ill-mannered men and women were to be found engaged in trade and commerce, but vulgarity and lack of conduct were to be found in the loftiest circles. Who had not come up against a duchess with appalling table manners, an outspoken countess who put the company to the blush, a duke too high in the instep to notice his inferiors, an earl given to drunken debauchery?

Watching closely, she noted that those members of the government and the *ton* present seemed disposed to mix freely, even intimately, with their hosts. But then, of course, so many of the landed aristocracy had invested in roads and canals and other commerical ventures their forefathers would have disdained. And government depended heavily on the taxes paid by the merchants and financiers. Of course, there would always be those who considered that anyone making money in any way other than through the land was beneath their notice, but times and opportunities were changing and perhaps, eventually, it would be they who were considered strange.

Social revelations were not the only ones to be offered to Hero that evening. Drew came to claim his waltz and she found herself in his arms for the first time since he had consummated their marriage.

She had danced often with Mr Reynolds, perfecting her expertise in the waltz, and being in his arms had not affected her in the least. But the moment Drew laid a hand in the small of her back and took one of hers in his warm clasp, a tide of such self-consciousness overtook her that Hero found herself stumbling over his feet.

'I am sorry,' she mumbled, her face scarlet.

'Do not concern yourself,' murmured Drew. 'You lack practice, that is all.'

No, she didn't, thought Hero desperately. She knew she would be able to dance the waltz faultlessly with any other man. It was being close to Drew that was causing her to perform badly. But he seemed entirely undisturbed.

In truth Drew was regretting the impulse that had made him request the pleasure of a waltz with his wife. For weeks now he had kept his distance, her presence in his house, in a bedroom so close to his own, a constant irritant, a source of unending temptation. He carefully kept the prescribed foot of space between their bodies as they danced but that did little to prevent his desire from rising to an almost disastrous level. He had been a fool to think that he could partner her calmly and assess her ability.

But as his agitation, well-disguised, grew, hers appeared to subside. He found himself guiding an accomplished, feather-light creature among the throng of other dancers. Reynolds must be a miracle-worker unless, as he began to suspect, she had hidden her talent in the face of his admittedly autocratic assumption that she was without any of the finer accomplishments required to move easily in society. He remembered again that purposely awkward curtsy and knew he was correct. Against his will a smile twitched the corner of his mouth. He wanted her, he admired her. She was his wife. Why should he not take her?

The music speeded up, signalling the end of the dance. He drew her close, whirling her into a finishing spin, felt her soft body mould to his. Her nearness intoxicated him and he resolved that tonight he would deny himself no longer but taste again of her sweetness...

As the music died away he smiled down into her flushed face to murmur, 'You confound me, ma'am. I must congratulate you. I have not enjoyed a dance so much this age.'

She was quite out of breath and for an instant he saw an answering lilt tip her lips before she seemed to recollect herself. She stiffened and quickly evaded his encircling arm. Her face lost its animation, became an inscrutable mask.

'Your approval overwhelms me, my lord,' she returned sarcastically. 'We are not entirely without accomplishment or conduct in the country. 'Tis I who should congratulate you. I believe my situation afforded me a superior opportunity to acquire the necessary graces than did yours. Or were you able to find the chance while you were...abroad?'

His face closed up and he answered her with cold civility. 'There is always someone able to play a fiddle while others dance. We made what pleasures we could.'

Hero immediately felt a vast wave of shame engulf

her. She had not meant to taunt him so but his presence was compelling, his nearness so overwhelming that she had been in danger of succumbing to his charm as easily as Mrs Rudge, of allowing him to see that she did not hold him in such abhorrence as she once had. That she would welcome his presence in her bed... So she had reacted badly, had struck out blindly and delivered an unintentionally telling blow.

But she could not apologise as she should or she would give herself away. 'I am certain you did,' she answered stiffly. 'As did we in local Devon society.' Before she had been forced to withdraw from it.

Back at her seat, he bowed. 'I shall be in the card-room should you want me,' he informed her. 'I ordered the carriage for two of the clock. I will return for you then.'

Hero inclined her head. She could not have spoken to save her life. Mrs Rudge saved her from having to do so by chiding Drew on being like all the gentlemen, more inclined to favour the gaming tables than the ballroom.

Drew made some smiling reply and walked away. Hero watched his tall figure for as long as it was in view.

'He is such a charming, fine-looking gentleman,' observed Mrs Rudge chattily. 'On his way to ruin another luckless gamester, I collect. As I said to Mr Rudge, it is difficult to imagine a member of the nobility being transported. I'm sure he did not deserve it. It must have been a mistake.'

She was, of course, probing. Hero had no intention of discussing her husband's past with a self-made merchant's wife, however agreeable. She swallowed and forced herself to speak calmly.

'I know nothing of it, ma'am. I look to the future, not the past.'

'And quite right too, my dear. But Mr Rudge says it don't do to cross a man like him. His experiences have made him a hard man. No mercy on those as owes him money, so he's heard.'

'I really would not know,' said Hero faintly.

'It's the talk of the City,' said Mrs Rudge confidentially. 'He's been the ruination of at least two important men. One of 'em, old Grimshaw, was a justice of the peace, too. Not that many had much room for either of the poor creatures, as they wasn't liked, but still, you can't help feeling some pity for 'em, can you?'

'I didn't know,' murmured Hero, attempting to hide her shame at being wed to a man who showed such lack of compassion. But had she really imagined her father to be the only victim of Calverstock's machinations? She simply hadn't thought about it until gossip forced her to.

'Well, I suppose I shouldn't be gabbling on embarrassing you,' admitted Mrs Rudge with belated finer feeling, 'but there you are, don't take no notice of me. *I* don't hold him any the worse for it. In my opinion a man shouldn't get into debt, not if he can't pay up. Mr Rudge is forever having to sue customers who don't pay their accounts. Think he's made of money, they do, and I'm not denying he has plenty,' she added somewhat smugly, 'but he wouldn't have if he let them get away without paying. Business is business. He don't deal direct with the *ton* if he can help it,' she confided loudly, 'they depend upon their tradesmen for all their fine things yet they take it as an insult if you ask 'em to pay.'

'Yes,' said Hero, bereft of other words.

At that moment an elderly alderman claimed her for a dance. Hero performed the steps automatically, kept a smile fixed on her face and said yes and no in what she hoped were the correct places.

Mrs Rudge's utterances revolved around her distracted mind. Was Calverstock really the dreadful creature he sounded? Was he really ruining one man after another? She had seen and heard him deal with her father. She had no doubt he could be equally ruthless with others. Yet, normally, he appeared to be an essentially honest, amiable man, a charming gentleman still languished over by the younger ladies despite his changed marital status, frowned upon by previously ingratiating mamas but otherwise popular with most in the circles in which he moved. Harrington would surely not consort with him if he thought him in any way dishonest or overly ruthless in his dealings, for Archibald Dalmead was the most chivalrous of creatures. He often hovered near by to rescue her from the attentions of dubious gentlemen and the questions of formidable peeresses when Drew was otherwise engaged. And Mrs Rudge had not sounded censorious. Just curious.

Yet she knew to her cost that her husband could be harsh and unforgiving. He was a puzzle she would dearly like to solve.

She longed to leave the ball before the time Drew had set but refused to be so weak as to seek him out and ask him to take her home. She spent as much time as she reasonably could in the room set aside for the ladies to replenish their toilet. After what seemed a lifetime Drew came to escort her to their carriage.

The dancing was still in full swing as they took their leave of Mr and Mrs Rudge. Hero looked in vain for any hint of censure in their manner towards her husband but could detect none.

'We are sorry you have to leave so early but quite understand, since you have a long journey home,' said Mr Rudge after Drew had expressed their appreciation of the hospitality of the City. The many others to whom they made their parting devoirs appeared quite affable towards him.

If government ministers, members of the *ton* and city gentlemen all accepted his behaviour, why should she feel at odds with him? Because, she realised, his conduct had turned her life upside-down, had unsettled her and made her face realities about her father she would rather not have admitted. And because she did not wish to grow fond of a wolf in sheep's clothing.

In the darkness of the chariot she pressed close into her corner. She did not think she could bear for any part of Drew's body to touch hers. It had been difficult enough to depart the ball on his arm, her fingers all too aware of the living flesh beneath the fine, silky cloth. But Drew, too, had withdrawn, sat close to his side of the carriage. A chilly space separated them. The moment the step was lowered Hero descended quickly and, without waiting for Drew, fled into the house. She wanted no cosy tête-à-tête with her husband and anyway it was far too late.

'I am tired,' she threw behind her as he entered the hall. 'I will retire immediately.'

'As you wish, my dear. I shall not expect to see you at breakfast.'

Since both so often rode early they met in the breakfast parlour afterwards. They spoke little, yet a quiet companionship had developed as both perused the morning papers. Drew could not know how much she had come to cherish those moments of shared interest. Occasionally one or the other would remark on some item of news and a short discussion would ensue. Hero was learning about government and politics, things she had never dreamt of studying in the isolation of Devon. News had come second-hand, for her father was no reader and newspapers were not delivered to the house. Although Drew had not as yet taken his seat in the House of Lords, he evinced a remarkable knowledge of what was transpiring in the country and the world. Small wonder that government ministers were happy to discuss matters with him.

'No,' agreed Hero. 'I shall instruct Jackson not to disturb me until noon. Goodnight, my lord.'

'Sleep well.'

The words floated up the stairs after her. Did she detect a hint of mockery in his tone? He knew very well that the events of the evening had disturbed her. That she was fleeing his presence. That she would probably lie awake most of the remaining hours of the night thinking about him.

What she did not know was that five minutes later Drew left the house again to walk off his frustrations by beating the bounds of his extensive grounds.

She slept eventually but not until the late winter dawn had brought faint grey light to filter round the edges of the window drapes. She woke again, heavy-eyed and listless, just before nuncheon. She instructed Jackson to bring out a simple house dress of dove-grey muslin, over which she wore a fine cashmere shawl to ward off the chill and the draughts. She almost always partook of the light meal in her boudoir, for Drew was seldom at home during the day. Any more than he was in the evenings. With the nuncheon came the news that his lordship had taken his horse to Kent shortly after breakfast, with Benbow in attendance. Jackson had received the news from the butler and been enjoined to convey his lordship's regrets, but he did not know how long his business would keep him away.

Hero's spirits dropped even lower at the news. She should have been glad to know that she did not have to face him again so soon yet instead she felt nothing but disappointment and a sense of being abandoned. Her appetite quite deserted her.

But she really must pull herself together. The low sun cast an alluring brightness over the park and the promise of fresh air drew her. She pushed her food to one side and ordered the barouche brought round. Changed into a warm blue carriage dress and pelisse, wearing a deep-brimmed velvet bonnet over which she tied a silken scarf to protect her ears so that she could drive with the hood down, she descended to join the last of the throng who paraded in Hyde Park at the fashionable hour. Meeting a few acquaintances and exchanging greetings might remove some of the loneliness from her heart.

She drove alone in the carriage, for she could not subject Matty to the rigours of a chilly promenade. Tribble knew her favourite route by now and proceeded at a sedate pace, drawing up beside another carriage the instant she indicated her wish to stop.

'Why, Lady Calverstock!' The greeting came from one of the many matrons with whom she had acquaintance and although this one was a duchess Hero wished her at Jericho, for Duchess Fanny was one of the most determined of the gabble-grinders among the *ton*.

There was nothing she could do to avoid the encounter. Tribble had already reined in the horses in response to the duchess's gesticulations.

'Your grace.' She greeted the woman with a polite inclination of her head. 'I fear we must not linger, or the horses will take a chill in this weather.'

'I will not keep you, my dear Lady Calverstock, but I simply had to ask! Is your husband ill?'

'Ill?' Hero looked as bewildered as she felt. 'Why do you ask?'

'I was in Harley Street this morning, visiting, you know, and I saw the earl coming from a doctor's consulting-rooms there. Or perhaps it is one of your servants who is suffering from some malady? He did have a young woman with him. They appeared well-acquainted.'

'Not that I know of, ma'am.' Hero kept her countenance and control of her voice by sheer will-power. 'I will enquire the moment I return home. But he has said nothing to me.'

'Don't want to worry you, very likely,' said the duchess. 'But I see he ain't driving with you today. I do hope he does not ail. Wish him well for me.'

'I will, ma'am. Thank you for your concern, but I am sure there is a simple explanation. Some lady who fainted in the street, perhaps, whom he felt bound to help.'

'Of course, that is most probably the case,' agreed the duchess, her manner conveying the impression that she did not believe a word of Hero's explanation. 'His man was holding two horses. I should not have worried you, perhaps, for I could have been mistaken—it might not have been Calverstock at all.' That, it was plain, she believed even less.

Hero did not believe it either.

The carriages continued on their ways and Hero ordered Ned to drive straight home. He and the footmen had heard the exchange but all their faces remained expressionless.

As she dismounted from the barouche she addressed Tribble. 'His lordship must have found it necessary to visit Harley Street before he set out for Kent.'

'Yes, ma'am,' said Ned.

The footmen's faces remained impassive.

Of course, she would be the last to know, poor Miss Hero, thought Ned as he drove the carriage back towards the stables. But you couldn't keep secrets from servants. He'd been regaled with all the gossip. His lordship had a number of women he visited on a regular basis. Benbow always accompanied him and clamped his lips together when questioned, only opening them to insist that there was nothing wrong in what his lordship did. But he would volunteer no explanation, so what was everyone to think? And that house in Kent he had most likely gone to visit now. Young Jem had been sent there once with an urgent message. He'd been told not to linger but he'd seen enough. A woman and kids, he reported. This had fuelled gossip for weeks. Perhaps the earl was secretly married! But then he'd arrived home with Miss Hero as his bride. So, unless he was a bigamist, that couldn't be the answer. For all the speculation no one really believed he was up to no good. Just a bit of a libertine, they'd decided with sly smiles. And why not, after the terrible time he'd had in the penal colony? They enjoyed the scandal and didn't blame the master for keeping a number of mistresses. He was generous and they all liked him far too much to want to lose their places. So they were careful with whom they gossiped. Servants who did so outside their own households were likely to end up without a job. Ned and Matty, concerned as they were for Miss Hero, kept their own counsel. Matty, he knew, was far from convinced that what they all suspected was true. His lordship had gained a stout defender in her.

For Hero the next week dragged past. She heard no word from Drew. She continued to ride when the weather allowed, to attend functions to which she was invited and to receive callers, but there was no pleasure in any of it.

Drew had a mistress. There could be no other explanation for what Duchess Fanny had observed. And discreet enquiries had revealed that the doctor he had visited specialised in women's complaints, particularly pregnancy. He had a mistress and she was increasing. That seemed to be the only logical explanation of his presence there. She had heard whispers about his former mistress, Lady Willoughby, of how spiteful she had become now he had dropped her. So it was only to be expected that he would seek satisfaction elsewhere. And this time he had chosen someone from the lower orders, for the duchess had taken the woman for a servant and she would not have been mistaken.

Misery ate at Hero's heart. Why had he not turned to her to satisfy his needs? Because, common sense told her, she had as good as rejected him.

And she'd reject him again! He'd forced her into a marriage doomed to failure, for quite apart from anything else she disliked the life she was expected to lead in London. Oh, it was exciting for a while and her presentation to the Regent at Carlton House in October had been an event she would not have missed. But to live the life for long would soon push her into a fit of the dismals.

She was already in a fit of the dismals. She could not deny it. And Drew's defection was the chief cause.

And then, on the seventeenth of the month, the Queen died and on the Saturday Drew returned to London.

CHAPTER SEVEN

HERO's joy at seeing Drew was quickly swallowed up in resentment at the aggravation he had caused her. She longed to confront him with what the duchess had seen but prudence won. He was back, even seemed a little glad to see her again, judging by the manner in which he greeted her. And the news of Queen Charlotte's death swamped every other consideration.

'Did you ever meet her?' asked Hero of her husband.

He nodded. 'I was presented at a drawing-room soon after my return to this country. Under her guidance the court remained both grand and decorous. She was a most gracious lady and devoted to King George. I doubt he will live long now she is gone,' he added sadly.

'So we shall have a new king. We already have him in all but name.' She sighed. 'I cannot like the Regent and I doubt very much whether he will maintain his mother's high standards.'

'He lives sumptuously and spends lavishly—his debts are huge—but his schemes provide work for many of his subjects, you know. He is an inveterate builder and a great connoisseur of the arts. Think of the men employed on building his palace at Brighton and on the works going on now to build the road to join Carlton House to Portland Place and Marylebone Park.'

'I suppose so. If rumour is correct the park will soon be renamed Regent's Park.'

'The road will be named after him too, no doubt. I know he is unpopular with the people because of the manner in which he treats the Princess of Wales, but he was forced by his position to enter into the dynastic marriage when he had already been through a form of service with the woman he has always loved, Mrs Fitzherbert. She is his true wife and by all accounts the Princess is an impossible woman. I have no great liking for him myself, but he has great charm and will be no better and no worse than many of the men who have sat on the throne of England.'

Hero grimaced. 'Despite their high birth, our kings and queens are all but men and women trying to perform a difficult task. Shall you attend the funeral?'

'That is my intention. Do you wish to accompany me?'

'I had thought I might. The procession will proceed from Kew Palace to Windsor, but not until the second of December. We have time enough to procure mourning. I have already bespoken a suitable gown, since court mourning is ordered. It will be delivered on Monday.'

Drew nodded approval. 'I visited Weston on my way here. Everyone will be wearing black, not just the court, and all entertainments will cease until after the funeral. We shall have a quiet ten days. I shall not be sorry.'

'Nor I.'

'You have been well-entertained during my absence, I trust?'

'Excellently, I thank you. I have been out almost every evening. Matty accompanied me.'

Drew's brows rose. 'As a married woman you scarcely need the services of a chaperone!'

'No, but a congenial companion is of great value. And her presence staved off the worst of the improper advances made to me during your absence.'

Let him make what he liked of that, both a prick of his conscience at deserting her and a reminder that while he chose to absent himself others vied to attract her attention.

For Archie's prediction had been vindicated. She was a success; to her surprise, men did gather round her eager to dance and flirt. And more than one had hinted at their desire for a liaison. Archie stood in for Drew as protection when he could but he was not always available. So she had taken Matty with her and Matty had thoroughly enjoyed herself watching her mistress attract so much attention.

'I cannot understand his lordship,' she had said on one occasion, 'going away and leaving you alone! He should be here with you.'

'He would be,' Hero had rejoined bitterly, 'except that he prefers to be elsewhere. He did not marry me for love, Matty, and there is no use your trying to pretend otherwise. Ours is a marriage of convenience, nothing more. I do not expect him to pay me much attention.'

'Then he's more of a fool than I thought him to be,' Matty had muttered darkly, but had said no more.

But now he was back and frowning at her words. His aristocratic nose lifted and he regarded her down its length. 'Am I to understand that you have suffered annoyance, ma'am? Tell me who has presumed on my absence to trouble you and he will answer to me!'

'Oh, no, my lord,' said Hero hastily. She had momentarily forgotten her husband's possessive streak, though why he should react the way he did when he did not want her himself was beyond her imagination. 'There has been nothing I cannot deal with myself. But Matty's presence was an insurance.'

Drew looked doubtful but pursued the matter no further. 'I see. I will dine here,' he said. 'It looks as though there may be a fog later.'

They spent a reasonably amicable evening together, though his response to Hero's enquiry as to whether his business had been completed satisfactorily brought merely a vague response. He had, it appeared, ridden back from Gloucestershire, not Kent.

'Well enough. I will not regale you with the details. They could be of no possible interest to you.'

His reticence did not surprise her but it did infuriate her. As though she had no claim to any knowledge of his affairs! Again she almost confronted him with the duchess's report but again did not. What did it matter? A wife had to expect such peccadilloes. He was with her now and she had the legal claim to him. The idea came to her to try to cut out his woman—or women. Other men appeared to find her attractive, so it should be possible... But that would be a fool's game. For if he rejected her advances she would never be able to respect herself again.

Drew had been right about the fog. The next day a remarkably thick yellow pall blanketed London. Even in Kensington one could scarcely see one's hand before one's face. Neither Drew nor Hero ventured out in the murk even to attend church, and afterwards were glad, for London had never known so many accidents. People were knocked over at crossings, carriages clashed with each other despite the torches used to guide them and the pickpockets were out in force.

The fog cleared by dawn but there were no routs, suppers, balls or performances for them to attend together during the week of clear weather that followed. Hero saw little of her husband. He dined at his club with Archie while she ate in her boudoir with Matty. He might just as well have remained in Gloucestershire.

On the Wednesday of the funeral they started out early. Carriages had already begun to pass through Kensington on their way to Kew and soon they were caught up in a mass of carriages, horseback riders and pedestrians, all intent on watching the procession start out for Windsor. The Calverstock carriage, with many others, would follow the cortège all the way.

Progress was slow. It took all day to reach the castle and as darkness fell the way was lit by torches held by soldiers lining the route. The flames made their helmets gleam with fire, illuminated the hearse, flickered on every part of the long, solemn procession of coaches and horses bearing all the trappings of death. Both the Calverstocks wore weepers, Hero a black veil over her face, Drew a band with streamers tied round his hat. The coachmen and liveried footmen all wore mourning. For the entire length of the route door knockers were wreathed in black crêpe. And the people lining it, half hidden behind the line of soldiers, had all assumed the same sombre garb. Everyone mourned and many were in tears as they bade farewell to a much respected Queen. It was a state occasion Hero would not forget in a hurry.

At long last they arrived at Windsor and the coffin was carried into the Royal Chapel of St George. The internment took place in the dim light of the vaulted crypt. The Regent and close family and friends followed the coffin down to observe the final committal, as did the prime minister and other statesmen. Hero and Drew remained in the chapel with the bulk of the mourners.

Afterwards refreshments were offered to all the guests. Hero was both thirsty and hungry, since she had eaten nothing since dawn. Drew remained by her side, plying her with food and replenishing her glass with lemonade the moment it became empty. He himself ate well but drank sparingly of the wine.

Then began the long journey back, faster than the funereal pace out but still slow because of the press of traffic. By the time the carriage arrived at Calverstock House in the early hours of Thursday Hero was fast asleep in her corner.

Even the bustle accompanying their arrival failed to wake her. Not until she felt herself being lifted in strong arms did Hero stir, to realise drowsily that it was Calverstock who held her, Calverstock who was carrying her easily up the steps and into the house.

She should, of course, have forced herself awake, demanded to be put down and walked up the stairs to her room. But she was far too comfortable. She could feel the steady beating of Drew's heart against her side and with a sigh of content her arms reached up to wind about his neck as she settled more securely into his embrace.

His heartbeat quickened and began to race as Hero's fingers teased the hair at his nape. She seemed to have no will to stop her seductive caress and why should she, when he had picked her up and his hold was having such a devastating effect upon her? Why, she wondered drowsily, did she always tremble when he touched her? Why did she feel that if she did demand to be put down and attempt to walk to her room her legs would refuse to carry her? Why did she feel so relaxed, so comfortable, so *at home* in her husband's arms? Why, when in fact she despised him for a heartless, manipulating creature incapable of any of the softer feelings, let alone love?

They reached her room before she had even begun to answer her own questions. Both Matty and Jackson were waiting for her though both had obviously been sleeping in chairs and had woken reluctantly. Calverstock took no notice of either but strode straight over to the bed and laid his burden down. He raised Hero's veil and untied the bonnet-ribbons beneath her chin. She saw his fingers shaking, the result of his racing heart. He was not the cool, controlled man of the image he liked to project. He wanted her, wanted her badly, there could be no doubt of that. So she did have the power to rouse him. The surge of jubilation at the realisation of her feminine power brought her fully back to her senses and for a delirious moment she toyed with the idea of seducing him.

But she could not. Could not bring herself to invite his attentions. The memory of that first night, when he had all but forced her to his will, flashed blindingly across her mind. No, she could not. But were he to ask, to woo, to suggest. . .

Then she would become a compliant wife, taste, perhaps, the pleasure other women found in the marriage act. For undoubtedly they did, if not with their husbands then with their lovers. That much she had most assuredly discovered since coming to London.

The scale of the infidelity practised by both men and women in what had become her circle both astonished and disgusted her. To Hero, marriage vows, however reluctantly made, were inviolable. So because she had been forced into this marriage if she did not find pleasure in Drew's arms she would never know the joyous depths of passion that others hinted could be experienced between a man and a woman. This dismal fact was already clear to her. Yet she could never easily allow herself to surrender to him as her body seemed to demand.

The decision was taken from her. Drew sucked in a harsh breath, straightened up and spoke, his expression cold, his voice curt.

'You are tired, my lady. Jackson, undress your mistress immediately. She has had a long and exhausting day. I shall not expect to see you at breakfast, my dear. Goodnight.'

Hero watched him leave with eyes heavy not so much with sleep as some other emotion which, she realised with some dismay, must be longing. If only he had sent the others away and remained with her. But he had not. He could not want her as much as she had imagined. Or as much as she wanted him.

But as Jackson came forward to tend her and Matty bombarded her with questions Hero's main emotion was one of deep disappointment. Quickly followed by equally deep resentment against the man who had caused it.

London burst back into life the next day. People continued to wear mourning but attended the reopened theatres and other entertainments, taking up the social round again with undiminished enthusiasm.

It was during the interval at the threatre the following evening that Hero overheard a conversation from the next box. Drew and Archie, who had accompanied them, had gone to fetch refreshment, leaving her blessedly alone for a few moments. They had closed the door of the box behind them and Hero sat back in the shadows, unwilling to invite intrusion from anyone. The group chattering behind the thin partition must not have realised her presence.

'So Blacklock is ruined,' came an accusing female voice.

'So I hear, my dear. He has been trying to raise money to pay off his debts but of course no one is willing to risk their fortunes to come to such a blackguard's aid.'

'He will lose his estates, I collect.'

'All but the house in Gloucestershire and a few acres, which are entailed to his son,' answered a gentleman Hero assumed to be the lady's husband.

'I feel sorry for Gatby. He does not deserve to lose his inheritance.'

'Sons often suffer for the excesses of their fathers,' responded the male voice grimly.

'Gatby is an effeminate fool. To think he will become a marquis one day! And you surely must not hold Calverstock responsible,' chimed in a much younger female voice. 'Blacklock is an odious man who has squandered the family wealth and in order to restore it is trying to wed his useless son to a fortune, as you must know since he tried to negotiate for my hand. I would never marry a man like Gatby, for I do not believe he likes women. It is my guess he does not wish to take a wife.'

'You would have wed the man had I chosen to order you, miss!' rapped the gentleman.

'But you did not, dearest Papa, and for that I thank you. Blacklock deserved to be brought to ruination. I can feel no sympathy with him at all and very little for Gatby. I admire Calverstock for bringing him down.'

'But who will be next?' demanded the father rhetorically. 'We know nothing of Calverstock except that he has found an unusual way of adding to his own property, which must be extensive by now.'

'I think him a positive benefactor,' declared the young voice firmly. 'I would have had no objection to wedding him had he not chosen that Polhembury girl. Why he did I cannot imagine. It cannot have been a love match, for they are merely polite to each other.'

'You foolish chit!' came the girl's mother's sharp voice. 'To cherish a *tendre* for such a man, and a married man at that! The sooner you are wed yourself the better. You could do worse than young Harrington.'

A silvery laugh rang out. 'Do not worry, Mama, I do not refine over Calverstock! I like Harrington enormously, but it will take a better woman than I to bring him to a declaration! He positively shudders whenever the question of marriage is mentioned!'

'Then he has something in common with Gatby,' observed her father drily.

'Oh, no, Papa.' The young voice sprang quickly to Archie's defence. 'It is not the same at all. Harrington adores women. He is known to keep a mistress. It is simply the thought of being leg-shackled that horrifies him.'

A wistful note had crept into the girl's voice and Hero longed to know who she was. Archie was much sought-after by all the mamas and had long ago learned to evade their scheming and the daughters' lures. But he needed a wife, and the girl sounded as though she had a sensible mind of her own as well as a good dowry.

At that moment the door of the other box opened and a hearty, booming voice rang out.

'What a squeeze! But I have your lemonade, my dear Lady Felicity. I have only spilt a little.'

'Thank you, sir,' came the girl's voice, all animation wiped from it. 'I apologise for sending you on such an onerous errand but I was exceedingly thirsty.'

'Not at all, not at all. Pleasure to serve you, my dear.'

'I believe the curtain is about to go up again. You should return to your seat, Harcourt.'

'Indeed, my lord, so I should. I will return to pay my respects again in the next interval.'

Receiving no response to this, Hero presumed, unwelcome promise, Harcourt departed just as Drew and Archie returned with refreshment, the lamps were dimmed and the curtain went up on the second act.

Hero accepted her lemonade and tried to concentrate on the play but found her thoughts wandering irresistibly back to the conversation she had overheard.

So Calverstock had not deserted his mistress to travel to Gloucestershire to administer his estate, but to ruin another man. Lady Felicity had seemed to admire him for it, but Hero could not convince herself to do the same. She knew, at first hand, how much misery his actions caused. Few people deserved to be pursued in the way Calverstock was hounding his victims. Her father had not been blameless in his dealings but had surely not deserved the harsh punishment Calverstock had administered.

But even as she fulminated over her husband's misdeeds her mind wandered back to the girl in the neighbouring box. Did Archie realise she cherished a *tendre* for him? He must know her. Hero determined to make the girl's acquaintance as soon as possible and the next interval seemed as good a time as any.

As the illumination in the auditorium increased she shot a sideways look at the people occupying the neighbouring box and glimpsed a young woman with fair hair cut to a fashionably short length. Like everyone else, she wore mourning and the black enhanced the fragility of her appearance.

'Are you acquainted with a Lady Felicity, my lord?' Hero enquired as soon as the applause for the second act had died away.

'Lady Felicity Charteris? Of course,' responded Archie airily. 'Daughter of the Earl of Beltinge. Kent, y'know. In the next box, as a matter of fact.'

'So I believe. I heard her mention your name.'

Archie shifted uncomfortably. 'Did she, now?'

'You must have seen her,' put in Drew, glancing

towards the next box and giving her a quizzical look. 'Tall chit, quite a beauty, sizeable dowry. Must have received plenty of offers.'

'But not from you or Harrington, I collect,' said Hero drily.

'Lord, no!' exlaimed Archie with a shudder. But his colour remained high.

Poor Lady Felicity, thought Hero. But Archie, she deduced from his manner, was not entirely indifferent to the lady's charms. With a little assistance from her...

'I should appreciate being presented to the Beltinges,' she informed Drew. 'I liked the sound of Lady Felicity's voice.'

Drew shrugged. 'Now? Why not? You would meet her before long in any case. The family returned to town for the funeral, no doubt.'

'Coming, Lord Harrington?' asked Hero sweetly as she prepared to leave the box on her husband's arm.

'Don't think I will,' muttered Archie. He had risen when Hero had and left the box with them but hurried off in the opposite direction on some unspecified errand.

'He is shy of her,' murmured Hero.

'Shy of any woman who shows an interest in matrimony,' chuckled Drew. 'Archie has a horror of being snared.'

'He has never fallen in love, then.'

Drew did not reply to this remark for he had rapped on the door of the Beltinges' box and a call came for them to enter.

By this time Hero was quite used to the interest she created upon being introduced by Calverstock as his wife. Having overheard so much of the earlier conversation, she was a little embarrassed, watching for any sign of censure in Lord, but particularly Lady, Beltinge's attitude towards her husband. She did detect a certain coldness in the latter, which seemed to disturb Calverstock not one whit. He maintained his most charming manner throughout. Lady Felicity greeted him in a calm, open fashion which greatly appealed to Hero and the smile the girl turned upon her was both appraising and friendly.

'I have been longing to make your acquaintance, my lady,' she told Hero confidentially as the others spoke together. 'The female who could persuade Calverstock to enter into matrimony earns my greatest admiration!'

'My hand was part of a bargain he struck with my father to save him from ruination,' Hero told her honestly, since everyone must suspect as much. 'I gather that both he and his friend, Lord Harrington, had been given up by most mamas long since.'

'Perhaps, now Lord Calverstock is wed, Lord Harrington may come up to scratch,' murmured Felicity.

'He shows little sign at the moment, but I do not despair of him.' returned Hero with a smile. 'Lady Felicity, would you do me the honour of taking tea with me one day? I feel we could become friends. I knew no one in London when I arrived and so far have made only acquaintances.'

'I should be delighted, Lady Calverstock,' cried Felicity, so warmly that Hero could not doubt her sincerity.

'Then let it be soon,' she said, smiling. 'Are you engaged tomorrow?'

'I do not believe so. I must consult Mama.'

It was agreed that Felicity should visit Calverstock House the following afternoon. As the third act was called Drew escorted Hero back to their own box and soon afterwards Archie rejoined them.

Hero scarcely heard a word of the last act. She was too busy planning—what she would say to Calverstock regarding his dealings with people who had fallen into debt, and how she could advance the cause of Lady Felicity Charteris with Lord Harrington.

They arrived home late. Hero went straight to her room, removed her black dress and wrapped herself in a dressing-gown.

'I will see myself to bed, Jackson. I wish to sit up for a while. You may go.'

'Very well my lady.'

Jackson curtsied and left. Matty had already departed for bed, having seen her chick safely home. Hero went through to her boudoir intending to recline on her day bed for a while but after a few moments sprang to her feet and began to pace the floor.

It would be prudent to wait until the morning before tackling Calverstock over the matter of his dubious activities in using his money and position to ruin people but she knew that she would never sleep if she did. She had to get it over with. She had been bottling up her resentment for too long, putting off the moment because she hated the thought of the unpleasantness which must follow. But her discoveries that evening had brought her feelings to the boil and not even the prospect of Felicity's visit the next day could calm them. She must speak with Calverstock now.

He had not come upstairs yet. He was most likely in the library, his favourite haunt while in the house. She would go down and tackle him this instant!

The thought was no sooner formed than she was out of her door and descending the stairs. The servants were all abed apart from Benbow, she supposed, and a boy on duty, dozing by the front door. He did not see her as she flitted across the staircase hall and entered the library without knocking.

Calverstock was there. He had removed his jacket and lay back in a comfortable chair, his newly fashionable closely trousered legs ending in pumps which rested on a brocaded footstool before the leaping flames of a revived fire. Their light gave the snowy sleeves of his shirt a pink tinge while nearby candles illuminated the rumpled waves of his brown hair, turning it almost golden. Hero's heart fluttered in appreciation of the sight of him.

Perhaps he was dozing. It took him an instant to realise that someone had entered the room. When he saw who it was he sat up and rose languidly to his feet. As she advanced towards him Hero saw his eyes lose their sleepy look to focus upon her dishabille. Too late, she realised that she should not have appeared before him so scantily clad. The nerves in her stomach quivered.

But she had not come to admire or dally. She steeled her resolve. 'My lord.' She addressed him coldly, hoping to kill off any sign of ardour before it had time to develop. 'I desire a word with you.'

He bowed slightly. 'Indeed, ma'am, I am at your service. To what purpose do you wish to speak?'

Hero moistened suddenly dry lips. But she had remained silent too long.

'I was forced to wed you for my father's sake, to save him from ruin, and now I must listen to tales of your contemptible behaviour towards others. I wish to make it plain that I find your activities despicable. I had thought my father your only victim but I discover this is not so. That there have been several other persons, even magistrates, brought to the end of their ropes, and that while you were in Gloucestershire last week you bankrupted Lord Blacklock, forcing him to make over all but his entailed lands to you.'

Calverstock's spine stiffened and his expression hardened. 'You judge harshly, ma'am. You know nothing of the circumstances——'

'No circumstances could exonerate you from shame at the way you set out to buy up a man's—or a woman's, for I believe at least one of your victims has been a woman—debts and then demand their property, their very livelihood, in recompense. Shame on you, sir! This is not the behaviour of a gentleman!'

'But then,' retored Calverstock in his most top-lofty manner, 'I have little to recommend me as a gentleman. I make no pretence. You know what I am,' he went on, bitterness suddenly edging his voice and stripping it of hauteur, 'an ex-convict. From the age of fifteen I was reared in a strange, harsh environment where every man and woman had to fend for himself or herself. What else, ma'am, should you expect of me?'

Hero swallowed, suddenly regretting her attack. The bitterness in Drew's tone spoke louder than his words. And he had proved himself considerate on occasion, could be most agreeable when he liked. The harshness was surely a veneer adopted to cover his true, softer nature.

'A little pity,' she whispered.

'Pity? Who has ever shown me pity? You may expect none from this quarter, madam. I see now that I have been too lenient with you thus far. It is time you realised I am no society fop to be twisted around a woman's finger!'

Hero gasped as he took two long strides to reach her. His fingers dug painfully into her shoulders as he shook her. Her head nodded violently so that her frilly nightcap, tied loosely beneath her chin, became dislodged and fell back and pins scattered, releasing a tumble of lustrous brown hair.

Drew's breath caught. Next instant his hard mouth came down on hers. Taken by surprise in the middle of a wild, involuntary nod, her lips parted in protest, Hero felt the impact shudder through her. His hands left her shoulders as his arms clamped her body to his while long, powerful fingers tangled almost painfully in the mass of waves hanging down her back. She had no time to think, no time to protest—the assault was too sudden.

His proximity, his touch, always a threat to her nerves, devastated her. To be held so closely, kissed so fiercely, his tongue filling her mouth with his essence, threatened imminent disintegration. Hero felt her resolution to resist diminish with the same speed as the strength in her limbs. She sagged against him.

Needing air, Drew released her mouth and looked down into her drowning face. With a soft curse he swept her up into his arms, strode from the library and began to ascend the stairs.

Hero lay completely limp in his arms, lacking the ability to even hold on, let alone resist. Yet by the time he reached the door of her bedroom and flung it open she had regained enough of her normal equilibrium to utter a hoarse protest against what she instinctively knew was about to happen.

'No, Drew. Not like this!'

Breathing heavily from the exertion, 'Like what?' he almost snarled. 'What other treatment can you expect from someone as uncivilised as a convicted felon? My God, woman, you have been driving me demented with your untouchable presence in my house. I am wearied of playing the gentleman. You are my wife. And tonight you will once more fulfil your marital obligations.'

While he was speaking he had flung her on the bed and stripped off his waistcoat. His shoes and trousers followed so fast that Hero had no time to collect herself before, still breathing heavily, he was on the bed with her, his fingers at the fastenings of her dressing-gown. He threw it back and dealt expertly with the buttons on her snowy cambric nightdress. Hero did not resist. Apart from calling for help, which was unthinkable, she knew there could be no escape. And a part of her rejoiced.

He moved over her, his weight pressing her down into the feather mattress. His head descended and his mouth began a merciless attack on first one bared breast and then the other while his hands roved at will over her body. Possessively, roughly, but not bruisingly as she had feared.

The first time he had made love to her Hero had not known what to expect. Now she did and a half-hearted attempt to suffocate at birth the response he was evoking failed. She was already too deeply under his spell, lost in the painful pleasure of her body's awakening. The excitement gripped her, would not be quelled. She had wanted him to come to her for weeks. Now she could no more resist the longing that had been building up in her than fly to the moon.

Her senses reeled, her brain ceased to function. She could only feel and respond with mindless abandon as tumultuous sensation took control.

She did not notice when Drew began to woo rather than demand, when what had been a passion born of anger and desperation became something quite different. No less intense, but sparked by new, softer emotions. Yet in the end uncontrollable desire swept them both up in its irresistible tide so that Hero welcomed the hard, deep, penetrating thrusts which eventually sent her whole being spiralling into uncharted regions of ecstasy.

As she descended once more to cold reality she discovered Drew lying on her as one dead. She could detect no trace of a breath. In a panic she began to push at him, to call his name in frightened tones.

To her infinite relief he gave a great shudder and came to life. In the light of the candles she had not extinguished she saw the bewildered look in his grey eyes give way to one of awed realisation. And then the shutters came down.

'The devil, wife, when you are roused you are a wanton piece!' he declared as he rolled from her to retrieve his discarded clothing.

His crumpled shirt and tousled hair bore silent witness to the truth of his words. Shame burned brightly on Hero's cheeks. He was disgusted with her behaviour. With a half-suppressed sob she turned over and buried her flaming face in the bedcovers.

CHAPTER EIGHT

A DISCONCERTING surge of shame almost swamped Drew as he allowed Benbow to prepare him for bed. His servant knew where he had been, of course, and would later go down to the library to make the fire safe and extinguish the candles left burning there. It was not his loyal servant's knowledge of his recent activities that caused his discomfort but the anguished look in his wife's eyes as she had turned away to hide her face from his derisive accusation.

He had censured her for wantonness for no better reason than to hide his own remorse. Guilt so overwhelmed him that he doubted he would recover in a hurry.

He had lost control. He, who had prided himself on his coolness under extreme pressure and provocation as a convict, had allowed himself to be propelled into such immoderate behaviour that he undoubtedly owed her an apology.

But did he? She had first roused his anger by repeating ill-informed gossip and accusing him of dishonourable intentions, and had been in no mood to listen had he attempted to explain. *His* feelings, *his* point of view were the last things she would ever consider, for she had thought him despicable from the first. Except on that one occasion when she had not known he was a convicted felon and had accepted him at face value. As he had accepted her and fancied she would make him an admirable wife. But on discovering his identity she had allowed his past to colour her opinion of him, had condemned him unseen.

And for her to appear before him so temptingly, so scantily clad! Unless she was a complete innocent she must know the effect such a sight would have on any man! Yet, he acknowledged, almost groaning aloud, in many respects she *was* an innocent, especially in the ways of men. Her feelings must have been strong enough to bring her to his presence on a surge of such righteous indignation that she had forgotten all else.

Once again he was moved to reluctant admiration for her spirit in pressing her opinions, misplaced as they were. If only he had not overheard those words of hers spoken before the wedding he might have found her perfect in every way. But he could not forget them, or forgive her for condemning him out of hand. He might have much of which to be ashamed, but she had more. He had no need to apologise. Besides, an apology would allow her the whip-hand.

On this comforting thought Drew closed his eyes and immediately fell into the slumber of a man released from physical frustration, not waking until Benbow came in to open the curtains.

The dull grey light which invaded the room did nothing to indicate the time of day. Yet instinct told him he had slept late.

'Ten o'clock, my lord,' Benbow informed him upon being asked.

'The deuce! Why did you not wake me, man?'

'You have no urgent appointments today, sir. You have not rested well for several nights now. Since you did not wake I left you to sleep your fill.'

Devil take him, Benbow was right. He had slept badly while away and even worse since returning to London. He had spoken nothing but the truth when he had accused Hero of driving him insane by her presence. And it was of no use his attempting to relieve his frustrations by turning to another woman. He had tried that and found himself impotent for the first time in his life. He remembered the occasion with deep mortification. Damn Hero Langage!

But he would, he *must* recover from his obsession. Quite apart from anything else, he would no longer deny himself the pleasures of the marriage bed. There could be no valid reason for him to refrain from intimacy simply because they despised each other. He despised whores but in the past he had used them effectively. His body stirred at the memory of his wife's unexpected capacity for passion, the feel of her, deliciously soft, feverishly responsive in his arms. Superior to any whore or mistress he had ever known.

And he had foolishly made her ashamed of her desire. But no matter, he reassured himself confidently, there would be plenty of opportunity in the future for him to teach her that a man seldom objected to active participation by his wife during the act of love, whatever young females might be taught to the contrary.

Meanwhile he must control his deuced libido or it could betray him at an inconvenient moment. The very thought of Hero threatened to render him a trembling wreck. Thank heaven he wore a nightshirt or he would be *afraid* to get out of bed, not simply reluctant! Deuce take the woman, what had he done to deserve entanglement in such a coil?

Knowing his master well, Benbow bore the brunt of his ill-temper stoically as Drew snapped, 'You take too much upon yourself, Benbow! You know I am out of sorts for the rest of the day if I do not gallop early in the park!'

'Indeed, my lord.' Benbow inclined his head in acknowledgement of the reprimand. 'I have your shaving water in the dressing-room. It will lose its heat if you do not use it soon.'

'Then you will have, perforce, to send for more! You have already informed me that I have little need to stir myself today.'

'Breakfast is on the table in the parlour. With respect, you should rise now, sir.'

'Do you think I brought you back here to bully me, man?' demanded Drew.

'No, my lord.' Benbow, imperturbable as ever, paused before adding, 'I believe her ladyship was up and about betimes.'

'Was she?' growled Drew. His reluctance to rise grew with the prospect of facing his wife. Perhaps she would choose to remain in her boudoir. 'Has she taken breakfast yet?'

'Not as far as I am aware, my lord.'

'I shall go to my club,' decided Drew abruptly, flinging back the covers to reveal a striped nightshirt. 'Damn thing,' he grumbled, turning his back to strip it off. 'Can't think why I allow you to persuade me into wearing it.'

'Because you know it is expected of you, sir,' rejoined Benbow, the faintest of grins touching the deep lines of his face. 'Supposing a maidservant were to enter and discover you naked?'

'I slept naked in the Colony,' Drew reminded him.

'Not the same thing at all, sir. We even worked half naked most of the time.'

'True. We would freeze to death clad like that here.'

Drew remembered the heat, the sweat which had poured from his back beneath the coarse cotton shirt he had sometimes, in sheer desperation, thrown off—but seldom in the full heat of the burning sun. One dose of sunstroke and agonising sunburn had been lesson enough. Eventually his skin had hardened, as had his muscles, until he could work stripped for long periods and toil all day without undue exhaustion.

With the prospect of a confrontation with his wife shelved, Drew's temper recovered. Having pulled on the underwear Benbow had laid out for him, he wandered through to his dressing-room and sat patiently while his valet shaved him. No sound came from the room beyond. Hero must either be in her boudoir or down in the breakfast parlour. By the time he met her again at dinner that evening, after which they were due to attend a rout, he would be fortified, his irrational sense of guilt pushed firmly where it belonged—out of his mind. When he finally took up the ribbons to drive his curricle to St James's he was whistling under his breath.

He returned in time to change for dinner and the evening engagement, to find the house in uproar.

Grindley, the butler, greeted him as he entered the door, his normally expressionless face lined with worry.

'My lord! Thank goodness you are returned home!'

'Why? What is amiss?'

'It concerns her ladyship, my lord. Lady Felicity

Charteris called earlier. She had engaged to take tea with the countess at three o'clock.'

'Yes, I heard her make the arrangement.'

'But her ladyship was nowhere to be found in either the house or grounds and on enquiry I discovered that she had not been seen at all today. Jackson says that when she went in to attend her ladyship she had already dressed and left her room but she thought nothing of it, as her ladyship often rises early without calling her. She is a considerate mistress.'

'But her ladyship did not return?'

'No, my lord. But even then Jackson was not concerned, having discovered that Miss Bright was also missing and must be with her.'

Drew swore under his breath. 'Foolish woman! Did she not think to inform me? Benbow knew I was at my club.'

'She did not believe it necessary to trouble you or anyone else, my lord. It was not until Lady Felicity arrived that she began to question her ladyship's absence.'

'The devil!' Drew's hands clenched into fists and the hard lines of his face settled into a look of such cold displeasure that Grindley flinched.

'Lady Felicity waited a full hour before leaving, so certain was she that her ladyship would return,' he hastened to add uncomfortably.

A scowl descended on Drew's brow, adding to the formidable expression already on his face. 'But she did not.'

It was a statment, not a question, but Grindley answered it just the same. 'No, my lord. She is still absent, as is Miss Bright.'

'Then where the devil are they?' barked Drew.

'I have ascertained that they departed before dawn, about six-thirty, my lord. A housemaid cleaning out the grates saw them leave the house. She thought they were embarking on a walk in the grounds.'

'At that hour? By God, but I am served by idiots!' Drew's voice rose to a shout. 'Benbow! Where the deuce are you?'

'He went out, my lord. To question hackney drivers, I believe.'

Drew's scowl deepened. What in Hades was Benbow up to? 'Send him to me the instant he returns. I shall be in her ladyship's rooms,' he snapped.

No one had mentioned a note but if she had intended to disappear—as Benbow must suspect—she would surely have left him some word—of reproach, most likely. For he had no doubt that his wife's defection could be attributed to his own behaviour the previous night. She had determined to teach him a lesson, he supposed. Well, he thought as he searched her boudoir and bedroom in vain for any missive, when she did reappear he would not offer an apology.

Her absence had revealed to him that the idea of living in the house without his wife's presence was even less agreeable than with it. She might frustrate and irritate him and drive him to dementia but she was there. Without her to share it his life would stretch ahead like the outback, which had claimed the lives of so many absconding convicts. It was an unwelcome revelation. He had not realised the extent to which he had come to rely upon her company, how much he enjoyed watching her take society by storm. How jealous he was of any man upon whom she smiled.

How much he admired the manner in which she conducted herself as hostess or guest. How proud he had become of his countess. But he would never admit as much to her.

And his concern was unnecessary. She would not dare to disappear for long. She would return in time to dress for dinner and the evening engagement, he assured himself. She must simply have forgotten her arrangement to take tea with Lady Felicity, or been delayed. Otherwise she would have left a note.

Jackson appeared and he wanted to berate the woman for not raising the alarm earlier, but refrained. Hero was a free agent; she could go out without telling her maid if she so wished. And, unlike him, what reason could Jackson have had to suspect that her mistress had run away?

'I expect her ladyship will return at any moment,' he said, affecting a casual air upon Jackson's bobbing him a curtsy and expressing her puzzlement over her mistress's disappearance. 'What was she wearing?'

'Her black gown and bonnet, my lord, and the cloak she wears in the rain. All her lovely things are here, except that I think she took a change of underwear and a few personal items, slippers and a comb and suchlike, in a small valise.'

Drew's lips firmed and a cold hand seemed to clutch at his vitals as Jackson delivered her blow. Benbow's search for a hackney driver who had taken up his wife began to make more sense, as did the general air of panic among the staff. For no doubt Jackson had disseminated her discovery to everyone.

Only he had not known. 'Why was no one sent to

inform me when you discovered this?' he enquired acidly.

'Mr Grindley sent a footman to your club, my lord. He returned to say that you were not there, had left an hour since.'

A grunt was Drew's only answer to that. He had driven round to call on his lawyer, having thought of some business he needed to discuss. Of course no one had known where to find him.

'I must change. I'll be in my room,' he told Jackson as he opened the communicating door and left her standing irresolute in his wife's empty bedroom.

Where had Hero gone? Back to Polhembury? She had dressed in her simplest clothes, taken little with her. He had checked her jewel case and the pieces he had given her were still there. But she had no need to sell her jewels—she probably carried with her enough cash drawn from her allowance. And she had access to what remained in her account at the bank. She would not starve and had enough funds to buy herself out of trouble or to pay her way to Devon if she wished.

He no longer believed she would be back in time to dress for dinner. She had gone.

A stab of fury pierced him. How dared she? She was his wife! And despite her possession of money and the presence of Matty she must have been aware of the dangers of travelling alone and unescorted by a man. The two women had walked from the house, apparently to take a stroll in the garden, or so the stupid housemaid had thought. How far had they wandered through the streets of London before finding a hackney to carry them? Not too far, for Matty could not have walked a great distance.

Drew discovered anxiety coupled with anger to be a heady, painful mixture. He wanted to shake her until her teeth rattled and yet, at the same time, he wanted to hold her safely in his arms, close to his heart. And then to make passionate love. . .

His imaginings were cut off at that moment by Benbow, who presented himself breathing heavily, as though he had been hurrying.

'Any news?' demanded Drew without preamble.

Benbow shook his head. 'No, sir. None of the hackneys I could find was on duty early this morning. We shall have to wait until tomorrow and try again.'

Drew punched a balled fist into his other palm. 'We cannot do that, man! She may be in danger!' Fearful pictures of the two women being set upon by footpads or lured into some den of iniquity filled Drew's mind and he sounded quite desperate as he growled, 'I must know where she went and how. Besides,' he added, 'I want her back here before anyone discovers her to be gone.' It would do neither his nor her reputation any good were her escapade to be discovered. He would have to make sure that Lady Felicity was given a believable explanation for Hero's absence earlier. He must scribble a note, but not now.

'It may not be possible to discover anything quickly——' began Benbow, only to be cut off by an impatient oath.

'I will send a reliable footman to enquire at all the nearest post houses. She may have hired a chaise.' Benbow nodded and moved to the bell-pull as Drew went on, 'And I'll order our horses saddled. We will make all haste to the Gloucester Coffee Tavern in Piccadilly. The mail coaches will not leave until eight.

We may find her still there if she waited to travel in more comfort and safety on the Quicksilver to Exeter rather than take a slower, crowded stage. Though I doubt it.' Common sense told him she would have departed on the first stage coach available, whatever he might hope. 'We will enquire about the passengers who have left on them, too.'

'You think she may have gone back to Devon?'

'Where else?' enquired Drew grimly. 'If we have no further news by tomorrow night I shall depart for Polhembury early the next morning. Help me to change. Move, man!'

'Yes, sir,' answered Benbow, a thoughtful look in his eye as he went to lay out his master's riding clothes. He had rarely seen his lordship so disturbed. 'The Exeter coaches pass the door,' he pointed out. 'She may have hoped to board one further out from London. Hounslow perhaps?'

'Then someone must enquire in that direction, too,' decided Drew.

The senior footman knocked and entered at that moment and instructions were given, together with admonitions of secrecy. 'If I hear a word of this outside the house I shall seek out the culprits and have them dismissed without a reference,' declared Drew sternly.

Seeing the look on his master's face, the footman knew the threat to be real. 'Mr Grindley and Mrs Deacon have already warned the staff against gossip, my lord,' he said as he made a dignified withdrawal and went to pass on the orders he had just received.

'Help me off with this,' said Drew as he began to struggle out of his blue superfine coat. 'We have little enough time to spare if we are to find her.'

'Should I inform Monsieur Vodin to hold dinner, my lord?'

Drew shook his head as Benbow, having removed his shoes, presented him with a pair of shining hessians. 'We will do that on our way out. Curse these things!'

The struggle with the boots over, Drew stood to draw on his riding coat. Cut more generously than the garment he had discarded, it required little assistance to don.

'The weather is foul,' remarked Benbow, handing his master a many-caped greatcoat. 'It was wise of her ladyship to wear her thick cloak.'

'Huh!' snorted Drew, glaring at his servant. 'I account it nothing but the height of foolishness for her to embark on such an irresponsible venture in whatever garb she chose.'

'She is a spirited young lady, sir,' murmured Benbow.

Drew glared. 'I have no need of you to tell me that, curse it!'

After a sleepless night Hero knew that she must leave Calverstock House and her husband as fast as she could. She had no clear idea of what she wanted to do and decided to seek refuge with her Aunt Augusta and so remain in London.

She could not fly straight back to Polhembury. There, she would have to face her father's wrath. For her leaving Calverstock might mean his debt being called in. Besides, she was not certain that she did want to leave him, not for good. But she must make some protest at the way he had treated her, the aspersions he had cast upon her character.

And she simply could not face him. She couldn't even face herself in a mirror. How could she have behaved with such abandon that Calverstock had thought her wanton? Her cheeks burned anew. Yet while it was happening it had seemed the most natural thing in the world to return his caresses, to cry out her need, to welcome the release his possession had brought. The first time, an inexperienced virgin, she had managed to remain calm and impassive under his skilful assault. But last night she had been unable to sustain a similar coolness because her body, having known it once, had longed for his touch, the fulfilment of his final possession, had responded automatically to his ardour.

She knew instinctively that he had enjoyed the encounter as much as she. But he had acted in a cloud of anger, had been punishing her for daring to accuse him of the pitiless accumulation to himself of others' wealth. She, while protesting her wish not to have him take her in such a mood, had made but a feeble protest; her resistance pitifully weak, she'd tumbled headlong into a trap set by her senses. Had responded to a passion born of anger and lust rather than love and respect, and been punished for it.

If she remained with her husband the same scene would be re-enacted again and again. He would take her, despising her, and she would respond, unable to help herself. So, unless his attitude changed, she could not remain. But could not, for long, continue to draw upon her allowance.

Unwelcome choices lay ahead. Unless she returned

to an impoverished Polhembury she would be forced to find some remunerative position as governess or companion in order to live. And if she returned there and Polhembury was taken from her father, she would be faced with a similar dilemma. And she must ask Matty to uproot herself again. Dear, loyal Matty, who scarcely argued when she invaded her tiny room long before dawn and begged her to leave Calverstock House immediately.

'Why, my chick?' she asked, rubbing the sleep from her eyes. Then she sat up suddenly, her nightcap askew, to demand. 'Has your husband ill-treated you?'

'Not really. But. . .he said things. . .Matty, I simply cannot remain here any longer.'

Matty grunted as she threw back the covers and left her warm bed. 'I don't know how I came to be so deceived by him,' she muttered. 'I'd have sworn he was an upright, honest gentleman, kind-hearted despite his manner at the wedding. And I thought he held a *tendre* for you, my chick, though he seemed determined to hide it. But there,' she finished as, roles reversed, Hero aided her to don her warmest clothes, 'he's not an easy man to read.'

'He holds me in disgust,' Hero said, her voice quivering. 'So, you see, I must leave him.'

Matty said no more. She packed a few of her things in a similar valise to the one Hero carried and together they left the house, the bags concealed beneath their cloaks. She knew her aunt's address in Dorset Square, knew it was located north of Oxford Street, north even of the new road linking Paddington with the City.

They walked to Hyde Park Corner and through the toll gates before, for Matty's sake, she hired a hackney to Portman Square. From there they walked aimlessly for a while before taking another hackney to Dorset Square.

They arrived at Aunt Augusta's front door as the family was taking refreshment with two other callers.

Hero regretted her lapse in not calling on her aunt before. Such a politeness would have saved a great deal of commotion now. Having been announced and ushered into a cheerful room overlooking the square, a much gratified Mrs Edward Dashper greeted her niece with astonished delight, introduced her daughters and friends, and extended an immediate invitation to her to sit down near the fire and partake of refreshment.

Hero indicated Matty, standing quietly at her shoulder. 'Miss Bright is my companion, Aunt,' she explained as she removed her cloak and handed it to a hovering maidservant. The valises had been left in the hall. 'She may join us?'

At this suggestion Aunt Augusta's face lost its look of effusive welcome. 'Matty Bright?' she murmured, recognition dawning. 'Was she not our nursemaid, your mother's and mine?'

'She was, Aunt, and mine, too. Now she is become my dearest friend.'

'I see,' murmured Augusta. 'Very well,' she agreed reluctantly, 'Matty may join us.'

'Thank you, Aunt Augusta,' smiled Hero, wishing with all her heart that her aunt had been alone, that she could have told her at once of the circumstances surrounding her visit.

'We saw the announcement of your marriage, my dear Hero,' Mrs Dashper declared as her new guests took their seats and accepted dishes of tea. 'Just fancy, I said to my dearest daughters, didn't I, girls? Just fancy, your cousin is become a countess!'

A murmur of approval came from Mrs Dashper's friends, both of them matrons, both clad splendidly but tastelessly in black of the latest fashion and appearing quite overset at meeting a real live countess. At least Aunt Augusta and her daughters, although in deepest mourning, were dressed with more taste, thought Hero, smiling at cousins Dorothea and Chloe. Aunt Augusta, the daughter of a baron, despite having made a poor marriage by society's standards, since her husband had no expectation of a title and little money, had retained much of the benefits of her upbringing.

Dorothea, the eldest of the sisters, who looked to be almost at her last prayers, smiled back shyly and quickly lowered her rather prominent pale blue eyes in confusion. A shy, lumpy girl, ill-suited by the black she wore, she would make little impression on the gentlemen, thought Hero with pity.

Chloe, younger by several years, fashionably fair and of a more lively disposition, exclaimed, 'Oh, yes, cousin. We were so excited. We did so hope that you——'

'Chloe!' cut in her mother severely. 'Guard your tongue!' She turned to Hero with an apology. 'Dear Chloe is so inclined to chatter. I tell her that forward, boisterous young ladies are not admired, that in company she should behave with the utmost decorum.'

'You must not count *me* as company, Aunt, I am family, though I am afraid that I have called in a most uncivil fashion——'

'Oh, but my modest establishment is honoured by

your visit, as are my friends! And one has no need to follow form when calling upon relations!'

Eventually the two matrons rose to depart, no doubt to spread their new, enlivening *on dit*. 'We will leave you to have a comfortable coze with your niece, my dear Mrs Dashper,' said one, while the other nodded assent, her head bobbing and wobbling her several chins.

Adieus were said and the ladies seen out. Aunt Augusta hurried across to the tall window and peered through the lace curtain to watch them descend to the road. She turned back to Hero with disappointment written all over a thin face which, in repose, could look discontented. Beside her stout friends Aunt Augusta had looked positively elegant.

'Did you not bring your own carriage?' she asked.

'No, we came by hackney,' explained Hero, realising that her aunt's disappointment stemmed from the fact that her friends would not see a crested coach drawn by splendid horses being walked outside her door. Its not being there would reflect badly upon the consequence of Mrs Edward Dashper.

'I suppose his lordship required its use,' speculated her aunt archly.

'No, Aunt, we have more than one carriage for our use should it be required. I owe you an explanation, but I would prefer to make it to you alone. Is there somewhere. . .?'

She allowed the question to trail off. Her aunt frowned in perplexity but immediately told her daughters to leave the room. They departed reluctantly.

Matty stood. 'I will wait in the hall, my lady,' she informed Hero. Hero nodded and Matty left the room.

'Now,' said Aunt Augusta, frowning austerely, seating herself opposite Hero. 'What is it you have to explain?'

'I came here hoping you would give me refuge, Aunt. I found it necessary to leave Lord Calverstock, no matter why.'

'And you wish to stay here?' demanded Augusta, unable to disguise her shock at this turn of events.

'If I may, Aunt. Matty, too. You are the only relation I have, apart from my father, and you live near by. I did not wish to return to Polhembury.'

'Well, I have no desire to pry,' declared Aunt Augusta in the manner of one denying her dearest wish, 'but I have never heard of anything so addle-witted! Left your husband indeed! My duty must be to send you straight back!'

Hero paled. She had not expected her aunt to welcome her with open arms, but had not foreseen opposition. 'Pray do not, dear Aunt. I may return in due course, but for the moment I need to escape Calverstock House while I decide what to do. The world is privy to my husband's past. The marriage was arranged by my father. You must realise that I had no say in the matter.'

Augusta exclaimed, 'Naturally not! No chit of a girl knows what is best for her! Your father's choice was impeccable. Since inheriting the title his lordship's reputation has been second to none. You should be the happiest of creatures!' She shrugged bony shoulders. 'But I can tell that you are in some distress. For your mother's sake I shall not turn you away.'

'You have my deepest gratitude, Aunt.'

'Honoured as I am to have a countess under my

roof, you must realise that this is not a large house. Matty will have to share the room with you. Have you any objection to that arrangement?'

'None at all.' Hero knew she would be glad of her old nurse's company.

Augusta's sharp eyes studied Hero's exhausted face thoughtfully. 'And the earl has no idea where you are?'

'None, Aunt. I was careful to leave no trail he could follow.'

Augusta pounced on this statement. 'So you believe he will wish to find you?'

Hero plucked at the folds of her skirt, her fingers trembling; not with fear, but some other emotion she could not name. Of course he would search for her. He considered her his property, part of a financial bargain. Perhaps the sentiment causing her such distress was resentment. Or disappointment that he would not seek her out for herself. 'I fear so.' Unconsciously, she sighed. 'He is not a man who likes to be crossed.'

Her aunt nodded. 'I dare say he is not. Well, my dear, you must stay here until your future is decided. Mr Dashper will be surprised to find you here when he returns. You have not seen him since you were a child.' She stood up. 'Dorothea will show you to your room. You will have time to get to know your cousins before dinner, which we take early.'

'Thank you, Aunt. I will try not to be a nuisance to you. I hope my stay will not be of long duration.'

'I doubt it will be,' replied Augusta somewhat ambiguously.

CHAPTER NINE

DREW paced the floor of the library, unable to relax.

'Do sit down, my dear fellow,' pleaded Lord Harrington, who, informed of Hero's disappearance, though not of the reason for it, had come to support his friend in his hour of need. 'Walkin' up and down like that will only wear a hole in an expensive carpet. I doubt she is at any hazard.'

'It's fine for you,' muttered Drew. 'She is not your wife.'

'And I ain't in love with her.'

At this blandly spoken observation Drew stopped his pacing to stand and stare coldly at the speaker. 'Meaning what, pray?'

'Nothin', nothin' at all,' drawled Archie with a bland smile. 'You ain't, of course. You can't be, you'd never be in such a takin' if you were.'

This irony was not lost on Drew. 'She is my wife,' he informed Archie with unnecessary violence. 'Her action, if it is discovered by the gabble-grinders, will reflect upon us both.'

'Never known you to care what the gossips said before.' With deliberate unconcern, Harrington took out his snuff box, flicked it open and offered it to Drew.

Drew waved it away. 'This is different. They will invent a lover where there is none.'

'You are certain of that?'

'Of course I am, damn you!' Drew controlled his reaction to Dalmead's deliberate provocation with difficulty. Archie knew as well as he that Hero was not the sort of woman to fly to another man's arms for solace. Archie simply wanted him to acknowledge the fact, a point borne out by the smug quirk on his friend's lips. 'She is new in society,' he went on more calmly. 'It will prejudice her position. The hostesses may not receive her. She will be ruined.'

'Stop tormenting yourself, Drew.' Archie sniffed up his pinch of snuff before adding comfortingly, 'All will be well, you'll see.'

Drew turned on his heel and walked over to stare out of the window, the fine vista an unfocused blur. 'At least we can now believe she is still somewhere in London. She was not seen boarding any West Country stage or mail in the capital.'

'And this mornin' you found a hackney driver who took her to Portman Square,' soothed Archie. 'Benbow and the others will soon be back from searching that area for further news.'

'Their enquiries can only increase the risk of her disappearance being discovered.'

'Perhaps we should visit our club and behave as normal? Put 'em off the scent, you know.'

Drew shook his head at this eminently sensible suggestion. 'I must remain here. But you could do me a service, if you would.'

'Anything within reason, my dear fellow.'

Drew sat at his desk and began to sharpen a pen. 'I have just remembered I must make my wife's excuses to Lady Felicity. She failed to keep their engagement yesterday afternoon.'

He scribbled quickly, read through what he had written, then sanded the sheet before folding it, reaching for wax and flame, and fastening it with his seal.

'Deliver this, if you will.'

Harrington looked down at the paper thrust into his hand as though it might bite him, the look on his face bringing a faint smile to Drew's lips. Even caught up in his own turbulent preoccupation, he could not miss Archie's reluctance to execute the commission.

'You do not need to hand it to her personally,' he drawled. 'Unless, of course you would welcome the excuse to call upon her?'

'Couldn't you send a footman or a groom?' asked Archie anxiously, his normally languid air quite deserting him.

'They are all otherwise engaged, as you know. Come, now, my dear fellow, you are surely not afraid to knock upon the door of the Beltinge residence?'

Archie rose stiffly to his feet. 'No such thing. But I do not wish to place myself in a position to be caught in parson's mousetrap.' He blushed. 'I have paid her quite enough attention recently. The gabble-grinders will begin their work.'

'If you like the girl wed her,' advised Drew. 'She cherishes a *tendre* for you, you know. You could do a lot worse.'

Archie shuddered. 'I have no desire to wed,' he declared in a pained voice.

'The wedded state is not the end of the world,' revealed Drew.

'Even when your wife leaves you?'

'Not even then. Do get along there, Archie, there's a good fellow. Just hand the letter to a footman if you must. By the way, I've said that Lady Calverstock was taken ill while out shopping and sends her apologies. That she will be in touch when she is fully recovered.' He grinned. 'In case you should see anyone to speak to.'

Archie grimaced. 'Devious devil! You simply want to see me as leg-shackled as you are yourself!'

'I want to see you happily wed,' said Drew sincerely. 'It can be the most felicitous of states.'

'But you ain't found it so!' Archie pounced on Drew's inconsistency to defend himself, moving towards the door. 'I'll see myself out. But,' he said, his hand on the knob, 'your lady is a diamond of the first water. Thought so from the first, and now we are better acquainted I'm sure of it. If you ain't happy, then ncither is she. Pity.' He shrugged one shoulder languidly. 'She missed you while you were away, y'know. Should do something about it. I'll call back later to see if there's any further news.'

He closed the door behind him without giving Drew a chance to answer. Drew slumped into his chair and buried his face in his hands.

Could he make himself forget those searing words of hers? Could he change her opinion of him? Unless he could do both, happiness would elude them.

A short while later a locally recruited housemaid, doing duty for an absent footman, knocked and entered. By this time frustration with his enforced inactivity had Drew pacing again.

'Yes?' he barked.

'There's a lad 'ere, me lord. Come to the back door, 'e did. Says as 'ow 'e 'as a messidge for the earl, must give it into 'is own 'and, 'e says.'

'Then send him in!'

As the girl turned to obey Drew strode impatiently towards the door. The boy, who had been waiting just outside, appeared on the instant. A grubby urchin with a running nose. Drew stopped short.

'What is it you want, boy?'

'Got a messidge for the earl. You 'im?' demanded the boy with a noisy sniff and gulp.

'Course 'e is!' put in the housemaid, but turned and sped off as she met Drew's imperious glare.

"I am,' confirmed Drew, holding out his hand for the soiled paper clutched in the lad's fist. 'Is that it?'

'The lady said as 'ow you'd give us a tanner,' muttered the boy, parting with the note reluctantly.

'You'll get it.' Drew broke the seal and perused the letter's contents with rising exhilaration. His first real smile of the day lit his face as he placed the note on his desk and took out his purse. 'Here is a shilling for you,' he said, dropping the coin into the boy's filthy palm.

'Cor!' The boy bit it to be sure it was genuine before tucking it safely into a pocket. 'Ta, guvner!'

'Thank you for delivering the letter so promptly.' Drew tugged on the bell ribbon. 'Someone will come to see you out.'

Hero sat, sharing a sofa with Matty, in the room where she had first met her aunt and cousins the previous day. She had slept badly for the second night running. Bruised circles had already made their appearance beneath her eyes. She wondered when she would enjoy a good night's rest again.

Her aunt chattered on, asking innumerable questions Hero did not wish to answer. Mrs Dashper occupied a position on the fringes of society, moving in a lower circle than that of her niece. Despite a certain restless jumpiness of manner, she was anxious to hear all the latest gossip and scandal circulating in first circles.

Hero did her best to respond but her mind was elsewhere. What was Calverstock doing? Was he angry? Worried? Indifferent? Or merely piqued that she should dare to leave him? Where was he? He could, she supposed, be on his way to Polhembury, thinking she would return there. Her aunt's address had been held in her head, she had left no written record behind, so he would have no immediate way of finding her here in Dorset Square.

Her head ached. She would be glad when the light nuncheon Aunt Augusta had promised for two o'clock was served, though she doubted whether she would have the appetite to eat. But a dish of tea might ease her malaise.

The morning seemed interminable. At every rattle of carriage wheels outside her aunt jumped up to peer from the window. Hero watched resignedly as she leapt up yet again. She had never known anyone so inquisitive about her neighbours' movements.

This time, however, Mrs Dashper gave a little cry. 'Girls, tidy yourselves! We have a visitor! No, do not rush to the window, Chloe, it is unbecoming behaviour in a young girl. Sit where you are. We will wait for Lily to announce the visitor in form.'

She returned to her own seat, arranged her skirts and sat, hands clasped in her lap, listening for the knock on the door.

'Who is it, Mama?' asked Chloe.

'Patience, my dear. A gentleman, I believe.'

Her aunt's expression held a mixture of excitement, guilt and triumph. Foreboding made Hero glance anxiously at Matty, who shook her head, frowning and giving a slight shrug. Only one thing seemed certain: Mrs Dashper had been expecting a caller. She was up to something.

A few moments later a familiar voice in the hall confirmed Hero's worst fears. She turned angrily to her aunt.

'You betrayed me!' she accused in a low tone.

'For your own good, my dear,' replied her aunt self-righteously.

The door opened on a knock and Lily, the parlour maid, announced Lord Calverstock.

He strode into the room, his eyes immediately seeking Hero's stricken face, but she refused to meet his gaze. Remembering his manners, he made his bow and addressed himself to his hostess.

'I must thank you for your communication, ma'am, which I received but an hour since. We are not acquainted but no doubt my wife will be pleased to make the introductions. My dear?'

The buzzing in her ears, caused by anger and mortification, not to mention the frantic leap of her pulses at sight of her husband, made it almost impossible for Hero to respond. Had it not been for Matty's reassuring squeeze of her arm she would probably have failed to find her voice altogether. As it was she managed to make the introductions, though in accents she scarcely recognised as her own.

'Do please be seated, my lord,' gushed Aunt

Augusta. 'A tea tray and some light refreshment will be with us in but a moment. You and my dear niece are both most welcome in my humble abode. My daughters are enchanted to have renewed acquaintance with their cousin. Are you not, my dears?'

'Yes, Mama,' they responded in unison.

'Both Dorothea and Chloe are "out", of course, but our social circle here is restricted. Perhaps, with their cousin's influence. . .?'

Hero cringed for her relation. How could she be so obvious?

'They could extend their expectations.' Drew finished the sentence for his hostess. 'Quite so, ma'am. When we return to town for the next season we must consider introducing them into our circle, must we not, my dear?'

Drew's tone was dry. In due course both he and Hero would be expected to pay for the services rendered them by Mrs Dashper. His wife looked quite crushed by her aunt's presumption. But in the euphoria of finding Hero again he really did not care.

The refreshments arrived. Hero drank her tea thirstily and nibbled dutifully at a scone. Drew ate with relish. But then, it took a lot to put him off his food. She watched him surreptitiously, seeking some indication of his attitude towards her. She could detect no trace of softness in his manner, which had been courteously polite from the start, but no anger, either. And he had come after her. Perhaps he had been just a little worried.

He had given no indication of his intentions. He may simply want to confirm her whereabouts. Hero did not really believe that and waited for his next move, her nerves stretched almost to snapping point.

If he commanded her to return with him, as though she were his property, she would resist. Much depended on his approach. His feelings were well-hidden; she found it impossible to read his thoughts or divine his intentions.

With the refreshments consumed and the tray removed, Drew at last broached the reason for his visit.

'Ma'am.' He addressed Mrs Dashper with due formality. 'I would account it a great service if I could speak to my wife in private?'

Augusta jumped to her feet. 'But of course, Lord Calverstock! I personally will show you both into the drawing-room. You will be undisturbed there.'

Hero rose reluctantly. She had regained much of her composure but the prospect of facing Calverstock in private threatened a return of debilitating emotion. Yet she must stand up to him, must convince him that she was not a wanton, that his accusation had been false. . .except that, when she remembered her bewildering behaviour in bed, mortification swept back to render her helpless before his censure.

The door closed behind Augusta. Drew, denied the gentleman's normal tactic of warming his back in the heat of a blazing fire, stood before the empty grate with one foot on the ornate fender, a hand resting on the mantelshelf beside a ticking clock.

'Well, wife,' he began austerely, 'I trust you have an explanation for your peculiar behaviour?'

Hero, her hands clasped before her, drew a deep breath. Now was the moment. She must be brave. 'I could not remain to be insulted, husband.' If he could call her 'wife' she could address him so, midway between formality and intimacy. 'I wished for time to consider my future. Had my aunt not betrayed me. . .'

'She did her duty.' He paused only briefly before looking down at his boot and asking, 'Did you not consider the anxiety your disappearance would cause?'

'I had Matty with me. I did not think you would care.'

'Not care?' He moved swiftly to stand erect, towering over her. 'When my wife leaves me? What sort of a fool does that make of me, pray?'

'I would rather be called fool than wanton.'

Hero's voice, scarcely above a whisper, shook. In the face of her evident distress Drew's anger, largely induced by anxiety, crumbled. He had sworn he would not but. . .

He swung away from his position by the fireplace to stand with his back towards her. He spoke jerkily. 'I owe you an apology, Hero. If you will but return with me I will prove to you that my words were said in the heat of passion, that they were not meant.' He turned to meet her gaze full on. 'You must allow me to take you home.'

There was no humility in his voice. He had made a statement of fact. Yet he had used the word 'allow' and his tone held a touch of strain. Hero knew he was sincere.

The colour came and went in her cheeks as she struggled to control her wild emotions, to subdue a mortifying desire to cry. She wanted to return with him. Life had become so desolate since she had walked out with Matty. Would Matty think her foolish to give in so easily? Probably not, for she had always held Drew Challoner in high regard, despite his unfortunate past.

As she hesitated, Drew's voice came again. 'Madam, I will not plead but it is necessary that you return. Gossip may already be rife, although I have done my best to avoid it. I sent a note to apologise for your discourtesy in failing to keep your engagement with Lady Felicity——' At Hero's gasp he gave a grim smile. 'You had quite forgot?'

'Yes,' gasped Hero. 'Oh, how could I?'

'Easily enough, it seems. I made the excuse that you had been taken ill while out shopping. Whether she will believe this, since she waited a full hour for you to return and to the best of my knowledge no one mentioned where you had gone, for they did not know, I cannot say. However, if you wish to avoid scandal and its consequent effects upon your position in society, you should return at once and make your own apologies to Lady Felicity.'

'I care little for my own position,' murmured Hero, making a dismissive gesture with her hands, 'but I would not wish to offend Lady Felicity or to make a mock of you.'

Drew shrugged. 'As to that, I am accustomed to being the object of speculation, censure and, in some cases——' he made a grimace of distaste '—pity. I mislike it but am well able to ignore it. Other people's opinion does not concern me. I trained in a hard school.'

Beneath the bold assertion Hero, for the first time in their association, caught a hint of vulnerability. It stirred her deeply yet still she made no response. Drew took a step towards her. 'If you return we will leave for Ashworthy almost immediately. There, perhaps, we can begin again, learn to know each other and hope that affection will grow between us.' He drew a breath. 'I need you, Hero. I must provide an heir and as my wife it is your duty to bear me one. I believe that if we both try we can deal well enough together.'

An heir. Yes, she was the only person who could supply him with a legitimate son. And a baby might compensate her for the love her husband could not give her. She determined to fight for her marriage, not simply give it up.

She nodded. 'Very well, Drew. I shall enjoy to see Ashworthy. I like living in the country. I have missed Polhembury.'

He took her cold hand and kissed her wrist. A shiver ran up her arm to end as a quiver in her heart.

'We will inform your aunt.'

'I must ask Matty to pack. We did not bring much with us.'

In a dry voice he responded, 'So I have been given to understand.'

'Drew.' Hero hesitated, feeling guilty for imposing the problem her new-found relatives could present in the future. 'I am sorry you have been forced to recognise Aunt Augusta and my cousins. Shall you mind very much if I bring the girls out in society? I feel sorry for them.'

Drew shook his head. 'Edward Dashper is well-regarded in gentlemen's circles and both parents are nobly born.'

'You made enquiries,' said Hero flatly.

'Naturally. I wished to know with whom I might be

forced to deal. I discovered that the family is merely poor. I shall not object to anything you may be able to do for them.'

Hero smiled, if rather ruefully. Her hands had stopped shaking. Her husband was nothing if not thorough, but she could return to him with renewed confidence in the future. 'I had better have a word with Matty.'

Upon their return to Calverstock House the servants were given much the same explanation for Hero's absence as Drew had sent to Lady Felicity. They knew she had left the house early and so the story was elaborated a little and the note delivered by the urchin was said to have originated with her. Drew rewarded the men who had been engaged in the search for her with a bonus and the tongues of the staff were stilled by Hero's own cheerful reappearance.

Apologies were sent to several hostesses whose invitations had been accepted for the next week. Hero called upon Lady Felicity and invited her to visit Ashworthy for the Christmas festivities. Lord and Lady Beltinge gave their permission and so it was arranged. Hero believed she would enjoy Felicity's company. Her presence, and that of several other guests already engaged to spend two or three weeks at Ashworthy, might ease the strain between her husband and herself. That Lord Harrington would be one of the guests Hero had not thought it necessary to mention. But if Felicity could not fix Archie's interest during that time then she was not the young woman Hero took her for.

From the moment of her return Drew had shown

greater consideration for her welfare. He spent much of the slow journey down to Gloucestershire in the coach with her and Matty, leaving the driving to Tribble, who led a procession of lesser carriages loaded with servants and luggage. The removal of the household to Ashworthy took a deal of organisation, which was accomplished by Drew and Mrs Deacon with enviable efficiency.

Mrs Deacon had been left behind to supervise the annual cleaning of Calverstock House by the small staff retained there. That done, she would see it maintained in a state of readiness to receive its owner at a moment's notice, although the household would probably not return to London until April.

The housekeeper at Ashworthy, Mrs Pilcher, greeted Lord Calverstock with an unmistakable affection which she seemed ready to extend to Hero.

'We are delighted to welcome you here, my lady,' she cried, her round, cheerful face beaming with genuine goodwill as she bobbed a respectful curtsy. 'I do hope you will find everything to your liking. The notice of your early arrival was short but we were already almost prepared to receive you. The entire staff hopes you will be happy here, ma'am, and offers you their best services.'

'I like it here already,' Hero returned with truth.

The chef, the butler, their personal servants and several footmen and maidservants had travelled down with them. Except for Matty and Jackson they were all familiar with the place, most having served the Calverstocks for many years, and, like their masters past and present, had spent more time at the country estate than in London. Hero was glad to see a few familiar faces as she settled into the vast, draughty stone pile Drew had inherited so unexpectedly upon his uncle's sudden and heirless death.

The driveway to the house wound through undulating parkland, the views obscured in many places by trees and undergrowth. They had rounded the base of a low rise and emerged from surrounding woodland to see the mansion spread before them. Hero had given a gasp of pleasure and surprise. Even on that overcast winter day the Cotswold stone had appeared warmly welcoming. The sprawling building, built over many generations, looked picturesque and intriguing with its stone mullioned windows and steeply sloping gabled roofs dotted with dormers, the whole topped by a veritable forest of tall chimneys. Unlike Polhembury, Ashworthy looked to be in a good state of repair. Not until she stepped inside and traversed the various corridors and galleries had Hero realised how deceptive the aura of warmth given off by the cream stone had been.

The rooms were kept warm by blazing fires but no female dared venture into a draughty corridor without first wrapping herself in a shawl. The maids wore theirs folded into a triangle with the ends crossed over in front and tied behind. After the first evening Hero carried a fine woollen or cashmere shawl with her wherever she went. But despite this discomfort she quickly came to love Ashworthy.

Drew loved it, too. 'It needed complete restoration when I inherited,' he told her as he escorted her on a tour of inspection. 'Perhaps I was prejudiced, since I had always found my grandfather and uncle to be uncharitable, odious creatures, but I felt the place needed cleansing of their presence. I set about renovating it from basement to attic.'

'You did an excellent job,' acknowledged Hero.

Drew accepted the compliment with a smile. 'I hired the best help available. The servants were wonderful.'

'They did not object to the upheaval?'

'Scarcely any of them, and those who did were soon replaced.' He shrugged self-deprecatingly. 'They seemed inclined to prefer my rule to that of my predecessors. Mrs Pilcher, in particular, has blossomed since I took over.'

'She adores you,' grinned Hero without rancour. There was scarcely need to be jealous of the adulation of the stout, middle-aged woman and Drew seemed to attract all females, whatever their position in society. She could not forget the woman Duchess Fanny had seen him with, the covert speculation over his dealings with women of a lower class rife in London. No one had been overt in their accusations but the hints had been too numerous to ignore. She hoped that here, in his ancestral seat, his women left behind, she would be able to win his regard and satisfy his needs sufficiently to render all competition redundant.

Since her return he had played the charming considerate husband both in public and private but he had not come to her bed. They occupied the master bedroom as was expected of them but Drew had chosen to sleep in the bed made up in the large adjoining dressing-room. Hero did not understand this. He had said he needed an heir. He must surely come to her soon. And when he did, how was she to behave?

She feared she would be unable to maintain the unresponsive modesty required of a woman of fashion being favoured with her husband's attentions. Drew had promised to prove to her that he had not meant the words he had spoken. He would teach her how to respond. But what if, she having once demonstrated passion, he asked for more than it was possible or decent for her to give? Some gentlemen, she knew, visited houses of ill repute or kept a mistress to slake the baser instincts their wives could not, or would not satisfy. She did not like to think of Drew being driven to such lengths. No one had suggested that the women he visited were other than normally obliging. Surely he would not need to indulge in behaviour she could not condone?

He had suffered a rough upbringing during his growth from youth to manhood. Had mixed with the lowest classes of criminal society, could have sunk to depths she could only dimly imagine. He had emerged, apparently, as a perfect flower of the nobility, but she could not be certain of what lay beneath his smooth exterior.

He had proved himself capable of harsh, even vindictive behaviour. In London he visited Jackson's gymnasium and he enjoyed watching a good mill. According to Benbow, who was inordinately proud of his master's capabilities, the earl possessed a useful bunch of fives, could plant a facer and acquit himself well in a brawl if necessary. And, quite apart from his acknowledged mistress, Lady Willoughby, he reputedly kept a harem of other women.

He gave no sign of dissolution. He looked hard, tough, yet she now knew of his kindess, the consideration with which he treated his inferiors. And he had only to smile. . .

Hero sighed. She seemed no nearer to fathoming her husband's personality than when she'd married him. Doubts still plagued her but did not stop her from experiencing emotions which bordered on love.

Leaving him had been like tearing herself apart. If it had taught her nothing else it had made her realise how deep her feelings for her husband had gone. Despite all his faults, real and imagined, she had begun to hold him in deepest affection and to feel tenderness towards him. Add passion, and surely that amounted to love?

She wanted to tell him, show him, but how could she when he did not want her love or even his marital rights?

She could not take the initiative. He had branded her wanton once. She would not lay herself open to that charge again. Patience and quiet affection, her only weapons, seemed singularly frail.

She lay that night, their second at Ashworthy, in the large canopied bed in which generations of Calverstocks had been born—including Gerald, Drew's father, but not Drew—the glow from the dying fire the only light to alleviate the darkness. The candle by the bed had long since guttered out.

The already comfortable room had been improved by new silken hangings to cover the walls and the addition of thick rugs, heavy curtains and a draught roll at the bottom of the door. It was one of the cosiest rooms in the house—the library and her small sitting-room being others—and she wished Drew would come and share it with her instead of banishing himself to the far less agreeable dressing-room. But he could not know how much she so longed to be held in his arms, to hold him in hers. . .

She must have dropped off as her mind wandered in the realms of fantasy. But she was not so deeply asleep that the slight sound of a door opening failed to wake her. No one should intrude at this hour. Matty and Jackson were both long abed. In her confused state she did not at first realise that it was the opening of the door to the dressing-room that had woken her.

She lay still, feigning sleep, ready to scream for help if the intruder proved hostile. One of the servants, perhaps, intent on theft? Or a stranger who had broken in with the same objective? Every nerve tense, her mouth dry, her hearing strained for any sound, Hero lay waiting.

Footsteps brushed across a rug, approaching the bed. She made herself lie still, breathing steadily, until, suddenly, she realised who it was. The familiar scent of her husband, compounded of sandalwood and his own distinctive odour, filled her nostrils.

Her heart began to hammer. Almost, she said his name but something stopped her. Somehow she controlled her breathing. He had come to her like a thief in the night. Why?

She could hear his breathing as he leant over her. It seemed to catch. A touch came on her forehead, so feather-light that she thought she had imagined it. But then, as fleeting as the brush of a butterfly's wings, she felt his lips on hers. On a breath he whispered, 'Sleep well, my wife.'

Hero's eyes flew open. 'Drew!' she gasped and reached up for him.

He came down into her arms with a small grunt. 'I

thought you would be asleep. I did not wish to wake you, my dear.'

'Then why did you come?' she whispered.

'Because I could not sleep,' he admitted ruefully. 'I have tried to give you time but I lay in the next room wanting...' He broke off and took a deep breath. 'I came in to look, to touch, to go away again and hope to sleep.'

Such an admission! Hero's arms tightened about his shoulders. 'Did you not realise I would welcome you, my lord? I have waited, it seems, so long...'

'Then you have forgiven me? You will allow me to make amends for my previous mistakes?'

'If you will forgive mine,' whispered Hero.

'You made no mistake that night, never think it. A man whose wife exhibits the passion you honoured me with is fortunate. I knew it and was overwhelmed. My reproof was born of other causes. But now, my wife, allow me to teach you how to please me as much as I hope to please you. You agree?'

'If you wish,' murmured Hero.

CHAPTER TEN

Drew threw off his gown and nightshirt, slid under the covers and took her in his embrace. For long moments they lay quite still, absorbing each other's nearness.

Hero could feel his heart hammering, as was her own. It seemed to have swelled and risen inside her breast, blocking her windpipe so that she could scarcely breathe. When Drew at last moved it was to untie the strings of her nightcap and remove it, spread her hair upon the pillow and bury his face in its fragrance.

Fascinated by the hard contours of his muscular shoulders, Hero allowed her fingers to smooth over his silky skin and felt a shiver run through his body. She stilled at once.

He groaned. 'Don't stop!'

'You shivered. I thought I had offended you.'

'You must learn to recognise the difference between revulsion and delight.' His finger traced a line down her spine and despite the presence of intervening cotton she could not repress a shudder. 'You see?'

She nodded, although he would not see in the darkness, but he must have felt the movement. 'You really don't need this nightgown, you know,' he whispered, his fingers beginning to undo the buttons it had taken Jackson so long to fasten. 'It separates us. I want to feel you. . .'

'But—'

He interrupted her protest with gentle firmness. 'Do not fear for your modesty, my dear. Between husband and wife there should be no shame. One day I shall stand you before me in all your naked beauty. There can be no sin in that.'

A blush suffused her whole body. Memory flooded back. She had glimpsed him naked and, despite her misery at the time, still saw him so in her dreams, glorying in the remembrance of his strong, manly body. She remembered, too, the anguish of knowing he had taken her merely from duty. And the only other time he had taken her it had been in anger, though desire had been there, too, in full measure. But now he seemed willing to give tenderness and passion, even if he could not give her love. To allow him to remove her nightgown did not seem too depraved. She made no further demur as he continued with his task, turning the operation into an erotic adventure.

They lay close again, skin to skin, and Hero luxuriated in the feel of him, the rough texture of his body hair against her tender flesh, the awareness of bunched muscles and spinal indentations under her fingers as she explored the length of his back until she reached his taut buttocks and experienced an explosion of pleasure.

He had probed the secrets of her body before, but not in the careful, almost adoring fashion he did now. His mouth closed on hers in the way she had longed for, demanding yet tender, in a kiss which drew from her the willing response he sought.

He followed the kiss by tracing a searing trail of salutes down her throat to the hollow between her breasts. As he ran his hot, moist mouth over the swelling mound then bit gently at a peak, his hand found hers and led it to the part of himself she had not dared to touch. Hero's hips reared involuntarily as spears of sensation from his suckling pierced through to her core just as her hand discovered his throbbing flesh.

Her senses spun. 'Yes!' she gasped. 'Please, Drew! Please!'

Drew lifted his head just enough to murmur, 'Patience, my wife,' his voice thick, his breathing fast and hard. On a kind of desperate laugh he added, 'I shall not be capable of pleasuring you for long.' She wondered what he meant as his head dipped again and his mouth claimed her other breast.

Hero could not stop herself. She shifted and moaned, clutched at him urgently as he pursued his passionate assault with mouth and hands. When at last he turned her under him and entered her clamouring body she let out a cry of exultation. His groan of satisfaction chorused with it as her warmth closed about him.

To hold him became impossible. Her limbs had no strength, she lay under him like a rag doll, the enervation like nothing she had known before. She wanted Drew to remain exactly where he was for ever and ever...

His weight bore down on her, a welcome burden, until he stirred to prop himself up on his elbows.

'I'll last as long as I can,' he promised softly, 'but I have waited so long for this that I may not be able...'

He trailed off and began to move. As the new, exquisite sensations began to ripple through Hero the strength returned to her muscles. She moved under and with him, wound her legs to twine with his, clutched him with urgent hands, pulled him closer, strained to take him deeper to fill the void inside her.

How long they coupled she did not know but it was over too soon. Sudden frantic movement, a huge groan and Drew jerked and collapsed on top of her. Great shudders shook his body. Hero realised that he had lost control and understood what he had meant. He had not been able to carry on. And she had driven him to this abandon!

The emptiness inside disappeared as tenderness for her husband filled her. She held his inert body tightly in her arms and, without any conscious thought, pressed a flurry of hot kisses on his neck and shoulder.

The shudders subsided and he stirred at length to kiss her gently on the forehead, then on her nose and, lastly, on her soft, vulnerable mouth.

'I behaved like a starving youth, grabbing all the food on the table for myself,' he apologised ruefully, 'but next time, I promise you, it will be different, my dear. Next time, we will share in the feast.'

'What feast?' queried Hero, and added shyly, 'Husband, I have never known such pleasure.'

'Nor I.' He sounded surprised at the admission. 'It was so great, the need so urgent, that I failed to carry you all the way with me. You had less of a climax this time than last.'

Hero flushed at his reminding her again of the humiliation she had suffered. But she knew he was not throwing it in her face. Man-like, having apologised, he had already wiped his offence from his mind.

'Was that a climax?' she asked in surprise. 'I did not

know. And tonight I experienced so much more delight in every way.'

He stroked the hair from her face as he slid to lie beside her. She felt his withdrawal as a loss. But he gathered her close again, pulling her to nestle against him. 'I am happy you should feel so. But you will reach greater heights of enjoyment, that I can promise you.'

'I felt shockingly wanton,' she confided in a small voice, daring to use the word with which he had once condemned her.

He laughed, no trace of censure apparent, and Hero sighed her content as her confidence returned.

'And so you should, my wife,' he murmured deeply. 'I shall not. . .object. . .as long as you confine. . .your wantonness. . .to your dealings. . .with me.'

This statement he punctuated with several kisses to her face. Instead of melting under this tender barrage Hero stiffened and tried to withdraw. 'You may have no fears on that score, my lord. I am fully aware of the duties imposed upon me as your wife.'

His arms tightened possessively. 'Oh, Hero! Don't ruin the mood between us by climbing up on your high ropes! Can you not recognise a tease when you hear it?'

Hero relaxed only slightly. 'Not from you, husband. You have already shown a tendency to indulge in quite irrational jealousy.'

'Irrational?' Indignation gave way to a rueful laugh. 'A natural emotion, wife, when your beauty drew the attention of every man in a room and I was uncertain of your response to me. But I know you better now, my wife. You will soon, I pray, become the mother of my heirs. I shall not doubt you again.'

So her abandoned response had not offended him but negated his fears. He did not know she loved him and could therefore never betray him. His jealousy had been, and would be, rooted in possessiveness, not love. That was the crux of her lingering sorrow but something she would have to learn to live with. She sighed and curled into him again.

'You have no need.'

To her shock she felt his body rear against hers, waking immediate response. She gave a small moan and when he murmured into her hair, 'Again?' she breathed,

'Yes.'

The household was astir before they slept. A little housemaid crept in to clean the grate and light a new fire. Screened by bed-curtains, they lay still and silent while she went about her task. As the door closed behind her Drew rose to turn the key in the lock. Her eyes being accustomed to the dark, Hero watched unashamedly, revelling in the pale gleam of the male body that had brought her such pleasure. He had kept his promise and taken her with him to that place where thought ceased and the world became a cocoon of sensuous ecstasy, making her forget that he did not love her.

He went briefly through to the dressing-room before rejoining Hero in the bed.

'I've left a note for Benbow. We shall not be disturbed until we ring,' he informed her, running a hand over the swell of her breast, down into the valley of her waist, over the rise of her hips to rest on one slender thigh. But for the moment passion was spent He turned her so that her back was against him, clasped her about the waist and murmured into her nape, 'Sleep well, my wife.'

Hero made a sound of assent, pressed his hands against her with her own and, secure in the knowledge that he did at least, quite unmistakably, desire her, complied.

They stirred at noon. Hero left the bed and drew back the curtains to find the countryside enjoying a bright, frosty December day. Drew rang for Benbow and Jackson and ordered breakfast to be served in the bedroom.

'Put on your riding habit,' he ordered as he disappeared into the dressing-room. 'After we have eaten we will ride round the estate.'

He looked relaxed, happy, energetic. Hero wished she did not feel as though she had been through a mill. He had been gentle but even so she ached in places she had never ached before. Still, she would enjoy the fresh air and the exercise might help.

With her usual efficiency Jackson, well-trained to be inscrutable whatever the master and mistress got up to, soon had her dressed. Matty had no doubt drawn her own conclusions and was keeping out of the way until called for. Not having been happy about their flight in the first place, she had been delighted at the reconciliation and Hero knew she held out strong hopes that here in the country everything would come right between the earl and her chick. After the night they had just spent together Hero began to hold out some hopes herself.

Drew led her to the stables, situated a few hundred yards from the house and covering an extensive area. The yard was busy. Hero saw Ned Tribble and immediately recognised Cuthbert, who crossed the yard to greet his master.

'You have the horses saddled?'

'Aye, my lord. I hope your lady approves of the gelding.'

Drew smiled. 'So do I!'

Several horses had been sent ahead from London, Drew's beautiful bay stallion, Samson, among them. A groom led him forward. Following behind came another, smaller but, to Hero's admiring eye, even more beautiful animal, a bright bay with white socks and a star on his forehead, carrying a new lady's saddle.

She gave a little cry and went straight up to the strange horse. He seemed to share her delight at the meeting, blowing into her palm and arching his graceful neck under her stroking hand.

'You like him?' asked Drew from close behind her.

Hero turned to him, her eyes shining. 'How could I fail? He is for me to ride?'

'He is yours, since you approve of him. I promised you a horse and both Tribble and I thought a gelding would suit you best. Cuthbert agreed and this one's temperament made him ideal. He is still young, but not too skittish. Many of my neighbours breed and I found him when I was last here.'

'Oh, Drew!' Even when he had left her alone in London he had not entirely forgotten her. Just in time Hero remembered the audience of grooms and stablehands and stopped herself from flinging her arms round her smiling husband's neck and kissing him. But her eyes said it all as she murmured demurely, 'Thank you for the most wonderful gift I have ever received. What is his name?'

Drew's hand touched hers as he, too, fondled the bay's muzzle. 'His stable name is Samson's Boy—he was sired before I purchased Samson a couple of years ago—but you may call him what you like.'

'Boy will do. Hello, Boy!' She kissed the white mark between his eyes and Boy whickered his pleasure.

'Allow me to help you mount. Samson,' Drew pointed out with a grin, 'is becoming restive. He is jealous at all the attention being given his son and wants to be off.'

'Does he know. . .?'

Drew gave a delighted laugh as Hero put her foot into his laced hands and he tossed her into her saddle. 'I think not! Only human fathers recognise their progeny and even they would fail were they parted before the child had grown. Boy is just another horse to Samson and not even a threat where the mares are concerned. So they should give no trouble when we ride together.'

He left her then to mount himself and soon had Samson alongside. The two animals, no doubt used to riding out together on stable exercise, took little notice of each other as their riders proceeded from the yard and took a path leading through lawns and gardens and across the park towards the farmland and open countryside beyond.

Boy's muscles rippled beneath Hero as they came to a field and kicked the horses into a canter, making for the crest of a rise. Never had she felt such immediate affinity with a horse, not even her beloved mount of old. She leant over his withers and crooned softly into his ear as he carried her effortlessly up the hill.

At the top Drew called a halt. As the horses blew to regain their wind and jangled their harnesses to show their exuberance he swept an arm to indicate the fertile land stretching away before them, dotted with buildings and small wooded copses and criss-crossed with hedges.

'The Ashworthy estate stretches as far as you can see in every direction,' he informed her, quiet pride in his voice.

Hero looked about her in wonder. Some of the myriad fields contained herds of cows, others flocks of sheep. Many lay bare of any apparent crop yet were clearly under cultivation. A man plodded his way along a furrow behind a plough drawn by two huge horses. A narrow ribbon of water, shrouded in places by lingering mist, wound across the landscape to disappear behind a belt of trees.

She turned to Drew, sitting his mount with erect dignity, hard and proud, exhibiting as always that lack of soft effeteness which set him apart from his peers. He stood out in London society because of it. But the last vestiges of town affectations had dropped from him and, by the way he was eyeing them, these acres held first place in his heart. He employed stewards to help, but she had already discovered that he largely administered his estates himself.

'Have you always loved this place?' she asked.

He glanced at her quickly, then away again. 'I did not know it in my childhood.'

'Oh?'

'You have not heard?'

His tone had taken on a grim tone. Hero shivered without knowing why. She was almost afraid to ask, but she did. 'Heard what?'

'My father was banished from Ashworthy, cut off without a penny for choosing to follow his heart and wed for love, a penniless girl, a mere gentleman's daughter.'

The bitterness in his voice brought quick sympathy from Hero and a flood of sudden understanding. No wonder he had sounded grim. There was little she could say to assuage his hurt, but she tried.

'I feel the greatest admiration for your father, Drew. And it must be a comfort to know you were conceived in love.' Unlike me, she wanted to add, but instead observed, 'Your grandfather must have been a hard man.'

'You cannot imagine.' He gathered his reins. 'Come, let us go down to the river.'

He had changed the subject. Hero hid her disappointment and almost forgot it in the joy of exercise. They reached the river and Drew led the way along a track which followed its bank. Before long they entered the belt of trees she had seen from above so that, although not far from the house or the driveway, they were invisible from both. The track widened into a grassy bank and Drew again brought them to a standstill.

He dismounted and slung his reins over a nearby branch. Turning, he held out his arms to help her down. Hero did not demur, although she could have managed perfectly easily without help. She let him catch her, knowing the pleasure it would give them both as she slid down his body to reach the ground.

'It is lovely here,' she remarked rather breathlessly as he let her go and she turned to look about.

'I shall look upon it with more favour in the future. Until today it has been a place to bring me nothing but unhappy memories.'

He had led the horses to the river and stood waiting for them to drink. Hero followed after him and asked, 'Why? What happened here?'

He gazed broodingly into the water. 'This is where my grandfather's gamekeeper caught me and so where my journey to the penal colony began.'

His voice held no bitterness now. Hero waited, almost holding her breath, for him to continue. But the horses had finished drinking and he led them back to the path and tied their reins to low branches. As they began to crop the lush grass he indicated a fallen log. Hero sat down and he came to prop his boot on the bark beside her. Elbow resting on his braced thigh, he clasped his hands together as he spoke again.

'I had better tell you my story. I had hoped not to have to but it will not be long before you hear it from others and I had rather you had it from me. My version will be accurate.'

'Only if you want to tell me, Drew.'

He sighed. 'It is time I did.' He paused a moment and she knew he was still reluctant to confide in her. But he did go on. 'My father, Gerald Challoner, was the Earl of Calverstock's younger son. As so often happens with younger sons, he was bought a commission in the army, the 28th Foot. My mother's parents were clinging to their small estate by the skins of their teeth so his chosen one had no dowry to bring him except her love. But still, he defied the old man and married her.'

'He must have loved her very much.'

'He did; they loved each other. Living on a captain's pay was not easy. However, they managed it. Mother rented rooms near his barracks so that they could be together as much as possible. She took in needlework to pay for my education, the best available wherever my father happened to be stationed, as long as it was in England. But when he set sail for Egypt she had to remain behind and eke out a living for us both by her needle. We returned to this part of the world, where they had both been born.'

He paused and Hero asked, 'Could you not have lived with your other grandparents?'

The definite shake of his head made it clear that that had been impossible. 'No. They were both dead and her brother had squandered what remained of the family fortunes. He sold the estate, spent the proceeds and took himself off to the West Indies to make a new fortune but died of a fever. There was nothing left.'

'And she had no other relatives?'

'None with room or money to spare for us.'

'And your uncle, your father's brother? Surely he——?'

Drew broke in, 'He was worse than his father. Papa had betrayed his class, they would have nothing further to do with him. And then,' he went on sombrely, 'word came that Captain Gerald Challoner was dead. No wonder we had heard nothing from him. He died of wounds in March 1801 after the battle under

Abercromby near Alexandria. Mother was prostrate for weeks.'

Hero swallowed. 'How old were you, Drew?'

'Thirteen. Mother had worked herself almost blind to send me to a minor public school. She had to work even longer hours then and she lacked the stamina. Less than two years later she went into a feverish decline. I had not realised... I left school at once, of course, and took a casual job in the local forge to bring in a shilling or two each week. We had nothing saved, I had to look after Mama, the parish paid out a pittance, but quite simply we were starving. The rent had to be paid or we'd be thrown out and that would have killed her. I collected firewood from round about but there was never enough money to feed an invalid properly or to pay a doctor. So I came here to beg help from my grandfather.'

A picture of Drew as a half-starved youth desperate with worry for his mother brought quick tears to Hero's eyes. 'Did he give it?'

'He laughed in my face.' The bitterness was back in Drew's voice now. 'How I hated him! I'd walked ten miles or more on an almost empty stomach to see him and all he did was laugh!'

'Oh, Drew!'

Hero put her hand up to touch his clasped hands. She wanted to put her arms about him to give him comfort but she could feel the resistance in his taut body. Indeed, the instant he saw the tears in her eyes he took his foot from the log and turned away.

Head flung back, he declared, 'I demanded no pity then and I wish for none now. I decided to take matters into my own hands. Instead of leaving the property immediately I scouted round and found what I had been looking for. Rabbit traps. Rabbit broth would do my mother a power of good and if I was to provide for her I needed something solid and warm inside me. I found a couple of prize specimens struggling to free themselves and released the poor creatures, put them out of their misery by wringing their necks, hid them under my coat and began to make for home.' He glanced towards the undergrowth beyond the path. 'The traps have gone now.'

'Did you have them removed?'

He shot her a sardonic smile. 'How did you guess? I could not bear to see them every time I passed this way. I was unfortunate, you see. Midgley, the gamekeeper, happened along and caught me with my prizes. Stealing game is, of course, a heinous offence. And I made matters worse by trying to fell the fellow and escape. I did not know he had assistants within call.'

'But surely the estate belonged to your family——?'

'But not to me. I told Midgley who I was and he took me before my grandfather. He refused to acknowledge me. Told Midgley to hand me over to the law. The rest you know.'

She did not, not really. How could she possibly imagine what it must have been like for a boy like Drew to be thrown into gaol, convicted, transported to the other side of the earth to work for slave wages in a harsh penal colony? And what had happened to his mother?

Hero sensed that he wished to say no more, so she suppressed most of the questions burning the tip of her tongue. All she said was, 'Your mother?'

He paced to the river's edge and spoke with his back

turned. 'They allowed me to send her a message. At least she knew what had happend to me. I wrote from time to time and her letters came like a breath of fresh English air.' He drew some deeply into his lungs before swinging round and grinning wryly. 'It seems I was well-liked in the area and my misfortune awakened the charitable conscience of the doctor and others. Thanks to them she survived and continued to make a living with her needle. I worked as much overtime as I could and sent the money home. She is still alive.'

Hero frowned. 'I did not notice anyone who could be your mother on the list of Christmas guests. Is she not coming to Ashworthy?'

'No. She prefers to remain quietly at her home.'

'What a pity. I'd like to meet her.'

He turned. 'You will, one day. But not yet.'

Hero wanted to ask why not, but didn't. He was releasing Boy and held him ready for her to mount, making it clear that confidences were over for now.

'Tomorrow we will ride to the village. You must meet some of the tenants who live there. The farmers will all come up to the house to pay their rents after church on Christmas morning, since it is quarter day. You will meet them all then.'

'Mrs Pilcher mentioned the Christmas feast you give for them. They bring their families, I believe. I shall look forward to it.'

He untied Samson and sprang into the saddle. 'We help to serve them,' he informed her with a sideways, interrogatory glance. 'You will not mind?'

'No! I wish I had thought of doing the same at Polhembury!' A slight sadness crossed her features. 'I wonder how they will all fare there this year.'

'Your Mrs Blackler will dish up something special for the household, I'm certain. They will manage. There will be sufficient income from the estate if your father manages it well.'

'And if he does not?'

His shrug said it all. 'That is his concern, not yours.'

Drew disliked Baron Polhembury for some reason and she did not wish to make matters worse, so she could not mention the drafts she had sent to Mrs Cudlip or the report she had received of her father's neglect. Perhaps, one day, when the shadow lying between them had quite gone, she would summon up the courage. Ask his help. But not yet.

'I came to know them well,' she explained her concern. 'I would not like to think of them suffering because of my absence.'

'You are quite unlike your father,' Drew surprised her by saying as they emerged from the wood and turned along the drive, heading towards the house. 'You did have a care for your people.'

'I always did my best for them,' she assured him quietly.

'I believe you did. Our servants already adore you. The tenants will soon learn to do the same.'

She looked at him quickly, searching for mockery, but found none. He meant it. The unexpectedness of his praise set her nerves tingling and her heart singing. Could it be that he no longer despised her?

CHAPTER ELEVEN

In just over a week the guests would begin to arrive at Ashworthy for the festivities. Hero spent much time in conference with Mrs Pilcher discussing the merits of venison—deer roamed the park—chicken, mutton, rabbit and partridge and whether to serve trout from their pond, fish from the sea—would it be fresh enough?—smoked salmon from Scotland, salt cod or pilchards, or something of everything, baked, boiled or stewed. The varieties of soup for the remove, of pies, puddings and custards had to be decided upon. Ice stored in the ice house made iced puddings a possibility, fruit and vegetables grew in abundance in walled garden and hothouse, and the estate could provide flowers and plants to decorate the table and rooms.

Despite all her training and years of experience, Hero found the decisions difficult, for they had seldom entertained at Polhembury and she scarcely knew some of the people Drew had invited. The party would not be large, just a dozen guests including Earl Bathurst and his countess, a young viscount, Lord Edding, and his mother Lady Edding, Archie and Felicity and, most alarming to Hero, Lord and Lady Castlereagh. Most would stay until the New Year. But, she consoled herself, if the choice on the table was wide enough, surely there would be something to please everyone!

The guest rooms had already been prepared and

allocated according to precedence. It remained only for her to arrange flowers in them on the day of arrival. Drew was showing an efficient aptitude for organising the entertainment. Card tables, billiard-room, smoking-room and library were all inspected and dispositions planned. A small ensemble of piano, violin and flute had been engaged to entertain the company with music on Christmas Day and to provide the music on St Stephen's Day, a Saturday, when they planned to introduce a little dancing. The older guests would surely stand up in such circumstances. And on New Year's Eve they were to throw a ball to which many of the local gentry had been invited.

In addition to the invited guests and the servants they brought with them, the musicians also had to be accommodated, but Ashworthy was large enough to house twice the number.

In her new role as Hero's companion, Matty helped in any way she could. She dined with them now, for Hero considered it her due, but Matty refused to join them when they entertained.

'I've not been bred to it, my chick,' she protested when Hero suggested that she should do so during the coming festivities. 'I'd be that nervous—I'm fine with just you and his lordship, since you've been so kind as to ask me, but I shouldn't feel right sitting at table with Lord Castlereagh! No, I'll have a tray in my room, or eat with Mrs Pilcher. I'll be much happpier, never you fear.'

'But you'll join us at other times, won't you?' Hero pressed. 'I'm relying on you to help me to entertain the guests. And to act as chaperone to the young ladies! We must allow no misconduct under this roof or I shall be ostracised from society!'

Matty grinned, showing her gappy teeth. 'I'll do that right enough, my chick,' she promised.

Hero retired each night tired but, on the whole, happy with the arrangements being made. Drew joined her in the master bedroom, where they shared hours of warm intimacy and passion.

She learnt to know his body as he knew hers. One night she had stood naked, proud and unashamed, while he circled her, a branch of candles held high, feasting his eyes on the firm roundness of her hips, the fullness of her breasts, the neatness of her waist. Afterwards he had shown particular passion during his lovemaking.

Yet she knew that although Drew wanted her he did not love her. He was still witholding part of himself. But so was she. Despite her growing respect and regard, she could not forget the ruthless way he ruined those he had taken in dislike. Nor, despite his having left them behind in London, could she ignore his consorting with all those women others hinted at—in the nicest, most tactful way, of course.

Subsequent to that first morning they rose at their usual early hour and rode about the estate before breakfast, calling in at remote farmhouses to meet Drew's tenants. Hero discovered that he was universally liked and respected. No one hesitated to tell him of necessary repairs and all were willing to discuss the latest methods of farming with him, even if, like the elderly, weatherbeaten Farmer Wellow, they scoffed at them.

Drew cared for the people, as well as the land, and was knowledgeable about both. This fitted ill with his treatment of her father and others, with the bargain he had made to make her his bride. Could it be that he was not as ruthless and without finer feeling as she had thought? He had certainly softened in his attitude to her.

'He were that good last spring when Mr Wellow were took bad,' confided Mrs Wellow, a comfortably built woman, mother of four married daughters and a longed-for son, as the men wandered out into the yard to inspect one of the oxen the farmer used to draw his plough. 'When the apothecary's medicine didn't seem to be doing any good he sent for the doctor and paid the bill. And he came over every day to see that young Alfie, our youngest—he's only sixteen—was managing to get the work done. Not above taking off his coat and doing a bit himself, is the new lord. Not like those that went before him. Mean devils, the lot of 'em. His lordship knows Mr Wellow'll be needing that animal fit before 'tis time to plough after Christmas and he'll see that it is.'

'Where is your son?' asked Hero politely.

'Alfie'll be in the milking shed. They'll be off there after, I don't doubt. Will ye be taking a dish of tea, my lady? I've a mite of fruit cake here if you'd care to sample it.'

'Thank you, Mrs Wellow. The exercise has made me quite hungry.'

'Haven't had breakfast yet, I'll be bound.' The motherly face beamed at Hero as Mrs Wellow placed a large wedge of succulent-looking cake in front of her. 'You look fair bonny, my lady, if I may say so.

Just the kind of wife a nice gentleman like his lordship needed.'

Hero took a large bite of the cake to cover her confusion. Drew had another admirer in Mrs Wellow, for most women found him irresistible, with his athletic build, light brown, sun-bleached hair, clear grey eyes and the smile which banished all trace of harshness from his features. She certainly did, she acknowledged as a wave of warm, weakening emotion swept through her.

'This is delicious,' she pronounced a trifle breathlessly, having swallowed the cake in her mouth. 'Would you allow me to have the receipt?'

After that the two women chatted like old friends until their husbands reappeared, by which time Hero had subdued her wayward thoughts. Drew accepted the refreshment offered by Mrs Wellow, a wedge of her cake and a jug of home-brewed ale.

As they rode back to the house Hero reflected that each day revealed some new facet of her husband's character. The disquiet she felt over his buying up of debts and his subsequent dealings with his debtors began to fade a little. Most of the time she could forget even the way she had been forced into marriage. She supposed he must have his own reasons for such behaviour. One day he would tell her. Until then she would try to trust the man she was coming to know so much better, who, in every other way, was very like the one she had instinctively judged him to be.

To Hero's relief the house party proved a great success. It did not pass without one or two moments of anxiety, however.

Archie Dalmead, faced with the appealing presence of Lady Felicity, at first sought refuge in the company of his friend.

'Devil take it, Drew! Couldn't you prevent your wife from inviting the Beltinge female?'

Drew merely lifted his brows. 'Hero has few friends. She wished to advance the acquaintance. Why should Lady Felicity's presence here concern you?'

Archie, regardless of his careful coiffure, ran agitated fingers through his hair. 'Because, as you are perfectly well aware, that female is out to trap me into wedlock! I won't have it, d'you hear?'

'I hear,' replied Drew, ostentatiously covering his ears against Archie's indignant bellow. 'But, my dear fellow, all you have to do is ignore her. Do not follow her into empty rooms, avoid dark and chilly terraces——'

'Don't play the fool, Drew! You know very well I'm fond of the chit! I believe this is a conspiracy to throw us together.'

'How can it be? You are perfectly free to leave,' observed Drew equably.

'And miss your Christmas party?' Archie flicked open his snuff box and took a large pinch, sniffing deeply and with great deliberation. He snapped the box shut and remarked with studied languor, 'No, I shall not leave, I shall simply treat her with the utmost courtesy when we meet but otherwise ignore her.'

'Lady Calverstock,' began Felicity breathlessly.

'Please call me Hero,' put in her hostess quickly. 'I know we are not well-acquainted yet, but I feel we are to be friends.'

'Thank you! So do I! But. . .' Felicity hesitated and began again with more determination. 'But Hero, had I known his lordship would be here—'

'Which lordship?' enquired Hero innocently.

'Lord Harrington! It is so very difficult. He pays me every courtesy, of course, and I thought he liked me, but he seems to be avoiding me. It is most lowering to be treated with so much indifference when I. . .I admire him so much,' confessed Felicity, colouring. 'I fear I shall find myself much exercised to hide my embarrassment in company.'

'Archie is a perfect gentleman,' observed Hero. 'He will not make his avoidance noticeable, you may depend upon it. Have you considered, Felicity, that it may not be due to indifference at all? That he may simply be running scared? He fears that you may well be able to fix his interest and wear down his resistance to the idea of matrimony.'

'Oh! But then, how much more. . .?' Felicity's breathless words trailed off.

'Just be your charming self, my dear,' smiled Hero. 'Ignore his coolness. Treat him as you would any other young gentleman. In fact, you could concentrate your attention on Lord Edding, could you not? He is a personable young man if a little tied to his mother's leading strings. Make Harrington a little jealous, perhaps?'

Felicity suddenly giggled. 'Hero! I believe you planned this! But how could you know that I cherish a *tendre*. . .?'

'I must confess to eavesdropping at the theatre. You thought our box empty and so did not lower your voice. I do apologise.'

'Oh!' Felicity looked a little confused. 'You mean that evening after the Queen's funeral, before you were taken ill?'

'I do.' Hero firmly repressed her guilty blush and hoped Felicity would not remember the remarks she had made about Calverstock and herself. 'You told your parents you would wed Archie were he to declare himself. We are merely giving him the chance, that is all.'

'No wonder he looked as though he wished to turn and run the instant he saw me here!' A small smile had begun to play about Felicity's mobile lips. 'Poor Harrington! I shall be sweetness itself. But, you know, I do believe I have suddenly discovered that I cherish a *tendre* for a certain young viscount!'

'Well done,' chuckled Hero. 'Archie is struggling against his feelings for you, you know. If that doesn't bring him to the point I cannot imagine what will!'

Presents were exchanged on Christmas Eve. Hero exclaimed over gloves and fans, a lavish writing box from Archie, sundry exquisitely worked handkerchiefs, papier-mâché and enamelled boxes and trays, together with baubles and other offerings from the servants. Members of the staff had all been presented with their Christmas boxes in the form of money, which both Drew and Hero had agreed would be of most use to them. The carefully chosen gifts presented to their guests were received with at least surface pleasure.

Hero had debated the question of what to give Drew for weeks past. While still in London she had decided upon and purchased a leather-bound volume, a first edition, for his library. As the last of the gifts were distributed and opened it became painfully clear that she was to receive nothing from him.

Her disappointment knew no bounds. He had given her Boy, of course, and the new saddle, but had said nothing about those being for Christmas. Surely he would not leave her out, not in front of their guests. It would be too pointed and quite at odds with his more recent behaviour. The omission must be an oversight.

Every parcel had been opened and exclaimed over and Drew had thanked her for an addition to his library that he would always treasure with what she knew to be sincerity. His teasing grey eyes rested upon her with something like real affection as he bowed elaborately before her.

'I fear I could not wrap my gift to you, my lady. If you will call your maid to bring your cloak and bonnet, I will take you outside and present it.'

Hero's eyes began to sparkle. Just the knowledge that he had not passed her over was enough, but to have to go outside—whatever could it be?

Matty had already murmured, 'I'll fetch them,' and left the room. Hero guessed she would bring her own things, too, for she would expect to accompany her mistress.

'May I come with you?' asked Archie, presuming on his friendship with Drew to be the first to speak. Everyone in the room was agog.

'Cannot we all come?' cried an older couple's young daughter, who had been ogling Archie ever since the family's arrival. Hero had not anticipated such a complication and hoped Miss Dickens would not spoil her plans for Archie and Felicity. But Archie seemed disinclined to encourage the chit even to defend himself against Felicity's charms and Hero had only to consider the girl's unfortunate looks and notice her forward manners to understand why.

'Of course,' agreed Drew expansively. 'The more the merrier!'

A rush ensued to fetch or ring for outdoor garments. Drew, in anticipation of the moment, had his caped greatcoat and beaver already waiting in the hall. Matty returned quickly with Hero's things, including gloves and muff. Thereafter Hero's patience was sorely tried as they waited for others to ready themselves to brave the crisp December air.

Eventually all were suitably garbed and the expedition set off, Drew leading the way with Hero on his arm. He conducted them right round the house, quite a long trek, since the building had, over the centuries, tended to sprawl as wings and extensions were added.

'It is a fine afternoon for a stroll, don't you agree?' he murmured, glancing down at Hero, a roguish look in his eyes.

'Where are we going?' she asked. 'Is this some kind of trick?'

'Not at all. Patience, my dear. I am just ensuring that our guests take some exercise.'

He was being mischievous. Perhaps he had not really wanted an audience when he presented his gift, but had felt unable to refuse the escort.

Having almost circled the house, they came at last to the stables. Hero began to tremble with an excitement she could scarcely contain. What could he have for her here? Another mount? A hunter, perhaps?

The others were all talking and laughing, making

jokes and playing a guessing game. As they entered under the stable arch Hero stopped in her tracks, while a concerted cry of astonishment came from those following behind.

Waiting in the yard stood a delightful little open carriage, painted black and gold, with scarlet cushions and a folding hood in case it should rain. Two-wheeled like a cabriolet or curricle, it was neither, for a cabriolet used only a single horse and a curricle had no hood. Harnessed to it, covered by blankets to keep them warm, were two superb black ponies she had never seen in the stables before, their headstalls beribboned and garnished with sprigs of holly. Tribble, his nose pink with cold, stood holding their heads, a wide grin on his face.

Hero looked up at Drew, her eyes enormous. She could hardly speak for the lump in her throat.

'Is that my gift?' she gulped.

He nodded. 'You will need your own conveyance here at Ashworthy. It may not always be convenient for you to ride Boy.' A note in his voice told her he was anticipating a time when she would be increasing. 'In this you may travel to the village or anywhere on the estate in comparative comfort. You can drive? If not, I shall be delighted to teach you.'

She hadn't driven for years, any more than she had ridden a horse. That skill had come back without effort and she supposed that that with the ribbons would too. But did he want to teach her?

'Only a very little,' she answered, moving forward at last to take a closer look at the extravagant gift the others were all admiring.

What must they be thinking? That it was the kind of

gift a rich and noble lord might give to his new and beloved wife? But she knew she was not beloved.

The first shock gave way to excited chatter and cries of congratulation.

Very softly Drew asked, 'Would you like to take a short drive now?'

She looked up and answered the quizzical smile in his eyes. He wanted to shake off their retinue.

'I should like that above everything.'

'Then I'll help you up.'

A groom removed the blankets and Tribble released the ponies' heads. Drew flicked the whip and they left the yard to the sound of a ragged cheer, leaving the others to make a leisurely way back to the house. Sitting close, because the carriage was small, Drew drove at a brisk trot, reminding her of the techniques involved in driving a carriage and pair. With the gates in sight, he handed her the whip and offered the reins.

'Drive to the entrance and then pull up.'

She did as bidden, the thrill of holding the ribbons again showing in the delighted concentration on her striking features. The gatekeeper ran out to open the gates but Drew beckoned him to come to them.

'We are not leaving the grounds,' he explained. 'Lead the ponies round, will you?'

So the carriage was turned and Hero began the drive back. Following Drew's instructions, she diverted into a crossing path which would lead them on a circular route back. Round a further bend, shielded from prying eyes by thick trees and undergrowth, Drew told her to stop again.

With the ponies obediently stationary, Hero looked at him, a question in her smile.

'Was that satisfactory, my lord?'

'Certainly. As in everything else, you are an apt pupil.' He grinned a trifle wryly. 'Is there nothing I can teach you?'

Hero blushed and lowered her eyes. 'You know the answer to that, my husband.'

'Then I shall require proof,' he responded, sending a thrill winging through her. Then, 'You have not properly thanked me,' he complained, injecting a plaintive note into his voice.

Hero, daring to look up again, caught the gleam in his eye but pretended not to notice it.

'I did,' she protested. 'You cannot have forgotten——'

Her words choked off as Drew put an arm round her shoulders, turned her face up and lowered his lips to within an inch of hers.

'Kiss me,' he instructed.

With becoming modesty, Hero complied.

'Mmm. After all my tuition you can do better than that.'

'Will this do, my lord?' she demanded and, abandoning all pretence, gave him the kiss dictated by her heart.

That evening, gathered in the drawing-room, several of the ladies entertained the company at the pianoforte. To Hero's amusement, Lady Felicity, in a pretty manner, persuaded Lord Edding to turn her pages for her. She performed so excellently and looked so delightful with the light of the candles mounted on each side of the instrument playing on her features that Hero felt sure Archie must be captivated. When he strolled across and replaced Edding at her side for an encore, she was convinced of it. Felicity played with greater spirit but less accuracy, which few except Hero noticed.

And then someone, Lord Castlereagh in fact, demanded that Hero should take her place at the pianoforte. She could, of course, have continued to decline, not protesting an inability but by her expression allowing everyone to infer it, as she had in London. But here, in what was now her own home, she thought she would not. She had not dared to practise since leaving Polhembury because Calverstock would surely have found out. She would be rusty, but that could not be helped. The deception had gone on long enough. He had so easily seen through her others that to discover his wife to be a talented musician should scarcely surprise him now.

He did look slightly aghast as she rose to her feet in compliance with the request. Archie and several others who had seen her decline before looked surprised. But Hero, bathed in new assurance of the felicity of her marriage, glided gracefully over to the instrument and settled herself on the stool. She had, surreptitiously, examined the music and knew there were several pieces she could play, as well as those she already knew by heart. As she searched for a suitable sonata by the late Mr Mozart a shadow fell across the music.

'Something else you have no need to learn?' asked a soft voice in her ear.

'I fear so,' murmured Hero.

'Why did you allow me to go on believing you so ignorant of the social graces?'

'Because you assumed it without condescending to ask.'

'Forgive me. I prejudged you, my dear,' Drew admitted. 'Are you able to sing?'

'Not as well as I could wish,' confessed Hero with a laugh. 'My voice is slight, though tuneful, I believe. I will try this.'

She handed him a sheet of music and he placed it on the stand between the candles. Hero flexed her fingers, as she did every day to keep them supple, and began to play the elegant sonata.

The applause when she finished sounded more than merely polite. On being persuaded to play an encore Hero launched into a lively country dance.

Then Drew said, 'Play this.'

He placed a song sheet on the stand. Hero looked up enquiringly and he grinned. 'I, too, have a concealed talent I am at last ready to display,' he teased.

And so he had—a strong, pleasant tenor voice. He had chosen a song with a chorus which Hero joined in, encouraging everyone else to do the same. Afterwards, by request, Hero played Christmas carols and the company raised their voices in joyful harmony.

Soon the village minstrels could be heard outside rendering, rather raggedly and somewhat off-key, the same old tunes. Peering from the windows a group of warmly wrapped figures could be seen, illuminated by the light thrown from the lanterns they carried. However untutored their performance, they had brought with them the spirit of Christmas. Arm in arm, Drew and Hero went to open the door, dispense some largesse and invite the singers in for refreshment.

It was, considered Hero, the best eve of Christmas she had enjoyed since her mother's death.

After church on Christmas Day the tenants followed Lord and Lady Calverstock and their guests back to Ashworthy in gig and cart, some walking their families in procession behind.

With his steward in attendance to keep the records, Drew personally received the rents, wished his tenants prosperity and happiness in the New Year and sent them through to the splendidly festooned dining-room, where preparations for refreshment had been made.

Felicity helped Drew and Hero to entertain their guests while Archie dispensed ale and lemonade with considerable dexterity and charm.

The tenants, subdued by their surroundings, scarcely spoke as they cleared the platters of ham, turkey and salmon, pigeon and lobster patties, fruit tarts and iced plum cake. Even the children, scrubbed and warned not to misbehave, spoke in whispers. Matty, at home in this company, chatted easily with them all, especially the children, encouraging them to eat heartily of the kind of food they seldom enjoyed at home. No one on a Calverstock estate would starve, and some tenants were quite prosperous, but most lived on more simple fare from day to day.

It astonished Hero, changing for their own festive meal, to discover how much she was enjoying the house party. Its success proved that one did not have to remain in London to take pleasure in society. She would enjoy to spend a part of the season in London each year, but much prefer to reside most of the time at Ashworthy. She suspected Drew felt the same, although duty took him to London and to other Calverstock estates from time to time.

And how she would have loathed entertaining if she and Drew had still been at cuffs, if behaving as a happy bride in public had still been all pretence! But the worst of their differences seemed to be over. Memories of their first disastrous weeks together were fading. They had found mutual enjoyment of each other as husband and wife and their attitudes had softened over matters of dissent. Understanding and companionship were growing between them. So, although she was not in fact quite the happy bride others imagined, it took little to maintain the fiction. Perhaps 1819 would bring the child they both desired. That event would give them a common purpose, a small creature they could both love without stint or reservation.

By New Year's Eve the house guests had settled into a routine and, if all had not immediately become bosom friends, no discordant note had so far been struck. The gentlemen spent much of the daylight hours outdoors hunting or shooting or indoors in the billiard-room, while the ladies pursued more decorous occupations, strolling in the gardens when the weather permitted, taking short carriage rides to view the surrounding countryside, or simply sitting before a cheerful fire reading, painting or embroidering.

But the bustle of preparation disturbed the peace and routine on the day of the ball, and not only in household matters. Maids dressed hair, pressed ball-growns, made last-minute alterations and added trimmings for their mistresses' approval, while valets attended to their masters' coiffures, brushed and pressed evening attire, ironed frilled shirts and prepared snowy cravats.

As the first carriage bringing guests rattled up the drive, Drew entered the bedroom where Jackson was putting the last touches to Hero's toilet.

'There, my lady. I think that will do.'

Hero took a last glance in the mirror and smiled approval.

'Thank you, Jackson. I think the new hairstyle suits me.' She rose from the dressing-stool and turned to greet her husband. 'What do you think my lord?'

Drew strolled across the room, took both her hands in his and spread her arms wide, holding her off to sweep his eyes down to the satin slippers peeping from beneath the heavily decorated hem of the shimmering, daffodil-yellow gown glowing through a mist of chiffon, and back up to linger on the swell of her bosom above the waist, on the creamy texture of the skin of her shoulders—the contemplation of touching which sent a remembered thrill through his own body—and on to study the abundant brown hair piled on top of her head with curls spilling out to frame her oval face.

'Capital,' he declared. 'I particularly approve of that ribbon and gauze affair on your head.' Gently, resisting the temptation to run a finger along the low neckline of the gown, he touched instead the delicate material nestling among her curls. 'You look beautiful, my dear.'

Hero fingered the exquisite heirloom necklace about her throat, the one he had given her before the lord mayor's dinner. 'I did not wish to wear the matching tiara and thought it went well with this.'

'To admiration,' agreed Drew. So saying, he pulled

her close and kissed her lightly upon the mouth, careful not to cause damage to her gown or coiffure. 'It is time to proceed downstairs. I hear our first guests arriving.'

Arm in arm, they descended to the hall to greet them.

Half an hour later, the receiving line having diminished to a trickle, the dancing was about to begin. Drew and Hero hovered by the door of the ballroom for a moment, absorbing the sight of their guests mingling in its restored splendour, the ladies' gowns and jewellery shimmering and glittering under the brilliant yet soft illumination offered by the hundreds of candles flickering amid the scintillating rainbow crystals of the chandeliers. Several long windows and a couple of doors graced the length of the opposite wall. One of the doors led to an orangery and the other directly to the terrace, beyond which lay the formal gardens.

'Ashworthy has come alive at last,' murmured Drew. 'You have worked a miracle, Lady Calverstock.'

His tone rendered the formal title as an endearment.

'I?' demanded Hero, startled. 'I have done very little.'

'Mrs Pilcher would not have managed half so well without your suggestions and encouragement. I could scarcely have entertained such a house party or given a ball alone. Your presence has made it all possible, my dear, and I am grateful.'

Hero, her heart leaping at the compliment, covered her quite inordinate pleasure by fluttering her lashes at her husband. 'I am glad you are satisfied wtih your bargain, my lord,' she responded with a smile half teasing, half sober.

'I am beginning to believe,' murmured Drew seriously, 'that my choice of wife was more admirable than I had ever anticipated.' How, he wondered, could he have guessed that the engaging creature he had met for such a brief moment yet had, on the strength of that slender acquaintance and despite her parentage, decided to wed, would turn out to be an incomparable? His fingers tightened on Hero's arm as he escorted her into the middle of the floor to lead the first dance. If only the marriage had not begun so badly. But he must put from his mind those scathing words he had overheard before the ceremony.

They took their places in the quadrille. As he bowed to acknowledge her curtsy he could not forbear to drink in the sight of her, to acknowledge that the overheard words did not represent the Hero Langage he had come to know. And her present attitude indicated that she might have changed her mind about him as much as he had changed his over her. Which thought gave him, a man who had long since ceased to care for the opinion of any but his dearest family and friends, a quite unwarranted degree of pleasure.

Felicity took to the floor partnered by Lord Edding. Harrington, looking less languid and decidedly less affable than usual, led a simpering Miss Dickens out to take their places in the measure. Hero noted Drew's sardonic eye fixed on Archie.

'Do you think he is suffering from jealousy?' she whispered as the steps of the dance brought them together.

'Lady Felicity has been doing her best to make him so, I believe. She cannot seriously be trying to fix the interest of that milksop Edding.'

It was several moments before Hero was able to answer. 'Of course not,' she maintained stoutly as they came together again. 'I do hope her campaign is successful.'

Drew chuckled. 'So she is mounting a campaign, eh? The designing creature! Poor Archie! But by the way he is glaring across at her, I believe she may be making an advance.'

During the next hour or so Felicity gracefully accepted Harrington's determined efforts to secure her hand and stood up with him on two occasions.

The supper dance ended. The company went through to the room set aside for the purpose to take refreshment. Hero was passing from guest to guest when Lord Edding fussed up to her.

'Lady Calverstock, have you seen Lady Felicity recently? I have been searching for her to take her in to supper, but she is nowhere to be found.'

Hero realised that she had not seen Felicity for some time. 'Had you secured her promise of the supper dance earlier? No? Then she has probably retired to her room to effect some repair to her toilet,' she suggested. 'I should not concern yourself, Lord Edding. I am certain she will return before long. She has a healthy appetite and will not wish to miss the refreshments.'

'I suppose not,' muttered his lordship irritably. 'I cannot search any longer. I must go and wait upon my mother. She will not be pleased at my not securing Lady Felicity's company.'

'You must not neglect Lady Edding,' agreed Hero, noting that his lordship was pursuing the heiress on his mother's instructions and hoping that neither they nor anyone else had noticed the simultaneous disappearance of Archie Dalmead.

She was not much worried. Matty had been given the task of acting as chaperone to any young lady who did not have her mother with her, and to Felicity in particular. Matty had stationed herself on a chair beside the door leading to the orangery. The couple were probably out there enjoying its shadowy privacy. Hero knew Matty would not allow any seriously improper conduct to take place and would do her best to divert anyone who threatened to intrude on the young couple. Though should she fail and the pair be discovered, Felicity would be compromised and Archie in honour bound to do the decent thing...

She forgot Felicity as she became absorbed in conversing politely with guests who, until that evening, had been strangers to her. As a good hostess this was demanded of her but she wanted to become acquainted with those who had their homes near by. If she and Drew spent much time at Ashworthy these people would constitute her social circle, and from them would come her closest friends.

Both Felicity and Archie reappeared before the end of supper. For the remainder of the evening it seemed to Hero that, for a man determined not to be caught in parson's mousetrap, Lord Harrington, in paying most particular attention to Lady Felicity Charteris and standing up with her yet again, was behaving in a manner calculated to spring it. He would end the evening heavily compromised.

On the stroke of midnight the year of 1819 was greeted with cheers and toasts. The dancing resumed. Drew had done his duty and danced with almost all their guests and Hero had not lacked for a partner all evening. Drew claimed his wife as the last waltz struck up.

'A most successful evening,' he murmured.

'In more ways than one, I predict,' answered Hero.

Drew did not have to ask what she meant. His hand pressed into her waist, pulling her imperceptibly closer. 'They are admirably suited. It should prove a felicitous union.'

Hero, as was usual when she danced a waltz with Drew, found herself short of breath. 'Archie needs a wife. He is already looking a changed man.'

'Marriage changes most men, whether they like it or not. Which is perhaps why most men try to avoid it.'

'It is as well for us poor females that gentlemen need to wed in order to breed an heir!'

He made no response to this tart observation for the music was speeding to a finish. Hero clung for a moment while she regained her balance and then reluctantly withdrew from Drew's embrace. He tucked her hand under his arm as they moved over to bid their departing guests goodnight.

As the house guests made their various ways upstairs Felicity hung back for a word with Hero.

Her excitement barely suppressed, she gave Hero such a radiant smile that there could be no doubt that Archie had been persuaded to declare himself at last.

'You have won your campaign?' smiled Hero, taking her friend's arm as they mounted the stairs.

Felicity giggled. 'He says it drove him wild to see me hanging out to catch such a poor fish as Edding. I pointed out Edding's pliable nature and his wealth, and Lord Harrington said that if I was going to make a cake of myself over the viscount he could see he would have no choice but to rescue me from future unhappiness by marrying me himself.'

'He didn't!'

'He did! I then confessed that, if he was offering, I would much rather marry him than Edding. I would prefer to have his mother as my in-law.'

Hero was laughing outright as they reached her bedroom door. 'What did he say to that?'

'He caught on that I was roasting him! Said I was a shocking tease, grabbed me and kissed me.' Felicity blushed. Her eyes shone softly. 'Then he said he would travel to London immediately and seek my father's permission to pay his addresses.'

'Lord Beltinge will not object?' asked Hero anxiously.

'No. He simply wishes to see me settled. Oh, Hero, how can I thank you?'

Hero leant forward and kissed Felicity on the cheek. 'By being happy.'

'Like you and Calverstock. I wondered once why he married you. But anyone can see he is in love with you. And you with him. You are fortunate, Hero.'

Hero passed no direct comment on Felicity's words. She hid the sharp pang of regret they brought, for of course Calverstock did not love her. Instead she remarked, 'You love Harrington. I think he loves you, though he may not realise it yet. You suit each other to admiration.'

Felicity smiled and as they parted threw her arms about Hero. 'I do hope so! And I must remember to thank Matty for not pursuing us into the orangery!'

Drew and Archie lingered in the library waiting for

Castlereagh and Bathurst to retire. The two politicians had much of interest to discuss but at length rose to leave.

The door had barely closed behind them before Archie announced that he must take his leave early the following morning. 'Urgent business in London,' he explained.

'You intend to restore Lady Felicity's reputation?' enquired Drew lazily.

'What?' Archie caught the twinkle in his friend's eye and grinned sheepishly.

'I warned you against dancing too often with the lady or taking her into secluded corners.'

'Found I didn't mind bein' caught,' admitted Archie. 'She's a deuced fine female. Throwin' herself away on that ass Edding. Couldn't allow her to do that.'

'Of course not,' agreed Drew. 'So you are off to seek Papa's approval, is that it?' Archie nodded. Drew sighed. 'I may well see you in town in a few days. I have to go up on business myself next week.'

'Does Hero know?'

'Not yet,' admitted Drew and added, 'It's a cursed nuisance. I've no desire at all to leave Ashworthy.'

Or my wife, he might have added.

CHAPTER TWELVE

BY MONDAY afternoon all the guests had departed.

'We could ride again tomorrow morning,' suggested Drew that night, drawing Hero into the curve of his body as they settled down to sleep.

'Oh, yes! Boy will be missing the exercise as much as I am. He must be feeling neglected.'

'Neglected? Why?'

'Since Christmas we have left him in the stables several times while we took the carriage out!'

Drew laughed and tightened his arm. 'Boy will have been exercised, never fear.'

'I suppose so, but I believe he will have missed me.' As his clasp drew her nearer she snuggled her back closer against the solidity of his warmth. 'I shall look forward to our riding out together again in the mornings.'

She felt the touch of his lips against her nape. 'I fear I must make a short visit to London on Wednesday.' He sounded regretful. 'Just a short visit. I should be back on Sunday. Then we may continue our excursions uninterrupted.'

Hero's disappointment was palpable. She shifted slightly in protest. 'So soon in the New Year?'

'Unfortunately, yes. The business will not wait.' His regret seemed genuine. He kissed the nape of her neck again and said lightly, 'I shall look forward to my return rather more than has been usual.'

He was flirting with her, recognised Hero as sleep overcame her. If only she could believe it was love he was expressing and not just affection based on desire. But even affection was better than contempt, was her last conscious thought.

The morning proved damp and rather chilly but, wrapped up in her thickest riding costume, Hero prepared to make the most of the occasion, since she would have to wait several days before it could be repeated. She wondered what his business in London could be; he had not said. A man's affairs were considered to be no concern of his wife, who must be protected from all financial and other worries. Fustian! Had she not largely administered Polhembury for years? She must make him see that she was interested, wished to take her place at his side...

However, he was not visiting one of his estates to solve a problem of administration, but journeying to London. He consulted his lawyer there quite regularly, she knew. Perhaps he had to see him urgently in connection with investments or some legal matter concerning an estate. It was of no use speculating. Just so long as he was not making an excuse to leave in order to visit that woman—or another about whom she knew nothing.

Hero thrust that thought aside as Drew, attentive as a lover, assisted her to mount, waving the groom aside. She could not doubt his recent desire to please her, for whatever reason. His Christmas gift had been nothing short of lavish. A bribe, a sop to stifle her doubts, a gesture to still his bad conscience?

Were that so, she did not know how she could continue as his wife. The hurt would be too great. She recognised the fact but stopped short of asking herself why.

Her spirits rose as the horses cantered and then increased speed to a full gallop in a race around a large field presently lying fallow. Afterwards they rode companionably side by side, walking their mounts, giving them time to recover their winds, before turning to trot for home.

As usual they returned via the thicket by the river, where the horses could rest and drink while they enjoyed a quiet, secluded moment or two before returning to face the day's demands. Tanner, the groom who always followed at a discreet distance in case his services should be required, knew their habit by now and remained well out of sight but within call.

They entered the clearing and prepared to dismount but before they could do so a deafening bang made Hero jump in alarm. For a bewildered moment she did not realise what the explosion meant. Then, as she glimpsed a stocky figure among the trees from whence a flash had come, she gave a great cry of outrage.

She heard a harsh shout of, 'Die, damn you, die!' but by now her attention had flown back to Drew, who had first slumped over and then fallen from his saddle. Panic gripped her as she watched the man she loved crumple to the ground. She knew in that instance that if he died she would not wish to live.

She threw herself from her horse's back and rushed to his side as Tanner, hearing the commotion, galloped up.

She pointed distractedly through the trees. 'A man! He went that way! After him! But be careful, he has a gun!'

'But his lordship——'

'I'll see to his lordship until help arrives.'

The man did as she said without further demur, riding off to circle the copse and cut off the assassin's retreat.

Hero anxiously examined Drew for signs of blood, her heart in her mouth. She had a little knowledge of how to deal with accidents, gleaned during her years as mistress of Polhembury, but if the wound was serious. . .

He could not die! Not now she knew exactly how much she had come to love him.

'Drew,' she whispered, 'oh, my love, please don't die!'

He was insensible yet she could see no blood on his coat, no hole where the bullet had penetrated his clothing. She knelt by his head and gathered it against her breast, murmuring endearments. Only then did she see the shallow furrow parting his hair and the oozing blood matting the strands to a sticky red. A trickle had begun to drip down his brow. Scalp wounds always bled profusely, she reassured herself. There was no need to worry about blood.

Upon closer examination she could see that the shot had done little damage. The bullet must have stunned him as it grazed his scalp. She had heard of that happening to others. Relief washed over her, leaving her shaking. She dug into one of his capacious pockets, found a handkerchief and began to mop up the mess.

In the distance she could hear men crashing about and shouting, the sounds of pursuit. The groom must have found help and be after the intruder. Nearer at hand heavy footsteps pounded along the path towards them and soon two groundsmen burst into the clearing.

By this time Drew had begun to stir. Grey eyes, fogged by pain, gazed up into anxious hazel ones. A ghost of a smile twitched the lips which had taught her how to respond to passion, how to love. 'What happened?' he demanded in a faint tone, content to lie a few moments longer in his wife's embrace. 'Were we attacked?'

Hero kept him pressed to her as he raised a hand to his damaged head. Her voice shook with reaction as she told him.

He struggled to sit up, wincing with pain at the movement, and Hero helped him.

The two groundsmen were making a hurdle, presumably to carry him back to the house, and he called across, his voice much stronger, 'You will not need that, as I am perfectly able to ride.'

'Oh, Drew, are you sure?'

Hero's eyes, huge and glowing with anxiety, met his. For a long moment they stared at each other, seemingly unable to break the contact. Dimly, Drew recalled a soft voice murmuring words of love in his ear. But he had been insensible. He must have been dreaming, imagining words he wanted to hear. At bottom, his wife despised him. He must remember that, or he might become completely entangled in her toils.

Hero watched the bemused expression in Drew's grey eyes harden into resolve as he dragged his gaze away from hers. 'I am perfectly sure. Cannon!' He addressed the groundsman by name, Hero noted. 'Come and help me to my feet.'

Cannon obeyed immediately, taking his master's elbow. Hero refused to relinquish her hold and between them they helped Drew up to stand on shaky legs. He muttered a low-voiced imprecation as he realised his weakness and felt the stab of a twisted knee, then apologised stiffly for speaking so before a lady.

Hero snorted. 'You need have no fear for my sensibilities, my lord! I have heard worse from my father, under stress.' Or the influence of drink. But she did not say that aloud.

Drew swayed as he stood. If only he did not feel so damnably giddy! But Samson had finished quenching his thirst and, sensing something amiss, had come over to nuzzle his master. Drew leant his weight against the bay's flank and felt better. He fished for a clean handkerchief and asked Hero to secure it round his head to stop the blood from running into his eyes. That done, he brushed off some of the leaf mould adhering to his clothing, discovering a few bruises about his person as he did so. Removing the mud and grass stains would require sterner measures. In an apologetic manner, Cannon handed him his hat, which had fallen off and rolled aside. Drew took it, gave it one look and grimaced in disgust. He could hardly put it back on his damaged scalp and in any case it was not fit to be worn again. The bullet had made a mess of it.

'Dispose of it, will you?' he grunted, handing it back. Then, 'Where is Tanner?' he asked, missing the groom for the first time.

Hero, brushing at the skirt of her riding habit, which had collected damp patches and grassy stains where she had knelt, told him, 'He went after your assailant. I hope he is all right. Oh! Listen! Is that not another shot?'

A single, grim word came in response. 'Yes.'

Hero shuddered. 'Pray God none of the servants has been wounded.'

Drew seemed in no hurry to mount up and make for the house. He was, Hero guessed, still feeling extremely shaky, however much he protested the contrary. So they stood listening intently as the distant commotion gradually died down.

Before long they heard hoofbeats drawing nearer and Tanner rode into view, his anxious expression giving way to one of relief and pleasure when he saw his master standing.

'What news?' demanded Drew.

Tanner dismounted and touched his cap. 'Well, my lord, I went after the man who attacked you as her ladyship instructed and soon found Cannon and Ward and told 'em to come to your lordship's help. I kept on after that villain, my lord, calling to a couple of other groundsmen who were working near by to come with me.'

As he paused to regain his breath, 'Go on, man!' urged Drew.

'Well, my lord, the knave gave us a good run but the truth is, my lord, he couldn't escape because of the high wall. He must've climbed in off the back of his horse, I'd guess. When we cornered him he turned a loaded pistol on himself. He had a pair with him, my lord; he'd used the other on you.'

'He's dead?' demanded Drew. 'Did you recognise him?'

'Aye, my lord.' Tanner hesitated, as though reluctant to proceed, but, seeing his master's impatient look, he swallowed and went on, 'Lord Blacklock, my lord, dead as a doornail. Begging your pardon, my lady.' He touched his cap in anxious apology.

Drew's already pale face lost all trace of colour. The deeply etched lines stood out on suddenly gaunt features. 'The marquis? The confounded fool! And dead on my land?'

Tanner nodded, his face sombre. 'Just so, my lord.'

'The devil! I am sorry, my dear, but this is bound to cause talk. The scandal-mongers will say I drove him to it.'

Blacklock. A near neighbour. One of the men gossip said had been ruined by Lord Calverstock.

'Perhaps, in a way, you did,' Hero said quietly. It was clear to her that Drew had not envisaged any such result of his actions but even to comfort him she could not deny the obvious. She still did not know why Drew did what he did, but was more than ever convinced that in his own mind he had excellent reasons. And because she loved him that was good enough for her. 'I do not blame you, my lord, but ruined men often take the only honourable course left open to them.' She thought of her father. It could so easily have been him. . .but he would simply take refuge in the bottle. 'Did you not consider such a possibility?'

'Honourable?' snorted Drew. 'Dastardly and weak, you mean!' He shut his eyes for a moment as though against the pain of his wound. When he went on it was in a calmer tone of voice. 'Perhaps I should have seen the weakness beneath the bluster. But it is done now.

Tanner, help me into the saddle and then see if you can round up that loose horse you spoke of.'

Drew walked Samson steadily back to the house, the jolting to his head causing him obvious pain. An anxious Benbow ran down the steps to assist his master while Matty hovered in the doorway.

'Where have they laid him?' Drew demanded shortly, waving aside Benbow's concern.

'In the gun-room, sir. It seemed. . .'

'Appropriate.' Drew nodded and then looked as though he wished he had not. 'Has the magistrate been sent for? Good. I must see the body.'

No one objected when Hero followed her husband as he headed for the gun-room. At the door, however, Drew seemed to recall the proprieties.

'Stay away, my dear. This will not be a sight fit for your eyes. Why do you not retire to your room with Matty and change?'

Hero did not argue. She had no wish to inspect the body of the dead marquis, only to remain near her husband in case he needed her. So she signalled to Matty to wait and remained by the door as Drew and his henchman entered the room.

Benbow's low voice only just reached her ears. 'You've nothing to reproach yourself with, sir. He deserved to die.'

'I know.' Drew's voice was grim. 'But I would it had not been almost by my hand.'

'He chose his own way out. Not like those poor creatures he condemned——'

'Enough!' Drew cut across Benbow's words, leaving Hero frowning over who Blacklock had condemned and to what. When he continued she could hear the weariness in her husband's voice. He must be operating on sheer will-power. 'I trust Sir John will not be long in coming. This business cannot be cleared up too soon. I must be away tomorrow.'

Benbow, perhaps Drew's closest confidant, whose complete discretion could be relied upon in all circumstances, never wavered in the deference he accorded his master. He murmured, 'Just so, sir. May I suggest you change your clothes and allow me to tend your wound while we await Sir John's arrival?'

'Very well. I must confess to a confoundedly painful headache.'

Hero waited for no more but hurried to join Matty. Together they mounted the nearest stairs. She knew Drew, a man who had survived who knew what privations and injuries during transporation, would resent being fussed over by her, however much she might wish to do just that. His moment of real need, of unconscious weakness, had passed. She had held him in her arms and ministered to him then. That would have to be enough. Benbow was quite able to provide him with all the attention he now required.

Besides, if she sought to nurse him she would be unable to hide her newly discovered love. He might detect her true feelings and, because he could not return them, withdraw some of the warmth from the relationship they had enjoyed since coming to Ashworthy. She might lose him altogether.

The remainder of the day passed in a flurry of official activity which gave Drew little time to recover from the shock and pain of his wound, slight as it had mercifully turned out to be. No one doubted the reason for Blacklock's attempt on Drew's life or that he had subsequently taken his own. There would have to be an inquest, but the verdict, said Sir John, was a foregone conclusion. Drew, who would be required to give evidence, should be back from London in time to attend. Some scandal was bound to ensue from the events of the morning but Sir John assured them that Lord Calverstock's position in society would not be threatened.

Drew chose to sleep in his dressing-room that night. He had the excuse of his scalp wound and a few bruises from the fall but in truth his decision rested on deeper motives which he himself could scarcely explain.

He was on the verge of falling headlong in love with his wife. To share her bed in his present state might precipitate matters and he was not ready to acknowledge the inevitability of his capitulation, since he could not be certain of her regard. For a fleeting moment he had imagined... But although she had softened her accusation by protesting that she did not blame him for Blacklock's death, she had said she believed him responsible. And once back at the house, while showing the correct degree of concern, his wife had evinced no sign of the tenderness he had imagined immediately after the attack. He needed to be sure of her feelings before he acknowledged his own and allowed them free rein.

To Hero, caught in the throes of an agonising unrequited love, his absence from the bed spelt desolation. They had shared it since their second night at Ashworthy. Now, for no good reason that she could descry, Drew had chosen to sleep apart from her. Of course, he was indisposed and had the worry of the inquest on his mind, but he could have found solace in her embrace had he so desired. It came as a lowering shock to discover that he had not.

Having endured a restless night, she was sitting up in bed drinking her chocolate when he entered her bedchamber early the next morning, dressed ready for his journey.

'You are feeling better? You are certain you are fit to travel?' asked Hero as he leant over to kiss her cheek.

'I am well enough,' he informed her shortly. 'Cuthbert and a groom will drive. I expect to be back in time to dine on Sunday.'

Hero nodded and then, unable to stop herself despite the presence of Jackson, fussing with the washing water, reached up to frame his face with her hands and bring his mouth to hers. For an instant he seemed to stiffen and a deadly coldness began to seep into her being, but then his lips took hers in a hard kiss which told of latent passion fighting to explode into brilliant life. 'Sunday,' he murmured hoarsely as he tore himself from her embrace and strode purposefully from the room.

'Take care, Drew.'

Hero's voice echoed after him as she sank back against the pillows. His kiss had bruised her lip, she realised as she stretched it in a wry smile of satisfaction he might have absented himself from her bed but, however unwillingly, he still desired her.

Since that second night at Ashworthy he had been anything but a reluctant lover. She wondered anxiously what could have caused the change last night.

She had almost five days in which to ponder and

worry over the question. To sit about doing nothing would drive her to distraction. An idea came to her while she dressed. Matty had long since found out where his mother lived—it was no secret among the servants. She occupied the restored dower-house on the edge of her small family estate of Hawes, some ten miles distant. Drew had purchased the estate from its new owners, offering them a price they could not refuse, and installed tenants in the main house, a family he could rely upon to look after the property and farm the land profitably. Why the Honourable Mrs Gerald Challoner had chosen not to spend Christmas at Ashworthy, and why Drew did not wish Hero to meet her mother-in-law as yet, were mysteries that teased her mind.

It was a fine day for travelling, crisp and sunny after yesterday's dampness, and she determined to take a drive in her carriage to find the place where his mother lived. That could do no harm. She formed no definite plan as to what she would do once there. She would wait to decide whether to call on Mrs Challoner or not.

Well wrapped up against the cold, with Matty, smothered in rugs, beside her, Hero set off. Ned Tribble rode escort, chosen to accompany her because he could be relied upon to keep her destination secret and could also find the way, having discovered the location of the dower-house from other grooms.

The Gloucestershire countryside positively sparkled under the wintry sun, the ponies responded readily to her hand on the ribbons, eager but biddable. Despite the cold Hero had seldom enjoyed a drive more. The fact that her excursion held a mysterious, almost forbidden element lent added excitement. She rested the ponies whenever Ned advised it, and less than two hours after starting out walked them slowly past a pretty, stone-built house surrounded by a large, well-stocked garden with its own gate to the lane, leaving it part of the estate yet independent of it. A little further up, where the road widened slightly, Ned helped her to turn the carriage. As she passed the house again the front door opened and a black-clad woman emerged, flapping a duster.

Hero gasped. Despite the years since she had last seen her, she had no difficulty in recognising Mrs Foster, Ben's and Bessy's mother. She drew the ponies to a halt.

She called across the hedge, 'Mrs Foster! It is you, is it not? I heard you had removed to Gloucestershire, but never expected to run across you here!'

The woman stared, frowning, until recognition brought a glad smile to her worn features. Hero noticed that the hair escaping from her plain cap was plentifully streaked with grey, but she looked better fed and more healthy than she had when living in Polhembury.

'Miss Hero!' she exclaimed, then, flustered, dropped a respectful curtsy. 'I beg pardon, my lady! I did hear that you'd wed the mistress's son.'

'Remember me and Matty, Mrs Foster?' demanded Ned with a grin, presuming on his old relationship with Hero to speak, which she did not in the least mind.

'You are still with Miss Hero!' exclaimed Mrs Foster. 'I didn't know that; I haven't heard from my Bessy since last summer.'

'Who is it, Martha?' demanded a soft, cultured voice

from inside the house, and a slender woman appeared at the door, walking stiffly with the aid of a stick and peering short-sightedly towards the road.

''Tis Lady Calverstock, ma'am,' explained Mrs Foster eagerly. 'She was passing by and recognised me.'

'Passing, eh?' said Drew's mother sceptically.

Hero coloured with guilt. Mrs Challoner must know that few people passed the house by chance. The lane, Tribble had assured her, led only to some farm buildings.

She put her whip in its holder and motioned for Ned to hold the ponies. 'I had hoped to visit, ma'am,' she called, preparing to descend from the carriage. 'If it would be convenient?'

'By all means,' answered Mrs Challoner. 'Come along in. Your groom and maid may keep company with Martha in the kitchen while we have a comfortable coze. The ponies may safely be tethered in the lane.'

Drew's mother was in her fifties, Hero judged, short to have given birth to so tall a son, but he had inherited her grey eyes and probably her hair, which was now a mixture of gold and grey, pepper and salt, beneath the lacy cap tied beneath her chin.

She wore a neat gown of blue merino wool with a patterned shawl fastened about her shoulders for warmth. As Hero began to tread the path to the door Mrs Challoner turned and disappeared inside. Hero entered the house and Martha Foster, with a quick smile, relieved her of her travelling rug.

'Have you heard from Ben recently?' Hero enquired. 'Is he well?'

'I had a letter at Christmas, my lady. He's well enough, he says, and he's much happier than he was with his first master. Mr Challoner—as was, that is, begging your ladyship's pardon—managed to get him with a good master just afore he came home himself.'

'I see,' said Hero, who did not.

Mrs Foster led her through to a room at the back of the house, comfortably furnished and warmed by the blaze from an ingle-nook fireplace. One of Mrs Foster's younger girls was engaged in piling logs on the glowing coals and bobbed a curtsy as she left the room with her mother.

Mrs Challoner had settled herself into a padded, high-back armchair and, as Hero advanced, waved her to its twin on the other side of the fire. But before she could sit Drew's mother changed her mind and beckoned her visitor nearer.

'Come close so that I can see you properly,' she ordered with a sweet, warming smile. 'My eyes are not very strong these days; I have spent too many hours over close needlework.'

Obediently Hero went to stand before her mother-in-law, enduring her scrutiny with what self-possession she could muster.

'I have been longing to see the young woman my son married——' Mrs Challoner spread her hands helplessly '—but he has been reluctant to bring you to see me. He said there were matters to be settled between you and he wished to wait. I suppose he does not know that you are here?'

'No, ma'am,' admitted Hero. 'I wished to meet you, had hoped you would join us at Ashworthy for Christmas, but he said you preferred to remain here.'

'And so I did; I dislike to travel and am not happy in grand company. I have been too many years on my own. But I would have welcomed you both on a visit to my home.'

The dim grey eyes examined Hero's face beneath the brim of her bonnet, and Mrs Challoner appeared satisfied by what she saw. She gave a little nod and motioned Hero to her chair.

'So,' she said as Hero settled herself, 'you are the young female my son married in such an irregular fashion, without even informing his own mother of his intentions!'

Hero did not avoid her mother-in-law's eyes. The woman deserved nothing less than absolute honesty. 'I fear so, ma'am. It was a sudden business arrangement between Lord Calverstock and my father. I had no say in the matter.'

A frown descended upon Mrs Challoner's brow and her tone sharpened. 'You did not wish to wed my son?'

'No, ma'am. I knew nothing of him apart from the fact that he had inherited the earldom unexpectedly and returned from the penal colony, to which he had been transported, to claim it. My father was in debt to him. He would have lost Polhembury had I not agreed to the match.'

'Polhembury.' Mrs Challoner eyed her shrewdly. 'Ben Foster worked for him, I believe, before he was transported.'

'Yes. Oh!' A dawning comprehension made Hero cry, 'Was that why Drew behaved towards my father as he did?'

'I do not know, my dear. My son does not confide

such things to me. But he did bring Ben's mother here and see his brothers and sisters settled.'

'Yes,' whispered Hero. Everything began to fit together. Those other men he had ruined. . .was there a Ben Foster in their lives? Her heart lifted. She could not be certain, but believed she had been right to trust in his integrity.

'I wonder why he made you part of the arrangement,' Drew's mother mused. 'He would not have done so had he not wanted you as his wife. Had you met before the bargain was struck?'

Hero, remembering, locked her fingers together in her lap. 'Once, briefly, in Polhembury village. We bumped into each other, literally. Neither of us knew who the other was. I confess it was a great surprise to me to discover that the agreeable gentleman I had met so briefly was the man demanding my hand in marriage on such harsh terms.'

Mrs Challoner nodded. 'That explains it. He must have taken a fancy to you. I cannot say that I blame him, my dear.'

'But afterwards he seemed to despise me!' burst out Hero.

Mrs Challoner gave her another shrewd glance and a small smile appeared on her face. 'Did you not despise him, knowing nothing of him except that he was an ex-convict? And for the way he was persecuting your father, perhaps? You did say that was what he had done, did you not, my dear?' Hero nodded and Mrs Challoner smiled. 'Most women would have felt the same, I dare say, if they did not know my son.'

'Yes, but. . .'

Hero tried to gather her wits, to remember her

attitude, and realised that his had been a reflection of her own. Or hers had been a reflection of his. They had despised each other. But no longer. On her part at least—and she thought not on Drew's either.

She took a deep breath. 'I am so glad I came to see you, ma'am! I do not know why Drew wants to keep us apart. I shall not tell him I have been here. I beg that you will not either.'

Her mother-in-law shook her head. 'It would be wiser not to mention it. My son has strong reasons for most of his actions and would not like to be thwarted in his plans.'

Hero nodded, comprehending that Drew had not wanted her to meet his mother before the understanding between them was complete. And so far, due to her own censorious attitude, he had felt unable to confide in her. She smiled across at the small woman opposite.

'Drew has gone to London on business. He was injured yesterday—oh, not badly——' she hastened to reassure his mother '—by a man he had ruined, Lord Blacklock. Blacklock killed himself after the attack. There is to be an inquest on Tuesday.' Hero's eyes began to shine. 'I do not fully perceive his motives but I do believe that he is too fine a man to set out to ruin others from carelessness or spite.'

'You had already discovered that, my dear?'

'Yes. And he told me only the other day of the crime for which he was sentenced to transportation. That his grandfather and uncle could be so without pity or mercy...' Hero's words trailed off into a shudder.

'Then he is beginning to trust you, Hero. I may call you Hero?'

'Of course, gladly, ma'am!'

At that moment Mrs Foster knocked and entered with a tea tray loaded with muffins and cakes.

'Thank you, Martha. Martha, of course, came to me on my son's recommendation, and I have never had cause to regret his choice of housekeeper and companion.'

'His lordship saved me and mine from near-starvation, my lady,' Mrs Foster told her. 'He did it for Ben's sake. He saved my boy from ill-treatment while he was a ticket-of-leave man himself. We are all that grateful, my lady.'

'I'm certain you are,' acknowledged Hero, her voice choked.

Mrs Foster left them. Drew's mother busied herself pouring the tea while Hero regained her composure.

'Will you have a muffin, Hero?'

'Thank you.'

Hero was not particularly hungry but the hot, buttery bun proved delicious. The silence between the two women who loved Drew lengthened.

At last, 'Are you estranged from my son?' asked Mrs Challoner softly.

Hero shook her head. 'Not now. Not completely. We have come to an understanding.' She blushed. 'I am hoping to conceive his child.'

Even if Mrs Challoner could not clearly see the softening of Hero's features she could not fail to hear the yearning in her voice. A small sigh of satisfaction escaped her lips. Her voice was gentle as she enquired, 'Have you come to love him?'

Hero swallowed. How could she deny it? 'Yes,' she admitted. 'But I have misjudged him so and he does not love me!'

Again, her voice told Mrs Challoner all she wanted to know.

'Come here, child.'

Hero rose and went to kneel at the older woman's feet. Mrs Challoner put a hand under her chin and lifted her face.

'You are beautiful, loyal and loving. Drew would be a fool not to love you, my daughter. He is not a fool.'

'Pehaps, if I bear him an heir——'

A decisive shake of the head met this tentative hope. 'Long before that. I imagine he does so already but is probably too stiff-necked to admit it because he has been hurt by your attitude. He tries to hide it but he is defensive about his past. Understandable as it might have been, your censure will have hurt him deeply. But, believe me, he would not have asked for your hand in marriage had he not fallen a little in love with you when you bumped into each other. Keep faith, my dear. He came here just before Christmas and spoke of you with admiration and affection. You will win his love.'

'I do hope so,' muttered Hero, and buried her face in Mrs Challoner's lap to hide her tears.

CHAPTER THIRTEEN

HERO returned to Ashworthy determined to win Drew's complete confidence. She needed him to confide in her fully, an essential step if they were to have a real future together. To know that he trusted her would compensate in some measure for the lack of his love. Sunday could not come soon enough.

When Drew did arrive home late in the evening, having started out at an inconceivably early hour—Cuthbert and his assistant had accomplished the entire journey in an incredible eighteen hours—he looked weary to the bone. Hero welcomed him without reserve, waited while he took a much-needed bath, then, when he descended casually dressed in trousers and frilly shirt topped by a dressing-gown, settled him by the fire and ordered the tray of refreshments to be brought. He leaned his head back and closed his eyes. She regarded the face of the man she loved, the strong, experience-worn features, the shadows about his eyes.

'How is your head? Does it still pain you?'

He stirred slightly but spoke without moving his head or opening his eyes. 'I fear so, from time to time, although not at this precise moment. Unfortunately I found the journey, which normally I take in my stride, excessively trying.'

'I am not surprised, considering how soon you set out after your injury!' Hero tried to keep concern from her voice. 'You should have taken more rest along the way. You could have lain in an inn overnight.'

His eyes opened and his face broke into a smile that set her pulses racing. 'And broken my promise to be back today? Are you not glad to have me home?'

'Husband! You know I am! Has my welcome been lacking? But I would rather delay the pleasure of seeing you than have you tire yourself out and perhaps prejudice your complete recovery. That is the thing I pray for, my dear. You had a narrow escape and my heart fails me every time I think on how close you came to death.'

Drew noticed that, for the first time, she had used an endearment. Unconsciously, he thought. And her voice had shaken slightly on her last words. He watched closely as he asked, 'You would have cared?'

The refreshments arrived at that moment, allowing her time to collect her thoughts. His eyes, for all the tired lines about them, regarded her keenly. Hero met his look with a candour which yet managed to hide the overwhelming love welling from her heart. She must guard her tongue, not give herself away by over-enthusiasm. She had once suffered the unwelcome devotion of a youth she admired but could not love. His unwanted ardour had embarrassed her and she could not subject Drew to such an irritation.

As the servants left them alone again she answered his question. 'Can you doubt it?' she enquired, lifting her brows in smiling query and spreading her hands to indicate the domestic warmth she had organised to greet him.

He grinned wryly. 'I believe a brandy would suit me better than a dish of tea but the food will be welcome.

I was anxious to make haste back to Ashworthy. We barely stopped for refreshment on the journey.'

Rather than call a servant, Hero rose and went over to the side-table, which held glasses and decanters, to pour the drink. She handed the brandy to him, saying, 'Then relax now. Satisfy your appetite and then we may retire.'

Drew swirled the spirit round in the balloon goblet and inhaled appreciatively before drinking with evident enjoyment. Only then did he enquire, with a suggestive lift of one brow, 'To satisfy a different appetite?'

Hero's blush would not be denied. Drew watched his wife's delicious confusion, his confidence growing. He had left the house unsure of her feelings towards him, determined not to fall victim to her growing appeal, which he recognised was composed not simply of physical attraction, which had always been there, but of something deeper, more fundamental and lasting which, was he to allow it, would render him her slave for life.

But her warm welcome, her pleasure at seeing him again, a subtle change in her attitude, gave him reason to hope that one day she might come to feel for him as he did for her. He believed her when she said she would have cared had he died. He could see something in her eyes now which had not been there before. And, despite his undoubted fatigue, he felt stronger mentally to resist her deepest lures for as long as necessary. He could make love to her without the danger of emotional involvement, just as he had to many women over the years.

Hero gathered her wits and managed to answer him

calmly. It would not do for him to believe her abandoned to all modesty. 'I had hoped you would return to our bed,' she told him somewhat stiffly. 'But I would fully understand if you wished to delay the full resumption of marital relations.'

'Very delicately expressed,' he teased, and, lifting his arms, stretched his splendid body from top to toe. 'I feel revitalised already. We shall have to see what the night will bring.'

Hero replaced her empty cup on its saucer. 'Have a muffin or a meat patty,' she suggested. The small table stood between them and she shifted the plates nearer to him. She felt less aware of his powerful attraction when he was occupied in something other than testing her responses. She wondered belatedly whether she would, in the heat of passion, be able to disguise the new tenderness she felt towards her husband. But no matter. It seemed he intended that they should sleep together again and nothing could destroy her anticipation of the night ahead.

Servants removed the refreshment tray. Drew accepted another brandy. It was cosy in the small red drawing-room, warmed by the fire. Hero felt no immediate urgency to move but Drew quickly finished his drink, rose to his feet and held out his hand. 'Come, wife, are you ready? Shall we retire?'

Hero placed her fingers in his warm clasp and smiled up into his face as he drew her up, noting that the lines of weariness had already begun to disperse. Whatever pleasures he may or may not have experienced in London, he did appear content to be home.

'Perfectly ready, husband.'

Upstairs, Drew dismissed both Benbow and Jackson

with an imperious wave of his hand. A small shiver of anticipation ran down Hero's spine. Drew had emerged from the strange mood which had possessed him immediately after his near encounter with death and returned, it seemed, intent on making up for his recent neglect.

The moment they were alone he gathered her in his arms. Their lips fused in a long, rapturous kiss which left Hero with the impression that her limbs had lost all substance. Her eyes closed. Yet through the languorous torpor which invaded her mind she was aware of Drew's fingers working at her back on the row of hooks and eyes fastening the bodice of her gown.

At last he lifted his lips and released her just enough to allow her to slip her arms from the sleeves. The gown fell to form a pool of blue at her feet.

The interruption was enough to restore strength to Hero's muscles and direction to her mind. Boldly, she pushed the dressing-gown from his shoulders, delighting in the feel of the smooth musculature beneath his shirt, and eased his arms from the loose sleeves to drop that garment to the floor as well. Next, her breathing quickening by the moment, her fingers worked at the buttons of his shirt while he untied the strings on her petticoat and chemise. Her undergarments joined the gown at her feet and he gave a rather breathless laugh as, naked apart from stockings and slippers, she pressed a kiss on the gold-tipped fuzz covering his bared chest and set to work, her fingers shaking, on the waist fastenings of his trousers. He had already flung off his shirt and now he removed his slippers and stepped out of his nether garments.

Easing off her own slippers, Hero gazed in fascinated admiration at the roused body of her husband. She had glimpsed him like this once or twice but he had never stood before her in all his magnificent glory. Mesmerised, excited, she forgot what she had been doing. The blood pounded through her veins, an excruciating throb of desire making her gasp. Before she could remove her stockings he had swept her up into his arms and laid her on the bed.

With a growling laugh he came down beside her, claiming her lips in another enervating encounter which he followed with a trail of worshipful kisses down her body until his lips met the tops of her stockings. These he rolled back in a series of long, sensuous caresses.

Moaning in protest, Hero sat up, unable to bear distance between them, and tangled her fingers in his hair, pulling his head towards hers.

A yelp of pain greeted this impassioned manoeuvre and Hero let go, crying out in distress.

'My dear love! I'm so sorry! I had quite forgot your wound!'

'So had I,' he growled, his heart leaping at the endearment as he finally removed the silk cladding her legs and pressed his lips to her toes, first one foot and then the other, while Hero wallowed in exquisite sensation.

He came back up the bed and lay close beside her. Trembling, Hero placed a feather-light kiss upon the still-tender scar which Benbow had left uncovered to aid scabbing.

'I would not hurt you for the world,' she whispered.

'I know, my dear.'

His lovemaking that night held a different quality

from any that had preceded it. Perhaps because of his impaired condition fierce passion gave way to tender ministrations which forced Hero into articulating meaningless sounds in response. Words of love rose to her lips but she forced them back. He was showing unexpected gentleness, an intensity of feeling she had not noted before, but that did not mean he would welcome a declaration of love.

His long, slow, sure strokes proved so ravishing that her climax broke over her like a tidal wave, washing her to some far shore where even ecstatic sensation seemed lost in sheer, insubstantial delight.

Drew had found his nirvana, too. She knew it because, even as she woke to awareness again, he gave a last convulsive shudder, heaved a great, gasping sigh and buried his face in her neck.

Hero's arms crept round him, holding his shoulders close. For long, long moments they lay, exhausted, all passion spent. . .yet there had been no fierceness of passion. What they had just shared had been beyond the normal bounds of coupling. She knew it and could not explain it. They might never achieve such wonder again. But they had known it and the experience could never be lost. In some indefinable way it must bind them together. Come what may, it was something she would hold close to her heart for the rest of her life. For, during those moments of union, she had known that Drew had loved her.

February, wet and chilly, did not encourage outdoor exercise and for some days during its third week Hero, feeling unaccountably sluggish, had remained abed rather than join Drew in his regular morning ride. He did not appear unduly upset and returned, exuding the aromas of horse, leather and fresh air superimposed upon his own seductive scents of sweat and sandalwood, in time to change and join her for breakfast.

Occasionally, if he was late back he would make straight for the breakfast parlour, apologising for eating in all his dirt while knowing that she did not object. That mixture of healthy odours suited him better than the false perfumes and clinging reminders of snuff and tobacco smoke that he picked up in drawing-room or club.

That morning he had not returned in time to change and Hero made her way to breakfast thinking to find him already there. She had heard a light carriage, probably a trap, arrive earlier but had taken little notice, for tenants often called at the house on business. After a few minutes it had driven off again. Because of this she was surprised to hear voices coming from the small reception-room off the hall. Drew's unmistakable tones, followed by those of a woman.

The door remained ajar. A footman stood sentry by the front door and a maid scuttled by carrying duster and mop. Drawn by curiosity, Hero crossed the hall intending to enter the room and greet the caller. Visitors at this time in the morning were rare, so the matter upon which the woman had come must be urgent.

As her hand went out to push the door wider she came to an abrupt halt. Chaotic emotions swamped her, leaving her breathless, her mind in revolt. She swayed as she stood.

The voices had stopped. She could see why. Drew

held a woman in his arms. Her hands rested confidingly against his chest. His head was bent to her upturned face. He lowered it further and Hero knew he was kissing the woman, although she could not precisely see their lips meet.

Something exploded inside Hero's brain. She spun on her heel and ran up the stairs to the sanctuary of her room, leaving a gaping footman staring after her. Jackson was there. She dismissed the maid with a brief word.

It was that woman the duchess had seen him with, Hero was certain. The description fitted. She was not dressed as a lady although respectably attired. She had followed her lover all the way from London to his home and he had welcomed her, kissing her while under the same roof as his wife.

After the last weeks of felicity Hero could not bear it. How could Drew think of another woman when she—?

She had made a fool of herself. That much was obvious. Imagining that on occasion he loved her! Giving herself to him so fully! A dry sob escaped her. She sat on, dazed, feeling sick and shaky.

Sounds below roused her and took her to the window. Peering down, she saw the Calverstock travelling chaise draw up before the door, a pair of Drew's best horses put to, indicating a modest journey ahead.

Someone knocked on her door and a footman entered.

He bowed. 'I am to inform you that his lordship sends his apologies, my lady. He has been called away on urgent business and cannot say precisely when he will return. He hopes to be back in time to change for dinner.'

She managed to thank the man, who left. Hero took up station by the window again and watched as Drew handed the woman into the chaise and Cuthbert, riding postilion, drove off. Benbow had not accompanied his master, a most unusual circumstance.

Drew must wish to be alone with that woman. On a sudden resolution she sent for Benbow, for he enjoyed more of Drew's confidence than she did.

By the time he presented himself she had herself firmly under control. She smiled.

'His lordship did not have time to explain the business on which he was called away. Do you know what it was?' she asked, trying to keep her voice casual, hoping Benbow would not detect her sick despair through the mask of normality she had pasted over it.

Benbow, impassive, shook his head, but Hero saw an evasive look in his eyes. He knew; but he would protect his master with his last breath. She had wasted her time and dignity by asking.

'I am sorry, my lady, I cannot say. But I understand his lordship does not expect to be away above a few hours.'

'So he implied. I did not see him myself; he sent a message by a footman.' She prayed she did not sound as hurt as she felt. 'The matter must have been urgent.'

'So I understand, ma'am.' Hero knew her pain had shown through, for he added, warmly for him, 'Do not concern yourself, ma'am. He will deal with the matter with his usual efficiency and return as promised, of that you may be certain.'

A new attempt to keep the distress from invading her voice failed dismally. 'But what *is* his business?' she asked, almost pleading for an answer.

Benbow shrugged, helpless to allay her fears without betraying his master's confidence. 'He will no doubt inform you upon his return, my lady.'

She doubted that. He had never told her anything in the past. She made an effort and pulled herself together. 'Very well, Benbow. You may go. Ask Miss Bright to come to me, please. She is probably taking breakfast.'

'Very well, my lady.'

Benbow bowed himself out. She liked the man and she thought he liked her but his loyalty to Drew came first. She should have known he would tell her nothing without Drew's express permission. Yet she had learned something from the interview. Benbow was aware of what Drew was about and had not liked having to keep his knowledge from her.

By the time Matty arrived Hero's mind was made up. She could no more sit about all day waiting for Drew to come home than fly. When he did return he would tell her only what he wanted her to believe, not the truth. Where had he taken that woman? To a nest somewhere on the estate? At least he had had the decency not to take her to bed in the house.

'Calverstock has gone off with another woman,' she informed Matty the instant her friend appeared. 'I am returning to Polhembury. Instruct Tribble to harness a team to the travelling coach. He can drive it back afterwards.'

'But Miss Hero, you cannot——'

'Cannot leave an unfaithful husband? Did I not say that he has gone off with some woman?'

'What woman?' demanded Matty suspiciously. 'It might be anyone, and him gone off for any number of reasons. He hasn't left you, my duck.'

She spoke with an absolute assurance which brought a grim laugh from Hero.

'Of course he has not! He will return to his dutiful wife as though his mistress did not exist!'

'His mistress? What makes you so certain the woman is his mistress?'

'She is the one the duchess saw him with in Harley Street.'

'How do you know? You've never seen her——'

'I just know.' She had been obviously pregnant, and perhaps that had been the most painful part. He had taken her to see that doctor because she was carrying his child. 'Stop prattling, Matty, and help me to put a few things into this bag.'

Matty did not move. 'You cannot run away again, my duck. He will not forgive you a second time. And I do not believe a word of it. He is too fine a gentleman to betray you so.'

'Gentlemen,' said Hero bitterly, 'especially noble gentlemen, think nothing to keeping a mistress. You know that.'

'And I also know that if their wives are wise they ignore the fact and make the best they can of their marriage. Not that I think you've any need. He's fond of you, my duck, is growing more fond by the day. Anyone can see it. Why should he trouble himself with a mistress?'

Hero shrugged, but did not stop bundling underwear

into her valise. 'Men are men. He is no different from any other. But I cannot live with him if he is unfaithful.'

Suddenly she was in tears. 'I love him so much, Matty. I cannot stand it!' she wailed.

In the end Matty had comforted her and agreed to their leaving. It was still early and although Hero had not eaten she refused to waste time in partaking of breakfast. She simply wanted to escape.

Thanks to Drew's generosity she had a purse filled with gold sovereigns, enough to meet any expense the journey might entail. She would think about repaying him later. She would think about her whole future later.

Why she should be so upset over Drew's infidelity she did not know. As Matty had pointed out, such peccadilloes were normal. In the first months of the marriage she would not have cared. Even after admitting her love to herself she had been ready to face the possibility of Drew's keeping a mistress. She had not liked it but had not felt compelled to run away.

The change had come after that wonderful night they had experienced together. That and the companionship they had enjoyed since. To discover him to be faithless now was something she could not endure.

It would take two days to reach Polhembury. At the first change of horses she ordered Drew's team to be stabled pending Tribble's return. They spent an uncomfortable night in an inn in Glastonbury, having reluctantly left the prospect of better accommodation behind with Bath. Late on the second day the coach rumbled up the neglected drive to draw up before the familiar, crumbling façade of her old home.

A youth she vaguely recognised ran out to hold the horses' heads. He grinned up at Ned and Ned called a greeting and she realised it was Dick, the stable lad, grown taller and more manly in her absence. An excited maid, a stranger, was dispatched to tell the master that his daughter had arrived.

The emotional upset had affected Hero physically. Her normally strong constitution had quite let her down. Exhausted by the journey, she allowed Tribble to lift her from the coach and Matty to support her indoors, where a beaming Mrs Blackler, looking less smart than when Hero had last seen her, waited to welcome her home, greeting her with a deep curtsy.

'Why, my lady,' she cried, 'I've never seen 'ee looking so fine! His lordship will be that pleased to see 'ee!'

One glance around had told Hero that things at Polhembury had slipped badly since her departure. The old oak lacked its former polish. The carpet had gained several new holes. Remembering the state of the drive and the decrepit appearance of the outside of the house, she deduced that her father had abandoned any pretence of keeping the place up.

'Where is my father?' she demanded, addressing the maid. 'Was he not told of my arrival?'

The girl bobbed a curtsy. 'He'm in the library, my lady. I did tell he but. . .' She trailed off with a shrug.

Without another word Hero strode towards the library door. Her giddiness had gone, banished by the need to discover why her father, since he was at home, had not stirred himself to come to meet her.

Her growing suspicions were confirmed the moment she entered the library. Lord Polhembury sat slouched in his armchair. A hand rested on his knee, an empty glass held loosely in it. On a small table drawn up beside him stood a brandy bottle.

'Papa!'

Hero crossed the room and stood looking down upon her parent. Things were far worse than she had imagined. A wave of anger swept over her, at her father for allowing himself to sink so low and at Calverstock for driving him to such despair. However badly he had treated young Ben Foster, her father scarcely deserved to be made to suffer so harsh a punishment.

'So you've come back to shee how I'm gettin' on, eh?' he slurred. 'Quite the lady now, ain't 'ee? Looksh as though you've done all right for yourshelf, my girl. Kind to you, ish 'e?'

'Papa! Much you would care if he were not! You sold me like one of your prime cattle!' She could not confess that she had left Calverstock. Not yet. However perfidious she thought him, he did not deserve to be denigrated before her father. He was, basically, a fine man, if mistaken in some of his actions and unfaithful, like so many others.

The pain jerked at her heart again but she ignored it.

'Pull yourself together, Papa! How could you allow Polhembury to fall into rack and ruin after you'd sacrificed me to keep it? The least you could have done was to make the best of your bargain!'

'What with?' growled her father and poured the last of the brandy into his glass. His hand shook so much that the liquid slopped on to his breeches. He gulped it down.

'Hard work!' snapped Hero, her patience exhausted.

She turned and left the room. She did not feel strong enough to deal with her father at the moment. She went through to the kitchen, where Matty and Tribble were recounting their experiences since leaving Polhembury.

'Companion, eh, Matty?' Mrs Blackler was saying enviously.

'Have you seen to the horses, Tribble?' Hero asked the groom.

'Aye, my lady, they're in the old stable. But I'd better go and rub 'em down now I've had my refreshment.' He put his empty beer mug on the table. 'Thanks, Mrs B. That was most welcome.'

Hero turned to Matty. 'Will you see that my room is ready? Get that new maid to help you.'

'Very well, my lady,' said Matty respectfully. Gratefully Hero realised that Matty would see that everyone at Polhembury heeded her new status.

With Bessy Fowler, still the kitchen skivvy, dismissed to the scullery, Hero questioned Mrs Blackler over her stewardship of the household.

'Without the money you sends through Mrs Cudlip we wouldn't have managed at all,' she told Hero. 'His lordship is always short, so it seems. On its own, what he do give me for housekeeping wouldn't keep a body and soul together.'

'He's paying the wages?' asked Hero.

Mrs Blackler shook her head. 'We've not had any for weeks now. Everyone has left except those ones you've seen already. Young Dick looks after his lordship as well as the horses and makes hisself generally useful. 'Cepting for the gardener, that is. His wife's got herself a job in the village and he grows his own produce on his plot; that's how they manages.'

'I see. So there are just you and two maids to keep the house in order?'

'That's right, my lady. And I'm nearly always busy cooking. So Joan does most of the housework, with a bit of help with the grates from Bessy, and Dick does the heavy work.'

'No wonder the place looks neglected. Something must be done. I'll see to it while I'm here.'

'Will his lordship be coming, my lady? Only I'll have to make a special effort with the meals if he is.'

'I'm not sure, Mrs Blackler. He may follow me here if he has no urgent business to keep him elsewhere. We left the question open.'

'He'll not be here tonight, then. You'll want supper, no doubt, my lady. Will Matty eat with you?'

'Yes, and my father if I can rouse him sufficiently. No doubt Tribble has told you that he will be taking the coach back tomorrow. His lordship may need it.'

'Aye, ma'am. You'll be staying a few days, then.'

Hero nodded, unwilling to commit herself in words. 'Supper in half an hour?' she enquired.

'I'll do me best, my lady. It won't be anything fussy.'

'I am not feeling like anything fussy. Hot soup would be welcome.'

'I've plenty of rabbit stew, that's no trouble.'

'Half an hour, then.'

Rabbit stew reminded her of Drew's nightmare experiences. Would he follow her? She had made no secret of her destination this time. A visit to her father could easily be explained away should their differences be resolved.

Matty had said he would not follow her a second time. But then, Matty was not wholly aware of the more recent relationship which had sprung up between them.

Perhaps she had been rash. Perhaps there was an innocent explanation for Drew's conduct. If so, would he ever forgive her for doubting him?

CHAPTER FOURTEEN

DREW did not arrive the following day as Hero had been dreading—and hoping—that he would.

'I warned you he wouldn't follow you a second time,' said Matty grimly. 'Mark my words, a proud man like his lordship does not run after his wife more than once.'

'I am glad he has not come after me. It is he who needs forgiving,' asserted Hero defiantly.

'Huh,' grunted Matty as she swept a final stroke of the brush through Hero's brown waves. 'Well, there you are, my chick,' she went on after a moment, letting the topic drop as she laid down the brush, picked up a nightcap and gathered the hair into it. 'You've only to tie the strings and you're ready for bed. Sleep well, my chick.'

'Goodnight, Matty. And thank you. It is like old times to have you to tend my needs again.'

'You'll be missing Jackson,' said Matty dourly. 'I haven't half her skill.'

'But you have a hundred times more feeling, dear Matty. Whatever should I do without you?'

'Go your own foolish way as usual,' muttered her old nurse, turning away.

Hero grasped her hand, holding her back as she prepared to leave for her own bed.

'Am I so foolish, Matty? Did I not have reason to be upset?'

'Maybe,' conceded Matty, 'but you should've given his lordship a chance to explain. I still can't believe he's acting wrong.'

Hero sighed. 'You always did favour Lord Calverstock. I remember the day we were wed. He bamboozled you with his charm from the start.'

'If you say so, my chick. But I thought you'd given up your foolish notions about his character and been won over yourself. Especially after meeting Mrs Challoner. Martha Foster couldn't speak highly enough of her or his lordship.'

Hero closed her eyes, squeezed Matty's hand and let it go. 'I don't know any more, Matty. But I mustn't keep you up any longer. I'll decide what to do tomorrow.'

Alone in her old bed, Hero could not sleep. The previous night exhaustion had overtaken her and she had quickly dropped into welcome oblivion. During the day she had kept herself busy trying to restore order to the chaos into which Polhembury had fallen. Mrs Cudlip, word having reached her of Hero's visit, had arrived in her husband's trap to give an account of her stewardship of Hero's remittances, after which the two women had caught up on their gossip. Hero had given a lively account of life in London and the pleasures of Ashworthy, hiding her distress at being forced to leave it all.

Mrs Cudlip, ten years Hero's senior yet youthful, amiable and romantic enough to interest herself in her young friend's affairs with enthusiasm, exclaimed as she was leaving, 'I am so glad the marriage has turned out well!'

Hero had given her no reason to suppose otherwise.

Time enough to confess her unhappiness when all hope had finally gone. She merely smiled in acknowledgement of the remark.

'When the little one arrives your happiness will be complete.'

Jerked from her morbid reflections by these words, Hero allowed the smile to fade from her lips and stared at her friend, a conscious blush and frown taking its place. 'We are hoping——' she began, only to be cut off by the other's surprised laugh.

'But my dear, surely you realise you are breeding? The signs are all there.'

'They are?' murmured Hero, bemused.

Mrs Cudlip, used to confinements, her own and those of her parishioners, had been right, Hero realised. The lethargy, the nausea, even the dizziness. Counting back, Hero wondered how she could have missed the absence of her monthly flow. Except that, since that wonderful night, she had been living in a euphoric haze disturbed only slightly by the necessity for Drew to attend the inquest on Blacklock. But that hurdle had been passed without trouble, no blame had been imputed and no question had arisen over the cause of death. A verdict of suicide had been returned as expected and Hero had been able to relax again.

As she thought of the baby growing inside her tears blurred her eyes, making a star of the flame of the candle left burning by her bed. She could not be absolutely certain yet, but it did seem likely that she was to bear Drew a child. The knowledge brought both joy and pain.

And she wondered whether, perhaps, her condition had been responsible for her shattering reaction to seeing Drew with another woman. Females could become very emotional in such circumstances.

Had she over-reacted? Matty thought she had. Confused thoughts jumbled about Hero's brain as she tried to work out what to do. Only one thing seemed certain: although she had thought she could not bear to remain with Drew, the thought of living without him now seemed infinitely more distressing.

The prospect of residing permanently at Polhembury filled her with apprehension. Until her marriage she had known nothing else. Now she realised how unsatisfactory existing as she had before—isolated, the victim of her father's temper—had been. Her horizons had widened. Living here, even with Drew's child to care for...

But she could not imagine Drew allowing a child of his, particularly his heir, to be brought up anywhere but at Ashworthy. She would not wish it, either. The child would deserve the best she could provide. And that meant a return to her husband; but he must not think she had returned simply because of the child. If only he had come after her, given her an excuse to change her mind and allow him to take her back...

The indubitable fact was, he had not come. Tribble had already left and must be halfway to Ashworthy by now. Perhaps when the groom arrived back without her and he knew for certain that she intended to stay at Polhembury, Drew would come...

Should she wait? Three more days, possibly——

But no! That would be the coward's way out. She had made a mistake and must face the consequences. It only remained to plan how her return could be accomplished.

Her father's hack was still in the stables, a poor beast sadly lacking in exercise. At the earliest moment tomorrow she would send Dick to the nearest post house to hire a chaise. The only vehicle for hire in the village was an old trap drawn by a lazy pony and Dick would have to travel further afield to find a suitable conveyance.

Having settled on her course of action, Hero settled down to sleep, hoping that, once back at Ashworthy, she could pretend that her flight had always been intended as no more than a filial duty visit.

In the morning she woke retching and feeling like death. She could eat nothing and refused her normal cocoa but drank several cups of coffee and felt slightly more human. Not to be deterred from her purpose, she sent Dick off on his errand. It would take an hour or so for the post chaise to arrive.

Matty dealt with their few possessions with rather more alacrity than she had shown when packing to leave Ashworthy.

'So you've come to your senses, my duck,' she commented when Hero told her of her decision. 'His lordship will welcome you back, I dare swear.'

'He might not realise I ran away,' suggested Hero hopefully.

'Benbow knew.'

'You told him?' cried Hero, outraged.

'Of course I didn't, ninny. But he knew. And Tribble knows.'

'Tribble would not say anything——'

'Not if you could get to him before his lordship does.'

Deflated, Hero sighed. 'In that case I shall simply

have to bow my head and apologise. I cannot allow pride to ruin our lives.'

'That's the spirit, my chick.'

While Matty packed, Hero went to see Mrs Blackler and leave instructions for the future. 'I shall make a point of visiting every few months,' she told her. 'I will see what can be done about the back wages meanwhile. Lord Polhembury has promised to pay you regularly in future.'

'Huh.' Mrs Blackler, fists planted on her ample hips, looked doubtful. 'Maybe he will, maybe he won't. Depends on whether he goes off on one of his sprees or not.'

Hero pictured the scene with her father the previous evening after supper. He had been truculent but also, she thought, a little ashamed. 'He has promised——'

'Aye, my lady. But promises don't buy food and such.'

'You have managed well, Mrs Blackler, and things will improve in future, you may depend upon it. Just stand by my father and try to ensure that he does not go completely to pieces. I will see that you do not lose by it.'

'I'll do me best, my lady, seeing as how it be for you, and besides, this is the only home I've got.'

With that promise Hero had to be satisfied. Now to say farewell to her father if she could rouse him from his bed.

She wore her travelling gown but had not yet donned her pelisse and bonnet. Time enough for that when the chaise arrived. She came up from the semi-basement kitchen to cross the hall to the stairs, the handrail of which, on her instructions, Joan was polishing. The sound of hooves pounding up the neglected drive brought her up short.

It was too soon for the hired chaise to arrive and in any case she could detect no crunch of iron wheels on gravel. It sounded like a single horseman. Dick, perhaps? No, too soon and he would accompany the chaise. And neither he nor tenants, except in an emergency, would push their horses as this animal was being pushed.

Joan hurried to open the door. Hero glimpsed an unmistakable figure swinging from his saddle and her heart jumped into her throat.

Drew *had* come after her! Alone and on horseback.

He strode into the hall and she could see by the state of his boots, by the damp clinging to his capes and beaver, but above all by the tired lines etched about his eyes that he had not just mounted up and come from some nearby hostelry. He had been travelling all night.

She did not quite know how to greet him but willed her legs to carry her forward. 'My lord,' she murmured, since they were not alone, 'I had not expected you.'

'Had you not, ma'am? I debated whether to come.'

Her heart sank a little. But he could mean several things by that remark. 'Come into the library. The fire is laid—it only needs a light. Joan, bring brandy and ask Mrs Blackler to supply a tray. His lordship needs refreshment.'

'The master keeps all the spirits locked away in a cupboard in the library, my lady.'

'You know where he keeps the key?'

Joan nodded. "Tes in his room.'

'Then go and fetch that and a glass.'

Joan hurried off on her errand and Hero led Drew through to the threadbare library. Being here, in the house where they had been married, must evoke memories for him as well as for her, she thought, and wondered whether they were kind or otherwise.

He laid his gloves and stock on the desk then placed his beaver alongside. Apart from the weariness he could not hide, he appeared quite unmoved. Hero took a tinderbox from the mantelshelf, bent to strike a spark and watched as the paper and kindling caught and flames began to lick up the chimney.

She turned to find that he had discarded his heavily caped riding coat and was standing watching her, his expression unreadable.

'Drew,' she began, but he shook his head.

'Wait until we are served. What we have to say to each other should be said in private.'

'Then sit,' she invited. 'You look weary. How long have you been in the saddle?'

He took the chair she indicated, her father's, drawn up before the fire. She sat on a stool on the other side of the hearth.

'Fourteen hours,' he said. 'It was no hardship. I worked harder for longer periods in the penal colony.'

She was saved having to reply to that—and what could she have said anyway?—by the arrival of Joan with two glasses on a tray and the key.

'His lordship still sleeps?' asked Hero.

Joan nodded. 'Yes, my lady. Dick had told me where he hid the key. That's the cupboard, my lady.'

'Thank you, Joan. You can help Mrs Blackler with the refreshments now.'

'Right 'ee are, my lady.'

Drew rose, took the key and unlocked the cupboard. Several stone bottles stood on a shelf.

'Contraband, I'd hazard,' he murmured as he took one out. 'Will you have some?'

Hero nodded. She felt in need of a stimulant. Drew was behaving with perfect courtesy but impersonally, as though they were almost strangers. She hoped it was because they might be interrupted at any moment.

She took the glass he handed her and took a sip of the stinging liquid. It passed down her throat like fire, warming her chilled insides. Her hands were icy, where a few moments ago they had been warm enough, coming as she had from the kitchen. One thing Polhembury did not lack was fuel for its stoves and fires. The estate abounded in old trees and it was all too easy to find a fallen branch, or even a trunk, to saw or chop up and burn.

They sat with their drinks in strained silence until Joan brought in the tray of refreshments. Mrs Blackler had been baking and the aroma of hot bread made even Hero's mouth water. She accepted a thick, fragrant slice, spread it with butter, and nibbled as Drew consumed his, together with slices of cold chicken and a wedge of fruit pie.

'Well, wife,' he said as he swallowed the last bite and wiped his fingers on a napkin, 'here I am, come after you again, as you can see.' Suddenly the strain showed itself on his face. Desperation laced his tone as he asked, 'Why did you leave me, Hero? What did I do to make you run away this time? Do you still trust me so little that you could imagine for one moment that I had taken Elizabeth Warner as my mistress and was off to some place with her?'

'Is that what Benbow said?' whispered Hero, shivering despite the flames now leaping up the chimney.

'It is what he deduced from your questions and your attitude. I could not believe. . .after all we have been to each other——'

'I saw you kissing her,' gulped Hero. 'She is breeding, is she not? I thought she was bearing your child.'

The sight of Drew's ravaged face made her catch her breath. 'What a confounded fool I have been!' he groaned. 'If only I had confided in you earlier! My darling, do you not realise that I love you?'

'Love me?' croaked Hero. What was this he was saying? Could she truly believe her ears?

He was on his knees before her, clasping her cold hands in his warm grasp. 'My dearest girl, you must have known! You have me completely in your toils. I cannot imagine life without you as part of it.'

'I did not know. How could I? You despised me from the first.'

'Not from the first, my love. I fell in love, I think, when we met so fortuitously in Polhembury. Your maid addressed you as Miss Hero and I knew you must be Polhembury's daughter. Him I did and do despise, and I had already determined to take my revenge on Ben Foster's behalf, but you, I thought, were different. For your sake I would let Polhembury off the hook to the tune of ten thousand pounds, more than the estate was worth.'

'Then why. . .?'

'Did I treat you so harshly?' His fingers tightened. 'I heard you talking with someone, Matty, I afterwards discovered. You condemned me unseen. Talked scathingly of me as a convict, someone obviously beneath contempt. And called my mother a common woman. That, in particular, I found it difficult to forget or forgive.'

Hero closed her eyes. Then, resolutely, opened them again, meeting his grey gaze without evasion. 'What a pity you overheard that nonsense. Matty put me right immediately. But Drew, how would you have felt had you just been informed by your father that you had no choice but to wed a man you had never met and whose reputation, even you must admit, was not of the best?'

A faint glimmer of a smile touched his lips but his eyes remained intent. 'Indignant, despairing and aggressive, I dare say.'

'Exactly so. Especially as I had so recently met the gentleman of my dreams in Polhembury——'

His hands now gripped hers so hard that she winced with pain. 'You cannot mean...'

'The attraction was mutual, Drew. But I heard my prospective bridegroom dealing brutally with my father and entered the room furious and disgusted for, although Papa had brought his troubles upon his own head, he did not deserve to be dealt with so severely. And I quickly discovered that the person I must marry to save my father from complete ruin was both the heartless creditor I held in contempt and the gentleman I had so briefly met in the village. Imagine my confusion!'

'And mine, when I heard you talking... My dear, have we truly wasted all these months despising each other over nothing?'

'Not over nothing,' asserted Hero bravely. 'I could

not understand why you chose to ruin certain gentlemen.'

'Have you not guessed, my dear? They have all been instrumental in condemning comparatively innocent people to the terrible trials of transportation. I met all their victims out there and tried to ease their lot if I could. That became easier once I obtained my ticket of leave. But none of them deserved such harsh measures to be taken against them, any more than I did. Or than you did,' he added with his first real smile, a roguish one that caused a jolt in Hero's heart. 'In the view of many a landowner, magistrate and judge, you would have deserved transporation for stealing my plums!'

'Your plums?' choked Hero, gazing at him in guilty astonishment. 'You own Wanleat now?'

He grinned openly. 'I must plead guilty as charged, my dear. But although I recognised my plums I did not have the heart to prosecute such an attractive thief!'

'Oh!' Hero's breath quite deserted her and for a moment, as colour flooded her cheeks, she was nonplussed. Then she decided to ignore his teasing and press on with what she had been about to say.

'I admit my father merited punishment for his intransigence over Ben,' she went on earnestly. 'I pleaded with him at the time to have mercy, but to no purpose. But Drew, did he deserve to be ruined? And Blacklock? Did he deserve to be driven to the point of murdering you in revenge, and finally to suicide?'

'That incident gave me pause for thought,' admitted Drew soberly. 'I shall review my methods for the future.'

Hero's eyes sheened with tears. 'I am glad of that. No man should think himself worthy to be both judge and jury of the actions of others.'

Drew nodded. 'I realise that you have a point.'

Hero went on with her explanation, speaking gently. 'Also, the rumours of your involvement with other women persisted. You seemed to be two different men.'

He let go of her hands and stood up. Now she had offended him. Hero yearned to have him close to her again. But he stood apart, looking down on her with a strange glow in his eyes.

'You thought I had betrayed you with Elizabeth Warner. Dare I believe that you were jealous?'

'As the very devil!' declared Hero with unladylike forthrightness. 'What was your business with her?'

'You noticed that she is pregnant. I was not kissing her, merely offering comfort. Her husband was arrested before she realised her condition and was finally transported last week. She was distraught and came to me for help once again. You see, I seek out those left behind to starve, and do what I can for them. I have opened a home in Kent to house some of the families who would otherwise be begging on the streets.'

'Oh, Drew! Why did I not trust you? My love, can you forgive me?'

He pulled her to her feet and encircled her with his arms. Secure in his embrace, Hero lifted starry eyes to his, her mouth soft and vulnerable, expecting his kiss. His lips curved into a mischievous smile.

'I can forgive you anything as long as you call me

your love. Am I truly so, my dearest girl? Do you feel for me as I feel for you?'

'Oh, yes,' breathed Hero. 'I believed it was just a desire to have you again in my bed. I despised myself for my weakness. I did not want to love the kind of man I thought you were.'

Drew groaned. 'You, too? What fools we have been!'

'But I just could not help myself,' confessed Hero.

'Nor I,' admitted Drew, just as a knock at the door disturbed them. Reluctantly he allowed Hero to leave his arms.

'Come!' she called.

Dick peered in, his face rosy from fresh air and exercise. He bobbed his head in a respectful greeting. 'The chaise be here, my lady.'

'Oh, the chaise!' she glanced uncertainly at Drew. 'Thank you, Dick. I won't keep it waiting long.'

Drew eyed her somewhat warily. 'You were intending to travel?'

Hero blushed. 'I intended to return to Ashworthy. I left in a fit of anger and despair. I had already decided that, whatever you had done, life with you would be more agreeable than without. Shall I retain the chaise? We could return at once.'

'Now I am here I would prefer to stay for at least one night. I have, as you deduced, missed my sleep. And there must be estate matters which need my attention. Shall I pay off the post boy and send him away?'

'Yes. You could arrange for him to return tomorrow.'

'No need, my love. I crossed paths with Ned Tribble

on the way here. He has turned round and is following me back. Between them, he and Benbow persuaded me that I might hope for your return.' He took her hand and told her softly, 'They both informed me, though in different words, that my lack of thought, my failure to repose confidence in you, had caused you great unhappiness. Tribble said it had made you ill.' He touched the shadows under her eyes. 'He did not exaggerate.'

'Why did you not confide in me, Drew?'

He shook his head. 'I will explain. First I must dismiss the post chaise.'

Hero sank into the chair by the desk as he left the room and, elbows on its surface, rested her face in her hands. The relief was almost overwhelming but it was the knowledge that Drew loved her that brought joy bubbling to the surface. And renewed her strength. She could face anything, any further revelations he might have to make, confident in his love.

He was not absent for long. When he returned he sat in the baron's armchair and held out his hand.

'Come here.'

Hero obligingly went over to him and was immediately drawn down on his knees. Wrapped once again in his arms, she sighed contentedly. He kissed her and she almost forgot that she had asked him a question. But the answer seemed important and so, when she was able, she repeated it.

'How could I confide in you?' he murmured. 'You are your father's daughter. And what I had heard...'

'You thought I was like him.'

'Not for long.' He kissed her again. 'But speaking about my past, explaining my attempts to mete out retribution and confessing my other activities are things I find it difficult to do. Benbow knows everything, of course—he has been with me throughout—and so does Archie Dalmead. We struck up one of those friendships which seem predestined and he divined my true purposes almost at once. He helps where he can, but I exacted his promise not to reveal his knowledge to anyone. Anyone at all.'

'And as a man of honour he could not ease my mind! Neither could Benbow! Really, Drew——'

'Do not berate me! Even my mother does not know!'

'Well, I will berate you! For laying yourself open to a vindictive attack like that of Blacklock's. Do you not think, my lord, that to take up your seat in the House of Lords and to mount a campaign against transportation from there might be a safer and better way forward than to continue to take individual revenge on people? You could be another Wilberforce. He is winning his battle against the slave trade—it is already illegal here and will soon be banned throughout all our possessions. You could expose all the horrors of transportation and no one could accuse you of not knowing what you were talking about!'

Drew looked quite struck. 'No, though they might think me prejudiced! And the stigma might rub off on you, Hero. Would you not mind?'

She shook her head. 'I would join your campaign.'

'My darling!'

'And you should tell your mother, Drew.'

He grimaced. 'I suppose I should. And speaking of her, I did not wish you to meet her until I had assured myself that when you did you would not despise her.'

'Drew! Did you really think me such a snob?'

'After what I overheard I found it difficult to believe otherwise. I know better now. I think you will like each other and I will take you to see her very soon, I promise. I have told her all about you.'

Hero almost confessed to her visit then, but decided to keep to her original decision. Nothing would be gained by admitting to the acquaintance and she would deprive Drew of the pleasure of bringing his wife and his mother together.

So she merely said, 'I am certain I shall love her, as you do.' She grinned impishly. 'I do not imagine she is like Lady Edding. Felicity told Archie that she would rather marry him than Lord Edding because she would prefer his mother as an in-law!'

'And brought him to the point, the devious chit!'

Hero chuckled, her happiness overflowing to embrace their friends. 'I quite look forward to seeing Archie leg-shackled in June!'

'The wedding will be a large one. Not like ours. Would you have preferred a society affair, my love?'

'No. Just one in which I had some choice! But truly, as long as I am married to you I do not now care how it happened.'

He smothered a yawn but his declaration was none the less heartfelt. 'Nor I.'

'You must go to bed!' exclaimed Hero, all concern. 'We can talk of the future later. I would like to think Polhembury will receive better management than my father seems capable of giving. He has not paid the wages for weeks.'

'Do not concern yourself, my dear. Polhembury shall have a steward and will be restored to its former glory.

It is your inheritance, and must be protected as such. I had thought it necesssary to take matters into my own hands long ere this. I receive reports and they have not been good. Without your financial support——'

'You knew!'

'Little escapes me where you are concerned, my love. Only my stubborn blindness prevented me from acknowledging the truth about you months ago. When you went to your aunt's I realised just how much your presence meant to me. I tried to make things up to you. I thought you were happy, although you did not love me.'

'I was happy, until I saw you with Mrs Warner. And because I loved you so much I could not bear to see her in your arms!'

'Yes, that. And, since I was all innocence, I could not imagine why you had left me again! I determined not to follow you, to let you go if you must, but Benbow's disapproval and twenty-four hours of missing you were enough to send me galloping *ventre à terre* to win you back.'

'I am glad you came after me. I was returning to you, but it would not have been quite the same if you had not.' She stopped to kiss his tired eyes. 'You really must sleep, my love. But one more thing before you do. Mrs Cudlip, the vicar's wife, thinks I may be breeding. It would explain how dreadful I have been feeling recently.'

'My dearest love! That is the best news you could have given me! After news of your return to me, of course!' He looked at her, suddenly anxious. 'Did her revelation have anything to do with your decision to return?'

Hero stroked his rough, unshaven cheek. 'Only to confirm what I already knew. Child or not, I could not live without you.'

With every breath he became more certain of her love. He had only to look into the depths of her lovely hazel eyes to see his own emotions reflected there. Content, he kissed her again, a ravishing kiss, the effects of which went with him as he sought a bed in which to catch up on his lost sleep.

Hero had no doubts left, either. 'You may unpack again, Matty,' she informed her companion as she skipped into her bedroom. 'You were wrong for once! His lordship did come after me again and we have finally come to a complete understanding. He is resting now and we will be staying for at least one more night.' Despite all her experience, all the confidences she and Matty had shared, she could not stop the blush which suffused her features. 'He will, of course, sleep here with me.' Oh, how she longed for the night to come! 'Ned,' she went on, 'is on his way back and we will all return to Ashworthy together in the Calverstock coach.'

'Humph,' muttered Matty dourly, though her face was wreathed in smiles. 'I thought it was about time you two realised you were meant for each other.'

The parlour door opened yet again.

Sarah watched a tall, broad-shouldered man enter the room. He came purposefully, yet gracefully, towards her, and she found herself staring up at a far-from-handsome and unsmiling countenance.

'I understand from the lady of the house that you have been gracious enough to permit me to share your private parlour, ma'am,' he remarked in the most attractive deep masculine voice she had ever heard. 'My name is Ravenhurst.'

Her lovely smile of greeting fading, Sarah sat rigid on the wooden settle, as though turned to stone. Ravenhurst. . .? It couldn't be!

Anne Ashley was born and educated in Leicester. She lived for a time in Scotland, but now lives in the West Country with two cats, her two sons and a husband who has a wonderful and very necessary sense of humour. When not pounding away at the keys of her typewriter, she likes to relax in her garden, which she has opened to the public on more than one occasion in aid of the village church funds.

THE NEGLECTFUL GUARDIAN

Anne Ashley

Harlequin Mills & Boon

SYDNEY ❀ AUCKLAND ❀ MANILA
LONDON ❀ TORONTO ❀ NEW YORK
PARIS ❀ AMSTERDAM ❀ HAMBURG ❀ MILAN
STOCKHOLM ❀ MADRID ❀ ATHENS ❀ BUDAPEST
WARSAW ❀ SOFIA ❀ PRAGUE ❀ TOKYO ❀ ISTANBUL

First Published 1997
First Australian Paperback Edition 1998
ISBN 0 733 51355 7

Published by
Harlequin Mills & Boon
3 Gibbes Street
Chatswood, NSW 2067
Australia

Printed and bound in Australia by
McPherson's Printing Group

Chapter One

The perfectly matched greys, admired by many of those august members of Society known as Corinthians, turned under one of the finest examples of an Elizabethan archway to be found anywhere in the County of Wiltshire, and came to a halt in the stableyard.

Marcus Ravenhurst, the much envied owner of the coveted pair, waited only until his trusted head groom had jumped down from the smart racing curricle, and had taken a hold of the spirited pair's heads, before alighting himself with the agility of a healthy, finely tuned athlete.

As Marcus stalked towards the house, the cold February wind caught at his many-caped driving-cloak, sending it billowing about his tall, powerful frame, and dead leaves swirled about the path in front of him before adding to the ever-increasing decaying piles dotted about the grounds.

His dark brows drawing together in one of his famed, heavy scowls, he cast the tall trees shrouding the fine building in a depressingly gloomy blanket a look of staunch disapproval before entering the relative protection of the stone porch.

Reaching out one gloved hand, he raised the highly polished brass door-knocker, and administered several short, sharp raps. It was a minute or two before his summons was answered, and the solid oak door was opened by an ageing, grey-haired retainer.

'Why, Master Marcus!' he exclaimed with genuine warmth, and a familiarity granted to loyal servants of longstanding. He moved to one side, allowing the unexpected visitor to pass into the hall.

'Her ladyship never said she was expecting you, sir.'

'She isn't, Clegg. I'm on my way to Somerset, and on the spur of the moment took it into my head to pay a call. The visit is a very brief one. I shall be staying only one night.'

After placing his curly-brimmed beaver hat and his gloves on the hall table, Marcus removed his cloak to reveal a blue superfine coat of impeccable cut, a snowy-white neckcloth and a pair of tight-fitting buff-coloured pantaloons, which encased his muscular legs without so much as a single crease. His plain double-breasted waistcoat was free from fobs and seals; the only embellishment he ever wore, in fact, was a plain gold signet ring, which emphasised his strong, shapely hands.

As always the elderly retainer was impressed by the sober, yet elegant, attire, and thought there couldn't possibly be a dozen gentlemen in the length and breadth of the land who could carry their clothes so well as his mistress's eldest grandson.

'Her ladyship is in her private sitting-room, sir,' he informed him, relieving him of the cloak and placing it almost reverently over his arm. 'I'll go up and inform her you're here.'

'Save yourself the trouble, Clegg. I'll announce

myself.' Marcus's harsh-featured face was transformed by a rare smile. 'Having no desire whatsoever to see a member of my own sex put out of countenance, I shall spare you the embarrassment of having to stand by while she rings a peal over my head for not having taken the trouble to visit her for some months.'

'As you wish, sir,' the butler responded gravely, but with a betraying twitch to his lips. 'I'll arrange a bed-chamber made ready for you.'

'Thank you, Clegg. And see to it my groom has everything he needs.'

At the head of the stairs Marcus turned to his right, and went along the narrow passageway leading to his grandmother's private apartments. After a perfunctory knock, he entered the room to find the Dowager Countess seated in a chair by the fire, a rug over her legs and a book lying open on her lap.

'Was that a caller I heard, Clegg?' she enquired without bothering to turn her head to see who had entered.

'I cannot tell you how relieved I am to discover there's still naught amiss with your hearing, Grandmama.'

'Ha! Ravenhurst!' She frowned dourly up at her favourite grandchild as he came striding in his usual purposeful way towards her. 'Haven't set eyes on you in a twelvemonth. Was beginning to think you were dead!' she remarked with morbid humour.

'Three months, to be exact, ma'am.' There was a suspicion of a devilish glint in his dark eyes as he placed a chaste salute on one pink cheek. 'And, as you are no doubt overjoyed to discover, I'm still sound in wind and limb.'

A wicked cackle answered this. 'Nothing wrong with your limbs, Ravenhurst. You're the finest specimen of manhood in this family by a long chalk. You've no looks to speak of,' she went on with brutal frankness, thereby eroding her former compliment somewhat, 'but, then, not all women are beguiled by a handsome face.'

He positioned himself before the fire, warming his coat tails, and looked down at her with lazy affection. Apart from the fact that she walked with the aid of an ebony stick, and that the hair beneath the fetching lace cap was completely white, there was little to betray that she had five-and-seventy years in her dish.

Her skin retained a satiny smoothness, her grey eyes were still brightly alert, and she had, much to her eldest son's discomfiture, and his wife's acute embarrassment, a mind as sharp as a meat cleaver and a tongue as corrosive as acid. Many had quailed beneath her blunt manner and astringent comments, but not so Ravenhurst. His grandmother numbered amongst that small handful of people he admired.

'I have never aspired to be an Adonis, ma'am.'

'Just as well,' was the forthright rejoinder. 'But, then, when a man's as rich as Golden Ball, looks are a minor consideration to any discerning female of marriageable age.'

'Not quite that rich,' he countered.

'Don't try to pull the wool over my eyes! You're one of the richest men in the land.' She scowled up at him for several moments before enquiring irascibly, 'And how much longer do you intend standing there, warming the seat of those tight-fitting breeches of yours at my fire, boy? Go get yourself a glass of Madeira! It's from Henry's cellar. The only evidence of intelligence I've ever found in my eldest son is in his ability to pick a wine. And you can pour me one whilst you're about it.'

One dark brow rising sharply, he obediently went

across to the table on which the decanters stood. 'I understood Dr Pringle to say, the last time I was here, that you were to drink only one small glass of wine with your evening meal.'

'A pox on all physicians!' the Dowager responded crudely. 'What does that fool know! And if you think I'm mutilating my insides by drinking a dish of tea at this time of the day, you're far-and-away out.'

Knowing from long experience that to remonstrate further would be futile, Marcus dutifully filled two glasses, handing one to his irascible grandparent before seating himself in the chair placed on the opposite side of the hearth. After sampling the excellent Madeira and settling himself more comfortably in the chair, he enquired politely whether the Earl of Styne was in residence.

'No,' the Dowager responded, not without satisfaction. 'He's taken that whey-faced wife of his to Kent to visit her mother. Don't expect them back for a sennight or, with any luck, two. Why, did you wish to see him?'

'I cannot recall ever having evinced a desire to see my estimable Uncle Henry,' he returned blandly, much to his grandmother's intense amusement. 'But I really think he ought to do something about the trees surrounding this place. They make the interior dratted gloomy, ma'am. And the grounds are a disgrace. Nothing short of an eyesore!'

'I'll thank you not to interfere, Marcus!' she snapped. 'Not one of those trees is being felled whilst I reside in the Dower House. They grant me privacy from all those prying eyes up at the mansion. And Wilkins will soon have the garden in order once he's recovered from his rheumatism.'

As the ancestral home of the Earl of Styne was situated in the centre of the vast park, a quarter of a mile or more away from the Dower House, someone wishing to spy on the Dowager Countess from there would need to possess quite miraculous eyesight. Yet, here again he knew that to argue further would be a complete waste of breath, and so changed the subject by enquiring politely, if with precious little interest, into the health of the other members of the family.

As the Dowager Countess of Styne had seen fit to bless the late Earl with six pledges of her affection, it was some little time before she had finished casting aspersions on her five remaining children and their numerous offspring.

'Agnes was my first chick, and my favourite, Ravenhurst. I've never made any secret of that. Your mother was the best out of the lot of 'em by far.'

'Perhaps I'm prejudiced, but I certainly thought so, too,' he responded, a rare note of tenderness creeping into his voice.

'Never thought I'd outlive any of mine.' She shook her head sadly. 'And it had to be my little Agnes taken from me. I don't think she ever truly recovered from your father's death, Marcus. They were a rare couple, your parents. A real love match.'

He did not respond to this, and after a few moments of dwelling on the deep sadness of loss, which for her had not lessened in six years, she gave herself a mental shake, and looked frowningly back at her favourite child's sole offspring to enquire what had prompted him to pay this unexpected call.

'I'd never hear the end of it if you discovered I'd almost passed your door and didn't pay a visit. I'm on my way to Somerset.'

'Oh?' She cast him an enquiring glance. 'Are you calling on that ward of yours in Bath, by any chance? Strangely, I was only thinking about her the other day. Agnes and her mother were great friends.'

The shapely hand raising the glass to his lips checked for a moment. 'No. I hadn't intended doing so.'

The slight inflection in his deeply resonant voice was not lost on her, and she stared at him for several thoughtful moments before asking, rather censoriously,

'Do you never visit that child, Ravenhurst?'

Placing his glass down on the table conveniently situated by the side of his chair, he rose abruptly to his feet, and took up his former stance before the fire. 'She has been well cared for,' he said in a tone bordering on the brusque. 'I placed her in that seminary in Bath, and then settled Cousin Harriet in Mama's old house in Upper Camden Place to look after the chit. I make her a quarterly allowance. She has everything she needs—my secretary sees to all that.'

The reproachful look remained in his grandmother's eyes, and he found his ready temper coming to the fore. 'Confound it, madam! What more could I have done? I know nothing of schoolgirls.'

'Schoolgirl?' she echoed blankly. 'Where have your wits gone begging, Marcus? Sarah Pennington may have been a schoolgirl, once, but her mother was knocked down by that runaway carriage not four months after your dear mama was taken from us. She must be nineteen, now, at least.'

'Well? And what of it?'

She stared up at him in exasperation. 'She was Agnes's godchild, Marcus. I don't think it would be expecting too much of you to pay some attention to your ward's future well-being. Why not fund a London Season for the girl? Bath is all very well, and I know dear Agnes preferred it to London, but Sarah is far more likely to find a suitable husband if she goes to the capital. And if she favours her mother, I expect she's a very pretty girl. Was she well provided for?'

'She's no heiress, if that's what you mean, but her portion isn't contemptible.'

'There you are, then! I shall speak to your aunt Henrietta when she returns from Kent. She's bringing your cousin Sophia out in the spring, so it wouldn't hurt her to chaperon Sarah as well. Or, I might even do so myself.'

'No need to put yourself out, ma'am,' was his almost indifferent response. 'If I do decide to fund a Season for Sarah Pennington, and I have decided nothing yet, then Harriet can chaperon her. That's what I pay her for.'

'Pshaw! That pea-goose!' the Dowager scoffed. 'If you're not careful, Ravenhurst, you'll have that woman your pensioner for life. She came perilously close to ruining that husband of hers with her gambling, you know.' She looked thoughtfully beyond him to stare down into the fire. 'I suppose, though, at the time you had little choice but to enlist your cousin's aid. I wish I had done more, but it was so soon after Agnes's death. I would have been poor company for the child.'

A tender look erased the annoyance from his eyes. 'Believe me, ma'am, there's no need to suffer pangs of conscience. Sarah is well enough. I've received ample very long and exceedingly boring letters over the years from Cousin Harriet to leave me in little doubt of that. And as far as a Season is concerned. . .?' He paused for a moment, looking thoughtful. 'Of course, I'm not against the idea, but a lot depends on circumstances.'

'Oh?' The Dowager looked questioningly at him again. 'What circumstances?'

'There is every possibility, as you'll no doubt be pleased to hear, that I might be getting myself leg-shackled in the not too distant future,' he confided somewhat crudely.

'And high time you were setting up your nursery, Ravenhurst!' Only a sudden glint in her grey eyes betrayed her delight at the news. 'And who is the lucky gel? Do I know her?'

'You may do. It's Bamford's eldest daughter. She was engaged to be married to my friend Charles Templeton. You may recall he died several years ago in a riding accident, not many weeks before the wedding was due to take place. Broke his neck.'

'Yes, I do remember that. But I cannot say I recall the girl. Is she pretty?'

'Pretty?' he echoed, frowning at an imaginary spot on the far wall, as though having difficulty in bringing a clear image to mind. 'No, I wouldn't call her so. She's handsome enough, and has a deal of self-assurance and reserve. Some think her aloof, but I don't consider that a fault.

'She's six-and-twenty. Not in the first flush of youth, you understand, but then a chit out of the schoolroom who expected me to dance attendance on her all the time wouldn't suit me. We've been acquainted long enough to be sure we'd deal comfortably together. Yes,' he went on as though trying to convince himself, 'Celia Bamford will make an ideal wife. She knows what is expected of her. Once she's provided me with a son or two, there's no reason why we should see very much of each other.'

He sounded so coldly dispassionate that it seemed almost as if he had chosen his future bride with the same impassive discernment as he would have used when selecting a brood mare. The Dowager stared up at her favourite grandchild in silent dismay, her delight, now, ashes at her feet.

'But do you love her, Marcus?' she enquired with unwonted gentleness.

'Love?' His thin-lipped mouth twisted into a cynical smile. 'I don't look for that overblown emotion. I have learned over the years, ma'am, that most members of your sex become extremely loving especially when I am about to loosen the strings of my purse. . .no, mutual respect will suffice.'

Unlike the Dowager, who passed a very troubled night, Marcus was up early the following morning and, after writing a brief note of farewell to his grandmother, set off on his journey to Somerset.

The wind had dropped considerably during the past twelve hours, and the day was bright, though very cold. Like their owner, the powerful greys were strong and healthy, and they reached the turn off to Trowbridge in good time. Ravenhurst, however, did not take this turning, much to his groom's intense surprise, but continued along the road to Bath.

It was most unlike his master to take a wrong road; those sharp, dark eyes, ever alert, seemed never to miss a thing. The groom debated for a moment, knowing that their eventual destination was a few miles east of Wells, then said,

'Did you not notice the signpost back along, sir? Trowbridge were off to the left.'

'Yes, I saw it, Sutton, but I've decided to make a slight detour,' was the only explanation forthcoming, but the groom, quite accustomed to his master's abrupt manner, was satisfied with that.

Mr Ravenhurst was renowned in polite circles for his sharp tongue and blunt language: traits undoubtedly inherited from the Dowager Countess. But those who knew him well knew him to be a just and honourable man: the sort of solid, dependable individual whom one naturally turned to in a crisis.

All his servants were devoted to him, and with good reason. Since his father's death he had proved himself to be a considerate and caring master who, in return for diligence and loyalty, paid every attention to his employees' well-being. So, naturally, it had irked him immeasurably when the Dowager had been censorious over what she saw as neglect of duty, but later he had had to own, if only to himself, that there had been some justification for the criticism.

He had just turned six-and-twenty when he had found himself in the unenviable position of guardian to a young girl still in the schoolroom. In the swift and decisive manner that characterised him, he had dealt with the situation promptly. Enlisting the aid of a recently widowed distant cousin, Harriet Fairchild, he had installed her in his late mother's Bath residence in order to take care of the orphaned Sarah Pennington, and then had conveniently forgotten the child's very existence, except on those rare occasions when he had taken the trouble to cast his eyes over one of his cousin's exceedingly boring letters.

With very few exceptions he held the entire female species in contempt. He was never vulgar, nor would it ever enter his head deliberately to embarrass any member of the fair sex, but he was a plain-spoken man with little patience for false gallantry.

His astringent comments and heavy scowls had sent many a hopeful young debutante scurrying back to the protection of her fond mama's side. He was impatient of vapours and megrims, and feminine tears rarely moved him. So what good would he have been in the rearing of a young girl?

None whatsoever, he told himself. It had been in Sarah Pennington's best possible interests for him to have kept his distance and not to have interfered. His heavy frown descended. But he could, he knew, at least have taken the trouble to write to the child from time to time, and it would not have hurt him at all to have visited her once in a while.

His conscience smote him. It was a rare experience, and one, furthermore, which he did not care for in the least. Consequently, by the time he had drawn his greys to a halt before a certain house in Upper Camden Place, he was not in the best of humours.

After giving orders to his groom to walk the greys until his return, he mounted the stone steps and rapped sharply on the front door. The young servant girl who answered the summons took one look at the forbidding countenance glowering down at her, and stuttered nervously that her mistress was not receiving any more callers that day.

'Oh, is she not?' he ground out, his tone as alarming as his expression, as he stepped, uninvited, into the hall. 'Well, she shall most certainly receive me. You may tell her Ravenhurst is here.'

After closing the door, the girl disappeared into a room on the right. Marcus, impatiently tapping one highly polished boot on the floor, heard a low murmur of voices before a high-pitched shriek rent the air.

Waiting no longer, he stalked into the room that the young maid had entered to discover his cousin, prostrate, on the *chaise-longue*, the young maid wafting burnt feathers under her mistress's nose and a middle-aged woman, dressed in a very becoming dark blue walking dress and matching fur-trimmed pelisse, kneeling on the floor beside the couch, murmuring soothingly to his highly distraught cousin, who had taken one glance at him and then had promptly dissolved into tears.

'Good heavens, Harriet! What the deuce ails you?'

'You. . .? Here. . .? Today of all days!' came the muffled response from behind the lacy edging of a fine lawn handkerchief. 'Gone, Ravenhurst. Eloped! Oh, the wicked, ungrateful child! How could she do this to me? And after all I have done for her, too!'

'I have already told you, ma'am, that Sarah has not eloped.' The assurance came from the lady kneeling on the floor. She then cast her intelligent grey eyes up at the tall stranger and, easily recognising the signs of a gentleman containing his temper with an effort, hurriedly rose to her feet.

'Sir, you must be Sarah's guardian. May I introduce myself? My name is Emily Stanton.' She held out her hand and found it taken for a moment in a warm, firm clasp. 'Perhaps it might be best if we repair to another room.'

Casting a final impatient glance at his, still, hysterically sobbing cousin, Marcus followed the lady across the hall and into a small parlour overlooking the street.

'Do I understand correctly from my sorely afflicted

relative's somewhat garbled utterance that my ward has eloped?'

Mrs Stanton looked at him consideringly. 'Would it disturb you if she had, sir?'

'Most assuredly it would! She was my mother's godchild. I would be failing in my duties if I permitted her to fall into the hands of some fortune-hunter.'

'Fortune?' she echoed, failing completely to conceal her astonishment. 'Are you seriously trying to tell me that Sarah is a young woman of some means?'

His dark brows rose sharply, betraying the fact that he found the question an impertinence. 'You seem surprised, ma'am? Why should you doubt it?'

'Why, indeed!' she muttered.

He could easily discern the frown of puzzlement before asking her politely to sit down. 'Perhaps you would be good enough to tell me what has been going on here this day? And, if you are able, enlighten me as to the whereabouts of my ward?'

'Be assured, Mr Ravenhurst, that it is not Sarah who has eloped, but my own daughter.'

Again his brows rose, but in surprise this time. 'You will forgive me for saying so, ma'am, but you do not appear unduly concerned.'

She smiled faintly at the dry tone. 'No, sir. I am not,' she frankly admitted. 'My daughter Clarissa and Captain James Fenshaw have known each other since childhood. His family owns the property adjacent to our own in Devonshire. We enjoyed extremely cordial relations with our neighbours until my husband and Mr Fenshaw quarrelled over an unimportant strip of land.

'Since that unfortunate episode, my husband has strictly forbidden Clarissa to have any further contact with James, even going so far as to stop the poor child writing to him.' She paused for a moment, absently twisting the strings of her reticule round her fingers. 'Several weeks ago James returned home from the Peninsular, injured. As soon as he had recovered sufficiently, he travelled with his mother to Bath to benefit from the health-giving waters, you understand.'

He saw the betraying twitch of her lips.

'But I was not fooled for a moment. He struck up an immediate friendship with your ward, and was a frequent visitor to this house, as was my own daughter.'

'Are you trying to tell me, ma'am, that my ward actively encouraged these clandestine meetings between your daughter and this man?'

Mrs Stanton raised her eyes to stare unblinkingly into angry dark ones. 'Yes, she did. Sarah and my daughter have been close friends since they attended the seminary together. Why, they are more like sisters! Your ward has stayed with us in Devonshire on several occasions. I am extremely fond of her. She's a very intelligent and sweet-natured girl.'

'After her involvement in this affair, it shows a generosity of spirit that you still think so, ma'am.' He cast his eyes briefly in the direction of the clock on the mantelshelf. 'Do you wish me to go after the runaways?'

A slight frown creased her forehead as she rose to her feet and stared up at him, almost assessingly. 'Would you do that if I asked?'

'I am at your service. You have only to say the word,' he assured her, and her frown deepened.

'No, sir. I do not wish to stop this elopement,' she surprised him by responding. Moving over to the window, she stared down at the street to see a groom walking a pair of fine horses harnessed to a curricle.

'You must think me a most unnatural parent, but I hope with all my heart that they are successful and reach the border. It was cruel and unjust of my husband to try to keep them apart. They are well suited, and I know James will take good care of Clarissa. I was, unfortunately, duty-bound to adhere to my husband's wishes. Now, thankfully, all that has changed.

'First, I must pay a call on Mrs Fenshaw, and see what can be done to smooth things over here. Unlike our husbands, we have remained on friendly terms. I know she will be of a similar mind. I must, of course, write to my husband and inform him of what has occurred, and if he is foolish enough to go chasing after the pair. . . Well, so be it!'

She turned round to look at him again. 'But all this is of precious little interest to you, Mr Ravenhurst. Your concerns are for Sarah, only.'

'You may take a light view of her involvement in this affair, ma'am, but I most certainly do not! I shall have a word or two to say to that young woman when she returns here,' he remarked ominously.

'But, sir!' Her expression betrayed her complete astonishment. 'Sarah won't be returning here. She, too, has left Bath.'

'What!' Disbelief was clearly writ across his face. 'Do you mean to tell me that she is accompanying the star-crossed pair on this bolt to the border?' and much to his intense annoyance Mrs Stanton dissolved into laughter.

'Do forgive me,' she apologised when she was able. 'You do not know your ward at all well. That much is certain. Of course she hasn't gone with them.'

'Then where the devil has she gone, ma'am?' he demanded, not mincing words.

As her husband, too, had something of a peppery temperament, she did not bridle at the strong language, and once again regarded him rather consideringly. 'Before I answer that, I should like to ask you a question. Why, after six years, have you suddenly taken it into your head to visit your ward?'

She smiled at the lofty glance he cast her. 'Yes, naturally, you find it a gross impertinence, and wonder what on earth it has to do with me. Well, sir, as I've already mentioned, I'm very fond of Sarah, and tell you plainly that I shall not help you to discover her whereabouts if your only reason for doing so is to berate the child for her involvement in my daughter's tiresome affair.'

A noise, something akin to a low growl, emanated from his direction. 'Let me assure you, ma'am, that I came here for the sole purpose of ascertaining whether or not my ward would care for a London Season.'

'I see.' Once again Mrs Stanton subjected him to a long, penetrating stare. 'I think there is much that warrants investigation,' she remarked at length, and somewhat cryptically. 'And I think I shall help you.'

'Do you know where my ward has gone, ma'am? And why, if it were not through fear of the repercussions of her involvement in your daughter's elopement, she found it necessary to leave this house?'

'I believe I understand fully your ward's reasons for leaving this place. With my daughter gone there would be precious little joy for her here if she remained. But I am no tale-bearer. You must discover the truth from Sarah yourself. As to where she has gone. . .? I'm afraid she did not see fit to confide in me. I wish I had been in a position to do more for the child, but. . .'

A deep sigh of regret escaped her. 'Sarah left letters for both your cousin and myself, but in neither did she explain where she intended going. In mine she merely begged forgiveness for her involvement in the elopement. Silly, silly child!' she went on, an unmistakable catch in her voice. 'As though I blamed her!'

She paused for a moment, as though striving to regain her composure. 'I have learned already that two ladies and a gentleman left the city early this morning in a hired post-chaise. One of the ladies was my daughter, and the other, by the description given to me, was undoubtedly Sarah. It's my belief she has asked my daughter to take her as far as the Bristol to London road, from where, I sincerely believe, she intends to travel into Hertfordshire.'

His expression betrayed his incredulity. 'What the dev—deuce does she want to go there for?'

Her smile was a trifle crooked. 'You perhaps do not remember, sir, but before you became Sarah's guardian, she was in the charge of a certain Miss Martha Trent, who was employed, so I have been led to believe, as a sort of companion-governess. They were very close.

'After you dispensed with Miss Trent's services, she found employment in Hertfordshire as governess to two motherless little girls. Subsequently, she married her employer. Mrs Alcott, as she is now, visited Bath last year. I have never seen Sarah so happy! I overheard Mrs Alcott say on numerous occasions during her stay that she wished her former charge would make her home with her. And it is my belief that that is precisely what Sarah has decided to do.'

'Do you know Mr Alcott's precise direction, ma'am?'

'I am sorry to say I do not. But what I can tell you is

that he lives in a village not far from St Albans. He owns a sizeable property, and is a well-known figure in those parts. You should have little difficulty locating him.'

'Thank you for your help, Mrs Stanton. You will forgive me if I leave you now, but the need is pressing. I must not delay in searching for my ward.'

'Please do not give me another thought. I shall remain here with your cousin a while longer.' She arrested his progress to the door by the simple expedient of placing her fingers on his arm, and looked up into a face betraying deep concern. 'For some years I have considered you a most neglectful guardian. I am beginning to think my judgement was at fault. Your ward is a capable young woman, but I shall not rest easy until you've found her.'

'Be assured, ma'am, I will!'

'Having now met you, Mr Ravenhurst, I do not doubt that for a moment. But—but, I beg of you do not return her to this house. If you have nowhere suitable to take her, then bring her to me.'

He refused to commit himself on this, but said, 'Be assured I shall not neglect my duties again. Something has induced my ward to leave this house. Why the devil she didn't write to me if she was so unhappy, I don't know. But I mean to find out!'

Mrs Stanton, watching him collect his hat and gloves from the hall table, felt untold relief knowing that dear Sarah was being sought by such a very capable and obviously very concerned gentleman.

Her relief would have been short-lived, however, had she been standing in a certain inn yard not fifteen minutes later to witness the same gentleman stalking into the hostelry with a face like thunder.

The establishment's owner, a conscientious, hard-working man, had, through his own efforts, turned the hostelry into one of the city's finest. Before his marriage to the late innkeeper's daughter, six years before, he had worked since boyhood on the Ravenhurst estate. He had been devoted to the family, but after his beloved mistress's unexpected demise, he had decided to turn his hand to something new, and had never looked back.

He was manfully struggling with a large barrel of ale when he heard a loud voice raised in the tap. Unruly behaviour in his inn was something that he would not tolerate, and had not infrequently been called upon to evict disorderly customers by rough-and-ready means. Breaking off from his task, he strode purposefully into the tap-room, only to stop dead in his tracks, his belligerent look vanishing instantly.

'Why, Master Marcus, sir!' He came forward to clasp Mr Ravenhurst's hand warmly. 'Haven't set eyes on you since. . .well, not since that sad time. How goes it with you, young sir?'

'Well enough, Jeb. But I need your help.'

'Anything, sir. You know that.'

'I had intended travelling to Wells, but have been forced to change my plans. Could you loan me a fresh team and look after my greys until I can arrange for their collection?'

'Course I can, sir! I'll let you have my bays. Wouldn't trust 'em to just anyone, you understand, but I know with you they'll be in safe hands.'

They walked out to the yard and, whilst a young stable lad was harnessing the bays to his curricle, Marcus looked down the long row of stalls. Although the inn was not a posting house, several of Bath's residents stabled their horses here, knowing they would be well cared for.

'Which is my ward's mount, Jeb?' Marcus asked suddenly, his eyes resting on a particularly fine dapple mare. When he had received that letter from his cousin, requesting a horse for his ward, he had not left the matter in the hands of his efficient secretary, but had dealt with it himself.

In his reply he had requested her to seek Jeb's aid in finding a suitable mount. He had thought the price she had paid rather steep, and the cost of a riding habit exorbitant, but had not quibbled, and had increased Sarah's quarterly allowance to cover the costs of stabling. 'Is it that mare?'

'No, sir. Miss Pennington don't stable her horse here. Fact is—' he scratched the side of his head '—don't ever recall seeing her ride. But I 'appen to know that the owner of the mare is wishful to sell her, if you're interested?'

Marcus did not respond to this, but looked at the ex-groom thoughtfully. 'Are you acquainted with my ward, Jeb?'

'Well, I know of her, sir. Naturally, she don't come 'ere, but I've seen her about the city. My wife knows her right enough. Says she's a sweet-natured lass. Not too proud to stop and chat when they bump into each other whilst out doing a bit of marketing.'

'Marketing?' he echoed, not hiding his astonishment. 'But surely my cousin has servants enough to—' He broke off abruptly, his heavy frown descending, as he accompanied the innkeeper outside into the yard once again.

'Don't like the look of that sky, sir,' Jeb remarked, glancing over to the west where dark clouds were gathering ominously. 'Looks as though we're in for a spell o' bad weather. I hope your journey don't prove to be a long un.'

'And so do I!' Marcus responded with feeling as he sat himself beside his groom in the curricle. 'I'll return your bays as soon as I can. Thanks again,' and with that he gave the horses the office to start.

The borrowed team were certainly not in the greys' class, but were, none the less, sturdy animals, and Marcus soon reached the London to Bristol road. Although he had tactfully refrained from divulging the nature of his errand to the innkeeper, Bath being a positive hotbed for gossip, he had explained to his groom the reason behind the change in plans.

Sutton cast a concerned glance at his silent master as the first flakes of snow fell to earth. 'I do hope we find the young person, sir. I reckon we're in for a heavy fall.'

'I'm determined to find her,' Ravenhurst responded grimly. 'Not even a snowstorm, Sutton, will deprive me of the exquisite pleasure of wringing my sweet ward's confounded neck!'

Chapter Two

Sarah Pennington entered the inn's infrequently used private parlour, and sat herself down on the wooden settle conveniently placed near the inglenook fireplace. The homely innkeeper's wife would not hear of a gently bred young woman remaining in the coffee-room where she might be forced to associate with the locals.

'Good enough people in their own way, ma'am,' she had said, 'but a little too rough-and-ready at times.'

She had been all kind consideration for the poor young 'widow's' plight. Sarah's lips curled into a wry little smile. How different her reception had been, here, at this small wayside inn!

When she had entered that busy posting house earlier in the day, she had been subjected to a display of hostile disapproval from the landlady who, after informing her in no uncertain terms that the common stage did not stop at that superior establishment, had begrudgingly furnished her with a cup of coffee before sending her on her way.

Odious woman! Sarah thought angrily, still nettled by the icy treatment meted out to her. How was she supposed to know where the London to Bristol Accommodation

Coaches stopped to change horses and pick up passengers? She had never travelled by that means of transport in her life. But she ought, she knew, to have known that a young unmarried lady, travelling without so much as a maid to give her consequence, would certainly be viewed by many with staunch disapproval.

Fortunately, however, Mother Nature in her wisdom had seen fit not only to bless Sarah Pennington with a very pleasing countenance and a perfectly proportioned figure, but to bestow upon her a sunny disposition, a lively sense of humour and a good deal of no-nonsense common sense. She had, therefore, swiftly rectified the little oversight on her part.

As soon as she had been out of sight of any prying eyes watching her from the windows of that posting house, she had rummaged through her reticule, and had slipped her mother's wedding ring on to her finger. It was, of course, quite respectable for a married lady to be travelling about the country alone. More so a widow! she had decided, quickly placing the handsome husband of her fertile imagination six feet beneath the earth without suffering the least pangs of conscience.

Soon afterwards Fortune had chosen to look favourably on the young 'widow'. Sarah had not walked above a mile or two when she had been taken up by a kindly carrier who had generously offered to convey her to Chippenham to await the arrival of the Accommodation Coach from Bristol or, if she preferred, as far as Marlborough, where he was to have delivered his load of furniture.

As her purse was woefully slim, Sarah had not hesitated in accepting the generous offer of a free ride. Then, of course, cursed ill-luck had seen fit to demand its turn!

They had travelled no more than a few miles past Calne when snow had begun to fall.

The carrier, a seasoned user of the roads, knew the vagaries of the weather, and had predicted a heavy fall. Marlborough, now, was out of the question. He had fully intended to seek immediate shelter with friends, and had advised Sarah to take refuge at the wayside inn clearly visible from the main road.

He had assured her that the landlady kept a good, clean house, so she need not fear damp sheets, nor poor fare; and she was, now, very glad that she had taken his sensible advice, for the snow was falling harder than ever, rapidly adding to the three inches already covering the landscape.

Her reverie was interrupted by the landlord who entered the parlour, his arms laden with several substantial logs.

'Getting mortal bad out there, Mrs Armstrong,' he remarked, piling the logs on the huge hearth. 'You mark my words—there'll be more than one unwary traveller stranded afore this day is over.'

'I dare say you're right. When I arrived at Calne, where my brother was to have met me,' she remarked, her fertile imagination coming to her aid, and not for the first time that day, 'the clouds were, even then, looking rather threatening. It was rather foolish of me not to have remained there, but it's such a busy posting house, and all the noise was giving me the headache, so I thought some fresh air would do me good. I expected, of course, to see my brother's chaise coming towards me at any moment.'

By the sympathetic look on the landlord's craggy, weatherbeaten face, the explanation she had offered for her present predicament, accompanied by a forlorn little sigh, had sounded very convincing.

'I'm so very glad I noticed the smoke billowing from your chimneys from the main road, and had the sense to come here, instead of trying to return to that posting house at Calne.'

'Would that be The White Hart, ma'am?'

'Er—yes, that's right.'

'Did you leave the rest of your baggage there?' he enquired, recalling clearly that the young lady had arrived carrying only a smallish wooden case and a rather old and battered cloak-bag.

'No, my trunk was sent on ahead,' she improvised quickly. 'I've been staying with friends, just a few miles from here. I thought the few clothes I had brought with me would be adequate for my journey home. But I'm afraid I made no allowances for a deterioration in the weather and any possible delays on the road.'

'Don't you worry your head on that score, ma'am. My good lady will provide you with any—er—little necessities you might need. And don't worry about your brother, neither. Stands to reason he won't be travelling far this day. As soon as the weather improves, I'll take you back to Calne in my old gig. No doubt we'll find him awaiting you at the posting house.'

Sarah thanked him, and then watched, a flicker of regret in the depths of her lovely aquamarine-coloured eyes, as he left the room. How she hated lying to these kindly folk! But what choice had she?

She could not bear to be stranded here and be treated with contempt, her presence nothing more than a hindrance, a tiresome burden. She had endured more than enough years of feeling nothing more than a troublesome millstone about someone's neck. No, that wasn't strictly true, she amended silently. She hadn't been made to feel unwanted, at least, not by Mrs Fairchild. And her wretched guardian simply hadn't concerned himself about her at all!

She turned her head to stare down at the logs hissing and crackling noisily on the hearth, and began to recall the events in her life that had led to her present very sorry predicament.

Her father had been a courageous man, a captain in His Majesty's Navy, who had given his life for King and Country during the Battle of the Nile. Sad to say she could hardly remember him at all. She had been just a child when he had died; but she had almost reached the age of fifteen when her dear mother had been so cruelly and unexpectedly taken from her.

Keeping her tears firmly in check, she began to dwell on those idyllic childhood years when she had resided in her father's charming house near Plymouth, and those happy times when she had visited her dear godmother at Ravenhurst, that beautiful stone-built mansion situated in its many acres of Oxfordshire parkland. She retained many fond memories of her kind godmother, but her godmother's son she could not bring to mind at all.

In those early years, whenever she had visited Ravenhurst with her mother, he had been away at Eton, and then, later, at Oxford. The only vague memory she retained of him was on that day he had visited Plymouth shortly after her mother had died.

A hazy vision of a hard-featured face swam before her mind's eye. At the tender age of fourteen, she had been too afraid to look at the tall stranger in whose hands her future well-being had been placed, let alone disagree with any arrangements he may have undertaken on her behalf, and had kept her eyes glued to his highly polished top-boots, and her lips firmly compressed.

Honesty promoted her to admit that she had not disliked the idea of attending a seminary in Bath; she had not even objected to being placed in the care of his cousin, who had turned out to be quite a kindly soul, though slightly scatty and prone to fits of the vapours when things had not gone her way; but she had bitterly resented being separated from her beloved governess.

'No, my dear. It will not answer,' Martha Trent had responded gently, yet firmly, to Sarah's pleas for them to remain together. 'Your guardian is right. It will be much better for you to go to school and have the companionship of girls your own age. And with you attending a seminary, I would have no role to play in your new home. Mr Ravenhurst's cousin will, I'm sure, take very good care of you.

'I cannot live off your guardian's charity, Sarah. I must look about for a new position. And Mr Ravenhurst has very kindly insisted that on no account am I to take the first one offered, but am to look for a situation where I think I would be happy.'

Sarah frowned slightly as Martha's words came back so clearly. Yes, to be fair, she had to own that her guardian had displayed some consideration for her beloved governess. Which was more than he had ever done for her! He was, by common report, a very rich man, and yet he had never seen fit to send her a little money of her own with which to buy a few little luxuries. What dresses she possessed, good quality garments, but sadly unfashionable, had been chosen for her by Mrs Fairchild.

Unlike other girls her age, she had never attended the balls held at the Assembly Rooms, and had rarely been invited to any private parties. The only times she had ever been truly happy were during those few short months each year when Mrs Stanton brought her daughter Clarissa to Bath, and those wonderful summer visits she had made to their home in Devonshire.

The weekday ventures to the Pump Room, where Mrs Fairchild sampled the waters and gossiped with her middle-aged cronies, and the twice-monthly card parties held in the large salon at Upper Camden Place, where Sarah had donned her best pearl-grey gown and had served Mrs Fairchild's guests with wine and tiny sweet biscuits, had proved to be the only slight relief from the tedium of living all year round in that, once, very fashionable watering place.

But it wasn't until Martha had paid that unexpected visit to Bath the year before that Sarah had become totally discontented with her lot. Her ex-governess had assured her that she would be most welcome to visit her in Hertfordshire, and to stay for as long as she wished, and had gone so far as to furnish her with enough money to hire a post-chaise for the journey.

Martha, also, had not attempted to hide her shock and dismay at her ex-pupil's drab, unfashionable attire, giving Sarah reason to hope that, perhaps, she wasn't so poorly circumstanced as she had been led to believe.

'As to that, my dear, I'm not perfectly sure,' had been Mrs Fairchild's vague response to her charge's blunt enquiry. 'Mr Ravenhurst has never seen fit to discuss your financial situation with me.'

'But surely, ma'am, I was left some money?' Sarah had persisted. 'We lived in a charming house near Plymouth. What has become of that? And my mother's family was certainly not poor. My grandfather was, after all, a baronet.'

'Very true, Sarah. But what you, perhaps, do not realise, is that your mother became estranged from your grandfather when she chose to go against his expressed wishes and marry Captain Pennington. Worthy man though your father undoubtedly was, he hardly belonged to your mother's social class. And as far as your old home is concerned. . .? Well, I really couldn't say. Perhaps your mother left debts and Mr Ravenhurst was forced to sell it.

'And I cannot understand just why you have suddenly taken it into your head to concern yourself over such matters,' she had gone on to say. 'You reside in a charming house, have good food to eat and are expected to undertake only the lightest of tasks for your keep.

'I'm sure Mr Ravenhurst has your best interests at heart, my dear. And it most certainly wouldn't do for you to go parading round Bath in a lot of finery and giving the totally wrong impression to any eligible young gentlemen, now would it? But I'm sure that your guardian would not object to purchasing anything for you if it were really needful?'

'In that case, ma'am,' Sarah had retorted, bitterly resentful at what she had deemed an unnecessary slight on her father, 'perhaps you would be good enough to enquire, when next you write to my excessively wealthy guardian, whether he would be willing to furnish me with a suitable mount, so that I am able to accompany my friend Clarissa on her rides whilst she is in Bath. I do not think that that would be too much to ask!'

Of course, Sarah had not left matters there, and had written to Mr Ravenhurst requesting information regarding her circumstances, but had never received a reply, nor had the horse she had craved ever been forthcoming; not that she had been particularly surprised about that. After all, a man who could not even bring himself to respond to the few letters she had written over the years was hardly likely to put himself to the trouble of purchasing a suitable mount for his tiresome ward.

Sighing, Sarah rose from the settle, and went across the room to stare out of the window. The snow was continuing to fall heavily in the rapidly fading late afternoon light. It was impossible, now, to discern the road from the grass verges.

She released her breath in a tiny sigh. Perhaps it had been rather foolish of her to leave Bath at this time of year, but she was not sorry she had. After all, with her friend Clarissa gone, and dear Mrs Stanton no doubt feeling quite out of charity with her daughter's conspiring friend, there was nothing left for her there.

Added to which, in June, when she attained her majority, her indifferent guardian would no doubt be only too eager to wash his hands of her completely. His obligations would then be at an end, and she would be forced to make her own way in the world. So, why wait until the inevitable was forced upon her?

It was as well to be prepared, she told herself, and look for a position as governess, or companion in some genteel household, and she felt certain that her dear Martha would aid her in finding a comfortable situation.

A smart racing curricle, making very slow progress along the road, caught her attention. The driver, his hat and cloak covered in white, put her in mind of a rather large and misshapen snowman; and she might have derived a deal of amusement from the spectacle had it not recalled to mind certain other travellers abroad that day, and she prayed with all her heart that dear Clarissa and James were not stranded on the road but, like herself, had found shelter at some inn.

The door opening broke into her disturbing thoughts, and she turned her head to see the innkeeper's kindly wife enter the room.

'Mrs Armstrong, we've another traveller just arrived wishful to shelter from the weather. Would you object if the gentleman joined you in the parlour for dinner? It's more fitting dining in here, him being a gentleman an' all.'

'Of course I don't object,' Sarah assured her. 'Is he, perhaps, the person I saw just now tooling a curricle?'

'Aye, ma'am. Though what possessed him to go careering round the country in an open carriage in the month of February beats me. Mind, I thought it wisest not to ask. Didn't look in the best of humours when he walked in. But I dare say he'll cheer up and feel a deal better once he's got a decent meal inside him.'

Sarah, her mind still dwelling on the long journey to the border her eloping friends had ahead of them, gave not another thought to the stranded gentleman traveller until, some fifteen minutes later, the parlour door opened yet again.

She watched a tall, broad-shouldered man, immaculately attired in a coat of blue superfine, tight-fitting pantaloons and shining top-boots—whose brilliance, no doubt, was attained from using a secret mixture containing champagne—enter the room. He came purposefully, yet gracefully, towards her, and she found herself staring up at a far-from-handsome and unsmiling countenance.

'I understand from the lady of the house that you have been gracious enough to permit me to share your private parlour, ma'am,' he remarked in the most attractive deep masculine voice she had ever heard. 'My name is Ravenhurst.'

Her lovely smile of greeting fading, Sarah sat rigid on the wooden settle, as though turned to stone. Ravenhurst. . .? The name echoed between her temples like some thunderous peal of bells. It couldn't be! Surely Fate could not be so wickedly capricious as to bring them face to face this day, of all days!

'Are you all right, ma'am?' The modicum of concern in his deep voice was lost on her. 'You are very pale. I'll summon the landlady.'

Sarah could not have responded even had she wanted to, and could only watch in a kind of trancelike state as he hurriedly left the room.

Placing a suddenly trembling hand to her throbbing temple, she tried to make some sense out of her frantically disordered thoughts. Was it, in truth, 'the' Mr Ravenhurst? She hadn't recognised him, but that was in no way remarkable, considering she had set eyes on him only once in her life before, and then had taken precious little interest in his outward appearance.

Her finely arched brows drew together in a deep, thoughtful frown. Even supposing, by some cursed ill-luck, that the stranger did turn out to be her guardian, then what in the world was he doing in this part of the country? Although, she reminded herself, didn't Mr Ravenhurst have relatives residing in Wiltshire? A grand-mother, or uncle, or some such? She felt certain that Harriet Fairchild had said as much.

If he had not been visiting his relations, then it must be pure coincidence that had brought him here, surely? He couldn't possibly have received word so soon of her leaving Bath. And even if by some mischance he had discovered her flight, he certainly wouldn't put himself to the trouble of coming after her. . . Or would he?

No, she thought, quickly thrusting this foolish notion aside, and focusing her mind on what course of action to take. Firstly, she must discover if the stranger was, indeed, her guardian; then, if the worst came to the worst, and it turned out to be so, she must try to discover what he was doing in this part of the world. She felt certain he had not recognised her and, given the circumstances, it might be wisest if she allowed him to remain in blissful ignorance.

By the time the object of her thoughts returned, with the very concerned landlady in tow, Sarah had regained full control of herself and was determined not to lose it so foolishly again. After hurriedly assuring the good woman that she was perfectly well, and that her 'queer turn' had no doubt stemmed from a singular lack of nourishment since breakfast, she, once again reverting to her widowed status, introduced herself to the severe-looking man who then drew up a chair, and seated himself.

'Have you far to travel?' she enquired when the landlady had left them alone together.

His deep-set dark eyes held hers from the opposite side of the hearth. 'As to that, ma'am, I couldn't say with any degree of certainty.'

'You are not from around these parts, sir?'

'No,' was the clipped response, but far from being annoyed by his abruptness, Sarah was amused.

He was, undoubtedly, a man prone to frequent bouts of ill-humour, the permanent crease between those almost black brows being adequate confirmation of this; and she recalled being told, on more than one occasion, that her guardian was a brusque, testy individual, much the same as her friend Clarissa's father.

Unlike Harriet Fairchild, however, who certainly entertained a lively dread of her untitled aristocratic cousin's unpleasant temperament, Sarah, strangely, experienced no such trepidation when in the company of such irascible gentlemen, and could not resist the temptation to goad him a little.

'No doubt you are feeling slightly peevish at having your journey interrupted, sir. Some gentlemen, I know, cannot brook the least deviation from their original plans, and fly into the boughs at the slightest hitch,' and it took every ounce of self-control she possessed to stop herself from bursting out laughing as he regarded her much as he might have done a rare specimen in some fairground freak-show.

'But as there is nothing either of us can do to improve the weather,' she continued, her voice not quite steady, 'I suggest we try to make the best of our enforced stay here.'

A sound, somewhere between the noise a gentleman makes when clearing his throat and that of a predatory beast's suppressed growl, reached her ears before he said, still with an unmistakable trace of annoyance in his voice, 'Forgive me, ma'am, if I seemed—er—peevish, but the day has not turned out at all as I had expected. There hasn't been so much a small hitch in my original plans as a total abandonment, instigated by the completely unwarranted and feather-brained actions of my—'

He stopped abruptly, his lips for a moment compressed into a thin, angry line, though when he spoke again it was in a distinctly milder tone. 'But as you correctly surmised, I do not reside in this part of the country, although I do have relatives living not far from here. My home is in Oxfordshire.'

Oh, God, no! Sarah could have screamed in vexation. There wasn't a doubt about it. The wretch was her guardian!

It was perhaps fortunate that the landlady and her buxom rosy-cheeked daughter chose this auspicious moment to enter the room: one laying covers on the table; the other going about the room lighting the various candles and closing the curtains, offering Sarah time to calm herself down and rethink her strategy.

From what he had let fall, it was abundantly obvious that he was searching for her. But how on earth had he discovered, so quickly, her departure from Bath? There was only one possible explanation: against all the odds, he must have visited Upper Camden Place that morning. Wretched man! Why, today of all days, had he suddenly taken it into his head to visit Bath?

Not that that was of any relevance, she told herself, turning her head to stare down into the fire once more, blissfully unaware that he was studying the play of different emotions flit across her face. It was unlikely that Harriet Fairchild would have realised where her charge had intended going and, to be fair, Sarah knew she had given little away in the note she had left her. But Clarissa's mother might well have guessed Sarah's destination.

If Mrs Stanton had happened to be present when Ravenhurst arrived, how much information had he gleaned from her? Certainly enough to bring him thus far. Therefore, it stood to reason that he had learned of Martha Alcott's home in Hertfordshire. What beastly ill-luck!

'Something appears to be troubling you, Mrs Armstrong.'

'W-what?' Sarah drew her head round with a start. 'No, not really, sir,' she managed in a moderately convincing voice, while silently cursing his astuteness. She forced herself to stare into those intelligent dark brown eyes. No, her guardian was certainly no fool.

Ought she to tell him who she really was? She dismissed the notion in an instant. His sole purpose in trying to locate her must be to return her to Bath. And she would not go back there! she thought determinedly. But she would need to be so very careful from now on, giving away no clue as to her true identity.

Had she mentioned that her destination was Hertfordshire to either the innkeeper or his wife? No, she felt certain she had not. Therefore, her destination now, if anyone should enquire, would be. . . Surrey. Yes, Surrey would serve very well, but she must ensure that she stuck to her original story, for if she made one slight slip, and he learned something different from either the innkeeper or his wife, she felt certain he would be on to her like a cat after a hapless mouse.

'I was just thinking about my brother. My friends left me at The White Hart in Calne where I was to have awaited his arrival.'

'Then why didn't you?'

It was on the tip of her tongue to tell him to mind his own business, but she refrained, and said, instead, 'I grew tired of waiting. I expected to see him at any moment coming along the road towards me in the chaise, but in the end was forced to seek shelter here. It was foolish of me not to have remained in Calne, I suppose.'

'Exceedingly so, ma'am,' he returned bluntly, the

forlorn little voice that had gained the sympathy of the innkeeper earlier having no such effect on him. 'Quite feather-brained, in fact!'

The green in her eyes became more prominent. 'Yes, as totty-headed as driving about the country in an open carriage at this time of year, I dare say,' she parried, and was astounded by the appreciative smile that curled his lips and completely erased the hard lines of his face, turning him into a most attractive man.

'*Touché*, madam.' He rose to his feet. 'I believe we are served.'

Sarah accompanied him over to the table, not quite knowing what to make of him. He was certainly abrupt, and exceedingly rude, but he was not totally ill-mannered, for he did pull a chair out for her, and then proceeded to carve several slices of chicken on to her plate.

'I'm relieved to see that you have a healthy appetite, ma'am,' he remarked after watching her help herself to the various contents of several dishes. 'I cannot abide females who insist upon chasing morsels of food around their plates for the duration of a meal, and then have the crass stupidity to wonder, after eating so little, why they are prone to fainting all over the place.'

She could not forbear a smile at his scathing tone. 'Then you must be relieved to see that you are not in the company of such a one. I enjoy my food, and can assure you that I have never fainted in my life.'

'You came perilously close to doing so earlier,' he countered, and she cast him a wary look, but gained her composure almost at once.

'And that is precisely why I am rectifying that near-transgression on my part. I really could not bear the humiliation of having you step over me whilst on your way about the inn.'

Once again she was privileged to see that rather wonderful smile. 'I would never do anything so ungentlemanlike, I assure you.'

He surveyed her for a moment over the rim of his glass, noting the strands of gold in her rich brown, plainly though neatly arranged hair, and the finely arched black brows and long black curling lashes that framed her lovely and unusually coloured blue-green eyes.

There was nothing classical in the lines of her small straight nose, but her lips were pleasantly formed and curled up slightly at the corners, and there was certainly more than a hint of determination in that softly rounded chin. All in all she was an exceedingly pretty young woman who, he suspected, possessed a great deal of lively wit and charm.

'Your husband must be concerned about you, ma'am. Were you expected home this day?'

'I'm a widow, sir,' she responded evenly, and just for an instant thought she could detect a flicker of sympathy in his eyes as they rested for a moment on her plain grey gown. 'Are you married, Mr Ravenhurst?'

For some reason his dark straight brows snapped together, and his tone once again was clipped as he said, 'No, ma'am, I am not!'

'No, I didn't think so.'

'Oh? And what gave rise to that assumption?'

'Because you had not long entered this room before I became fairly confident that I was in the company of a confirmed misogynist.'

His deep rumble of laughter filled the air. 'My word, but you're forthright, ma'am! If that were, indeed, true,

I think I can safely say that I'm rapidly losing my hatred.'

For one dreadful moment she suspected him of flirting with her, but then he changed the subject, and she felt certain she must have been mistaken.

Unlike his cousin Harriet Fairchild, who rarely cast her eyes over a printed word, and then only those set between the hard covers of a Gothic romance, Sarah was an avid reader who scanned the daily newspapers from cover to cover, and so kept abreast of happenings in the world. She was, therefore, able to converse with Mr Ravenhurst on a wide variety of topics, from the progress of the war with France to the Prince of Wales's inauguration as Regent the previous year.

It transpired that her guardian had been amongst the two thousand guests who had attended the celebration party held at Carlton House; but from his scathing condemnation of the traffic blocking many of the capital's busy streets that day, and his caustic remarks on the oppressive warmth and the cluttered and vulgar opulence of the Regent's town dwelling, it was quite apparent that he had not enjoyed the experience very much.

They had no sooner eaten their fill of the excellent dinner than the landlady's daughter returned, carrying a bottle and a glass on a tray.

'Ma said as how you being a gentleman, sir, you'd be wanting this after your meal,' she offered nervously, setting the tray down on to the table.

'What's your name, girl?' Marcus asked, reaching for the port and pouring himself a glass.

'Daisy, sir. . . Daisy Fletcher, sir.'

'Be good enough to convey my thanks to your mother, Miss Fletcher. That was an excellent dinner.'

'Oh, thank 'ee, sir! Ma do know how to look after

gentlemen, right enough. She were in service when she were a girl. She do keep a good, well-stocked larder, so you needn't afear to go 'ungry whilst you're 'ere. And if the weather do stay bad for a few days to come, Pa be willing to slaughter the goose, and his favourite suckling pig, which'll do for several meals if you make use of the innards an' all. No, you won't be going 'ungry, sir.'

Marcus, a look of comical dismay on his face, watched her leave the room, and then turned once again to his dinner-companion to see her shoulders shaking with suppressed laughter.

'Has no one ever told you, ma'am,' he said in a voice of mock censure, 'that it shows a decided lack of breeding to laugh at rustics?'

'I was not laughing at her!' Sarah refuted hotly, but not quite steadily. 'It was you who very nearly sent me into whoops. If you could have seen the look on your face when she mentioned slaughtering the pig.'

'Dear me, yes. She spoke as though it were a pet. And do people consume the insides of a pig?'

'Some parts of it, certainly. The liver, and the chitterlings, I believe.'

'Oh, God spare us! Let us hope it doesn't come to that. Though I'm sure if you're willing to tackle such fare, I can steel myself to do so. Where are you going?'

Sarah, who had risen, placed her chair neatly beneath the small table. 'I was up very early this morning, sir, and am rather tired. So, I'll bid you good-night, and leave you to your port.'

Picking up a candle, Mr Ravenhurst surprised Sarah by escorting her to the door, and then across the deserted coffee-room to the foot of the narrow staircase where he handed her the candle.

'Good-night, Mrs Armstrong,' he said, his features once again softened by that warm smile. 'I look forward to the pleasure of your company at breakfast.'

Feeling not just a little confused, Sarah made her way up the narrow staircase and along the passageway to the spotlessly clean, low-ceilinged bedchamber that she had been shown into soon after her arrival at the inn.

At some point, while she had been in the parlour, someone had entered the room to fold down the bedcovers and to pull the floral-patterned drapes across the window. The candle on the small table in the corner had been lit and the fire had been made up, making the room pleasantly warm and cosy.

After going about the room lighting the other candles, she set the light Mr Ravenhurst had given her down on the chest of drawers by the bedside, and then went across to the table in the corner on which she had placed her wooden writing-case. She had been able to bring so few possessions with her—not that she had that many to bring—but she had refused to leave this, the last present her mother had ever given to her, behind in Bath.

She ran one finger lovingly over the delicate gold leaf of her initials, exquisitely carved into the fine wood, before flicking the catch and opening the lid. It was so beautifully made, having sections for ink bottles and pens.

There were two small drawers, one set in each of the back corners: the right quite inocuous; the left hiding a cunningly made secret compartment for billets-doux. There was also ample room in the centre of the box for several sheets of paper, the top one of which already contained several lines in Sarah's neatly flowing hand.

Lifting the sheet from off the pile, Sarah ran her eyes over the letter to her guardian that she had begun to write, ironically enough, shortly after her arrival at the inn, and groaned inwardly. The cool formality had seemed just the correct tone to adopt, but now, having met Mr Ravenhurst again after so many years, it seemed totally inappropriate, rude almost.

She raised her eyes to stare blindly across the comfortable room. And what an enigma the man had turned out to be! She had been given every reason to suppose, from remarks Mrs Fairchild had made over the years, and from snippets of information gleaned from visitors to Bath who were acquainted with her guardian, that Mr Ravenhurst was nothing more than an abrupt, unfeeling individual who had no consideration for his fellow man.

A wry smile curled her lips. He was most certainly abrupt, but his caustic remarks, far from giving offence, had amused her. She had enjoyed his company very much during dinner; and the simple thanks he had offered to the landlady's daughter had afforded a glimpse of his true character. He was far from the care-for-nobody she had thought him. Which made his seeming indifference towards her over the years even more puzzling.

She shook her head, genuinely perplexed. Something just didn't ring true. Added to which, he had come searching for her. Was that the action of an indifferent guardian? No, of course it was not! And, now, having come to know him a little, she felt she ought to tell him who she really was. After all, sooner or later he was going to discover the truth; and she felt certain that, once he understood her reasons for leaving, he would not force her to return to Bath.

Yes, first thing in the morning, she decided firmly, she would confess all. And who could tell, he might even be kind enough to escort her the rest of the way to Hertfordshire!

A sudden commotion below reached her ears. She could clearly hear the sound of several raised voices, and wondered what on earth was going on.

Curiosity got the better of her and, quickly thrusting the letter back into the writing-case and closing the lid, she picked up a candle and made her way back down the stairs to discover that a strange assortment of dishevelled travellers had invaded the coffee-room: some arguing amongst themselves; others calmly watching proceedings; and the very distraught landlord trying desperately to make himself heard above the din.

'What the devil is going on out here?'

The authoritative voice had an immediate effect. The hubbub ceased instantly as all eyes turned to stare at the imposing figure framed in the parlour doorway.

'Sir!' The landlord hurried towards Mr Ravenhurst, realising at once that here was a man born to command and, unless he was very much mistaken, accustomed to having those commands obeyed.

'These be the passengers from the London to Bristol Accommodation Coach. From what I can make out their vehicle be in a ditch, sir, a mile or so back along the main road. The driver and guard are walking the horses to Calne. And I been trying to tell 'em that that's what they should o' done, instead o' coming 'ere. We ain't a posting house, sir. We can't cater for such a large number.'

'Now, Frederick—' his wife came forward '—you can't send these poor folk back out on a night like this. Why, it's blowing a blizzard out there. It would be positively unchristian!'

'And I for one won't walk another step!' declared a very fat woman who, much to Sarah's amusement, substantiated the statement by plumping herself down in the middle of the coffee-room floor.

Marcus, not so easily diverted by the action, shot the woman an impatient glance before casting his eyes over her fellow-travellers, his gaze coming to rest on a sandy-haired young man who was gaping back at him in astonishment.

'Ravenhurst! What the deuce are you doing in this out-of-the-way place?'

'I should have thought that that would have been patently obvious to anyone of the meanest intelligence, Nutley,' he responded dampingly before addressing himself to the innkeeper's wife. 'How many of these persons are you able to accommodate?'

'Well, sir, if some wouldn't mind sharing, I dare say we can fix them all up.'

'One of the ladies could, perhaps, come in with me,' Sarah offered kindly.

'No, there's no need for you to put yourself out,' Marcus intervened before the landlady could accept the generous offer. Unlike Sarah, he had taken stock of the passengers.

Apart from the fat lady, who was still stubbornly seated on the floor, and who looked to be travelling with the thin man hovering nearby, there were only two other females amongst the passengers: a spinsterish-looking woman who bore all the appearance of a governess, and whose face was hidden by a large and rather ugly bonnet; and a twinkling-eyed female in a dashing red confection, whose saucy smile gave him a fair notion of what her particular calling might be.

'If you would be willing to change rooms with me, ma'am, I shall be happy to share with one of these gentlemen,' he continued, raising a questioning brow at the tall young man whose broad shoulders were propped against the wall, and who had been silently viewing proceedings with an amused glint in his tawny-coloured eyes.

'Very decent of you, sir,' he said coming forward. 'My name is Carter—Captain Brin Carter.'

Marcus acknowledged him with a nod before turning to the innkeeper again. 'I leave the rest of the arrangements to you and your good lady.'

Although having been granted little say in the matter, Sarah did not object to the new arrangements, and accompanied Mr Ravenhurst back up the stairs.

It took but a few moments to repack her meagre belongings into the cloak-bag and carry it across the narrow passageway into her newly allotted and much smaller bedchamber. She was genuinely fatigued after the events of the day, and long before the harassed innkeeper and his wife had the remainder of their unexpected guests accommodated, she had fallen sound asleep.

Marcus did return downstairs for a short while. He joined Captain Carter and one of his fellow travelling-companions in the tap to sample a tankard of the innkeeper's excellent home-brewed. The Captain, it transpired, was on his way to Bristol to board the next vessel leaving for Spain, and Mr Stubbs was merely paying a visit to the city to stay with his daughter.

Mr Stubbs's explanation for travelling at such a time of year sounded plausible enough, and Marcus might have accepted the reason at face value had the middle-aged, stockily built individual not betrayed an inordinate interest in the other customers: locals who had braved the elements for their evening tipple.

'An odd character, Stubbs,' the Captain remarked later, when they entered their bedchamber. 'Friendly enough, but a mite inquisitive, wouldn't you say?'

Marcus's lips twisted into a crooked smile. 'Yes. Our friends at Bow Street do travel far and wide these days.'

'A Runner?' The Captain's brows rose. 'That would account for it, then! He was very chatty during the journey, asking a great many seemingly innocent questions. In fact, that weasel-faced fellow in the black coat, who started all the commotion earlier, was quite put out when Stubbs asked him what he did for a living. Can't imagine why. Turns out he's only some damned clerk in a lawyer's office.'

Marcus did not respond to this, for his attention was focused on the gold letters carved into the lid of the very handsomely made wooden box resting on the small table in the corner of the room. Without experiencing the least qualms he calmly opened the lid, ran his eyes over the unfinished letter lying on top and, much to the Captain's unholy amusement, suddenly uttered a string of decidedly colourful and unrepeatable oaths.

Chapter Three

Sarah awoke with a violent start the following morning when the daughter of the house, entering the bedchamber, thumped a pitcher of warm water down none too gently on the top of the wash-stand.

'Sorry, Mrs Armstrong, did I wake you?'

'Oh, that's all right.' Rubbing the sleep from her eyes, Sarah watched the flat-footed Daisy stomp across the room to draw back the curtains. The morning looked remarkably bright, and for a few elated moments she retained the hope that she might be able to continue her journey, until assured that nothing had passed along the road that morning.

'I overheard one of the locals saying last night that there be drifts ten foot deep in parts, blocking the main road,' Daisy voiced dampingly. 'Although the sun be shining, there be precious little warmth in it, and Pa reckons there'll be more snow afore long. You won't be leaving 'ere today, Mrs Armstrong. Nor tomorrow, I don't reckon.'

'Never mind. It cannot be helped,' Sarah responded, resigning herself quickly to remaining at least one more day at the inn. Fully awake, now, she sat up and pushed her tousled brown hair away from her face. 'Did you manage to accommodate all those passengers off the stagecoach?'

'Aye, we did that, ma'am, but it were a bit of a squeeze. I had to give up my bed to that farmer and his wife. The young sprig and another man had Ma and Pa's room, and Mr Ravenhurst's groom kindly agreed to share with our Joe, so the lady in the pretty red bonnet could 'ave 'is old room. And the spinster lady and that man who be forever carping on 'ad to make do with the smallest rooms down the far end of the passageway.'

Having always taken an interest in the welfare of others, Sarah looked up in some concern. 'But where on earth did you and your parents sleep?'

'We bedded down in our parlour next to the kitchen. But from tonight I'm to sleep at me aunt's 'ouse, just down the road. And we're to 'ave me cousin Rose 'elping out.' She pulled a face. 'She be a right flighty little wench. And as sly as bedamned. I'd never trust 'er. She'll come to a bad end one o' these days, ma'am. You see if she don't.'

So, Daisy evidently didn't care for her cousin very much, and most certainly wasn't looking forward to her presence at the inn. Sarah regarded her with an understanding smile. 'I expect you could do with the extra pair of hands, though.'

'Aye, we could that. Ma's been up since daybreak, baking and the like. Which reminds me. She wants to know if you'd like your breakfast brought up on a tray, or are you wishful to eat in the parlour again?'

'Definitely in the parlour, Daisy. You will have enough to do without running up and down the stairs with breakfast trays all morning.'

After washing in the contents of the pitcher, Sarah donned her detested grey gown, and stood before the wash-stand mirror to tidy her hair, twisting it in a long plait before securely pinning it to the back of her head. Vanity, thankfully, had never been one of her failings.

Yet she was feminine enough, as she stood there staring at her reflection in the mottled glass, to crave pretty dresses to wear and to long for the ministrations of an abigail, whose skilled fingers could arrange those silky brown tresses in a more becoming style.

A sigh escaped her. Elaborate hairstyles and elegant gowns were not the hallmarks of a governess, she reminded herself and, desperately trying to resign herself to her possible future station in life, left the bedchamber, blissfully unaware that her unfashionable attire and plainly arranged hair did not diminish her prettiness one iota.

Young Captain Carter was most certainly favourably impressed with what he saw, and cast an appreciative eye over both face and figure as Sarah entered the parlour a minute or two later. Unlike Mr Ravenhurst, who remained seated and merely acknowledged her with a curt nod, the Captain politely rose to his feet and, after introducing himself, thanked her for so generously giving up her bedchamber the night before.

'Not at all, sir. It was no inconvenience, I assure you.' She sat beside Mr Ravenhurst at the table but, after a quick glance at his forbidding profile, decided to address herself to the far more amiable Captain. 'I trust you both slept well?'

Captain Carter shot a wicked glance in his bedfellow's direction. 'I'm quite used to sharing, ma'am. In Spain one is forced to adapt to many things, but I don't think our friend, here, is similarly accustomed.

'And it certainly didn't improve matters by being awakened this morning by a young lass who threw open the door so violently that it crashed against the wardrobe, and then added insult to injury by tripping up over the mat at the bottom of the bed and very nearly drowning us both with the contents of the water jug she was carrying.'

'Clumsy wench!' Ravenhurst muttered, his eyes narrowing fractionally as he detected the slight movement of slender shoulders shaking in suppressed laughter. 'By the by, Mrs—er—Armstrong, I believe you left that box in our room last night.' He gestured to the small table by the window on which he had set the writing-case a little earlier. 'At least I assume it's yours. It has the initials S.P. carved in the lid.'

'Oh, yes. It is mine,' Sarah confirmed after casting the briefest of glances at her most treasured possession, and cursing herself silently for leaving it behind in the room for him to find. 'My maiden name was Postlethwaite,' she managed after only the briefest of pauses. 'Serafina Postlethwaite.'

Marcus very nearly choked on his coffee, and hurriedly got to his feet. 'If you will both excuse me, I think I shall take a wander outside and see for myself just how bad conditions are.'

The Captain, frowning slightly, watched him leave. 'He's an odd fellow. Don't quite know what to make of him. One minute he's as considerate as can be, and the next—' He broke off abruptly, and cast Sarah an almost apologetic smile. 'I'm sorry, ma'am. Are you well acquainted with the gentleman?'

'No, sir, I am not,' she responded truthfully. 'He arrived here late yesterday afternoon, and we dined together. He is certainly a puzzling creature, though. I cannot make up my mind whether I like him or not.' She considered the point as she bit into a deliciously warm buttered roll. 'Last night he was a charming companion, and yet, this morning. . .'

'Temperamental, I should say.'

'Oh, he's most certainly that, Captain. I suspect he was thoroughly spoiled as a child,' she went on, experiencing no qualms whatsoever at discussing her guardian with a complete stranger. 'Needless to say he belongs to the aristocracy and is incredibly wealthy. So, I suppose, he's accustomed to having his way in all things.'

'Ah, yes. Our privileged aristocracy. Where would we be without them?' he responded bitterly, but then seemed to collect himself and hurriedly rose to his feet. 'I hope you'll not think me rude if I leave you to finish your breakfast in peace, ma'am. I think I, too, shall take a wander out of doors to indulge in a reprehensible habit I picked up in Spain.'

'Not at all, sir.' Sarah watched him leave, wondering why he should bear such an ardent grudge against a certain social class. There had certainly been more than a touch of acrimony in the attractive Captain's pleasant voice.

Shrugging, she quickly dismissed it as her own immediate problems came to the forefront of her mind and, rising from the table, went over to her writing-case, once again silently cursing for leaving it behind in that room.

Could her guardian possibly suspect? she wondered, staring down at those beautifully carved initials. After all, S.P. could stand for—well—almost anything. More importantly, thought, why hadn't she been honest with him when the opportunity had arisen? She shook her head. No, she couldn't have confessed, then, not with the Captain present. Added to which, Mr Ravenhurst had not been in the best of moods, most unlike the convivial companion he had been the evening before.

She was still determined to tell him the truth, but she must choose just the right moment, catch him in a more agreeable frame of mind. In the meantime, though, it wouldn't do to add to any suspicions he might already be harbouring by hiding the case away. No, it made sense to leave it in full view for the time being, but she must certainly remove that damning evidence.

Quickly opening the box, she screwed the half-written letter into a tight ball and threw it into the fire.

The once intended recipient of that, now, burning missive was at that precise moment standing just inside the stable block, with his faithful groom beside him, gazing frowningly at the depth of snow in the yard. Captain Carter, who had emerged from the inn a few moments before, was standing by the door leading to the kitchen, enjoying a cheroot, and the innkeeper's massive son was busy with a shovel, trying to clear a path round the hen-coop.

'Not a hope in hell of us getting away this day, sir,' Sutton remarked, gazing up at the sky. 'Nor tomorrow, neither, by the looks o' them clouds yonder.'

'No, there's certainly more to come. We must resign ourselves to remaining here for two days, possibly more.' Marcus glanced down at his trusted, middle-aged henchman. 'How did you manage last night?'

'What a carry on, eh, sir? Never seen the likes before! You'd think folks'd be thankful to find shelter anywhere rather than be out on a night like that.' He looked across at the innkeeper's son. 'Joe be a big beef-witted lad, but there's no 'arm in 'im. And how did you cope, sir?' he asked casting his eyes in the young Captain's direction.

'Well enough. But I don't doubt we'll all be sick and tired of one another's company before too long, and be more than ready to leave here when the time comes. Which reminds me. . .' Ravenhurst stared down in silence at the stable's earth floor for several thoughtful moments, then went on, 'I've changed my plans, Sutton. When the roads do become passable, I want you to go to Sir Henry Bamford's place with a letter of apology from me. I most certainly shan't be staying with him now.

'You'll no doubt be able to get a seat on the stagecoach with this lot. Take it as far as Chippenham, from where you should have no difficulty hiring a horse to take you the rest of the way. Bring Quilp and my carriage to my grandmother's house.'

The groom's brawny shoulders shook with wicked amusement. He had scant regard for his master's pernickety valet. 'I reckon old Quilp must be miffed 'cause we ain't turned up, sir.'

'I do not pay Quilp to question any change of plan I may choose to make,' was the curt response. 'I employ him to take care of my gear.'

Sutton cast his master a surreptitious glance. 'Will you be going after the girl again, sir?'

A not-unpleasant smile erased Marcus's heavy frown. 'Be assured, Sutton, my darling ward isn't so very far away.'

'Aye, sir. But where?' He shook his head, genuinely perturbed. 'I don't like to think of the young lady about on 'er own. Why, anything might 'appen to 'er!'

'Come on, man! Use your head! How far away can

she be? You know full well that that farm labourer saw a young female getting out of a post-chaise at the junction. The coach turned north on the road to Stroud, and she, on foot, went east.

'The landlady at that posting house gave us an accurate description, and we know a female answering that description was seen in a carrier's cart by that toll-gate keeper at Chippenham. We traced her as far as Calne. The carrier couldn't possibly have gone much farther.'

'Aye, sir, but supposing it weren't your ward, but some other little lady riding in that cart.'

'It was extremely remiss of me, before leaving Bath, not to have attained an accurate description of my ward and what she might possibly be wearing. But I harbour no doubts whatsoever, Sutton, that the young woman in the grey cloak and bonnet and my ward are one and the same person. Believe me, I shall have Miss Sarah Pennington safely installed in my grandmother's house long before you arrive there with the carriage,' and with that positive assurance Marcus went back into the inn.

He was halfway across the tap when he was accosted by the innkeeper, who kindly enquired whether he would care to browse through a copy of the *Morning Post*. Marcus accepted politely and, with the briefest of nods to acknowledge the stagecoach passengers consuming a hearty breakfast in the coffee-room, carried the journal into the private parlour to discover Sarah still there, seated at the small table near the window, busily writing a letter.

She didn't look round to see who had entered, and for a few moments he studied her, his expression a strange mixture of exasperation and gentle appreciation.

'It's good to see you are able to keep yourself occupied,

Mrs Armstrong,' he remarked, seating himself at the dining-table.

'I think boredom will prove to be the malady of us all.' She looked out of the window. The snow was so deep that it almost came up as far as the window-sill. The only tracks were those of tiny birds, braving the elements to search for scraps of food. Nothing, not even a farm cart, had risked travelling along the road. 'How long do you think we shall be stranded here, sir?'

'By the look of the sky, I should say we're in for a further fall.' No sooner had he spoken than the first flakes began to flutter to earth. 'Certainly not tomorrow. Perhaps the day after, if we're lucky.'

'Ah! May we join you?' The stylishly attired young gentleman who, Sarah noticed, had addressed Mr Ravenhurst by name the evening before entered the room, accompanied by a stockily built middle-aged man with penetrating grey eyes set in a kindly face. 'Or do we intrude?'

'Not at all, sir.' Sarah's warm, friendly smile encompassed them both. 'I did not hire this parlour for my private use. You are welcome to use it whenever you wish.'

'That is most gracious of you, ma'am,' the younger man responded. 'Ravenhurst, be kind enough to introduce me to this charming young lady.'

His dark eyes appeared above the printed page. 'Mrs Armstrong, the Honourable Mr Cedric Nutley and Mr—er—Stubbs. Mrs Armstrong, I should mention,' he went on after the gentlemen had made their bows, 'ought not to be here at all. But as she chose to go jaunting about in a snowstorm, found herself, like the rest of us, stranded here.'

Sarah, wisely, ignored the gibe, and merely satisfied herself with casting him a darkling look before resuming her seat at the small table. After exchanging a few pleasantries with Ravenhurst, Mr Nutley came over to her.

'What a charming writing-case, Mrs Armstrong!'

'Yes, it is, isn't it.' Sarah surreptitiously covered the letter that she had just begun writing with a plain sheet of paper. It was destined for an elderly lady, whom she had been in the habit of visiting regularly, and she did not wish him to catch sight of its contents, which might give rise to mention of a certain city.

'It's beautifully made, and has a secret compartment, here,' she explained, pressing one of the tiny carved squares that decorated the sides of the drawers, and a small flap sprang open, revealing the hidden section. 'Needless to say, it is empty. I never use it. In fact, the spring is a little stiff, I notice.'

Mr Nutley looked at it keenly for several moments. 'Why, unless one knew its secret, one would never suspect it was there! Which little square did you press?'

'This one—third from the end.' Closing the flap, Sarah obligingly repeated the procedure before putting away her letter and closing the case.

'Heavens above!' Marcus ejaculated suddenly, drawing everyone's attention. He turned to the front cover of the journal. 'This newspaper's over a week old. I thought the articles seemed familiar. Wait a moment, though. . . I've not read this before.'

His eyes scanned the few lines at the bottom of one of the columns. 'The Felchett diamonds have gone missing. There's a reward being offered for information leading to their return.' He raised his head, fixing his eyes on Mr Nutley. 'Did you know about this, Cedric?'

'I thought everyone knew,' the young man responded casually, before joining Mr Stubbs on the settle. 'Their disappearance was discovered on the morning after the betrothal party. You were there, Ravenhurst. Surely you cannot have forgotten?'

'I attended the party, yes,' he concurred, 'but I left early for London the following morning, and haven't been back to Oxfordshire since.'

'Oh, well, in that case—' Mr Nutley shrugged one slim shoulder '—you probably wouldn't have heard. Deuce of a to-do about it the following day when the maid discovered the necklace wasn't in her mistress's jewellery-case. Been left open all night, apparently, on the dressing-table.

'My beloved sire had gone off with Lord Felchett and a few of the other gentleman guests for a spot of shooting. By the time they returned to the house, Lady Felchett had already sent poor Harry hot-foot to London to call in the Runners. Old Felchett was furious when he discovered what his good lady had done. Well expected him to burst a blood vessel the way he went ranting on. Didn't want any fuss, you see.'

'That seems rather odd, Mr Nutley, don't you think?' Sarah remarked, frowning in puzzlement. 'You would have thought Lord Felchett would have applauded such swift action on his wife's part.'

'Perhaps. But half the gentry in the county had been invited to their son Harry's betrothal party. Some of them were staying on for the weekend, my family included. Wouldn't do to have the Runners sniffing round, asking a lot of fool questions. Might give offence. One cannot go about accusing one's neighbours, ma'am.'

'No, I suppose not,' she agreed. 'Is the necklace very valuable?'

'Lord, yes! Worth a small fortune, wouldn't you say, Ravenhurst?'

'It is certainly reputed to be very valuable, yes,' he responded, gazing fixedly at an imaginary spot on the floor. 'I wonder if there's a connection?'

He looked up to find three pairs of eyes regarding him questioningly. 'Several valuable and well-known items of jewellery were stolen in London during the Season last year. And the famous Pelstone pearls were taken when the family was in Brighton during the summer. I was just wondering if the same person or persons were involved in the robberies.'

Sarah frowned. 'But how do they dispose of the items, sir? If they are all well-known pieces, surely they would be easily recognisable?'

Marcus looked directly into the grey eyes of Mr Stubbs, who had been listening intently to the conversation. 'Now, there's an interesting point, sir, do you not think?'

Mr Stubbs's gaze did not waver. 'No honest merchant would touch 'em, of course, so I would very much think that the items must find their way into the hands of some unscrupulous dealer who would, then, either sell them abroad, or separate the stones, melt down the gold, or whatever, and have them made up in some other form.'

'I, for one, think that is monstrous!' Sarah exclaimed, appalled by the mere thought of such callous actions. 'Those jewels have probably been in the respective families for years. They must be of great sentimental value, too.'

'But not to the thieves, my dear lady,' Marcus countered, getting to his feet. 'It's turned out to be only a small flurry this time. Looks as though the sun is trying to come out again. I think I'll lend a hand at clearing the yard.'

'What an odd fellow he is!' Mr Nutley remarked when the door had closed behind Mr Ravenhurst. 'Helping servants to clear away snow? Whatever next! Do you know, Mrs Armstrong, I've known that man all my life, and yet I still don't understand him at all.'

'You live near him in Oxfordshire, Mr Nutley?' she enquired.

'Yes. My father's Sir Giles Nutley. Our home is some four miles from Ravenhurst.' Slightly effeminate arched brows drew together above insipid blue eyes. 'Deuced odd his being here, though.'

'I don't see why, sir,' Sarah responded in what she hoped was an indifferent tone. The last thing in the world she wanted was for Mr Nutley to start asking awkward questions. 'I'm sure Mr Ravenhurst mentioned that he has relatives living not too far away from here.'

'That's right, he has! I'd forgotten that.' He giggled suddenly like a schoolgirl. 'Lord! He must be smarting, having to put up at a place like this. Ravenhurst's accustomed to the very best. Well, he can afford it, not like some of us,' he went on, his tone decidedly resentful. 'Lucky dog! He's independent. He isn't forced to travel on the common stage because of the miserly allowance his father gives him.' A glinting sparkle brightened his eyes. 'But it won't be like that for much longer.'

Evidently Mr Nutley was expecting to come into money. Sarah cast a brief glance over his fashionable, yet slightly dandified attire. He was certainly able to clothe himself in the first style of elegance on his miserly allowance, if nothing else. She decided she didn't care for this sulky young man very much, but masterfully disguised her feelings as she made an excuse to leave the gentlemen to their own devices, and went out into the coffee-room to find Daisy busily clearing away the breakfast dishes.

'Here, let me help,' she offered.

'Oh, no, ma'am. There's no need for that. We've plenty of 'elp, now. Me cousin's 'ere. And that farmer and 'is wife offered their services if Pa could see 'is way to knocking a bit off their bill. They expected to be back in their own 'ome by now, and are a bit short of the readies. They've turned out to be good workers. Which is more than can be said for 'er,' she added, gesturing to the archway by which one gained access to the stairs.

Sarah caught a glimpse of a golden-haired girl in a blue dress and white apron. From what she could see of her, the slender girl appeared to be rather pretty, and Sarah could quite understand, as she looked back at Daisy's plump figure and homely face, from where poor Daisy's dislike of her cousin stemmed.

Jealousy seemed a common affliction amongst certain inhabitants of this inn, she mused as she mounted the narrow flight of stairs. Mr Nutley was definitely envious of Mr Ravenhurst's wealth, and Daisy, Sarah suspected, her cousin's good looks. Captain Carter, too, had certainly betrayed a deal of resentment, earlier, to a certain class of persons.

As she reached the top of the staircase, she saw the spinsterish-looking female who had been among the passengers off the stagecoach hurrying purposefully down the passageway towards her.

'Good morning. I am Mrs Armstrong.' Sarah stood at the head of the stairs, effectively preventing the woman's further progress. 'I, too, have been forced to seek shelter here.'

'Grimshaw. Miss Tabatha Grimshaw. Pleased to meet you,' she responded in clipped tones. Which betrayed the fact that she was anything but!

'I find all this most vexing, Mrs Armstrong,' she went on in a most agitated manner. 'As I particularly asked for peace and quiet, I did not object to being placed at the very end of the passageway in what is, I suspect, the smallest room in the house, but when I requested that no one should enter my room on any pretext, and find upon my return from breakfast that my belongings have been tampered with. . . Well, it is just too much!'

'Oh, dear. Have you discovered something missing?'

'Missing? On, no, no! Everything is there.' The icy-blue eyes behind the pince-nez shot Sarah a furtive glance. 'It is just that I have not been well of late. An irritation of the nerves, you understand. The slightest little thing seems to overset me. I am better on my own. I shall insist upon all my meals being brought up to me on a tray from now on. I must have my solitude. And I won't have my belongings touched!'

Sarah had come across many highly strung people during her years in Bath, and Miss Grimshaw gave every sign of belonging to their number. She was a tall, thin woman, whose greying hair was confined in a tight bun at the back of her head, and whose pallid complexion was evidence of poor health, as were the dark circles round the eyes.

Moving aside, Sarah cast her a sympathetic smile. 'I'm sure when you explain that you have been unwell, Miss Grimshaw, the landlady will be only too pleased to send your meals up to your room.'

'Dried-up old stick!' a voice behind her snapped, and Sarah, after having watched Miss Grimshaw scamper down the stairs with quite remarkable agility for a middle-aged woman who professed to be unwell, swung round to find the female who had been wearing the bright red bonnet the evening before regarding her from one of the bedchamber doorways.

Sarah's eyes began to twinkle. 'Who. . .? Me?'

The woman gurgled with laughter, a light tinkling sound which instantly brightened the atmosphere. 'No, Miss Grimstone, or whatever 'er name is. She never spoke a word to anyone from the moment she entered the stage at Marlborough. And when I asked, friendly like, if we'd met before, she deliberately snubbed me. Miserable old fossil!'

'Well, perhaps there's some excuse for her behaviour. She hasn't been well.' A sudden frown creased Sarah's forehead. 'And I don't think she's as old as she appears.'

'She's certainly a lot older than you or me. My name is de Vine, by the way. Dorothea de Vine.'

Sarah went smilingly towards her. 'Mrs Serafina Armstrong.'

'Is that your real name?'

'W-what?' Sarah was rather taken aback. 'Of course it is! Why do you ask?'

The young woman entwined her arm round Sarah's and drew her into the bedchamber. 'My name ain't really de Vine,' she confessed in a conspiratorial whisper. 'That's me stage name. Me real name's Dottie Hogg.'

'Oh, you're an actress. How exciting!'

'It ain't all it's cracked up to be,' Dottie confessed with a plaintive sigh. 'I'm between jobs at the moment, as you might say. Tried me 'and in London, but it didn't work out, so I'm going back to Bristol. Me old mother still lives there, so I'll move back in with 'er until I can gets m'self fixed up, like.'

'How I envy you! You must meet some interesting people,' Sarah remarked, accepting the invitation to sit down beside Dottie on the bed.

'You come across all sorts, that's for sure. Like that lot off the stage. Mr *Stubble* is a good sort. Nice and friendly, not like old Grimlock and that weasel-faced clerk.'

'I haven't met him yet.'

'You ain't missed much, Mrs *Armitage*. What a fuss he were creating last night! The young sprig's not so bad. Kept giving me the eye, though, but I'm used to that. And I ain't just anyone's for the asking,' she confided, much to Sarah's puzzlement. 'But that 'andsome Captain, now. Cor! I bet he could show a girl a good time. Like that gentleman friend of yourn. He's a bit stern-looking. But I like a man to be a man, if you knows what I mean. I bet he knows 'ow to treat a girl, eh?'

'Gentleman friend?' Sarah echoed, still somewhat confused by Dottie's perplexing utterances. 'Oh, you mean Mr Ravenhurst! He isn't a friend of mine. He arrived late yesterday afternoon, and we dined together.'

Dottie looked slightly nonplussed. 'Well, if that's so, you watch out, Mrs *Armshaw*. He's right taken with you. Believe me, I know the signs. The way he looked at you just before you went off to bed last—'

'You're mistaken, Dottie,' Sarah cut in. She found herself, unaccountably, blushing and hurriedly rose from the bed. 'Mr Ravenhurst isn't interested in me in the least.'

'No offence intended, I'm sure.' Dottie, too, got to her feet. 'Anyone can tell you're a lady. It was just. . . Oh, well, never mind.' She began to rummage through the contents of her cloak bag, which she had scattered across the bed. 'Here, would you like to read this? A friend give it me. Trouble is, me eyes ain't what they were, and I can't make out the print too well.'

Sarah accepted the well-thumbed volume with genuine gratitude. 'Thank you, yes. It will certainly help to pass the time.'

'And I've a letter, somewhere,' Dottie announced, arresting Sarah's progress to the door. 'Drat the thing! Where the devil did I put it?' She delved into the pockets of a rather garishly coloured red-and-green striped gown. 'I know I brung it with me. Oh, well, when I do come across it, will you be kind enough to read it to me? It's me dratted peepers, you see.'

'Of course I shall. And thank you again for the book.'

Sarah wandered along the passageway to her own room, which had been tidied in her absence. The fire had been made up, and she was about to draw the chair nearer to its comforting warmth when the sound of voices caught her attention. As her bedchamber was at the front and very end of the house, she thought at first the voices were filtering up from the private parlour situated directly below, but then she realised that they were coming from outside.

Curious, she went over to the window to discover Mr Ravenhurst, Captain Carter and two other men she did not recognise busily clearing a path along the front wall of the inn. By the deep rumbles of masculine laughter that from time to time reached her ears, the four were enjoying their task hugely. She gazed at each man in turn before her eyes became fixed on one head of dark, slightly waving hair.

Discourteous and surprisingly thoughtful by turn, Mr Ravenhurst was, as his young neighbour had remarked, a very perplexing man. Unlike Mr Nutley, however, who evidently thought it beneath his social standing, Mr Ravenhurst did not hesitate to lend a helping hand at clearing away snow or, she reminded herself, to say a simple 'thank you' to an innkeeper's daughter for a meal enjoyed.

She experienced a sudden feeling of deep regret that they had not become better acquainted during those years of his guardianship. It was unlikely now, given the over-crowded confines of the inn, that this omission would be rectified. But somehow she must contrive to attain a few precious minutes alone with him in order to declare her true identity.

The opportunity was destined not to be granted that day, however. Mr Ravenhurst was not among those who partook of a light luncheon, and Sarah did not see him again until the evening, when she entered the coffee-room to join her stranded fellow-travellers just before dinner.

She had spent most of the afternoon in the company of Dottie who, after skilfully arranging her own blonde tresses in a riot of bouncy curls, had contrived to arrange Sarah's hair in a more becoming style.

Donning her best pearl-grey gown, which she had worn on the occasions of Mrs Fairchild's exclusive little card parties, Sarah thought she looked quite presentable until Mr Ravenhurst, breaking off his conversation with Captain Carter and Mr Stubbs, came over and greeted her with,

'Oh, God! Not half-mourning again!'

She flashed him a look from beneath her long curling lashes. 'You forget, sir, I am a widow, after all.'

'You err, child. I forget nothing.' His dark, intelligent eyes looked her over from head to foot. 'The hair is a definite improvement, though.'

'Why, thank you!' Sarah felt inordinately pleased by this mild compliment. 'Miss de Vine arranged it for me. She's very clever with—'

'Miss who?' he cut in sharply.

'Miss Dorothea de Vine. Haven't you been introduced yet, sir?'

He clapped one shapely hand over his eyes. 'No, I haven't. And you can spare yourself the trouble of introducing me to the "Divine" Dorothea. Pure fabrication if ever I heard it! Still,' he tutted, 'there's plenty of that going on here.' He removed his hand and cast a brief glance at the lively and not unattractive damsel who had positioned herself at the Captain's side. 'What's her real name, by the way?' he asked, not giving Sarah the opportunity to assimilate his former remark.

'Dottie Hogg.'

'Oh, dear me, yes. I suppose there's some justification for it, then. Only slightly worse than Serafina Postlethwaite, I should say.'

This time Sarah couldn't mistake the underlying implication, and looked at him sharply, but his expression gave nothing away. In fact, he stared down at her with such a depth of warmth in his dark eyes that for some obscure reason her pulse became quite erratic, and she swiftly forgot her suspicions.

Whether or not by his contrivance, Mr Ravenhurst was seated beside her at dinner. She had suggested to the landlady earlier in the day that it would be more convenient, and involve less work, if everyone ate together in the coffee-room, after which they could all repair to the parlour, enabling the staff to clear away in peace.

The landlady had welcomed the idea, and had placed two tables together to accommodate everyone. Only the farmer and his wife, whom Sarah assumed were eating in the kitchen, and Miss Grimshaw did not join the group.

Mr Ravenhurst, as had happened the night before, proved to be an ideal dinner companion, and only twice came close to oversetting her. The first occasion was when he asked Mr Nutley, who seemed for some reason in a very subdued frame of mind, to move the branch of candles further along the table as the light was catching his young neighbour's brightly coloured waistcoat and dazzling him.

The second occurred when the middle-aged clerk, Mr Winthrope, whom Sarah had met for the first time at luncheon, began to bemoan the fare, declaring the beef overcooked and the chicken tough. Mr Ravenhurst turned his head and spoke just one soft and very idiomatic sentence. Sarah did not quite catch what he had said, but knew it must have been extremely rude, for Mr Winthrope coloured to the roots of his sparse, greying hair, and said not another word throughout the remainder of the meal.

Apart from the chastened clerk, who sought immediate refuge in his bedchamber, everyone else repaired to the parlour once the enjoyable meal was over. The innkeeper had managed to provide them with a pack of decidedly sticky and dog-eared playing cards, and Sarah found herself making up a foursome at whist.

Mr Ravenhurst elected himself her partner, leaving Mr Nutley to join forces with Captain Carter as their opponents. Sarah and her partner won the first rubber, and then went on to win the second very comprehensively, which won her a modicum of praise from Mr Ravenhurst.

'However,' he went on to say, his tone decidedly censorious, 'it does lead one to suppose that your upbringing was not all that it might have been, Mrs Armstrong, if you were permitted to while away your formative years in the pursuit of gaming.'

'Oh, yes. Such wanton dissipation! You cannot imagine to what extent I indulged myself. I became thoroughly depraved, in fact,' she responded airily, much to the Captain's amusement and Mr Nutley's astonishment.

'The lady is but jesting, Cedric,' Ravenhurst assured him. 'Your deal, I believe.'

'I'll sit this one out.' Mr Nutley rose from the table, offering his place to Mr Stubbs. 'I think I'll track down that rascally landlord. I have a fancy for a glass of rum punch.'

When he returned to the room, after what seemed a very long absence, he was bearing a tray upon which stood several glasses and a large bowl. Pushing Sarah's writing-case a little to one side, he set the tray down on the small table by the window, and began to ladle out the warm liquor. 'Who'll join me?'

Only Sarah and Mr Ravenhurst declined, but the others were happy to imbibe in the warming drink, though the Captain, Sarah noticed, grimaced at his first mouthful. She offered her place to Mr Nutley, who seemed far more convivial than he had earlier in the evening, and for a while she sat talking with Dottie before being the first to retire for the night.

She could hear, quite clearly, the murmur of voices from the room below as she curled up in the comfortable bed. She found the sounds reassuring, and was soon fast asleep.

* * *

She awoke with an almost violent start sometime later. What on earth was that? A table being overturned. . .? A chair, maybe? For a few moments she lay there, not daring to move, her frightened eyes darting about the room, expecting at any moment to see a shadowy movement, but all remained still, all was quiet; not even the murmur of voices, now, from the parlour below.

Then, as the grandfather clock near the foot of the stairs struck two, she understood why. She had been asleep for several hours, not the few minutes she had first thought.

Cautiously, she eased herself into a sitting position, and felt for the tinder box. It took a moment before she had the candle on the bedside table lit; then she cast her eyes about the small bedchamber once more, just to reassure herself that there was truly no one there. All was as it should be, and yet she felt certain she had heard something. . .but what?

Wide awake now, she abandoned the notion of trying to get back to sleep for the time being, and decided to finish the letter she had begun writing the previous morning, but recalled that she had left her case downstairs in the parlour. She hesitated only for a moment then, throwing the bedcovers aside, she slipped her woollen shawl round her shoulders, and picked up the candle.

Her bare feet made hardly a sound as she tiptoed lightly along the passageway, but she was powerless to prevent the eerie creaking of the narrow stairs during her descent to the coffee-room. She had never been afraid of the dark, not even as a small child, and yet, without quite knowing why, something in the atmosphere of the place unnerved her.

It did not help matters when she bumped into one of the chairs, sending it scraping across the wooden floor, but when she began to imagine every shadow had a life of its own, and a dozen pairs of villainous eyes were watching her every move, she took herself roundly to task for such childish fancies.

Consequently, when she opened the parlour door to discover a darkly cloaked figure standing by the window, she was disinclined to believe the evidence of her own eyes, and it was only when a sudden blast of cold air blew out her candle, and the shadowy figure perched itself on the sill and swung its legs out of the open window to disappear into the night, that she realised her imagination had not been playing tricks on her after all.

Her first impulse was to turn tail and run, but she checked it, and with the self-possession that characterised her she flew across to the windows and securely fastened them, lest the intruder return.

The terrifying possibility that she still might not be alone, that the intruder might have had an accomplice, now waiting in the shadows, ready to pounce on her at any moment, crossed her mind, and she stood perfectly still, not daring to move, hardly daring even to breathe; but the only sounds she heard were the heavy pounding of her own heart, and the solemn ticking of the grandfather clock in the other room.

Slightly reassured, she very slowly turned her head, darting quick glances about the room, trying desperately to pierce the gloom. The only faint light came from the dying embers of the fire and, after taking several deep breaths in a desperate attempt to steady her fraught nerves, she made her way cautiously towards it, very nearly tripping over something lying on the floor.

With trembling hands, she felt along the high shelf until her fingers came into contact with a taper. It was her duty to rouse the landlord, but she flatly refused to venture one more step without the aid of a light to guide her way.

Quickly thrusting the taper into the embers, she relit her candle and only just managed to stifle the hysterical cry that rose in her throat. It was not a chair leg that she had almost tripped over, but a man's leg, a thin leg encased in fashionable primrose knee-breeches, and she instinctively knew, even before she had edged her way round the end of the settle, and had forced herself to look down into those strangely staring insipid blue eyes, that Mr Nutley was dead.

Chapter Four

For a few moments it was as much as Sarah could do to stop her knees from buckling and to remain standing, then without conscious thought she made all haste back up the stairs and along the passageway to the room situated directly opposite her own. Pausing only a second or two to catch her breath, she scratched lightly upon the door.

'Mr Ravenhurst. . .? Mr Ravenhurst, are you awake?' she called softly, her heart pounding against her ribcage, but only silence answered her. She raised her hand, about to knock again, when she detected the distinct sound of a bed creaking. The next instant the door opened a fraction, and that heavily scowling countenance, blessedly, appeared in the crack.

'What is it? What's wrong?'

How comforting, how reassuring that curt voice sounded! 'It's Mr Nutley, sir. He's downstairs in the parlour. He's dead. . .I'm certain he's dead'

His heavy frown, if possible, grew more pronounced. 'Wait there! I'll be but a moment.'

The door closed, but opened again almost at once, and Mr Ravenhurst, looking surprisingly younger with his dark hair tousled by sleep, emerged from the room, dressed in a strikingly patterned brocade robe; and it was only by exercising the firmest self-control that Sarah suppressed the almost overwhelming urge to throw herself on that broad expanse of chest.

'Hold the dratted thing steady, girl!' he scolded, after trying unsuccessfully to light his candle from hers.

She had not realised she was trembling. She suddenly felt so very cold, and so very vulnerable standing there in just her nightdress and shawl, and with her hair tumbling down her back, but managed to gain control of herself sufficiently for him to achieve his objective at the second attempt. Then, without another word, he stalked along the landing, and Sarah almost had to run to keep up with his massive strides.

She followed him down the stairs and across the coffee-room, but flatly refused to re-enter the parlour and remained by the door, watching anxiously as he knelt down by Mr Nutley's body.

'He's dead right enough,' he confirmed, after a brief examination. 'His neck is broken.' He turned his head, saw Sarah still hovering by the door, her face as white as her nightgown, and went slowly towards her, shielding her gaze from Nutley's body.

'What happened, child?' he asked in the gentlest tone she had ever heard a member of his sex use.

'I—I came in here to collect my writing-case.' She remembered everything in minute detail, and yet it seemed so unreal, like a terrible dream. 'There was someone standing over there by the window. Before I knew what was happening, he'd disappeared.'

'Where? Through the windows?'

'Yes. I closed them. The draught blew out my candle,

you see. That's why I went across to the fire. And it was then—it was then that I saw. . .'

As her voice trailed away, Marcus went over to the windows, checked that they were securely fastened and then drew the curtains. He came back towards her, his expression thoughtful. Then he suddenly became aware of her state of dress.

'Where the devil is your dressing-gown? And you've nothing on your feet!' he admonished.

'W-what?' The scolding tone did manage to penetrate that veil of unreality which seemed to be shrouding her, but she still felt somewhat dazed by it all. 'Oh, no, I know. There wasn't room in my cloak-bag for things like that.'

He muttered something under his breath as he placed his candle down on one of the tables, and before Sarah could utter more than a stifled protest, he had lifted her into his arms.

'What on earth do you think you are doing, sir?' she demanded, indignation bringing colour back to her cheeks and restoring her self-possession with a vengeance.

'I'm putting you back to bed where you belong,' he ground out, striding purposefully back across the coffee-room, and sublimely ignoring her continued demands to be put down at once. 'And that is precisely where you are going to stay, my girl! And, for heaven's sake, hold that candle steady! I don't want covering in hot wax.'

He carried her effortlessly up the stairs and along the passageway, just as though she had weighed no more than a child, and he was not even breathing heavily, she noticed, as he lay her gently down on her bed.

'You're absolutely frozen, girl!' he continued scolding, after briefly clasping one slender foot in his warm fingers, which had the effect of sending her pulse rate soaring. Casting her a far from approving look, he straightened the bedcovers, relieved her of the candle, and then went over to light the one on the wash-stand.

'Now, I'm going to leave you for a while, but I'll be back. And don't concern yourself if you hear people moving about.'

'What are you doing?' she asked in some agitation as he removed the key from the door.

'I'm going to lock you in.' Both expression and voice were much softer now. 'But don't be alarmed, child. I shan't forget you.' He made to leave, but turned back to ask, 'You don't happen to know which room Stubbs is in, do you?'

'It's down the far end. First door on the right after the stairs, I think.'

She heard the rasping of the key being turned in the lock, the reassuring sound of his firm tread moving along the passageway, and then nothing more for what seemed an interminable length of time, but was perhaps no more than a few minutes.

Then all was action: doors opening and closing; heavy feet descending and mounting the stairs; and a continual muttering of voices. The sounds of people talking below in the parlour eventually reached her ears, but she could not discern just what was being said. She felt certain, though, that one of the voices belonged to Mr Ravenhurst, and smiled to herself as she lay her head back against the pillows.

She felt, oddly, very comforted knowing that he was there. He was so capable, so dependable. It was strange, too, the way she had instinctively gone to him in those moments of panic and confusion after she had discovered poor Mr Nutley, as though to do so were the most natural act in the world. She closed her eyes, trying ineffectually to blot out the memory of Mr Nutley's twisted body and wildly staring eyes.

Her hand trembled as she gripped the bed covers. Reaction, at last, was beginning to set in. She wished desperately that Mr Ravenhurst would return, but the grandfather clock in the coffee-room had chimed three before she heard the blessed sound of the key being fitted back into the lock, and turned her head on the pillow to see him, a cup in one hand and her writing-case in the other, enter the room.

'Ah, good! You're still awake,' he remarked in an almost conversational way, just as though nothing untoward had occurred. 'Here, sit up and drink this.'

Sarah automatically obeyed. Taking the cup of warm milk he held out, she took a large swallow, and then grimaced at its taste. 'What on earth have you put in it? It's vile!'

'Only a little brandy, my dear.' He placed the writing-case down on the floor and then sat himself on the edge of the bed. 'Now drink it up. You've had a nasty shock, and it will do you good.'

He could not prevent a smile at the suspicious glance she cast the cup's contents as she tentatively raised it to her lips. 'Why, anyone would think it was drugged!' His smile faded. 'Drugged. . .' he murmured. 'I wonder?'

'What do you wonder?'

'Nothing, child. I was merely thinking aloud. Come, down with that milk.'

Feeling fairly sure that he would not let her get away with leaving any, and that he wouldn't balk at forcing the issue by pinching her nose and tossing the contents down her throat himself, Sarah gulped down the rest, and shuddered as she placed the empty cup on the bedside table.

'What has been going on?' She lay her head back down on the pillow once again, perfectly composed, as though it were quite the norm for her to be alone with a man in her bedchamber. 'I heard a lot of moving about downstairs.'

'Nutley's body has been removed and placed in one of the outhouses,' he explained. 'The parlour has been tidied, and a thorough search has been made of the downstairs rooms, and those bedchambers we were able to enter.'

She frowned up at him. 'Why? Surely the intruder wouldn't be foolish enough to return?'

'I should think that highly unlikely, child.' His voice was very reassuring, as was his smile. 'So rest easy. What we were endeavouring to discover was just how he managed to get in here in the first place. Although we found no sign of a break-in, the landlord freely admits that several of the window catches do not fit properly and could quite easily be forced.'

'Then, if he did not break in,' she said after a moment's thought, 'he must have been in the inn already, or. . .'

'Or someone let him in,' he finished for her. 'Yes, child. They seem the only logical alternatives. In the ordinary course of events, a magistrate would have been summoned without delay. Unfortunately, the nearest lives some three miles from here. Getting a message to him is out of the question for a day or two, so we are obliged to deal with the investigation ourselves.'

'Oh, dear.' A wickedly mischievous twinkle brightened her eyes. 'How tiresome for you, sir! You didn't expect to have anything like this thrust upon you when you sought shelter here, did you?

'No, I most certainly did not! Nor have I any intention of taking responsibility for the unfortunate affair,' he said determinedly. 'And that, my child, is precisely why I did not hesitate to rouse Mr Stubbs.'

'Mr Stubbs?' she echoed, perplexed.

A wry smile curled his lips. 'Our friend Mr Stubbs is none other than a Bow Street Runner.'

'Good heavens!' Sarah was astounded. 'Well, it just goes to show one should never take people at face value.'

'It does indeed,' he concurred, his twisted smile returning. 'He wanted to question you tonight, but I wouldn't hear of it. But if you're not too tired, perhaps you could explain to me exactly what happened, precisely what you saw?'

Sarah was silent for several moments, her brow furrowed in deep thought.

'Something woke me,' she began. 'At first I thought there was someone in my room, but now, of course, I realise the sound must have come from the parlour directly below. I heard the grandfather clock chime the hour, and lit my candle. I knew I wouldn't go back to sleep, so I decided to finish a letter I had begun yesterday morning. Then I remembered I had left my writing-case in the parlour and went down to collect it.'

'Go on,' he prompted when she fell silent.

'It might have been my imagination, but there was something in the atmosphere of the place. . .something eerie.' She shuddered at the memory. 'I kept imagining there were people lurking in every shadow. So, by the time I did enter the parlour, and saw someone by the window, I was fully convinced I was seeing things.'

'Were the windows open at this point?'

She frowned in an effort to remember. 'Yes. Yes, they must have been, because the draught blew my candle out.'

'I imagine, then, our intruder must have heard your approach.'

'Well, I'm not surprised,' she responded frankly. 'I bumped into one of the coffee-room chairs, sending it skidding across the floor.'

'That must have been what I heard. Go on,' he urged again.

Sarah shrugged. 'You know the rest, sir. He escaped through the window, I relit my candle, and then. . .and then discovered Mr Nutley.'

'You said "he", child. Are you sure it was a man?'

'Oh!' Sarah fixed her eyes on the strong column of his neck. Some detached part of her brain registered that there were dark hairs clearly showing between the lapels of his dressing-gown, but so hard was she concentrating on trying to conjure up a clear vision of the intruder that she paid little heed to this rather startling discovery. 'I assumed it was a man. Whoever it was was certainly not as tall as you, sir, more Mr Nutley's height, or maybe an inch or two taller. I cannot be sure because he was wearing a dark cloak with the hood drawn over his head, which might have made him appear taller. He was certainly wearing boots and breeches—which, of course, would suggest a man—and yet. . .and yet something struck me as rather odd at the time, but for the life of me I cannot think what it could have been.'

'All right, my child, that's enough for tonight.' Marcus rose to his feet. 'You'll need to repeat what you've told me to Stubbs in the morning, but do not worry—I fully intend to be present when he questions you.'

The fact that he should insist upon being with her during the interview did not occur to her; she was just grateful that he was offering his support. She watched him move across to the window to check that it was securely fastened. 'What's Mr Stubbs doing here, sir? Is he on the trail of some villain?'

'In a manner of speaking, yes.' He picked up the candle on the wash-stand before moving back over to the bed, and looked down at her with his attractive smile. 'But, unless you are a jewel thief, my dear, you've nothing to fear.'

'Oh, I see.' Her eyes glinted like those of a child who was about to indulge in some new and exciting game. 'The diamond necklace you were discussing yesterday, I should warrant.'

'Amongst others, yes. He's learnt of a certain gentleman in Bristol who doesn't bother asking too many questions about items brought to his establishment. Now, that really is enough for tonight!' he said authoritatively, like a strict uncle dealing with a recalcitrant child. 'Try to get some sleep. I shall lock your door again, but don't worry. I shall sleep with mine open, and shall hear you if you should call.'

It never entered her head to protest. The brandy was beginning to take effect, and she had no troubling in dropping off to sleep.

When she opened her eyes again it was to discover that it was morning and to find Daisy standing beside the bed.

'Ooh, ma'am, what dreadful goings on, eh? That poor young gentleman. Me and Rose learned all about it when we arrived. Ma and Pa's right upset. Never 'ad anything like this 'appen 'ere afore.'

'Yes. It will be a shock to everyone.'

'Aye. And you most of all, I'll warrant. It must of been terrible finding 'im that way. How are you feeling, Mrs Armstrong?'

'Dreadful!' Sarah placed her hand to her throbbing temple. 'Mr Ravenhurst laced my milk with brandy. And now I have the headache!'

'You ain't the only one, ma'am,' Daisy informed her, her plump face breaking into what Sarah considered an extremely callous smile. 'Apart from Mr Ravenhurst, everyone seems to 'ave a sore 'ead this morning.'

Sarah watched Daisy draw back the curtains, and then screwed up her eyes against the painfully bright light. 'What time is it?'

'Getting on for ten, ma'am. Mr Ravenhurst said as how you weren't to be disturbed any earlier.'

The dratted man seemed to be taking an awful lot upon himself! Sarah felt quite out of charity with him as she eased herself into a sitting position so that Daisy could place the tray on her lap. She found she had little appetite, but managed to force down a buttered roll and to drink a cup of coffee before placing the tray back on the bedside table.

When she went down to the coffee-room, half an hour later, it was to find Mr Ravenhurst and Captain Carter seated at a table. Mr Ravenhurst had his face buried between the printed sheets of a newspaper, but raised his head at her approach, and rose to his feet, his dark eyes scrutinising her face.

'How are you feeling this morning?' he enquired gently, and could not mistake the flash of annoyance in her eyes before she seated herself at the table.

'But for you, sir, I think I would have been perfectly well. He took it upon himself to force brandy down my throat,' Sarah explained in response to the young Captain's puzzled look.

'If it's any consolation, child,' Marcus drawled, sounding sublimely unconcerned, 'there are others similarly afflicted.'

'So I have been reliably informed. But it is scant consolation.'

He smiled at the pettish tone as he turned his attention once again to the journal. 'How riveting!' he remarked in an attempt to change the subject. 'It would seem the Fair Langley is rivalling Sarah Siddons in popularity.'

'I have never been to the theatre, so have never been privileged to see either of them,' Sarah admitted, placing her elbows on the table and resting her chin on her hands. 'But I believe Mrs Langley is considered a very handsome woman.'

'Like yourself, ma'am, I have never seen the lady perform,' the Captain responded, 'so cannot comment on her degree of beauty, but can safely say that although men may appreciate handsome women, we much prefer pretty ones. Eh, Ravenhurst?'

'Infinitely,' he answered, his eyes resting on Sarah's delicately featured profile.

It wasn't necessary to look at him; she instinctively knew those dark eyes were turned in her direction, and could feel the heat glowing in her cheeks. There had been an unmistakable teasing quality in the Captain's voice, but not in Mr Ravenhurst's, and she felt untold relief when there was the sound of a door opening, and Dottie emerged from the parlour, holding a highly perfumed handkerchief to her temple.

'Oh, Mrs *Armitage*! What a to-do, eh?' she wailed. 'It were bad enough waking up with the worst 'ead I've 'ad in years, but then to be questioned as though I was a common criminal. And 'ere I thought Mr *Stebbs* were such a nice man, too!'

'He is only doing his duty, madam,' Marcus responded, displaying not a ha'p'orth of sympathy.

'I know that, Mr *Ravenleigh*, but the whole business 'as sent me quite unnecessary, and I think I'll lie down for a bit.' She cast an appealing glance at the more sympathetic younger man. 'Would you assist me up to my room, Captain? Me legs feel all queer.'

Rolling his eyes in Mr Ravenhurst's direction, the Captain rose from the table. 'It will be my pleasure, Miss de Vine.'

Sarah frowned in puzzlement as her eyes followed their progress towards the stairs. 'Do you know, sir, I do not think Dottie can be a very good actress. She cannot even remember people's names. So how on earth does she memorise her lines?'

His lips twitched as he rose from the table. 'I think the theatre plays only a small part in our "Divine" Dorothea's life, my little innocent. Her talents, unless I'm very much mistaken, lie in quite another direction. Now, do not let us keep Mr Stubbs waiting.'

Only for an instant, as Sarah entered the room, and stared briefly at that portion of floor where Mr Nutley's body had lain, did she experience any slight trepidation. Mr Stubbs, looking very efficient, sat at the table with several sheets of his hand-written notes in front of him. She answered all the questions he put to her clearly and without hesitation, but she was unable to tell him any more than she had told Mr Ravenhurst the night before.

'And nothing else has occurred to you?'

The question came from her guardian, and she turned her head to look directly into his eyes. 'Yes, sir, it has. Why do so many people appear to be suffering from the headache this morning? Mr Stubbs, here, appears similarly afflicted.'

The Runner had, indeed, been massaging his forehead on several occasions, but his perceptive grey eyes had remained fixed on Sarah throughout the interview. He turned his gaze on to Mr Ravenhurst, one greying brow rising. 'I think we can tell her that, sir, don't you?'

'I don't think there's any need,' Sarah put in before Mr Stubbs could explain. 'With the exception of Mr Ravenhurst, everyone was drugged.'

'Clever girl!' Marcus's lips curled into an appreciative smile. 'Stubbs and I had come to that conclusion.'

'Normally, ma'am, I am a very light sleeper. It is essential in my line of work. But last night I slept heavily. I heard nothing. In fact, it took Mr Ravenhurst, here, a full five minutes to rouse me.'

'The drug could not have been in the wine,' Sarah voiced after a moment's intense thought, 'because I had a glass with my dinner. Therefore, it must have been. . .'

'In the punch,' Marcus finished for her. 'I did notice yesterday evening that although Nutley poured himself a glass, it remained on the table by his elbow, untouched. It's a pity, in this instance, that the lady of the house is such a diligent person. She cleaned both bowl and glasses before retiring for the night, so we are unable to confirm our theory.'

'I see.' Again Sarah became thoughtful. 'Wait a moment, though. What about Miss Grimshaw and Mr Winthrope? They did not join us yesterday evening.

Have you had the opportunity to question them?'

'Yes, I have, ma'am.' Mr Stubbs referred to his notes. 'Miss Grimshaw is in the habit of taking a few drops of laudanum in water last thing to help her sleep, and so heard nothing. And Mr Winthrope came down to request more candles, as he'd been reading throughout the evening, and was accosted by Mr Nutley who, having just finished preparing the punch in the coffee-room, persuaded the gentleman to sample a glass.

'Mr Winthrope assures me that ordinarily he doesn't imbibe in strong liquor, but isn't averse to the occasional glass of rum punch. And as for the others. . .' Again he referred to his notes. 'Not one of them heard a thing until roused by Mr Ravenhurst and myself. Although Mr Ravenhurst's groom mentioned that Nutley did try to persuade him and the innkeeper's son to sample a glass of the punch whilst they were keeping each other company in the tap, but they both declined.'

Sarah's frown returned. 'But why should Mr Nutley have attempted to drug everyone? Unless, of course, he had arranged to meet the man in the cloak and didn't want anyone to witness that encounter.'

'A distinct possibility, child,' Marcus agreed. 'Or his intent was quite otherwise, and he was disturbed by our mysterious cloaked figure. But whether or not his death was accidental, we can only speculate at this juncture.'

Sarah shuddered convulsively as she rose from the table. 'Unless you've any further questions, Mr Stubbs, I think I shall return to my room.'

She closed the door behind her, leaving the two men in private. Although Mr Ravenhurst had flatly refused to take any responsibility for the enquiry into the sad affair until a magistrate could be summoned, it was evident that, perhaps because he was acquainted with Mr Nutley's family, he felt obliged to take some interest in the proceedings.

And as Mr Ravenhurst had proved, beyond a shadow of a doubt now, he was not a man to shirk any obligation. So why, then, a tiny voice reminded her, had he behaved so out of character during his guardianship of her? It just didn't make sense.

Sarah pondered anew over this rather puzzling circumstance as she made her way back to her room. At the head of the stairs she heard one of the bechamber doors close, followed by the sound of humming, and turned to see Daisy's pretty golden-haired cousin tripping lightly along the passageway towards her.

The girl cast her a rather furtive glance as she brushed past and Sarah's eyes narrowed suspiciously as she watched her progress down the stairs. Perhaps Daisy's dislike of her cousin was well founded, after all: there was something decidedly sly about that girl.

Dismissing the thought from her mind, she went along the passageway and into her own room. Although there were no signs, yet, of a thaw, there had been, thankfully, no further falls of snow during the night, and the day was dry and bright.

Sarah decided that she had had more than enough of being cooped up in the inn, and collected her cloak from the wardrobe. As she swirled it about her shoulders, the folds caught Dottie's book, which had been placed on the bedside table, sending it tumbling to the floor.

Bending to retrieve the volume, Sarah noticed a folded sheet of paper lying beside it and, believing it to be her own, cast her eyes over the few lines written in a rounded childish scrawl: *I am glad you did that to the little worm,*

Dottie. He had it coming to him. Hope everything turns out well for you. Eliza.

Why, this must be the letter that Dottie had been searching for the previous day! She must have slipped it inside the back cover of her book for safekeeping, and then forgotten where she had put it, Sarah decided, and so took it along to Dottie's room.

After scratching lightly upon the firmly closed door, and waiting in vain for her summons to be answered, Sarah pondered on what she should do, for she could clearly detect soft moaning sounds and the creaking of bedsprings, so knew there was someone within.

Fearing Dottie might be unwell, she very gently turned the doorknob, opening the door sufficiently for her to poke her head into the room, and then promptly coloured to the roots of her hair at the sight that met her naïve, incredulous gaze.

She had often pondered with her friend Clarissa on the mysteries of the marriage bed, those untold, secret dealings between men and women that married ladies carefully avoided discussing with their younger and less experienced counterparts. Sarah realised in those few brief moments of acute embarrassment and stupefaction that she was witnessing, first-hand, those veiled relations between the sexes.

Then, before either Dottie or Captain Carter could detect her presence, she quietly closed the door, thrust Dottie's letter beneath, and flew down the passageway, only to collide moments later with a solid, immovable object at the head of the stairs. Strong fingers grasped her arms, steadying her, and she found herself staring up into laughing dark brown eyes.

'Anyone would imagine the devil himself were after

you. Steady, child!' Marcus then noted the heightened colour and slightly erratic breathing, and his smile faded. 'What is it? What's occurred to distress you?'

'Why, nothing! Nothing at all,' she managed, but not very convincingly. 'I'm just going out for some air,' and before he could detain her further, she broke free from his gently steadying hold and rushed headlong down the stairs.

The cold air on her burning cheeks was refreshing, and it was such a relief to be out of doors after the previous day's confinement. The day looked set to remain dry and bright, giving one reason to hope that the thaw would not be long in commencing. No vehicle, though, had braved a journey along the road; the snow remained a furrowless thick blanket of white, sparkling brightly like some glinting bed of crystals.

A sudden gust of the biting northerly wind sent the brightly coloured inn sign swinging to and fro on its rusty hinges, drawing her attention, and she looked up to see the painting of an old man making his weary way towards a building whose windows were ablaze with welcoming light.

'The Traveller's Rest,' she murmured with a wry little smile. There had been precious little rest for the weary travellers who had sought shelter beneath this roof, and she certainly didn't envisage that state of affairs changing after the tragic events of the previous night.

'Ah! So there you are.'

Sarah swung round to see Mr Ravenhurst, seemingly oblivious to the icy conditions underfoot, striding towards her. Evidently, he had doubted her assurances that she was perfectly all right, and had come out in search of her. How very thoughtful! She felt strangely touched by this obvious concern for her welfare.

'Not that we can walk very far, but permit me to show you round the outside of our temporary dwelling place,' and without giving her the opportunity to acquiesce or not he reached for her hand.

In those moments when those long shapely fingers, strong yet gentle, curled about hers to entwine her arm through his, a vision of yet another long-fingered, shapely hand fondling a large white breast flashed before her mind's eye. What must it feel like to be caressed like that? she wondered, as Dottie's image was replaced suddenly by one of herself lying on a bed, a lean, muscular frame stretched out alongside her.

She was aware of a strangely powerful craving developing deep within. Only it wasn't the image of the tall Captain's well-muscled frame pressed against her soft white nakedness that aroused this frighteningly powerful yearning, but that of the man beside her.

A further gust of icy-cold wind brought her out of her reverie with a start. What on earth had come over her to imagine such things? she wondered, appalled at having had such abandoned thoughts. Surely she couldn't possibly be attracted to this man? No, unthinkable! Ravenhurst was her guardian, for heaven's sake! He stood in place of a. . .a father.

She cast a tentative glance up at that hard-featured profile. The trouble was, though, she just couldn't bring herself to see him in that light; and only hoped, as they set off on their stroll round the rambling old building, that if he should happen to notice the renewed scarlet flush mounting her cheeks he would put it down to nothing more than the frosty nip of the cold north wind.

The men had stuck to their task the previous day, and

had managed to clear a path all round the inn, but Sarah's stout boots slipped occasionally on the exposed stones, and she was glad of that supporting arm. They inspected the exterior of the many outhouses, but Sarah carefully avoided enquiring into which Mr Nutley's body had been placed, and they ended their tour in the long stone-built barn, which contained only three horses and one cow.

They sat themselves down on the wooden stools placed near the open doorway, and after a few minutes Sarah realised that Mr Ravenhurst, who had been conversing quite amicably during their short tour, had grown very quiet as his dark eyes scanned the rear aspect of the inn.

'What are you studying so thoughtfully, sir?'

'That lean-to roof.'

Sarah turned her attention to the single-storey construction, which had obviously been added to the original building at some later date, and which ran along the whole length of the inn's back wall. Its sloping roof was tiled, and at its highest point was only a matter of a foot below the four bedroom windows.

'Are you thinking the intruder might have entered the inn that way?'

'It's a possibility, certainly. Climb on that water butt at the end there, and you can get on the roof without any trouble. Why, even a child could do it! If there is a loose catch on any one of those windows, it would be a simple matter to insert a knife or some other thin implement and flick open the catch.

'It's a great pity the landlord and his son cleared the snow off that roof yesterday. We would have seen footprints and known for sure, then. But as some of the timbers are not too sound, it's quite understandable why they did so.'

'Supposing our intruder did enter by one of those windows, he was taking an awful risk. After all, he wasn't to know that most of the occupants of those rooms had been drugged,'

'Very true.'

'And if that were, indeed, the case, surely the motive for doing so must have been robbery, and not to meet Mr Nutley.'

'It certainly looks that way.'

'More importantly, though, where did he go after climbing out of the parlour window? Travel is nigh impossible, even on a horse. Nothing has passed along that road for a day and a half. I know one can manage to walk into the village because Daisy and Rose have done so, but—' She gave a sudden start. 'Oh, Lord! You don't think it was one of the local inhabitants, do you?'

'That, too, is a distinct possibility.'

She looked searchingly at him. 'But you don't think so, do you?'

'I'm not sure what I think, child. But Nutley drugged the rum for some purpose. And if we could uncover why he did that, it might give us the answers to a great many questions.' He stood up and assisted Sarah to her feet. 'Come, let us return indoors. It will soon be time for luncheon.'

Leaving Mr Ravenhurst to quench his thirst with a tankard of the landlord's excellent home-brewed, Sarah made her way up the stairs, blushing slightly as she hurried past Dottie's room. She had only just hung her cloak back in the wardrobe when there was a knock on the door, and she turned, surprised, to see Miss Grimshaw quietly enter the bedchamber.

'Mrs Armstrong, I thought it my duty to come and see

you. How are you feeling? What a terrible thing to have happened!' She slumped down, uninvited, on to the only chair. 'Why, we might all have been murdered in our beds!'

'I'm fine, ma'am,' Sarah assured her. 'It was kind of you to take the trouble to enquire.'

'You saw who killed poor Mr Nutley, so I've been told.'

'I certainly saw the intruder, ma'am. But whether or not he was responsible for Mr Nutley's death. . .'

'Yes, yes. I suppose it might have been an accident, but. . . Oh, dear! My poor nerves won't stand much more of this. I can hardly wait to be away from this wretched place!'

'I think we all feel the same.'

Miss Grimshaw cast her a rather penetrating glance before staring fixedly down into her lap. 'Yes, yes. I dare say. But I expect you will need to stay to see the magistrate or—or someone. After all, you're the only one who saw the intruder.'

'I saw a figure, yes, but I didn't see his face. I could pass him in the street and wouldn't recognise him.'

'Oh, I see! Well, in that case, there would be little point in your remaining.' Miss Grimshaw placed a hand to her temple. 'I long to be with my sister in Bristol, Mrs Armstrong. Even though I didn't really know the young gentleman, I'm afraid this dreadful business has quite overset me. Did you know Mr Nutley at all well? Did you become acquainted yesterday?'

Sarah thought this rather an odd question to ask, but didn't hesitate to respond. 'Naturally we had some conversation. It is rather difficult to avoid one another in this inn. But we had never met before. Mr Ravenhurst knew him, however. I believe he lives not too far away from Mr Nutley's parents. I suppose that is why he has taken an interest in proceedings.'

'A very proper attitude!' Miss Grimshaw remarked, rising to her feet. 'Well, I shan't detain you further, Mrs Armstrong. It will soon be time for luncheon, and you are no doubt eager to join the others downstairs.'

'Why not eat with us yourself, ma'am?' Sarah suggested. 'It might help to keep your mind off things.'

'That is kind of you, but I'm not very good in mixed company. I think gentleman find me a little trying. No, I'm better on my own.'

Sarah, watching the woman leave the room, experienced the most peculiar feeling of unease. Had that visit really been made out of the purest motives? She could not help thinking that it was quite otherwise.

Chapter Five

Sarah was rudely awoken not by Daisy this time, bringing in the morning pitcher of warm water, but by a bedroom door being slammed, quickly followed by the sound of heavy footsteps hurrying along the passageway. It was in all probability only the farmer and his wife rising early as usual in order to help in the kitchen. In which case, it would be quite some time before the pitcher arrived, she thought and, turning on to her side, promptly went back to sleep.

When she awoke again, it was to see a bright ray of sunlight filtering though the chink between the patterned drapes. Swinging her feet to the floor, she padded across to the window, and could have wept for joy at the sight that met her eyes as she drew back the curtains.

Some time during the night the wind had changed direction from a biting-cold northerly to a much friendlier westerly. Although the landscape was still covered in its blanket of white, droplets of water were running down the window panes. The thaw had begun!

Deciding not to wait for Daisy, Sarah washed in the contents of the previous day's pitcher. It was unpleasantly cold, but she didn't care. The only thing that mattered was that she would soon be able to leave this place; perhaps not that day, but certainly the next, providing, of course, the wind continued to blow from its present direction and, perish the thought, there were no fresh falls of snow.

She refused, however, to be pessimistic and, hurriedly finishing her toilet, went downstairs, expecting to join the other no doubt equally jubilant stranded travellers, only to discover the coffee-room, surprisingly, deserted.

She frowned as she went over to the table at which they usually ate their meals. Not even the covers had been laid. How very odd! Although her stay at the inn had been far from pleasant, she had no fault to find with the landlady, who always had meals prepared on time. A quick glance at the grandfather clock, solemnly ticking away in the corner, confirmed that she was far from late in coming down to breakfast. So where was everyone?

It was then that she detected the sound of voices in the parlour. Surmising that breakfast for some reason was once again being served in there, she was about to enter when a noise behind her caught her attention and she turned to see Daisy, carrying a large tray, enter the coffee-room. One swift glance at those red-rimmed eyes was sufficient to warn Sarah that all was not as it should be.

'Why, Daisy! Whatever's the matter?'

'Oh, ma'am!' Depositing the tray on the table and herself down on a chair, Daisy sniffed loudly. 'It—it's our Rose. She—she were found behind the hen-coop this morning by our Joe. She's been done for. . . Her throat's been cut!'

Sarah, joining her at the table, could hardly believe it, didn't want to believe it. 'When did it happen?'

'During the night, they reckon.' Daisy drew out her handkerchief and blew her snub nose vigorously. 'I overheard Mr Stubbs say as 'ow she'd been dead for several hours.'

Sarah frowned. 'But I understood that you and Rose walked back to the village together, directly after serving dinner here in the evening.'

'Aye, Mrs Armstrong, that be right. And we walked back to me aunt's house together last night. I been sharing Rose's room. We ate our supper, and then went to bed at the usual time, but when I wakes this morning she weren't there. I thought it odd, but didn't pay it much mind. I thought she'd just got up early and come 'ere by 'erself. Our Joe found 'er when he went out to collect the eggs for breakfast.'

'So, at some point during the night,' Sarah remarked after a moment's intense thought, 'Rose got out of bed, dressed and came here. She must have arranged to meet someone, surely?'

'Aye, ma'am, that's what we all thinks. I know its wrong to speak ill of the dead, but she were a right flighty piece. There be no getting away from it. Our Joe were right fond of 'er, but she weren't interested in 'im. Kept calling 'im a slow-top and the like. You can bet your life she came 'ere to meet some man. She were forever teasing the village lads, setting one against the other. I reckons one of 'em 'ad 'ad enough, and did for 'er.'

It was certainly a possibility, especially if Rose's disposition was flirtatious. But why arrange to meet someone here? Sarah wondered. It just didn't make sense. Surely if Rose had wanted the meeting with this man kept secret, she would hardly select directly outside her aunt's house as a trysting place?

Reaching for the coffee-pot, Sarah was about to pour herself a cup when the sound of hysterical sobbing reached her ears, and she turned her head in the direction of the parlour's closed door.

'Who on earth is in there?'

'Mr Stubbs carted Miss de Vine in there quite some time ago, ma'am,' Daisy disclosed in a conspiratorial whisper. 'Summat to do with a letter found on our Rose. Though what Rose were doing with it, I can't imagine. Couldn't read a word, she couldn't!' The pathetic sobs continued. 'Sounds right upset, don't she? Wonder what they're doing to 'er in there?'

'I don't know, but I mean to find out!' Without a moment's hesitation Sarah stormed into the parlour to discover not only Mr Stubbs, but Mr Ravenhurst too, and poor Dottie, her elbows resting on the table, and her face buried in her hands. 'What on earth is going on?' she demanded, the light of battle in her eyes.

'You should not be here, child.' Marcus's tone betrayed his annoyance at the interruption, but Sarah stood her ground.

'I have as much right to be in here as you have,' she countered and, ignoring that, now, all-too-familiar low growl, calmly closed the door and moved towards them.

Dottie grasped Sarah's hand in pathetically trembling fingers. 'Oh, Mrs Armstrong!' she wailed, for perhaps the first time in her life remembering someone's name correctly. 'They say I done it, but I didn't. I swear I didn't!'

'We're saying nothing of the sort, you foolish creature!' Marcus snapped as he continued to stare in a far-from-friendly fashion at Sarah. 'We are merely trying to discover why a letter written to you was in that servant girl's possession.'

'And I keep telling you it ain't mine!' Dottie cast her blue eyes up to Sarah in wide appeal. 'They won't believe me, but I ain't never seen it before in my life.'

Sarah turned to Mr Stubbs. 'May I see this letter?' and without the least hesitation he handed it across to her. The ink was smudged, but the writing was still legible, and she had no difficulty in recognising it as the letter that had fallen from the book, and which, subsequently, she had slipped beneath Dottie's door. As the note had her name clearly written on it, it was extremely foolish of Dottie to deny ownership, unless. . .

Sarah gave a sudden start as a suspicion crossed her mind. Raising her eyes, she held Mr Ravenhurst's angry gaze above Dottie's head, and then quite deliberately turned the letter the other way up before handing it to Dottie. 'Just have one more look to make sure. I know your eyes aren't too good, and the ink is rather smudged. But, just to be certain.'

Sarah saw enlightenment dawn on the men's faces as Dottie, without turning the letter the right way up, cast her eyes over its contents, just as though she were reading every word.

'No, I ain't never seen it before,' she confirmed.

'No, but I most certainly have,' Sarah astonished them all by admitting. She calmly took the letter from Dottie and handed it back to Mr Stubbs, who was regarding her with intense interest now. 'Dottie loaned me a book the day after we all arrived here. Yesterday morning I accidentally knocked the book on to the floor, and that letter fell out. It wasn't until after I had apprised myself of its contents that I realised it wasn't mine, and so took it along to Dottie's room.'

'But you never gave it to me!' Dottie stated flatly.

'No, I know I didn't. You—er—were not alone at the time. I believe Captain Carter was with you, so I pushed it under your door.' Sarah could feel the heat rising in her cheeks, and carefully avoided looking in Mr Ravenhurst's direction.

'There are one or two other rather important facts you ought to be aware of, Mr Stubbs. . .I have it on the best authority that the poor dead girl was illiterate. Furthermore, how did that letter come to be in her possession? More interestingly, though, the letter, I noticed, has been deliberately altered. It was signed by someone calling herself Eliza, not A Well-wisher.'

'Eliza Cooper!' Dottie exclaimed. 'She were working at that theatre with me.'

Sarah cast a look of comical dismay at Mr Ravenhurst. 'You're certain her name is Cooper?' she asked tentatively, knowing all too well the lively damsel's propensity for getting names wrong.

'Course I am!. . .or it might be Hooper,' Dottie amended after a moment's thought. 'Something like that, anyhow.'

Sarah could not prevent a twitching smile. 'And the—er—little worm your friend Eliza refers to is. . .?'

'Oh, 'im! He were the boss o' that rubbishing place. Dirty old demon! He were always after us girls. Wouldn't leave us alone.'

Tears forgotten, Dottie gurgled with laughter. 'I got 'im a bit tipsy one afternoon, took off all his clothes and got one o' the lads to 'elp me carry 'im on to the stage. Brought the house down, it did, when he stood up stark naked in the middle of the first act.' She raised her shoulders in an indifferent shrug. 'Course, he gave me the push afterwards, but it were worth it.'

'I dare say all this can be confirmed, Mr Stubbs,' Sarah remarked airily. She felt rather pleased with herself for coming so successfully to Dottie's aid and, although Mr Ravenhurst's brows remained fixed in a disapproving scowl, Mr Stubbs, before she went out, looked far from displeased with her interruption.

Her appetite having deserted her completely, Sarah went directly up to her room to collect her cloak. As she stepped outside the inn, the rapidly melting snow squelched beneath her boots. There were large puddles everywhere, and several wheel tracks, now, along the road. Life, it seemed, was getting back to normal.

But would life ever be the same at The Traveller's Rest? she wondered, walking across the yard. Certainly not for some considerable time. She shook her head in disbelief. It seemed incredible that such grisly events had taken place in this idyllic rural setting. Two deaths in as many days! A frisson of fear feathered its way down the length of her spine as the gruesome thought of who might be next crossed her mind.

'Oh!' She gave a sudden start as she walked into the stable. 'I didn't see you standing there, Captain.'

'Sorry if I startled you, ma'am.' He stepped out of the shadows. 'Came out to blow a cloud, as there were no signs of breakfast being served.'

'It is ready now,' she informed him, sitting herself down on one of the low stools. 'What do you make of this sad business, Captain? I must confess it has me puzzled.'

Flicking the cigar butt into the yard, he sat beside her on the other stool. 'I don't know, ma'am. Nutley's death might well have been an accident. He might have fallen awkwardly, and hit his head on the edge of the settle, and it was that which broke his neck. But the young girl. . .?' He shook his head. 'That was murder. . .cold-blooded murder.'

'But why on earth should anyone want to murder a—a servant girl?'

'She might well have discovered something about Nutley's death. When Stubbs examined the body, he found a fragment of a five-pound note clutched in the dead girl's fingers.'

'Blackmail?' Sarah's eyes widened for an instant, then she became thoughtful. 'Yes. Yes, I should say Rose would have been capable of that. After all, where else would she have come by such a large sum of money? I wonder just what she had discovered. . .and, more importantly, about whom? Surely not someone staying at the inn?'

'It certainly looks that way, Mrs Armstrong. The weapon used in the attack was lying in the snow beside the body. The landlady recognised it as one of her own kitchen knives.'

'Oh, my God!' Sarah's stomach lurched violently at the mere thought of someone at the inn being the culprit. 'I know Dottie's letter was found in the dead girl's possession, but. . . No, I cannot believe Dottie would ever do such a thing!'

'Oh?' His russet-coloured brows rose. 'And why not? Women are as capable as men of committing dastardly, underhanded deeds.'

Sarah stared at him sharply. His tone had been flat, indifferent almost, as though it would not have mattered a jot to him if the murderer did turn out to be none other than Dottie. Yet, how could he remain so impassive after what had taken place between them only yesterday? Surely he must care something for the woman? Or could a man share those experiences with a female and remain totally unemotional. . .? Apparently, yes.

She felt, unaccountably, annoyed, and found herself saying, a touch of censure creeping into her voice, 'But I thought you liked Dottie, Captain Carter?'

'I neither like, nor dislike her, ma'am,' he responded with brutal frankness. 'I have learnt the hard way that people are not always what they seem. And have been given little reason to trust your sex.'

Sarah's annoyance faded and she regarded him thoughtfully. His voice had remained level enough, but she had easily detected the bitterness and underlying hurt. She gazed at his strong, attractive profile.

She had liked Captain Carter from the first and, had circumstances been different, had she not been forced to play the part of a recently widowed young woman, friendly but slightly aloof, wary of every word lest she give her true identity away, she would not have objected to getting to know him a little better. He was still a young man: twenty-four; twenty-five at most. Yet, already, life had begun to etch unmistakable lines of cynicism in his young face.

'So, you have been let down by a lady, Captain. And rather badly, I suspect. And now you have scant regard for the rest of my sex.' She saw his strong hands clench, the knuckles growing white. She had no intention of prying, and was tolerably certain that he would not satisfy her curiosity if she did, but could not prevent herself from adding, 'There is a great deal of bitterness in you, sir.

And, I suspect, it does not all stem from unhappy dealings with women.'

He looked at her then, his tawny eyes questioning. 'What do you mean?'

'You made it abundantly clear, the very first morning we met, that you bore a grudge against our privileged class.'

His well-shaped mouth twisted into a begrudging smile. 'And with good reason, ma'am. Although, I suppose, you might say I number amongst them.'

'Oh?'

'My father was a younger son of a Viscount. But my mother, God bless her, came from rather different stock.'

'Really? Then we have something in common, sir,' Sarah responded, completely forgetting to put a guard on her tongue. 'My mother was a baronet's daughter, and my father a naval captain.'

'Well, well!' There was not a trace of bitterness, now, in his pleasant voice. 'Tell me, ma'am, do you ever feel that you belong in neither one class nor the other?'

She shrugged. 'To be honest, I've never given it much thought. I am what I am, sir, and there is nothing that can be done to change that. But it does anger me sometimes when people suggest that my mother married beneath her. My father was a courageous man. And I'll not hear a word said against him!'

'Good for you, ma'am!' His smile was full of appreciative warmth, and there was more than just a hint of respect in his tawny-coloured eyes, too. 'And you are wrong, by the way. . .I do not hold all members of your sex in contempt.'

'Do I intrude?' Mr Ravenhurst suddenly appeared in the doorway, his expression anything but warm. 'Stubbs is looking for you, Carter,' he informed him curtly. 'Wants to ask you some questions.'

'Lord! It's worse than the Spanish Inquisition in this place! In fact, I'll be glad to return to that country. It's a dashed sight more restful.' The Captain reluctantly rose to his feet. 'May I escort you back inside, Mrs Armstrong?'

'I am more than capable of performing that courtesy!' Marcus snapped out. 'Therefore, do not let us detain you.'

Sarah saw the Captain's smile fade and his eyes narrow, and hurriedly intervened. 'You go on ahead, sir. I shall be along presently.' For a few moments Sarah watched his progress across the yard, and then turned a reproachful look up at the man glowering above her. 'Are you always in such a disagreeable mood before noon?'

'Only when I'm put into one by damnably foolish actions!' he retorted. 'What do you mean by remaining out here alone with that man?'

How dared he adopt such a high-handed tone with her! Sarah rose from the stool, her bosom heaving. 'And what, pray, has that to do with you, sirrah?'

'God give me strength!' he rasped through clenched teeth and, before she knew what he was about, he took a firm hold of her upper arms and shook her none too gently. 'You brainless creature! A young female has been brutally murdered here within the last twelve hours, possibly by someone residing at this inn, and you wander about aimlessly, just as though nothing untoward had occurred.'

'Oh, how dare you!' Sarah gasped, breathless from the shaking. She had never been so ill-used; nor could she ever recall feeling so angry with anyone in her life before.

'Kindly remove your hands from my person. I dislike it excessively!'

Her lofty tone drew a ghost of a smile to his lips. 'You might need to accustom yourself, my girl.'

'Now you are being ridiculous! As ridiculous as suggesting Captain Carter is the murderer.'

'I was suggesting nothing of the sort!' He released her then, his smile vanishing as he ran an impatient hand through his dark hair. 'But, unlike you, I possess some discernment, and do not accept people at face value.'

'And neither do I. But unlike you,' she mimicked him with wicked sarcasm, 'I try to look for the best in people.'

'In the circumstances, my girl, that is singularly foolish. You would do better to cultivate the opposite standpoint. What do you know about Captain Carter? What do you know about any of them?'

'Not very much, I'll admit. But I know I am as safe with Captain Carter as I am with. . .with you.'

'Oh, is that so?' he purred silkily. The sudden glint in his dark eyes should have warned her, but she took little heed. 'So, you think you are safe with me,' and before she knew it, she was in his arms and his lips had fastened securely on to hers.

Only for an instant did she struggle against the pressure of his mouth and the firm clasp of those muscular arms, then quite suddenly, unexpectedly, she found herself responding. Of their own volition her lips parted beneath his, and his kiss deepened, demanding and receiving a response.

Her imaginings of the day before were becoming a reality. That powerfully exhilarating sensation deep within began to stir once again, and her body seemed suddenly to have acquired a will of its own.

Her young breasts, pressed against that broad expanse of chest, grew hard, and she experienced an almost overwhelming desire to raise her arms, to entwine them round his neck, to run her fingers through that dark waving hair and to keep those tantalisingly disturbing lips securely fastened to her own, but his arms continued to encircle hers, restraining, keeping her his firm, but far from unwilling, captive.

When at last he released her, she was achingly aware that her traitorous body yearned to be pressed against that hard muscular frame once again, and could only stare up at him in wonder, in disbelief, almost.

'Now, let that be a lesson to you,' he said in strangely hoarse tones, his breathing as ragged as hers. 'It is unwise to be alone with any man. No matter how honourable he may be, given enough provocation, he might not always behave as he ought.'

Sarah did not wait to hear more. Reality had returned with a vengeance, and she felt the red-hot heat of shame rising rapidly to the roots of her hair. Swirling round, she hurried back inside the inn, not stopping to catch her breath until she had attained the relative sanctuary of her bedchamber.

Slumping down on to the bed, she placed her hands to her burning cheeks. What must he think of her? She had behaved no better than a wanton! And yet she seemed, even now, powerless to quell that strange yearning in her newly awakened young body. If she were to grant the opportunity, could any man have such a devastating effect on her? She quickly thrust this disturbing thought aside, for she knew it couldn't possibly be true.

On one occasion when she had been staying at her friend Clarissa's home, she had been caught in the shrubbery by a neighbour's son. She had found his advances repugnant, and had boxed the spotty youth's ears soundly when he had tried to kiss her.

Yet Mr Ravenhurst's kiss had aroused no desire for such retaliatory actions, a taunting little voice reminded her. He, of course, was a man of experience. He had probably kissed scores of females, and had no doubt enjoyed the charms of many a beautiful mistress over the years, she thought bitterly, experiencing for the first time in her life that gnawing pain of jealousy.

She released her breath in a heartfelt sigh. It was a lowering realisation, but one much better faced—he had kissed her merely to teach her a lesson. It had meant less than nothing to him. And yet, her brows drew together in a deeply puzzled frown, if that was, indeed, the case, why then had he seemed just for one unguarded moment as disturbed by the experience as she had herself?

As no logical explanation came readily to mind, Sarah tried not to dwell on the disconcerting interlude, but this proved no easy task. In the end she decided she could not possibly come face to face with Marcus Ravenhurst again until she had herself, mind and body, well in hand. She remained incarcerated in her room for the remainder of the morning, and for the first time since her arrival at the inn requested a meal brought up on a tray.

Having not partaken of breakfast, she consumed every last morsel on her plate, and had only just set the tray back down on the bedside table when there was a knock on the door, and her tormentor, himself, walked boldly into the room, just as though he had every right to do so and, what was worse, as though he hadn't a care in the world.

'Over your sulks yet?' he enquired with a wickedly

provoking smile, and that was all it needed to restore Sarah's equilibrium.

She glowered across the small room at him. 'I have not been sulking!' she retorted. 'And kindly close the door again on your way out,' she added pointedly.

'Now, that is most impolite, my girl. Especially as I came here to see if you would care to leave.'

'Leave?' she echoed, forgetting to be angry with him. 'Do you mean the roads are passable?'

'Certainly. The Mail was spotted travelling along the main road quite early this morning. The local magistrate is here now, and I've cleared it with him for us to be on our way.'

'How wonderful!' She was on her feet in an instant. 'The landlord very kindly offered to return me to—'

'I know all about that,' he cut in. 'I've already told him I'll escort you. Do you think you can be ready in half an hour? I'll meet you downstairs.'

Without giving her the opportunity to disagree with the arrangements he had undertaken on her behalf, he left the room. Not that Sarah had any intention of wrangling over who took her back to Calne. She was too excited at the prospect of continuing her journey to worry her head over such an insignificant detail, nor did it cross her mind to wonder why the magistrate had not insisted upon seeing her before she left.

It took no time at all to pack her meagre belongings, and after returning Dottie's book and bidding her farewell, she went down to the coffee-room where she discovered Captain Carter sitting quite alone.

'It would seem, sir, that I have been given permission to leave, and Mr Ravenhurst has kindly offered to escort me back to Calne. So, I must bid you farewell.'

He rose to his feet and took her outstretched hand in both his own. 'Godspeed, ma'am. I hope the remainder of your journey may pass without incident.'

'I sincerely hope so, too.' She looked earnestly into his attractive tawny-coloured eyes. 'But do you know, Captain, I should dearly love to discover just what has been going on here.'

'Probably no one ever will. But if by some chance the truth is ever unearthed, Ravenhurst has promised to write and let me know. Apparently he is acquainted with my commanding officer, Colonel Pitbury. So a letter should reach me.'

Sarah's smile was full of gentle warmth. 'Well, good-bye, Captain Brin Carter. Don't get yourself killed, will you?'

'I shall do my utmost not to.' His smile was a carbon copy of her own. 'And let us say, rather, farewell. Who knows, my dear lady, our paths may cross again. . . I, at least, sincerely hope so.'

He made to pick up her cloak-bag, but she forestalled him by grasping the handle first, and as she walked away, she had the oddest feeling that they would meet again, and perhaps more than once, in the not too dim and distant future.

The landlord, awaiting her in the tap, informed her that Mr Ravenhurst had paid her shot, and then insisted upon carrying her belongings out to the curricle. Sarah thanked him for his hospitality, said all that was proper in respect of the death of his niece and then, after requesting him to pass on her farewells to the other members of his family, scrambled up beside her escort while the landlord placed her belongings beneath the seat.

'Is it not wonderful to be on our away again, sir?'

Sarah remarked, as Mr Ravenhurst gave the bays the office to start. 'But where is your groom? Surely you're not leaving him behind?'

'Sutton is taking a seat on the stage as far as Chippenham, and then hiring a horse. I've sent him on an errand.'

'Oh, I see!' Sarah, then, bethought herself of something else, and began to rummage through her reticule. 'You paid my bill, sir. How much do I owe you?'

He cast her an impatient glance. 'Nothing.'

'But, sir, I cannot possibly permit you to—'

'If you think I'm stopping this carriage,' he cut in sharply, 'so that you can grease my palm with a few paltry coins, you can think again. Put that confounded purse away, child!'

For some reason, best known to himself, he had fallen into one of his more disagreeable moods. Sarah cast him a furtive sidelong glance. Ought she now, at this the eleventh hour, to divulge her true identity? It wasn't that she had deliberately avoided doing so; it was simply that just the right opportunity had never presented itself. Which was hardly surprising, considering the tragic events that had taken place in the past days.

A tiny sigh of indecision escaped her. He was hardly in a particularly approachable mood, and yet. . .

She was still debating with herself when they arrived at the main highway. Instead of turning right, which would have taken them to Calne, Mr Ravenhurst confounded her by turning in the opposite direction.

'Sir, you have gone the wrong way!' she pointed out in some urgency.'

'No, I haven't.'

'But, sir, Calne is the other way,' she reiterated,

slewing round in the seat to look back at the signpost.

'I'm fully aware of that, child. I know this part of the country very well.'

'Then why have you come this way?' she asked, not unreasonably, and watched a wickedly slow and infuriatingly smug smile curl his lips.

'Because, Mrs Serafina Armstrong, *née* Postlethwaite. . .alias Miss Sarah Pennington, my troublesome ward, I am taking you to a place where I can keep my eye on you!'

Chapter Six

For several moments it was as much as Sarah could do to gape at him, hoping against hope that she had misheard, but his smugly satisfied smile was proof enough that she had not. The wretch had deliberately tricked her into going with him! And she, idiot that she was, had climbed willy-nilly into his carriage like a trusting fool!

'How long have you known?' she asked at length, striving to remain calm.

'Since that first night,' he answered truthfully. 'And I cannot tell you how relieved I am that you are not foolishly trying to deny it.'

A little late for that, now, she thought wretchedly before cursing herself silently for a fool. What a complete and utter ninny-hammer not to have realised long before! Almost from the moment of his arrival at the inn he had shown such marked consideration for her welfare, and she had foolishly put it down to nothing more than a gentleman's concern for a young widow.

She raised puzzled eyes to stare blindly at the road ahead. But how on earth had he discovered her true identity? Had she foolishly given herself away? She cast her mind back, trying to recall in detail all of their many conversations, but could think of nothing she had said that might possibly have betrayed her. Curiosity got the better of her and she found herself asking outright how he had found out.

'The instant I saw those initials on your writing-case I became suspicious,' he did not hesitate to admit. 'And, of course, that damned impertinent letter confirmed it.'

'What? You mean you read. . .?' Sarah regarded him in silent dismay for a moment, remembering all too clearly the pompous, not to say condescending, tone she had adopted when composing that half-finished missive, but then the sheer effrontery of his actions brought her temper to the fore. 'How dared you rifle through my belongings, sir! How dared you! Stop this carriage at once!'

'No,' he responded with infuriating calm. 'And do not attempt to jump out,' he continued while expertly overtaking a lumbering coach. 'You might achieve your objective without suffering a sprained ankle, but you'll certainly end up with a sore rear. I'll see to that!'

He caught the tiny gasp of outrage, but missed the calculating look she cast him.

'That you would stoop so low as to lay violent hands on a defenceless female does not surprise me in the least,' she informed him loftily. 'But don't you think you've left it rather late to play the heavy-handed guardian? Or to take on the role at all, come to that?' she finished bitterly.

'So that rankles, does it?' He did turn to look at her then, and noted the stubborn set of the softly rounded chin. 'Believe it or not, child, I refrained from interfering in your upbringing because I believed you would go on much better without it. But I see, now, I was wrong.' He cast a scowling glance over her dull grey garb. 'Confound it, girl! Have you no dress sense at all? That dratted colour don't suit you in the least!'

'Dress sense?' she echoed, anger stirring once again at the unjustified criticism. 'How was I supposed to dress anywhere near decently on the paltry allowance you gave me?'

'Paltry. . .?' His brows snapping together, he drew the curricle to a halt at the side of the road, and then turned in the seat to face her squarely. 'Right, it's high time you and I sorted a few things out, young woman. Why did you suddenly take it into your head to run away?'

'I didn't run away!' she refuted staunchly. 'I left. . . well, I left because I saw little point in remaining. I shall attain my majority in June, in case you have forgotten,' she reminded him, a hint of sarcasm edging her voice. 'Your guardianship will then be at an end, and I shall need to make my own way in the world. I thought to seek some genteel occupation—a companion, or governess.'

'Governess?' he echoed, not hiding his consternation. 'What foolishness is this?'

'It might seem foolish to you, sir,' she retorted, flashing him an angry look from beneath her long, curling lashes, 'but not everyone is blessed with a vast fortune. Most of us need to work in order to live.'

'And what makes you suppose that you number amongst them?'

'I should have thought that was obvious!' she snapped. 'I have no money.'

'Who told you that?'

Sarah opened her mouth, closed it again, and regarded him questioningly. 'Are you trying to tell me that I do have money of my own?'

'Of course you have, you silly chit! Surely you cannot have forgotten your home near Plymouth? Which I have rented out, incidentally, on your behalf. And I suppose you have in the region of twenty-five thousand pounds on top of that, or perhaps a little more.'

'Twenty-five. . .?' Sarah's jaw dropped perceptively. It was a fortune! And all these years she had assumed she was little more than a pauper. 'Why didn't you tell me?' she queried, a touch of censure creeping into her voice now. 'Surely I had the right to know my financial situation, sir?'

'You had only to ask.' he responded airily.

'Ask? I did ask! Well, I wrote to you,' she amended. 'But you never once bothered to take the trouble to reply to any of my letters.'

He did not respond to this, and after a few moments Sarah turned her head to look at him. There was a strange intensity in his gaze. He was looking directly at her, but she sensed that he was seeing something else. Then suddenly she saw it too. Everything became crystal clear. He had never received her letters, not one, simply because Mrs Fairchild had never sent them.

She realised, too, in those moments of astonishing enlightenment, that the allowance he had made her over the years must have been a generous one, but most of it had gone into Harriet Fairchild's pocket or, rather, had been squandered on her ruling passion—gambling.

The woman had been so very cunning, keeping her charge away from the assemblies, and denying her the pleasure of attending many parties where she might just possibly meet some eligible young man, because her comfortable existence would then have come to an end. As long as Sarah had remained in Bath, Mrs Fairchild could continue to indulge in her vice at her wealthy cousin's expense.

'The lady I met in Upper Camden Place told me there was much that warranted investigation,' he said ominously. 'And she wasn't far wrong!'

'So, you did meet Mrs Stanton,' Sarah remarked, instinctively knowing to whom he referred. 'I thought you must have done. Your cousin wouldn't have realised where I intended going.'

'Yes, I met your friend's mother.' His expression was one of staunch disapproval as he gave the bays the office to start again. 'And I shall have a word or two to say to you in the not-too-distant future, young woman, regarding your involvement in that elopement.'

You carry on, then. See if I care, Sarah thought blithely before a thought struck her. 'Why did you suddenly take it into your head to visit Bath? Did you go there especially to see me?'

'Of course I did, silly chit! Why else should I go to that confounded place?'

'Well, there's no need to snap my nose off! How was I supposed to know?' she retorted, having come to the conclusion long since that there was little point in trying to hold a polite conversation with him. 'You've never bothered to pay me a visit before. Did you have a specific reason for doing so?'

'I intended asking whether you would care for a Season in London.'

'Truly?' Sarah was startled by the admission.

'Yes. But, given your recent conduct, I'm not so sure the offer is still open.'

For a few elated moments Sarah allowed her mind to dwell on the heady delights of a London Season, but then realised that it might be best if she didn't accept his offer. She had been confined for so many years, and the thought of being encumbered with yet another chaperon did not appeal in the least. During the past few days she had experienced the sweet taste of freedom, and had no desire to relinquish her new-found liberty.

No, she told herself, it would be better to stick to her original plan and stay with the Alcotts in Hertfordshire. Thankfully, having money of her own, she would not now need to seek a position, and once she had attained her majority, she could return to her home near Plymouth.

'It's kind of you to offer, sir, but I don't think I shall go to London.'

'I-beg-your-pardon!' he ground out, turning the curricle off the main road and down a narrow twisting country lane. 'What makes you suppose that you'll be given any say in the matter? If I say you'll go to London, you'll go, my girl! And that will be an end to it!'

'I have decided on exactly what I am going to do,' she returned, completely unruffled by the autocratic tone. 'And why have you turned down here?'

'Because I'm taking you to my grandmother's house until I can make more suitable arrangements.'

'No, I won't go there!' Determination was very evident in her voice. 'I am going to Hertfordshire.'

'Sarah,' he said with careful restraint, 'you will do exactly as I tell you.'

'Oh, do you really think so?' she parried sweetly. 'I wouldn't be too sure of that if I were you.'

He gave vent to one of his low growls, but managed to bite back the threatening retort that rose in his throat.

They continued the journey in chilling silence, but from time to time Marcus cast a suspicious glance in her direction. She kept her gaze firmly fixed on the road ahead, and her hands in her lap, looking for all the world quite innocently angelic, but he was not fooled. They had not spent those three days in close proximity without his gaining a fair knowledge of her character.

His eyes narrowed. The little minx was definitely plotting something: how to give him the slip, no doubt. He would need to watch her like a hawk for the next few days, he decided grimly.

Entering his uncle's vast Wiltshire estate by the north gate, Marcus turned the curricle on to the driveway leading to the Dower House. As soon as he had brought the team to a halt in the stableyard, and an aged groom had taken a hold of the horses' heads, he leapt out the curricle and, before she had time to alight herself, grasped Sarah's slim waist and swung her to the ground.

Ignoring the indignant look she cast him, he took a firm grasp of her wrist and almost hauled her behind him along the path to the front entrance; and only when Clegg had opened the solid oak door in answer to the summons, and they had stepped into the hall, did he release his hold.

'I take it my grandmother is in her sitting room, Clegg? Good,' he went on in response to the nod. 'This is my ward, Miss Sarah Pennington. And I should be grateful if you would keep an eye on her while I have a brief word with her ladyship.'

While he was speaking he removed his hat and coat, and promptly handed them to the bemused butler, who was regarding the very pretty, but indignant young lady with considerable interest. Then, without so much as a glance in Sarah's direction, Marcus mounted the stairs, and went directly to his grandmother's private apartments. He entered the room without knocking to find her seated in her favourite chair near the hearth.

'Ah, good! You're awake.'

The Dowager gave a start. 'Heavens above! Must you creep up on a body like that!' she greeted him crossly, but with unmistakable warmth in her grey eyes, as he came towards her chair. 'Well, and am I to congratulate you? Am I looking at a betrothed man?'

'What?' He looked nonplussed for a moment. 'Oh, no. Never got as far as Bamford's place. Been careering about the country after that ward of mine. Little baggage had the temerity to run away from Bath! Caught up with her, though. She's here now. And that's what I've come to speak to you about.'

'And so, too, have I.'

They both turned to see Sarah framed in the doorway: the Dowager's expression one of surprised interest; her grandson's one of scowling disapproval.

'I thought you knew to await me below!'

Sublimely ignoring the reproof, Sarah turned and calmly closed the door before taking several paces into the room. She had removed her grey bonnet and cloak, and was embarrassingly conscious of the Dowager's shrewd eyes scrutinising the plain grey gown, but did not betray her discomfiture, and even lifted her chin slightly.

'Your grandson, ma'am, has brought me here for some perverse reasons of his own and, I might add, against my will. Unless I am very much mistaken, he was about to persuade you to house me under your roof—an arrangement, I'm sure, which would please you as little as it would please me.'

The Dowager tapped her ebony cane on the floor. 'Hoity-toity, miss! I shall say what pleases me and what does not.' She looked up at her grandson. He was still staring fixedly across at his ward. There was more than a touch of annoyance in that gaze, but something else, too.

She looked back at Sarah. 'Come here, child. Let me look at you.' Sarah meekly obeyed, and stood before the Dowager, gazing solemnly down at her. 'Why, you do look like your mother! Except prettier, I think. And you certainly did not get those lovely eyes from her, nor those dark brows. What unusual colouring!'

'No, ma'am. From my father, so I understand.' Her lips curled into a shy smile. 'Did you know my mother well?'

'Yes, child. Your mother and my Agnes were great friends since the days they both attended the seminary together. Your mother frequently stayed with us when she was a girl, but I saw little of her after she married your father.' She turned to her grandson. 'I cannot imagine why you are still standing there, Marcus. Go away and leave me to talk to Sarah in peace. You'll find brandy in the library.'

'I could certainly do with one after what I've had to contend with during these past days!' he responded with feeling. He went over to the door, but turned back to add, 'And don't you dare try to slip away, my girl! The library is downstairs. And I fully intend to keep the door open.'

'Infuriating man!' Sarah muttered, much to the Dowager's intense amusement, as the door closed behind him.

'Has my obnoxious grandson been giving you a hard time? Do sit down, child, and tell me all about it. What induced you to run away from Bath?'

Sarah raised her eyes heavenwards as she settled herself in the comfortable chair opposite. 'As I told your grandson, though he seems determined not to believe me, I did not run away, ma'am. I simply chose to leave.'

She then went on to explain the reasons for her actions. The Dowager leaned back against the chair, listening quietly for the most part, but occasionally interrupting to ask a question. Her shrewd grey eyes never wavered from the lovely, expressive face as she learned a little of those years Sarah had endured in Bath.

Her grandson's arrival at the inn, and the subsequent events, brought more than one wickedly amused chuckle to rise in her throat, and Sarah's astringent comments on her guardian's perfidy at tricking her into accepting a ride in his curricle afforded the Dowager unholy amusement.

'The cunning wretch!' she exclaimed when she had learned all. 'Little wonder you feel quite out of charity with him, my dear. But he is right, you know,' she went on seriously. 'You cannot go wandering about the country on your own. Look at what has befallen you already!'

There was a clearly discernible glint in Sarah's eyes. 'Naturally, I was saddened by the tragic deaths, but I could not help being excited by it all,' she freely admitted. 'Nothing like that has ever happened to me before!'

'You poor child. You did have a very dreary time of it all in Bath, didn't you?'

Sarah could feel the colour rising in her cheeks, and was unable to hold that shrewd gaze. 'Well, I—I. . .'

'There is no need to explain,' her ladyship said gently. 'That is all in the past. Now, we must look to the future. But first, you may go across to the decanters over there, and pour me a glass of Madeira. And pour yourself one whilst you're about it,' she added as Sarah rose gracefully from the chair 'It won't do you a mite of harm.'

The Dowager watched her intently, scrutinising every fluid movement of the slender young body, and was more than satisfied with what she saw.

'My dear child, I'm beginning to like you already,' she remarked, taking the glass held out to her. 'You have a steady hand and you can fill a glass. Which is more than can be said for some people.' She sampled the wine, then continued, 'Now, we must decide what is best to be done with you. I can fully understand your being piqued at my grandson's high-handed attitude. Sadly, it is his way, and you must grow accustomed.

'For my part I see no reason why you shouldn't stay with your old governess. It is evident that you have a great fondness for each other. I shall certainly have a word with Marcus about it. But it is out of the question for you to travel to Hertfordshire alone, and on the common stage. So, until some arrangements can be made, would you object very much to remaining here with me?'

Sarah had the grace to blush. 'I'm sorry if I appeared rude when I came in here, ma'am, but I thought Mr Ravenhurst might try to, well, bully you into housing me here.'

A wicked cackle answered this. 'Oh, my dear child! When you come to know me better, you will realise that even my dictatorial grandson is incapable of that feat.'

She became serious again, and looked across at Sarah intently. 'We are very alike, Ravenhurst and I. There are those who might disagree, but I believe I have mellowed over the years, and my grandson might well do so, given the incentive. But we're both plain-spoken, and spoilt enough to want our own way in all things. You might not find it easy staying here with me, and I shall not force it upon you, but I should very much like to have you as my guest, Sarah Pennington.'

Sarah did not doubt the sincerity, and felt touched by the invitation. 'Well, I—'

'Decide nothing yet, child,' the Dowager interrupted. 'Take a little time to think it over. Now, be good enough to go over to the bell-pull.'

Sarah obeyed and, at the Dowager's request, gave it several sharp tugs. A few minutes later a gaunt middle-aged woman, with the most frighteningly piercing and almost black eyes, entered the room. She cast Sarah the briefest of glances before turning to her mistress and enquiring, quite disrespectfully, Sarah thought, what she required.

'Sarah, my child, this obnoxious creature you see before you is my personal maid, Buddle,' the Dowager informed her with wicked amusement. 'Don't be alarmed. She might not appear so, but she is quite human, I assure you. She has been with me for more years than I care to remember.'

A loud snort answered this, and her ladyship turned to her maid without any visible signs of having taken offence. 'Has a bed chamber been prepared for Miss Pennington, Buddle?'

'Naturally.'

'Which one?'

'Master Marcus always has the largest guest chamber, as you very well know,' the maid answered impatiently. 'Miss Pennington's belongings have been placed in the other guest room.'

The Dowager was silent for a moment, then said decisively, 'Then remove them! Put Miss Sarah in the room next to mine. See that she has everything she needs, then come back here to me.'

Only for one unguarded moment did the maid betray surprise. 'Very good, my lady.' She turned to Sarah. 'If you would care to come with me, Miss Pennington, I'll show you the way.'

Sarah wasn't so very sure that she did care to go with the forbidding-looking woman but, after hurriedly finishing the contents of her glass, rose to her feet, and followed Buddle down the narrow passageway and into a room where the drapes had been pulled halfway across the window. She was immediately aware of the delicate fragrance of lavender and rose petals sweetening the air, and turned her head to see a good fire burning welcomingly in the grate.

Buddle went over to the windows, and opened wide the drapes, allowing the fading afternoon light to filter fully into the room, and then turned to see an unmistakable look of delight on Sarah's face as her eyes wandered over the room's decor, picked out in delicate shades of blue.

'It is a pretty room, isn't it, Miss Pennington?' she remarked, with a modicum of warmth in her voice.

'Yes, it is,' Sarah answered, running her fingers lightly down the pale blue velvet bed hangings.

'I'll just go along and collect your things from the other room. Now, is there anything else you'll be wanting?'

'If it isn't too much trouble,' Sarah replied, casting the abigail an apologetic smile, 'I'd dearly love a bath. I've not had one since leaving Somerset.'

As soon as the door had closed behind Buddle, Sarah examined her surroundings more closely. The drapes at the windows matched the bed hangings exactly, and the pale blue wallpaper was patterned with delicate bunches of flowers in shades of pink, and white. A beautifully made lace cover with scalloped edging adorned the dressing-table, on which stood several dainty scent bottles, a comb and a silver-backed hair brush.

It was undoubtedly the boudoir of a lady of fashion. And she was anything but! She grimaced at her reflection in the dressing-table mirror, disliking more than ever the dull grey gown and her plainly arranged hair. Her appearance seemed even dowdier in these lovely surroundings. But why, suddenly, did it matter so much to her how she looked? Her appearance had never worried her unduly before.

She was still pondering over this when Buddle re-entered, carrying the battered old cloak-bag and writing-case. As a result of the hasty packing back at the inn, her best pearl-grey gown was badly creased, and she looked at it in dismay. Everything, but everything seemed to be going wrong for her that day!

'Don't you worry your head over that, Miss Pennington,' Buddle said, noting the forlorn expression. 'I'll soon have it pressed. The bath is on its way. Ring when you've finished, and I'll come back to you.'

Later, when Sarah emerged from the rose-scented water, clean and refreshed, and having washed her hair, she felt slightly less disgruntled. Wrapping herself in the robe a young maidservant had brought with the towels, she rang for Buddle, and then sat at the dressing-table and studied her reflection in the glass.

The Dowager Countess had said that she had unusual colouring. Sarah turned her head on one side, considering this, as she dragged a comb through her long wet tresses. She had never given it much thought before, but she supposed she had. The finely arched dark brows and long dusky lashes made a striking contrast with hair that looked more golden than brown when touched by sunlight or a candle's glow.

Her features were regular and, looking at them dispassionately, she supposed her blue-green almond-shaped eyes were her most striking feature. She did not consider her small straight nose anything out of the common way, nor did she realise that many men found her sweetly curving lips very provocative and extremely kissable. But she had been given reason to suppose that Mr Ravenhurst considered her a pretty young woman.

She found herself, unaccountably, blushing, and was angry with herself for the unalloyed pleasure his appreciation gave her, especially as she still felt completely out of charity with him for his duplicity and high-handed treatment earlier in the day.

Buddle entering the room, accompanied by the young maid carrying several dresses over her arm, gave Sarah's thoughts a new direction, and she gazed across at the vibrantly coloured garments in wonder as the maid laid them very carefully down on the bed.

'Her ladyship said you were to make use of these, miss, until you have more suitable garments of your own to wear,' Buddle informed her, picking up the blue velvet gown and casting an expert eye over Sarah's slim, shapely figure. 'Yes, I think this will do nicely for this evening. Her ladyship has decided to eat downstairs in the dining-room, miss. So we'll need to look lively. The mistress has always kept early hours when in the country.'

'But—but who do they belong to, Buddle?' Sarah asked, gazing longingly at the dark blue velvet gown with its high neck and long tight-fitting sleeves, and wishing fervently that it was hers.

'They belong to Miss Caroline, one of her ladyship's

granddaughters. She visits every year, and left a trunk full of her belongings here after her last visit. More hair than whit, that one, Miss Pennington, but she does know what suits her. Now, while Betsy's bringing the rest of the things in, I'll see to you.'

Sarah had grown accustomed to doing most everything for herself during the past six years, and found it more than a little embarrassing to have someone else in the room while she scrambled into freshly laundered underthings. Buddle, however, seemed not to take the least notice, and set about drying the long hair on a fluffy towel.

'You have very pretty hair, miss, but it's rather heavy and is in desperate need of cutting,' the abigail remarked in her usual forthright manner and, without giving Sarah the opportunity to acquiesce, or otherwise, whipped out a pair of sharp scissors from the pocket of her starched white apron and made several judicious snips.

Sarah glanced down apprehensively at the growing pile of prettily waving long strands of hair about her feet, and earned herself a severe reprimand, much as her old governess had given her on more than one occasion when she had been a child; but she could not prevent a reluctant smile as she sat obediently rigid on the chair.

For the next few days, at least, she would find it difficult not to be in the company of at least one of three very domineering people; and unless she was prepared to make a stand right from the start, she would no doubt find herself scolded and bullied and far from gently persuaded into doing precisely what she had no earthly desire to do.

So, it would be far more comfortable in the long run if she made it abundantly clear, right from the start, that she was a young woman with a mind of her own, and had no intention whatsoever of becoming submissively docile and kowtowing to the unreasonable demands of the members of what could only be described as a despotic household.

Raising her eyes from the contemplation of the dressing-table's lacy covering, she promptly forgot her resolve to be assertive as she gazed in astonishment at her reflection in the mirror.

Buddle had gathered her hair high on her head, twisted and pinned a large portion of it into a tight circlet, and then had pulled the remaining hair through, so that it hung over one white shoulder like a silken pony's tale. She had also cut several strands very short at the front, and tiny curls now feathered across her forehead and on to her cheeks.

'Oh, Buddle, what clever fingers you have!' she enthused, still somewhat in awe over the result. 'I could never achieve anything half so elegant.'

The compliment had been spontaneous, and had sounded so sincerely meant that a suspicion of a smile hovered about the abigail's thin-lipped mouth. 'It's quite a simple style, Miss Sarah, but effective. And it's as much as I can do for you this evening. Now, let us get you into that dress. They will be awaiting you downstairs.'

Quickly hooking up the velvet gown, Buddle barely gave Sarah time to cast her eyes over the finished result in the full-length mirror before she whipped a blue-and-white silk shawl about her shoulders, and then showed her the way downstairs to the drawing-room where the Dowager and her grandson sat talking.

As the door opened, Marcus broke off what he was saying to turn his head, and for one unguarded moment could only stare in rapt admiration of his ward's transformed appearance as she moved gracefully towards them.

He rose to his feet. 'Certainly an improvement,' was the only mild praise he offered, however, before turning to his grandmother. 'Where did the dress come from?'

'It belongs to your cousin Caroline. She left one of her trunks behind the last time she paid me a visit. I doubt the silly chit has missed it.' She smiled up at Sarah. 'My dear, you look charming. Don't feel uncomfortable about making use of the other things, but we must not delay too long in purchasing some new garments of your own. There's quite a respectable little establishment in Devizes that might be worthwhile visiting.'

'I should dearly love to, my lady. Unfortunately, I have only sufficient funds to cover the rest of my travelling expenses to Hertfordshire.' She bestowed a rather sweet, but slightly provocative smile on her, now, frowning guardian. 'Unless, of course, I may have a little of the money my mother left me.'

'No, you may not!' was the unequivocal response. 'You secure your inheritance upon marriage, or attaining the age of five-and-twenty. Whichever comes first.'

'But—but that is monstrous!' Sarah was hard pressed not to scream at the injustice of it all. What had her mother been thinking of? Under the terms of the will she had been effectively prevented from becoming an independent young woman. And, what was worse, she would be virtually tied by the caprice of another for a further four years. It really didn't bear thinking about!

The Dowager could easily discern the resentment in Sarah's eyes, and cast her a sympathetic smile. 'It is in no way unusual, my dear, for matters to be settled thus.

But it need not prevent us from acquiring a new wardrobe for you.'

Scant compensation! Sarah thought bitterly, but it was not in her nature to agonise over what could not be altered, and resigned herself very quickly to making the best of it.

During dinner the Dowager and her grandson kept up a lively conversation. It soon became abundantly clear to Sarah that they were very fond of each other, and their pithy remarks and bantering exchanges caused more than one chuckle to rise in her throat.

As soon as the meal was over the ladies returned to the drawing-room. The Dowager wasted no time in extracting a promise from Sarah that she would be willing to remain at the Dower House for the time being, and then her ladyship made plans to go on the shopping expedition the following day.

'Of course, you cannot expect a provincial dressmaker to rival a London modiste, Sarah, but I do not think you will be disappointed.'

'Oh, I shan't, ma'am. I assure you. Anything has to be better than what I have at present.'

'That much is certain,' Marcus concurred, earning himself one of his ward's darkling looks as he came back into the room. 'In fact, I think I shall accompany you when you go on this trip to Devizes, just to ensure that you do not continue to tog yourself out in half-mourning.'

'If I thought that by doing so I could annoy you, I would be almost tempted,' Sarah retaliated.

'Now, now, Marcus,' the Dowager intervened quickly. 'You are not to tease the child. Sarah has agreed to stay with me for a while. But what plans have you for her future?' She saw a ghost of a smile hovering about his mouth. 'Do you intend that she should go to London for the Season?'

'Perhaps,' was his non-committal response.

'Well, you had better hurry and make a decision, my boy. It will soon be March. Precious little time to organise everything.'

At this he turned to his ward. 'Would you care for a Season, Sarah?'

His polite enquiry surprised her: she wasn't accustomed to such courtesy from him. Then her eyes began to twinkle rather wickedly. 'The object of a Season being to find a suitable spouse, I rather think I would, sir. If I am successful in my endeavours, I shall then be free of your pernicious influence.'

'Hornet!'

Sarah rose to her feet, and merely curtsied in response before turning to the Dowager. 'If you will excuse me, ma'am, I think I shall retire early. What with one thing and another, it has been a rather trying day.'

'Oh, Sarah,' Marcus said in suspicious tones, arresting her progress to the door, 'do I need to lock you in your room tonight to prevent a furtive midnight departure?'

She turned her head on one side as though giving the question due consideration. 'No, I do not think there is any necessity for that. I rather have a fancy to lull you into a false sense of security, and then abscond when you're least expecting it. That would be far more rewarding.'

'Little baggage!' he muttered after the door had closed behind her.

'Do you know, Marcus,' the Dowager remarked, highly amused, 'that gel ain't in the least afraid of you.'

'Of course she isn't! Why the devil should she be?'

'Well, you're not exactly renowned for your polite drawing-room conversation, you know.'

He dismissed this with an impatient wave of his hand. 'Sarah's not such a wigeon as to boggle at a bit of plain speaking.'

'Just as well,' responded the Dowager, eyeing her grandson for a moment with a mocking glint in her eyes, but then she became serious. 'What has been going on, Marcus? From the snippets Sarah let fall earlier, the child has had a pretty poor time of it all in Bath. And those dreadful clothes she brought with her. . .they are positively dowdy! Why, even my servants are better clad!'

'You may well ask,' he responded grimly.

She looked at him with interest, but when he offered nothing further, she changed the subject by remarking, 'I'm glad Sarah has agreed to a Season. I don't think you'll have the least trouble in getting her off your hands, Marcus. She's a lovely, prettily behaved young woman.'

'Prettily behaved?' he echoed, incredulous. 'It's quite evident that you do not know her very well, ma'am. You've no notion of the worry she's caused me. She's the most outrageous little minx! She's friendly to a fault, she'll mix with any raff and scaff and she's as trusting as bedamned! And when I think I shall need to keep an eye on her every minute throughout the Season, just to make sure she doesn't fall into any more scrapes, I'm almost tempted to retract the offer!'

The Dowager considered his remarks a trifle inflated, but refrained from further comment. In fact, during the rest of the time she remained downstairs with him, she did not mention Sarah's name again, but that night as she lay in her bed, sipping her customary cup of warm milk, she had a very thoughtful expression on her face.

Buddle, who was in the process of hanging her mistress's gown back in the wardrobe, looked suspiciously across at her. 'I know that look of old,' she remarked, coming across to the bed to relieve the Dowager of the cup. 'You're up to something.'

The Dowager did not so much as blink; her eyes remained glued to an imaginary spot on the far wall. 'What do you think to Sarah Pennington, Buddle?'

'Ah! So that's it, is it! I knew as soon as you wanted her put in Miss Agnes's old room you were up to no good. If you want my advice, you'll leave well alone, and not interfere in Master Marcus's concerns.'

'But he likes her, Buddle,' the Dowager murmured, almost to herself. 'There is that in his eyes when they rest upon her. . . There is such—such tenderness there. It is unmistakable. I've never seen him look at anyone that way before.'

Her lips curled into a satisfied smile. 'And he hasn't offered for that Bamford chit,' she went on to divulge to the woman who was not only her personal maid but also a friend and confidante. 'And I cannot say I'm sorry. Sounds a cold, heartless chit to me. Wouldn't suit him at all!'

'Be that as it may, Master Marcus still wouldn't thank you none for meddling in his private concerns. And you know it!'

The Dowager's brows snapped together as she fixed her gaze on her maid. 'Do you know, Buddle, you are becoming quite testy in your old age. Cannot imagine why. Now, go away, and leave me in peace! I need to think.'

Chapter Seven

Sarah, too, had much to ponder over before she eventually fell to sleep that night. Her main concern was not her immediate future. The Dowager Countess seemed genuinely eager to have her as a guest, and Sarah was not unhappy at the prospect of remaining in a place where she knew her presence would be welcome. But her stay here could not be an indefinite one.

Once she had attained her majority, of course, she could seek shelter with the Alcotts, and her guardian would be powerless to remove her from their sphere, but he still retained control of her fortune for a further four years. Curse him! That still rankled, but she forced herself to swallow her chagrin and concentrate her thoughts on the options open to her.

She was still determined to go to Hertfordshire and remain with dear Martha and her family for a few weeks, but, here again, to impose upon the Alcotts' hospitality for any great length of time was unthinkable. Independence had effectively been denied her until she had attained the age of five-and-twenty.

So, unless she stuck to her original plan and tried to

seek employment as a governess, or was prepared to bind herself to Mr Ravenhurst's will, which would no doubt involve living quietly somewhere with yet another female of his choosing acting as chaperon, the only other course open to her was marriage.

Sarah frowned as she stared up at the velvet canopy above her head. Strangely enough, she had never considered marrying. She didn't quite know why this should be, because all the young females of her acquaintance thought of nothing else. Perhaps, she mused, it was because she had had precious little experience of men.

Her father had died when she was very young and, with the exception of James Fenshaw, whom she had liked very much, but who had never figured in her thoughts as a prospective husband, the only other men with whom she had ever had any real dealings were the middle-aged husbands of Harriet Fairchild's friends.

Naturally, she had come into contact with many young men during her years in Bath. The Pump Room was a favourite meeting place for ladies of all ages, many of whom were dutifully escorted by some young male relative; but with very few exceptions, Sarah had considered those budding sprigs of fashion empty-headed nincompoops, who had little thought for aught else other than the latest vogue in tying a cravat, or the way to achieve a looking-glass shine on a pair of boots.

Her frown grew more pronounced. Perhaps the only man she had ever been attracted to on sight was Captain Brin Carter, and yet her feelings for him had been—well—more sisterly, really, like her feelings towards her friend Clarissa's beau. . . And the only other man, of course, with whom she had ever had more than a passing contact was. . .

Sarah's frown grew so heavy her brows almost met above the bridge of her nose. No woman in her right mind would ever consider Marcus Ravenhurst as a prospective husband! He was rich, certainly, but all the wealth in the land could never compensate for being joined in wedlock to such an arrogant, dictatorial creature! He was without doubt the rudest man she had ever met in her life. It would be impossible to find another ruder! And yet. . .

A soft, reminiscent little smile erased the scowl as her mind returned to those days spent at that inn. Her guardian could be quite kind at times, touchingly so in his little acts of thoughtfulness. Beneath that hardened exterior lay a benevolent, generous spirit. The right sort of woman, one who would not be cowed by his sharp-tongued brusqueness, could, she felt certain, mellow him in time, allowing the real essence of the man to surface.

She could do it; she felt certain of it! His caustic remarks never upset her; annoyed her sometimes, certainly, but for the most part she found his acerbic tongue highly diverting. Yes, she mused, she most certainly could sweeten the masterful Marcus Ravenhurst's vinegary disposition, and. . .

Releasing her breath in an almost imperceptible gasp, Sarah brought her wayward thoughts to heel sharply. What on earth was she thinking of? Marry Marcus Ravenhurst. . .? Why, it was unthinkable! Ludicrous! Besides, he would never take to wife someone so beneath his own station in life. Only the daughter of a duke or marquis would be good enough for him. Added to which, she didn't even like the man. . .did she?

Dressed in another borrowed gown, a pale blue dimity this time, with a high neck ending in a tiny frill, and long sleeves buttoned at the wrists, Sarah went into the room where they had dined the evening before to find her guardian sitting alone at the table, consuming a hearty breakfast. He acknowledged her with a nod, and then politely enquired whether she had slept well.

After responding that she had, which wasn't strictly true, but rather better than admitting that thoughts of him had kept her awake until the early hours, she proceeded to place several wafer-thin slices of ham on her plate and pour herself coffee; but each time she raised her eyes from the food on her plate, it was to discover her guardian staring at her in a rather disconcerting and quite unreadable way.

She tried her best to ignore him, and carried on eating in silence, but after several more minutes of this continued scrutiny she found herself asking, rather testily, 'What on earth is the matter with you now? I know more often than not you're in a churlish mood in the mornings, but must you keep staring at me as though—as though I'd a smut on my nose?'

His lips twitched in response to the waspish tone. 'You've no smut, but you do have two or three rather pretty freckles. No, no! Don't rip up at me, you little shrew!' he went on hurriedly when she looked about to do just that. 'Instead, tell me if you've a riding habit amongst those borrowed clothes of my cousin's?'

She was rather taken aback by the unexpected enquiry. 'I'm not certain. Why?'

'You can hardly go riding without one.'

'I can hardly go riding without a horse, either, come to that,' she parried, sweetly sarcastic. 'And as I do not possess a mount, the question of whether or not I can lay my hands on a habit is completely irrelevant, wouldn't you say?'

Leaning back in his chair, he regarded her from beneath hooded lids. 'Remind me to beat you some time.' He saw the slender shoulders shaking with suppressed laughter, and could not prevent a twitching smile himself. 'You really are the most provoking little witch at times, Sarah Pennington,' he informed her with gentle censure. 'Now, do you think we could possibly continue this conversation with a little less flippancy? Can you ride, child? If not, would you like me to teach you?'

For a moment Sarah regarded him in astonishment, then quickly lowered her eyes. If she had needed more proof of Harriet Fairchild's artfulness, she had been given it now. His cousin had never written to him requesting a mount for his ward, or if she had, the money had been squandered elsewhere. Sooner or later he was going to discover the full extent of his cousin's chicanery, but she had absolutely no intention of turning informer.

After quickly searching her mind for a suitable response, she said, 'Yes, I do ride, sir, but I'm a little out of practice, I'm afraid.' Which was true enough, as she had not been in the saddle since staying at her friend Clarissa's home in Devonshire during the previous summer.

'Never mind that,' he replied dismissively, rising from the table. 'I'll see what cattle my uncle's got in his stable. He's bound to have something suitable for a lady to ride. We'll soon have you up to scratch. Meet me outside in an hour. And if you cannot lay your hands on a habit, wear that deplorable grey gown of yours. It won't matter a whit if that gets ruined. In fact, it'll be a blessing if it does!' was his parting shot on closing the door.

Sarah was too excited at the prospect of riding again to concern herself over that completely unnecessary gibe. She did not linger long over her breakfast, and hurriedly made her way back up the stairs, but stopped outside the Dowager's room.

Her guardian might be quite mannerless at times, but she was not prepared to allow his shortcomings to rub off on her. She was a guest in his grandmother's house, and it was only polite to enquire if there was anything required of her before setting off on her ride.

Buddle answered the summons, admitting Sarah with a modicum of warmth in those almost black eyes which, had Sarah but known it, meant that the highly discerning middle-aged servant had made her assessment of Ravenhurst's ward and had already awarded the young person the stamp of approval.

The Dowager, still abed and propped up against a mound of frothy while pillows, was sipping a cup of sweet hot chocolate.

'Good-morning, child. I trust you slept well?'

'Quite well, thank you, ma'am.' Sarah came to stand beside the elaborately carved four-poster bed. 'Your grandson has kindly offered to take me riding this morning, but I wondered if there was any service I might perform for you before I leave?'

'My dear, you are not here to dance attendance upon me,' her ladyship responded gently, yet firmly. 'You are a guest in my house and, as such, may do precisely as you wish. Besides,' she went on, her grey eyes twinkling with wicked amusement as she cast them briefly in her formidable abigail's direction, 'Buddle might become jealous if I conferred her privileged duties on to another.'

'Ha! Privileged, indeed!' Buddle scoffed before turning

a much friendlier countenance on to Sarah. 'You'll be needing a habit, miss. I believe there is one hanging in the wardrobe in the spare bedchamber. Hardly ever been worn, as I recall. I'll go and fetch it and bring it along to your room.'

'Yes, that is something else we must attend to when we go shopping later, Sarah,' the Dowager remarked as Buddle went out. 'We'll order a habit made, and a few other gowns, but I'm sure you would much prefer to wait a while for the bulk of your new clothes, and deck yourself out in the latest fashions when we go to London.'

'We?' Sarah echoed, lips twitching. There seemed to be much the Dowager had decided upon since the evening before. 'Are you proposing to act as my duenna, ma'am?'

'Yes, my dear, I rather think I shall.' Her ladyship, looking for all the world like a very contented cat, patted the bed, and Sarah dutifully sat herself down on the edge.

'I haven't been to London for some years—not since your godmother passed away, so it's high time I bestirred myself and did a little socialising whilst I'm still able to get about reasonably well. I shall enjoy visiting my old friends. I had considered asking Henrietta to chaperon you, as she is bringing Sophia out this year, but I think you'll find it more amusing with me.'

Sarah frowned slightly. 'I'm sorry, ma'am, but I do not perfectly understand. Who is Henrietta?'

'She is the Countess of Styne, my dear, my son Henry's wife. And Sophia is their eldest daughter. Their eldest son, Bertram, is up at Oxford. The boy's an impertinent nincompoop, but harmless enough. And I shall not bore you with details of the four other children who are all still in the nursery and all equally silly.'

'I look forward to meeting them,' Sarah responded

politely, though slightly unsteadily.

'They are due home at the end of the week, so I don't expect it will be long before I receive a visit from them,' the Dowager remarked with scant enthusiasm. 'Henrietta's a wigeon, but a kind-hearted soul. I expect you'll like her—most people do. But I don't relish the prospect of spending several weeks under the same roof as my daughter-in-law. I'll have a word with Ravenhurst. I'm sure he'll grant us the use of his town house in Berkeley Square for the duration of the Season.'

The Dowager glanced across the room at the clock as she placed her empty cup on the bedside table. 'You run along now, my dear. You don't want to keep my grandson waiting. And don't be late back from your ride. I want to leave for Devizes directly after luncheon.'

Buddle was awaiting her in the bedchamber, and it took Sarah no time at all to change into the stylish gold-coloured habit, and to have her hair neatly confined in a snood before a beaver hat, dyed the exact same shade as the habit, was placed at a jaunty angle on her head. From somewhere Buddle had acquired a pair of black gloves and a riding crop, and as Sarah emerged from the house, she felt for the first time in her life quite the young lady of fashion.

She found to her surprise that the stableyard was deserted, and so decided to fill the time while awaiting her guardian's arrival by inspecting the exterior of what was to be her dwelling place for the next few weeks.

The late February sun was doing its best to brighten the setting, picking out the pinkish hues in the Dower House's grey stone and striving to cast its rays into those numerous shadowy areas of what could only be described as a very neglected, overgrown garden, but it was battling against overwhelming odds. Sarah cast a frowning glance up at the tall trees. Even now, still bared of their greenery, those stately beeches and elms managed to make their presence felt by blocking out most of that much-needed light.

She had noticed the evening before that Clegg had gone about lighting the candles very early because the rooms on the ground floor were so gloomy. It was such a shame, really, Sarah thought, looking along the front aspect of the fine Elizabethan building.

It was a charming house, not large, but elegantly appointed and very comfortable. Two or three industrious men would soon have the gardens in order, and if a few of those trees were felled the light could filter into the rooms, making them much more cheerful.

The sound of hoofbeats reached her ears, and she turned to see Ravenhurst, astride a large bay and leading another mount, disappear under the archway. Picking up her skirts, she hurried along the path to the stables to catch him in the act of dismounting.

'Ah, so there you are!' His expression was one of approval as he watched her approach. 'I was just about to go searching for you. I cannot tell you how relieved I am to discover you're a female who can be on time!'

'I came out a few minutes ago. I've been taking a look at the garden.'

His expression changed dramatically. 'It's damned disgraceful!' he declared, not mincing words. 'I've already told the Dowager she ought to have these confounded trees chopped down, but she won't listen.'

Sarah could not prevent a smile at this. 'And what would you say, sir, if people tried to tell you what you should do with the gardens at Ravenhurst?'

'Tell 'em to mind their own business!'

'Precisely! You are very like your grandmother, you know.'

'Hornet!' he responded, but far from nastily, as he helped her into the saddle.

It took Marcus a few minutes only to satisfy himself that his ward was a very competent rider. She sat the hack gracefully and had good light hands.

'I wish I'd sorted you out something with a bit more spirit, child,' he remarked, casting her sluggish mount a frowning glance, 'but I thought it wisest to be cautious as you gave me the impression that you ride infrequently. Which I find very strange,' he went on matter-of-factly, 'considering I received a letter from my cousin requesting funds to purchase a horse for you, as riding was one of your favourite pastimes. And I have been paying stabling costs for almost a year.'

Sarah kept her gaze firmly fixed between her horse's ears, but instinctively knew her guardian was staring at her. Only honesty would serve, now. Ravenhurst was no fool, and had probably worked out for himself where her allowance had been going.

'As soon as I came to know you a little, I knew you would never have quibbled over furnishing me with a mount,' she said at length.

'Where has your allowance been going, Sarah? Gaming?'

'I think so.' She heard him muttering something under his breath, and found herself coming to Mrs Fairchild's defence. 'You mustn't think I have been ill-used, sir. Your cousin was always very kind to me.'

'Kind!' he ejaculated. 'I'll give her kind when I see her! Squandering your allowance on her own pleasures, whilst you went about in clothes fitted only for a servant. No wonder the confounded woman very nearly swooned when I turned up unexpectedly! She realised the game was up!'

Knowing that in his present mood it would be a waste of breath trying to make him view his cousin in a less derogatory light, Sarah encouraged him to vent all that pent-up condemnation on a different source by quite deliberately asking how Mrs Stanton had taken her daughter's elopement. It had the desired effect.

'And well may you ask, my girl!' The dark brows snapped together. 'What the devil do you mean by getting yourself involved in that disgraceful affair?'

'Clarissa has always been my closest friend, sir,' she answered, far from cowed by his staunch disapproval of her actions. 'And I'm very fond of James, too. I couldn't bear to see them made unhappy because of the selfish caprice of their respective fathers who, I might add, before a silly difference of opinion, actively encouraged their children's close friendship.'

She turned her head to look at him, and he could not mistake the flicker of combined sadness and regret in her eyes. 'Was Mrs Stanton very angry with me?'

He quickly discovered he was not proof against that look, and didn't hesitate to reassure her. 'No. In fact, I gained the distinct impression that she was more disturbed by your sudden flight than her daughter's.'

'I knew it!' Sarah exclaimed triumphantly, her aquamarine eyes sparkling again. 'I always thought that deep down Mrs Stanton was not happy with the state of affairs. She thinks a great deal of James, so I guessed she was far from opposed to the match.'

'Be that as it may, my girl!' he countered, his

disapproval returning. 'You ought not to have become involved. I well expect to receive a visit from your friend's father after my blood!'

'Oh, I shouldn't worry, if I were you,' she said dismissively. 'He's a blustering, bad-tempered individual at times but, believe me, you're more than a match for him, sir.' Sarah, the perfection of her forehead suddenly marred by a deep frown of concern, kept her eyes firmly fixed between her mount's ears, and so missed the look of almost comical outrage on her guardian's face. 'I think it most unlikely that Mr Stanton will seek you out. No, he's far more likely to go after Clarissa and James.'

A tiny sigh escaped her. 'I cannot help worrying about them, sir. James said it would take five or six days to reach the border. But, of course, he wasn't making allowances for a deterioration in the weather.'

Once again he found sympathy coming to the fore. 'Then you can stop worrying, child!' he ordered with a kind of rough gentleness. 'Before we left the inn yesterday, I learned from the magistrate that only the southern counties were affected by snow. No doubt your friends had a very tedious, but quite uneventful, journey to Scotland. And who knows, they might at this very moment be standing before that infamous anvil!'

He cast her a reassuring smile. 'If it will ease your mind, I shall try to discover the outcome when I collect my greys from Bath in a few days' time.'

He then changed the subject and, as they continued their ride, pointed out various features of interest on his uncle's vast estate. When the huge Restoration mansion came into view, he caused more than one amused chuckle to rise in Sarah's throat by his scathing condemnation of the imposing ancestral home. He stigmatised the building as a great draughty barn of a place.

It was his considered opinion that the addition of the two new wings during the previous century had ruined what little architectural beauty the house had ever possessed; and as if that were not bad enough, his great-grandfather, apparently terrified of a fire breaking out, had instigated the construction of a new kitchen area, which was only accessible through miles of corridor. Consequently, by the time meals arrived at the dining-room they were always cold.

Secretly, Sarah, too, thought it rather an unprepossessing structure with little to commend it, but was far too well-bred to comment. The park, on the other hand was very much to her taste. With the exception of a small area near the eastern boundary, the landscape was quite beautiful with its sweeping lawns, rippling streams and large clumps of majestic trees.

She frowned as they began to skirt the overgrown area. 'Why has this part been allowed to develop into a wilderness, sir?'

'A couple of centuries ago a woman accused of being a witch was dragged here by some of the villagers. Before she drowned, she was heard to put a curse on this place.'

He raised his eyes heavenwards. 'Complete nonsense, of course! Still, I suppose there's some justification for the superstition,' he added fair-mindedly. 'An ancestor met his death near this very spot, and my uncle came perilously close to drowning here himself when he was a youth. There's a good-sized lake hidden behind that wall of overgrown shrubs and brambles. If you like, we'll try to find a way through and I'll show it to you.'

Possessing an inquisitive rather than a fanciful nature, Sarah did not hesitate. After tethering their horses to the branch of a tree, they forged a way through the shrubbery, Sarah finding the brambles' wickedly clawing thorns more threatening than any supposed curse. When they did eventually arrive at the lakeside, she looked about her in dismay at the sheer neglect of what once must have been an idyllic spot.

Taking a hold of one slender gloved hand, Marcus led the way along the overgrown path round the water's edge. 'You can't deny, Sarah, it's an eerie place. Listen to that high-pitched wailing! The witch, I suspect.'

'That's the wind,' she scoffed.

'You think so? Well, you may be right. But what about those ghostly forms rising from the lake?'

'Mist. And you know it.' She detected the slight movement of broad shoulders shaking with suppressed laughter. 'You can stop trying to frighten me because you won't succeed! Tell me, instead, what that building is just ahead?'

'It's the old boat-house. Not used now, of course. Since my uncle's unfortunate experience, no one ever comes here.'

'Well, someone most certainly does,' Sarah countered as they arrived at the stone-built structure. A raised wooden platform had been constructed along the front wall, from which one gained access to a rather rickety-looking jetty that reached out some distance into the lake. 'And has been here quite recently, I should say,' she added, staring down at the clearly visible wet footprints.

Ravenhurst walked across the platform to the far side of the boat-house. 'Well, well, my dear! We evidently disturbed a trespasser. He's left his catch.'

Sarah looked down at the four large fish lying in the grass. 'A poacher?'

'More than likely. He must have seen or heard us approaching, and made himself scarce.' He scanned the dense area of shrubs to his right. 'No doubt he's watching our every move at this very moment.'

'Are you going to inform your uncle when he returns?' Sarah asked tentatively, but instinctively knew what his response would be even before he said,

'Certainly not! That lake must be teaming with fish. The Earl makes no use of them, and if some unfortunate wretch can provide himself with a decent meal, I shan't be the one to throw a rub in his way.' There was certainly more than just a hint of devilment in the smile he cast her. 'Come, let us away, so the poor fellow can collect his dinner.'

Their arrival back at the Dower House a short while later coincided with that of a very elegant travelling-carriage. Sarah watched with interest as a sparse man in his forties, dressed in a suit of severe black cloth, alighted. He then took a few rather mincing steps away from the equipage before bowing with studied elegance to Mr Ravenhurst.

'Ah, Quilp! In good time. Two pairs of my boots are in urgent need of your meticulous attention. You know your way.' Thus disposing of his valet, Marcus then acknowledged his stable lad who had driven the carriage to Somerset before turning his gaze on to his head groom who had not, even by the slight raising of his bushy, greying brows, betrayed the fact that he had recognised Sarah.

Ravenhurst's thin lips curled into a not unappreciative smile. 'I trust your journey passed without incident, Sutton. This young lady, whom you've never met before, is my ward, Miss Pennington.'

Although she had had little conversation with the groom during her stay at the Inn, only ever passing the time of day, Sarah flatly refused to partake in her guardian's rather childish and totally unnecessary game of pretence. She acknowledged the head groom with her friendly smile, asked him how he went on, and then returned to the house to change back into the dress she had been wearing earlier that morning.

When she returned downstairs, Clegg informed her that luncheon was not quite ready to be served, so she took herself off to the library and began writing a letter to Mrs Stanton.

She had felt untold relief to learn that her friend's mother bore her no ill-will. After apologising once again for the part she had played in Clarissa's elopement—which, in fact, had been woefully small—she began to relate what had befallen her since she had left Bath, which had been a mere five days, but which seemed like a lifetime ago.

She had just reached the part where Mr Ravenhurst had arrived at the inn when she was disturbed by a tapping sound, and turned her head to see the man himself standing on the other side of the window, beckoning to her with an imperious hand.

Rising from the desk, Sarah went across to open the windows, and Marcus, lifting one muscular, booted-leg over the sill, stepped into the room.

A frown of disapproval creased her brow. 'Why you cannot use the door like anyone—' Sarah caught herself up abruptly as his actions struck a chord of memory. 'Do that again!'

'Do what again?'

'Climb out of the window.'

He regarded her suspiciously. 'You're not going to close them by any chance, so that I have to walk round to the front door?'

'Of course not! Just do as I ask!'

He looked far from convinced, but obediently repeated the procedure. 'Satisfied, now?'

'That's it!' Excitement brought a sparkle to her eyes. 'That's what I found so odd on the night of Mr Nutley's death!'

Chapter Eight

Marcus regarded her in frowning silence for a moment. 'What precisely struck you as odd?'

'The way that intruder climbed out of the parlour window at the inn. I knew there was something peculiar about the action at the time, but it wasn't until I watched you just now that I realised precisely what had puzzled me. Here, let me show you.'

Brushing past, Sarah sat on the window-sill. Then, gathering the folds of her skirts beneath her, she swung both legs over the ledge together. 'That is how our intruder did it, just as any female would perform the feat.'

'Are you trying to tell me that you think, now, our mysterious cloaked figure might possibly have been a woman?' He helped her back inside, and then securely fastened the windows. 'The evidence on which to base such a judgement, if you'll forgive me saying so, child, seems rather flimsy.'

'Yes, perhaps it does,' she conceded. 'But the intruder's actions appeared so natural, just as though he—she was accustomed to wearing skirts. If my memory serves me correctly, that window at the inn was about the same distance from the ground as this one. The intruder was wearing breeches, so why didn't he simply step over the sill as you did? I could quite easily do so if I wore breeches.'

Marcus moved across to the small table on which several decanters stood and, at Sarah's shake of the head, poured out just one glass of wine. He sipped the rich dark liquid meditatively, then said, 'Assuming you're right, and I'm far from convinced myself, who are we looking at? Your actress friend, that middle-aged spinster and the farmer's wife.'

'I think we can safely rule out the farmer's wife,' Sarah responded with a twitching smile. 'She was, as you no doubt recall, a lady built on generous lines. Although that cloak concealed the intruder's identity, it couldn't possibly mask a person's size, at least not to that extent. Our intruder was much slimmer and rather taller, if my memory serves me correctly.'

'Could it have been the "Divine" Dorothea, then?'

Sarah gave the question due consideration as she resumed her seat at the desk. 'It's certainly possible, yet my instinct tells me otherwise.'

'What makes you so sure that it wasn't her?'

'Because Dottie is my height, and although I saw the intruder for a few brief moments only, I feel certain she was taller than I. And then there was that letter found on the murdered servant girl. It was rather a clumsy way of trying to incriminate Dottie in Nutley's death, don't you agree?'

Tossing the contents of his glass down his throat, Marcus came across to sit himself on the edge of the desk. 'Given what we now know—yes, I do. No doubt Stubbs will not fail to check out Dottie's story when he returns to London, but I for one do not doubt the truth of it.'

He was silent for a moment, absently swinging one well-muscled leg to and fro. 'Like Dottie, that servant girl was illiterate. Even supposing the girl did come across that letter, it would have meant nothing to her. But she certainly discovered something about someone, and evidently didn't hesitate in stooping to a little blackmail. And I think whoever murdered her planted Dottie's letter on the dead girl's body.'

'And you think the intruder and the person who murdered the servant girl are one and the same person? And that that person was someone staying at the inn, don't you, sir?'

'Yes, child, I do.' He stared down into her troubled eyes. 'Let us go through events step by step. I think you would agree that no one putting up at that inn did so by design. Taking that fact into account, it's highly unlikely that Nutley arranged to meet anyone there. Also, taking into account the state of the roads, it was impossible for our cloaked figure to have travelled very far.'

'But don't forget that it was possible to walk into the village,' she reminded him.

'True. And I'm sure it didn't take long for word to spread that the inn was filled with stranded travellers—easy pickings for someone willing to take a few risks, you might say. Very well, let's deal with that possibility first, and assume someone from the village did break in. His motive for doing so must have been robbery, wouldn't you say?' and he watched her nod in response. 'Yet nothing was stolen.'

'I know.' Sarah looked up at him intently. 'But Mr

Nutley's appearance would have put a stop to the burglar's intentions, surely?'

'You would certainly have thought so, wouldn't you? We still cannot be sure whether Nutley's death was an accident, or not. But let's assume for argument's sake that it was. There was a scuffle between him and the intruder. Nutley slipped, possibly knocking over the chair that we found upturned, hit his head on the settle and broke his neck. The noise woke you. How much time elapsed, after you had woken, before you entered the parlour?'

She shrugged. 'Perhaps five minutes, not much more.'

'And yet our villager, bent on a little petty theft, was still there.' The look he cast her was openly sceptical. 'Theft is one thing—being accused of murder is quite another. Had our intruder been some petty thief, I feel certain he would have departed, instanter!'

Sarah chewed these particulars over for a few moments and quickly came to the same conclusion. 'So why did our intruder remain, sir?'

'That's exactly the point! Why, my dear Sarah? Petty theft certainly wasn't the reason. Nutley had a purse in his pocket containing several sovereigns, there was a timepiece attached to his waistcoat and he was wearing a gold signet ring. All could have been quite easily filched in the time it took for you to get downstairs.'

'How very odd!' Sarah's brows drew together in a puzzled frown. 'What on earth was our cloaked figure doing, then, during that time?'

'I doubt foolishly trying to revive Nutley.' Marcus moved across to the decanters once more to refill his glass. 'Let us leave that for now and move on to yet another very interesting fact—the quite deliberate drugging of that rum punch. Nutley's intention, I feel fairly certain, was not to drug everyone. If that were the case, he would have tried harder to coax both you and me into accepting a glass. But he didn't. . . Why?'

Sarah gazed up into his intelligent dark eyes as he resumed his former position on the desk. 'I suppose it might have aroused suspicion had he done so.'

'Very true. . .or,' he continued after the briefest of pauses, 'it was of little importance to him whether we imbibed or not because his intended victim had already accepted a glass.'

He watched her lovely, expressive face closely and knew the instant enlightenment had dawned.

'Of course! Mr Stubbs!'

'Clever girl!' he remarked approvingly. 'Nutley was sharing a bedchamber with the Runner, and it's my belief that some time during that day he got wind of Stubbs's profession. But ask yourself this, Sarah—why should this knowledge bother him? Why should he want Stubbs drugged, dead to the world?'

Her puzzled frown returned. 'Well, we can be fairly certain that it wasn't because he had arranged to meet someone at the inn and didn't want Stubbs to witness that meeting. So, perhaps, he had something to hide? Something in his possession that he was terrified of Mr Stubbs discovering.'

'Precisely! And that is what I believe took Nutley back down to the parlour. I think he was endeavouring to hide something until he was able to continue his journey. Now, nothing incriminating was found on his person, nor amongst his possessions, and Stubbs and I searched that parlour thoroughly and discovered nothing out of the way.'

'So, you think our cloaked intruder took whatever it was Mr Nutley was endeavouring to hide?'

'I think he, or she, was searching for it, certainly, but without success, because you, my dear, inadvertently interrupted proceedings. Stubbs and I are positive that someone searched our rooms, possibly during the time we were interviewing you in the parlour. If our cloaked friend had found what Nutley had hidden, there would have been no need to search further.'

'You know, sir,' Sarah said after several moments' intense thought, 'the more I think about it, the more convinced I am that you are right, and that cloaked figure was amongst the guests staying at that inn. He or she must have heard Nutley leave his room that night, and followed him downstairs. Though, precisely who it was I cannot imagine. What is more, it seems he or she knew that Mr Nutley had something to hide. And if Nutley was involved in something underhanded, do you think this person might have been, well, an accomplice?'

He shrugged. 'It's possible, but we can only speculate on that, child. I'm just glad we're well out of it now.' He dismissed it from his mind, and gazed down at the letter she had been writing, one dark brow rising when he caught the name of the intended recipient. 'Ha! Guilty conscience, I see!'

She cast him a disapproving frown. 'You appear to have a propensity for reading other people's letters.'

'And those destined for myself!' he countered, his frown as pronounced as her own, as he recalled clearly the contents of the letter that he had found in her writing-case. 'How long did you intend keeping me in the dark as to your true identity?'

'I had every intention of informing you the day after

our arrival at the inn. But you were in such a disagreeable mood at breakfast. And then finding Mr Nutley that way. . . Oh, I don't know! The right moment just never seemed to arise.' She received not so much a growl in response to this as a grunt. 'Well, you could just as easily have informed me that you knew who I was,' she added in her defence.

'What? And risk your doing something bird-witted like loping off in the dead of night? Not a chance!'

She satisfied herself with casting him a look of impatience, and as Clegg entered the room a moment later to inform them that luncheon was about to be served, the topic of conversation ceased.

After they had all eaten, the Dowager was all eagerness to set off on their trip to Devizes. Mr Ravenhurst had mentioned that he might well accompany them on the shopping expedition, but Sarah, having by this time acquired a fair knowledge of his character, was not in the least surprised when he informed them quite bluntly that he had no intention of doing so, as he had one or two urgent letters he must write.

She was not very surprised, either, when he took it upon himself, in his usual high-handed manner, to organise their transport. Refusing point blank to permit his ward to travel even a short distance in what he stigmatised as her ladyship's antiquated bone-shaker of a berlin, which might easily become stuck in the inches of mud still lying on many of the minor roads after the recent thaw, he ordered his grandmother's team of handsome bays harnessed to his own well-sprung and far more comfortable carriage.

Not surprisingly, neither lady objected to these arrangements, and the short journey was achieved swiftly and without mishap.

Naturally, the small town could not offer those elegant establishments to be found in Bath, but Sarah was far from disappointed. For years she could only stare longingly at the pretty, frivolous bonnets and elegant gowns offered for sale; now, however, she could enter shops, confident in the knowledge that anything that happened to take her fancy would be hers for the asking.

She quickly discovered that the Dowager Countess of Styne was well known. No sooner had they entered the town's most fashionable shop, owned by a lady who had for a time worked under one of London's most famous modistes, than chairs were swiftly found for the distinguished customer and her young protégée. She quickly discovered, too, that her notion of an adequate wardrobe was certainly far removed from the Dowager's.

Lengths of silks, satins, muslins and velvets were brought out for inspection, whilst Sarah was pulled this way and that and her measurements taken with ruthless efficiency. Day dresses, walking dresses, pelisses and spencers were ordered to be made as quickly as possible and sent to Styne, and several lengths of material, including a very pretty turquoise silk, which the Dowager considered ideal for an evening gown, were parcelled up and placed in the carriage.

All Sarah's protestations fell on deaf ears. In the other shops the Dowager's reckless spending continued. A more than adequate supply of undergarments and nightwear was purchased before bonnets, shoes, gloves and many, many more 'absolute necessities', according to the Dowager, were chosen by her with blatant disregard for cost.

When they eventually arrived back at the Dower House, Sarah could only watch in silent dismay as the servants, having to make several journeys, collected the multitude of packages from the carriage and carried them up to her room.

Marcus emerged from the library to find his ward, a look of combined anxiety and guilt on her face, and the Dowager, a look of pleasurable satisfaction on hers, divesting themselves of cloaks and bonnets.

'What's the matter, child? Has my indomitable grandmother worn you out?'

'No such thing!' her ladyship put in before Sarah could open her mouth. 'She's been all of a twitter for most of the afternoon. Can't imagine why. Unless she's worried that you'll come the ugly, Marcus, at laying out blunt for a few little necessities.'

'A few little. . .?' Sarah placed a restraining hand on her guardian's arm as he made to follow the Dowager into the drawing-room. 'Sir, I couldn't stop her,' she told him, real perturbation sounding in her voice. 'I tried. Truly, I did! But she just wouldn't listen.'

'A family failing, I'm afraid,' he responded, casually pulling her arm through his and guiding her into the room his grandmother had entered. 'So don't waste your breath in trying, my child.'

Sarah knew that that was his rather tactful way of telling her that he simply wasn't interested in how much money had been squandered that afternoon. He was so wealthy, of course, that the day's expenditure represented a mere drop in the ocean, but Sarah could not reconcile her conscience with such wanton extravagance.

That night, dressed in one of her new nightgowns, she sat at the small table in her room, and poured out her thoughts in the letter she had begun earlier in the day to her friend's mother.

The words flowed so easily from her pen as her reflections centred on her guardian. What a surprisingly complex creature he had turned out to be! she wrote. He bore no resemblance whatsoever to the mean-spirited tyrant of her imaginings.

And just why his cousin Harriet Fairchild held him in such lively dread she could not imagine, because he was, for the most part, an agreeable man who could be quite touchingly thoughtful at times. The quill in her hand stilled suddenly, and she raised her eyes to stare blindly at the delicately patterned wallpaper.

Yes, why had she heard so many bad reports about Marcus Ravenhurst during her years in Bath? she wondered. Most of what she had been told was complete and utter nonsense. True, he could be very abrupt at times, and he certainly didn't suffer fools gladly, but he was far from the unfeeling monster she had been led to believe.

His appearance was against him, though, she mused. One glimpse of that heavy scowl would send the timid scurrying away even before he had opened his mouth, and she could quite understand why many a faint-hearted female might find his brusqueness a trifle off-putting. He could hardly be described as handsome, either, or of having a kindly face, but he did have a rather wonderful smile.

And there was no denying he was a fine figure of a man. Broad shouldered and muscular, he was ruggedly attractive and, therefore, must surely appeal to many members of her sex. Added to which he had many fine qualities. So, why then had he never married?

The thought, unbidden, came into her head, and she

absently brushed the feathers of her quill back and forth across her chin while pondering over this rather surprising circumstance. He had no title, it was true, but he was excessively wealthy. Could it be this fact alone that had kept him a bachelor? Was he wary of being coveted only for his great wealth?

If that was the case, she could quite understand why matrimony held no appeal for him. Why, it was despicable to marry someone merely for money! Yet, she was worldly-wise enough to know that both men and women did just that.

But supposing he did meet someone who loved him for himself; what sort of husband would he make? Her lips curled into a wicked little smile. Well, he would certainly wish to rule the roost. Which was only right and proper, she decided fair-mindedly. A man ought to make the decisions, and shoulder the responsibilities.

Sadly, though, given Mr Ravenhurst's temperament, if he eventually married some milk-and-water miss who hadn't the courage to stand up to him, he would be in grave danger of degenerating into nothing more than a rather unpleasant autocrat. On the other hand, though, if he married a girl of spirit, and one who, moreover, coveted the man and not his money, she felt sure he would be a devoted husband, attentive to his wife's every need.

She felt certain, too, that he was a man capable of deeply tender feelings who, when parted from his love, would no doubt write long and affectionate letters, letters intended for her eyes alone, which she would keep safely hidden away.

Instinctively, Sarah's fingers sought the little device which opened the secret compartment in her writing case, but nothing happened. She frowned as she set aside her quill. The spring was stiff, she knew, but it seemed almost as if something was jamming it, preventing the flap from opening. She tried again, but it took several more attempts before she eventually succeeded, and the flap reluctantly opened

'What on earth. . .?'

Very carefully she eased the tightly wedged object out of the compartment, and laid it across her hand. For several moments it was as much as she could do to stare down at it in astonished disbelief, then, throwing on her robe, she rushed from the room, almost colliding with Buddle in her headlong flight along the passageway.

Ravenhurst, comfortably established in bed, propped against a mound of pillows, hardly had time to raise his eyes from the book he was reading, and answer the imperious tattoo, before the door was thrown wide and Sarah charged into the room.

'Great heaven's, child!' He regarded her keenly. 'Whatever's the matter?'

'Oh, sir!' Breathless more from excitement than from her headlong dash along the passageway, Sarah plumped herself down on the bed, and almost threw her incredible find on to the coverlet in front of him. 'Just you look at that!'

Setting aside the book, he obeyed the command, casting only the most cursory glance at the necklace before raising enquiring eyes to hers. 'Well, and what of it?'

'But, sir, don't you see? It isn't mine!' she informed him in some agitation, slightly nettled by his lack of interest. 'I found it wedged in the secret compartment of my writing-case.'

At this his attitude changed abruptly. 'Did you, now?' Spreading the necklace out, he studied it more closely.

'I've seen you before,' he murmured. 'But where have I seen you?'

He looked back at Sarah, who was in the process of making herself more comfortable on his bed by tucking her slender feet beneath her. Her robe was unfastened, and the movement caused the material of her nightgown to pull taut, clearly revealing the tantalising outline of young, firm breasts.

He cleared his throat, made a mental note not to leave it very much longer before he made a trip to London to visit his mistress, and then forced himself to concentrate on the mystery in hand. 'So, your writing-case has a hidden compartment, has it? Have you no idea how long this gaud has been in there?'

'Well, no, not really,' she confessed. 'You see, I don't ever use it, so I—' She broke off, her eyes narrowing. 'No, wait a moment! The morning after we arrived at the inn, I was showing it to Mr Nutley, and the necklace certainly wasn't there then.'

He did not respond, and after a few moments she raised her eyes to find him regarding her rather quizzically, and the reason for the look was obvious.

'Oh, no! You don't think that this was what Mr Nutley was so afraid of a certain someone discovering in his possession, and so hid it in my case?'

'That is precisely what I think, child, because I've just recalled where I've seen this necklace before. . . The last time I set eyes on it, it was adorning the neck of Lady Felchett.'

He picked it up, studying the glinting jewels beneath the candle's glow. 'I don't know, though. I'm certainly no expert, but it looks to me—' He checked on what he had been about to say when he noticed Sarah staring in unblushing fascination at his naked torso. 'Something seems to be puzzling you, child?'

'Yes, it's that.' She didn't hesitate to respond, pointing rather rudely at the triangular mat of dark hair covering his chest. 'Are all men similarly cursed with all that hair on their bodies?'

'Cursed with. . .? You really are the most outrageous little baggage, Sarah!' he scolded, slightly affronted by this slur on his manliness but, far from cowed, she dissolved into laughter.

'I'm sorry,' she apologised, wiping her streaming eyes with the back of her hand, 'but it came as rather a shock. You see, I've never seen a man without his clothes on before.'

'Good God! I sincerely trust not!'

A further gurgle escaped her. 'You know very well what I mean. I shouldn't have been surprised, though,' she admitted. 'I did notice when you came to my bedchamber, that time at the inn, that you had hairs at the base of your throat, but I didn't realise just how far they spread.'

She watched as he, with all the modesty of an embarrassed virgin, pulled the bedcovers further up his chest, and chuckled again. 'Do you never wear a nightshirt, sir? Not that I suppose there's much need,' she went on, not giving him the opportunity to answer. 'With all that on your person you must be warm enough.'

'God in heaven!' He clapped a hand over his eyes. 'What will the outrageous chit say next? And kindly move yourself—you're sitting on my feet!'

Sarah altered her position. 'I think it might be best if we concentrate on the diamond necklace,' she suggested with what he considered the most provocative feminine smile he had ever witnessed. 'What do you intend doing with it? Are you going to return it to Lord Felchett?'

He scratched the side of his head, ruffling his dark hair into disarray. 'No. I suppose I'll need to pay a visit to Bristol, and see if I cannot locate Stubbs,' he responded without much enthusiasm. 'I intended making a return trip to Bath in a few days, anyway. So I shall go to Bristol first, and then go on to Bath afterwards.'

He could clearly read the unspoken question in her eyes. 'Yes, Sarah, I fully intend to pay a visit on my swindling cousin. And I shall also call upon Mrs Stanton while I'm there, and discover if she has heard anything from your runaways.'

Sarah brightened at this. 'Oh, would you give her my letter, sir? I've nearly finished it. I'll return to my room and do so now.'

She had only just slipped her feet back on to the floor when the door was thrown wide, and the Dowager came purposefully into the room. 'What is the meaning of this?' she demanded in outraged tones. 'Sarah, return to your room at once!'

'Yes, you run along now, child,' Marcus urged gently before she had time to open her mouth and explain the reason for her presence in his bedchamber. 'Finish your letter, and then give it to one of the servants to bring along to me. I intend leaving early in the morning, so I'll bid you farewell now.'

The Dowager bade her a curt good-night, and then waited for the door to close behind Sarah before moving towards the bed where her far from penitent grandson regarded her with a wickedly mocking gleam in his eyes.

'What do you mean by permitting that child to visit

you in your bedchamber, Marcus? Have you such scant regard for her reputation?'

'Oh, for heaven's sake!' he responded in combined exasperation and amusement. 'What the devil did you think I was proposing to do. . .ravish the girl?'

She could not prevent a twitching smile at this. 'No, I did not. You have faults enough, but despoiling innocent damsels isn't one of them. But Sarah is an exceedingly pretty young woman, and—'

'Yes, I had noticed.'

'And you are a man.'

'I wouldn't be at all surprised if Sarah hasn't come to that conclusion, too.'

'Marcus!' The Dowager rapped her cane on the floor. 'This is no time for flippancy! Who will believe her innocent if she continues to visit you in your bedchamber?'

He regarded her for a moment in brooding silence. 'Yes, you're right, of course,' he admitted, rather reluctantly it seemed to her. 'I'll have a word with Sarah when I get back. But in the meantime,' he went on, giving her back look for look, 'I won't have you scolding the child. The last thing in the world I want is for her to be afraid or embarrassed to come to me.'

She assured him that she had absolutely no intention of doing so and, satisfied, he turned his attention once more to the necklace, requesting her to take a look at it, and explaining how it came to be in his possession.

'I don't care for it very much,' the Dowager remarked when she had learned all. 'The setting is rather heavy. Quite ugly, in fact! No doubt the Felchetts will be relieved to have it restored to them, though. Which is more than the Nutleys will experience when they learn about the goings-on. One cannot but sympathise, Marcus. It is one thing to discover your offspring is dead, and quite another to learn he was nothing more than a common thief.'

'Nutley was a nincompoop, ma'am,' her grandson responded, betraying his scant regard for the deceased. 'I should be very surprised if his was the brain behind the robbery.' And that is precisely what concerns me, he added silently.

The following morning Marcus was up early, and went out to the stableyard even before his ward had left her room. He had sent a message for Jeb's bays to be harnessed to his curricle and for his young stable lad to accompany him, and everything was in readiness for his departure.

Sutton cast a rather petulant look up at his subordinate, who was already seated in the carriage, keeping the bays well under control, before slanting a rather hopeful glance in his master's direction. 'Will you be collecting the greys, sir? Cause ifen you are, I could quite easily go wi' young Ben 'ere, and save you the bother.'

Marcus could not prevent a smile as he climbed up on to the seat beside the young groom and took the reins from him. He knew Sutton must be feeling peeved at not being the one to accompany him, but this time he had far more important work for his head groom.

'I have business in Bristol first, Sutton. Then I shall go on to Bath. I don't know just how long I'll be away, but it's important you remain here. I need you to watch over my ward whilst I'm gone.'

Sutton's ears pricked up at this, and he looked up at his master in some alarm. 'Lord bless me! She ain't likely to lope off again, is she, sir?'

This drew another smile from his master, but it seemed much softer this time. 'No, Sutton, rest easy. Now having come to know my ward, I can safely promise you that she wouldn't do that. That isn't my Sarah's way. But I want you to accompany her whenever she ventures out of doors. Never let her go off on her own, whether on foot or horseback. I don't care what excuses you need to make, so long as you never let her out of your sight.'

There was no semblance of a smile, now, and his eyes grew flint-like as he stared down at the ground. 'Guard her with your life, Sutton. . .I would not be best pleased if aught ever happened to my Sarah.'

Chapter Nine

It was difficult to believe that within the space of less than two weeks there could be such a marked change in the weather. But so it was. February with its biting-cold winds and snowstorms was well and truly a thing of the past. March had arrived, bringing with it pleasant days of mild sunshine and almost cloudless skies, though the nights continued to be cold and there was always a light covering of hoar-frost by morning.

Spring seemed to have arrived, surprisingly, quite early. Everywhere the light greenish hues of new growth were to be seen, and Sarah, having always been an avid walker, ventured out of doors much more often. Her strolls around the Dowager's garden, however, soon began to pall. Like Ravenhurst, she found the overgrown grounds rather depressing, and decided to venture further afield.

The previous day she had walked across the Earl's vast estate and had spent a very pleasant afternoon exploring the home wood; and today she had decided to inspect the pretty village that she had passed through on the day her guardian had brought her to the Dower House.

She had almost reached the main driveway leading to the big house when she became aware of the sound of heavy footsteps, and turned to see Sutton striding purposefully in her direction. Since Mr Ravenhurst's departure, six days before, Sutton had ridden out with her each morning, and she most certainly didn't object to his company.

The groom made a cheerful companion, and his rather dry sense of humour never failed to amuse her. Apart from this, he knew the county well, and had shown her some of the more pleasant rides, and had escorted her to several places of interest round about.

She had been rather surprised, though, suddenly to come across him in the home wood the day before. Her eyes narrowed suspiciously. Yes, that encounter might well have been purely accidental. But for it to happen twice in as many days was just too much of a coincidence!

'Well, well, Sutton,' she greeted him as he reached her side. 'What a surprise! I expect, like me, you decided on the spur of the moment to enjoy this rather pleasant afternoon sunshine and go out for a walk.'

'Aye, that's it, ma'am!' He made a sound suspiciously like a sigh of relief. 'There ain't much for me to do back at the stables with the master away.'

'No, quite. You'll no doubt be pleased to return to Ravenhurst and your own domain.' They reached the main driveway, and Sarah's lips curled into a wicked little smile. 'Where were you thinking of walking? Up to the big house?'

As this seemed the most obvious goal, Sutton did not hesitate. 'Aye, that's right, ma'am.'

'In that case, I'm afraid we must part company. My destination lies in quite another direction.' The expression on his face was so ludicrous that Sarah dissolved into laughter. 'Oh, Sutton! You must consider me the veriest dunderhead! How long did you suppose it would take me to work out your little ploy?'

The suspicion of a blush showed beneath the weathered skin, and he looked so uncomfortably guilty, like a child caught in some mischievous prank, that Sarah took pity on him.

'Oh, come along with me. I don't mind in the least if you accompany me to the village. Though just why your master should have asked you to keep an eye on me I can't imagine.' She cast him a rather thoughtful glance. 'Unless, of course, he suspected that I might try to leave in his absence.'

'Oh, no, miss. It weren't 'cause he were afraid of owt like that,' he hurriedly assured her. 'And that I do know. But he did ask me to keep me eye on you, right enough,' he freely admitted.

Did he, now? Sarah thought, eyes narrowing again, and it didn't take many moments before she had worked out the possible motive behind the request.

'Sutton, was anything else discovered about those unfortunate happenings before you left the inn?'

'What inn would that be, Miss Pennington?'

'Don't prevaricate!' she snapped. 'I have no intention of indulging in one of your master's foolish games of pretence.'

A spark of respect glinted in the groom's grey eyes. He had swiftly come to the conclusion that his master's ward was a sweet-natured filly, but she certainly didn't lack spirit. Anyone who could stand up to Mr Ravenhurst the way she did must have considerable pluck, and Sutton admired her for that. Added to which his master was clearly very fond of her. And that in itself was good enough for him!

'No, nothing, miss. 'Cepting I did overhear someone complaining that someone had been in their room, going through their things, like.'

'Who was complaining?'

'Can't be sure, but I reckon it were that gangling wench that put me in mind of a school-ma'am. They were in the parlour at the time. . .her and the magistrate, I think it were. Only just caught a snippet as I passed the door. The magistrate arranged for Nutley's body to be sent back to Oxfordshire. But apart from that,' he shrugged, 'nothing much else 'appened. We were all allowed to leave not long after you and the master went.'

'And did Mr Stubbs resume his journey with the other passengers?'

'Aye, miss, that he did. Though whether he went as far as Bristol, I couldn't say. I left the stage at Chippenham as I 'ad to go and collect the master's carriage and old mincing bree—Mr Ravenhurst's valet,' he amended quickly.

Sarah could not prevent a smile at this. It had not taken her very long to discover that the head groom and valet had scant regard for each other. She had heard Quilp sniff rather pointedly at mention of the groom's name; and Sutton's rather vulgar response to any mention of the valet was to spit on the ground.

It had not taken Sarah very long, either, to discover that Sutton, in particular, was touchingly devoted to his master. Ravenhurst could do no wrong in the head groom's eyes. There wasn't a better master in the land, according to Sutton, nor a more idyllic spot to be found anywhere than the Ravenhurst estate.

His master's word was law, and Sutton had not hesitated to carry out Ravenhurst's orders to the letter, though Sarah suspected that time hung heavily on the groom's hands as he had been only too eager to ride out with her in the mornings. But Ravenhurst had not commanded him to go with her whenever she ventured forth in order to keep the groom gainfully employed, nor to provide her with some genial company.

Oh, no, her guardian had done so because he feared that the mysterious cloaked figure would, by a simple process of elimination, work out who must have the diamond necklace.

By the time she had arrived back at the Dower House, after having toured the quaint little village that lay just beyond the estate's boundary wall, Sarah had still been unable to work out who Mr Nutley's possible accomplice might have been.

If, as Sutton had suggested, Miss Grimshaw had suspected that someone had been going through her belongings, and if the cloaked figure had, indeed, been a female, there was only one possible candidate. Sarah shook her head in disbelief. If Dottie Hogg turned out to be the malefactor, then she was the most accomplished actress alive. And that was something Miss Dorothea de Vine most certainly was not!

On entering the hall, Sarah was informed by the butler that the Countess of Styne, accompanied by her eldest daughter, had called, and that she was to go straight up to the Dowager's private sitting-room. Sarah had learned from Buddle the day before that the family had returned from Kent, and she was eager to make their acquaintance.

Delaying only for the time it took to remove her cloak and bonnet and to tidy her hair, Sarah entered the room to discover a rather colourless female in her mid-forties, and a rather pretty girl, with large brown eyes and a riot of dusky locks, sitting side by side on the sofa, and the Dowager in her favourite armchair, making not the least attempt to stifle a yawn.

'Ah! Sarah, my dear. Come, let me introduce you to my visitors,' the Dowager said, brightening perceptively.

After the introductions were made, Sarah seated herself in the chair on the opposite side of the hearth and politely thanked the Countess for the use of her horse.

'Not at all, my dear. I ride so infrequently these days that my mare gets little enough exercise. You are most welcome to make use of her whenever you wish.' The kind offer was accompanied by a warm smile. 'It is rather a pity that Sophia is not fond of that form of exercise, otherwise I am sure she would have been delighted to accompany you on your rides. Unfortunately, she sustained a bad fall some years ago, and is disinclined to get back in the saddle again.'

'Very understandable, ma'am,' Sarah responded, ignoring the Dowager's unladylike snort of disapproval, and bestowing a smile on poor Sophia, who had grown quite pink with embarrassment at her grandmother's all-too-evident derision. 'It would be unkind to force her to sit a horse if she was disinclined. Perhaps she may overcome her fears, given time.'

Her sympathetic understanding earned her a warm look of approval from the kind-hearted Countess. 'Mama-in-law has been telling me that you are to spend a few weeks here, and then go to London in the spring. I have been endeavouring to persuade her to stay with us in the town house for the duration of the Season. You and my daughter would be company for each other.'

Sarah steadfastly refused to look in the Dowager's direction. 'That is most kind of you, ma'am. But I believe my guardian is wishful for us to stay at his house in Berkeley Square.'

'Perhaps he can be persuaded to change his mind.'

'I shouldn't bank on that, Hetta, if I were you,' the Dowager put in bluntly. 'You know Ravenhurst.'

'Yes, yes, I do.' The Countess responded, casting a sympathetic look in Sarah's direction. 'He's grown so very like his dear papa. . .well, in looks, at any rate,' she amended.

Sarah regarded her with interest. 'Does he resemble his father, ma'am? I remember dear Godmama very well, but I cannot bring to mind my guardian's father.' She shrugged. 'But then I was very young when I paid those visits to Ravenhurst.'

'Yes, Marcus resembles his father,' the Dowager confirmed. 'Warren Ravenhurst could never be described as a handsome man, either. But, like his son, he had a presence. Eyes instinctively turned in his direction. Just as they do when Marcus enters a room.'

'Yes, that is certainly true,' the Countess agreed, flashing Sarah an unmistakable look of concern this time. 'Your guardian, though, does have a rather more forceful nature than his father had.'

'He certainly does have that, ma'am, but one grows accustomed. Added to which I don't let it worry me. If he tries to become too high-handed, I merely take him down a peg or two by giving him a scold.'

The Dowager's eyes glinted with unholy amusement as both visitors gaped in amazement, just as if they had suddenly discovered that Sarah had descended from another planet.

'Your sympathy is quite misplaced, Hetta. I'm pleased to say that Sarah isn't afraid of Marcus in the least. It is so very refreshing!' She looked approvingly at her grandson's ward. 'It is Sophia's birthday next week, and the family is celebrating the occasion with a party. Remind me to have a word with Buddle. I want your new evening gown finished in good time.'

The following afternoon Sarah had to forgo her walk as Buddle, having worked hard on it for many hours, brought the gown along to Sarah's room for the first fitting. The dress needed only a few minor alterations, the abigail decided before kneeling on the carpet to pin up the hem.

From her position Sarah was unable to catch sight of her reflection in the full-length mirror, but thought the turquoise silk had made up quite beautifully, although she did consider the square neckline had been cut indecently low, but refrained from comment. She soon grew tired of looking down at Buddle's bowed head and turned her own to stare out of the window, her eyes narrowing as she caught sight of a fair-haired young man busily raking up dead leaves.

'Who's that outside in the garden, Buddle? I cannot see his face clearly, but I can tell that it certainly isn't Wilkins.'

'It's probably the new lad who came round the other morning looking for work. Wilkins could do with the help. He isn't getting any younger. The lad will be here only a few weeks, though. He's hoping to find work in London for the Season, so Clegg tells me.' Buddle's brows snapped together suddenly. 'Will you keep still, miss! How am I supposed to get this hem straight with you fidgeting away?'

Sarah looked down again at the abigail's bent head, and her lips curled into a fond smile. For all her snappishness and impatience the woman really was a dear. 'Do you know, Buddle, you're a wonderful abigail. You arrange hair beautifully, and you're an excellent seamstress. Pity you're such a scold. . .and a tale-bearer,' she added meaningfully.

Not once since the night she had been discovered in her guardian's bedchamber had mention been made of her presence there, a circumstance which she considered most strange. Although she had sought him out in all innocence, and nothing improper had occurred, she was fully aware that she had committed a scandalous breach of conduct by being alone with a man, guardian or not, in such intimate surroundings.

She was very well aware, also, who had alerted the Dowager to the possible dangers, and raised a quizzical brow as Buddle lifted guilty eyes to meet hers.

'Now, Miss Sarah, don't you go holding that against old Buddle. What was I supposed to do? I knew there was no harm in it, even before I learned about you finding that necklace an' all. But others might have viewed things different. You were lucky I spied you. Had it been one of the other servants seeing you slip into Master Marcus's room that way, I shudder to think of the gossip.'

Sarah had never supposed that Buddle's actions had been prompted by anything other than the purest of motives, but could not resist the temptation to tease her further.

'I've learned from her ladyship that you began life with this family as nurserymaid; have learned, too, which among those many chicks placed in your capable hands was your undoubted favourite.'

One finely arched brow rose again. 'Whose reputation were you trying to protect, Buddle—his or mine? I can only imagine,' she went on, suddenly finding the fingernails on her right hand of immense interest, 'that you must have feared I had gone to that room with the intention of compromising your favourite nursling.'

Buddle rose to her feet instantly, and was halfway through voicing a staunch denial when she noticed the mischievous twinkle in blue-green eyes. 'Why, you little monkey!' she scolded, just as though Sarah had been one of her former nursery charges. 'You never thought nothing of the sort!'

'No, I never did,' Sarah confessed, not in the least shamefaced. 'But I have frequently wondered why the Dowager didn't take me roundly to task. Do you know, Buddle, she has never said a word.'

'Ah! Well, I know why,' she responded, forgetting to be cross. 'Master Marcus told her in no uncertain terms that she wasn't to do so.'

'Did he, really? Well, was that not kind of him!' Sarah frowned suddenly. 'Unless, of course, he wishes to have that privilege himself, and intends to scold me when he returns. . . Yes, that sounds much more likely, much more like him,' she decided finally, and drew a surprising gurgle of laughter from the maid.

'I knew it! Knew the instant I set eyes on you that hidden behind that sweet face was the mind of a wicked minx.' Buddle's disapproving shake of the head might have looked convincing had her thin lips not twitched slightly. 'I know what signs to look for, you see.'

Sarah's eyes glinted in response. 'Oh, I knew it would be fruitless trying to fool you. You're quite right, of course. I am utterly depraved. Quite beyond the pale, in fact!'

'Well, I wouldn't go as far as to say that,' Buddle's lips twitched again as she resumed her former kneeling position. 'But it will be no bad thing when Master Marcus returns and takes you in hand again.'

Sarah became serious, and raised troubled eyes to gaze sightlessly across the room. 'Yes, I wonder what can be keeping him? It's been a week since he left.'

'Aye, miss. But Master Marcus has always been one for keeping his own counsel. Mayhap he hasn't been able to locate that Bow Street Runner, or maybe other errands have kept him busy. Either way, there's no need for you to fret none. Master Marcus is quite capable of taking care of himself.'

Sarah wasn't so much worried as just eager for news. No, she amended silently, she was eager for his return. The simple truth of the matter was that she was missing their bantering exchanges; missing his caustic remarks and heavy dark-browed scowls. . . She was, quite simply, missing him. Which was really quite silly when one came to think about it, she reflected. After all, she had known him for such a short time, and yet it seemed as if she had known him all her life. How very strange that was!

As the days passed and still no word reached them of his possible return, Sarah's discontentment increased, but she was careful not to show it. She found some relief in her continued daily rides with Sutton, and although she enjoyed the groom's company, he was no substitute for Ravenhurst.

She also derived much pleasure in the evenings when she would sit with the Dowager, either reading aloud to her or playing cards; and she, at least, looked forward to the regular afternoon visits made by the Countess and her eldest daughter, both of whom she considered friendly and charming; but no matter how much satisfaction she attained from these varied interludes, she began to feel increasingly that there was something fundamentally missing from her life.

As the second week drew to a close and there was still no word from Ravenhurst, Sarah had resigned herself to attending Sophia's birthday celebration without the comfort of his escort.

As Buddle had warned her that she wished to create a more elaborate hairstyle for the occasion, Sarah repaired to her room in good time, and sat obediently still on the chair before the dressing-table mirror, watching in fascination as the experienced abigail's artistic fingers busily worked away. Buddle piled the golden-brown hair high on Sarah's head so that it cascaded down in a shower of long ringlets, and then intricately weaved a turquoise ribbon through the silken locks.

When at last she was permitted to stand before the full-length mirror to see the finished results, Sarah stared at her reflection with scant enthusiasm. The dress was lovely, and Buddle had added a flounce, decorating it with tiny rosebuds fashioned from the same turquoise silk.

Her arms were covered in the first pair of long evening gloves she had ever owned, and the Dowager had insisted that she wear a lovely string of pearls and matching ear-rings, which had once belonged to Sarah's godmother. Never had she been so elegantly attired. She ought she knew to feel overjoyed. But the simple fact remained that she felt anything but.

'What is it, miss?' Buddle's shrewd dark eyes had not missed the forlorn expression. 'What is it that doesn't please you?'

'Oh, nothing, nothing! Everything is just perfect!' she hurriedly assured her. 'The dress is beautiful, and I simply love the way you have arranged my hair.'

There was a moment's silence, then, 'Come, on, miss. You can tell old Buddle. What is it that you're not happy about?'

Sarah's forced smile faded. 'I'm not happy about Mr Ravenhurst's continued absence,' she admitted at last. 'I cannot help thinking something must have happened to him.'

Buddle stared deeply into the blue-green eyes for an endless moment. 'You'll do,' she surprised Sarah by remarking softly. 'Yes, you'll do very nicely, I think.

'Now, come along, miss,' she went on in her usual no-nonsense manner, 'otherwise you'll be late. Let's get this shawl round you, and you'll need make do with your old cloak for the carriage drive as your new one hasn't arrived. And, miss,' she added, arresting Sarah's progress to the door, 'don't you go worrying your pretty head over Master Marcus no more. He'll turn up safe and sound. You see if he don't.'

A little of Buddle's optimism must have rubbed off on her, for as Sarah entered her guardian's elegant carriage, awaiting them at the side entrance, she experienced a tinge of excitement at the prospect of attending Sophia's seventeenth birthday celebration which, according to the Dowager, was not likely to be a small affair.

Although she rarely had a good word to say about her eldest son, her ladyship had had to own that the Earl was far from miserly on these occasions. She had mentioned earlier in the day that musicians had been hired for the evening, and that she wouldn't be in the least surprised to discover half the county had been invited.

Sarah was unable to confirm whether this was true or not, but as they neared the mansion, only a matter of a few minutes later, she could see a long line of carriages waiting to deposit their passengers at the front entrance.

The early March evening was dry, with a starlit, cloudless sky, but there was that inevitable frosty nip in the air. None the less, with their legs covered with a fur-lined rug, and with hot bricks at their feet, the Dowager and Sarah remained comfortably warm until the carriage reached the front entrance and it was their turn to alight.

This was not Sarah's first visit to the ancestral home. She had been invited to dine twice since the family's return from Kent. The Earl, a rotund little man in his late forties, had made her feel most welcome, and the evenings had passed very pleasantly, though she had found herself unable to mask a chuckle on the first occasion when the meal had arrived at the table far from warm, and she had been reminded of her guardian's scathing condemnations.

He had been right, too, about the large, high-ceilinged rooms being draughty; but she had no fault to find with the furnishings, which managed to combine both elegance and comfort.

The ballroom, however, was not so very comfortable. Many of its windows were ill-fitting, and the large fireplace had an unfortunate tendency to billow out smoke at regular intervals. Therefore, the Countess, very wisely, had decided not to hold the party in there, but had thrown open two connecting ground-floor rooms for the occasion.

Sophia, dressed in a very pretty gown of white sarsenet, adorned with the most delicate pink rosebuds round the sleeves and neckline, stood shyly beside her parents at the entrance to the first salon. After receiving the warmest of greetings from the kindly host and hostess, Sarah complimented Sophia on her lovely gown before following the Dowager into the room where chairs had been placed all along the walls.

They had only just seated themselves when a tall, rather handsome young man, sporting a dazzling waistcoat embroidered with bright crimson poppies, approached them. He bore too strong a resemblance to his younger brothers and sisters for Sarah not to know, instantly, who he was, even before he said,

'Grandmama! What a pleasure it is to see you looking so well!'

'Bah! Jackanapes!' was the Dowager's rather charming response, and her grandson's finely chiselled lips twitched as he winked rather cheekily in Sarah's direction.

'Now, now, ma'am, you know you don't mean that. You like me, really, you know you do. Not as well as you like Cousin Marcus, but I come a close second.'

Her ladyship gave vent to one of her unladylike snorts, but there was a decidedly appreciative gleam in her eyes as she said, 'If you have not already guessed, Sarah, this impertinent young chub is the Honourable Bertram Stapleton, the Earl's son and heir. Bertram, this is Ravenhurst's ward, Miss Sarah Pennington.'

His bow was a study in elegance. 'Would you do me the honour, Miss Pennington, of standing up with me for the next set of country dances?'

Because she had frequently practised with her friend Clarissa, Sarah knew the steps to most country dances, and did not hesitate to accept the invitation.

'I cannot tell you, sir,' she remarked as they made their

way towards the wide open doors leading to the salon where people were already forming sets for the next dance, 'how refreshing it is to discover someone who isn't afraid of the Dowager. The other members of your family seem almost terrified of her. Poor Sophia never dares to open her mouth when in the Dowager's presence, and even your father appears to be somewhat in awe of her.'

'Yes, madness, ain't it?' He raised his eyes heavenwards. 'The only way to deal with the old lady is to stand up to her, give as good as you get. Cousin Marcus told me that years ago.'

Sarah decided she liked Sophia's elder brother. He seemed a friendly young man with pleasant, easy-going manners, and she found herself saying, 'Yes, and he's another many seem in awe of.'

He slanted a quizzical glance. 'Are you?'

'It would be a little unpleasant if I were, considering I am his ward. But, no,' she admitted. 'No, I'm not in the least afraid of him.'

'Pleased to hear it! Marcus is a great gun. Pulled me out of a scrape or two, I can tell you.' His glance down at her this time was almost apologetic. 'It wasn't until I arrived yesterday that I was aware of your existence, Miss Pennington. I cannot recall my cousin ever mentioning that he had a ward.'

Far from offended, Sarah admired his honesty. 'I suspect, sir, that that was because he had forgotten himself.' Her eyes danced with wicked amusement. 'How very glad I am, now, that I took it upon myself to leave Bath, and put him to the trouble of scouring the country in search of me. I can safely promise you that he won't forget my existence again in a hurry.'

The Dowager, following their progress into the other room, saw her grandson suddenly throw back his head and roar with laughter. She was not in the least surprised that Sarah had captured his interest so soon. She was a lovely girl whose rather wicked sense of humour would appeal to Bertram. Her grandson was, the Dowager secretly thought, a charming rascal, both handsome and good-natured, but rather too young yet to pose any real threat.

She continued to watch them, a satisfied smile curling her lips, as Sarah performed the dance's intricate steps with effortless grace. As the evening wore on her charge returned to her side from time to time, but Sarah was in great demand. Many of the young men, and some not so young, requested her as a partner, and so she spent much of the time on the dance floor, leaving the Dowager quite happily conversing with her numerous acquaintances.

The evening was almost half over when she became aware of a large dark shape looming at her side, and broke off her conversation with her daughter-in-law to turn her head.

'Ha! So, you've returned at last, have you? And high time, too!'

Chapter Ten

Marcus gazed down at his grandmother in his usual lazy affectionate way. 'The warmth of your greeting, ma'am, never ceases to affect me deeply.'

'Ha! When has there ever been need for wordy sentiment between you and me, Marcus?' Her tone was indifferent, but the look in her eyes as she cast them over his tall figure, immaculately attired in satin knee-smalls and a long-tailed coat of black cloth, was anything but apathetic. His bearing was always impressive, but in full evening garb he looked magnificent. 'How long have you been back?'

'Only long enough for me to freshen up, change and come here.' He turned to his aunt, who was gazing up at him with the customary mixture of admiration and awe which he always managed to instil in her. 'I hope you will overlook my late arrival, ma'am, and my arrogant presumption that I might descend upon you without invitation.'

'Oh, no, no! Not at all,' she hurriedly assured him, slightly breathless in her confusion. She had grown accustomed over the years to a man whose conversation was frequently blunt to the point of rudeness, and never in her wildest imaginings had she believed him capable of such courteous charm. 'You are always most welcome, Ravenhurst. You should know that.'

'Your graciousness, madam, is only just matched by your excellent taste in dress,' he responded, which had the effect of sending her quite pink with pleasure, and even caused his grandmother to blink several times. 'As always, your appearance is faultless.'

'Well, you've certainly made her day,' the Dowager remarked a few minutes later when her daughter-in-law, still with a suspicion of a gratified glow in her cheeks, moved away to mingle with her other guests.

'I have never rated my aunt's intelligence very high. But you will need to go a very long way to find a woman with better dress sense. She is always immaculately groomed. I believe in giving credit where it's due, ma'am.' His eyes scanned the salon. 'Where's my ward?'

'She's in the other room, dancing. The poor child must be quite exhausted. She's hardly sat down all evening. Which is something I wish you would do, Marcus. I am getting a crick in my neck looking up at you all the time.'

He obeyed automatically, seating himself in the chair his aunt had just vacated, while his dark eyes continued to scrutinise the dancers in the other room. 'Is that her?' he enquired, suddenly frowning. 'The one in the bluish-coloured dress?'

'Of course it is!' The Dowager cast him an impatient glance. 'Don't tell me you've forgotten what the poor child looks like already?'

'Of course I haven't forgotten! But her hair has been arranged differently. And what the devil do you mean by letting her wear such an indecent gown?'

'Indecent?' she echoed, rather taken aback by the unjustified criticism. 'It's nothing of the sort! It is cut no lower than most of the other gowns the young ladies are wearing. Besides, Sarah has nothing of which to be ashamed. She has a charming figure. Quite delightful, in fact!'

'I can see that!' he retorted. 'And so can every other man in the room!'

The Dowager refused to comment further, for it had suddenly dawned on her what lay at the root of his ill-humoured remarks. She smiled to herself as she watched the dancers leave the floor, and knew by the undisguised delight that suddenly sprang into a pair of aquarmarine-coloured eyes the instant Sarah had caught sight of her guardian.

'Oh, sir! It is so very good to see you again!' Almost running the last few steps towards him, she held her hands outstretched and, standing up, he took them eagerly in his own.

'And it is good to see you again, my child. I do not need to ask if you are well. Your delightful colour informs me clearly enough.'

He then dispensed with the services of the young man who had kindly restored Sarah to the Dowager Countess by casting him a slight smile, and then turned his attention back to his ward.

Having nearly attained the age of two-and-thirty, he was certainly no stranger to feminine charms. He had seen many beauties over the years, many lovelier than Sarah, but he had never glimpsed a figure to better hers. Slender yet shapely, she was perfectly proportioned. He allowed his gaze to wander over the slim waist and hips before raising his eyes to dwell for an appreciative moment on the delightful swell of the firm young breasts.

Sarah had received numerous compliments on her appearance that night, and countless admiring glances from the many gentlemen present, but Ravenhurst's swift appraisal had felt more like a soft caress, causing a pleasurable tingling sensation to feather its way over her skin, and bringing added colour to her cheeks.

When, however, he did finally raise his eyes to meet hers, she was unable to tell whether he approved of her appearance or not, nor was she able to account for the strangely disturbing intensity in their dark fathomless depths.

'Why not ask your ward to dance?'

The Dowager's suggestion broke the mesmeric hold of that ardent gaze, and Sarah looked down at her, and then rather shyly back at her guardian in hopeful expectation, but he disappointed her by saying in his usual blunt way,

'Because I never dance, as you very well know. I leave all that prancing about to the young nincompoops. And talking of which,' he added, noticing someone heading in their direction, 'who's this tailor's dummy about to descend on us?'

Sarah glanced round. 'You know very well who it is. And don't you dare to say anything rude to him, sir!' she ordered in an undertone. 'He thinks very highly of you, and he has been very kind to me this evening.'

'By all that's wonderful!' Bertram gave his cousin an affectionate slap on the back. 'So you made it after all, Marcus!'

'As you see. But what the duece are you doing here?'

'Came down for m'sister's birthday. What do you think?'

'Came down?' One dark brow rose suspiciously. 'Or sent down?'

'Now, now, cuz! You know I don't get into scrapes any longer. Well, none that I'm admitting to, at any rate.' He noticed those dark, intelligent eyes move fleetingly to the bright red poppies adorning his waistcoat, and puffed his chest out rather proudly. 'What do you think of it, Marcus? Wonderful, ain't it?'

'Believe me, young man, I should take the greatest delight in telling you exactly what I think of it,' he responded with feeling. 'Unfortunately, though, I have been forbidden.'

'Do not take any notice, Bertram,' Sarah hurriedly intervened before the young man was foolish enough to prompt further. 'The musicians are striking up, and I have promised you this dance.'

She whisked him on to the dance floor with unseemly haste, and soon afterwards noticed her guardian escorting the Dowager into the room set out for cards, where most of the older people present had sought refuge well away from the the younger and more boisterous guests.

She was impatient to discover what had been decided with regard to the diamond necklace, but as she had promised to take supper with Bertram, and as Ravenhurst spent the remainder of the evening in conversation with many of the other people present, most of whom were known to him, she was unable to broach the subject until the evening had drawn to a close and they had climbed into the carriage awaiting to take them the short distance back to the Dower House.

She looked across at him eagerly. 'Now that we're alone, sir,' she said, with sublime disregard for the lady seated beside her, 'you must tell me what happened in Bristol. I'm simply bursting with curiosity.'

'Bursting. . .? Bursting! What sort of language is that for a young lady, may I ask!' the Dowager admonished crossly. 'Why, if such a word had ever fallen from my lips when I was your age, I would have been soundly whipped.'

Marcus caught the mischievous twinkle in the lovely blue-green eyes before Sarah cast a look of mock censure at the Dowager. 'Now, ma'am, that is a shocking untruth,' she admonished, mimicking her ladyship's disapproving tone to a nicety. 'And well you know it! No one would ever have dared to do such a thing to you.'

The Dowager gave a shout of laughter before wrapping Sarah across the knuckles with her fan, and then turning to her grandson, whose dark eyes were alight with amusement. 'You see how incorrigible the chit is, Ravenhurst. You have been away far too long.'

'Yes, far, far too long,' Sarah agreed. 'What happened in Bristol, sir?'

Leaning back against the plush velvet squabs, he regarded her indulgently. 'Not very much, child. It took me several days to locate Stubbs's whereabouts, and only did so because I had the great good fortune to run in to your friend Captain Carter.'

'Oh, is he still in Bristol, sir?'

'Not now, no. The delay on the road caused him to miss his boat. He has departed for the Peninsula now, however. But whilst he was kicking his heels in the city, he offered his services to the Runner. Stubbs, as I believe I mentioned once before, was sent to Bristol for the sole purpose of keeping watch on certain premises owned by a man suspected of dealing in stolen goods.

'However, being a conscientious individual, Stubbs

wanted to check the information given to him by our stranded fellow-travellers. You will no doubt be pleased to learn that he never for one moment suspected Carter of being responsible for either Nutley's death or the servant girl's, and didn't hesitate, therefore, to make use of him. He set him to keep watch on those premises I mentioned, whilst he went about verifying the information he had been given by the other stagecoach passengers.'

'And did all the stories turn out to be true?' she prompted eagerly when he fell silent.

'All but one, yes. You'll no doubt also be relieved to hear that the "Divine" Dorothea does have a mother living in Bristol. She is residing with her at present. A couple of days after they had arrived, Stubbs followed her when she left her mother's house, and saw her enter a theatre, presumably looking for work.

'The clerk's story also turned out to be authentic. He lives and works in the city. But I'm afraid of the Grimshaw woman there is no sign. Her sister's address turned out to be a church, of all things!'

Sarah frowned, remembering clearly what Sutton had disclosed. If Miss Grimshaw had, indeed, suspected that her belongings had been searched, then she was hardly likely to turn out to be the cloaked intruder. But why had she deliberately given Mr Stubbs false information? There seemed no good reason for having done so unless, of course, she had something to hide.

'How very odd!' she murmured.

'Quite!' he agreed laconically. 'Well, as you have probably gathered, all this was discovered before I turned up with the Felchett diamonds. Which really did start things moving. Stubbs wanted to return here with me, but felt he couldn't leave his post. So he sent an express to

London, and whilst he was awaiting reinforcements, I went on to Bath, leaving the—er—diamonds in his safe-keeping.'

He refrained from mentioning that he hadn't remained long in that city, and had taken the opportunity to travel to London to pay a much-needed visit to his mistress. The night of unbridled passion had certainly assuaged his bodily needs, but that was all. His heart and mind had been quite otherwhere, and he had left the house the following morning feeling strangely hollow inside, and experiencing not the least desire to spend a further night in the arms of his skilful light o' love.

'Did you call in to see your cousin?'

Sarah's tentatively spoken enquiry drew him out of his reverie. 'I had a word or two, certainly.'

She eyed him gravely. 'Yes, I can imagine.'

'Sarah, surely you didn't expect Marcus to permit all his cousin's underhandedness to go unpunished?' the Dowager put in in her grandson's defence. 'Why, the deceitful, conniving wretch has been fleecing him for years!'

Sarah wasn't in the least surprised to discover that the Dowager was in full possession of the facts, although she herself had never breathed a word. She did consider any actions her guardian had taken completely justified in the circumstances, but the fact remained that she could not help feeling sorry for Mrs Fairchild, for the woman had been neither cruel nor even mildly unkind to the little orphaned girl placed in her charge.

'Yes, you're both right, of course,' she conceded at last. 'It's just that. . .'

'I did not turn her out on to the streets, Sarah, if that is what concerns you,' he assured her, much to her intense relief. 'But I have made it abundantly clear that, if she chooses to remain in that house, she will pay me rent, and at the going rate. If she falls behind with her payments, then I have left her in no doubt whatsoever that she will be evicted. And I shall suffer no qualms in doing so, either.

'But rest easy, child,' he added, casting her a rather crooked smile. 'I know for a fact that she was left adequate funds by her husband to live quite comfortably. If, however, she wishes to indulge in her particular vice, then I'm afraid she will need to find another source of income to cover the expenses, for she will get not a penny more from me.'

Silently, she was forced to admit that he had been really most lenient, and looked at him approvingly before asking him if he had also found the time to call on Mrs Stanton.

'Certainly. And you will be overjoyed to learn, no doubt, that the runaways were successful in their endeavours, and that Mrs Clarissa Fenshaw, as she is now, has been restored to the bosom of her family, for the time being at least.' He smiled at her exuberant expression. 'I have brought letters from both Clarissa and her mother, which will no doubt explain events far better than I ever could.'

'I must say, Sarah,' the Dowager remarked after listening quietly to her grandson's tidings in increasing dismay, 'you're a dear sweet girl, but it would appear you have a propensity for becoming involved with the most unsavoury characters—runaway couples, jewel thieves. . .and murderers, no less! I should imagine you find the peace and quiet at the Dower House quite a refreshing change.'

No sooner had she spoken than the carriage pulled up

in the stableyard. Without waiting for the groom, Ravenhurst jumped out, and had only just let down the steps when the elderly butler, carrying a lantern, emerged from the house.

'Oh, Master Marcus, sir!' Clegg, looking decidedly distraught, hurried across to the carriage. 'Thank heaven's you've returned! I was on the point of sending a message up to the big house to bring you back.'

'Why? What's happened?'

'We've had a break-in, sir. And poor Mr Quilp has been attacked. We've laid him on the sofa in the drawing-room, and I've already sent for the doctor.'

'Attend to your mistress!' Ravenhurst commanded, and then went striding into the house without another word

'Well, well! It would seem I spoke too soon, child,' her ladyship remarked as she stepped down from the carriage. 'It would appear that the gods have ordained that you won't be experiencing peace and quiet whilst you reside with me. How very enlivening!'

Clegg, raising the lantern aloft, saw them safely across the few feet of yard and into the house. They paused briefly by the drawing-room door, saw that not only Ravenhurst but Buddle, too, was attending the injured Quilp, who was now, thankfully, sitting up on the sofa, holding a cloth to his head.

As neither of them felt they could be of any help, and might possibly be in the way, they went straight upstairs to the Dowager's private sitting-room where a fire still burned welcomingly on the hearth. At her ladyship's request, Sarah poured out two glasses of Madeira, and then sat herself in the chair opposite and stared down into the glowing flames.

It would be comforting to think that the break-in had

been perpetrated by some opportunist thief, but Sarah could not delude herself. Foolishly, she had believed that, once the diamond necklace had been handed over to the authorities, the unfortunate affair would be at an end. How wrong could anyone be! Thankfully, though, her guardian had not been so simple-minded, and that was precisely why he had taken the precaution of ordering Sutton to watch over her in his absence.

She closed her eyes, recalling vividly the look in Ravenhurst's when Clegg had given him the unfortunate tidings. There had been such a strange mixture of anger and foreboding in their dark depths. Two people had died and another had been injured because of that wretched necklace! But why? Robbery, as Ravenhurst had pointed out, was one thing; murder quite another.

What on earth was so significant about that particular diamond necklace? she wondered. Surely there was more to it than just a simple case of robbery and greed? More importantly, how many more people would suffer before the mystery was finally solved?

A heartfelt sigh escaped her as she raised her eyes to gaze across at the Dowager. 'It would seem, ma'am, that I have, unwittingly, brought trouble to your house. It might have been better had I never come here.'

'Nonsense, child!' her ladyship responded, realising at once what had prompted the suggestion. 'Who is to say it wasn't some local rascal who, learning that there was to be a party at the mansion, thought to try his luck at a few houses in the vicinity.

'Not that I have much here worth stealing, you understand,' she went on matter-of-factly. 'There's my jewellery, of course, and a bit of silver. But not much else. I must ask Clegg to check and see just what is missing.' She sipped her wine, and a contented smile hovered about her mouth as she savoured its taste. 'I must say I prefer this to the champagne served earlier. Never could stomach the stuff myself. Weak and insipid, I call it!'

It was quite evident that the Dowager did not wish to discuss further what had occurred in their absence, and so Sarah followed her lead.

'It was a lovely party, ma'am, didn't you think so?'

'Yes, most enjoyable. Although I've never held my daughter-in-law in high esteem, I have to own she is a very gracious hostess.' A wicked cackle of amusement escaped her. 'Ravenhurst sent her quite pink with pleasure this evening. You are a very good influence on him, my dear.'

Sarah was not given the opportunity to enquire what she meant, for the door opened and the man himself entered the room to inform them that the doctor had arrived, and to assure them that Quilp, thankfully, was not too badly hurt. He then went on to warn them that they would shortly be disturbed by the sounds of hammering as he had ordered the broken window in the library boarded up until a new piece of glass could be installed.

'Thank you, Marcus, for seeing to everything. You are always to be relied upon.' The Dowager finished the contents of her glass and rose to her feet. 'Well, it has been a long evening and I'm rather tired, so I shall bid you both good-night. No doubt Clegg will present me with an inventory of exactly what is missing in the morning.'

Sarah watched her guardian close the door behind his grandmother, and then walk across to the table on which the decanters stood. He lacked none of his natural athletic grace, and yet she detected a suppressed tension in those fluid movements as he seated himself opposite in the Dowager's favourite chair.

'Nothing has been taken from the house, has it, sir?'

He looked at her for a moment above the rim of his glass before tossing the contents down his throat in one large swallow. 'No,' he said at length.

'No, I didn't think so.'

'Don't jump to conclusions, child. One cannot rule out the possibility that it was some local bent on a little petty theft. It is not an infrequent occurrence, after all.' He placed his empty glass down on to the table before looking directly across at her again. 'And do not forget the intruder was disturbed only a matter of minutes after he had gained unlawful entry. Which would hardly have given him time to relieve my grandmother of any of her belongings, now would it?'

Sarah chewed these remarks over in silence for several moments, and had to own that his suggestions were not unreasonable, but she remained sceptical and asked him to explain exactly what had occurred.

All the servants with the exception of the valet, it transpired, had congregated in the kitchen to enjoy a late supper. Quilp, having a fastidious nature, had insisted upon tidying his master's bedchamber before joining them. He had been descending the stairs when he had thought he detected the sound of breaking glass and, suspecting the footman of dropping a decanter whilst helping himself to its contents, had gone into the library to investigate.

The only light in the room had come from the fire which, apparently, had still been burning quite brightly in the grate. Even so, he had seen no one. The next instant, he had been struck from behind.

'Apart from the table, which had been overturned,' he went on to inform her after a thoughtful pause, 'no doubt by Quilp himself when he fell, and the broken window, everything seems to be in order.'

'So it might well have been an opportunist thief, but, personally, I do not think so.' She held his eyes with her own. 'And neither do you.'

He did not attempt to deny it, and said, taking her completely by surprise, 'We'll discuss this evening's incident, and our views on the matter, with Stubbs in the morning.'

'Mr Stubbs?' She was startled. 'Did you bring him back with you?'

'Yes. I made a return trip to Bristol to collect him. He's putting up at the village inn. I deposited him there earlier before I came here.'

'Then you both must think that an attempt will be made to retrieve the necklace, if this evening's fiasco was not, indeed, the first attempt to do so.'

His mouth set in a grim, straight line. 'One person has already been murdered, possibly two. And tonight there might easily have been a third fatality. . . Yes, child, I do think that this night's occurrence was perpetrated by our mysterious cloaked figure,' he admitted at last. 'Furthermore, I fear that whoever it is will not stop now.'

'But why, sir? Why?' she demanded urgently. 'What is so important about that particular necklace that someone is prepared to commit murder just to get their hands on it?'

'I have asked myself that very same question,' he admitted. 'And with perhaps more reason than you have had for doing so,' he finished rather cryptically.

Chapter Eleven

A hundred years before all the people inhabiting that tiny village nestling in the hollow just beyond the estate's boundary wall had had some connection with Styne. There was not a family living there that did not have at least one member working on the vast estate, either in the house or gardens; in the stables, or on the land itself. Generations had lived and died there without so much as travelling the merest five miles from home.

Over the years the tiny community had thrived, attracting outsiders. A blacksmith from Devizes had purchased some land off the previous Earl and had built his forge on the outskirts of the village, serving the community itself and people from miles around; and the inevitable inn had been erected where the men could relax and enjoy a tankard of ale after a hard day's toil.

The improvement in the roads during the second half of the previous century had inevitably brought changes. Where once everyone had known everyone else, now, many strangers came into their midst, either putting up at the inn, or merely passing through the village on their travels. It was quite a common sight to see sporting carriages of all descriptions bowling along the main street.

Consequently, when Sarah and Mr Ravenhurst, seated side by side in his curricle, entered the peaceful community, they aroused little interest, attracting no more than a fleeting glance from an elderly woman busily working in her front garden, and from the group of children playing happily together in the road.

Like most of the other buildings, the inn had whitewashed cob walls and a charming low thatched roof. At this time of the morning there were few, if any, customers. Marcus brought his curricle to a halt in the stable yard, and the sound of wheels on cobble stones so early in the day brought the innkeeper's inquisitive son out of a side door to investigate. He took immediate charge of the equipage, allowing the Dowager's grandson, whom he recognised instantly, to alight.

Sarah, who was looking perfectly charming in one of her new outfits, a pale blue walking dress and matching pelisse, and a very becoming bonnet lined with blue silk and with a matching silk ribbon tied in a coquettish bow beneath her chin, gratefully accepted her guardian's helping hand to alight. It never crossed her mind to demur when he tucked her arm through his, even though she was acutely aware of the latent rippling strength beneath the faultless sleeve of his blue superfine coat.

The instant she entered the inn the sweet smell of lavender, mixed with tobacco and spirits, assailed her nostrils, reminding her vividly of The Traveller's Rest. Here, too, the landlady seemed an industrious person, for already the wooden tables had been polished to a looking-glass shine and the floors swept clean.

As soon as her eyes had grown accustomed to the dimness, Sarah could see that the inn was deserted except for one customer, sitting at the table in the corner, casting his grey eyes over a copy of the *Morning Post*.

After ordering two tankards of ale, and a glass of wine for Sarah, Marcus wasted no time in apprising Mr Stubbs with details of the previous night's incident. The Runner listened intently, but from time to time would cast his eyes in Sarah's direction, a look in their shrewd depths that was hard to interpret.

'Well, sir, it would appear that it has happened rather sooner than either of us had expected,' Mr Stubbs remarked after learning all. 'The wretch certainly didn't waste much time. It would be a grave mistake to underestimate her.'

'Her?' Sarah echoed. 'Oh! Did Mr Ravenhurst inform you that I had come to the conclusion that the intruder that night at The Traveller's Rest was a female?'

'He did, Miss Pennington. And may I say it was an excellent piece of deduction. However, I already knew we were looking for both a man and a woman in connection with a series of robberies that took place last year.'

'Really?' Sarah's eyes began to twinkle as a rather amusing thought struck her. 'Did you never suspect that I might be that woman? After all, I did discover Mr Nutley's body.'

'In my line of work, one needs to question the authenticity of everyone. But one also, in time, becomes a fairly shrewd judge of character. And Mr Ravenhurst was sensible enough not to waste any time in apprising me of your true identity, and the reason why he had found himself at that inn.'

Sarah cast her guardian a reproachful glance, and he reciprocated with a rather mocking one.

'Yes, I don't doubt you would have preferred I

remained silent. Knowing you as I do, I feel certain you would have derived a deal of wicked amusement had you been carted back to Bow Street by Mr Stubbs.'

'Oh, I wouldn't go as far as to say that. But I would certainly have enjoyed putting you to the trouble of journeying to the capital in order to rescue me.'

Sarah could not prevent a chuckle at the look of exasperation on her guardian's face, but then became serious again as a thought struck her. 'You said you were looking for both a man and a woman in connection with certain robberies, Mr Stubbs. Did you know all along that Mr Nutley was the thief? Were you following him?'

'Oh, no, miss. It were pure coincidence we were both passengers on that particular stage coach.' Leaning back in his chair, he regarded her for a moment in silence, then said, 'Do you recall that morning when we were all in the parlour, Nutley included, and Mr Ravenhurst here mentions, quite innocent-like, that several items of jewellery had gone missing in recent months, and wondered whether it were the work of the same person or persons?'

'Yes, yes, I do, Mr Stubbs. I remember it quite clearly.'

'Well, he weren't far wrong. We at Bow Street had suspected for some time that at least two people were involved in the thefts. In each case a large party had been held at the house. Sometimes the jewellery wasn't discovered missing until days later. But in every case a recently employed maidservant would take exception to being questioned, and would soon afterwards leave in high dudgeon.

'During a London Season, miss, most of the large houses employ extra help. Most get staff from reputable agencies, but not always. And folk are so careless. You wouldn't believe it! Often they don't even bother to check references.

'It were the same in the case of the Felchett diamonds. Local girls, at least they were thought to be all local, had been hired for the occasion. The following day, after the diamonds had been discovered missing, one of the women took umbrage at being questioned, and upped and left.'

'But surely she was searched before being allowed to leave?'

'Yes, miss, she were. But the family assured us that nothing was discovered on her, nor amongst her belongings. Each robbery were the same.'

Sarah drew her brows together in profound thought. 'So, unless the searches were not thorough enough, the stolen items must have been handed over to someone else.'

'Precisely, Sarah!' Marcus concurred. 'Not another servant, however, but someone above suspicion. . . One of the guests attending the party, perhaps?'

'And was Mr Nutley among the guests at these parties?'

'He certainly was, miss,' Stubbs answered. 'But there were a dozen or more names that kept cropping up. Mr Ravenhurst were at three of 'em.'

'But what about the maidservant?' she enquired, resisting the temptation to goad her guardian on this very interesting circumstance. 'Surely you managed to get an accurate description of her?'

'Lord bless you, miss!' The Runner looked genuinely amused. 'In two cases she has black hair. In the others, seemingly, fair or brown. She were a Londoner, a Northerner or a West Country lass. She were described as a 'andsome wench—sometimes quite plain. The only things that never varied were height and build. She were taller than average for a woman, and of slim build.'

Sarah fell silent, digesting what she had learned. The woman was evidently an expert at disguise. An actress, perhaps. . .? Yes, she might well have been just that at one time, and had evidently been putting her considerable talents to a more profitable use during the past twelve months. And Dottie Hogg was an actress, of course. But Dottie was not tall, nor did she have a particularly slim build.

No, only one person putting up at that inn fitted that description. An image of the middle-aged spinster appeared before her mind's eye. That greying hair could have been a wig, and the dark circles round the eyes and the sallow complexion might easily have been effected by artificial means. She recalled, too, the way Miss Grimshaw had run with such agility down those stairs, just as though she had been years younger.

And how very cunning the woman had been, too! She had quite deliberately kept herself to herself as much as possible, and had remained in her room for fear, perhaps, that someone discerning enough just might penetrate the disguise.

'I think you've perhaps worked out for yourself who Nutley's accomplice must have been,' Mr Stubbs remarked after watching her expressive face closely. 'But, as I mentioned a while back, I didn't take a seat on that stage coach in order to follow Nutley. One of those stolen items of jewellery had turned up in Bristol, and I were being sent to that city to keep watch on a certain pawnbroker's shop that we at Bow Street had been getting some rather disturbing reports about.'

He paused to take a large swallow from his tankard. 'Nutley told me he were travelling to the West Country to visit an aunt, and until his death, and the subsequent events, I had no reason to disbelieve him, nor to think he was involved in the robberies.'

'But after his death, did you begin to suspect Miss Grimshaw, or whatever her real name is, of being his accomplice?'

'Oh, aye, miss, I suspected her right enough, but I couldn't go arresting her just 'cause she 'appens to be quite a tall wench.'

'One cannot go about accusing people and carting them off to Bow Street without good reason, Sarah,' Marcus put in gently, amused by the look of frustration on her face. 'Citizens do have their rights. If Stubbs had been able to discover her in possession of the necklace, then that might have been a different matter, but he knew it would avail him nothing to search either her, or her room.

'Remember what I told you,' he reminded her. 'Both Stubbs and I were convinced someone had searched our rooms. It was obvious that Grimshaw couldn't have been in possession of the diamonds.'

She looked at her guardian intently. 'And did you suspect her all along?'

'No, I didn't. Our friend, here, kept his own counsel. I had made it clear right from the start that the only person I was concerned about was you. I really did not want to become involved, Sarah, in something that was, after all, none of my affair. But your discovering that confounded necklace has changed all that. When I eventually succeeded in locating Stubbs's whereabouts in Bristol, I did, then, insist upon knowing all the details.'

His expression was suddenly very grim. 'And there's little point in trying to delude ourselves. We all feel fairly sure that she'll come after that necklace again. The trouble is, if I passed the confounded woman in the street, I'm certain I shouldn't recognise her. The only time I saw her was on the evening she arrived at the inn, and that bonnet she was wearing at the time hid most of her face.'

'And the only occasion I got a close look at her was when I interviewed her.' There was a faint rasping sound as the Runner stroked his chin thoughtfully. 'The dratted wench is so good at changing her appearance, though. I still can't be certain that even I'll recognise her again.'

'You might not be able to, Mr Stubbs. But I'm fairly confident that I should.' Both men looked at her sharply. 'You see, I spoke to her twice. On the second occasion she came to my room. I recall thinking at the time that there was more behind that visit of hers than mere solicitude. I realise, now, that she had sought me out for the sole purpose of ascertaining whether I had recognised her the night before. I had not and, therefore, didn't hesitate to admit to it.

'If my memory serves me correctly, I believe I also gave her the impression that I thought the cloaked intruder was a man. Which, of course, is precisely what I did think at the time.'

'Then that, Miss Pennington, is what saved you.' The Runner looked gravely across the table at her. 'I had thought for some months that we were dealing merely with a pair of harmless thieves. One of them was most certainly just that, but the other is a very different proposition. She has murdered once. . .and I think she wouldn't hesitate to do so again.'

He moved his head slightly to stare directly into a pair of dark brown eyes betraying deep concern. 'Well, sir, it's up to you. As you know I was hoping for more time, but in the circumstances I think it might be best if we do what you suggested.'

'Which is?' Sarah prompted when both men remained silent.

'Remove you to Ravenhurst, where I can better protect you,' her guardian answered softly, 'and the necklace will, of course, be returned to its rightful owner.'

'No!' Both men were startled by the vehemence in her voice. 'I will not hide away like some frightened child for weeks, possibly months.'

Marcus's sigh was audible. 'Sarah, you don't understand the peril you're in.'

'On the contrary, I understand perfectly.' Sarah began to twist the strings of her reticule absently round the fingers of her left hand. 'Naturally, if you are concerned for your grandmother's safety,' she went on after a moment's thought, 'then I shall go. But don't ask me to do so for my own sake.'

She looked across at the Runner again. 'Returning that necklace to its rightful owner might well put an end to the affair. On the other hand, though, it might not. Added to which, don't you think we owe it to that servant girl, and possibly Nutley, too, to bring this woman to justice?'

There was more than a hint of respect in both men's eyes, but in Marcus's it was compounded with grave concern and something else, too—something so deeply disturbing in its intensity that Sarah was startled by it.

'Well, sir?' Stubbs prompted, drawing those unsettling dark eyes on to him. 'What do you say?'

Sarah waited with bated breath, knowing full well that, if her guardian insisted that she be removed to Ravenhurst, she would be unable to prevent it, and almost sighed with relief when he said,

'I say, as no doubt Captain Brin Carter would phrase it, we stand and fight.'

A faint smile of understanding touched the corners of the Runner's mouth. From the first moment he had set eyes on Mr Ravenhurst at The Traveller's Rest, he had respected his no-nonsense attitude, and had quickly grown to respect his judgment, too. Unlike Sarah, he had interpreted that look in those dark eyes and knew just how much that decision must have cost him to make.

He gave nothing away, however, as he said in his usual businesslike manner, 'Very well, sir. Firstly, we must try and discover if there have been any strangers about in recent days. I've already had a word with the landlord, and he assures me that no one, apart from myself, has put up at this inn in the past three weeks.

'I'll wander down to the smithy later, and hire a horse. I don't want to spread my profession abroad, but it might be worthwhile having a chat with the blacksmith. It's a fair bet he'd notice anyone not local hanging about the place.'

'And I shall not delay in paying a visit on my uncle, and discover if he has hired any new staff of late.'

Sarah gave a visible start. 'Good gracious! I'd forgotten about that. Your grandmother hired someone to help Wilkins in the garden.'

'Did she, now? Right, I'll look into that first.' Marcus tossed the contents of his tankard down his throat, and rose to his feet. 'I'll get back to you today, Stubbs, if I learn anything of significance.'

Throughout the short journey back to the Dower House, Ravenhurst maintained a flow of inconsequential chatter that masked quite beautifully the almost unbearable anxiety he was experiencing over his ward's safety.

Even now, the temptation to spirit her away to Ravenhurst, where he could place complete reliance on his trusted servants to watch over her every minute of the day, remained a highly tempting solution to his immediate problems. But deep down he knew that Sarah had been right. Even supposing the necklace was returned to Lord Felchett without delay, there was no guarantee that that would bring an end to the affair.

The Grimshaw woman had already committed murder, therefore, it was not beyond the realms of possibility that she might try to extract some petty form of revenge for having been thwarted. A sigh escaped him. How could he expect Sarah to live for weeks, possibly months, forever looking over her shoulder, watching, waiting for that harridan to strike? Of course he could not. It was unthinkable! Inhuman! Yes, he reiterated silently, Sarah had been right: the woman had to be caught and brought to justice.

As soon as they had arrived back at the Dower House, he suggested that Sarah change into her riding habit and meet him again in the stableyard in half an hour, and they could ride over to see his uncle together. He then wasted no time in going in search of his grandmother's newest employee. There was not a soul to be seen in the garden, which he noticed was beginning to look much tidier, but he did eventually run the old gardener to earth, busily at work in the potting shed.

'Why, Mr Ravenhurst, sir!' Wilkins grinned broadly as Marcus entered the gardener's private domain. 'Ain't often I sees you about the grounds.'

Marcus would never have dreamt of hurting the old man's feelings by informing him that he avoided entering whenever possible what was probably the worst maintained and most depressing garden he had ever had the misfortune to see. Wilkins had worked loyally for the family all his life; and it was hardly his fault that the Dowager stubbornly refused to have some of the trees chopped down, which would not only make his job much easier, but would instantly make the grounds much pleasanter.

So, he merely made some light response, and then wasted no time in asking where the young assistant was to be found.

'Wish I knew, sir. Sent the lad up to the big 'ouse first thing this morning with the barrow to pick up a few bits and pieces, and ain't set eyes on 'im since.' He raised his hat to run a grimy hand over his balding pate. 'Eh, sir, you don't think he'd owt to do with the break-in last night, do 'ee? Heard all about it when I arrived this morning.'

'That's what I am endeavouring to find out.' He looked at the gardener sharply. 'What do you know about the lad, Wilkins? Where's he from?'

'Over Devizes way, I reckon he said. Came strolling into the garden a week or so back, asking if there be any work going up at the big 'ouse. Told 'im I reckoned not, as the family were away at the time. We got to talking, and 'ee seemed a nice enough young fellow, so I tells 'im I'd ask if 'er ladyship would take 'im on for a few weeks as I could do with the 'elp.

'Seemingly, that were all 'ee wanted as 'ee were 'oping to work as a footman or the like in Lunnon. Which would suit 'im better, I'm thinking.' He shook his head. 'Never seen 'ands blister up so easy. Only got to pick up a shovel an' the poor lad's suffering.'

Marcus's eyes narrowed. 'So, he hasn't done much hard manual work?'

'Ha! Wouldn't o' said so, sir. Got 'ands as soft as a woman's, so the lad 'as.'

'Has he, now. . .? How very interesting!' The sinister smile that curled his thin-lipped mouth sent a frisson of fear to scud its way down the length of the old man's slightly twisted spine. 'Where does he bed down for the night?'

'Wi' me, sir, in the cottage. Lad didn't 'ave nowhere else to stay.' Wilkins cast his mistress's grim-faced grandson a sidelong glance. 'The lad's a good worker, sir,' he added in his underling's defence. 'Look' ow much better the garden be looking. And he be right 'andy in the cottage. Cleaned it up right fine!'

But Marcus's expression did not alter. 'What did you do after finishing work yesterday?'

'Went back to the cottage, 'ad a bite to eat and then wandered down to the inn.'

'Did the lad go with you?'

'Aye, sir. That he did, but he didn't stay long. Said he weren't feeling too good. Didn't even finish is ale, now I come to think on it.'

'What time did you leave the inn?'

'About nine, or thereabouts. The lad were fast asleep when I got back. And he were still there, tucked up in bed, as snug as yer like, when I gets up this morning.'

Marcus realised, even if the old gardener did not, that this proved nothing. The lad, if indeed he was a lad, could quite easily have waited until Wilkins was asleep, slipped back here and returned to the cottage without the old man being any the wiser.

If anything, his expression was grimmer than ever as

he returned to the Dower House to change his clothes, but when he met Sarah in the stableyard a short time later, he looked for all the world as though he hadn't a care, his face a perfect mask of sublime unconcern.

For her part Sarah, too, was doing her level best to put a brave face on it all. From that moment at the inn, earlier, when Mr Ravenhurst had freely admitted that he hadn't wanted to become involved, she had suffered pangs of conscience. And the simple truth of the matter was that he would not be involved at all but for her.

Common sense told her that she could not be held responsible for the actions of others, but at the same time she was very well aware that, had she remained in Bath with her guardian's cousin, the lives of those residing at the Dower House would not now be in peril.

Her depressing thoughts were for a moment set aside when she entered the stableyard, and was surprised to discover only the big bay that Mr Ravenhurst had commandeered from his uncle's stable saddled and tethered to the post.

'Oh! Did her ladyship request the return of her mare?'

'No. But I asked Sutton to take her back. I have something rather more suitable for a lady of your ability to ride.' Ravenhurst nodded to his groom, who disappeared into the stable, and emerged again moments later leading a lovely dapple-grey mare. 'I thought it time you had your own mount,' he told her, smiling at the look of combined astonishment and delight on her face.

'Oh, thank you,' she said huskily, the lump that had suddenly lodged itself in her throat making speech difficult. 'She's beautiful!' Sarah introduced herself to the mare very gently, talking softly while stroking the sleek neck. 'Where did you find her?'

'When I discovered your flight from Bath, I called in at The King's Head to hire a fresh team of horses. The landlord there used to work for my family. I noticed this lovely lady in one of the stalls. Jeb mentioned that the owner was wishful to sell her, so when I returned there last week, I made an offer for her, and brought her back with me yesterday. Now,' he went on, leading the mare to the mounting block, 'let's put her through her paces.'

Sarah quickly discovered that the horse was a gentle-mannered creature, but thankfully far from sluggish. She was delighted with her, and for a short while she managed to forget that fearful cloud under which she now lived, but cruel reality returned all too quickly as her guardian, after an extended canter across the park, headed towards the mansion, and she recalled the reason behind their visit.

As they rode into the stableyard, they discovered Bertram in the process of mounting his horse.

'Hello there!' he greeted cheerfully. 'I was just about to ride over to see you all.' His pleasant smile faded. 'Heard all about the break-in. Do you know what was stolen?'

'Nothing, thankfully.' Marcus dismounted, and handed the reins over to a waiting groom. 'As you intend paying a call, perhaps you would be good enough to escort my ward back?' He turned to Sarah. 'There's no reason for you to remain, my dear. Tell Clegg that I won't be home for luncheon. I'll eat with Stubbs at the inn.'

Sarah did not object, for Bertram was an amusing rascal, and the journey back to the Dower House was very pleasant and over far too quickly as far as she was concerned. They learned from Clegg that the Dowager was in her private sitting-room and, after passing on her guardian's message, Sarah went straight up to the room, without changing her clothes, to discover the Dowager seated at the escritoire, engrossed in writing a letter.

'I have brought you a visitor, ma'am,' she informed her brightly. 'And I apologise for coming to you without first changing out of my habit.'

'Do not trouble yourself over that, my dear. I do not object to the smell of the stables.' Placing down the pen, the Dowager turned to see who it was Sarah had with her. 'Oh, it's only you, Bertram.'

By his cheerful expression it was apparent that he was completely undaunted by his grandmother's total lack of warmth. 'Yes, it is I. And a bottle of Madeira purloined from my father's cellar. Thought you might like it.'

Her ladyship's attitude changed abruptly. 'My boy, you rise further in my estimation each time I see you! Open it up, and let's sample a glass!'

Although the day was dry and bright, and quite warm for the time of year, the Dowager always had a good fire burning in the grate, even on the warmest summer's day. She settled herself in the chair by the hearth, and bestowed a rare smile of approval on her grandson as she sampled the wine.

'I'm not sorry you came now, my boy,' she remarked handsomely. 'Though I'm sure it wasn't just to bring me a bottle of wine.'

'No. I've come to take my leave of you, ma'am. I'm returning to Oxford this afternoon.'

She shook her head. 'My poor old brain must be going soft, for I feel sure your mama told me you were staying until the end of next week.'

'And so I was, until I learned that she's invited her eldest brother to stay. Uncle Horace will be arriving late this afternoon. And I fully intend to be well away from the place before he gets here.'

The Dowager's wicked cackle echoed round the room. 'Can't say I blame you, Bertram! Who wants to sit down to a sermon each mealtime?'

'Is your uncle a cleric?'

'Not just a cleric, Sarah, my dear. A bishop, no less!' He rolled his eyes in a very disrespectful way. 'And the most prosy old bore who ever drew breath! I'll probably come down again at the end of the month when I'm certain he'll have left. Will you still be here then, Sarah?'

'No, she won't,' the Dowager put in before Sarah could reply. 'I'm taking her to London, and we need to arrive before the Season begins, so that we have plenty of time to add substantially to her wardrobe,' she added with a meaningful glance at her future charge.

'Is Cousin Marcus escorting you?' There was more than just a hint of devilment in Bertram's wickedly glinting eyes. 'I shouldn't worry too much about finding Sarah a suitable husband, ma'am, if I were you. You'll have no trouble there. Why, I might even marry her myself! I think we'd suit admirably,' he remarked handsomely, and earned himself a flashing look of annoyance from his grandmother, but he was not deterred.

'I think your time will be better employed in finding Marcus a suitable wife. He ain't getting any younger, you know. And he ain't every woman's idea of a suitable spouse, rich as he is.'

'I shall take leave to inform you, you impertinent young jackanapes, that your cousin is not on the look out for a suitable wife, because he has already found himself the ideal mate,' the Dowager retorted in defence of her favourite grandchild. Then, realising she had been goaded into a foolish indiscretion, added, 'It so happens he—er—informed me a few weeks ago that he was considering offering for Bamford's eldest gel.'

Bertram was highly delighted with the unexpected news; Sarah was anything but. It felt almost as if an iron band had been clasped about her, and was slowly tightening, causing the most excruciating pain in a certain region beneath her ribcage.

Throughout the remainder of Bertram's visit and, later, when she sat down to luncheon with just the Dowager for company, she was able to maintain a reasonable flow of light-hearted conversation, but it was an effort. She felt anything but light-hearted, and as soon as she was able, she sought the solitude of her bedchamber.

She couldn't deny that the Dowager's disclosure had come as a bitter blow, both painful and totally unexpected. But why should this be? she wondered, sitting herself on the edge of the bed, and trying desperately to make some sense out of her wildly conflicting and surprisingly agonising thoughts. Her guardian would very soon attain the age of two-and-thirty. It really was high time he was thinking seriously about settling down.

He was a very wealthy man, and it was only natural that he would want his own offspring, children begot from a legal union, to inherit the Ravenhurst fortune. And there was no doubt in her mind that he would make a wonderful father, strict when necessary, but loving and devoted too. No matter what the world at large said of him, she knew that behind that hard, cynical exterior lay a deeply caring and very considerate man. But he was also, she reminded herself, extremely astute.

No, she reflected sombrely. He would never contemplate marriage without very serious consideration. The woman he had chosen must, therefore, have complied with all his ideals. She was no doubt a female of unimpeachable birth, a lady of grace and charm whose faultless manners and good breeding made her the perfect mistress for that lovely house at Ravenhurst. Sarah closed her eyes against the painful image of that oh, so faultless and, no doubt, very beautiful woman.

She ought, she knew, to feel overjoyed that her surprisingly kind and thoughtful guardian had at long last found the woman with whom he wished to spend the rest of his life. But the simple fact was that she hated the mere thought of his marrying.

A heartfelt sigh escaped her. She was, of course, simply suffering the reactions of an over-indulged child who had learned that its pampered existence would soon be coming to an end. Not since before her mother's sad demise had she experienced that comfortable feeling that comes from knowing there is someone close by who really cares about one's well-being.

For a brief time she had sampled the joys of a certain someone's undivided attention, and she was honest enough to admit that she resented bitterly the prospect of that certain someone bestowing his thoughtful considerations on another. Yes, that was why she felt so miserably depressed, so hollow inside, she decided, trying desperately hard to convince herself that there couldn't possibly be any more to it than that.

Well, this childishness must stop! she told herself bracingly, rising from the bed, and going across to the door. She had always prided herself on being a level-headed young woman. And she must continue to behave like one!

The Dowager, she knew, had retired after luncheon to the small downstairs parlour where the sun's rays did manage to penetrate the wall of trees and filter into that west-facing room. She would join her there, and they could discuss plans for their removal to the capital, and talk about the heady delights awaiting them in the forthcoming London Season.

Sarah was halfway down the stairs when the front door opened, and her guardian stepped into the hall. She stopped dead in her tracks, as though held by some intangible force, and watched him place his hat and gloves on to the table. As if sensing he was being watched, he looked up suddenly, and that wonderful smile reached his eyes.

His reaction at seeing her seemed so natural, so wonderfully spontaneous, that Sarah could only stare back down at him in wonder, in disbelief, almost, as the true state of her feelings hit her with such frightening clarity that it was as much as she could do to stop herself from gasping.

Then, without giving him the opportunity to address her, she swung round on her heels, and fled back up the stairs to her room, unable to believe, not wanting to believe the state of her own heart. It was all too new, all too frighteningly incredible to be true!

For a few moments she remained with her back firmly pressed against the door, trying desperately to listen for the sound of his footsteps above the deafening pounding in her ears. When she considered enough time had elapsed for him to have reached his bedchamber, she flew across to her wardrobe to collect her cloak. Thankfully, she saw no one lurking in the hall as she crept back down the stairs, and she hurried across to the front door and let herself quietly out of the house.

Both the small parlour and her guardian's bedchamber

were situated at the rear of the building. If her guardian was not still in his room, then the chances were he would have joined his grandmother downstairs. Which would be a blessing if he had. The last thing in the world she wanted was for a pair of sharp, dark eyes to catch sight of her.

So, Sarah hurried along the path at the front of the house that led to the large and rather overgrown shrubbery, and hid herself behind the dense foliage of a large clump of rhododendrons.

After a few minutes, when she saw no one coming along the path in pursuit, and felt fairly confident that she had not been spotted from the house, she began to relax a little: her breathing became slightly less erratic, and the all-too-betraying flush of colour that had mounted her cheeks from the moment she had made that startling discovery slowly began to fade. But she still felt unequal to facing him.

No, not yet, she told herself as she forged her way further into the dense area of shrubs. It was too soon, and he, the astute devil, would know instantly that there was something wrong. A shudder ran through her. She couldn't bear his knowing the state of her feelings, for if he for one moment suspected, it would lead to constraint, embarrassment, even, and the camaraderie that had existed between them right from that first night at The Traveller's Rest would be gone forever.

But when had it happened? More importantly, how had it happened? Even now she found it difficult to accept the simple truth that she loved him, and yet it had to be true, otherwise why should she feel the most intense dislike for this unknown female whom he had chosen for his future wife? Added to which, she couldn't deny that she was consumed with jealousy, virulent and agonisingly painful. And where there was no love, of course, there could be no jealousy.

Her lips trembled into a wry smile. How on earth could she have allowed herself to do such a foolish thing as to fall in love with that overbearing and frequently irritating man? After all, when had there ever been aught of the ardent lover in him throughout his dealings with her? True, he had kissed her once, but that had been merely to punish her. Why, he behaved towards her more like some strict uncle, forever scolding, than a gentleman wishing to fix his interests.

And therein lay the crux of the matter. His only interest in her was that of a concerned guardian, nothing more, nothing less. He liked her well enough. She did not doubt, either, that he found her attractive. She was definitely to his taste. . .as he was to hers. . . But his heart, unlike hers, belonged to another.

A sudden sound behind her brought her out of her despondent thoughts with a start, and she swung round, praying that her guardian had not, after all, seen her go out into the garden, and chosen to follow her. She just couldn't bring herself to face him yet. It was too soon-far, far too soon. She needed more time to get her emotions under control, to come to terms with the almost unbelievable state of her own heart.

Her eyes scanned the length of the overgrown path, and for a few moments she saw nothing at all, but then she detected the movement of foliage, and watched in horrified silence as a shadowy figure stepped out on to the path.

'Oh, my God!' she croaked, from a rapidly constricting throat. 'It's you!'

Chapter Twelve

'It is, indeed, Mrs Armstrong.' A far from unpleasant smile curled the attractive mouth. 'Or should I say, Miss Pennington.'

Quite surprisingly, Sarah suddenly felt very calm, mistress of her emotions once more, as she looked the woman over from head to foot. It was quite remarkable—there was no denying that it really was the most marvellous disguise. Anyone, Mr Stubbs, her guardian included, would never have suspected for a moment that the person standing before her now wasn't, indeed, a youth.

With short-cropped fair hair, and with her slender figure clad in workman's rough clothes, the woman bore little resemblance to that dithering middle-aged spinster who had resided for a time at The Traveller's Rest. Only those ice-blue eyes, so cold and calculating, remained the same. And Sarah hadn't forgotten those eyes.

For a moment or two she allowed her gaze to waver as she glanced fleetingly at the lethally formed piece of metal clasped in the slender fingers. 'Is there really any necessity for that?'

'I sincerely trust not, Miss Pennington.' The educated

voice, too, was far from unpleasant. 'Believe me, I have no desire to harm you, but I most certainly shall if you do not do exactly as I say.' She gestured with the pistol. 'Now, we shall leave this deplorable wilderness that I have been forced to work in these past days. And no more talking for the present, if you please.'

It took Sarah a moment only to come to the conclusion that little would be gained by crying out for help. Even supposing someone did happen to hear, she felt fairly certain she would be lying on the ground with a piece of lead shot in her long before any help arrived. So, she decided, for the time being at least, it was in her own best interests to do exactly as she was told.

Without a word, and yet so very conscious of that pistol pointing directly at her back, she turned and ventured deeper into the shrubbery. It was far from easy trying to forge a way through the tangled mat of branches, which snared at her hair, dislodging most of the pins, but eventually, looking very dishevelled, she came out on the far side where a rough wooden fence separated the Dowager's garden from the parkland.

Ordered to climb the fence, and then to keep as far as possible to those clumps of trees dotting the landscape, she continued to lead the way across the open stretch of land towards the wood.

Her young eyes, ever watchful, scanned the rich green acres in the hope of seeing one of his lordship's many estate workers, but, sadly, she detected no other human soul. Only sheep and cows, feeding on the lush pastureland, turned inquisitive eyes in their direction, but soon lost interest and lowered their heads again to continue grazing.

Once they had entered the relative privacy of the wood,

Sarah sensed the woman behind her relax slightly, though her abductor still made no attempt to speak, except to tell her in which direction to walk.

Keeping well away from the main tracks, where the gamekeeper might well be found patrolling, they headed in an easterly direction, but it was not until they had reached that part of the estate that had been left to deteriorate into a wilderness that Sarah had some inclination of where their destination might possibly be.

She had long since realised, of course, that she was being used as a means to attain the Felchett diamonds. Just how her abductor intended going about this, however, defeated her completely, for she suspected that the necklace, by this time, had been taken to London, and was probably safely locked away in a drawer somewhere at Bow Street.

All things considered, it might be wisest in the circumstances, she decided, her eyes narrowing assessingly, as the stonebuilt boat-house came into view, to allow this woman to believe that the necklace was still at hand.

'Be kind enough, Miss Pennington, to remove that wooden bar from across the door and place it against the wall,' her abductor said politely, stepping back a pace to enable Sarah to carry out this feat, which was no easy task as the wood happened to be a stout piece of oak and far from light.

She then gestured to Sarah to go inside and, without giving her the chance to take stock of the dim and musty-smelling interior, ordered her to sit on a pile of empty, evil-smelling sacks, and then promptly bound her hands with a strong piece of cord before tethering her like an animal to a stout metal ring fixed into the wall above Sarah's head.

'I apologise for all this melodrama,' the woman remarked with a wry smile. 'I think there's little chance you'll escape when I leave and secure the door. The bars at the window are pretty stout as well. But one cannot be too careful. I hope you are not so very uncomfortable?'

'Not at all,' Sarah responded with equal politeness as she studied her abductor, who had seated herself on a wooden box placed a few feet away. She made a strikingly handsome youth, and was, no doubt, an exceedingly pretty woman when dressed appropriately. She was not in her flush of youth. Nearing thirty, Sarah judged. Her features were regular, although there was a rather aristocratic line to her nose, and her hair was a soft, pretty shade of blonde.

'You are taking stock of your abductor, Miss Pennington,' she remarked after watching Sarah closely for a few moments. 'No doubt so that you will be able to give a detailed description to your friend from Bow Street.'

Sarah was unable to prevent a smile at this. 'With your undoubted talents I rather think that would be a complete waste of time.' She held the woman's gaze steadily. 'But may I be permitted to know your real name?'

One slender shoulder rose in an indifferent shrug. 'I don't see why not. It is Grant, Miss Pennington. Miss Isabella Grant.'

Sarah sighed as she looked down at the musty-smelling sacks beneath her. The woman had committed murder, and yet, now, having come face to face with her again, she could not find it within herself to hate her, or dislike her, even.

'What do you intend doing with me, Miss Grant?' she asked, raising her head to stare into those calculating blue eyes once again. Then, after a moment's deliberation, added, 'I think you ought to know that I am no longer in possession of the diamonds.'

'I don't doubt that for a moment.' A glimmer of something resembling respect added a sparkle to those ice-blue eyes. 'I was far from certain that you had the necklace, of course, even though I had managed to search everyone's room but yours back at that inn.

'But as soon as I saw Stubbs last night, I knew for sure that at one time it must have been amongst your possessions. Unlike me, you are an upstanding citizen. Upon discovering the necklace, you handed it over to your guardian who, in turn, wasted no time in making contact with the Runner.'

Sarah digested this in silence before a thought struck her. 'But how on earth did you know where to find me? And how did you know Mr Ravenhurst was my guardian?'

'As soon as I discovered you and Ravenhurst had left the inn, I made an excuse to see the magistrate. Stubbs wasn't with him at the time, but he had conveniently left all his notes on the table. The magistrate left me alone for a few minutes, and that was all it took for me to glean the necessary information. Ravenhurst very obligingly had even informed Stubbs where he intended taking you.'

She frowned suddenly. 'Now, may I ask you a question? Out of pure interest, where did you find the necklace?'

'It was in the secret compartment of my writing-case,' Sarah did not hesitate to tell her. 'I presume Mr Nutley must have placed it there.'

For a moment her blue eyes seemed to take on a faraway look, then she smiled. 'Of course! The case was on the table in the parlour. Well, well, well! I should never have credited Nutley with such ingenuity. He truly was a halfwitted buffoon, you know, Miss Pennington. I should never have become involved with him, but—' she shrugged again '—for a time our liaison proved worthwhile.

'But that is neither here nor there. As I was saying—I saw Stubbs last night at the village inn. He didn't see me, or didn't recognise me, one or the other. Pity your guardian brought him back. It forced my hand, somewhat.'

'So, it was you who broke into the Dower House last night.' Sarah looked across at her gravely. 'Do not underestimate Mr Stubbs or my guardian. They are not fools.'

'I realise that, Miss Pennington. It was foolish of me to have broken in last night in the slim hope that Ravenhurst had retained possession of the necklace, but as you know I was foiled in the attempt, and have only succeeded in alerting Stubbs and your guardian to the fact that I am, indeed, in the locale.' She waved her hand airily as though this fact was only of minor importance. 'But the trinket I covet far outweighs any possible danger. . .I must have that necklace!'

There was no mistaking the determination in the voice, and Sarah experienced a strange sense of satisfaction knowing that she had not been merely fanciful when she had suspected as much. That particular necklace meant everything to this woman, much, much more than just its material value. She was consumed with curiosity and was unable to curb it. 'Why, Miss Grant. . .Isabella? Why does that particular necklace mean so much to you?'

'Oh, it's a long story, my dear,' she responded, her mouth twisting into a bitter smile, but the enquiring look remained fixed in Sarah's eyes, and after a moment's indecision Isabella relented. 'Well, and why shouldn't I tell you? It can do no harm, after all, and it will help to pass the time. I don't intend leaving here until it begins to grow dark.'

She rose to her feet and went over to the window to stare out between the iron bars at the rippling grey water beyond. 'I have never learnt to swim, Sarah, have you?'

'No, I haven't.'

'Then we have something in common. . . But that is all, I suspect.' Thrusting hands into her pockets, and standing with feet slightly apart, she looked every inch the swaggering youth. 'You see before you the result of my poor mother's one foolish indiscretion, her one night of all-consuming passion. She was the only child of a country parson. Like you, she was sweet-natured, virtuous and very lovely.

'My grandfather lived close to a large estate, not unlike this one. He and his daughter were frequent guests at the house. On one occasion when they were invited to dine there, my mother met a young man of noble birth who was staying with the family. He charmed her and, foolishly believing him to be in love with her, she gave herself to him.'

Her bitter laugh was mirthless. 'The following day she discovered he had left without even so much as a note of farewell. Once my grandfather learned of my mother's unfortunate condition, he sent her to stay with his sister in Bristol. My mother died giving birth to me.'

Sarah, her eyes now filled with compassion, looked up at Isabella, who continued to stare resolutely out of the grimy window at the fading light. There had been no bitterness in her voice as she had related her mother's sad story. If anything, she had sounded quite matter-of-fact about it all, but then, Sarah reminded herself, it must be difficult to feel any sense of loss at all for someone you have never known. Isabella began to speak again, and she forced herself to listen.

'Needless to say, I did not enjoy a happy childhood. My great-aunt was a self-righteous, narrow-minded creature who never allowed me to forget for one moment my mother's shame. But she did educate me, and well enough for me to obtain a position as governess with a well-to-do family residing on the outskirts of Bristol. Before I had been with them a month, I was violated by the master of the house.'

Sarah's gasp of anguish seemed to hang in the air for endless moments.

'Yes, Sarah. I was raped. I doubt you have any real notion of what that means. . . And I hope to God you are never forced to find out!'

Isabella's sudden shout of laughter was a hollow sound that echoed round the cold stone walls. 'My grandfather never wanted anything to do with me. I was an embarrassment, you see—a blot on his stainless reputation. My father was and still is, for that matter, a womanising wastrel, who cares for nothing and for no one. . . And my first employer initiated me so tenderly into the gentle art of lovemaking. It is little wonder, is it not, that I have scant regard for the male sex?'

'No, it isn't any wonder,' Sarah agreed sombrely when Isabella fell silent. 'What did you do? You didn't stay with the family, surely?'

'Oh, no, my dear. I sought refuge again with my oh, so very loving aunt. Needless to say, she didn't believe my side of the story. She happened to be a friend of the family, and was firmly convinced I had encouraged her friend's husband to be unfaithful to his wife. She refused to take me back, so I joined a band of travelling actors.

'From childhood I had always been fascinated by the theatre. The world of make-believe is far more pleasant than cruel reality. And I was a good actress, a natural, even though I do say so myself, but being fairly tall, I was always given male roles to play. Which suited me very well. I think I should have been a boy. My life, I'm sure, would certainly have been less. . .traumatic.'

Sarah felt her sympathy coming to the fore once again, but concentrated her thoughts on the matter in hand by asking Isabella what made her turn to a life of crime.

'The theatre is not all joy, I assure you. But I shan't sully innocent ears by relating some of the more lurid aspects of an actress's life. Suffice it to say that, after eight years of travelling from place to place, I had had my fill. Besides—' she shrugged '—I was becoming a little too old to continue playing youths of sixteen and seventeen. So, I began to wonder how else I could make use of my undoubted talents.'

'How did you meet Mr Nutley?'

'I met him when our little company was giving a private performance at a large house in London. We talked for a while, and it became obvious that he was tired of trying to exist on the paltry allowance his father made him. He seemed an ideal choice at the time. He was invited everywhere, and he was certainly more than willing to make some easy money.'

Drawing her fair brows together in a deep frown, she shook her head. 'But it was foolish of me to have taken him as a partner. He was greedy, you see, and impatient to get his hands on the money.'

'So you started robbing the wealthy?' Sarah prompted when once again Isabella fell silent.

'Yes. I attained a position as a maid in different households. Sometimes I would work a week, maybe two, and then on the evening when a large party was being held, and the staff were fully occupied, I would steal the various items, and give them to Nutley that night, or the following day when he would call to thank his hostess for the pleasant evening.

'A week or so later I would take our ill-gotten gains to Bristol, hand them over to a certain gentleman I know, and deposit the money I received in the bank, to be shared between Nutley and myself at some later date. But as I mentioned before, he was eager to get his hands on the money. I warned him that if he started throwing brass about, people would wonder where it had come from and get suspicious. But he wouldn't listen.

'So, I made a bargain with him. If he helped me steal the Felchett diamonds, he could have all the money in that account of ours. He agreed, but insisted on retaining the diamonds and accompanying me to Bristol.'

'Did—did you kill him?' Sarah asked tentatively, and almost found herself sighing with relief when Isabella, a moment later, shook her head.

'No, I didn't kill him. We managed to get a few moments alone together at that inn, and he told me that he suspected Stubbs of being a Bow Street Runner. I asked him to hand the diamonds over to me, but he wouldn't. He said he would hide them somewhere safe until we were able to continue the journey to Bristol, and so I gave him that little concoction he put into the punch. But as I have already told you, he was a fool. I could never trust him to do anything right.'

Again she shook her head as though at some private thought. 'The close confines of that inn posed problems, though. I didn't want anyone to see me wandering about at that time of night, so I dressed in masculine attire and waited. I heard Nutley leave his room, and after a few minutes followed him down the stairs, but I waited too long, Miss Pennington. He flatly refused to tell me where he had hidden the necklace.

'I became angry, and took a step towards him. I must have startled him. He stepped back, fell over the chair, and hit his head on the settle. It was whilst I was searching for the necklace that you came down. I heard you in the coffee-room, and had only just enough time to open the windows before you came into the parlour. I went straight round to the back of the inn, climbed on to the lean-to roof, and managed to open my bedroom window and get back inside.'

'And the servant girl, Isabella. . .did you kill her?'

Isabella turned her head and looked down at her. 'Yes, I did,' she admitted, her voice emotionless, but Sarah could not mistake the flicker of regret in the blue eyes. 'It was never my intention to do so. . .it was never my intention to harm anyone. But the nosy little strumpet had been poking about my room. I believe I told you that, when we met for the first time at the head of the stairs, remember?

'She had opened the box where I keep my make-up and wigs, and knew I wasn't quite what I seemed. As soon as she had learned that Nutley had died, she came to me. Threatened to tell the Runner what she had seen in my room. The walls in that inn were paper-thin, and I was afraid our conversation might be overheard, so I managed to persuade her to meet me that night.'

Everything slotted so neatly into place, and Sarah might have believed Isabella nothing more than a victim of circumstance except for one or two rather damning facts. 'You said you never meant to harm anyone,' she reminded her. 'But you had one of the kitchen knives with you, Isabella, when you went to meet Rose. And you also planted a letter belonging to Dottie on the dead girl in a rather callous bid to implicate her.'

Isabella made not the least attempt to deny it. 'I saw the knife lying on the table when I returned my tray to the kitchen that evening. Truly, I meant only to frighten her, but I realised as soon as we met outside that I could never trust the conniving little harpy. Sooner or later she would have talked, no matter how much I paid her.

'And as for the letter...' There was a touch of malice in her smile this time. 'I went along the passageway, intending to search Dottie's room, as a matter of fact, when I saw that letter beneath the door.' She gave a shout of laughter. 'If my memory serves me correctly she was—er—rather occupied with the dashing Captain at the time. But then, she always was a flighty piece.'

This struck a cord of memory and Sarah, thrusting aside the embarrassingly vivid memory of that bedroom scene, said, 'Dottie mentioned once that she thought she recognised you. You did know her, then?'

'Oh, yes. We worked together some years ago in Bristol. Then I went off touring with the company. Can't recall what she did. She certainly didn't come with us.' Isabella moved away from the window, and was silent while she busied herself with lighting a candle set on one of the crates.

Then she turned to look at Sarah again. 'I'm afraid I must leave you now as I have certain arrangements to make. Wilkins assures me that no one ever comes here, and I must confess I have been here on several occasions and have never caught sight of a soul. You'll be safe enough for now, but I shall need to make arrangements so that I can hide you somewhere else early in the morning.'

She frowned heavily. 'That confounded Runner turning up out of the blue has caused me a great deal of trouble! It had never been my intention to abduct you, Sarah. But,' she shrugged, 'one must learn to be adaptable.'

'What makes you so sure the necklace is still here? All this might be a complete waste of time,' Sarah suggested, but Isabella shook her head.

'If your guardian hasn't retained possession of it, then you can be sure that Stubbs has it. He no doubt thought to use it in an attempt to draw me out into the open.' She picked up the candle and placed it on the crate nearest to Sarah. 'I'll return as soon as I can with some food, but I'm afraid it won't be for some little time, so I'll leave you the candle.'

'Isabella,' Sarah said softly, arresting the woman's progress to the door, 'don't do this. You'll be caught. They will hang you.'

The woman's laughter held a note of recklessness. 'Well, as my dear aunt was so fond of telling me, I was born to be hanged. But not in this country, my dear. I have a fancy to try my luck in the New World.'

'Then go, Isabella!' she urged. 'Go now while you still have the chance! The necklace cannot be that important to you.'

There suddenly seemed fire in those ice-blue eyes. 'Oh, but it is, Sarah,' she countered, her voice throbbing with emotion. 'It means everything to me. . . Had Lord Felchett been an honourable man, had he married my mother, those diamonds would eventually have been mine. They are mine by right!'

As soon as he had changed his clothes, Marcus took himself off to the library, and began to compose a long letter to his secretary. It had never been his intention to stay away from Ravenhurst for this length of time. Even had he stuck to his original plan and gone to the Bamfords, he would have remained with them for a week at most.

But, of course, Sarah had changed all that. And he certainly had no intention of leaving her now. In a week or two he would escort her to London. But would she be any safer there? He paused in the act of dipping his quill into the standish, his dark brows snapping together. No, confound it, she wouldn't! There could be no peace of mind until that Grimshaw woman had been caught and placed safely behind bars.

Thoughts of his ward continued to break his concentration, and it was quite some time before he had completed his task. After sealing the letter with a wafer, he left the library and went across the hall to the parlour, and was surprised to discover his grandmother the sole occupant of the room.

'Where's Sarah?'

The Dowager glanced up from her embroidery. 'I've no idea. I haven't seen her since luncheon. I thought she was with you.'

'Perhaps she's still in her room, then.' He sat himself down, and absently began to tap the arm of the sofa with his fingertips. 'When I came back earlier, she gave me a most peculiar look, and then shot up the stairs. It really was most odd. She looked at me just as though I were a complete stranger.'

'You do tend to have that effect on people, Marcus. I expect you said something beastly and upset the poor child.'

He cast her a glance of exasperation. 'I'll have you know I never so much as opened my mouth. Still—' he shrugged '—I expect it's nothing. Women do tend to take queer turns at times, as you know.'

'No, I'm afraid I don't know, Marcus. You'll need to explain yourself.'

'You know very well what I mean!' he retorted. 'Females tend to behave oddly at a—er—certain time each month.'

The Dowager placed her embroidery on her lap, and looked directly across at him. 'If that is your rather indelicate way of trying to ascertain whether Sarah is suffering from her monthly, then I can tell you with absolute certainty that she is not. That was over days ago. But if the poor child seems not quite herself. . .well, it's hardly surprising in the circumstances, now is it?'

Before going to see Stubbs that morning, he had taken the Dowager into his confidence, admitting freely that he suspected the break-in the previous night had been perpetrated by none other than Nutley's accomplice, after the Felchett diamonds. Her ladyship had betrayed not the least sign of surprise, nor dismay. Her only comment, in fact, had been to agree wholeheartedly with him when he had suggested that Sarah be removed to Ravenhurst for her own safety.

A ghost of a smile hovered about his mouth. 'By the by, Sarah refuses to leave. I tried to persuade her, but she won't run away.'

'A pity, but I cannot say I'm surprised, Marcus. It's in the child's blood, after all. Her father was a courageous man, and her mother was most certainly no shrinking violet.'

They were interrupted by Clegg, who entered to light the candles. When he had completed his task, the Dowager requested him to ask Buddle to go up to Sarah's room and check that all was well. Five minutes later the maid came in, her expression grave.

'Miss Sarah isn't there, my lady, and her cloak's missing from the wardrobe.' She cast anxious eyes across at her mistress's grandson. 'I know on fine days she's in the habit of going out for a walk with Sutton, so I checked. But he hasn't seen her, not since this morning.'

'It's probably nothing, Marcus,' the Dowager suggested, but not very convincingly. 'Sarah may have wanted to be by herself, that is all.' Out of the corner of her eye she caught sight of her butler hovering, uncertainly, behind Buddle. 'Yes, Clegg. What is it this time?'

He came forward, a note in his hand. 'I have just found this pushed under the door. It's for you, sir.'

The Dowager watched her grandson pale visibly as he cast his eyes over the single sheet, and nodded dismissal to her servants before saying, 'That woman has Sarah, hasn't she?' He did not respond, but then he really didn't need to, for his grim expression was answer enough. 'We must get every able-bodied man on the estate out searching for her,' she suggested in some urgency, but surprisingly he shook his head.

'No, we can't do that. Here, read it for yourself.'

Although the Dowager's eyesight was not good, the letter was written in a neat hand, and after a few moments she was able to focus sufficiently to read:

I have your ward, Ravenhurst. She is unharmed and shall remain so providing you make no attempt to locate her whereabouts. You know what I want in exchange for her safe return. I shall contact you again tomorrow with further instructions.

The Dowager looked across at her grandson, who had gone over to stare sightlessly out of the window. 'Do—do you think she will harm her?'

'She has committed murder once, I'm sure she's quite capable of doing so again.'

'Oh, Marcus, no!' The Dowager had been reared to consider any display of the weaker emotions quite vulgar. Not since the death of Ravenhurst's mother had tears been seen in her grey eyes, but they were clearly visible now. 'You must hand over the necklace,' she urged him. 'You have no choice.'

'I fully intend to.' His voice was impassive, but the look of cold fury in his eyes as he turned away from the window almost made her gasp. 'And if she has harmed so much as one hair on my little Sarah's head, I will kill that woman with my bare hands.' He went across to the door, but turned back to add, 'I must contact Stubbs and tell him what has occurred. For the time being, ma'am, I should be obliged if you keep your own counsel.'

Half an hour later Marcus, his expression as grim and as darkly threatening as a thunder cloud, rode into the inn yard. He was suffering agony over Sarah's well-being; but resentment at his inability to do anything positive to aid her only fuelled his rage. Throughout his adult life he had always been resolute, making decisions swiftly when necessary, no matter how unpalatable they had happened to be; and yet here he was, still, frustratingly in two minds.

If he sent men out searching for his ward, as his grandmother had suggested, he might well be placing Sarah in yet more danger. On the other hand, though, once that woman had the necklace in her possession, Sarah would be of no further use to her, would be a liability, in fact. Could he really trust a woman who had killed before to keep her word, and not harm Sarah? It was a risk he was not prepared to take.

And yet, where did he begin searching? Sarah might be anywhere: here in this very village, or miles away by now. He ground his teeth in vexation. The situation seemed hopeless!

As he entered the inn he suffered a further setback when the landlord informed him that Stubbs had ridden out of the village on a hired horse that afternoon, and had not as yet returned.

'Did he say where he was going?'

'No, sir, that he didn't.' The landlord scratched his head. 'I mind that he mentioned he'd be back for supper, though. So p'raps he won't be too long.'

'Very well. I'll have a tankard of ale whilst I'm waiting.'

Marcus sat himself at a corner table, his mind deep in sombre thought. He was vaguely aware that the tap was becoming crowded with locals, refreshing themselves after a hard day's toil, but it wasn't until the room suddenly echoed with hoots of raucous laughter that he ceased his contemplation of the logs burning brightly on the hearth, and gazed about the inn. Unfortunately, his sharp eyes caught no sign of Stubbs. It appeared he was in for a long wait.

Tossing the dregs of the tankard down his throat, he went across to the counter for a refill. 'What's all the commotion about?' he asked, after noting the amused expressions on several faces.

'Oh, it be only old Saul 'ere, spinning one of 'is yarns,' the landlord answered.'

'I tell 'ee I seen it!' vowed a near-toothless individual in a rough homespun jacket, and battered, misshapen black hat. 'Seen it wi' me own eyes, I did. And 'eard it too. Oh, m'lord,' he said, fixing his myopic gaze on Ravenhurst, 'the scream it were fearful, so it were. Like the cry of something un'uman.'

'Pay 'im no mind, sir,' the landlord advised. 'He always be in 'ere telling some tale. Reckons he saw the old witch up at the boat-house on your uncle's land.'

The hand raising the tankard to Marcus's lips checked in mid-air, and his eyes narrowed fractionally. 'So, you heard someone scream. When was this?' He caught the warning glance the landlord cast in the old man's direction. 'Come on, man! I'm not interested in what you were doing on my uncle's land. But I want to know if you genuinely saw or heard someone near that boat-house.'

'It were 'bout an hour ago, sir,' the old man said after a moment's indecision. He stared fixedly down into his empty tankard. 'Sometimes I takes a short cut across 'is lordship's land. Weren't doing no 'arm.'

'And you're certain you heard a woman scream?'

'It were the witch, sir! 'Orrible wailing it were. And I saw 'er ghostly shadow through the window. All bent and twisted she were. Weren't 'uman!'

Marcus was far from convinced. The old man looked just the type to say anything to gain a bit of attention, but on the other hand the boat-house would be an ideal place to hide someone. No one local, he cast a shrewd glance in the old man's direction, except perhaps someone engaged in an unlawful pursuit, would ever venture there.

Demanding pen and paper, he returned to his table. The landlord's writing materials left much to be desired. The single sheet he brought was decidedly grubby and dog-eared, the ink bore a strong resemblance to thick mud and the quill was in urgent need of sharpening. Nevertheless, Marcus managed to pen a note which was reasonably legible. He then folded the letter carefully and tucked the note he had received from Sarah's abductor inside before taking it over to the counter.

'It is imperative that you give this to Mr Stubbs the instant he returns, understand?' He handed the folded sheet over to the landlord, watched him place it for safety upon a shelf, and then turned to the old man who was regarding him rather suspiciously. Taking a handful of coins from his pocket, he tossed them down on the counter. 'Buy yourself another drink. And if I should discover this witch of yours, you shall be rewarded with the finest supper, fish or otherwise, money can buy!'

The old man watched Ravenhurst leave, not quite knowing what to make of him. If the Earl's nephew chose to go on a witch-hunt, that was his business. At least, he mused, he would be getting a decent supper at the end of it. Because he had seen her. As large as life, all bent double and swaying from side to side, and with hair all wild and tangled. . . Of a certainty he'd seen her!

Chapter Thirteen

The flame flickered yet again, casting weird shapes across the cold greystone walls. The candle would soon gutter, and then the only light would come from that, Sarah thought, staring up between the bars at the window at that bright crescent shape in the cloudless late evening sky. She shivered, but with her hands confined she was unable to draw her grey cloak more tightly about her.

As soon as the sun had gone down the temperature had dropped like a stone, and yet she tried desperately not to think of the comforting warmth of the Dowager's sitting-room, or of the pheasant pie that was to have been served for dinner that evening. She doubted very much if that delicacy had been sampled by anyone. Hidden beneath the Dowager's prickly exterior was a sweet old lady who would have had little, if any, appetite. And her guardian. . .?

Sarah blinked back the threatening tears. Poor Ravenhurst must be out of his mind with worry. Right from that very first evening when they had dined together at The Traveller's Rest, he had taken such good care of her, attentive to her every need. Dear God! What a fool she had been to go out into the garden alone! But she had done so, and it was entirely her own fault that she was now suffering the consequences of her own folly.

She gave herself a mental shake. Despondency certainly wouldn't aid her cause. Perhaps she ought to try again to free herself from her bonds? she thought, but then dismissed the idea. Her wrists still felt raw after her last attempt. And what a complete waste of effort that had turned out to be! She had succeeded in getting to her feet, but try as she might she could not pull the metal ring from the wall, and had screamed out in frustration.

The memory of her fruitless efforts drew a reluctant smile from her. She would scream her head off if she thought there was the remotest possibility of someone hearing her, but she doubted a search would be instigated until morning. By which time, of course, there was every chance she would have been removed from Styne.

The depressing realisation had just filtered across her mind when she thought she detected a sound outside, and turned her eyes towards the door. Yes—yes, there it was again! It was definitely a footstep. Isabella, no doubt, returning with some food. Well, that was something, at least! She was absolutely famished!

She heard the heavy piece of oak being removed from its confining metal brackets, and then the creaking sound of the rusty hinges as the door swung open. The inevitable pistol barrel came into view first. Isabella, evidently, was remaining cautious, no doubt fearing that her prisoner just might have released herself from her bonds, and was lurking, ready to attack.

Some hope! Sarah mused, glancing heavenwards. Then she realised that the dark shape filling the aperture was too large to be that of a woman. It couldn't possibly be. . .? Her heart seemed to turn a somersault. Yes, yes, it was!

A strange little sound somewhere between a sob and a squeal of joy escaped her, and then she heard that beloved deep masculine voice.

'Ah! So the witch does exist, after all. And, I might add, looking every inch the evil crone with her hair all wild and tangled.'

'Oh, sir!' Sarah was too deliriously happy to see him to pay any heed to his insults. Nor could she prevent an errant tear from escaping as she watched his approach. 'How on earth did you know I was here?'

'I hadn't a clue where to start looking for you, my darling.' Placing his pistol down on the wooden crate nearby, Marcus knelt down in front of her and began to undo the cord. 'It was whilst I was waiting at the inn for Stubbs to put in an appearance that I learned from our poacher friend that he had seen and heard someone, or—er—something, in the boat-house. He was firmly convinced it was the witch.

'And I must say,' he added, casting a wry glance at her grime-streaked face, and tussled brown locks, 'you do resemble one.'

'And you wouldn't be looking at your best, either, if you had done battle with your grandmother's shrubbery!' she retorted, her spirit returning, but couldn't prevent a tender little smile as she distinctly heard the half-smothered oath as he grappled with a particularly stubborn knot. 'You are like a knight of old, sir, riding *ventre à terre* to rescue the damsel in distress.'

'Loath though I am to disillusion you, my child, but I left my fiery steed back at the inn, and walked. As I was ordered not to go searching for you, I thought I'd be less likely to be seen if I came to the exceedingly foolish damsel's rescue on foot.'

As Sarah had cursed herself more than once for going out alone into the garden, she did not waste her breath trying to account for her actions. The criticism was entirely justified, after all. Instead, she asked him when he had heard from Isabella.

'Is that her name?' He untied the last knot, and was silent for a moment as he examined her sore wrists. 'I received a note from her shortly before we were due to dine. Which reminds me. I haven't eaten, and I'm slightly peckish.'

'You're not the only one! Oh, do let's hurry, sir,' she urged. 'Isabella said she would return.'

'Has returned,' a rather smugly sounding voice corrected.

A gasp rose in her throat, but everything happened so quickly that Sarah hardly had time to move. She saw Ravenhurst reach for his pistol, saw the sudden flash of light from the doorway before the deafening report echoed round the stone building and her guardian slumped down on to his knees, gripping his left arm just above the elbow. Then Isabella, with lightning speed, had his pistol in her hand and was levelling it at his head.

'No!' Sarah screamed. Scrambling to her feet, she placed herself between the pistol and her guardian without a thought for her own safety. 'You'll not shoot him again, Isabella. That I swear!'

'Get out of the way, Sarah!' Ravenhurst ordered in a far-from-gentle way, but she ignored him, and took a step towards Isabella to avoid his outstretched hand.

'I mean it, Isabella. You'll need to shoot me first.'

Ice-blue eyes looked deeply into Sarah's. 'Yes, I really

do believe you mean that. Well, well, well! What have we here?' She sounded genuinely amused. 'You're a lucky man, Ravenhurst. But a rather foolish one, too, for I did warn you not to go searching for her.'

The look he cast her, as he rose slowly to his feet, betrayed his utter contempt. His arm throbbed painfully, and already he could feel the stickiness of blood oozing between the fingers of his right hand as he held the wounded portion of flesh. 'You'll need me to get the diamonds.'

'Stay just where you are!' Isabella commanded, levelling the pistol threateningly as he made to take a step round Sarah. 'Although I would dislike very much to hurt your ward, I would think nothing of putting a period to your existence. You don't imagine for a moment that I would foolishly trust you. I'm not so gullible.

'You will get the necklace when I have Sarah safely hidden in some other place. She will be returned to you, unharmed, when you have handed over the necklace. Now—' she slowly backed away from them '—stay perfectly still, both of you.'

Sarah didn't need telling twice, and she prayed that the man standing beside her wouldn't foolishly make another sudden move, for the pistol clasped in those slender fingers was still levelled in his direction. Hardly daring to breathe, Sarah watched her bend to pick up something lying by the wall, and caught it deftly as it was hurled in her direction.

Then Isabella disappeared into the night, the door was slammed shut, and she almost sighed with relief when she heard the scraping sound of the wooden bar being fitted firmly into place.

'If I do not end by flaying your rear, my girl, it will

be no thanks to you!' Marcus ground out when the sound of Isabella's footsteps had died away. 'You have the crass stupidity to go out walking by yourself and, not satisfied with that lunacy, you then place yourself in front of a maniac brandishing a loaded pistol!'

Totally unmoved by the threat, and the scathing condemnation of her actions, Sarah set the small sack which Isabella had hurled at her on the wooden crate, and then persuaded her still seething guardian to remove his cloak so that she could take a look at his injured arm.

Tossing the cloak on top of the crate, he sat himself upon it. He felt more than one stab of pain as Sarah eased him gently out of his jacket, but he was gratified to note, as she rolled up his shirt sleeve, that she did not flinch at the sight of blood.

'I was fairly confident that she would not attempt to shoot me,' Sarah remarked after inspecting the wound, which thankfully was little more than a deep scratch, 'but quite certain that she would not hesitate to shoot you again. She doesn't like men, you see.'

'No, I don't see!' he snapped, far from appeased; then promptly forgot his anger as Sarah, unexpectedly, raised the hem of her dress and tore a strip off her underskirt, and he was afforded a tantalising glimpse of a neat ankle.

Sarah delved into the sack, wondering if it contained anything that might help clean her guardian's wound, and drew out a small flask. 'I wonder what's in this?'

He took it from her, deftly flicked off the lid and raised the flask to one thin nostril. 'Brandy,' he informed her, only to have the flask snatched from his fingers moments later as he was about to place it to his lips.

'In that case I'll have it. James Fenshaw told me that soldiers in Spain use this to clean wounds when they can get hold of it. At least,' she amended, pouring it liberally over his upper arm, 'I think he said brandy.'

'Here, don't waste it all, woman!' he ordered, snatching the flask back and taking a large swallow before she could reach for it again. 'Ahh, that's better! It'll do more good inside than out.'

He took no heed whatsoever of the disapproving look she cast him, and so Sarah concentrated on making a pad with her clean handkerchief, and wrapping the wound up deftly with the piece of material torn from her petticoats.

'Does that feel any easier?' she asked, rolling down his shirt sleeve, and helping him back into his jacket.

'Much. You make a capital little nurse, my darling,' he informed her, using the endearment for the second time, she noticed, and was glad the dimness concealed the pleasurable glow that rose in her cheeks.

Being a level-headed young woman, however, she tried not to read too much into those sweet words, and went back over to the small sack to see what other goodies it contained. Luckily, Isabella had had the forethought to bring more candles, together with a bottle of wine, a wholesome loaf of bread and a good wedge of cheese, and Sarah quickly lit a fresh candle from the remnants of the old before it finally went out.

Holding the new candle aloft, she gazed about their makeshift prison, and noticed something lying near the door. 'How thoughtful of Isabella!' she exclaimed, bending to pick up the item. 'She's brought us a blanket.'

His jaw dropping perceptively, Marcus gazed across at her as though she had taken leave of her senses. 'Thoughtful...? Thoughtful! I'll give her thoughtful when I get my hands on her!'

The look in his dark eyes boded ill for their captor as

he stalked across to the door. It was securely fastened by the wooden bar and did not so much as creak when he put his full weight behind it. He then went over to the window, but here again the metal bars were solidly in place, and he knew that it would be a complete waste of time and energy trying to prise one loose. It looked as though their only chance of escape lay firmly in the hands of the Runner.

He threw himself down on the pile of sacks, and sniffed suddenly, his threatening expression being replaced by one of distaste. 'Phew! What is that revolting stench?'

'I expect it's those sacks you can smell. One gets accustomed to it after a while.'

'Does one?' He looked far from convinced. 'Well, I'll take your word for that. What else did the darling creature see fit to provide us with?'

Sarah collected the food and wine and joined him on the pile of old sacking. While she busied herself breaking two goodly chunks off the loaf and dividing the wedge of cheese, Marcus picked up the wine, drew the cork out with his teeth and spat it on the dirt floor before offering her the bottle first. Sarah found that she was thirsty and swallowed the rich red liquid with gusto.

'Here, steady on, child!' He snatched the bottle from her. 'I don't want you tipsy. And have a thought for your bodily functions, for heaven's sake! There aren't too many places to hide in here when the time comes for you to relieve yourself.'

Sarah paused in the act of biting into her chunk of bread. 'Must you be so vulgar! I was just beginning to enjoy this candlelit supper, and now you've gone and ruined it.' She betrayed more than just peevishness in the look she cast him. 'Though I suppose it's hardly a new experience for you.'

'And what, precisely, is that supposed to mean?' he enquired, after taking a drink himself and wiping the back of his hand across his mouth.

Flatly refusing to admit that she had felt a twinge of jealousy at the thought of the many times he must have enjoyed an intimate meal with only his mistress for company, Sarah merely shrugged and began to eat the wholesome fare, but after a while broke the silence that had grown between them by saying, 'Isabella wouldn't have hurt me, you know. It's only men she dislikes.'

'Yes, so you've mentioned before.'

'And it's quite understandable really.'

She then went on to relate the woman's rather sorry life history, but the look on his face informed her clearly enough that he was far from sympathetic, even before he said, 'Others have suffered equally, Sarah, and have not resorted to murder.'

'I know,' she agreed softly, brushing the crumbs from her skirt, 'but I cannot help wishing, now, that I'd never given you that necklace. For all I care, Isabella is welcome to the wretched thing!'

'My sentiments exactly!' he astounded her by divulging. 'If I hadn't given it to Stubbs, I would have willingly handed it over to her already.'

'She won't rest until she has it, sir. She considers it hers by right. She told me she is Lord Felchett's illegitimate child.'

This ignited a spark of interest, and his brows rose. 'Is she, by gad? Well, I can't in all honesty say I saw any resemblance, but then, I was hardly looking for it.' He reached for his cloak and the blanket, and began to spread them over their legs. 'Let's hope Stubbs doesn't delay too long bringing it here.'

'Is it still in his possession then, sir?' Sarah was astounded, even though she recalled Isabella saying that this was possibly the case. 'I thought he wouldn't have hesitated in returning such a valuable item to Bow Street.'

The look in his eyes was decidedly guarded. 'Stubbs suspected that she would make an attempt to get her hands on it again, and so retained possession of it to—er—flush her out, as it were. Now, let's try and get some sleep. With any luck it won't be too long before Stubbs comes to our rescue.'

Sarah made to move a little way away, but was pulled roughly back against him, her head forced down on to his broad chest and firmly held there.

He felt her slender body stiffen, and could well imagine that that lovely face of hers had already stained to an embarrassed shade of deep crimson. Undoubtedly, this was the first time she had ever lain stretched out beside a man, and the knowledge brought a gleam of satisfaction to brighten his eyes.

'We'll keep each other warm this way,' he remarked in an attempt to assure her she had nothing to fear. 'We've little enough coverings, and it's beginning to get damned chilly.' As though to add credence to his words he shivered. 'There'll be a frost before morning.'

Sarah dared not move, hardly dared even to breathe. The latent strength in that hard muscular frame both frightened and aroused, causing her pulse rate to soar and awakening that strangely disturbing yearning deep within.

If the feel of his fully clad body could have such a devastating effect on her, how would she react if that image she had had of them lying together naked, their limbs seductively entwined, ever became a reality? She was powerless to prevent a little shiver of sensual pleasure running through her at the mere thought.

Misunderstanding completely the reason for the convulsive movement, Marcus removed his hand from her head, and pulled the blanket further up about her shoulders. The simple action brought her back down to earth with a jolt, and she did not know whether she felt reassured, or utterly disenchanted: perhaps a little of both.

No matter what her own private fantasies might be, her practical guardian was holding her this way for one reason only, and although it was grossly improper, it did make sense to give each other warmth if they could. So, she wriggled into a more comfortable position, moulding her slender body close to his, and was ordered in no uncertain terms to stop fidgeting. She could not forbear a smile; scolding was, after all, so much a part of his nature.

For a while she lay there listening to the steady pounding of his heart but, lulled by the steady rise and fall of his chest, and the comforting stroking of her hair, it wasn't long before her eyelids grew too heavy to keep open.

By the sudden deepening of her breathing Marcus knew the instant she had fallen asleep, but continued absently to caress the soft golden-brown locks. It had been a mistake to force her so close to him; he realised that now. He could clearly feel the soft roundness of her breasts through the thin material of his shirt and the warmth of her slender legs nestling against his own, and experienced that inevitable stirring deep in his loins.

He was a virile man, and not accustomed to curbing his very natural male desires. A string of experienced mistresses over the years had satisfied his needs whenever the mood had taken him; but he had never felt for one of them, nor indeed any other human soul, the tender emotions he experienced for this young woman.

Without conscious thought he raised his other hand to trace the sweet curve of her jaw, and Sarah stirred slightly, murmuring in her sleep. Yes, he could quite easily raise that lovely face and awaken her with softly coaxing kisses. He was experienced enough as a lover not to frighten her with urgent passion, but to arouse her with gentle caresses until she willingly gave herself to him.

Yes, it would be so delightfully easy, so intoxicatingly pleasurable to do so, too, but he knew he must not. Certainly not at the time, but soon afterwards she might regret what had taken place between them; might possibly become resentful, especially when the inevitable happened and they were forced to marry. And that, he reminded himself, far from concerned at this very real possibility, might well prove to be the outcome of this night's escapade if Stubbs didn't hurry and put in an appearance.

Sarah was the first to wake the following morning. For a few moments she was a little disconcerted to discover her head not resting on the accustomed softness of a comfortable pillow, but on what felt something very like a hard stone wall. Then memory returned, and she carefully raised herself so as not to disturb her guardian, who appeared to be resting, still, in the arms of Morpheus.

Her lips curled into a tender little smile. How different he looked when asleep, and yet the high-bridged aristocratic nose was just the same, as was that square determined chin; but the deep clefts on either side of his mouth seemed less pronounced, as were the tiny lines at the corners of his eyes.

Suddenly his eyes were open, staring fixedly up at her. 'Ah! So you're awake at last. You sleep as one dead, Sarah. I was beginning to get cramp.'

Not the most loverlike words from a man who had held her in his arms all night, she thought wryly. But how typical of him! She edged away a little, and turned her head to stare at the early morning light filtering through the grimy window.

'Mr Stubbs never turned up, then?' she remarked absently.

'Oh, he popped in for half an hour or so, but the sound of your snoring soon sent him away again.'

The fulminating glance she cast him before scrambling to her feet brought a deep rumble of masculine laughter to echo round the cold greystone walls.

'I am not an aggressive person by nature, sir, but there have been many occasions when I have experienced an almost overwhelming desire to box your ears soundly. Never more so than now!'

Raising his good arm, he rested his head on his hand, and gazed up at her with the most wickedly masculine smile she had ever seen. 'In that case I shall take leave to inform you, young woman, that you are a very disrespectful ward.'

'And I shall take leave to inform you,' she countered, 'that from the beginning of our acquaintanceship, I have never considered myself your ward. Nor have I ever looked upon you as a guardian, for that matter.'

'No? How very interesting!' The look he cast her was openly challenging. 'How do you look upon me, Sarah?'

As my love. . .my life, her heart answered. She turned

away lest he should glimpse the truth mirrored in her eyes, and said, in quite a remarkable interpretation of a frosty middle-aged spinster, 'I look upon you as possibly the most irritating man I have ever had the misfortune to encounter.'

He chuckled at this. 'Never mind, my darling. You'll grow accustomed to my little foibles in time.'

He made to rise, checking perceptively at a noise outside. Sarah, who had heard it too, looked back at him, but remained silent at the warning look in his eyes. She turned her attention to the door. Could it possibly be Mr Stubbs at last? Her hopes plummeted when the door opened, and she glimpsed that, now, all-too-familiar pistol clasped in slender fingers before Isabella came slowly forward.

'I trust you passed a not-too-uncomfortable night?' The smile she cast Ravenhurst was not pleasant, enmity clearly visible in her eyes. 'Sarah, if you would be good enough to come over here to me, we shall be on our way.'

'Enough of this tomfoolery!' Marcus ground out before Sarah had taken more than a pace or two towards the door. 'Take me, and let Sarah get you the diamonds.'

'Thank you for the offer,' Isabella responded, her eyes never wavering from his face for a second as she gestured Sarah to approach, 'but I think I'll stick to my original choice. Not only am I certain that Sarah would never willingly harm me, as you most assuredly would given half the chance, but I rather think that her company is more to my taste.'

Sarah noted the look of disgust flit across his features, and hurried forward before he could even think of trying to overpower Isabella. Her wrist was snatched, and the pistol was placed to her temple, and yet, strangely, she experienced no fear whatsoever for her own safety, only for the man's standing several feet away.

'Don't even think of moving, Ravenhurst,' she warned, pulling Sarah back and out of the door.

Once outside, Isabella released her hold to toss a folded piece of paper down on the boat-house floor, and then slammed the door closed in what seemed almost a triumphant gesture while signalling to Sarah to pick up the wooden bar.

She did not hesitate. The last thing in the world she wanted was for Ravenhurst to come charging out, and receive another bullet. He might not be so lucky next time. She bent, about to pick up the heavy piece of oak when she saw a sudden movement out of the corner of her eye.

Mr Stubbs seemed to appear from nowhere. The next instant he was cursing loudly as he grappled with Isabella for the weapon. Although they were both of a similar height, the Runner was far stronger; but Isabella, with a strength generated by stubborn determination, fought like a wildcat to retain a hold on the pistol. They swayed this way and that, almost toppling over at one point, then retrieving their balance.

Had Sarah not been witnessing it with her own eyes, she would never have believed it possible for a mere woman to put up such resistance. Two pairs of arms rose in the air, and then swung in a wide arc down again. There was a sudden deafening report, the boat-house door flew open and Ravenhurst came hurtling out, almost knocking into her as she watched Mr Stubbs fall to the ground, his face contorted in agony as he gripped his leg.

With lightning speed, Isabella ran part of the way along the jetty and drew out a second pistol from her jacket pocket to hold Ravenhurst once again at bay. She either did not notice, or was simply unconcerned that Sarah had gone to the Runner's aid.

Ripping yet a further strip off her already depleted undergarment, Sarah attempted to staunch the flow of blood pouring from the badly injured knee. She was vaguely aware that a conversation of sorts was taking place between Ravenhurst and Isabella, but so concerned was she over Mr Stubbs's welfare that she took little heed of just what was being said.

The remnant of petticoat was soon sodden, and blood oozed between her fingers. She raised deeply troubled eyes to Mr Stubbs's face, and saw him make a gesture with his own.

The silent message was discernible enough. Altering her position slightly in an attempt to hide her actions from the ever-alert Isabella, Sarah felt in the pocket of the Runner's jacket. Her fingers came into contact with cold metal, and something else, too.

Very slowly, she eased both pistol and necklace out, handing the pistol to the Runner before rising slowly to her feet. Ignoring his gesture for her to step aside, she turned and walked slowly towards the jetty, coming to a halt beside her tall guardian.

'Here, Isabella, this is what you want.' She held out the necklace in the hand coated in the Runner's blood, and felt heartily sickened by the unmistakable flash of triumphant delight in the woman's eyes. 'Here, then, take it! More than enough blood has been spilled already over the wretched thing,' and with that she hurled the necklace away from her in a gesture of revulsion, as though to handle it further would infect her with the same malignant obsession.

The sparkling stones, glinting with all the colours of the rainbow, seemed to hang suspended in the frosty morning air for such a long time. Isabella leaned against the wooden rail, her arm and fingers stretching out in a frenzied attempt to grasp the precious trophy.

There was the sudden sound of splintering wood, followed by a terrified, high-pitched scream as Isabella tumbled over the edge. And the last thing Sarah saw as she rushed forward were Isabella's fingers, still clasping the necklace, disappear beneath the murky grey waters.

'Oh, my God!' She turned imploring eyes up to Ravenhurst. 'She cannot swim, sir. . .she cannot swim!'

He seemed to hesitate, but only for a moment. His cloak and jacket were tossed on to the jetty, quickly followed by his boots; then he dived into the lake. Sarah waited, her heart pounding against her ribcage, her eyes frantically scanning the surface of the water for what seemed an interminable length of time, but what was possibly no more than two or three minutes. Then she saw bubbles rising to the surface, and Ravenhurst's head, blessedly, appear above the water.

His fingers blue with cold, he held on to the jetty with difficulty. 'God, it's freezing down there,' he gasped, trying desperately to catch his breath, 'and as black as pitch. I can't see a blasted thing!'

He took a deep breath, and looked as though he was about to submerge again, but Sarah, kneeling down, reached out and held on to his arm firmly, as though her very life depended upon it.

'No, sir! Please don't try again! It's hopeless, and maybe it's better this way. . . Perhaps it was the only way.'

Then she promptly dissolved into tears.

Chapter Fourteen

Setting aside the book, which had failed completely to capture her interest, Sarah went across to the window and stared down into the garden. It was set to be yet another dry, bright day. Everywhere looked quite normal, quite tranquil. It just didn't seem right somehow. Surely there ought to be something, anything, to betray the tragic happenings of a few hours earlier?

Isabella's triumphant expression as she had reached out and grasped that most coveted of objects flashed once again before Sarah's mind's eye, as it had so many times that morning. She shook her head in disbelief. Three people had been injured, and three others had died, including Isabella herself. . . And all because of that cursed gaud! Was it really worth all that carnage?

She gave an almost imperceptible shake of her head. Of course, it was not. . .at least, not to her. But to Isabella, of course, it had meant everything. To her, no price would have been too high. . .and she had paid the ultimate price: her own life.

Sarah closed her eyes, trying desperately to blot out the memory, but it would not leave her; perhaps it never would. But she remembered other things too: the way Ravenhurst had clambered on to the jetty, and had taken her in his arms, comforting her until all tears had been spent. Then, gentle understanding thrust aside by the domineering aspect of his character, he had insisted on being the one to summon help, leaving Sarah to do what she could for Mr Stubbs.

It had seemed to take no time at all before several of the Earl's men had arrived, bearing a stretcher. Sutton, appearing with her mare, had escorted her back; and no sooner had she set foot inside the Dower House than Buddle, at her most dictatorial, had whisked her upstairs, where a hip-bath, already brought up from the nether regions, had been awaiting her.

It had been bliss to soak in that rose-scented water and rid herself of the unpleasant odour off those evil-smelling sacks, which had clung to her like a second skin. Some time later Buddle had returned, bearing a breakfast tray, and had informed her that the doctor had arrived and that Mr Stubbs had had the bullet removed from his knee and was now resting comfortably in the guest bedchamber.

That at least was something, Sarah supposed, releasing her breath in a tiny sigh. But how long would poor Mr Stubbs be laid up? And, more importantly, would he ever be able to return to Bow Street if the injury left him a cripple? She shook her head in disbelief. Who would have believed it possible that putting up at such an innocuous-looking place as The Traveller's Rest would have resulted in such very grave consequences for so many people?

She felt even she would never be the same person again. When she had left Bath, believing the life of a governess would eventually be her lot, she had experienced at least some hopes for the future, but she experienced no such pleasurable expectations now. She had met Ravenhurst again and, incredible though it was, had fallen in love with him.

But it would not be too long now, a wickedly taunting voice reminded her, before she would see the only man she had ever loved, the only man she could ever love, married to someone else. . . No, her life most certainly would never be the same again.

The bedchamber door opening broke into her deeply depressing reverie. She did not need to turn her head to see who had entered: the loud tut-tutting reverberating off the walls informed her clearly enough.

'I don't know, Miss Sarah. You haven't eaten a morsel of that food I brought you.'

'I wasn't hungry.'

Buddle drew her disapproving gaze away from the untouched tray, and fixed it on Sarah's slender back. Her eyes softened at once. 'Come over here, miss, and let me see to your hair.'

Like an automaton, Sarah moved across to the dressing table, and sat herself down on the chair. Buddle piled the silky brown locks high on Sarah's head, her expert fingers working quickly, but from time to time her eyes would stray to the mirror to look at the reflection of the forlorn little face.

'It probably won't make you feel any better, miss, but his lordship's men managed to fish the body out of the lake. All twisted among the weeds it were, with the diamond necklace still clutched in the fingers. But at least she'll be buried proper, now. And she won't be placed in a pauper's grave, neither. Master Marcus has seen to all that. She's to be buried in the churchyard, and no one any the wiser. They'll just think the poor woman drowned in the lake.'

'That was kind of him to arrange that.'

There was a further long silence, then Buddle said, 'And poor Mr Stubbs is still sleeping like a baby. Mind, the doctor gave him that much laudanum he'll probably sleep the day through.'

'It might not be a bad thing if he does.'

'No doubt you'll be taking luncheon with the others, miss. Her ladyship and Master Marcus are in the downstairs parlour now, if you would care to join them.'

'No. I think I'll remain up here. I'm not very good company at the moment.'

Buddle's eyes narrowed as she pinned an errant curl into place. There was more behind all this apathy than reaction to the events of yesterday evening and this morning; Buddle felt certain of it. Time for a little harmless deception, she decided, casting her eyes ceilingwards in a brief request to the Almighty for forgiveness.

'Well, that's a pity, because I was hoping you'd take a look at Master Marcus. I passed him in the hall a while back, and it might have been my imagination, but he looked a little flushed to me.'

Sarah's eyes rose from their contemplation of the lacy covering on the dressing table and met those of Buddle's in the mirror. 'Didn't the doctor take a look at his arm?'

'Oh, yes, he did that, miss. Said the wound was good and clean, and put a fresh dressing on it, but. . .' Buddle shook her head, looking genuinely perturbed. 'I've known many a light wound turn very nasty, the patient becomes feverish, and then. . .'

Sarah was on her feet in an instant. 'I'll go down and take a look at him.' As she went over to the door, she missed the satisfied smile curling a pair of thin lips. 'And if I think it's necessary, we'll summon the doctor back at once.'

Sarah entered the parlour a minute or two later to find the Dowager sitting in the chair by the fire, busily plying her needle, and her guardian lounging on the sofa, appearing perfectly composed. He looked up as she entered, and rose at once. They moved slowly towards each other, each scrutinising the other's face.

'You are looking a little pale, child,' he remarked, grasping her hand and guiding her over to the other chair by the fire. 'Perhaps you should return to your room and try to rest.'

And you are looking. . .fine, she thought, deciding Buddle must have been imagining things after all.

'If the roses have faded from her cheeks, Marcus, it's hardly surprising after what she has been through.' A hint of respect gleamed in the Dowager's grey eyes. 'I saw you so briefly this morning, child. I'm afraid Buddle is the most wickedly overbearing creature alive, hauling you upstairs that way. But if it's any consolation, she only ever bullies people she likes.'

Sarah couldn't prevent a slight smile at this intelligence, and turned to look across at her guardian, who had seated himself on the sofa again, and who looked back at her with such a depth of warmth in his dark eyes that if she had been pale earlier, she felt very certain that that was no longer the case.

'It—it was very kind of you to arrange Isabella's funeral, sir,' she remarked shyly.

'I didn't do it for her, Sarah. I did it for you. I knew you would fret if she was placed in a pauper's grave. Very few know of the circumstances surrounding her death, and it shall remain so. As far as the local inhabitants are concerned, a woman merely drowned in the lake.' His lips twisted into a wry smile. 'Yet another fatality to substantiate that wretched curse.'

'And it is certainly more than the woman deserves,' the Dowager remarked. 'Yes, I know of her life history, child. Marcus has just been telling me all about it,' she went on as she received an unmistakable look of reproach from a pair of blue-green eyes. 'But it doesn't alter the fact that she was a murderess, and perhaps it is only justice after all that she died for what is little more than a piece of trumpery.'

Sarah caught the frowning glance her guardian cast in his grandmother's direction, and looked at him sharply. 'What does her ladyship mean, sir?'

He appeared slightly discomforted, but responded promptly enough with, 'The necklace was quite a remarkable imitation of the original. When you brought it along to my room, I was not perfectly satisfied that it was genuine, so when I went to Bristol I had a reputable jeweller take a look at it, and he confirmed it was paste.'

'I do not perfectly understand you, sir.' Sarah drew her brows together, genuinely puzzled. 'Are you trying to say that at some point after it was stolen someone switched the genuine article with a forgery? If so, where in heaven's name is the real necklace?'

'No, child, I'm not suggesting that at all.' He couldn't prevent a smile at her continued bewilderment. 'It's my belief that, some time in the past, Felchett himself had a copy made and sold the original to pay off his mounting debts. He's always been a gamester, always been heavily in debt, but whilst his wife was seen wearing that valuable necklace, he managed to fool his creditors into believing that he still had funds.

'That, I would imagine, was the reason behind his anger when a stir was caused over the necklace's disappearance. Any expert would have seen at once that it was a forgery. And he certainly didn't want any scandal attached to his name, especially not having just arranged his son's very advantageous marriage to a wealthy Cit's daughter.'

Somehow, the knowledge that the necklace was nothing but a worthless imitation seemed to make everything so very much worse: the loss of life; poor Mr Stubbs lying upstairs, his career as a Runner probably at an end. Sarah looked gravely across at her guardian, her eyes mirroring her concern. 'What will happen to Mr Stubbs, sir, if he doesn't make a full recovery?'

'It's too early to tell whether he will or not, but there's no denying his knee is badly damaged. In a week or two when he's stronger, I'll arrange for him to be taken to London to see my private physician.' He cast her a reassuring smile. 'Don't worry, child, I have no intention of abandoning him to his fate. He came to our aid. Rather later than I had hoped, but that was hardly his fault.'

The look of concern in Sarah's eyes was replaced by one of interest. Evidently, much had passed between Mr Stubbs and her guardian before the injured man had succumbed to the effects of the laudanum. She was curious to hear the Runner's side of the story, and didn't hesitate to ask.

'When I had luncheon with Stubbs yesterday, I informed him of the disappearance of my grandmother's under-gardener, and of my suspicions that he might not be a youth. Stubbs guessed that, if the gardener was the woman he was seeking, she would have put up at an inn not too far away.

'After I had left him, he hired a horse, and began visiting the villages round about. At a place about five miles from here, he struck lucky. The landlord of the inn had let a room to a lady, and had been paid to keep it until her return. Once the landlord discovered Stubbs was a Runner, he didn't hesitate to show him the room, and sure enough, tucked away at the bottom of the wardrobe was the damning evidence—a box containing wigs and make-up.'

'I wonder if she was proposing to take me there?'

'As to that, child, we'll never know. The note she threw on the boat-house floor merely informed me where to leave the necklace for her collection. However, to continue: Stubbs informed the local magistrate, and a round-the-clock watch was arranged to be placed on the inn. It was getting late by this time, so Stubbs dined there, and then set off on his journey back here.'

His lips twitched. 'Unfortunately his mount decided to cast a shoe, and poor Stubbs was forced to walk the best part of the way back. It was very late by the time he arrived at the village. Our landlord, roused from his bed by Stubbs's thunderous knocking, completely forgot about the letter I had written.

'Fortunately, the landlady, an early riser, was up before daybreak, spotted the note on the shelf and, thankfully, didn't waste any time in taking it up to Stubbs. And it was while he was making his way through the home wood that he had the great good fortune to spot Isabella and followed. . . The rest you know.'

'Well, that is all very interesting, I'm sure,' the Dowager remarked, breaking the short silence that followed her grandson's disclosures. 'But we have far more important matters to discuss. . . Your marriage for a start.'

A spasm of pain ran through her, and Sarah lowered her eyes, thereby missing the angry glance Marcus shot at his grandmother.

'Yes, it's all very well you looking at me like that,' the Dowager continued, completely unruffled by her grandson's scowling disapproval. 'But you know yourself that Sarah cannot possibly remain unmarried now.'

The surprising mention of her name brought Sarah's head up sharply. She glanced from her guardian's angry countenance to her ladyship's smugly satisfied one. 'W-what are you talking about, ma'am?' she asked, taken aback somewhat. 'I am not going to be married.'

'My dear child, you cannot possibly spend all night alone with a man and remain single. Why, it's unthinkable!'

'B-but I didn't spend all night alone with a man. I spent it with my guardian.'

The Dowager gave a cackle of wicked laughter at the look of outrage on her grandson's face, but Sarah, not quite realising just what she had said, rose to her feet in some confusion, and continued to look at them both in dismay. 'But nothing improper occurred, ma'am, I assure you.'

'I do not need your assurances over that, child,' the Dowager responded, still smiling wickedly. 'I am certain Marcus behaved like a perfect gentleman. But no matter what you may think, he is very much a man, and a marriage between you must be arranged without delay.'

'No!'

Sarah's staunch refusal echoed round the small room with devastating clarity, bringing Marcus to his feet. He cast a brief glance at the determined set of her lovely features and then turned to his grandmother in no little annoyance.

'Would you kindly leave us, ma'am?' His tone was clipped, making it abundantly obvious that he was more than just a little nettled over her interference. 'Kindly allow me to do my proposing in my own way.'

'Oh, very well, Marcus.' Setting her embroidery aside, the Dowager begrudgingly rose to her feet. 'But for heaven's sake don't be afraid to put it to the touch! You've been shilly-shallying long enough.'

Annoyed though he was, Marcus was powerless to prevent a grudging smile of admiration from curling his lips as he watched the door close behind his grandmother. She had probably known from the day he had brought Sarah to this house that his feelings for his ward went rather deeper than those of just an attentive guardian.

His smile turned rueful. Not that he had ever seen himself in that light. Right from that very first night at The Traveller's Rest he had been attracted to Sarah, and not only physically: her wit and intelligence had appealed to him too. Never before had he experienced such an overwhelming desire to protect; to cherish.

Discovering her true identity had certainly been a set-back—no, much more than that, a bitter blow; but he had taken comfort in the knowledge that the constraints placed upon him as her guardian were, blessedly, for a limited period only.

He had been fully prepared to indulge her with a London Season; he had owed her that much, at least, for all those joyless years she had endured in Bath. He might possibly have derived much pleasure himself from squiring her through the social whirl; and would certainly have attained much satisfaction from keeping all would-be suitors at bay.

In June, once she had attained her majority, of course, his guardianship would, thankfully, be at an end. Freed of encumbrance, he would then have been in a position to further his own interests, and woo her in earnest. Sadly, though, that delightful prospect had now been denied him; the events of yesterday had effectively destroyed all his well-meaning intentions and carefully made plans.

A deep sigh of regret escaped him. The Dowager had meant well, but she had probably quite unwittingly done more harm than good. Sarah, he felt sure, was still brooding over the events of the morning. It was hardly the most appropriate time to declare himself. . .but what choice had he now?

He turned to look at her. She was staring fixedly down at the brightly patterned carpet, as though to look at him were abhorrent to her. But he knew this wasn't so. She liked him well enough. . . But was liking enough?

'I'm sorry it had to happen this way,' he said softly, his voice sounding diffident, totally unlike his own, even to his own ears, 'but you must realise that we have little—'

'I realise nothing, sir!' she cut in sharply. He was right: her emotions were raw, and this on top of the battering they had received during the past twenty-four hours was almost more than she could bear.

She stormed over to the window, fighting to control the hot tears of biting anger that threatened at what she deemed a most unflattering proposal. She was being offered the one thing in the world she most desired, and yet she was being offered nothing at all.

If he loved her—yes—then it would be perfect, utter

bliss to accept; but he was offering her the protection of his name no doubt out of some misguided sense of chivalry and obligation. . . And for what? What had he done after all? Nothing! Well, she wouldn't permit it to happen!

'I believe the acknowledged mode is to thank the gentleman for his kind offer, but unfortunately I find myself unable to accept.' In a desperate attempt to appear politely composed, she had tried to keep her voice level, unemotional, but had only succeeded in sounding haughty, disdainful almost, and his eyes narrowed. 'After all, there is no need for such drastic measures. We have done nothing of which we need be ashamed. Nothing improper occurred between us.'

'I don't need reminding about that, my girl!' he ground out, both hurt and annoyed by what he took for indifference on her part. 'But I damned well wish it had, then you wouldn't be standing there now spouting out this flummery at me!'

Astonished by his vehemence, Sarah swung round and regarded that beloved scowling countenance uncertainly for a moment before an almost hysterical gurgle of laughter rose in her throat. 'Why, Mr Ravenhurst! I could almost believe you wish to marry me.'

'But of course I wish to marry you, you foolish creature! Why the devil else would I be asking you?'

For a few moments it was as much as Sarah could do to gape across at him, while trying desperately to suppress the surge of exhilaration coursing through her. He had sounded so convincing, as though he genuinely meant it. . . But how could that be? What of this other woman he wished to marry? Surely he was not prepared to thrust her aside without so much as a second thought like some worn out shoe?

No, he wouldn't do that; she felt certain of it. His disposition was far from fickle. He was not the kind of man to transfer his affections from one woman to another with callous disregard for anyone's feelings but his own. So, could the Dowager have been mistaken? Might it just be possible that his affections were not already engaged?

She watched him move with less than his usual athletic grace over to the decanters and reach for the brandy. She wanted nothing more than to believe that he truly wished her to be his wife and was not merely offering her the protection of his name, and yet a nagging doubt remained.

'It is kind of you to say that, sir,' she responded, managing to keep the hard lump which was trying desperately to lodge itself in her throat at bay. 'But I understood from the Dowager that you were as good as betrothed already to a certain lady whose name I'm afraid I cannot recall.'

The hand raising the glass to his lips checked for a moment as he turned his head to look at her, his expression unreadable, then he tossed the contents down his throat in one large swallow. 'So, she told you that, did she? Confound the woman!'

Sarah was not quite certain at whom this curse was directed, but she suspected it was at the poor Dowager. She watched him reach for the decanter again, his hand not quite steady. 'You do not deny it?' she prompted when he remained silent.

'No, it's true enough.' The contents of the second glass went the way of the first: down his throat in one swallow. 'There was a time when I foolishly considered marrying Celia Bamford. Thankfully, though, I never got round to asking her. You saw to that.'

Sarah felt as though she were on a see-saw, one moment her hopes plummeting, only to soar the next.

'How—how did I manage to do that?'

'It was while I was journeying to her parents' home in Somerset that I suddenly took it into my head to pay a call on you. I'll admit, I wasn't best pleased at the time to discover you'd absconded.' Sarah watched in fascination as a tender little smile curled his lips. 'But since, I've blessed you every waking moment. Your actions stopped me from making the biggest mistake I could ever have possibly made.'

Placing his glass back down on the tray, he turned to face her squarely. 'Look, Sarah, you and I get along very well. . . Come, couldn't you stomach me as a husband?' His voice, now, was like a caress: gentle; coaxing. 'I'd never hurt you, you know that. You could have anything you wanted—carriages, jewels, fine dresses. . . Anything you asked for would be yours. But I would want children, Sarah. I would try to be patient, give you time to come to. . .'

He caught the tiny sound like that of a suppressed sob, and saw the tears glinting on her lashes. He took an uncertain step towards her, wanting desperately to take her in his arms, and to assure her that everything would turn out fine, but checked himself. He didn't doubt the depths of his own feelings, only hers.

'Oh, confound it!' he cursed. 'I'm no damned good at this sort of thing. If you cannot bear the thought of me as a husband, then say so. I can't. . .won't have it forced upon you!'

Sinking her small white teeth into her bottom lip in an attempt to stop it trembling, Sarah watched him stalk across the room to stare down at the brightly burning coals on the hearth. Her spirits had soared to such dizzy heights, she felt as if she were floating on a cloud of pure happiness. He loved her. Against all the odds he loved her. . .and more. He loved her so much that he would not force her into marriage.

Once again she found herself having to do battle with that stubborn lump before she could manage in a voice barely more than whisper, 'I think I ought to make it perfectly clear right from the start, sir, that you cannot buy me. I want neither carriages, nor jewels. . .I only want. . .you.'

For a moment it seemed as though he had not heard, then very slowly he turned his head, and what he saw mirrored in those lovely blue-green eyes sent him striding wordlessly towards her.

With hands not quite steady, betraying the fact that he was still labouring under deep emotional strain, he took a hold of her upper arms and stared down at her intently, his dark eyes searching, devouring each lovely feature in turn. 'Do you mean that, my sweet Sarah? Do—do you mean you really care for me?'

She managed to raise one arm, and stroked his cheek with gentle fingers. 'Didn't you know? Didn't you even suspect?' she murmured before his mouth came down to cover hers in a kiss so full of loving tenderness that had there been any doubts left in her mind of the depth of his feelings for her they would have been instantly swept away.

'I felt sure you liked me,' he murmured, burying his face in her soft curls. 'But I never dared to hope that. . .'

'That I could ever have been foolish enough to fall in love with such an arrogant, overbearing creature,' she couldn't resist teasing. 'Yes, it quite amazes me, I can tell you. But I recall my dear mother telling me years ago that women are not always sensible when it comes to matters of the heart.'

There was little gentleness in him this time. Moulding her body to his so that she was frighteningly aware of every hard sinewy muscle in that powerful frame, he captured her mouth with a possessive hunger that left her lips slightly swollen, her senses reeling and her mind in little doubt of his very ardent desire for her.

'I think we had better sit down,' he suggested, rather breathless himself from the passionate exchange. 'I managed to contain myself last night, but much more of this. . .well, I cannot promise to continue behaving like a gentleman. I'm only flesh and blood when all's said and done.'

She laughed at his rueful expression as he drew her down beside him on the sofa, and looked down at the shapely hand still retaining a gentle hold on her own. 'When did you fall in love with me?' she asked shyly, resting her head against the comforting strength of his broad shoulder.

'I'm not perfectly sure, my darling.' His lips curled into a warm, reminiscent smile. 'I cannot say that I'm a believer in love at first sight, and yet. . .I knew for certain when I kissed you in the barn, remember?'

'Oh, yes. I remember,' she responded softly, smiling herself at the memory. 'I thought you had done so to punish me.'

'No, not to punish you, Sarah. I was merely trying to show you how dangerous it was to be alone with a man. And all I succeeded in doing was proving to myself that I had fallen in love for the first time in my life.' He dropped a kiss into her hair, and then, placing his hands on her shoulders, held her away from him so that he could look down at her enchantingly lovely face. 'And, of course, I was not best pleased over your obvious regard for the young Captain?'

She found this rather surprising confession extremely gratifying, but didn't hesitate to reassure him. 'I certainly liked Captain Carter, but I was never in the least danger of losing my heart to him. And he is certainly far from ready to form a lasting attachment. That is most definitely for the future.' She frowned suddenly as yet another memory returned. 'But you won't forget to write to him, will you, sir? You promised you would.'

'No, I shan't forget. And my name is Marcus, by the way.' He pulled her back into the crook of his arm. 'Now, when will you marry me, you abominable girl?'

'Whenever you like, Marcus,' she replied, finding his name came quite easily to her lips.

'Do you want to be married in London, or somewhere quiet?'

'I think I should prefer a quiet wedding.'

'And so should I, my darling. I'll leave for the capital in a day or two. I promised Stubbs I'd take that wretched necklace to Bow Street. Whilst I'm in London I'll obtain a special licence, and then we can be married as soon afterwards as you like.'

'Tomorrow wouldn't be too soon for me,' she responded and was rewarded for her good sense with a further demonstration of his masculine passion.

'Nor me, my love.' His mouth remained hovering above her sweetly parted lips, but before he could experience the considerable pleasure of kissing her again, the door opened.

'Good God!' He bestowed one of those famed, heavy

scowls upon the intruder. 'You've barely given us time to get acquainted.'

The Dowager, completely unmoved as always by her grandson's black looks, focused her attention on Sarah, noting the flushed cheeks and brightly sparkling eyes, not to mention the decidedly swollen lips. 'By the look of your future wife, I should say I've been away decidedly too long already!' She turned to her butler, still hovering by the door. 'Clegg, bring up a bottle of champagne from the cellar. I do believe we have something worth celebrating!'

'We do, indeed,' Marcus concurred, quickly setting aside his resentment at the interruption.

'And Sarah and I will need to put our heads together and work out the wedding arrangements.' The Dowager resumed her seat by the fire, looking a picture of blissful contentment. 'Have you decided where in London you intend holding the ceremony?'

'We've decided on a quiet wedding,' her grandson informed her.

She looked mildly disappointed at this, but brightened almost at once. 'Yes, that might be best. I dare say Sarah wouldn't care for hundreds of strangers milling round her on her wedding day.' She smiled warmly at the loving couple, who seemed to be experiencing the greatest difficulty in keeping their eyes off each other. 'Will you hold the wedding at Ravenhurst?'

This drew Marcus's attention. 'No, I think we'll be married from here, if you don't object. Then, afterwards, I shall take Sarah to Ravenhurst.' He looked at his intended with that wonderful smile that had won her heart. 'Unfortunately, my love, with that Corsican upstart still reigning supreme on the continent, a honeymoon abroad is out of the question. So I suggest we spend a few quiet weeks together at Ravenhurst, and then go to London.'

This sounded perfect, but before Sarah could voice her wholehearted approval to the scheme, the door opened again and Buddle entered.

Her shrewd dark eyes took in the situation in a trice, and a suspicion of a satisfied smile hovered about her lips as she looked across at her mistress. 'There's a footman here from the big house. His lordship's compliments. . .and would you, Master Marcus and Miss Sarah care to join the family for dinner this evening?'

'No, we would not!' the Dowager snapped. 'My son only wants to ferret out what has been going on.'

'He knows already,' her grandson countered. 'I explained everything to him this morning. No matter what your opinion of your son may be, ma'am, you cannot deny that he is extremely discreet, as, too, is Aunt Henrietta.' An arresting look suddenly took possession of his features. 'Wait a moment! Isn't my aunt's estimable brother staying with them?'

'Yes, he is. And that's even more reason for not accepting,' the Dowager muttered. 'Who wants to sit down to dinner with that prosy old bore?'

'I most certainly do!' He turned to Sarah with all the excitement of a schoolboy. 'The Countess's brother is a bishop. I can obtain a special licence from him. We will be married tomorrow!'

'What!' The Dowager looked across at her grandson as though he had taken leave of his senses. 'You must be mad! We cannot possibly arrange everything in so short a time. Surely you want all the family and your friends to be present?'

'No, not particularly,' he responded with brutal honesty. 'Of course I shall invite the Earl and Countess. But we can hold a big gathering to celebrate our marriage when we're in London.'

'Shabby!' The Dowager beat a tattoo on the carpet with her ebony stick, her usual method of informing people that she was vexed. 'And you Ravenhurst of Ravenhurst! Shabby, that's what I call it!'

'But, ma'am, it would suit me very well,' Sarah assured her and then, diplomatic to the last, added, 'And when we do go to London, you could join us there. I couldn't possibly arrange such a big party without your help. I would need you to advise me on who to invite, and to help me organise everything.'

This suggestion seemed to placate the outraged Dowager somewhat. 'Yes, yes, I think I could be of help to you, child,' she agreed, betraying more than just a little enthusiasm for the scheme; then her brows snapped together again. 'But that doesn't alter the fact that the ceremony itself would still be a paltry affair.'

She fixed her staunchly disapproving gaze on her grandson. 'And you haven't given any thought to poor Sarah,' she remarked in a last valiant attempt to make him see reason. 'She hasn't anything in the least suitable to wear for such an occasion. Though I don't suppose for a moment that it would bother you one iota if the poor girl turned up for her own wedding dressed only in her shift!'

He resisted the temptation to respond to this highly provocative suggestion, though Sarah noticed the wicked gleam that sprang into his eyes before he turned them towards Buddle, who was still standing silently by the door, waiting for a positive answer to pass on to his lordship's footman, and who had a suspicion of a wicked twinkle in her eyes, too.

'Buddle, you most admirable of creatures! I'm relying on you to come up with something suitable for my future bride to wear on her wedding day.'

'Well, sir, there's the cream silk gown and matching bonnet. If I furbish them up a bit, I think they would serve very nicely.'

'You traitorous wretch!' The Dowager waved her ebony stick threateningly. 'You dare to encourage them in this folly and. . .and I shall turn you off!'

Buddle thrust her scrawny bosom out to its farthest limits. 'Master Marcus, sir. . .I'll do it on that score alone!'

XAALL

Have a *Merry Christmas* with Harlequin Mills & Boon

With Christmas near HM&B is ready to spread some cheer and romance with a great line up of Christmas titles.

This years Christmas selection includes two anthologies - *Christmas Treats* and *Christmas Miracles*, the *Regency Historical Christmas Collection* and the always favourite *Harlequin Mills and Boon Christmas Pack*. Fantastic stocking fillers, these titles make the perfect gift idea.

Available from selected newsagents, bookstores and chainstores, including K-Mart, Big W, Target and Coles and www.romance.net au